BE

THE

SEA

BE
THE
SEA

CLARA WARD

Atthis Arts

BE THE SEA

Published by Atthis Arts, LLC
Detroit, Michigan
atthisarts.com

ISBN 978-1-961654-04-4

Library of Congress Control Number: 2023946349

To Ebeth, Erin, Charlotte, Amanda, Virjilio,
Melanie, Marissa, and the future

ACT ONE:

SAILBOAT

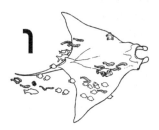

THE WATER PULSED, dim but clear.

The high cliffs enclosing La Baie des Vierges blanketed the seafloor in early morning shadows, while the rocking of meter-high swells comforted Wend. The press of warm water through their scuba gear meant safety. The drag of the air tanks, sample bot, and drybag on their back kept them grounded even while swimming through unfamiliar ocean.

A shining school of fish changed direction to swim alongside Wend. Their yellow-green backs and white bellies brightened the underwater world, making Wend smile behind their full-face mask. Only when the small fish turned and dove en masse, did Wend rise closer to the surface to reorient.

Five sailboats remained at anchor in La Baie des Vierges in November of 2039. Despite ten centimeters of sea level rise, looming rock features and tall palms still dominated the bay, viscerally reminding Wend of pictures posted decades before.

There it was. The reason Wend slipped uninvited through unknown ocean, now of all times. The purple hydro turbine on the double-ended cutter pierced the clear water, a bright human-made shape, easy to spot below the surface. *Nuovo Mar* gleamed in a coordinated violet script at the stern. Since no ladder hung over the *Nuovo Mar*'s signature purple rubbing strip, Wend timed their approach to swim up with a swell and throw an arm high to grab a metal stanchion.

Their shoulder yanked hard. They used the momentum and all the core strength they still possessed to kick one finned foot onto deck. The fin tip smacked hard and missed a solar panel by inches. Wend grimaced but carried on.

Rolling onto a boat's deck was never graceful or quiet, but Wend made it on the first try, which was as much of a success as they could ask from the day.

"Dites-moi qui vous êtes!" The stocky figure shouted something that was clearly not a request and brandished a knife while holding something unidentifiable in the other hand.

"Dites-moi pourquoi la vie est belle." Wend raised both hands and spit out their regulator as they responded impulsively, brain pattern-matching faster than it could decode a language Wend barely spoke.

"Tang ina!" The knife stabbed forward a couple inches, but with questionable intent.

Wend had no idea what that phrase meant but guessed it was a swear in some language other than French. "Hello? Hola? Ciao? Sawatdee?"

A taller figure rose from the shiny white cockpit into a slant of sunlight and responded in English, voice gruff but clear, "He doesn't care why life is beautiful or how this ocean features in some old musical you're quoting. But who you are seems like a fair question. Climbing aboard the wrong boat near dawn is a strange walk of shame."

Wend pushed up to sitting. The deck was well equipped for an older sailboat, with two solar panels braced on the foredeck and two more clamped to railings. Feeling exposed all of a sudden, Wend took a deep breath. They leaned against their air tanks and all their earthly possessions strapped to their back, as they stared in between the two backlit figures. Wend carefully displayed both empty hands before disengaging their scuba mask and raising it onto their bristly short hair. "Are you Viola Yang? I'd like to join your crew."

Only bird cries and lapping waves interrupted a long silence.

Then Viola laughed, deep in her throat, and asked, "I suppose you swam up from Atlantis to meet me?"

The man with the knife shook the item in his other fist menacingly. The shift revealed it to be a papaya. "Everyone on this island is loko-loko."

He stomped over to a drying rack spread with sliced fruit and covered with netting. A separate drying rack held only fish. Without the bright light of the rising sun directly behind him, Wend saw the man was compact, maybe five foot six, wearing shorts and a faded red tank top over medium brown skin. The stringy but well-defined muscles of his arms and shoulders flexed as he chopped the papaya with more force than necessary, having dismissed Wend as a threat.

"You still haven't said who you are." Viola kept her distance but moved around the cabin and the stowed mainsail to lean against the bow railing. Her tank top was less faded than the man's, batiked with mottled blues and greens on what might have been silk. It hung lose above threadbare denim cutoffs. Messy curls of brown and gray framed olive-skinned monolid eyes that matched what Wend could remember from the picture on Viola Yang's webpage.

The reality of what Wend had done hit them like an anchor dropped from above, but they found their voice and said, "I'm Gwendolyn Taylor. But please call me Wend, pronouns they/them. Your photos of attractive megafauna at the coral reef four islands over, in Anaho Bay, ran in the last issue of *Ocean Rescue* beside an article I co-authored with the Marine Census Project. I wrote the section on the reef microbiome." Most of that speech came out the way Wend had planned, and they counted it as their second success of the day.

Viola lifted her chin but held the rest of her body still and relaxed against the rail. "Okay, say I check online, despite the exorbitant local cell rates, and confirm you are who you say. Why are you boarding my boat like a pirate, then demanding to join my crew?"

Pirate? Demanding? Wend took a deep breath, wondering if the words were meant as a joke. They didn't feel like a lie, but there was a pressure behind each syllable. Wend wanted to explain that pressure and what had drawn them from several islands away, but couldn't. Not yet.

The amusement Viola displayed before had faded. Still there was a pull, a need to connect, that kept Wend talking, pushing well beyond their social comfort zone. "Someone on the local VHF net said this boat was headed to Hawai'i. They mentioned you were short a crew member." Wend wasn't acting completely on instinct. They'd checked up on the *Nuovo Mar* before spending the last of their francs convincing the only sailor passing nearby to drop them at the mouth of La Baie des Vierges. "I've heard the crossing from the Marquesas can be rough and you need someone on watch at all hours. I can take a watch. I brought a hammock I can tie on deck if that keeps me out of your way at anchor. I don't get motion sick. If you'll take me along to Hawai'i, I can offer stories to entertain you for several weeks."

"Not hearing a lot about your sailing experience in there." Viola didn't move and didn't invite Wend to.

Squinting into the sun, now fully risen above the surrounding cliffs, Wend tried not to squirm. "I haven't trained with a gaff rig like yours, but I've spent half the last decade on sailboats. I follow directions, am stronger than I look, and have advanced and deep dive certifications." Motioning with an elbow to the bundle at their back, Wend offered, "My sample bot is certified for the Marine Census Project. In case you want to do any science or reporting along the way, I could back you up with my writing and lab results. Well, the genetic and chemical results would have to wait until we reach a participating lab at the University of Hawai'i, but I'd be more than happy to take samples all along the way. My bot contains 600 pre-certified sterile and auto-sealing sample containers. It automatically sieves microbiome samples and tags each with the GPS coordinates, temperature, pressure, and salinity at collection."

When Viola still looked dubious, Wend added on instinct, "I was born in Hawai'i—June 20th, 1972."

With her first visible startle, Viola huffed and said, "You're one day older than me. I would have guessed you for at least a decade younger, and most people guess me as younger than sixty-seven."

Wend heard that a lot—about their own appearance. Some said they had the build and bearing of an adolescent, not someone in their sixties. The white in their hair was scattered amidst varied shades of brown, the lightest of which bordered on blond, and with their terracotta tan skin, people had trouble classifying Wend by age, race, or gender, something people were all too eager to do. Of course, Wend knew Viola's birthdate from the research they'd done online but didn't mention that now. They'd rather be called a pirate than a stalker. Mentioning dreams and mysteries that summoned them to this deck, flopping like a fish out of water, would have them cast back fast.

Wend tried not to lie or deceive, but they also knew to protect themself. "Salt water and sea air suit us both, I guess. I don't need to be paid, just food and water to stay alive, and air for my tanks if we're diving." Not that Wend didn't need money, and Viola was certainly rich enough, but beggars couldn't choose benefits. "I even brought my best cocoa, sugar, and powdered milk to contribute to ship stores, if that will sweeten the deal."

"Your only food supplies are ingredients for chocolate milk?" Viola was back to sounding amused, which made the interrogation, interview, or whatever it was, easier to bear.

"It's better as hot chocolate, and I have enough to make at least three gallons. That, stories, and my labor are what I can contribute." Wend shrugged and smiled. "Beyond that, I've got maybe a day's worth of nuts and a couple energy bars."

Viola turned to the young man who'd finished filling the drying racks, leaving a few bite-sized chunks of papaya on the cutting board. "What do you think, Aljon? Can you put up with two sixty-somethings all the way to Hawai'i?"

Aljon waved his chopping knife carelessly in a circle. "Whatever. You know I have the greatest respect for my elders."

Even Wend could recognize the sarcasm behind those words, but Aljon seemed more dubious, maybe even curious, than hostile now. Wend could live with that.

"I'll decide by dinnertime." Viola stood away from the railing, suddenly taller and very much the skipper. "Inventory what we'd need to add another person to our crew." Aljon nodded as Viola walked past Wend saying, "No promises. If you're lucky I'll leave you on shore rather than making you swim for it."

"Keep your shoes on. The rocks at the bottom are sharp." Viola gestured to the pool at the base of the waterfall, the sun now high overhead.

Wend was caught staring at the 200-foot-high, nearly vertical, fall of water. It thundered in isolation on the tiny island of Fatu Hiva with only five sailboats in the nearest bay and a couple of local farms along what passed as both road and hiking trail before the path led upriver. A multitude of plants, both broad- and small-leaved, surrounded the pool. The air hung heavy with pollen and slightly fermenting fruit smells, but most of all—it didn't smell of salt.

Island air settled sweet and hot compared to the marine layer that hovered offshore, never as hot but always salty. Wend tended to forget about the land when trying to save the oceans. But freshwater without cities and people called to Wend as strongly as the sea. The crashing waterfall reminded them of waves, and the pool at the base hid as many secrets as any tidepool. Those secrets echoed Wend's own. They squatted to dip their fingers in the fresh water and pet the soft mud and algae by the edge.

Viola stripped down to a black bikini and water shoes, leaving her phone hidden beneath her shorts, tank, and overshirt. She wore a single gold charm, a flat circle with a face in it, dangling from a thin chain around her neck.

Wend stepped into the refreshingly cool water wearing the board shorts and long-sleeved rash guard they'd arrived and hiked in, as well as sandals made from recycled plastic that they'd chosen for water wear. The freshwater pool offered what might be Wend's best chance to wash both skin and clothes in the next two or three weeks. Beside the falls, the water bubbled and rushed in a way no ocean could. Sinking deep, Wend scrubbed their own fingers back and forth through their centimeter-long hair and snorted out appreciative bubbles at the sensation of soft water and total non-stickiness. The sun filtered pink through their eyelids as they floated to the surface.

A shift in nearby currents let Wend know when Viola started treading water nearby. They blinked their eyes open and shifted to vertical to avoid looking into the sun.

Viola was studying their face, practically forcing eye contact. "You're an odd one, aren't you?"

Whatever comfort Wend had taken from the water ended then. Their eyes shifted to shore, mapping easy ways out. "Odd" was the least of what they'd been called. It could mean neurodivergent, queer, old; that their hair was too short, their skin too tan, their clothes too out of place; or a million other perceived transgressions. Wend hated trying to sort such things out. They only said, "Perhaps."

"At least you're not staring at my tits." Viola swept her arms in a move that couldn't even be called swimming but landed her where she could stand easily with her head out of the water. "You don't talk much for someone who wants to barter passage with stories. Come tell me something that will help me understand."

The invitation drew Wend to shallower water more surely than any current could. The potential to connect, to reach an understanding, practically radiated from the world-sailing photographer Wend had discovered almost by chance, the person they had changed all their plans to meet. It was easier to return Viola's gaze now, as they bobbed in the warm water, feet comfortably touching bottom.

Wend hadn't intended to tell this story, certainly not first, but the peace of the water and the word 'understand' drew it from them. "The last time I visited the tidepools on Lāna'i, I didn't understand what last meant. My dad stayed on the boat. Only Mom followed my sprint down the beach. We passed a couple other families that came in by boat. Sixty-three years ago, there was only one small hotel amid thousands of acres of pineapple farms on the island, but I don't think I understood that then. We always arrived and left from the beach."

Viola's eyes traced the lines and edges of Wend's face, which made Wend look away. As long as they pretended the focus was on their story and not their person, Wend was eager to continue.

"This last time, someone spoke to Mom, distracting her. I slowed down a little on the jagged rocks around the tidepools to let her catch up. The rocks were dark and hot but not too scratchy for the bottoms of my tough feet. The rocks had to be crossed. So I did.

"I didn't know the smaller child or the mom already at what I thought of as my tidepool, so I ignored them.

"I walked naked into the pool that was larger than our living room. Swimming naked in the ocean was the only time my skin felt right. Mom said I learned to swim in that tidepool, but I couldn't remember or imagine not knowing how to swim. She called what I did the 'frog paddle.' I hadn't seen many frogs, but jellies, salps, and sea cucumbers could push water out to move. I used the limbs I had to push the water out behind where I wanted to go." Wend wanted to frog paddle across this pool, to relive the feeling on their skin and through their body in this novel place. While they hadn't swum naked in years, water reached past clothes to bare skin better than air ever could. They settled for standing neck deep in front of Viola, head conveniently above water to tell their story.

"The tidepools on Lāna'i always seemed the warmest, and they always contained sea cucumbers. The He'eia Fishpond near my house on O'ahu had starfish, crabs, and fish, but not many sea cucumbers.

"I knew just how to touch the black ones. That day I rested four fingers against a full smooth body that reached almost to my elbow. It stayed soft, breathing in sand and water at one end, pushing it out the other. My whole body stilled to avoid moving my fingers or upsetting the sand underwater.

"The mom I didn't know complained, 'Why'd she freeze up like that? Is it a seizure?' There was something more about seizures and someone's brother.

"My mom shook her head and smiled. She felt and looked like static in those moments. The smile was a lie. Lies hurt to be around." Wend risked a glance to catch any sign of understanding or judgment from Viola, but the tightening of the woman's eyes could be a reaction to sunlight reflecting off the water.

Wend shivered despite the relatively warm water. What felt like a huge admission to them could pass as metaphor to others. Usually, letting others explain away Wend's idiosyncrasies provided camouflage, protection. If none of the hints they offered found purchase, then Viola was like all the others. Whatever drew Wend to Viola took hold and shook them in that moment. Viola ignored that as easily as Wend's previous shiver, let alone the mention of lies that hurt.

Wend wrapped one arm around their own waist underwater. "The steady, relaxed sea cucumber felt safe to me.

"Even at age four, I knew Mom didn't like questions about me, but I didn't understand the rest. Other times, when I moved fast like I usually did, people asked if I were hyperactive. When I picked up tiny crabs, people said I might hurt them. I don't think I ever hurt them. I didn't know why so many things I did seemed wrong to people."

Still no reaction from Viola, nothing Wend could interpret or build explanations around.

"The smaller child at the tidepool came closer and closer, splashing and making noise. Leaning forward to see what I was touching. They splashed a hand right down and through the water to grab the big black sea cucumber. It shrank, expelling a sudden plume of sand and water. Going leathery and rigid before sinking into a crack in the rock underneath.

"I missed touching the soft water-filled body.

"The other child squealed and laughed, shouting, 'Loli! Loli!' At least they knew the name for what they'd driven away. I knew that if the sea cucumber had been more frightened or hurt, there would have been trouble. It could have injured itself and poisoned the tidepool with its guts and toxins. But it just pooped out extra water and sand to shrink away. The littler kid didn't even get a warning for grabbing at it that way.

"It reminded me of how I'd pooped in a tidepool once, a big poop that floated to the surface, and made a mother scream and pull her kid away. After that, I figured it was okay to pee but not poop in the ocean. My mom explained it the same way she explained needing to wear clothes most places, not in terms of humans making other humans sick. The way I saw it, all the animals in the ocean must be pooping there. I didn't understand how I was any different."

Wend paused. Viola didn't interrupt or wrinkle her nose in disgust.

She shrugged and tilted her head, still listening and watching. It would have been comforting for Wend to sink fully underwater, but the pressure and currents from their shoulders down were supportive enough as they straightened and then flexed their arms. The fact Viola hadn't objected to the rambling nature of Wend's story encouraged them to keep trying.

"I didn't want to go back to the boat at all that last day. There were many things I didn't understand, but I knew I didn't want to leave. I could have slept in the ocean. It felt good on my skin. Even the sand felt fine so long as it was wet.

"When we had to get back on the boat, Mom rinsed me with a pitcher of fresh water. She tucked me into my tiny hammock with my fuzzy blanket. I always slept best there. Mom had tried putting a hammock in my room at home. But it didn't move right without the ocean underneath. That was my last night sleeping in my hammock on that boat." A loss Wend hadn't felt that day saturated the memory now. It emptied them from the inside, tugged at an emptiness already deep within Wend. They wondered if Viola saw the void behind Wend's lowered eyes.

"Wrapping up tight in my blanket was the best I could do for years after that. I thought I was like a sea cucumber. Or maybe I was the water and sand inside that could be pooped out to escape. But I learned not to tell people that."

Finally, the corners of Viola's mouth curved down and then up. Wend waited expectantly.

Viola didn't laugh, and it took a while for her to comment. "So your family had a boat with enough room to hang a hammock. Was it a yacht?"

The energy from storytelling deserted Wend in a rush. Viola hadn't connected with the story or glimpsed the larger forces Wend was struggling to convey. Instead, Viola had asked a useless rich person question.

Wend swallowed their disappointment. Communication took time. Explaining a puzzle Wend only half glimpsed could take many attempts and multiple stories. To generate time for all that, Wend needed to sail with Viola to Hawai'i. Wend hoped their averted gaze hid how the temporary setback stung. "It was a very small hammock and a very small yacht. But yeah, that's what they bought with all the money my mom saved up before she got married. And that's what the man I thought of as Dad kept in exchange for me in the end." They rushed to finish. Wend heard the flatness in their own voice, and that wasn't how they wanted to be with Viola. They struggled to meet her eyes, again.

"That sounds like a whole other story." Viola waved her arms beneath the water such that one barely brushed against Wend's arm, causing Wend to startle, but the current shifted around them in a pleasant way.

They calmed and held still as a line of tiny fish with iridescent blue stripes followed the sudden shift in the water to trace along Wend's arm and then circle around their other side before darting back toward some rocks. Viola squinted at the odd progression of the fish as if her eyes were taking a burst of photos.

"I'll tell you if you want," Wend offered, feeling again the scooped-out emptiness that would accompany that other story.

"Maybe later. For now, I'm wondering how you remember so much from when you were only four."

Wend shrugged, not wanting to explain how strong emotions linked back to memories from half that age. "I don't remember things word for word, not even from last week. But I couldn't forget that day on Lāna'i if I tried."

Viola studied Wend the way she'd tracked the parade of fish, and her focus seemed to shift as she asked, "Do some expressions or deceptions still feel like static to you?"

Wend bit down on their lips, hopes alight again, then fumbled for words. "I don't feel it the way I used to, but I still feel something I can't describe any better than static. Why, do you have some sense for when people are lying?"

"I thought I did," Viola said. She didn't try to hide her own skepticism. "I was wrong, a lot. Mostly, I've become lie averse myself. I tell people I'm too old to bother with lying or being lied to."

Breathing deeply, Wend impressed this moment of first real contact firmly into their memory. They'd said almost the same to others, and finding even one hint of similarity based on that first story suggested there could be more. The promise that had drawn Wend across the Marquesas might be fulfilled. "I bet people think you're wise."

Viola snorted. "Nope. Probably why it's only me and Aljon on the boat."

Looking downriver toward where they knew the *Nuovo Mar* waited, Wend said, "You could add to my application for crew that I won't lie to you."

Viola wandered to the side of the waterfall pool, swiping her arms back and forth through the water until she was halfway out. She didn't respond to Wend's promise. "Let's head back. You can tell me about your baby hammock. I sense there's more story there."

Wend twitched, a little raw from the last story and the vulnerability of hope. That hammock mattered to Wend in ways that had nothing to do with Viola or what Wend needed to communicate to her. Being directed to tell a specific story so soon made the sharing feel uncomfortably like an audition. For the last couple days, they'd worried over how to board a strange boat and talk their way onto the crew, but no preparation could make this easy.

Wend forced themself out of the pool and began speaking as Viola pulled her discarded clothing on over her wet bikini. "I know that first hammock was made by my Grandma Cora, who gave me my first lesson in fractions and genetics. While cutting up liliko'i she illustrated how she was half Seminole, which made my dad one quarter Seminole, and me one eighth Seminole. Years later, I started reading about the Seminole and learned about their baby hammocks, which looked nothing like mine. Eventually, I found out I wasn't really Seminole, not by culture or blood, certainly not from my supposed dad and Grandma Cora."

"Each of your stories leads into another." As she squeezed between tight rocks to reach a grassy path on the north side of the stream, Viola segued to a conclusion Wend hadn't expected. "You mentioned genetics with your robot, too. Is that your field?"

"I started in genetics, with a bachelor's and master's in the nineties, back when I thought I'd have all the answers by the time I reached fifty or sixty." Wend chuckled, then wondered where they'd learned to laugh at that, because it didn't feel real anymore. Maybe it never had. "I designed the sample bots when I went back for a doctorate in education in the twenties. I wanted citizen and student scientists to be able to collect samples fast and easy wherever they were. It's not the pinnacle of science or technology, but Pacific Tech later made, insured, and distributed hundreds of bots like mine. School groups can leverage micro-grants for various projects and gear based on having certified bots that take self-sealed samples that participating labs are guaranteed to accept. My thesis provided a roadmap for improving STEM education with simple tech programs more than anything to do with genetics. Most of my work since has been with the Marine Census Project, traveling to sites funded by various universities." They didn't mention that they generally earned the same pay as the students they worked with, as their education degree didn't translate into advancement as an educator.

"Wouldn't you rather be in the Arctic documenting what the first ice-free summer does to the marine microbiome there?" Viola made the question sound ordinary. To Wend it stretched like a test or a trap, but they tried not to dive down the rabbit hole of second-guessing.

After a slow breath of the cool creek-side air, Wend replied simply, "Not many people predicted that would hit this year, but groups trying to save or document the last polar bears and seals up there have been taking samples for the Marine Census Project for years. The microbiomes from their samples feed into files I track."

Viola huffed. "Sounds like you don't care much for megafauna."

"Polar bears and seals are cute, and losing the ice they live on is tragic. But melting permafrost upsets all the local ecosystems and releases methane with thirty times the impact of carbon dioxide on sea level rise and climate change in general." Wend cringed at pictures of sickly polar bears, but the loss of thousands of tiny species they hadn't had time to appreciate or even record left them bereft. "Besides, it's hard to race to the Arctic when I'm trying to travel with zero emissions and live as close to carbon neutral as I can, as you said you do in a bio I read." Unlike the Galapagos, Aotearoa, and Hawai'i, the Marquesas didn't have the international capital or local infrastructure to support all-electric or hydrogen-fueled zero emissions plane flights yet. Nor did they have carbon capture or biofuel options to supply long-distance flights. They met minimum international standards by offering fuel shipped in from France, along with other supplies. "There's no way to fly out of here without adding to the problem. You may have noticed I hitched a lift on a fishing vessel and then swam to your boat."

Viola listed to the left as she emerged from another scramble between rocks. Her joints hung loose, as if ready to leap or shift at a moment's notice. "Swear to me you'll only write about science and will never write a biography or exposé about 'reclusive photographer Viola Yang.'"

"I promise," Wend said as they landed on springy grass that trailed out from the rocks. Writing an exposé had never occurred to them, and they considered whether rambling about their education had made a bad impression or helped. Then they wondered if a few weeks of swapping stories on a boat would be enough to understand Viola's worries or answer the questions Wend most cared about.

Without looking back, Viola said, "I guess you still like hammocks, since you brought your own. You have any opinions on fruit? If you're joining the crew, we'll need to add what we can to our fresh food stores before setting out tomorrow."

All the breath left Wend's body, as they basked in the sudden relaxing of tense muscles and vigilance. Wend took their inclusion as crew to be their greatest success of the day.

2

WHEN THEY ROWED the dinghy back out to the *Nuovo Mar*, Aljon made them dunk all the fruit in the ocean before passing it aboard. Wend almost dropped a heavy stalk with over twenty bananas when fat black bugs swam off in all directions amidst the floating grit. They dunked the bananas a couple more times.

The crew—all three of them—ate dinner in the tidy white cockpit from metal bowls that stacked to form lids for each other. Aljon served up crepes stuffed with banana, papaya, starfruit, and guava. On the side, he provided small fish cakes. Viola smiled and hummed at him, then leaned toward Wend with raised eyebrows and a questioning noise.

"This is really good," Wend offered between bites.

Aljon nodded and looked away, but Viola said, "Don't sound so surprised."

Wend wondered how other people would have said it even as they noticed that Aljon wasn't eating any fish cakes himself. "I never had crepes on a boat before or anything this fancy." Wend struggled to express the appreciation they truly felt without misstepping again. "Maybe it comes from sailing with scientists, but even the research base on Nuku Hiva tended more to nutrition than taste."

"Well, Aljon has strong opinions about nutrition as well." Viola rested her knee against Aljon's as she once again spoke for the younger man. "I'd advise you not to ask about the vat of spirulina he grows under the dinghy when it's stowed on deck. Basically, if you don't like what we eat at sea, you're flat out of luck. That goes for a lot of things. You'll see, it's like living in the past—old school skipper, full keel boat, no nav, no motor, no luxuries."

Such a warning delivered over delicious crepes didn't make much sense to Wend, but they were used to the world not making sense. "Don't worry, I'm delighted to be on board a zero emissions boat." To Aljon, Wend added, "And I'm happy to help cook if you want."

Aljon only nodded again. It was unclear whether he'd welcome help or not. Wend's mind strobed though emotional images: being kicked repeatedly while babysitting by a kid who hated their tuna salad but wouldn't say why, having weevils fly up from a bag of flour the first time they tried to make pancakes for their mom, being laughed at for not taking the seeds out when asked to dice bell peppers at their first research posting. It wasn't as if they had much to offer in the kitchen or to appease Aljon.

Each time Wend changed locations, no matter how they tried to be their true self, they came out a little different. A week ago, Wend hadn't known they'd risk everything to swim onto Viola's boat. Aljon hadn't figured in their plan at all, and they clearly hadn't made a good first impression, flopping onto deck unannounced. Fear crept cold under Wend's skin at the thought of spending two or three weeks trapped with someone who might grow to hate them. Not that it hadn't happened before, but Wend wanted desperately to bridge that divide. They had no idea how.

"Why don't you tell us a story?" Viola prompted.

The plan Wend had formed ahead of time for communicating with Viola via stories hadn't taken into account the third person on their voyage. None of Wend's research had mentioned him, and without knowing his background, it was hard to guess which stories might be well received at this point.

The version of Wend that had hitched a ride on a passing boat and swam into La Baie des Vierges this morning had chosen to take risks. Now they had no way out. Wend took a deep breath and sent their mind back through the years. They'd give Viola the honesty they'd promised, hint at the questions they hoped to answer, and watch for any sign of how to make things right with Aljon. Another early story came to mind, one that described being different but also finding connection. It felt right, or perhaps some greater insight drew them there. They would trust it. After eating the bite of guava and crepe they'd saved for last, Wend began.

"After leaving Hawai'i, my mom and I ended up in Sacramento, California. Before I was born, she'd worked at the California Department of Motor Vehicles, in the main office downtown. I didn't understand until later how hard it was to fight her way back up through the ranks after four years away. She'd been the highest-level woman in management at the DMV before she left to have me." Wend thought about pointing out to Viola that it was money saved from over ten years of working at the DMV that had paid for the yacht mentioned earlier, but it seemed unfair to Aljon, alluding to a story he hadn't heard. Besides, Wend had enough to communicate without further asides or complications.

"All I understood when she went back to work was that she left me at Walnut Tree Preschool all day. Nothing there made sense. I went from living mostly outside with few kids my own age to everyone else being my age and knowing everything about rules and a strict schedule.

"My first week there, someone decided I had cooties. The kids who pointed and squealed in my direction radiated yellow to white, like flames burning my skin if I passed too close." Stiffening at the ghostly burn, Wend added, "I still associate certain feelings with those moments and those kids. But I was only four and didn't have the range of words from disapproval to contempt."

Viola's lips tightened, but she stayed silent. Aljon stared down, focused on his last bites of food, slow and pensive.

"A teacher sat me down in a quiet corner one day and asked if I were 'angry' or 'sad.'

"The burning on my skin had eased with distance. But my throat was too tight to swallow, to answer. My eyes squinted. Not with tears. I didn't know the word for that feeling either." Eventually Wend would call that a belly full of tears, but that came later, a different story. This one was hard enough to tell.

"The longer I failed to answer, the brighter and hotter the teacher became, until I was burning again.

"I turned my face from the heat and asked, 'Why? Are you mad?'

"She said, 'I'm not mad or angry. I'm trying to help you.'

"Static pricked across my burning skin. She was lying. I felt the heat of her anger and didn't know why she would lie about that. It confused me. I couldn't tell if she was lying about wanting to help.

"I shook my head and managed to say I was 'done.' Maybe I only said the one word. Maybe it would have been different if I'd said I was confused. I didn't know yet that other people couldn't feel or see lies or anger. I thought it must burn everyone the same.

"She told me to sit quietly until I was ready to talk about it.

"I didn't have the words. I sat rigid in a corner. The clothes I had to wear to school dug in at my waist and had huge, lumpy seams that ran down my ribs and legs. I kept shrugging my shoulders to make it less awful.

That only made me feel confined in a bad way. The tag in the back rubbed at a bump in my spine until it felt like it would bleed." Wend shrugged in remembered discomfort and their rash guard settled smoothly over their skin with serged seams, no tag, and the smoothest eco-friendly fabric available.

"I sat all alone until it was 'outside time.'

"Outside, I ran as far and as fast as I could. I sang the 'Chitty, Chitty, Bang, Bang' song loudly as I ran. When the words were only gasps, I climbed to the top of what we called a 'jungle gym' back then. It was a dome shape made of metal bars. No one else was using it. I sat on top and sang as loud as I could."

An explosive feeling of escape via shouting and loudness that Wend could only embrace in memory afforded them vicarious release now. They took a deep breath, half immersed in that moment, before continuing.

"A different teacher came over and said, 'We don't shout.'

"I replied, 'I'm singing.'

"She shook her hair in a long black wave that caught my eye. 'We don't sing like that.'

"I tried to guess what was wrong with the song. I liked Disney movies. I wondered if preschool could have a rule against Disney. I tried singing 'Oh! Susanna.' My mom had made it about coming to California rather than Louisiana when she taught me, so I figured it would be okay to sing in a California preschool.

"The teacher shook her head again. Her hair made a whispery, rippling sound, and she said, 'Still too loud.'

"That was useful information. I sang quieter. But I'd heard her hair swoosh. That meant I hadn't been singing too loud.

"She walked away without projecting any emotions I could feel.

"I sat on top of the metal structure swinging my legs beneath the bars and singing quietly to myself."

Vulnerable in the memory, Wend had forgotten their audience. When they glanced again at Viola and Aljon, they almost expected to feel the others' emotions buffeting their skin. Instead, Viola leaned calmly forward. Aljon set aside his empty plate. Wend couldn't read anything from their expressions but retreated back into the story, skipping ahead a bit.

"After that, hardly a minute passed without some problem I couldn't foresee. I sat in the wrong place at snack. I moved the wrong blocks and the other kids burned white hot with something like anger, something I might later call disdain mixed with rejection. Shrieks about 'cooties' kept me away from the puppets."

Wend hoped they'd conveyed enough of their childhood state of mind for the next part to be meaningful, but they couldn't force their eyes up to check on their audience. "By the time the teachers finally let us outside again, I was happy to sit by myself in the sand. I sank my hands into the dry grains. It scratched a little, not like wet sand in the ocean. But it was cool underneath. When I lifted handfuls, the sand poured through my fingers sort of like water.

"Some other kids had buckets and shovels. I didn't know if those were for everyone at the preschool or if they brought them from home. When kids started talking about the beach, I said, 'My mom and I used to live by the ocean.'

"They didn't answer me. One said to the others, 'Let's move over there.'

"I felt ashamed, like I was always wrong somehow. But most of the time I didn't know how.

"After they moved to the far corner of the sandbox, the next closest kid looked at me. His eyes met mine for a moment. It felt like a touch. I cringed and looked down.

"A while later, I noticed he was inching closer and closer to me. He had a metal scoop that he pushed through the sand to make a line. It could have been a river if filled with water.

"I heard him making a soft humming sound as he pushed the metal scoop.

"I pushed my fist through the sand to hollow out lines around me. I tried to make a sound like his humming.

"When his scoop came within a few inches of my lines he said, 'Want to connect our roads?'

"I said, 'Okay.' Not knowing what else to do, I let him run his scoop across one of the lines my fist had drawn.

"He started humming again as he ran across more of my lines.

"I sat in the middle like a stone that sent ripples out across the water. He drew lines inward like the rays of the sun. When there was no place left for him to move without messing up one set of lines or another, he said, 'My name is Mathew.'

"'I'm Wend,' I said. 'Do you want to be friends?'

"'Yes!' he said a bit louder. Then he quietly added, 'They like me less than you.'

"'Do you know why?' I asked. He wore pants. I wore shorts. His shirt had buttons. Mine did not. His skin was pale. Mine was tanned.

"His answer surprised me. 'You say "my mom and I" a lot. I stopped saying that. They teased me for not having a dad.'

"'Why?' I asked. When he shrugged, I said, 'I don't like lying.'

"Mathew jabbed his scoop into the sand. 'I don't lie. I say "my family." My mom and me are a family.'

"Then I understood. Kids who lived with two parents thought it was bad to only have one. I hadn't thought of my mom and me as a family yet, but it was obvious we were. 'You're right. It's not a lie. Thanks for telling me.'

"'Friends tell each other stuff.'

"After that, we talked every day. We talked in the sandbox. We talked hanging upside down on the bars.

"I told Mathew about how I could hold sea cucumbers.

"He told me, 'I talk to cats. I say meow or mew lots of different ways.' He demonstrated, and some of his sounds could have come from a real cat. 'Some cats like it. Sometimes they'll take turns saying meow to me.'

"'Have you seen that commercial where the cats sing, 'Meow, meow, meow, meow . . .'" I sang it for him, and he began to sing along.

"When we stopped to breathe, he said, 'I love that commercial.'

"We sang it in the sandbox and on the bars. We sang it while skipping around the playground and holding hands. Mathew was the first person, other than my mom, that I liked holding hands with. Sometimes other kids said we both had cooties or tried to trip us or roll balls in our way. Sometimes they said meaner things and burned with fiery colors, but never white hot. And we sang only loud enough to hear each other. The teachers didn't get mad at us for that. I noticed the teachers didn't complain as much when Mathew and I were together as when either of us was alone.

"We tried to be together as much as possible. Mathew wasn't at Walnut Tree Preschool as many hours as I was, but we helped each other figure out words and rules that people didn't explain. Mathew said it was like talking to cats. If you tried different ways of talking or acting, you could see what different people reacted to best. We both agreed to keep singing the meow commercial and skipping around holding hands, even if other kids didn't like it. Because we liked it.

"I didn't have words for it yet, but I trusted Mathew. There were many things we didn't understand about each other, but he saw me for who I really was. Maybe it was easier at that age, but he was my first true friend."

Wend looked up to see Aljon studying them. He looked away immediately, but his wide-eyed openness, as if he'd been caught up in the story, lingered like an afterimage in Wend's mind. They hoped his attention was a good thing. Wend didn't expect any visible reaction from Viola by that point but couldn't help checking. Viola gave only a nod that seemed to mean Wend should continue. After facing so many risks in one day to reach this point, Wend decided to offer up the corner piece of their puzzle.

"By the end of my year at Walnut Tree, I trusted Mathew enough to tell him one of my big secrets. We were sitting at the top of the dome-shaped metal bars that no one else came near if we were there.

"'I think that I can fly after dark,' I admitted." Wend watched Viola for any reaction as they said it.

She didn't even twitch.

Wend pushed forward with the story, unable to look to the other side to see Aljon. "Mathew met my eyes for a moment. We didn't do that much. He asked me, 'How?'

"'Sometimes it's like swimming,' I said. 'I have this way of pulling through water called frog paddling. At first I thought it only worked for flying at night because there's more water in the air then. But it turns out it only works if I fall asleep first. So maybe only the part of me that can't sleep gets to fly. It doesn't make my hair or sleep clothes damp. I wasn't sure for a long time whether I was only dreaming that I could fly, but I've seen some things I couldn't have seen otherwise.'

"'Like what?' Mathew asked.

"'When I fly to the grocery store or the gas station, the lights are still on when everything else is dark. And the streetlights stay on all night, too. Did you ever wonder about that?'

"'I can see a streetlight from my bedroom window,' Mathew said. 'It makes up for not having a nightlight like I did at my old house.'

"That was an interesting point I hadn't considered before. Some people had bedroom windows that faced streets. Mine faced our backyard, and beyond that, more backyards.

"'Yesterday, my family drove down a street that I'd only seen from the air before, while flying.' We said 'my family' when talking to each other because Mathew insisted it was good practice. 'The street went up a hill and curved away exactly as I expected it to. But I'd never been on it before. I couldn't have known how that street curved if my flying at night wasn't real.'

"Mathew nodded and said, 'I wish I could fly.'

"'Maybe you can learn,' I said.

"'I don't know how to swim either.'

"I tried to teach him to frog paddle by lying on our stomachs on top of the bars. I don't know if he learned enough for it to work for swimming or for flying. I think he believed that I could fly at night sometimes, but he never managed to do it.

"I told him about seeing and feeling when people were angry or lying or some other bad things. I'd only recently figured out that most people didn't see and feel such things.

"He asked, 'Do you see colors or feel heat or static from me?'

"'Never,' I said.

"'What about when I say I don't miss my dad?'

"'Nope,' I shook my head.

"'Then maybe you only feel it when you can guess someone is lying. Because I'm pretty sure that I'm lying when I say that.'

"I didn't know how to respond. I never missed my dad, as I still thought of him then. I didn't know why I hadn't felt that lie from Mathew. Maybe it didn't work with him, or maybe I only felt certain types of lies. Matt's disbelief devastated me. My mom hadn't believed me when I told her about sensing lies or about flying. That had hurt a lot, but I thought Mathew would be different.

"As we sat silently on the bars, I could feel sparks of yellow heat coming from Mathew. I knew he was mad at me, at least a little. But I didn't know why. I didn't want to tell him I could feel it, so I didn't say anything."

It wasn't how Wend had planned to end the story, but their throat was tight with equal parts hurt and emptiness. They still missed Mathew after all this time.

"Huh," Viola said, a while after Wend stopped talking. "Have you heard of synesthesia? I'm told I had that as a kid, although I barely remember."

The offer of connection, of recognition, was enough to push Wend into speaking again. "I've read some descriptions of color-mood synesthesia that are similar to what I experienced, but maybe not the same." The sun was setting, and Wend contemplated the oranges and pinks in the sky as if those hues could also share stories. They didn't burn or feel angry at all. "I stopped seeing the colors in the years after that. Some people with synesthesia say they lose it or parts change as they grow. I still sometimes feel like people's negative emotions radiate out from their skin to mine. I know there are plenty of subconscious mechanisms that could come into play, but . . . Did you ever feel anything like that?"

Viola paused long enough to think but showed no discomfort, perhaps even smiling as she leaned closer to Wend. "Not that I remember. The first portraits I drew, when I was five or six, showed people with impossibly big heads, the expressions on their faces never the same on both sides. When asked, I insisted that the people I drew never felt just one way. What you were saying about that first teacher, who asked if you were sad or mad, made me think of that."

Each person was different, but this was the sort of connection Wend had hoped to build with their stories. Finding commonalities one piece at a time. Before they could follow up, possibly ask if Viola ever had touch sensitivities or flying dreams, Aljon interrupted.

"Whatever." He tossed off the word in a tone he'd used before, and Wend couldn't tell if it was bored, sarcastic, or if something in the discussion had touched a nerve. As he stood and started to gather the dishes, Viola rose as well.

Wend bent to help tidy up but Viola said, "Let him do that. You can help me check the sails, solar, and hydro to make sure we're ready to sail tomorrow. You'll need to learn all our systems to work as crew, let alone take watch."

Aljon nodded. Wend would have preferred to help him, but it was clear Viola expected to have her way as skipper. Aljon didn't object, so Wend didn't either.

The solar panels were familiar to Wend. All four had been deployed during the day, latched to railings or jammers and feeding any power not needed immediately into a state-of-the-art silicon lithium-ion battery.

Waving toward the battery, Viola said, "People call these batteries sustainable, but the best I can say is they're less toxic and three times as powerful as previous versions."

"I have two small panels to charge my sample bot, but they could feed into your batteries the rest of the time." Wend brought the panels from their drybag, and Viola made a place to store them with the rest of the solar power system in the port-side cockpit locker.

Then Viola showed Wend the hookups and what they could check from above on the purple hydro turbine pulled behind the *Nuovo Mar*. "This is our newest addition, with sturdy brackets to withstand heavy seas." Viola pointed with her foot. "The pitch of the impeller should be adjusted for our expected speed. Right now, it's optimized for 5 to 7 knots, which would generate at least 240 amp-hours on a 12-volt system per day. That make sense to you?"

Wend nodded, eager to demonstrate technical competence. "My sample bot uses 100 watts for three seconds each time it takes and seals a sample, which is negligible compared to that. Your hydro turbine must be great at higher speeds or when you can't get solar."

Viola gave no indication of appreciating the compliment or anything else as she walked ahead checking sheets and lines. "You'll learn what you need about the rigging fast enough tomorrow. In an ideal world, all we'd need would be sails to move and solar or hydro for lights, GPS receiver, and cooking. Aljon's amazing at conserving power in the galley, so he makes all decisions there. If we were only sailing around French Polynesia or only around Hawaiʻi, that's all we'd carry. But I wanted to keep my options open, even before this trip around the world with Aljon. I'll show you the choices and compromises I've made. If you don't like them, I might even drop you off on land rather than make you swim ashore tomorrow."

Viola had made a similar joke earlier, before accepting Wend as crew. It hit harder now, after Wend had expended nearly all their emotional energy trying to fit in. Still struggling to decipher the meaning behind the words, Wend followed Viola down the stairs from the cockpit. Without comment, they passed the small galley, quarter berth, folded up chart table, and two berths on opposite sides that clearly looked slept in. In the thirty-one-foot boat, all of that shared one room, like the smallest of small studio apartments.

With a low hand motion, Viola said, "Starboard side's the head with a composting toilet and a foot pump for the sink. Other side's the hanging locker." Wend's wetsuit had already been hung beside two others, one of them a shorty.

Viola opened up a tightly but neatly packed forward locker and flatly pointed out the remaining electronic devices: GPS (with a spare in a sealed steel box), a self-sealed GPIRB emergency beacon, a small SSB receiver to pick up weather and marine warnings, a handheld VHF radio for busy ports, and electronic charts and anchorage information (accessible via Viola's phone when it was turned on, although Viola swore the paper copies they carried were more trustworthy). They didn't carry several common but power-intensive instruments, such as electric autopilot, radar, or AIS. Short of activating the GPIRB to summon search and rescue, they would be unable to communicate with the outside world once out at sea.

"Too primitive for you?" Viola asked.

"Not at all." Wend hadn't expected even that much tech on board.

Viola nodded. "I'll show you the backup system that a friend insists I carry, but I don't ever intend to use it and refuse to plan any trip that I couldn't make without it." Viola radiated annoyance, almost as clearly as Wend had felt it as a kid. Wend was curious enough to ignore the discomfort. In the forward locker, next to a bank of rechargeable batteries, sat a well-secured drybag containing a heat-sealed plastic bin with something metal and shiny inside, about the size of a 50-gallon aquarium.

When Viola frowned silently at the device for a full minute, Wend asked, "Do you want to tell me what it is?"

"A hydrogen fuel cell with a self-contained generating system, including its own desalination." Viola pointed vaguely to one side for the fuel cell and the other for the water siphon. It was hard to see any details through two layers of protective coverings. "Add seawater and solar charging and you can store clean power with only pure water, salt, and oxygen as byproducts."

Wend thought most skippers would brag about such a device. Wend had never heard of such a compact generator.

"The energy loss going in is less than with a battery and coming out is less than with a combustion engine. It won't lose charge in between the way a battery would." She patted the bin. "The greatest drawback to even the best new batteries is their weight. For skippers who want a backup engine when there's no wind, battery weight becomes prohibitive for a long voyage. For those using electricity only for lights, galley, and minimal equipment, smaller batteries can recharge from solar panels or wind or hydro turbines like ours. Those vessels and others that stay close to shore were the first to go green. That's how I sail."

Wend knew they were missing something, but Viola seemed reluctant to explain. "You said the fuel cell is more efficient than batteries and you have a way to recharge it."

Viola's hand tightened on the bin, and her knuckles turned white. "Hydrogen fuel cells became more common as nanoparticles increased their performance and efficiency. As transportation sectors shifted toward zero emissions worldwide, increased sales to high end markets brought prices down for older, bulkier fuel cells. Now used hydrogen fuel cells, still four or five times lighter than the newest batteries, let alone the older marine standbys, cost a thousand dollars, maybe two thousand depending on a boat's needs. The drawback is that they have to be refilled with compressed hydrogen, which isn't available for love or money in small ports like Fatu Hiva, and you can't make your own at sea if you run out. At least, most people can't."

Viola stared at the bin as if gazing upon a dead lover. A feeling of profound loss enveloped her, jarring Wend with the contrast to Viola's dispassionate speech. "Electrolysis is generally more expensive than reforming hydrocarbons to generate hydrogen fuel, and part of that is the need for purified water. But research fifteen years ago showed copper layers could repel corrosion to make direct generation from seawater economical. It's only cost-effective for small batches." Viola's voice hardened even further as she said, "In most developed areas, it's easier to refill your fuel cell commercially than to produce your own fuel. But on a boat, having the ability to make your own could be the difference between life and death. As a bonus, the byproducts include drinking water. This could be the technology that makes zero emissions long-distance sailing safe and economical."

"That's amazing." Wend believed the obvious needed to be stated in this case. "I've heard of government subsidies and programs to create larger systems for military and commercial vessels, but I didn't think there was any such thing for smaller boats."

"There isn't." Viola sighed and unclenched her fingers, shifting to pet the still-sealed unit instead. "This is a prototype my friend made and shopped around to philanthropists and NGOs. Her pitch was that anyone who committed to making 10,000 of them could bring the price down below $1000 for this generator. Then long-distance sailors like me could buy them as backup systems. She included dozens of other uses, from struggling coastal communities with uncertain supply chains to emergency services in areas endangered by flooding and sea level rise. Can you imagine having these available after a hurricane wiped out an island's entire power grid?"

Images of devastation at Marine Census sites from Indonesia to Puerto Rico cascaded through Wend's mind, recollections that made their eyes sting. Aid agencies often provided solar panels that could in theory be protected and re-deployed after storms and flooding, once the clouds cleared. But dams and wind farms weren't as easy to protect and restore. The one resource all the hardest hit areas had in common was an abundance of salt water. Generators the size of fish tanks might not save a nation, but if local sailors carried the generators for emergencies at sea anyway, most of those would be safe ashore when the worst storms hit.

"I'm guessing her pitch didn't succeed." Wend stared at the device, wanting to study blueprints or ask Viola's friend a thousand questions. Wend's sample bot was a simplified economy version barely resembling higher tech marine robots. This hydrogen generator represented a step forward, promising the full benefit of hydrogen fuel on a smaller scale for users who'd never have access otherwise.

"She stirred up some enthusiasm for a while. Never enough or from someone in a position to make a commitment on that scale. She left it with me when she swore off sailing forever." Viola's voice was dead flat again and didn't invite the sort of questions Wend wanted to ask.

"That must be the crew member you lost. Sorry." Wend knew better than to seek further details about the unnamed friend but went ahead and asked, "Why are you so reluctant to use it?"

Viola closed the locker and leaned against it. "The same reason you wouldn't fly to the Arctic. I sail a zero emissions boat and try to lead a zero emissions life. If I want other people, skippers, companies, and agencies to commit to the same, I can't cheat and use a system most of them can't have. Especially when I wish everyone could share this one-of-a-kind technology." Viola patted the tightly sealed device forlornly, and Wend remembered their discussion of dying polar bears earlier. Viola cared about the generator as much as Wend cared for unacknowledged microbes lost to greenhouse gas effects and rising sea levels. "She included instructions for converting the impeller on a hydro turbine into a propeller that could drive the dinghy or maybe even a boat this size for a short time. It could save lives. But like the GPS or the SSB, a lightning strike could take it out. And while it's designed for marine use, a crack could let in seawater. There's a reason the purists say never to trust electronics on the ocean.

Still, I promised my friend I'd keep this onboard and unseal it if it ever came down to life or death."

"I can respect that promise and your dedication to live carbon free without advantages others don't share," Wend said. The reasoning wasn't what Wend had expected from the wealthy globetrotting photographer. It inspired a whole new set of questions—that were probably better not asked, at least not yet.

Viola raised her eyebrows, opened her eyes wider than before, and blinked slowly. Her expression smoothed to neutral. "Well, that's a relief." Wend thought her tone was sarcastic, but let that go as Viola continued, "If you're staying, let's find a safe place to stow your stuff. You can hang your hammock between the shroud and backstay for tonight, but when we're under sail you'll have to make do with the quarter berth."

Wend was grateful to be accepted as crew and offered a bed at all. They didn't worry how it came across when they asked, "What did I do to deserve all of this?"

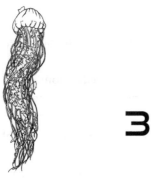

3

AS A SEA URCHIN, Wend was ravenous. The pale dead reef abounded with tasty brown macroalgae. The dinoflagellates that humans called *Gambierdiscus toxicus* lurked invisible to the light-sensitive cells in their tube feet. Light was only relevant for hiding. It hardly mattered when Wend-urchin feasted many body-widths deep below the ocean's surface.

Their tube feet worked better for walking and sampling than seeing anyway. The toxins in these dinoflagellates would not poison the urchin as they would a human. They barely affected the chemicals—the taste—as the urchin sensed and devoured huge swaths of plentiful algae. The milder taste of carotenoids translated to Wend's overmind as orange, hinting at their appearance, at least in brighter light.

Vast spans of dead reef offered excellent feeding grounds as the urchin's formerly favored seagrass beds became harder to find. Slurping rapidly, the algae stroked the sensory ring around their hidden mouth. The delightful texture triggered nerve responses all along their five radial canals and branched outward through finer nerves to make tube feet and spines alike twitch in response. Debris caught on their orangey spines rippled like tiny flags in the warm seawater, and Wend-urchin enjoyed the differing sensations derived from the fluttering bits that caused humans to dub their species "decorator urchins."

Wend-urchin used their stalk-like pedicellariae to remain attached to the algae. Their tube feet held onto the reef and captured food. They were always hungry, so very hungry, but as long as the dead reefs offered copious opportunities for red and brown algae blooms, Wend-urchin would be content and well fed.

A movement unlike the flutter of algae stopped their hundreds of tube feet, instinctively, in their tracks. The taste of octopus nearby could not masquerade as food, no matter how the tentacles grasping upward might camouflage for those with eyes. Long limbs and a bulbous head passed quickly upward in a rush of current, seeking cowrie, not prickly urchin. Wend-urchin barely changed direction before continuing their own grazing.

As they entered an area where two others of their kind fed, Wend-urchin was briefly anxious. But it was impossible to hyperventilate in this form. With respiration happening through their tube feet as they took in water and food, there existed no physiological parallel to accommodate Wend's more human reactions. They continued to feed; a pleasant rush of chemicals, fullness, rightness spread through them as they consumed algae along with seawater. They could live like this. The two new urchins need not be a threat to their survival or sustenance.

A spiky sense of companionship and shared algae shifted into startled, clinging tube feet—hands—as a steady flow of nutrients transformed into Viola calling out, "Sun is shining, time to get sailing."

Wend had slept well in their hammock cocoon. Any night when they dreamt as an ocean invertebrate provided escape from their annoying human spine and the multiple wakings it caused most nights. Now they peeked out from three layers of high-tech, lightweight, mostly eco-friendly fabric to find Viola studying them, head tilted.

"Is that mummy bag waterproof?" she asked.

As Viola's eyes traced the straps that held the outer sleep sack to the hammock, Wend wished they felt as settled in their waking world as with the two urchins feeding alongside them in their dream. "The outer layer that fastens to the hammock is. The inner is moisture wicking. The center is meant to retain body heat without overheating even when soaking wet."

"I want to include it in a photo," Viola announced as she turned away. "I won't sell or post any picture where you're identifiable without permission, but I have the right to any photos I take on my boat or while we're diving."

Wend disliked being in pictures, but those terms were better than they'd expected when asking to crew for a professional photographer.

Without waiting for a reply, Viola ordered, "Practice with the safety grabs to haul yourself in if you're ever caught outside in bad weather. Always puke over the downwind side, and tie yourself to the boat if you reach that point. Generally, you shouldn't be on deck at night without telling someone. For now, get this cleared and secured, and we'll be anchors aweigh."

The clang of a metal spoon striking a pan signaled that Aljon expected them to eat breakfast first. Wend wolfed down an eggy scramble and a banana before thanking the otherwise silent chef and getting to work.

They were soon underway with Viola shouting "short tack to starboard" and "sheet that mainsail in" from the helm with one hand on the tiller.

The mainsail served to maneuver out of La Baie des Vierges. While Wend didn't know much about a gaff rig, they knew the spar at the top of the four-sided sail was the gaff. The one at the bottom was still called the boom. The single mast on the cutter was also rigged for two staysails, the outermost called the foresail. Viola had assured Wend that was all they needed to know for now.

Together, Aljon and Viola performed the slow dance of leaving an anchorage under minimal wind with a grace born of familiarity. Wend stayed out of their way and took the opportunity to appreciate the shadowy bay, silently saying goodbye to the palm trees and towering volcanic rocks they hadn't had time to explore.

"Stop admiring the verges and tie that line to the starboard pin rod," Viola called.

Wend secured the indicated line, before asking, "What's a 'verges'? I don't know that term."

Catching the glare Aljon shot at Viola, Wend braced for derision. But they'd decided years ago to ignore the power plays that led to not asking questions.

Viola rolled her eyes and sent Aljon to set the staysail. "Missionaries renamed this anchorage 'La Baie des Vierges' meaning 'Bay of the Virgins' because they disapproved of the previous and much more apt 'La Baie des Verges.'" She gestured at the tall spires of rock to starboard as they exited the bay. When Wend failed to react, Viola clarified, "One letter in French is the difference between virgins and penises."

And one word would change how Wend saw those soaring pinnacles forever. At least Viola didn't laugh at Wend, just grinned like they were sharing a joke. Aljon didn't smile or laugh. His blank expression left Wend wondering, but the wind on their face as they left the shelter of the 'verges' and the beauty of Fatu Hiva was too sweet to ignore. Soon they were under full sail with the wind just forward of the beam.

"Weather forecast is clear," Viola volunteered as she slathered her face with sunscreen. They all wore long sleeves, polarized glasses, and well-secured hats, but when Viola set a tarp to shade part of the cockpit, everyone settled underneath when they could. The UV index maxed out across French Polynesia for all the weeks Wend worked there. Both air and water temperatures hovered around 27 degrees Celsius or 80 Fahrenheit. Wend wasn't any more tied to a measurement system than to a fixed address, but they were never fond of extremes.

"Want to play cards or tell a story?" Viola asked.

"I want to make pie," Aljon announced before taking off below decks.

"He'll bring stuff up here if he wants to be social."

Wend sifted through memories for a story that wasn't too serious for such a bright day and where it wouldn't matter if Aljon joined them in the middle.

"After Walnut Tree Preschool and a year of kindergarten, I tested into what would later be called a magnet school. Mostly I enjoyed the field trips, like staying overnight at an old fort or spending an entire week in Yosemite. We had math enrichment every week, where topics like basic algebra and standard deviations made for fun word problems, much like the creativity exercises that were popular at the time, where we'd brainstorm unusual ways to use a brick or an umbrella.

"I didn't have a new best friend or any way to keep in touch with Mathew, but I did have a new bully. She was two years older and named Nel. She had a way of twisting my arm up behind my back that she claimed was inescapable. I got out of it once in third grade, but it hurt for days afterward. She told me I was 'weird' and 'stupid' and would 'never have any friends.' I didn't understand why she targeted me. But even in a school filled with smart alecks and outside-the-box thinkers, people kept letting me know I was weird, pretty much every few minutes if I interacted with anyone at all." Wend pushed down the swell of bile that rose from their stomach to their throat. This wasn't intended to be that sort of a story.

They pretended to watch the billowing mainsail while checking for any reaction.

Viola casually scanned the ocean ahead, with one hand on the tiller and occasional glances at the compass, GPS, or a chart mounted beside her. She might as well have been listening to an audiobook for all the recognition she gave Wend.

"In third grade, our class received an extra week of education about 'Native Americans' because three students, meaning at least ten percent of the class, met the state definitions of 'Native American.' I was proud when my grandma's people, the Seminole, were mentioned. That's when I started reading up on them and learned about the baby hammocks. I also learned about the Trail of Tears. One thing led to another, and I dug in at the school and public library, finding out about the Holocaust, Apartheid, slavery and all sorts of bad things people had done to other people.

"One boy in my class, Robert, said something I thought was racist during the week that we studied Native Americans. In hindsight, I realize I didn't understand racism. Later I'd revise everything I believed about being Seminole. Whatever DNA I did or didn't have, I never had a claim on that culture or community. But in third grade, it was the strongest identity I had, and I set out to educate Robert.

"One day, while I was following Robert and testing out my latest arguments, Nel came after us both. I ran for the far side of the upper grade building. Robert followed me. When I looped back to the younger kids' side and hid in an upright giant tire, Robert hid in the other side of it.

"We were both panting. His cheeks were very pink. The rest of his face was so pale it almost glowed in the darkness of the tire." Wend glanced up apologetically. "That's how I saw it at the time." Their memories didn't change as Wend did. They hoped Viola would understand, but her face remained passive.

"So I blurted in a way that usually got me into trouble, 'What makes you so white?'

"'I'm albino,' he answered and then froze and closed his eyes tight. For the first time I empathized with him, because I knew he was wishing he could disappear and not have said that. 'My parents told me to keep it secret, because some people think it's a curse.'

"All I wanted was to keep the conversation going, and we were trapped together in a very small space, hiding from the same bully. 'I mostly don't believe in curses, although I can't prove they don't exist. Most people say space aliens aren't real, but there are old images carved in stone in South America that seem to show alien astronauts. There are reports the US government hid parts of a spaceship that crashed in Roswell, New Mexico. So I think aliens could be real. It's pretty hard to prove anything definitely isn't real.'

"Robert stared at me across the dim interior of that giant tire. 'I want to believe in aliens.'

"'Me, too.'

"Robert slowly became my friend, but not like Mathew. I never felt that sort of connection.

"He didn't tell his parents about me, so he didn't have to tell them I knew he was albino. I didn't tell my mom much about Robert either. She'd been diagnosed with depression after her boss forced her to go see a counselor. I thought hearing about Robert and curses, as well as all the bad things done to Black, Jewish, Indigenous, and other people might make her feel worse. That was also when I fully took over cooking and cleaning our house, since my mom wasn't doing much of either anymore. I didn't tell anyone about that, not even Robert."

Wend paused, not knowing why they'd thought this story light enough for a sunny day at sea. Their face heated as they worried none of their stories would fit this setting and audience. Aljon hadn't returned. Viola stared out to sea, with occasional glances at the compass and GPS. The *Nuovo Mar* had left land behind and entered a borderless space, surrounded by ocean. Wend rose and fell with the boat, powerless.

The familiar rhythm and smell of seawater seeped into Wend's thoughts and soothed them. There had been times in the past when they spoke to the ocean. They resolved to tell the story their way and see what came of it.

"I showed Robert my list of reasons for why I thought I might be an alien. You understand, that's what we called extraterrestrials." Wend was going to have to take Viola's lack of reaction as understanding for the terms used.

Then Viola shook her head. "I was there, you know. The Seventies. You're fine to tell the stories as they are."

Wend's arms released some tension and they felt momentarily disoriented.

"The list of reasons?" Viola prompted.

Wend nodded. "First on it was: Humans don't make sense to me. No matter how hard I try, I get funny looks. No one is interested when I tell them about things I find extremely interesting. The biggest tomboy in our school told me I couldn't be a tomboy because I sometimes wear dresses. I don't know what clothes have to do with it, since I only wear them to not be rude. Also, I can't imagine being part of a species that would allow slavery, the Holocaust, or Apartheid.

"Robert and I had talked a lot about my research by then, and I thought I'd convinced him not to be racist. He didn't object to that part of my list.

"Second, I listed: The characters most like me in stories are usually aliens or robots.

"Third: I have sniffles all the time but I don't get sick. I was told the sniffles might be an allergy, but I sniffle all year, so maybe I'm allergic to this planet. Also, when half our class had chicken pox, I didn't get it. When almost everyone on my school bus missed a day or two for a virus that caused a high fever, I didn't catch that either. I have never missed a day of school or run a fever, but still, I sniffle all year round.

"Of course, the idea that my near constant sniffles came from my mom's near constant smoking didn't occur to me until I left home for college and stopped sniffling. I don't imagine it occurred to Robert either.

"Fourth: Late one night, my mom said I wasn't really Seminole because the person on my birth certificate wasn't really my dad. She refused to tell me who else could be my dad, except that he was the only man she'd ever thought was a good person. That made me strongly suspect he could have been an alien, given what I thought of humans, but I wasn't sure if she was lying or joking in some way, and she denied the conversation later.

"That repudiated conversation started me thinking about my identity in ways I wouldn't put into words for decades. It wasn't just about not being claimed as Seminole in one way or another, but that other people shouldn't get to decide who was or wasn't my parent. But that's a whole other story.

"Fifth: My body bends more than others. In gymnastics, I figured out how to fall forward and roll all the way to backbend position. The teachers were horrified that I would break my neck. One of the teenage helpers said she'd seen someone do that before, but I think she was lying. I also got away from Nel once when she said no one who wasn't double jointed could get out of the arm lock she had me in. I got out of it, but there is no other evidence I'm double jointed."

Wend had never forgotten that childhood list. They'd hoped, especially after showing brief interest in it, that Viola would comment on parts or on ways she'd seen herself as different from others, even if some turned out to be false leads. But Viola was still staring out to sea. While Wend had mostly given up their childhood hypotheses that their sniffles, flexibility, or social differences might have extraterrestrial origins, they'd hoped Viola would volunteer some commonality, as she had about synesthesia and sensing lies. Stories were generally safer than questions, even if waiting for what others would volunteer left Wend starving for information. With the sort of conundrum Wend was facing, an open-ended approach might fill in areas they couldn't anticipate. After sixty-plus years, another week or three shouldn't matter much.

Viola finally opened her mouth to say something, but Wend never found out what. Aljon came up the stairs carrying two pie pans and a bladed device in a jar. He plopped down next to Viola and across from Wend before using his fist to rapidly pound the blades up and down, chopping nuts in the jar until they resembled coarse cookie crumbs. Wend couldn't help but stare at the carnage.

When Aljon began pressing the smashed nuts into a pie pan to form a crust, Viola said, "From the galley, I bet you heard Wend's story about bullies and childhood theories involving space aliens. Do you want to hear more or would you rather cook as a spectator sport?"

Aljon shrugged, and Viola gently kicked his foot. Then she tapped against the side of Wend's sandal and said, "Go ahead. Tell us more."

While the earlier lack of response had discouraged Wend, the way Viola knocked their foot the same as Aljon's and treated their storytelling as comparable to Aljon's cooking made Wend glad to oblige. "Robert tried to make his own list for why he might be an alien, but his theory rested on all albino people being related to aliens. We weren't sure if people would see that as better or worse than being cursed, so we both agreed not to tell anyone.

"Even when Robert stopped being my friend in fifth grade, he didn't tell people any of our ideas about aliens. He probably worried it would make him look bad, too. Some things he did to me after that should have seemed worse, but times were different, and that's another story.

"By fifth grade I'd also made a list of why I probably wasn't an alien. It referenced a life science textbook with fairly primitive language about genetics and different species not being able to interbreed. That seemed to rule out my mom being human and my dad not. I was also hit by a car while biking that year. There were x-rays and blood tests. I figured the doctor probably would have noticed if I were other than human."

"But you still weren't convinced?" Viola sounded amused, not dismissive. Her face gave away nothing that Wend could interpret.

"Anyone who could come up with over twenty extremely different ways to use a brick could come up with ways extraterrestrial or unknown tech might change the rules. So I made a list of why I still felt like an alien. I didn't know what it meant to be 'alienated,' but I was approaching adolescence by that point. No matter how well I managed to compensate and pass as normal, human individuals and society didn't fit well with me."

A single wrinkle deepened between Viola's brows. "You said your mom saw a counselor and was diagnosed with depression. Did anyone see you or suggest any diagnosis?"

Aljon's elbow bumped Viola's. It could have been an accident.

"Not then. My mom was ordered to see a counselor because of something that happened at work. I suspect it had as much to do with alcoholism as with depression or what was later labeled 'bipolar two.' But no, I never even saw a school counselor or nurse. As listed, I never got sick, aside from my near constant sniffles. Teachers and others called me 'hyper' in an offhand way, as people did back then. My mom warned them not to repeat it if she heard. So I never had any official diagnosis or label. But I wrote my lists, kept journals, and did my own forms of research. By fifth grade, I could have explained my neurodivergence better than any doctor, although I wouldn't hear the term 'neurodivergence' until the next century."

"And the part about not being accepted as a tomboy?"

Wend checked to make sure Aljon knew the term. A simple nod and half smile suggested more support than Wend expected.

Viola's questions were beginning to feel like an interrogation. Wend kept hoping she would volunteer similar memories, as she had about her early drawings, but Wend didn't know how to encourage that sort of sharing without feeling manipulative. "At the time, it stung like another rejection, invalidating another piece of who I was, losing another word. Later, it helped me to better appreciate this century and all the words the millennials added to public discussion. I don't think I understood how binary most people thought gender was until the word 'nonbinary' appeared on the scene. The first time I heard it was like a kick to the head, my head. It was the simultaneous feeling of 'isn't that obvious' and 'how did I not realize how not obvious it was to so many people'?"

"I'm not sure I ever grasped the full range of millennial terminology. But I don't think I'm a very binary thinker, about anything," Viola said with a smirk as she turned her attention to Aljon and asked, "What was it like growing up with millennial vocabulary?"

He shrugged. "Nobody says millennial anymore. I need to check on the sweet potatoes." Adding an exaggerated eye roll he left, taking two pie crusts with him.

In the silence after his escape Viola leaned forward and half whispered, "You can't expect a twenty-nine-year-old who chooses to live nearly alone on a boat for over a year to warm up quickly to new people. He'll come around."

Wend suspected that was far from the whole story but wondered if they'd caused Aljon's abrupt departure or Viola had. Either way, they shivered at Viola's breath on their ear, and the heat beating through the shade tarp felt more oppressive than before. "Are there triggers or stuff I should avoid?"

"Now *you* sound like a millennial." Viola waved the question off along with any further discussion of Aljon. Her hand brushed Wend's shoulder, causing a startle that brought them even closer together.

"What about you?" Wend asked with a pang. A lifetime of poorly received questions swarmed like bees in their head. They struggled, caught between wanting time alone to regroup and hoping to connect with Viola. "How do you see yourself and how you got here?"

Viola stared at the horizon, devoid of any boats and all but a single bird. The breeze that filled the sails stirred the air in the cockpit as well. "Hah, I'm not a storyteller like you. I'm a photographer. What you see is what you get."

Wend briefly caught Viola's eye and smiled. "I don't suppose you have a slideshow of your life you'd care to share?"

"My photos are all in the cloud," Viola said with her voice pitched higher in what might have been sarcasm, "and backed up on a couple of hard drives stored in Italy and the States."

"Italy and the US?" Wend prompted as Aljon returned with a bowl full of purple sweet potatoes and a tray bearing other supplies.

"Fine." Viola shifted to make room and plopped down on the bench beside Wend, close enough Wend could feel the heat from her skin. "Born in San Francisco, California, USA. Father is Italian and had a stake in a family farm back home, which I inherited. Before you get any grand ideas, it's mostly a net loss, with what I'm expected to pay into it, but I'm sure I'd always have a bed to sleep in if I found myself willing to live there. My mother was half Chinese and half Filipino. The Chinese part was three generations deep in California, and even my mom barely understood the Cantonese her grandparents spoke. The Filipino side still expects balikbayan boxes and for me to house younger relatives whenever I have a house, no matter how hopeless I am in any version of Tagalog. Aljon's the only one stubborn enough to follow me onto this boat."

"Tita Viola, you would starve without me." Aljon waved a purple potato in her direction.

"Just keep making me purple pie." She stretched a leg across the cockpit to jostle him with her foot, and he flicked a piece of sweet potato skin onto her lap. The sweet potatoes were even brighter purple inside.

"If you piss me off, I can turn it pink with lemon juice," he threatened.

Viola held both hands up, suddenly animated. "No, no. But you might write Wend's name on one to demonstrate."

Aljon didn't say anything more, but Wend was pleased to be handed a pie with their name marked out in bright pink capital letters that evening.

Wend awoke from a dream of burrowing deep in the benthic substrate to a sound of quiet singing they couldn't quite make out. Pushing their head free from three layers of sleep sack in the cozy quarter berth under the cockpit, they recognized Aljon's voice and a language they now guessed was Tagalog or some variant thereof. For a young man who seldom spoke, he had a surprisingly sweet singing voice. Wend kept their eyes closed and dozed to the sound and the rocking of the ocean until they had to get up to stretch and use the head.

The *Nuovo Mar* had a basic composting toilet, but at least it didn't stink. The head was beside the galley, and past the galley were Aljon and Viola's berths, with Aljon's currently empty. The board to keep Viola from falling out of her berth was high enough to hide whether she was asleep.

Viola and Wend had shared first watch the night before, with Viola speaking more than Wend for once—mostly explaining all the possible things that could go wrong, what to do, and when to wake the rest of the crew. She'd demonstrated her preferred method of sheet to tiller self-steering, how to balance the lines with bungee cords, and variations for different wind conditions. Unless the moon was very bright, they wouldn't be trying to travel far at night, so night watch was mostly about keeping them safe and as close to their intended course as possible. The stories Viola shared illustrated how changing conditions and the long draw of waves in the Pacific could send them off course or into dire circumstances, especially if someone fell asleep on watch. All useful advice, but Wend believed the trickiest part of seafaring would be keeping a crew happy when no one could leave the boat.

As Wend headed up the stairs, Aljon called out, "You could grab yourself some breakfast bread and fruit."

Turning around, Wend saw the galley white board said "eat me" over a secured metal container. Lifting the lid released a smell like carrot cake. Although the slices were more solid and unfrosted, a quick bite tasted deliciously of carrot and fruit. Wend took three slices and a banana and went to join Aljon in the cockpit. "You are by far the best ship's cook I've ever met."

Aljon froze at the words and then said "Thanks" without even a glance at Wend.

Possible stories of Aljon going to work as a seafarer and ending up ship's cook unfolded in Wend's mind. For most of Wend's life, Filipinos had dominated crews on commercial fishing vessels and cruise ships, but they didn't want to stereotype. The great pandemic had decimated the cruise industry even before carbon emission rules changed the face of commercial shipping and fishing. Labor protections in the Philippines had improved, and Wend didn't think many in Aljon's generation would have sought such careers.

Wend dared to ask, but tried to keep things light. "Did you discover you liked cooking or sailing first?"

From the brief look Aljon gave over his shoulder, he didn't appreciate even that limited probing. "I learned to sail first. I became a cook because it was better than other jobs on my first ship. I'm not sure I liked either until I came here."

Appreciating the effort of explaining as much as the food, Wend said, "Well, your breakfast bread is amazing."

"It's made with nutritional yeast and spirulina algae, both complete proteins to start your day." He watched Wend for some reaction, perhaps hoping they'd freak out or say, 'I ate what?'

Wend bit back the correction that spirulina was cyanobacteria and not algae. Instead, they asked what they were most curious about. "I see shreds of carrot and coconut, but what's the main fruit?"

"Pamplemousse, banana, and guava."

Pamplemousse were the large grapefruits common in the Marquesas. Wend had run into them before and didn't have to ask. "Did you add sugar, or is it naturally this sweet?"

Aljon's stance at the tiller relaxed while talking about cooking. "The guava and coconut are extremely sweet. Can you taste the cinnamon and mint?"

"Mint!" Wend exclaimed, finishing up their last bite. "I tasted but didn't recognize it. Thanks for telling me. And if you ever want help, I'd love to learn how to make stuff like this."

"Sometime," was all Aljon said.

"Want me to take the tiller for a while?"

Aljon shrugged off the offer and pointed out a red-footed booby flying overhead.

They were quietly passing binoculars back and forth when Viola arrived with her hands full of breakfast bread. She sprawled across the cockpit bench such that her feet landed on Aljon's knee and her head in Wend's lap.

"Have you tried this bread?" she asked. Viola's hand flashed up and tapped a bite to Wend's lips.

Wend had been taking a deep breath to control their startle at the sudden invasion of their personal space. There was nothing to do but take the bite offered before saying, "Yes, I already told Aljon how much I like it."

Rolling her neck back, Viola asked, "Blue skies, good company, and tasty treats. What more could I want in life?"

Aljon groaned and looked pointedly away.

Wend waited for Viola to say something, anything that might explain Aljon's reaction. Instead, the silence stretched until Wend's skin crawled and Viola's head weighed on their thigh like a cannonball. Wend didn't know how to restore the lost conversational ease and instead pulled away saying, "I'll set up the solar panels."

4.

WEND HUDDLED on the shady side of the cockpit updating a few sections in their waterproof notebook. Viola had the helm, and Aljon was catching up on sleep as the late morning sun burned bright overhead. Wend asked Viola, "Is this a good time to bring my sample bot up for a quick morning sample?"

Viola answered but did not turn around. "We're traveling faster today, northwest with about six knots of wind due north and a westward current. Would I need to change anything?"

Wend was sore, more from adapting to different sitting and sleeping positions than from their work as crew, but present conditions were no problem compared to previous runs where they'd had to take more frequent samples in all kinds of seas. "I should be able to lower and raise the bot myself with two lines attached so there's no chance of losing it. I'll have my hands full for about five minutes. You won't need me during that time?"

"Go ahead."

Wend retrieved their sample bot from a forward locker below decks, trying not to wake Aljon, who was sprawled on top of his blanket in the shorts and tank top he'd worn the day before. He didn't so much as twitch either time Wend passed by. It reminded them of sharing a bunk room with their students, either at sea or in small research stations, but felt strangely more intimate with only three people on board.

Back on deck it was second nature for Wend to attach two lines, double check both attachment points, lower the bot into the water, trigger one sample, then another. The water pulled hard enough that Wend had to put their back into hauling the bot out, but they had years of practice at keeping their spine straight and using both hands smoothly. They swung the bot up without a thump on the hull and left the lines attached as they braced the bot to dry in the sun before returning it to storage. It didn't need charging after taking two samples.

"You make that look simple." Viola looked back over her shoulder, an easy expression on her face as Wend returned to the cockpit.

Wend relaxed. "It's designed for even young students to collect scientifically useful samples in sterile, auto-sealing containers. Ease of use, affordability, and reliability—most of my work involves training others to take samples or make use of the bots or our database for local research. I also troubleshoot the microbiome portion of the Marine Census Project and do other analyses, primarily on marine invertebrates."

"How'd you end up in the Marquesas?" Viola asked.

"I usually choose among projects already funded under the Marine Census umbrella based on what's closest, trying not to wreck the planet while studying it and all that. The last couple years I went from Fiji to Tonga to Tahiti before landing in the Marquesas at Nuku Hiva."

"To document a dying reef." Viola slowly shook her head but didn't comment further.

"Every shallow water reef is dying or at risk. The one at Anaho Bay always had limited diversity due to its distance from other islands, but that also meant a high percentage of endemic species. With the recent discovery of a living mesophotic reef a few miles offshore, the Marine Census Project needed deep divers to study both and compare." It was second nature for Wend to demonstrate the relative depths of each reef with their hands, but Viola sat so close there was barely room.

"I did read the article that ran beside my photo," Viola said, literally looking down her nose at Wend.

"Sorry, I tend to speak as I think. I didn't mean any insult." Wend had offered that apology more times than they could count. It wasn't a very good apology, but they'd accepted it as a social nicety, not truly apologizing for how they thought. Communication always involved compromise.

"No worries." Viola smiled and met Wend's eyes before turning to face forward. "So you came to the Marquesas because of the mesophotic reef and because you were already in Tahiti?"

"More or less. I have a vested interest in supporting as much Marine Census sampling as possible, pretty much anywhere. Whatever other researchers are trying for, every sample includes the microbiome."

"Why Hawai'i?" Viola asked. "There must be plenty of people sampling there already."

"True. Some of the earliest research on endemic species populating both mesophotic and shallower reefs took place in the Hawaiʻian Islands. But I haven't been back since I started this work. As mentioned, I was born on Oʻahu." It was true. They'd been hoping for an excuse to return ever since they'd finished their doctorate at the age of fifty, over fifteen years before, but explaining their sudden urge to meet Viola and travel to Hawaiʻi this year might reveal too much about the mystery Wend was trying to solve. They risked asking, "What about you?"

The wrinkles around Viola's eyes and mouth deepened as she searched farther forward, perhaps imagining Hawaiʻi, 1700 nautical miles away. "I don't know," was all Viola offered for a long while. "Aljon's never been, and it felt right."

For all that Wend wanted to be their true self, they struggled to admit to such urges. Often, they struggled to even know what they truly wanted. "For a long time, I felt drawn to the ocean. Any part of the ocean. Seriously, I'll dive into the water at the slightest excuse if we stop."

"Me too." Viola laughed and turned toward Wend, lowering her shoulder in a way that made one strap of her pale gray tank top slide off. She was shiny with sunscreen and sweat.

Viola swayed well within the bubble Wend considered their personal space. They were trying to accept such intrusions as part of sharing a small boat with limited pockets of shade this close to noon. But when their fingers started to touch and Wend couldn't help flinching away, they made it into a motion to retrieve their sample bot. "Looks like this is already dry. I'll stow it below."

Wend woke close to dawn the next morning, despite taking the first half of night watch on their own. The usual comfort of their triple-layer sleep sack felt unbearably constricting. Their hands pushed open the drawstring and Velcro around their face with a motion that had moments before been swimming—no, flight by swimming through the air. They'd dreamt of flying off the bow of the *Nuovo Mar* to find a shining island to port.

Wend stumbled upstairs to the cockpit, where Viola rested with one hand lazily on the tiller, although the tiller was still connected to the mainsail for mechanical self-steering. "Viola, lend me the binoculars."

Handing them over without hesitation, Viola said, "You have a penchant for dramatic dawn entrances."

"You're the one who landed in my lap yesterday morning." Wend was too preoccupied with studying the ocean forward and to port to consider the tone or implication of Viola's next question.

"Did you like it?"

Wend answered with questions instead. "What's that, and can we steer closer?"

Taking the binoculars, Viola asked, "What is it?"

Trying not to flap their hands in frustration, Wend said, "I don't know. A shiny island?"

"Unless I'm misreading the waves and the distance, which I'm not, it's about the size of this boat and floating, therefore not an island. Not a boat either." Viola slipped the line holding the tiller and adjusted course to swing closer to whatever it was. The sail fluttered as Wend shifted it on Viola's orders.

Soon, Viola was shouting, "Aljon, are you awake?"

Aljon rushed onto deck in white boxer briefs. "Wazzat?" He instinctively followed Viola's gaze to the mound of shiny plastic they were rapidly approaching.

"Sheet in the mainsail. We'll heave to for a dive."

Aljon shifted the mainsail to the other side of the boat as they tacked into the wind.

After following a series of quick commands from their skipper, Wend shifted the foresail against the wind and Aljon took the helm on the now nearly stopped boat. If the wind picked up, the boat could lose position and strand Viola and Wend in three-mile-deep water. It would be up to Aljon to watch carefully and call them back fast or manage a rescue all on his own. For now, the *Nuovo Mar* held position about 50 meters north of a tangle of plastic and fishing nets that, as Viola predicted, covered about the same surface area as the thirty-one-foot cutter.

"I need to be in the water with my camera now." Viola was pulling on the shorty wetsuit as she spoke and had already tossed Wend's gear onto the cockpit bench beside them. "I saw a ray, maybe a giant manta ray if they still exist."

Viola's tanks were already in place as Wend struggled into their full-body wetsuit, the only one they owned. While Viola apparently wore a practical bikini under daily clothes or her wetsuit, Wend chose to strip off their rash guard but keep their boardshorts, fitted to allow this option. They'd never cared about modesty for their own sake, and Aljon and Viola didn't bat an eye.

As Viola pulled on her mask, regulator just short of her mouth, she ordered, "Wend, once you're in the water, stay as still as possible and out of my shot. Aljon, hold the boat at least this far north so you don't block my light. And pay attention in case some gyre of currents brought this mess here." The two cameras Viola strapped on next probably cost more than all Wend's gear combined.

Wend attached their air tanks and sample bot, then hurried to collect their own mask and fins as Viola shot photos both before and after leaving the deck.

To Wend's eye, it appeared someone had collected plastic bags full of disposable plastic water bottles before losing them or tossing them into the ocean. The entangling net might have once been meant to secure them to a deck. Now it formed a death trap for birds, turtles, and possibly a giant manta ray. Any feeling Wend had about that would have to wait for later.

In the water, Wend stayed a couple meters north of Viola, but triggered the bot strapped to their back to take a reference sample right away. This was their first time in the water after two days at sea. The ocean welcomed them, hugged them tight while seeping into their wetsuit. Pleased as a hermit crab acquiring a new shell, they swam toward the floating plastic.

From their new position underwater, with the morning sun shining low across the waves, the garbage patch again resembled a shiny island. It was exactly as Wend had seen it in their dream.

They froze and then relaxed, letting salt water and natural buoyancy hold them in place. No matter how ridiculous it felt at sixty-plus years to believe they could fly outside their body in dreams, this time Wend practically had proof. They'd have to be careful when talking to Viola later, but they'd hopefully planted the seeds with the story of their childhood dreams.

Thinking about that conversation threatened panic breathing and rash actions. Wend let those thoughts go.

Instead, they studied the jumble of plastic and followed the angle of Viola's camera lens to spot a large dark diamond shape flapping pectoral fins like wings on the far side of the plastic patch. It swam back and forth, as if pacing the perimeter of an oval, while keeping to the south side of the floating mess. The ray didn't approach or retreat. It seemed to be watching them as much as they were watching it.

The standoff stretched for several long minutes. Wend wondered if their presence would scare the ray off, possibly saving it from eating or becoming tangled in the plastic. As a journalist and scientist, they weren't supposed to interfere, weren't supposed to want that. But looking at the magnificent creature across from them, Wend yearned for it to leave. To escape. To survive.

Yet, the giant ray—and whatever species it was, Wend thought it must be at least three meters across—swam under the mass of plastic. Its mouth opened like a large round hole.

Something pushed out. A light-colored blob emerged. A mucosal membrane puffed outward like a balloon inflating.

Suddenly Wend understood. This ray was everting its stomach. Unlike a sea cucumber, there were no intestines visible. One smooth inner surface billowed into the water as the ray shook its head side to side. Then the stomach sucked back in, leaving a whiteish glob of mucus and several smaller pieces of detritus that rose into the garbage above.

The beauty—like an afterimage of what had been momentarily disgusting or alarming—resonated with the waves and reverberated through them. Witnessing this made Wend more at home in the sea, part of a greater whole beyond the explanations of humans.

Only as the ray flapped its fins and swam away did Wend notice Viola had dropped at least ten meters, either finding a better perspective on the stomach eversion or capturing the more identifiable marks on the ray's light underside.

Wend had forgotten there was another observer. They wondered how much of their experience could be captured in photographs, no matter the skill of the photographer.

When Viola swam up to join them, Wend couldn't see her smile around the mouthpiece but the lines by Viola's eyes were unmistakable.

After a moment of rest, they swam together to explore the mound of plastic debris. Viola took hundreds of pictures from all sides and underneath. She even found the mucus expelled by the ray and photographed that from different angles. Wend sampled the water from a few inches away and from a dozen other points.

When they headed back toward the boat, Viola found the exact angle where they'd entered the water relative to the garbage patch and repeated several shots she'd taken from there. The boat was now twenty meters north.

Swimming to it and climbing up the ladder from a relatively calm sea, Wend felt pleasantly tired.

Viola practically bounced into the cockpit, sliding her fins off and pulling up her mask. She scrolled through pictures on her camera screen with tanks still on her back. "Look at that caudal thorn! I just photographed a giant manta ray in the middle of the South Pacific displaying behavior I'm not sure anyone's documented before. I'm not even sure when the last verified sighting occurred outside of a marine reserve. This shot of the belly spots should be enough to identify if anyone's photographed this individual before. They live for decades, if humans don't hunt them down. Or kill them with plastics. Does that look like it was trying to vomit out plastic to you?"

Aljon smiled at her enthusiasm but said nothing. Wend volunteered, "I've seen pictures of gastric eversion with rays before. I don't know whether it's been documented with this species or not."

"You're sure that was its stomach and not a plastic bag?"

"Definitely. Sharks, frogs, and sea cucumbers also do it. Sea cucumbers are the only ones known to jettison their intestines, but the rest may use stomach eversion to expel bad or indigestible food." Wend was glad to have expertise as well as inexplicable dreams to contribute.

"Did it look like it ingested anything bad right before? It hadn't even opened its mouth. And the way it swam back and forth. I'll leave interpretations to the scientists, but my photos show it approached and then waited, watching us before going under that mound of plastic to do whatever it needed to do."

"I agree," Wend said, intending to write about the event with as little speculation as possible. Still, it was hard not to theorize about if or why the giant manta ray was drawn to the shiny island of plastic. Much like Wend had been drawn in their dream. They shivered, even though the morning was warm with little wind.

"Look at these pictures of the plastic on the side where we entered and left. It fades away in real time. Like it's being eaten. In the time we were visiting. There's something similar around the place where that blob of mucus floated up."

Wend hadn't noticed that, even swimming right beside the photographer.

"I'm going back in for another set of pictures," Viola announced.

"Eat first," Aljon said.

Glancing around, Viola checked for signs that the calm ocean or weather might change. "Okay, we can take a few minutes."

Aljon hurried below. No one wanted to waste the calm that let them swim with the boat heaved to and basically still in the water. Wend set out solar panels to catch the morning light and hooked up the bot to recharge. Taking dozens of samples with the bot strapped to their back used far less power than the self-steering sometimes needed near reefs, but Wend took the opportunity the moment presented.

Still smiling, Viola asked, "Okay, I'll bite. What pulled you out of bed and had you demanding binoculars to lead me to the photo opportunity of the year if not my lifetime?"

Wend froze. They wanted to tell, had set the stage with stories. While they'd never lied, they'd bided their time before acknowledging they still had flying dreams and believed they were real. If this morning didn't prove it, Wend didn't know what would, and yet, the words piled up, clogging their throat. A series of past rejections flashed through their head.

Despite a decade or more of deciding not to hide, compensate, or lie any more than necessary, Wend bit their tongue and almost choked before blurting out, "I dreamed I was flying there."

The staredown that followed lasted forever. It might have been under thirty seconds, but that amounted to an excruciating degree of direct eye contact for Wend.

"I admit, I'd never consider flying dreams an explanation if your stories hadn't hinted as much." Viola spoke calmly, but there was a twinge of staticky deception that Wend had never experienced before from Viola. The photographer shook her head slowly before shutting the fraught topic down. "We'll revisit this later."

Aljon emerged, wearing baggy blue shorts and a yellow long-sleeved tee shirt. He brought them large fruit smoothies and leftover breakfast bread that Viola and Wend both gobbled down fast.

"Thanks," Wend said before asking, "Do you want a chance to dive or at least swim?"

Aljon shook his head.

Viola looked up from reattaching her cameras. "I taught him to dive in case I needed a dive buddy, but he hates the equipment. Treats swimming like a chore. Don't know why he wants to live on a boat."

Aljon shrugged as he took her place at the helm. Wend viscerally understood the difference between boat and sea, even if their preferences differed from Aljon's. Under different circumstances, they might have offered support. But the halted exchange about flying dreams was all the conflict they could stomach mid-morning.

Viola and Wend hurried back into the water. They stayed a couple hours before the sea grew rougher and even Viola agreed that she'd taken enough photos.

Once underway with Aljon at the tiller, Viola showed off her pictorial evidence that the plastic was rapidly diminishing at the edges and from two central spots, one of which was where the ray's mucus had settled. Aljon only smiled. He'd probably viewed a huge number of photos as he traveled around the world with Viola. Wend on the other hand was almost as excited about seeing the discovery documented by a world-class photographer as by finding it in the first place.

"My background is more in genetics than biochemistry," Wend said from close beside Viola on a cockpit bench, "but I remember some scientist in Japan found what appeared to be naturally evolved bacteria breaking down plastic water bottles—PET plastic—in a dump, back around 2015. For the last couple decades, researchers attempted to develop similar bacteria that would act faster. The efforts I saw targeted recycling centers where the PET plastic could be heated to 75 degrees Celsius and they could use cutinase as a pre-treatment to cut polymer chains. Even then, they would be left with monomers to make into new PET plastic, rather than base components like water and carbon dioxide. I don't know of any natural or bioengineered organisms that could break down the entire carbon backbone in polyethylene bags."

"You're saying that whatever's eating the water bottles out there probably won't eat the shopping bags?" Viola asked, flicking between her earliest and latest pictures from the northern edge of the garbage patch. "You may be right."

"It should take months to break down PET plastic at 75 Fahrenheit rather than 75 Celsius, even if these were bioengineered bacteria—something that shouldn't be found on an isolated clump of plastic in the middle of the Pacific."

"We saw the giant manta ray push its insides out to expel mucus." Viola had given up on impressing Aljon with her photos and was pressed up against Wend with the camera resting on their inner knees. "What if that happened when it swallowed bits of plastic at some other trash island? It could have developed a conditioned response to evert its stomach whenever it finds plastic trash. Couldn't it spread bacteria naturally from one feeding site to another? Maybe it first came across a test site with some engineered bacteria and associates that plastic with what it found here. That ray could be returning to the site we found, adding more bacteria every few hours or days as it everts its stomach, until it spreads to the entire trash island."

Wend found that hypothesis more elaborate than necessary. "If we were in a lab, we could feed isotopically labeled plastic to a carrier species and check both the waste products and whether the bacteria survived in the stomach and spread from one feeding site to another. No one should be testing engineered bacteria in the open ocean without checking that first and taking precautions to keep the new bacteria from entering wild populations."

"Bet they wouldn't have tested for a giant manta ray everting its stomach. Anyway, won't your sample bot have collected any bacteria present?" Viola was practically speaking into Wend's ear when she turned her head, and Wend noticed Aljon frowning in their direction.

Wend answered as well as they could, having spent more time in teaching environments than in labs recently. "Isolating bacteria in a sample of seawater is a far cry from seeing what it does on a plastic substrate, especially in the wild. But my preserved samples might show if whatever is happening is shredding plastic into smaller bits or biochemically degrading the polymer. Luckily, there are no PET plastics or similar polymers in my sample containers or bot."

"Smaller pieces and microplastics can fill up marine animals' stomachs until they die from starvation as surely as larger animals can die from eating larger pieces, choking, or strangulation. But it's harder to capture the small-scale effects in photos." Viola leaned her head against Wend's shoulder, sounding sad.

Wend relaxed into the prolonged contact, finding it easier to handle at this point. The risk to sea life worried them more than they could process in science mode. Estimates that fifty to seventy percent of Earth's biodiversity had already been lost in their lifetime echoed through Wend's brain. They tried to focus on a larger picture, involving pollution, plastics, and what might be happening now. "Whatever is going on here, the fact it's happening fast enough for you to capture in photos an hour or two apart may be unprecedented—both in the wild and at natural temperatures. I wish there was a way to set up a monitor back there and take time lapse photos over days or weeks."

"Leaving cameras in salt water has been the downfall of many documentary filmmakers. I don't know of any that tried it in open ocean, and we're certainly not equipped for that." Viola sighed wistfully, as if discussing a fairy tale.

Wend's thoughts progressed along similar but more analytical lines. "Yeah, I looked into a lot of fancier marine bot designs when planning for an affordable sample bot. I gave up on good cameras first thing, but my bot tags GPS coordinates with each sample. What are the odds someone could use wind and current records to track this mass of plastic on satellite images, in case researchers wanted to follow up later and see which parts diminished or fell away?"

With a yawn, Viola pressed further into Wend's shoulder. "I'd say almost zero, unless they had a lot of money or military access. Even then, I don't think anyone is likely to come back and follow up during hurricane season. There's a reason we're making our crossing now."

"I know." Wend sank back on the bench seat to reclaim some personal space along with the latest disappointment.

Viola leaned forward and patted Wend's knee where the camera had previously rested. "I'm going to store the memory card with these pictures in a double sealed metal dry box. If you want protected storage for any notes or samples from your bot, let me know. We have no way to mail or share any of this until we reach Hawai'i."

Wend spent the next few hours writing notes, a couple articles to shop around, and both a teaser and a more complete blog post for Pacific Tech's marine education site. Some of their former students would be over the moon to see such unprecedented bacterial activity documented. Most others would prefer Viola's pictures, and Wend appreciated that photographic evidence more than ever.

5.

INCREASED MOTION that was more distracting than unpleasant woke Wend in the middle of the night. They lay awake, systematically flexing and releasing sore muscles, until their brain cataloged the dozen or more creaking noises throughout the *Nuovo Mar*. All were becoming familiar after four days at sea. Wend's body gave in to exhaustion.

For their next shift, they woke braced between the sides of their berth as a squall battered the boat.

Wend ached like they'd worked through the night as the deck rocked side to side in choppy waves.

Now seawater splashed over their feet or blew into their face. But there was still a brisk wind that Viola seemed to appreciate as she called out, "Have to keep the speed up to steer for the flatter spaces. We may have no port in this storm, but there's little to worry about hitting."

Viola stayed constantly at the helm, sometimes sharing her steering knowledge and tactics, and demanding the others be quick on the uptake. Often her voice, as well as the squeaking and grating noises of the boat, was nearly drowned out by the whistling and pounding of wind in the sheets.

As rain hit harder, Viola called to further reef the mainsail.

Aljon was busy securing the galley, so Wend shouted from across the cockpit. "Do I need to tighten the foresail first?"

"Yes. Then release the mainsail halyard to lower it down to the third reefing ring."

Wend took care of the foresail easily enough but had to grab the mast hard as the bow surged up on a wave and down into the trough behind it. They managed to hook the third reefing ring to the boom and retighten the mainsail halyard.

"Tighten the winch on the mainsail reefing line," Viola shouted.

"It's tangled!" Wend called before clambering leeward. The deck tilted thirty degrees down toward the water. A wave broke over Wend's back. For a moment they lost track of the boom and were sure they'd be struck in the head and thrown unconscious into the water.

But their hand grasped the railing and a minute later they reached the boom end and untangled the lines. Nearly swinging between handholds, they made it back to the winch to tighten the reefing line. As they tidied the lines, the boat steadied with the wind. Wend breathed in the elation of success, as a true member of a crew weathering a storm.

Thunder rumbled. Viola yelled, "We need to secure all electronics in case of lightning. Check if Aljon finished the galley. I'll try for one last weather update before we lock up the SSB."

Wend stumbled down the stairs, numb from constantly tensing their muscles even though it wasn't cold. They relayed Viola's message to Aljon before adding, "Could I ask you a favor?"

"I'm not taking the helm in a storm so you and Viola can cuddle or fool around."

Wend froze, wondering if that was a joke or if, yet another time, they'd totally missed social signals everyone else found obvious. They'd considered Viola's intent, but other than landing her head in Wend's lap or leaning against Wend while discussing photos and Aljon looking at them askance now and then, Wend couldn't construct any chain of evidence to support such possibilities. Still half numb and half shaking with adrenaline they stammered, "I—I can't even—I can't figure this out right now. Some other time, I will try to explain my boundaries regarding touch, let alone sex, if you want. I was only going to ask if there was any chance of hot water now or later for hot chocolate, but obviously you have more essential stuff to worry about. Never mind."

Wend headed topside without waiting for an answer. On the stairs, their mind reeled at the miscommunications implied in that conversation. Whatever alarms Viola had triggered by invading Wend's personal space had been nothing compared to working in "male-dominated" labs throughout the nineties. Not that the nineties as a decade excused a sixty-seven-year-old's behavior in the present. Wend could admit the shifting assumptions across time and individual people confused them, but they knew how to set boundaries and challenge Viola if necessary. Aljon had clearly misconstrued at least as much about Wend if he thought they would ask such a favor of him. Let alone during an emergency. Wend swallowed around the lump in their throat and forced their shoulders back.

The boat pitched to port, and Wend slammed an already bruised hip against the stair rail. They'd stopped midway up. They'd stopped mid-breath as well.

Breathing in to a count of five, Wend remembered the conversation about dreams that Viola had left hanging. Their plan to connect via stories, their belief from the day before that they would finally unravel the mystery of their flying dreams, was hanging by a thread. Again. They had to hold on.

Breathing out to a count of five, Wend forced another step. It was all too much. Wend had to draw a line between larger social goals and doing what needed to be done in that moment. They'd spent decades learning to compensate for whatever their mind threw at them.

Today, they'd focus on surviving this storm.

Viola spent the next hour shouting "reef another ring" or "grab that line."

Wend scrambled from task to task buffeted by shifting winds. They were the only crew on deck with Viola after the bilge pump broke and Aljon went below to fix it.

The bow was riding low. Waves broke over the side and washed across the deck constantly. Wend could feel where seawater had splashed up above their knees contrasting with the softer, smoother texture from rain showering the rest of them. Their eyes and head pounded faster than the waves. Their palms rubbed raw. But at least they felt useful as the third crewmember. Even if they were the least competent sailor onboard, they'd made a real difference in getting through this storm. So far.

Aljon called out from below. Wend rushed to open the door to make out his words and repeat them to the skipper. "He needs another pair of hands."

"Go. Hurry back," was all Viola said.

The floor below decks was wet, but not as musty or swamped as Wend had feared. Mostly, they noticed quiet. It couldn't be quiet in any real sense. The floor and walls thrummed with vibrations from wave and wind. The whole boat shook. All the creaks and screeches that had kept

Wend awake before were still present. Wend stood in awe of the relative silence as the pounding in their head took center stage.

Aljon had pulled up two boards from the cabin floor and was lying on his belly with both hands reaching down into water. One pressed on a rectangular strainer while struggling with a switch beside it. The other held a stiff wire that might once have been a coat hanger, now hooked around a hose. "Take the wire," Aljon said. "Secure it any way that keeps that hose in place."

There was no floor left for Wend to lie on. They braced their knees on one side of the gap and crawled their hands forward to grab the wire from Aljon. The hose pulled it down with more force than they expected.

As soon as Wend took the wire, Aljon grabbed a wrench and started attacking something under the switch. Not wanting to distract with questions but mindful of Viola's order to hurry back, Wend bent the upper end of the wire around the support for the removed floor board. If Aljon was planning to leave the wire in the new position, either he'd have to carve a notch in the bottom of the floorboard or the floor wouldn't lie flat. At the moment, that seemed the least of their worries.

Every bruise and scrape on Wend's fingers screamed as they bent wire with their bare hands. But it wasn't delicate work, and Wend's hands were still as strong and calloused as they'd ever been.

When they let go, both wire and hose stayed in place.

As the boat leaned hard to port, Wend pushed back onto their knees to keep from falling across Aljon. They asked, "Need anything else?"

"No, go help Viola."

Wend went. As soon as they were out in the wind again, they heard Viola yelling, "Trim the staysail." She didn't ask how the pump was coming, and Wend rushed to tend the sail.

Hours later the three of them ate a hasty meal and huddled in the cockpit for a brief discussion. Aljon reported the bilge pump was unstuck and doing fine. He'd bailed out the cabin to as good as it was going to get during a storm.

"I think we're in good shape for now," Viola stated calmly. The wind had eased to a constant growl, and the boat complained less forcefully than before. "We kept close to our planned course. This storm may yet push us past the doldrums. But that means we're sailing through a dark and cloudy night using the wind to keep us steady with near zero visibility. We may hit lightning and rough weather, and I need to sleep for at least a couple hours. I'm confident Aljon can handle the wind and the boat. Wend can keep watch for hazards and do what's needed outside the cockpit. Are you both awake enough? Anyone need to use the head first?"

"I set a thermos of hot water aside earlier," Aljon said. "Do you still want hot chocolate, Wend?"

It was ridiculous that something so simple should matter so much. Wend could barely find their voice to say, "That would be great, thanks."

"There's extra coffee I could add if you need caffeine," he offered.

"No thanks, unless you're mixing it all at once and want that yourself."

He shook his head as he ducked downstairs calling back, "I'll make some the way your mix says to make it, even if it's at least 25 degrees out and I've never served any form of chocolate on a boat before."

Viola raised one eyebrow and a corner of her mouth as she said, "Your influence on people is interesting, at the very least."

When Aljon returned with a pair of sealed travel mugs, he handed one to Wend and took the tiller with his free hand.

As Viola headed below, Wend took their first sip of hot chocolate in a week and couldn't help but moan in appreciation. The warmth flowed through them. Their insides practically hummed with pleasure.

Aljon rolled his eyes and said, "I might have misinterpreted that reaction as flirting if Viola was still around. Sorry for what I said earlier." He took a sip and nodded approvingly.

"You brought me chocolate. I couldn't hold a grudge even if there were something to hold onto." Wend savored the barely sweet but deeply chocolate flavor of their favorite drink in silence for a long while. Then they picked up a pair of binoculars and tried to sound casual as they said, "If I did something that bothered you, I'd appreciate knowing what. I think you heard me say I'm not neurotypical, or a bunch of other stuff. It helps me to learn from other people's perspectives."

They kept scanning an arc in front of the *Nuovo Mar* until Aljon said, "Fair enough. I'm asexual, or ace, since you seem familiar with 'millennial terminology.' When Shelly was still on board, the sex and flirting parts were always in my face. Drama like a teleserye. Not to fault them, but it's a small boat. Anytime Viola treats you the way she did Shelly, it reminds me."

Wend filed the name Shelly away as someone who Viola had been involved with and probably the friend who left the hydrogen generator. As Aljon continued to look anywhere but toward Wend, they tried to guess which of the million questions in their head were best to ask. "Had you seen Viola around anyone else?"

"Only family in the Philippines."

"To be honest," Wend said as they lowered the binoculars, "I was ready to trust your judgment over mine if you said Viola was testing me or trying to start something. But it sounds like neither of us may have the best radar for that. I'm mostly oblivious to flirting and demisexual, if anything."

Aljon shrugged and waved a hand over the boat's old-fashioned compass and complete lack of radar.

When Wend laughed aloud, he smiled.

"Did it bother you when she put her feet up on your leg or her head in my lap?"

"Not really. Before going to sea, I'd rant about every ad implying sex and about everyone I saw pairing up and hanging all over each other. But I know a lot of people want more touch and get it that way because it's easy. I'm not exactly sex averse or even touch averse. I just don't need it."

"No touch at all?" Wend asked.

"Not much, but I've always been around family who touch me pretty freely. Viola is the least of that. If I ever try sailing alone for a year, I'll find out if I need people or touch at all."

Nodding along, Wend tried looking through the binoculars to see if that encouraged Aljon to say more about his sailing or other experiences. Eventually Wend offered, "Some people might describe me as touch averse, and I can go without human touch for a long time. But with me it's that I'm hypersensitive and had to learn techniques to dial down my sense of touch and control startles and other reactions. That got easier as I aged. Not sure how much was biological and how much involved compensating or learning. Mostly, it was easier to avoid touch than to let someone close enough to learn how I liked to be touched. The way I understood myself before millennials rewrote the dictionary, I saw sex as a minor but interesting form of touch that was challenging for me to explore. I read up on terms like 'gray' or 'demi-sexual,' and I'm glad they exist as a starting point for explaining to others, but they didn't have the impact on my life that 'nonbinary' did."

"Do you have texture aversions with food that you didn't feel comfortable mentioning earlier?" Aljon asked softly.

"By necessity, I worked past most of those as a kid. Also, I sincerely appreciate having enough food and can stomach almost anything when necessary." Seeing that Aljon was waiting patiently for more Wend admitted, "Not that it will come up on a boat, but if I showed a lack of enthusiasm for cold milk or cold pudding, that wouldn't be anything personal."

The slight smile at the corner of Aljon's lips somehow reached his eyes as well. "Were you always so open in talking about this stuff?"

"No." Wend lowered the binoculars to better gauge Aljon's reactions. "I had a sort of 'oh, shit' moment in my forties."

"You want to talk about it?" Aljon asked with an exaggerated teasing tone, but he was watching Wend.

Their eyes met. "I'm fine with telling the story, but I hadn't planned to share it while sailing in case of superstitions or stirring up anxieties."

"It involves drowning?" The way Aljon said it was barely a question.

"Yeah." Wend hadn't planned to choose separate stories for Aljon or to seek out ways to connect with him individually. But he'd already shown uncommon insights, and Wend wondered about other areas where they might understand each other.

A wave crested high enough to splash the deck. Aljon spoke louder, above the rain and boat noises, "What better story for a night like this!"

Wend wasn't sure there was ever a good time for such a story, but they'd been surprised before by the moments that brought people together. Wrapping their hands around their knees, Wend began. "In 2015, I moved back to the California coast after twenty years away from the ocean. I spent my first weekend helping with a coastal clean-up, feet sinking into warm sand, but the water there is cooler. I'd had more than enough of people by the end of the day.

"As night fell, light gray clouds reflected indirect sunlight. They mirrored the white tips of the waves crashing along the beach. I'm not a very visual person, but I couldn't help staring. The symmetry of light framed the repeating sound of the waves."

Wend let the peaceful beginnings of the memory soothe them as they scanned the current night with binoculars. It was already much darker than the moment they described. No moon or stars were visible; only white tips on the choppy sea marked the border between ocean and storm clouds. Aljon's face showed as barely an outline, and Wend couldn't read his expression.

"I wandered farther and farther along the shore, climbing over small outcroppings of rock, then walking at the edge of the still wet sand. The tide had been going out for as long as I'd been exploring, leaving a long stretch of damp sand that made it easy to walk there.

"A giant wave came out of nowhere, crashing around my knees. It knocked me over and pulled me out to sea. In that instant, the water seemed colder than before, a thousand icy claws digging into my skin.

"I turned upside down, tumbling, arms and legs flopping, useless. As someone who swam before I learned to walk, I'd never felt so helpless in the water.

"My first rational moment gave me a glimpse of shore. I bobbed at least thirty meters from land, facing a shallow slope. When my feet hit solid ground, I pushed and paddled toward land. I'd lost my flip flops, but I was wearing jeans and a sweatshirt that dragged me down and were hard to remove. My hands grew numb until I couldn't feel my fingers."

It shocked Wend how clearly they remembered the feel of their hands, their clothes, and the ocean around them. This wasn't a story they told or even relived in dreams very often, but it was part of them in a way other traumas weren't. Even as they recalled the physical sensations, they felt empowered by having survived.

"I'd pulled myself a step or two forward when another wave crashed over me, grinding me through sand, tangling me with seaweed and something else slippery, then tossing me end over end like a washing machine. It pushed into my nose and mouth. I tried not to breathe it in and not to let the air in my lungs escape. For the first time ever, seawater hurt on my skin. I don't know if my touch sensitivity spiked or if the prickling sensations meant I'd lost too much body heat.

"My hands felt like frozen soda cans, blunt objects without separate fingers. My shoulders and legs ached as if I'd been beaten up. I knew I was weakening fast, either from the cold or from limited oxygen.

"Then my brain started processing in a different way." Remembering that moment settled Wend's breathing now. This was their story to tell, and they truly wanted to tell it to Aljon. He'd demonstrated a distrust of both the ocean and Wend that morphed into active curiosity, as he tilted his head to better hear this story even while watching the storm.

"During a break in the waves, I spotted a small delta where a stream flowed into the ocean and the ground rose soft between rocky outcroppings. Positioning myself to face the oncoming waves, I swam down under the next one. It worked, in that I wasn't tossed around. The water was calmer down there. I swam unseeing for as long as I could toward that delta. Something told me the waves hitting shore would be calmer there, with less undertow.

"Only as my breath was running out did I think about the consequences if I lived or died. I'd lost my shoes, my phone, and my keys. I was new in town and hadn't lined up a job yet. The old college friends I was staying with didn't know me well and might think I'd skipped out on them if I didn't return. I could only think of two people who would miss me, who would mourn if my body washed up later. But they were both friends I kept in touch with by email. They wouldn't know to worry for a couple days.

"If I survived, I'd have to approach strangers, ask for help. At the time, I tried hard not to be a burden, not to inconvenience anyone. I lived by a strict set of rules to compensate for my social anxieties, communication challenges, touch sensitivities, and other issues. I hadn't heard the term neurodivergent yet, but in the midst of my life and death struggle, while swimming underwater to reach a delta, I realized I was perpetually exhausted from forcing myself to accommodate everyone else's expectations.

"I could let go of all that, let the water hold me, even if it froze my body and mind." Wend was glad they couldn't see Aljon's reaction to that. They kept speaking without giving him a chance to interrupt.

"I got tangled in seaweed and whatever else was being tossed about by the waves. I swear I felt crabs and fish in there with me. Then I thought about their lives, how they were beaten about by waves every day. This was their life. They were living. Each in their own plant or fish or crab way.

"I pushed up for a breath of air and discovered I'd chosen to live, at least in that moment.

"As another wave crashed down, I barely managed to dive under.

"It tossed me around again. That time was more like being in an egg-beater than a washing machine. Honestly, it surprised me I wasn't choking or suffocating yet. It seemed like I'd been struggling through the waves for at least twenty minutes, but I couldn't trust my time sense.

"My body felt loose like a jelly. I thought about leaving it up to chance and wave patterns, whether I washed up on shore or was sucked out to sea. But the next wave pounded that notion right out of my head.

"I went up for air and spotted the delta.

"It was right there in front of me. All I had to do was follow the waves in without letting them suck me back out. I swam underwater until I could reach the seafloor to brace between waves. A couple times my feet slipped right out from under me and I was ground into the sand, using my clublike hands and the drag of my waterlogged clothes to cling to the progress I'd made.

"I crawled out onto the beach. Cold water and foam lapped under me. I knew if I fell face down, I could still drown. But I'd moved past the point of giving up and come out the other side."

The way Aljon nodded at that, without looking away from the course he was holding through the wind, was all Wend needed. Better in fact; they appreciated not having to make eye contact or answer questions and wondered if Aljon intuited as much.

"Pain like needles or icicles stabbed into my hands and knees with every move, but I kept going until I touched dry sand. I saw a path leading up from the creek and lights from houses at the top.

"I pushed up to standing. Every step stung like walking a bed of nails. I thought my feet must be cut open and bloody, but it was too dark to see. I kept walking, one foot in front of the other, until I reached the top.

"I stood in a grassy area at the end of a paved road. It even had a park bench where a young couple were sitting together, kissing. With who I was then, I would never have bothered them, never have interrupted. But I must have looked pathetic, coming up that steep path sopping wet and shoeless.

"When they looked up at me, I saw they were really young, probably teenagers who'd snuck out together. I worried I'd frighten them, but instead they asked if I needed help.

"I told them I'd lost my phone and car keys.

"They were amazingly understanding. I could barely string words together to explain that I was new in town and didn't know the address, only the names of the friends I'd been staying with and the beach where I'd left the car I'd lost the key to. One of the teenagers, who introduced herself as Marta, lived in the nearest house. She and her parents insisted I take a warm shower and put on dry clothes that they lent me. After warming up, I realized how incoherent I'd probably been. This teenager and her family took it all in stride, explained to me about sleeper waves, and got me sorted out. A couple years later I ended up working at the aquarium where Marta volunteered."

Wend stopped. They wondered at how naturally that story had poured out in the darkness above a portion of the same ocean where they'd almost drowned. Staring out into the stormy night from the cockpit with Aljon was like sharing a bubble fit for humans amid a natural environment that was mostly otherwise. They appreciated their bubble.

Aljon let the silence stretch as he and Wend shared a semi-peaceful moment amidst the dissipating storm. Finally, voice barely raised above the remaining noise of wind and rain, he said, "I'm glad you survived and that family took care of you, but how does nearly drowning lead you to openly talking about touch and sex and stuff?"

Wend remembered why they'd chosen that story, the points they still needed to connect to answer Aljon's question.

The old pain that knotted Wend's spine hadn't bothered them during the telling. Aljon didn't know about the medical debt Wend had built up in the decade before nearly drowning. Whatever Wend had to say about disability rights or their ineligibility for the "not so" Affordable Care Act would probably sound hollow to a twenty-something who'd grown up in the Philippines. Wend hadn't realized until the day after they chose to live, amidst their bruises and scrapes and an eye infection, how the tumble in the ocean had relieved their nerve pain and spine issues, more than any chiropractic treatment or physical therapy they'd ever tried.

Instead they explained, "When I decided to live, I only wanted to do it as myself. I gave up on making everyone else comfortable by hiding the ways I thought and felt and was different. Not that I'd ever been able to pass completely, but blending in and taking up as little space as possible—physical or mental—were second nature to me by then."

"What did you change first?" Aljon asked.

"I didn't replace my lost smartphone." Wend ducked their head as Aljon gave a snort that undoubtedly covered a laugh. "People called them that then! Instead, I bought a cheap burner phone and only turned it on when I felt like dealing with people. The only two people I'd thought would miss me if I drowned already communicated with me almost solely by email. Without me even asking, they'd realized I liked email better than calls or texting. They had no problem understanding I was nonbinary once I discovered the word. And neurodivergent. It was like I claimed pieces of myself, bit by bit, at that point in my life."

Aljon nodded along and then said, "It's not really the same, but I changed after rescuing someone from drowning."

"How so?" Wend tried not to sound too eager, but the idea of Aljon volunteering a personal story warmed them almost as much as the hot chocolate they'd shared before. The fact they were bonding over accounts of drowning might raise concerns for others, but Wend tended to trust wherever shared stories led.

"My first paid sailing gig was taking tourists around the Philippines on a luxury superyacht. The Philippine Green Goals for inter-island traffic required zero emissions for tourist and recreation boats. It was suddenly popular for rich families or parties of up to eighteen people to charter this hundred-foot zero emissions yacht that came with a six-person crew.

"I was the youngest, someone they'd tease about 'still having milk on my lips' in Filipino. That meant I spent sixteen or more hours a day clean-ing the deck, making up the guest rooms, fetching drinks. Whatever. Then this woman fell overboard, and I was the only person who saw. I hit an alarm button, grabbed a flotation device, and jumped in after her.

"It wasn't quite what they'd told us to do in training, but it worked. The woman and her extended family expressed over and over how pleased they were. They insisted I join them for cake and champagne that night. It was awkward, but it was my job to go along with whatever the custom-ers wanted. I thought I'd get a good tip at the end. Instead, the woman I'd rescued pretty much ordered me back to her room. I'm not going to describe what happened or all the things I said trying to get out of there. I claimed to have a very traditional fiancée and family and all of that, but nothing got through to her."

From his profile in the dark, Wend couldn't read Aljon's emotions. If anything, he intentionally kept his face at least half turned away as his words gained speed with every sentence.

"At the end of that cruise, the skipper insisted I hand over all my tip money or he'd tell management I was fraternizing with the guests. He had no respect for management or those rules and clearly thought any young man would have done the same in my place. He used it as an excuse, a threat. I gave him the money rather than explain that I was ace or how I'd felt trapped by the situation.

"Two days later I went to management and told them I needed to be transferred to a different ship and had trained to be ship's cook. I knew that if I made any sort of labor complaint, they'd exact retribution, eventually if not right away. Instead, I implied I had cause and was giving them the chance to buy me off with a transfer. Suddenly, I was another ship's cook. I barely had to interact with passengers at all, and when I did, it was from the far side of a table."

Aljon mostly watched the ocean as he spoke. When he looked to Wend, they were careful to meet his eyes as they said, "I'm glad you worked things out. But what that woman did after you rescued her and then the skipper's attitude, that was a terrible situation to be in. Were there people you could talk to? Get support?"

He looked very young in the next moment as he rolled his eyes, the only part of his face clearly visible in the inky dark of night. "Yes, I had ace friends, even a support group. You don't need to therapize me."

"Understood." Wend held up both hands in a gesture of surrender, realizing their knuckles had grown stiff while gripping the binoculars. They were relieved to know someone had been there for Aljon when he'd needed to tell that story for his own sake. "Your generation might be better about this than mine, but I spent a long time figuring out how to listen and support people who were working through experiences with non-consent and dubious consent, back when I didn't even know those terms."

"I don't speak for my generation. I know some good people—and a lot of others. After three years as ship's chef with a couple different crews, I'd reinvented myself. I wasn't out at work, but I'd earned enough respect to dodge most personal issues. I found ace friends online, even a couple where I lived. Of my relatives, I told Viola first, since she'd been openly and defiantly queer, independent, and thumbing her nose at any familial pressure to marry since before I was born. I don't think anyone was surprised by the time I announced I was going to take my turn to live with Tita Viola. It didn't hurt that she offered to pay a crew stipend I could send home to them."

"But this is what you wanted? What you want now?"

Aljon grunted. "Unlike my esteemed elders on this boat," he offered in a tone even Wend could be certain was playful sarcasm, "the extremely limited use of my phone was the closest to a deal-breaker for me. But sailing around the world with Viola is worth it. Now tell me, why did you seek out my Tita Viola?"

The tone of the question was light, but with all they'd been discussing, Wend knew he was serious. Aljon hadn't only been worried about sharing a boat during a seduction, he questioned Wend's motives in general, which seemed fair. "I appreciate you asking directly. If I had the words to answer, I would. When I can't find the right words, I tell people stories. The stories are my truth, and they carry words or concepts for a language I can't fully translate. You remember the teacher I told you about who asked whether I was 'angry' or 'sad'? I didn't have the words to answer, but my brain associated what I was feeling in that moment with times I'd felt something similar before. Even at four years old, I had patterns of associations that worked as a shorthand for me, like analogies or place-holders in a language without words. Sharing stories is my way of trying to communicate ideas that I don't otherwise know how to explain. When I saw Viola's pictures beside my article and looked at more of her work, I thought we might share a certain understanding or connection."

"Not entirely unlike a seduction," Aljon noted.

"Perhaps, but I'm not trying to hide it." Then Wend had a flash of social insight. They knew from experience they might be way off base or unable to explain, but they had to try. "If part of what made you uncomfortable with whatever came before was that I might end up hurting Viola, I'll try very hard not to."

Aljon looked at them sideways, but finally said, "Okay. That's good to know."

6.

THE FIFTH MORNING started late for Wend, with the boat as close to silent as it had been since they'd weighed anchor. In their dreams they'd been a bristle worm, yanked from the ocean floor when the holdfast for a giant kelp gave way. Both alga and occupants had ultimately crashed against a dark and stormy beach to their demise, which seemed somewhat ironic given the story of survival Wend had shared the night before.

When they staggered up on deck, Viola sat mending a line amidst newly polished and deployed solar panels and a nearly slack sail.

The skipper said quietly, "I sent Aljon to bed when the wind died before dawn. It's not quite the doldrums—Inter-Tropical Convergence Zone, ITCZ, or whatever you choose to call the hemispheric trade winds colliding as the air heats up—but we're going nowhere fast. I brought up some granola nut bars and bananas to snack on."

Wend ate.

Viola broke the silence to chat in a surprisingly gentle tone. "GPS shows we crossed the equator last night. Welcome to the Northern Hemisphere. Some flying fish landed on deck, so that's probably lunch or dinner. I photographed them as foreground for an otherwise cheesy dawn photo."

It surprised Wend when Viola set aside the line she'd been checking to retrieve a camera from one of the cockpit lockers and bring up the dawn photo on the camera display.

The picture made Wend blink, and they realized there were tears in their eyes. The photo captured one of the emotions Wend could never name, with the dead fish proclaiming destruction but the dawning light and open sea in the background as the epitome of hope. In the picture they were one, inextricably connected. "I guess that's how you tell your stories."

Viola cracked a small smile. "If you want a chance to hang your hammock again, the current is favorable and our sails are mostly useless right now."

"Do I have to pose for pictures?"

"Definitely not, but if I see a good picture, I'll take it." She winked, but with Aljon's commentary fresh in their mind, Wend turned away to pull their carefully rolled bundle from a cockpit locker.

In minutes the hammock hung from shroud to backstay again. Wend brought up their sleep sack and burrowed inside, trying to enjoy the roll of the waves and ignore the presence of a photographer nearby.

Most of the time, Wend ran cold and wasn't prone to overheating even in the tropics. But after half an hour of cozy hammock time, they peeled back the three layers of sleep sack, letting them hang in the fresh sea air. Still not wanting the sun on their face, they curled mostly face down with only a bare arm to block the remaining light.

It surprised Wend that they could hear a shutter clicking over the omnipresent ocean noises. They wondered if people who invaded personal space to touch casually were also freer about taking candid photos.

For several minutes they focused on breathing and tried to relax. Finally, they gave up and raised their head to say, "I'm probably the best-rested person on this boat right now. You want to try out the hammock and I'll keep watch?"

Viola stowed the camera and had evidently finished the maintenance tasks she deemed important. "Can't say no to an offer like that. Keep an eye on the compass and GPS. Wake me if there's wind." Viola took Wend's place and zipped the inner layer of sleep sack around herself. She appeared to fall asleep instantly.

Wend couldn't help watching Viola, as the hammock was strung in front of the cockpit. The outer two layers of sleep sack spread like a butterfly drying its wings. For once, Wend could understand the desire to take a picture, although the fondness they felt could be either for Viola or for their sleep sack.

As the sun rose higher in the sky, those drooping wings began to flutter. Wend was wondering whether to wake Viola when they took a final scan with the binoculars and noticed a plume of smoke, although Wend supposed it could be a vertical cloud formation peculiar to the ITCZ. Following the plume down, Wend spotted a boat near the horizon, flying an orange flag. They looked again and then shouted, "Viola, are you awake?"

Wend set down the binoculars.

Knowing they wouldn't want anyone to touch them in their sleep, Wend shook one end of the hammock instead. "Viola, wake up."

Instead of any response from Viola, Aljon came thumping up the cockpit steps. His eyes darted with panic until he took in Wend's hand shaking the hammock.

"She sleeps like a rock when given the chance. Why do you need to wake her?" Aljon asked.

"I spotted a boat near the horizon flying an orange flag. It looks like there's smoke rising from it."

Aljon grabbed the binoculars and looked in the direction Wend pointed. "That's definitely a distress flag and smoke. Not sure how much help we can offer, but we should try." He strode right up to the hammock and shook Viola by her shoulders. "Wake up, we need to check the radio and maybe help a superyacht."

All that saved Viola from flailing right out of the hammock while still tangled in one layer of sleep sack was Aljon's grip on her arm and the zipper of the sleep sack. As soon as she landed on her feet, Viola ordered Wend to pack up the hammock and Aljon to take the helm while she used the SSB receiver to check for emergency transmissions on all frequencies.

Wend had stowed their bedding and hammock by the time Viola announced, "I'm not picking up a distress call and can't hail them by VHF, but if they were hit by lightning last night, that could have fried their electronics. At the very least we can offer them our GPIRB if they don't have one of their own." Then she started calling out directions to set the staysail and mainsail as they slowly changed course to assist the larger boat.

With the light winds, it was an incredibly low-speed rescue effort. Viola took some pictures, whether as proof there'd been smoke and a distress flag or for some future sale, Wend couldn't guess. They used the slow-moving opportunity to lower their sample bot over the side for a quick test.

As they drew closer, Viola and Aljon commented on the superyacht in front of them with equal parts scorn and awe.

"Nicer than the ones I worked on," Aljon volunteered, "bet it's still twice the size needed for the supposed maximum occupancy."

"Zero emissions at least," Viola said, "probably to meet some ports' requirements."

To Wend, the superyacht's wide catamaran base looked like a giant water insect hovering on the ocean. Two wind turbines stuck up like antennae, over ten meters high, and most horizontal surfaces were covered with solar panels. They suspected there must be fuel cells, state-of-the-art batteries, hydro turbines, or other systems involved in powering something that massive without sails.

Aljon's appraisal was different. "The sales price for that yacht is more than my government spends on social services in a year. At least, that was true a couple years ago."

Viola snorted and shook her head fondly. "Hope you looked that up on company time. Prepare to tack to starboard."

Nearly half an hour after first sighting, they were heaving to beside the much larger boat as someone in a white button-down shirt covered in smears and stains shouted down from the higher deck. "Hello, I'm Hans Mehta. Do you have any spare batteries? We were hit by lightning and the electrical system is dead."

"I'm Viola Yang. We have minimal battery power. Were you able to issue a mayday?"

"Our radio is wrecked. Our GPIRB survived and activated three hours ago, but we have no way to hear if anyone calls back." Mehta pushed a wave of long bangs back from his sweaty forehead and groaned. "We have a medical emergency, and I'm draining the four marine batteries that serve as backup power. If you could spare even one standard marine battery, I could swap in and recharge my four one at a time from the surviving solar array. It might buy me a couple hours or more."

"We saw smoke. Were you on fire?"

Mehta's fingers clenched the rail, but his voice held steady. "Not directly. Some of the ruined electronics smoldered and caught fire, but I had an extinguisher nearby." He paused. "I hate to speak of it, but my father was already on life support when we lost power. We were heading back to Aotearoa after he had a stroke at sea." Belatedly, Wend placed the man's accent as Aotearoan, albeit with a melodic quality that they associated with Indian languages. He sounded agreeable even as dread practically radiated from every line of his body.

Viola did not seem to appreciate the urgency or the explanation. "You happened to have a life support system on board?"

Mehta raised his hands in the air as if he wanted to shout at Viola, but he lowered them to clutch the railing again as he patiently articulated, "Yes, I would not lie about this, but I do not wish to explain my father's health history or my qualifications to provide medical care. Will you help us? I do not know how long it will take for rescue services to reach here, but the battery power we have left will give him less than two hours and won't hold enough charge to last overnight."

Wend didn't understand why Viola was hesitating. While the silicon lithium-ion battery currently attached to their solar panels and hydro turbine might be low on charge after a day of storm and then doldrums, they had a backup battery that was close to fully charged. Did Viola think it would be wasted because rescue wouldn't come that day and their battery might not be enough? Or did she think Mehta was lying about his dying father?

Only then did Wend remember the hydrogen generator Viola had sworn to only use in a life-or-death situation.

"You don't think rescue will come fast enough for a spare battery to help," Wend said from right beside Viola, where only she could hear.

Viola answered as quietly, "There's nothing on any frequency about this emergency. The fuel cell could take the place of four marine batteries, and he could use solar to generate more hydrogen simultaneously. There might be enough extra to power his VHF transmitter and send a real mayday, if he can get that working." She shouted across to the other boat, "If we give you a power supply, is there any other assistance you need? Do you want help checking over your VHF or other systems?"

With a relieved shake of his head, Mehta said, "I am a medical systems engineer. I know the life support system and the workings of my boat as well as anyone could. Other than the power issue, we are provisioned and prepared to wait a day or more for medevac, depending on weather and who arrives to help."

"Throw across a secured line." With that, Viola took off downstairs.

Luckily, Mehta had a decent throwing arm, as the line landed with a fat coil on their deck when Wend failed to catch it. They scooped it up and temporarily secured it to a cleat.

Viola returned with the bulky drybag and called across to Mehta, "This is a prototype for a self-contained hydrogen generator with a desalination unit. You can attach it to your solar panels, siphon seawater, and refill the hydrogen fuel cells indefinitely. There are instructions inside for hooking it up, as well as contact information and a mailing address for Shelly Svoboda with the Green Energy Alliance. When you reach land, I'm trusting you'll contact her and return this. If you can't reach her, we'll be in Hilo on the island of Hawai'i within the month. I promised her I'd only part with this unit in a life-or-death situation. I'm not giving away her life's work, only lending it to you. Only to save your father's life. Do you understand?"

Wend had not heard this tone in Viola's voice before, and shivered with the sudden idea they'd not want to be on the wrong side of it.

"I do," Mehta said, much more calmly than Wend could have in his situation. "I and my family greatly appreciate what you're doing for us. If you want to secure the line to the bag and then throw the excess back, we can make a loop to transport it across more gently."

Viola tied the line to the bag. Then she wrapped it tightly around the bag and tied it again. When she tossed the line back and Mehta secured the ends to form a loop, Viola pulled with all her weight plus that of the prototype as a test before sending it across.

When the generator rested safe on his deck, Mehta opened the bag and glanced through the instructions inside. He nodded twice and called out, "Thank you. I cannot thank you enough, and I will return this to Shelly Svoboda with my thanks as well. Is there anything we might have aboard that you would like in the meantime? Food? Wine?"

Viola shook her head, voice rough with what could be contempt, annoyance, or more. "No thanks, I'm sure you're eager to set that genera-tor up for your father." She was already untying the line, clearly wanting the *Nuovo Mar* free to maneuver if needed. "Do you want us to stay until other help arrives?"

"You have already done more than I could ever expect. I know what it's like to depend solely on the wind, which seems to be picking up now. Fair winds and following seas."

Viola tilted her head as if surprised by the phrase, or surprised to hear it from Mehta on his modern superyacht. Perhaps it redeemed him as a sailor in her eyes. With a not too audible sigh she replied, "Same to you in the future, and my best to your father for now."

It was late the next day when Viola checked the SSB and announced, "Medevac picked up the Mehtas. Evidently the father is real, truly needed life-support, and made it out in stable condition."

"That's great," Wend said from where they'd been sitting alone on watch. The winds were still low, under ten knots, so the helm wasn't demanding. They'd been sailing sheet to tiller with little human intervention all day, even managing to lower the sample bot once without a second person on deck, but now twists of wind and rain gathered on the horizon. Another storm might be brewing as night fell.

Scanning the wide-open space in front of them, Viola frowned and said, "Sounds like the fancy yacht company got their emergency repair techs there first, believe it or not. They're going to have to tow that over-sized bath toy all the way in to dock. It's completely fried."

"If no one got there until today, that means you saved a life." Wend wondered if it was the right thing to say.

"Some rich old guy." Viola waved the comment off with a flap of one hand.

"Someone's father. An elder. A person." Wend couldn't help trying.

"I know." Viola plopped down beside Wend and slowly leaned into their shoulder. The motion was deliberate enough that Wend saw it coming and could appreciate the contact. "At least something good came from carrying that thing around, and it's better for me to be rid of it."

"You're okay?"

"About this, yeah."

Viola hadn't volunteered any insights about Shelly or why she'd left the crew. In fact, she'd hardly spoken about her. From Aljon's comments and the regret mixed with care that Viola displayed for the generator prototype, Wend suspected it had been Viola's last tie to someone she missed more than she wanted to admit. Despite blooming curiosity, Wend respected Viola's privacy and didn't pry.

"Would you like to hear a story?" they offered instead, hoping to break the tension.

The shake of Viola's head was clear, even as she said, "Perhaps it's selfish, but sometimes I like a quiet boat, even if I'm sharing it with other people."

"We could celebrate silently with hot chocolate," Wend offered.

"You think hot chocolate makes everything better."

"It's chocolate." Wend smiled in vindication and delight as Viola made her way to the galley. Wend wouldn't have dared without Aljon's express permission, but Viola insisted she was allowed free run of her own galley. At least when Aljon was asleep.

Unrelenting rain and unpredictable winds hounded them throughout the next day into late afternoon. Aljon convinced Viola to catch a few hours' sleep while she could. "If it stays like this all night, you know you'll need it."

The fact Viola gave in without argument spoke to how exhausted she was. Wend wondered if she felt unsettled or less safe after giving away her backup plan, even if she'd never consciously admit it. Today's squalls hardly seemed as bad as the last storm, but Viola had battled them all day as if taking personal insult.

Shifting weather kept Aljon glued to the tiller.

He issued detailed instructions to Wend to tighten lines and shift sails. "If either of us goes below to check GPS, Viola won't be able to keep herself from taking over. I can hold a course by compass alone as long as I never take my eyes off it."

"You're doing as well as any skipper I've known, and they all had GPS and usually landmarks as well."

"Out here, it's a whole different kind of sailing. Viola's better at it than I am, but I try. I grew up hearing how my family were born and bred to be the world's best sailors. It was a point of pride for many in the Philippines."

"You're just a fine upstanding patriotic healthy normal Filipino boy?"

Aljon raised his eyebrows and asked, "What are you quoting?"

"A musical called *Bye Bye Birdie*. It fascinated me when I was ten or eleven. As with many musicals, people found it humorous but seemed to hold tight to the very behaviors being parodied. That song has people promoting a young singer by telling all sorts of wild stories to the press and then coming back to the line calling him a fine upstanding patriotic healthy normal American boy. I struggled to understand all sorts of descriptors people used, even ones as seemingly innocuous as 'healthy' or 'normal,' so that song fascinated me.

"Most people would dismiss *Bye Bye Birdie* as dated and problematic, which it is. On the other hand, I learned the most from musicals now deemed problematic. I always found it easier to remember words set to music, too. I'd call them to mind in real life social situations and revisit my past interpretations to improve my understandings."

"I'm post-problematic, but as a white elder you don't have that privilege." Aljon smiled, and Wend was pretty sure he meant it kindly, or at least humorously, even before he said, "Please, educate me about this musical."

Years ago, Wend would have felt conflicted about being called white when they'd grown up feeling otherwise or at least uncertain. Now they tried to embrace just being themself and explaining what they could. "How many white elders can get over ninety percent of the lyrics right and stay mostly in tune?"

When Aljon opened his mouth to answer, or probably sass, Wend added, "From the cockpit of a small boat in the middle of weather like this?" Privately, Wend had to admit it was an odd stage for performing a sixties parody musical loosely based on Elvis Presley getting drafted.

"Hey. You're whiter and older than me. If you're willing to shout out lyrics in a squall, that's more plausible right now than reading a book, which used to be my primary source for understanding society." Aljon checked the compass and horizon before saying, "Musicals are simply another way of telling stories, after all."

Remembering how they'd appreciated Aljon singing on a previous morning, Wend asked, "You want one song or the whole musical?"

He looked up with a start. "You seriously remember whole musicals from your childhood?"

"Only the songs," Wend said with a shrug, "But I can tell you what happens in between."

Aljon laughed. "I'm happy to listen as long as your voice lasts. Only sing in the cockpit while facing me, so you can see when you need to be a sailor instead."

Wend suspected that as a sailor they should be singing *HMS Pinafore*, but that musical had never meant half as much to them. "I think the first song highlights much of why I found people confusing, and a trans woman I worked with in Monterey made a terrific burlesque routine out of it." They started in, singing "How Lovely to be a Woman."

Aljon was laughing by the end of the first verse when Wend sang, with a little extra lilt, about the happiness of having "grown-up female feelings."

In pain, flat on their back, every muscle tense, afraid to move—It took Wend a couple minutes to come fully awake. They couldn't remember any dreams, only storm and rain and pain. The familiar pinch in their neck traveled down their right arm, making sleep on that side impossible. Sleeping on their back to avoid that agony must have irritated nerves near the base of their spine.

It was their lower back that had them afraid to move before becoming fully conscious. The sacroiliac joint and lower vertebrae had seized up, an instinctive reaction to pinched and irritated nerves.

They drew a deep breath. Their eyes stung and their head throbbed. Remembering the disabling nerve pain they'd lived with for the decade covering most of their forties, Wend knew they could work through this. If they were careful, they could manage the pain and still function. Some small part of Wend's brain warned that one knock the wrong way could shift everything back to as bad as it used to be, but after years of practice, they knew better than to dwell on that.

Two different doctors had dismissed Wend's spine issues, told them double doses of ibuprofen would be enough, and only grudgingly sent them to physical therapy time and again when nothing improved for months that turned into years. Wend half believed they dreamed about being invertebrates so often because backbones caused too much trouble, but they'd had those dreams long before they'd learned to hate their spine and adjacent nerves.

Carefully, Wend curled their knees to their chest. They barely had enough clearance in the quarter berth to manage, but they did. After spending thirty seconds curled up, they tried lowering their feet and almost cried out as some vertebrae clicked and pinched a nerve, a literal stab in the back. When that pain faded, Wend planted their feet and lifted their hips, tightening their core.

It hurt. At first they could only manage a couple inches, but pushing their shoulder blades together helped. Within a few minutes they'd worked up to a suitable stretch. The way their knees braced on the top of their berth helped keep them steady as the ship still rocked fiercely from side to side.

They must have been pretty tired to sleep through the creaking and grinding noises all around. Either that, or they'd grown used to them as well as the pain. In that moment, Wend sympathized with the *Nuovo Mar*.

Whether through age or hard use, both of their bodies were struggling right now.

After several repetitions of stretches they'd learned long ago, Wend was mobile enough to get out of bed. They downed four ibuprofen, relieved no one else was there to see. With luck, they'd loosen up over the next few hours, rather than having their back fully seize up, leaving them useless as crew. By the time they'd used the head and swallowed a granola nut bar, Wend could stand upright and manage the stairs.

"Finally, took you long enough to get up here," Viola greeted them as Wend clutched a handhold at the top of the steps. "Help Aljon tighten the lines securing the dinghy over his precious spirulina. Then he needs a nap while you tend the sails."

If Wend was a little slower in their movements or careful to squat rather than bend by the dinghy, no one commented.

By the time they finished, Wend stood soaked to the skin with warm rain and splashes of ocean waves nearly as warm. If anything, it made Wend feel better to be part of the huge stormy water system, even when every motion hurt. Careful movements and ibuprofen would have to be enough for now, and knowing that let Wend relax in a way that might help their back even more.

Aljon ducked below to sleep, and Wend settled in to follow orders from a short-tempered skipper who clearly needed sleep more than anyone else on the boat. The way Viola held the tiller steady, keeping the compass in her peripheral vision as she scanned the horizon, highlighted her profound connection to the *Nuovo Mar*. Wend watched in awe and knew they'd never achieve that competence. For all they tried to play lookout, they weren't sure they could spot another boat in this weather.

For the first hour, Viola held to a steady course, and Wend did little. Later, winds gusted from two different directions. Wend scrambled to follow orders. There were twinges of renewed pain in their back, but nothing Wend couldn't handle.

Viola had all the electronics save for one GPS double sealed in the steel boxes below in case of lightning. Wend thought of the hydrogen generator more frequently than they ever had before. From Viola's snappy tone, she registered the loss as well. The absence of her previous crewmember and dissatisfaction with Wend's inexperience may have contributed to Viola's dour mood.

Large waves slammed the boat from every side. They dropped ten feet then stopped as the next wave hit and they surged up again. Wend's stomach lurched a step behind each vertical shift, despite never having been seasick before.

The wind jumped from zero to thirty knots, too unreliable to be useful. They didn't even try to adjust the hydro turbine blades to gain advantage from such limited bursts of speed. Still, wind in the sails gave Viola power to steer between surges, and she was reluctant to hand over the helm. She'd napped no more than three hours in the last thirty-six.

"Mainsail is flopping. Trim it in." Viola's annoyance cut through the storm the way durian fruit could out-onion onions.

Wend's eyes stung. They were tethered to the boat and fought the lines with numb fingers and heavy arms. It wasn't objectively cold, but they were chilled deep in their bones. They'd fretted in and out of sleep and didn't feel rested, even though they'd slept more than Viola. Hopefully, Aljon was managing to sleep well.

For the next hour, Wend struggled to keep the mainsail to port. Sudden shifts in the wind kept pushing it to starboard. Waves swept the deck repeatedly. Wend's feet slipped in their tightly strapped water sandals despite the grips on the soles. Their arms and shoulder ached and trembled from the constant need to grasp onto something as the boat leaned side to side.

As a sudden wave washed onto deck, Wend fell and lost their handhold and the line they were securing. They collided with the boom, hard on their shoulder, as it swung to starboard.

"Grab that line!" Viola shouted, even as she sprung from the helm to secure it herself. As she did, something clanked and skittered across the deck. "Shit! Grab the GPS!"

Wend threw both arms out at that, not sure which way the GPS had fallen, but terrified by Viola's sudden vehemence. The change in tone and language transmitted Viola's panic to Wend. They lifted their head and drew up to their knees but had no idea where to even look. Instead, they crawled to the line they'd dropped and Viola had only half secured, tying it back into place.

When they tugged it secure, Viola was back at the tiller, glaring down at the compass and muttering, "I never lost a GPS before." Then, she hadn't found it. After Wend hadn't caught it. Their skin turned cold.

"It was my fault. I'm so sorry," Wend offered as they slid back into the cockpit. Their body and mind grew numb as shame swamped all the rest.

"Have to keep the spare GPS locked up until there's no chance of lightning, and then we'll have to be extra careful with it, lock it up during every storm," Viola muttered. She glanced at Wend and dry as hardtack said, "You're bleeding."

Following her gaze, Wend saw their right calf was blooming in watery red. It might as well have been someone else's leg. Wend didn't feel a thing. They wiped the mess away to reveal a long scratch. The movement tugged where the boom had hit their shoulder. Their range of motion was limited and there would be quite a bruise tomorrow, but they weren't going to mention it today. "It's only a scratch."

Viola practically growled. "Go below and clean it. Send Aljon up and take your sleep shift."

"Really, I can—"

"Just go." The way Viola cut Wend off burned with barely hidden anger.

Wend untethered and clattered downstairs, dripping wet and miserable. They forced out the words, "Aljon, are you awake?"

"Sure." The rasp to his voice said otherwise. He'd been deeply asleep a moment prior. The way he said it sounded so much like Viola. "Is't my shift already?"

"I got a scratch and we lost the GPS, so Viola wants you to start early. Sorry."

He pulled on a shirt even as he stood from his berth. "Don't apologize. When I arrived, I said 'sorry, sorry, sorry,' until Viola made a rule against it."

Wend wasn't sure the same would apply to them, especially not today. But they'd known people, especially in the service industry or from certain families, who apologized for everything. While part of Wend once felt like they did everything wrong, that had never been one of their speech issues. Another time, Wend would have been eager to learn about Aljon, curious how he and Viola had changed each other in their time together. Now Wend could barely remember themself as someone who cared or wondered. They'd lost Viola's GPS.

"The first aid kit is here." He tapped the locker Wend was headed for anyway before he made a quick stop at the head, shoved a fruit bar and nuts into his pockets, and struck out into the howling rain.

Suddenly alone, Wend swallowed back a sob. The boat groaned and sighed from every direction, the thumps of waves and rain discordant and unpredictable against the pain in their back. The cabin smelled of sweat, and Wend would swear they tasted the anxiety of the crew. They wanted to fling open windows and breathe fresh sea air, but that wasn't what they'd signed on for.

Instead, they cleaned and dressed the long scratch on their calf and took another double dose of ibuprofen. They stowed the first aid kit and stripped where they stood before trying to dry off and then deal with their wet clothes and all the water they'd carried in with them.

It seemed pointless to pull dry clothes onto their damp and dirty body. They did it anyway before drinking some water and crawling into their sleep sack.

The layers that usually swaddled Wend stifled. Their feet were damp. Wet spots and drips pervaded much newer boats than this one. If the covered portion of their berth were damp, there was nothing they could do. Stabbing sensations like pins driven into the soles of their feet echoed nerve pain throughout their hips and spine. That ghost of their old injury told Wend they were freaking out.

They tried to breathe deeply and slowly but failed. They'd be unable to speak now, even if there were someone to hear, but they preferred to have no witnesses for this.

As their sense of touch spiked, Wend shifted restlessly in their sleep sack. They wanted to curl inward, but hips and shoulders pinched nerves on both sides. Flat on their back, they felt exposed, fragile.

They stilled beneath a looming figure. Someone they'd trusted back in college. Even believing they were fully consenting, they'd lost their words when hurt while laid out like this. They'd frozen and become a thing, unresponsive and unable to curl inward. But anxiety never stopped their breathing long enough for Wend to pass out. They waited until it peaked, and ended up gasping.

The loss of control barraged them with fear, adrenaline, panic. They tensed and choked under the bombardment.

But Wend wasn't a scared child anymore. They knew it would end. Even in the midst of an attack, they could mentally repeat over and over that it would end, that they would feel better later. They didn't have to believe it, just repeat and remember all the times they'd made it through in the past.

Fear always simmered inside Wend. The way it stayed hidden during a crisis reflected how constantly Wend had been terrified when younger.

To function they'd learned to put off bad emotions until later. People triggered them or played on their emotions enough that solitary coping mechanisms became an act of defiance. By learning the exact size and shape of each hurt, each crack in their armor, Wend could hold on to the fear and force it to wait until they had time alone.

The tears streaming from Wend's eyes didn't matter. That was a release.

They'd always ached when spikes of adrenaline accompanied negative emotions with no relief at the end. The world left them cracked wide open. Waiting let the adrenaline die down. Tears brought relief if not comfort. Once Wend started shaking, they could move again.

They rolled off their back onto the shoulder that hadn't been bruised by the boom. That side screamed with the pain that had shot through their nerves minutes before, and Wend struggled to find the position that hurt least.

They ended up deep in their sleep sack, face hidden and warm breath trapped. But in their imagined cold, the warmth helped. They stroked their own fingers over their knee—up, down, around—over and over until the skin beneath could barely stand the light touch. Then they reached farther and stroked their own calf, avoiding the scratch. The oversensitivity of their skin when out of control like this could wear down their defenses, trick their body into relaxing. Wend hoped their senses would reset if they finally fell asleep. At least if they slept, they'd have a break from it all, for a while.

7.

LIGHT RAIN transformed into warm humidity, but Wend could not shake the chill from their bones, despite wearing their warmest rash guard under their windbreaker. The sleeves on each layer clung, but the shoulders were comfortable, and there were no irritating tags or seams. They'd taken ibuprofen again, and felt much better than the day before, despite fresh bruises.

Viola wore a breezy leaf green romper and was mostly silent at the helm as Wend kept watch and followed orders. The wind picked up, inconstant and annoying, as was the variable damp and haze they sailed through for minutes or hours at a time. Whenever Wend spotted the back-up GPS beside the compass, they felt a twinge in their gut.

Aljon kept busy below, tending sprouts that he had been growing in dark trays ever since Wend boarded. The first were ready to harvest, and the cook was excited to add them to tabbouleh and some kind of soup. Wend wished they could watch and learn about growing sprouts and preparing meals on a boat, but in this weather, it made sense to have two people on deck whenever possible.

During a quiet spell, Viola surprised Wend by saying, "I've known you for ten days now, and I feel simultaneously very close to you and like I don't know you at all. Was that your intent? Aljon says you had no plans to seduce me. I'm not sure if I should be relieved or insulted about that, by the way."

Muscles along Wend's neck and spine tensed with unease, wondering what exactly had been discussed in their absence and where Viola would steer this conversation. "It's never occurred to me to seduce anyone in my life," Wend volunteered then stumbled over their words to add, "except maybe metaphorically as far as convincing you to let me sail with you and share stories." They wondered if Viola and Aljon had talked about them last shift or before Viola asked for a quiet boat two days ago.

"You offer to tell stories, but you only tell those from your childhood."

That implied Aljon hadn't shared the story of Wend's near-drowning, which demonstrated consideration at the very least. "Is there something wrong with that?" Wend asked, leaning against the side of the cockpit. They lowered the binoculars but were unable to fix their eyes on Viola's. "I present whichever stories seem most relevant, because I think by association. Otherwise, I'm rather bad at communicating."

"You speak as well as I do."

Spoken like a photographer, they couldn't help but think. She wondered if Viola could understand. "That's what you hear, now. Neither words nor social skills came easily to me. I put a lot of work into both. But every word and gesture is an act of translation. Behind those, I offer more context, and often more words, hoping the listener will meet me halfway, to build understanding." This speech lodged in their throat, each phrase requiring effort. Wend glanced up to find Viola staring at them, but without trying to make eye contact. There had been times in the past when such a look would have sent Wend scurrying away to hide, but right now being true to themself meant standing brave until they learned more.

"Some say art means what the viewer sees in it."

Wend wasn't sure if their words or stories were supposed to be art. "Okay, but is that still communication?"

"Sometimes appreciation is enough."

"To me it just leads to new communication challenges." They thought of the people who'd only wanted to hear their most painful or bizarre stories. Maybe that had been art or performance. Their audience had been rapt, but telling those stories without the others left Wend wrung out and inevitably more misunderstood. Thus far, they hadn't felt that way with Viola, but she might want those stories as well as the rest. "I'd like to hear any stories you want to tell. And I'd willingly tell you almost anything you ask about."

The skeptical raised eyebrow and tight mouth with which Viola greeted that confession hurt. Wend wondered whether they had revealed too little or too much. For most of the voyage, they'd felt accepted if not understood.

Now Viola sounded unfairly cold when she said, "You never did tell me why you and your mother left Hawai'i."

The way she asked, Viola clearly anticipated the hurtfulness of that story. She probably didn't realize the vise-like pain bearing down on Wend already, but as with talk of drowning during a storm, bad moments sometimes summoned hard truths. Wend made a slow scan with binoculars while breathing in through their nose and out through their mouth, as if filling their body with calm before beginning.

"I was four, and I already feared bright white walls. My dad's anger burned white hot beside me. I would not take his hand." The burn, emotions, and images flashed through Wend faster than they could speak. Later realizations about not having to accept or claim him as a parent were beyond the reach of the Wend in this story, along with so much more.

"This was the first and last time he drove me in the car alone. His older kids were all at school. The building he drove to was the biggest and whitest I'd ever seen. Taller than the palm trees beside it. They were very tall palm trees, and I knew palm trees. I did not know the building was the Kailua Hospital, the same one where I was born.

"I followed where my dad's shadow should have been. But the brightness inside burnt away all shadows. The smells stung my nose like washing white sheets. I was near running to keep up with him. I didn't know whether I was running away or running to something. I never knew why anything happened back then.

"Turning. Turning. Long halls and sunlight. Safe golden sunlight at the end of the hall."

Wend's hands tightened on the binoculars. They squeezed—right, left, right, left—trying to corral impressions into words, into a coherent story. "Mom sat in a metal chair with a yellow cushion. She was wearing her green and yellow pajamas. Her hair was back in a ponytail. She wore lipstick with her pajamas. She held her arms out to me, and I ran to her.

"'Why did you die?' I sobbed into smooth green satin by her neck.

"'He shouldn't have told you that, baby,' was what she said. 'I didn't die. I would never leave you on purpose.' She petted my hair and held me tight. She was the only one whose touch felt safe, brought comfort.

"'Now who's bending the truth,' my dad snorted behind me. 'You attempted suicide, and no court in the country would let you keep her if I protested.'

"'Little ears,' Mom said in the voice she used for me, but it sounded like she was talking to him. 'I said you could keep all the rest. We'll be gone in a week. Give us that. Don't say it out loud. One week.'

"'She'll forget it all anyway.' My dad's burning white anger sizzled my skin as he said it. I did forget. For a long time. He should have been right about that, but it ended up locked in my mind." Wend brought the binoculars to their eyes, to hide behind, not to see.

"Did he hit you?" was what Viola asked. Her eyes were fixed directly on Wend in a way they could feel without looking.

Wend refused to perform a series of stories linked by abuse. They lowered the binoculars as they said, "Not then. At that age I perceived other people's emotions as physical touch, especially harsh emotions."

"You sound less like yourself the older the memory you're recalling."

Wend wondered if that were true or in the eyes of the beholder. "Maybe I sound more like myself," Wend offered without even trying to meet Viola's gaze. "Those memories fit the way my brain works better than anything from later. I never had the right words and was confused almost all the time as a child, but those memories are the closest to a native language I possess."

After a long pause to use the binoculars to actually scan the horizon, Wend could feel Viola staring at them again. When Wend finally looked back, they imagined a flicker of understanding behind the suspicious and tightening eyes. "Why are you telling me all this?"

"If I knew how to answer besides sharing stories I would." Only as they spoke, Wend wondered if they were holding too much back. They shied from the hostility in Viola's voice, without knowing what caused it. They couldn't ask how much of her annoyance stemmed from the lost GPS and how much from misperceived romantic or other signals. When they justified that caution in their head, a thousand images—mom, dad, teachers, classmates, even Mathew when insisting Wend couldn't sense lies—reinforced their failings at direct communication.

"So you're going to tell me your whole life story?" Viola's question hung limp in the damp air, like a tiny gray rain cloud.

"It's not that long of a boat trip." Wend's voice broke in an unpleasant way as they said it. "The stories are like puzzle pieces that fit together in different ways. Fitting them together is an act of translation from my perspective to yours."

Viola shook her head and refused to talk beyond the necessities of sailing after that.

Wend spent half the time too choked up to speak. They fell asleep that night frozen but not cold. All their muscles clenched tight with exhaustion and worry, realizing how vulnerable they were, stuck on this boat for at least another week or two, wondering if they could find a better way to communicate.

"Wend, wake up."

The shouting faded from Wend's mind. They curled in a ball within layers of cloth between two hard walls.

"Are you okay, Wend?" The voice was Aljon's.

Wend's muscles clenched tight. Their body ached, battered and bruised. It took longer than usual to untangle from their sleep sack in the cramped quarter berth. "My turn on deck?" They'd changed into a dry short-sleeved rash guard and board shorts before bed and were ready to hit the deck at a moment's notice.

"No, we're past the rain and fog. Visibility's good, and Viola wanted some time alone." Aljon added in a softer tone, "You were making noises."

"Snoring?" Wend asked, despite knowing better. They only snored when their nose was stuffed up. Flashes of a dream, of their mother shouting and others joining in, combined with waking up curled in a tight ball, suggested what sorts of noises Wend had been making. They didn't think Aljon had answered. Maybe he shook his head. Without thinking, Wend said, "Sorry."

"Don't." He turned to the galley where he was tending his sprouts. He wet a cloth that hung over the trays as he asked, "Would you like some hot chocolate?"

"Am I that predictable?"

"I like people who can be cheered up with favorite foods. Viola calls it my 'love language.'" He wrinkled his nose. "I could do without that term."

"If you put it that way, I would looove some hot chocolate." Wend exaggerated the word "love" and smiled wide to make it clear they were joking. "Is there anything I can do to help?"

"This entire galley fits the span of my arms." He put water to boil on the two-burner stove and set the stacked trays of sprouts back in their locker in order to place a cutting board on the tiny counter next to a tray with fish and a bowl of sprouts he'd harvested.

Wend asked, "If I stay over here, will you tell me about what you're making?"

"Sprout patties."

Wend was fighting not to ask for more details when Aljon offered them anyway. He held up a few of each sprout as he named them. "I use lentil, bean, and sunflower sprouts. Chop the larger ones. Mix with onions, soy sauce, nuts, and homemade tofu. I'll serve them beside some dried fish curls that Viola likes." He waved to the fish and worked as he spoke. By the time he'd finished, he was mixing hot water with powdered milk, cocoa, and sugar.

"Thanks," Wend said, taking the cup of hot chocolate Aljon handed them. "I guess I'm not the only one you're trying to cheer up today. Do you even eat fish?"

He tilted his head, either surprised Wend had noticed or debating what to say. "I had far too much fish while growing up and learning to cook for tourists. I finally realized I could be a 'proud upstanding patriotic healthy normal Filipino boy' even if I'm vegan, ace, and dislike most traditional Filipino cuisine and ideas of masculinity."

Wend could practically hear the stories of hurt that lurked behind those declarations, but didn't dare ask now. They appreciated his *Bye, Bye Birdie* reference but felt a twinge of guilt for the hot chocolate they now held. "If I'd known you were vegan, I wouldn't have brought powdered milk into your kitchen or asked you to make hot chocolate. Do you mind if I say I'm sorry for that?"

Aljon rolled his eyes dramatically. "You saw me drying fish for Viola the day you arrived, and I worked as a professional chef for three years preparing whatever people ordered. I agreed to cook Viola's fish, but other than that and your powdered milk, everything served on this boat is vegan."

"Even the breakfast scrambles?"

At this, he grinned. "Made with soft beans and spices. My hot chocolate," he added, looking as though he imagined Wend had been wondering about it also. "Made with macadamia powder and a touch of coconut oil to help the cocoa blend better."

Wend knew their preferred cocoa was particularly hydrophobic but appreciated scientifically that phase-separated components could combine in an emulsion. "Did you like it?"

Aljon nodded and half-laughed through his nose. "You can try it next time."

Trying not to grimace, Wend said, "I've tried a lot of vegan chocolates and never really liked them."

Surprisingly, Aljon nodded. "Non-vegans overdo it with the coconut, or go right to soy or almond. There are plenty of alternatives, especially for hot chocolate, if you want to go vegan. I've also got dried cashews and some hemp seeds."

Wend nodded slowly, having struggled with this before. "I mostly eat what's served wherever I am, but when given options I try to choose foods lower on the food chain for environmental reasons. I'll go out of my way to buy lab-grown dairy, but it's still not available most places I work. You probably think I'm terrible."

Aljon sighed gently, and the sound carried more honest reassurance for Wend than any words that could follow. "I'm vegan for both ethical and environmental reasons, but I try not to judge people in absolutes. As if we don't all have things to work on."

"I would be happy to try your macadamia version next time." Wend lifted the warm thermos mug in their hands.

"Good." Aljon paused, taking a moment to form a tidy sprout patty between his palms. "You told me quite a story to explain how you stopped trying so hard to blend in. If you want to be vegan or pescatarian, just tell people. Most places offer a lot of good alternatives now."

Wend closed their eyes and took a long sip of their chocolate. They still struggled with asserting themself and with deciding when to push. Conflict around food was especially hard, but they vowed in that moment to do better.

Opening their eyes, Wend smiled and said, "You're quite the persuasive speaker when you want to be, and English isn't even your first language, is it?"

"I learned Tagalog, Filipino, and Bikol at home. Those are mostly genderless languages, in case that interests you. In school, I became a good student who loved to read. There was so much I wanted to read in English that I picked it up fast with fairly formal grammar. Traveling with Viola has improved my accent, and there's nothing like living on a small boat. Most people hate it, but I wouldn't give up the last year for anything." Aljon placed the last sprout patties in neat lines around the edges of a tray and filled a bowl with dried fish curls.

"Even with not eating fish and disliking scuba and swimming?"

Aljon shrugged as he placed the bowl of fish curls in the center of the tray. "Have you ever lived on a boat this long?"

"I've been on larger research vessels for several weeks at a time. Until this trip, I'd never spent more than two nights as part of a crew this small. Most often, we had a camp or some sort of housing to return to between trips."

With a chuckle, Aljon said, "You're lucky to have found us. So far Viola's on her best behavior, and everyone likes a cook."

Wend knew finding them wasn't luck but wondered what Aljon meant by Viola's best behavior. Or, they realized, 'so far.'

When they brought the food upstairs, Viola exclaimed, "Fish curls! I love those."

After a long time with the three of them eating in silence, Wend asked, "Would you like to hear a story?"

Viola answered abruptly, "No stories. Just quiet."

Wend sank into the cockpit bench. The weight of unresolved issues with Viola pinned them like the harshest wind. They'd found a brief respite while talking with Aljon, but the guilt from losing the GPS and their physical pain that day and since wore on their nerves. That overlaid the uncertainty they'd felt in every conversation since Viola asked how they'd spotted the plastic island and then put off discussing their flying dream with a hint of staticky deception.

Aljon snatched a fish curl off Viola's plate and waved it in the air, as far from her as he could reach.

"I know you're going to give that back." Viola held her hand out flat, mock solemn, and Aljon moved the fish curl a little closer. "Let me appreciate the food and good weather in peace for a while. I promise I'll be in a better mood by next shift."

Aljon returned the pilfered fish curl and finished all his sprout patties except one. He gave that one to Wend before going below to sleep.

For the next hour, the wind was steady; therefore the skipper wasn't barking orders. Wend heaved the hydro turbine out and adjusted the propeller blades on their own for the first time. They double-checked all the turbine's connections to boat and battery before heading back to the cockpit.

When the sun finally warmed Wend to the point of relaxing tense muscles, they were glad for their short sleeves even in the shade of the cockpit. They took some time to write out recent thoughts and events in their waterproof notebook. Those pages would become a letter when they landed, so it was almost like talking things through with an old friend. Hours passed in near silence.

Later, when Viola went downstairs to sleep for a full shift and Aljon emerged in a loose long-sleeved tee shirt and shorts, Wend remained silent out of habit.

Eventually Aljon pointed out dolphins speeding along by the bow of their boat. "They take advantage of us pushing the water to help them go faster."

There were at least two dolphins. Wend suspected there were more but could only ever spot two at a time. None were distinct enough to identify as individuals. They flashed silver in the sun, leaping fearlessly despite the much larger boat.

"Is that what you meant by 'attractive megafauna' when you first described Viola's pictures?" Aljon asked.

"You have an excellent memory for precise phrases." Wend almost laughed. "I was mostly referring to the photo she got on the cover. It was a common octopus, or *Octopus vulgaris*, probably the most prolific and most studied octopus around the world. Viola caught it half camouflaged amongst brown macroalgae with two tentacles turning deep red with rust-colored stripes as it lunged for prey. It was an exciting action shot, better than anything we had for documentation, and exactly what the magazine wanted."

"Did you expect them to use photos your group submitted?"

"It's not that," Wend said. "I understand the publicity value of good photos, and no matter how dire or fascinating my discoveries with the microbiome may be, I don't expect cover shots of microscope slides."

Aljon glanced at the dolphins still keeping pace as the boat sped along. "The dive where she took those photos wasn't fascinating. I don't like the breathing apparatus and mask anyway, so dive buddy is not one of my favorite roles. But with Viola that night, I had to sit perfectly still in the dark on the ocean floor for half an hour. The reef looked half dead and covered with algae not fit for human consumption. I only noticed the octopus because Viola was suddenly intent and taking bursts of photos."

Wend thought about how reassuring they found the weight and

enclosure of their diving gear and were glad their presence on the crew might at least give Aljon a break from one task he disliked. "The octopus did have one interesting mention in our research. Did you and Viola go diving at any of the deeper, mesophotic reefs around the Marquesas?"

"No." Aljon sounded apologetic. "With only two of us onboard, Viola passed up a lot of deeper dive opportunities. There wasn't a safe way for both of us to leave the boat, even if I were trained for those depths, and Viola won't dive out of my sight without a buddy."

Wend nodded, respecting Viola's responsibility as a diver and to Aljon. "There's an old system of reefs ninety meters down, probably buried since the Pleistocene but with a totally different ecosystem now. There's also a mesophotic reef at less than half that depth. In the early twenties, when I became involved with the Marine Census, some people hoped these deeper, more isolated reefs might preserve the species we were rapidly losing to coral bleaching, storms, and pollutant run-off from land into shallow waters. It turns out the mesophotic reefs are still degrading, albeit more slowly. They aren't going to help restock species lost from better-known shallower reefs because most species can't handle that range of depths."

Wend could tell from the blank look on Aljon's face that he found this description almost as dull as sitting on the ocean floor while Viola photographed a half-dead reef. They couldn't help watching as they dropped their own megafauna hook.

"The common octopus can handle the depth. They do it for foooood," Wend stretched the word until Aljon smiled as they continued speaking, "with a varied enough diet to feed along either mesophotic or shallower reefs. Their genetic adaptations handle acidity created by increased carbon dioxide as they travel between regions. Lower oxygen slows their metabolic rate and limits their growth, but the adaptability gives them an advantage most species don't have. When traveling between the different reefs, the octopuses carry representatives from the microbiomes. Much of what they carry can't survive in the new ecosystems, but some can."

Aljon shook his head, but his renewed interest lit up his face. "Is that a long way of saying that you're okay with Viola's photos being paired with your article?"

"I'm saying, I know how that octopus helped the microbiome." Wend shrugged. "Besides, it was an awesome picture. I would have happily taken your place, sitting still in scuba gear for half an hour to see it live."

"I'd have been happy to give you that chance."

"If you really want the things I have . . . " Wend slipped into song by the end of the line.

"What musical is that?" Aljon smiled as he asked.

"*Lost Horizon*, which you probably have to be post-problematic to appreciate now, although I don't think that song is too bad, and it passes the Bechdel test."

Aljon shook his head slowly. "Believe it or not, *Lost Horizon* was one of the books I read aloud to practice English, and perhaps to annoy my relatives. Aside from the inherent colonialism and racism, it did discuss aggression versus appreciation and acknowledge different points of view. Is the musical any worse?"

"I don't think I ever read the book." Wend ducked their head, then realized their true self wasn't at all ashamed of that and smiled up at Aljon instead. "I've told you I tested out concepts and remembered words better from songs." Aljon nodded. Wend continued, "Well, the song I quoted has two women with different perspectives comparing the things they will not miss and offering them to each other like gifts. Another song portrays a man and woman contemplating how they might scare each other away because they were brought up in two different worlds. Then there's a glee-fully American- and Anglo-centric song called 'Question Me an Answer' that is totally played for laughs as a reluctant teacher does about what you'd expect given the title."

"Sounds like you should question me a musical and maybe I can say what's different in the novel."

His expression lightened a touch, and for the first time since the storm, Wend's own weighty thoughts did as well.

8.

ALJON TURNED OUT to be an excellent storyteller when sharing what he'd read. Hours later, Wend and Aljon had dug deep enough to discover that they'd both read *Cry, the Beloved Country*, but Wend's singing voice wasn't up to something as operatic as the musical version, *Lost in the Stars*.

As the sun set and the wind began to falter, Aljon said, "Tell me something you liked to eat as a kid that sounds ridiculous now."

Wend knew the sort of food choices he meant. They'd known kids who ate jam on French fries or orange juice on Frosted Flakes. "I don't think I ate anything that unusual." When Aljon raised his eyebrows and waited, Wend tried again. "I do remember when microwaves were new and exciting. My mom brought one home in 1978 and told me they were how astronauts cooked their food. That turned out to be a myth. Raytheon had a lot of excess magnetron tubes that had been used for radar in World War II and some engineers almost accidentally discovered they could be used to heat food and pop popcorn."

Aljon leaned back, hand steady on the tiller, patiently waiting for Wend to bring food into the story.

"Once we had that microwave, I experimented until I found the perfect frozen dinner. It was Salisbury steak, mashed potatoes, and mixed carrots with peas. I'd never had Salisbury steak before, and I thought it was very fancy. My mashed potatoes had previously come from a box, and peas had always been frozen. Carrots were sweet for a vegetable, but mostly, all those foods cooked consistently all the way through if I followed the directions. I felt pretty good about making a real grown-up dinner for my mom when she came home from work."

Aljon smiled lazily in the fading light and told how he'd faked his way through making sinigang the first time it was requested by tourists, even though he'd never cooked it before. "My whole family said my lola made the best sinigang on the island. It had a sour taste that came from tamarind that you had to balance with fish sauce, radish, and onions. I had to eat it growing up whenever I was sick, as if it could cure the common cold. Lots of Filipinos find it comforting. I'd say it's an acquired taste that I never cared to acquire." He rolled his head side to side and continued. "Mine was terrible, but that boatload of tourists believed it was authentic and didn't dare complain. They'd asked for it after all. When I offered to make dishes better suited to the ship's galley, they were relieved to enjoy the simpler foods I knew how to make. Eventually, I did learn to make sinigang and all the foods tourists were likely to request."

"And now?"

"Be glad we're not eating spirulina at every meal."

It wasn't until later that night when Viola and Wend were alone under a steady wind that Viola said, "I don't like seeing Aljon try to cheer everyone up or play peacekeeper between us."

"Neither do I," Wend agreed immediately.

Viola glared at them. "Most people hate tests because they fear failure. At this point in my life, I'm used to failure. But I still don't like tests. Your plan, that I solve some puzzle to know what you're asking, it sounds too much like a test."

After two days of worry and mind-whirling uncertainty, Wend had at least considered this objection. "What if we don't approach it like a jigsaw puzzle? Maybe I'm trying to solve a crossword, and slowly but surely, I'm filling in words. If I share the clues with others, they might fill in words I don't know. Or they might challenge a word I put horizontally where nothing that intersects vertically fits with it."

"Your stories are like clues in a crossword puzzle?" Viola's raspy voice sounded harder than ever. It made Wend want to brace in their corner of the cockpit and retreat from the punishing soundwaves.

Instead Wend held their place directly across from Viola and said, "Maybe. I've had better luck with stories than analogies."

"Your stories aren't working for me." Viola shook her head and looked back out to sea, hand steady on the tiller. "I'll admit, when you came rushing out of your bunk and pointed to that patch of plastic, I couldn't help but remember your story about flying dreams and how you knew that a road you'd never been on would curve. But that could have been chance, a child remembering only when they guessed right."

Wend nodded in agreement.

Viola continued, "The tiny fish that came out from hiding when we visited the waterfall seemed to change course to swim around your arm and then all the way around you—that could have been chance too, but I remembered them when that giant manta ray hovered near the heap of plastic and then came even closer to us before turning its stomach inside out. That had to be an extremely vulnerable moment. As a photographer, I've been witness to more than my share of rare moments. I'm not going to attribute them to magic, or whatever, because you tell evocative stories." Viola kept her hands and feet tucked in close, and Wend realized the usually tactile woman hadn't touched them in days—since losing the primary GPS or whatever conversation she'd had with Aljon, Wend wasn't sure.

"You say you've witnessed more than your share," Wend began, "and at the waterfall you mentioned sensing when people lied, even if that later failed you in some major way."

Wend expected an interruption or an emotional reaction. When there was none, they said, "As an analytical thinker, I notice patterns. I look for explanations that are verifiable, because I know humans tend to see patterns even where there aren't any. I first went into genetics to learn why I was the way I was. But genetics couldn't pin down my neurodivergence or where my ancestors came from. That way of thinking is outdated. Even with all we've learned in the decades since then about gene expression and epigenetics, I don't think genetics is going to answer if dreams showed me where a plastic patch floated or how a street curved. I don't expect science to explain how you or I perceive lies or emotions. But if you have suggestions, either hypotheses we can test or observations that connect to mine like words in a crossword or pieces of a puzzle, I'd like to know. Even if you call something magic, I won't dismiss it without proof or at least a better model of reality."

"Even if I believed all this, that you can describe old memories with visceral eloquence, but somehow can't just tell me why you're here, on my boat ... Why should I get involved?" Viola asked in one smooth rush, as if it were nothing, but to Wend it sounded like everything. Viola might represent their last chance to reconcile the seemingly impossible flying dreams and lie detection to their true self and how they connected to others.

After taking a deep breath, Wend looked Viola right in the eyes. "My model of reality suggested you might already be involved. I'm offering you stories I thought you might want to know." At another time in Wend's life, they would have apologized for not managing that better. Now they held eye contact well beyond their tolerance, until they physically needed to look away. They left it at that.

Viola rubbed her temples and said, "Fine, tell me a story."

Wend knew what story had to come next. Whether it would help or not, they couldn't guess. "By my first day of junior high, in 1984, I thought I'd learned how to camouflage, at least physically. I'd sold stationery door to door over the summer to earn enough money for new clothes and a fancy haircut. I wore polo shirts and pedal pushers. I applied tinted lip gloss and then three shades of eye shadow following directions I read in a magazine aimed at teenagers. My hair was feathered on both sides from my forehead to my shoulders and required hairspray that made my eyes water. I learned to do that step before the eye makeup."

Viola nodded, either in recognition of the times or to show they were listening.

It surprised Wend to feel that tiny reassurance as a loosening in their chest. "I started at the overcrowded local school nearest to my house. I knew almost no one, but that seemed like an advantage to me. I kept quiet but did my schoolwork. I still felt like I was putting on a performance every moment just to avoid bullying and to get by socially, but I believed proving I was smart and a good student would be necessary to my later survival.

"For about two months, I did as well as any new kid in junior high could expect. But I didn't have any friends until Gabi, who sat across from me in homeroom, invited me to eat lunch with her group.

"I was more than surprised. Gabi never spoke in class. I'd noticed that she started wearing eye shadow and lip gloss like mine about a week into school. Her clothes were mostly tee shirts and jeans. I hadn't yet figured out the hierarchy of different brands of jeans or even that there was one, but Gabi's clothes fit her curves, and having curves was a big deal from what I'd seen so far in seventh grade.

"Of course, I joined her for lunch. Her friends were polite and welcomed me. They were all girls and none of the rest wore makeup. Two of them were trading rainbow stickers for their binders, and I wondered if eating with this group would make me a target for bullies again. I could accept that in exchange for having friends.

"By a week later, I'd decided Gabi was smarter than everyone thought and needed her vision tested. She wouldn't let me talk to our homeroom teacher about it, but she let me explain my reasoning to the school nurse who immediately ran a test with an eye chart on the wall. Then she ordered a follow-up test, which the school paid for, and a week later Gabi had glasses. She was shy about wearing them at first, but I told her they magnified and drew attention to her eye makeup, and that did the trick.

"I think the glasses were what led to me being invited for dinner and then sleepovers at Gabi's house. It turned out Gabi was an only child living with a single mom, just like I was. Her mom sold makeup door to door, but hadn't let Gabi wear any until she went on and on about me that first week of school. Her mom tried to teach me all about skin care and to discourage me from biting my nails. That didn't really take. But she also believed in home cooking, mostly beans, rice, tortillas, and soups. I never turned down a chance to eat at their house.

"Gabi's mom didn't really get along with my mom, but she was willing to let Gabi spend the night at my house, even if I fed her microwave dinners.

"It surprised me when the bullies at school picked on Gabi more than me. I taught her everything I'd taught Robert about avoiding them, and she taught me a few tricks of her own. But one day after school a bully came and put his hands under Gabi's skirt. He was saying something about wanting to go behind the gym and make like rabbits.

"Gabi froze, not saying a word. Her eyes got shiny, and the fear emanating from her made me shout, 'Keep your hands to yourself.'

"He said something like, 'You gonna make me?'

"I was a twiggy thing with no training to fight, but in that moment, all the fear I'd suffered at the hands of bullies turned into defending Gabi, who'd become my friend. The two thoughts that pushed me forward were that Gabi couldn't afford to break those glasses and for the first time ever I was bigger than a bully. I don't think my weight was even in triple digits, but I'd grown four inches over the summer. In every other way, I thought of myself as small or average in size. But in that moment, I believed I had to fight or give in to being bullied and letting my friends be bullied for the rest of our lives.

"Next thing I knew, that boy and I were rolling on the ground hitting with knees, elbows—I don't think I even knew to make a fist. But I ended up on top with one of his arms pinned under him and the other under my knee. He called me 'crazy' and maybe some worse words I didn't really know. I didn't call him anything back because I didn't swear and even then I wouldn't use the word 'crazy' like that, given my mom's issues.

"I made him promise never again to touch anyone who didn't want to be touched. I didn't think he'd keep the promise. I didn't expect him to even leave Gabi and me alone without several more fights. But he said the words I demanded and the fight went out of me. I let him go.

"At least a dozen kids were watching. It wasn't like in movies where kids stand around and cheer a fight on. It felt more like a freak show."

Wend fell out of the story for a moment, glancing sideways to see if Viola was offended or had any reaction to how Wend had seen themself in that moment. Viola sat rigid, staring out to sea. She nodded briefly, as if she knew Wend was checking but wouldn't want eye contact, or maybe Viola maintained that separation for her own sake. It took everything Wend had to continue.

"As soon as it was over, I was cold and started to shake.

"Gabi took my arm and led me back to her house, because it was closer. Her mom was out working, but Gabi heated up leftover soup. When we were done eating, she said she wished she knew how to fight like I did.

"I told her I didn't know anything about fighting and couldn't remember most of it, but maybe we could join the school wrestling team and both learn. That started a whole other type of fight with the school, because only boys were allowed to compete in wrestling at the time. Eventually, Gabi and I discovered triathlons instead and joined a city-wide club that was mostly adults.

"The surprising part for me was that neither Gabi nor I was physically bullied or attacked for the rest of junior high. All because of one fight where I could barely remember the violent details.

"That summer, Gabi spent almost every weekend at my house. Her mom had a new boyfriend who we both thought was creepy. We talked about how his creepiness practically oozed from him and felt slimy on our skin, even without touching. I was glad we both sensed that the same way, because I'd never had anyone to validate those feelings before.

"By the time Gabi and I both had our thirteenth birthdays in June, I knew her better than I'd ever known anyone in my life. I'd never felt such a

connection with anyone except Mathew. That's when I remembered that
Mathew and I celebrated our fifth birthday together. I wondered why the
two people I'd felt closest to in my life were both born within the same few
days." They paused. "In June, 1972."

Wend hadn't been brave enough to watch Viola's reactions as they rushed
to finish their story about Gabi. They'd waited days for this opportunity.
If Viola didn't feel the pull that had brought Wend to her or dismissed the
birthday connection out of hand, Wend would know they hadn't laid out
enough of the puzzle or presented it correctly.

Only after mentioning the shared birthday celebrations did Wend
fall silent, waiting for any reaction. The skipper gazed out to sea, which
admittedly Wend hadn't been doing, despite the *Nuovo Mar* maintaining
a relatively high speed even in the dark of a new moon.

Viola's face was well illuminated, clear and calm.

All she said was, "If there's more to this story, then finish."

Wend took a deep breath and endeavored to keep their eyes scanning
the sea. "I sold a bunch of my stuff in a garage sale and kept my room
spotlessly clean to make room for Gabi when she stayed over. My room
was ten feet by twelve feet, and we were not little kids by that point. We
had a sofa bed mattress that we pulled into my room for her to sleep on.
I tried to convince Gabi to rinse dishes before leaving them in the sink,
much as I'd tried to convince my mom, but suddenly with three people
in the house, I could be outnumbered in arguments. That sort of thing
annoyed me, but to be able to argue like that, and for Gabi to put up with
my mom when she was drunk or depressed, it opened a layer of reality I'd
never shared with anyone else.

"We'd made birthday cards for each other that included heart stickers
and were signed with 'love' before our names, but I didn't think anything
of it.

"One day, Gabi asked me, 'Do you think you're gay or straight?'

"I'd known the words for a long time. I'd known since I read about
the Holocaust and delved beyond the stories about Nazis and Jews. Our
school history text neglected to mention gays, Roma, Jehovah's Witnesses,
the disabled, and others. I'd figured out all on my own that pink triangles

on signs and pins were a reclaiming of that history, but until Gabi, I hadn't really talked about it with anyone.

"In the terms of the time I told her, 'That question never made sense to me. Even if I don't understand much about sex, I don't see how the other person's sex would matter to how people feel about each other. A lot of times you can't even know what's really under someone's clothes. I think it's creepy that our language makes everyone tell about private parts or have other people tell by saying he or she all the time.'

"She took a while to respond, but I'd come to expect that with Gabi. While I'd thought a lot about related issues over the last couple years, they were things I wouldn't have mentioned or asked about with anyone else. It would have been an entirely different discussion if we'd had millennial terminology or the internet, but at that point, I hadn't even realized that sex was supposed to be pleasurable. I figured it was an urge, like hunger or needing to pee, that I just hadn't experienced yet. When I'd suggested to my mom that I'd rather use 'it' pronouns, for myself and everyone else, she told me people would consider that rude. Honestly, I think my mom might have identified as nonbinary and ace if she'd ever known those words. I was thinking back to something my mom had said, without much explanation, about people being told to 'lie on their backs and think of England' by the time Gabi finally responded.

"'I don't understand sex either, but I think it only sometimes goes along with loving someone.' Gabi was picking at a fuzzy blanket on the mattress we'd pulled into my room for her. 'I think people are less likely to love someone who's opposite from them, but maybe that's why they want to have sex with them?'

"I know we revisited the subject other times, but as of that summer, neither of us really understood.

"Toward the end of eighth grade, Gabi's mom moved in with her creepy boyfriend across town. Gabi didn't want to go and didn't want to change schools a couple months before finishing junior high. We convinced both our moms to let Gabi live at my house during the week and go across town to her mom on weekends.

"The summer after junior high, Gabi spent less time at my house than the previous year. At first, she complained about her mom's creepy boyfriend, but after a while, she said he was very kind to both her and her mom. One day when the boyfriend let me come along for a picnic at a botanical garden with them, he told me all about his religion and how he'd been drawn to Gabi and her mom every time they were reincarnated, no matter what their ages or appearances. Then he told me I was like them and we'd all arrived on the same spaceship together a long time ago.

"My brain buzzed like it was full of bees. I knew he was lying, but I didn't trust my own instincts by that point. For years, I'd thought I might be an alien, only to put that idea away as childish and biologically implausible. Now an adult was telling me it was true and sidestepping any biological issues by claiming cycles of reincarnation. I'd been taught to respect other religions, and I usually longed to hear other people's perspectives and stories.

"But this was the creepy boyfriend. He still felt creepy to me in a way that pushed out and slimed across my skin. The story he told hurt my brain like static shocks across my scalp.

"As soon as we were done eating, I pulled Gabi down a different garden path than the adults were following. I headed for a grove with fruit trees that would hide us and offer shade from the hot Sacramento sun.

"'Doesn't it feel like lies to you, Gabi? Doesn't he still make your skin creep?'

"'I don't know,' Gabi said, leaning against an apple tree, the smell of warm fruit all around us. 'A lot of things you and I talked about sound kind of crazy. The other people from his church are nice, and they don't feel creepy. Maybe we were wrong about him and he's just a different kind of different from us.'

"After that day, I barely saw Gabi for two months. Then I received an invitation to her wedding. We were both fourteen. She was marrying her mother's boyfriend with her mother's permission. They were talking about soul bonds and how age didn't matter compared to something like that.

"When I asked my mom, she said it was legal for a fourteen-year-old to marry in California with a parent's permission. She claimed she didn't know enough about the family or their religion to judge them but recommended I send a gift and not attend the ceremony.

"I was heartbroken in ways I didn't come close to understanding. Gabi dropped out of my life, and I wasn't sure whether I was jealous, judgmental, or just a different kind of alien."

Viola shook back her curls. She set the lines for sheet to tiller, and let the boat mostly steer itself as the two of them watched the waves ahead and took turns with the binoculars. "While I was an only child, I never lived with a single parent."

That opening surprised Wend, but anything short of rejection felt soft and filled them with relief. "I can't explain why so many kids with single parents reached out to me, even as casual friends. For overnights, other parents hesitated to let their kids spend the night in single-parent households back then." Wend had that spelled out for them—in an unkind way—before the end of fourth grade. "I knew a disproportionate number of people whose parents were alcoholic or had mental health issues, but I don't presume either is true of you."

Not responding to that, Viola asked, "Did you ever see Gabi again?"

"I ran into her at a shopping mall a decade later. At first, she was angry and paranoid that I'd tracked her down, which I hadn't. She wasn't wearing glasses anymore, and I couldn't tell if she had contacts. She mentioned having a new name, which she wouldn't tell me, and not wanting outsiders interfering with her life or her kids. She had a six-year-old with her and implied she was still married to her mother's ex-boyfriend, but her mom had left their church and tried to take her grandkids. Once I assured Gabi that I had no connection to her mom, hadn't been stalking her, and only stopped by the mall while visiting the old neighborhood, she calmed down. She was quick to assure me she was happy. She hadn't had kids until after high school and had gotten an associate's degree while raising them, although she wouldn't name her field of study. Her anger at the beginning of the conversation had upset me enough that I couldn't tell if she was lying. She didn't feel like the same person to me anymore, not a trace, and I wasn't sure which of us had left the other behind."

Viola suddenly turned to face Wend and said calmly, her voice neither cruel nor kind, "And this is supposed to teach me what? That people born in June of 1972 share a special connection and can sense lies until they convince themselves they can't or are too upset to try?"

"I don't know." Wend shrugged even as they shuddered inside. Whatever they'd been trying to prove when they swam aboard this boat depended on Viola recognizing the connection that kept Wend seeking. They breathed in salty fresh air and watched waves roll silver and shiny in the dark as they searched for words to explain. "By the time I ran into Gabi with her kid, I wasn't sure what I meant when I said I was happy. I'd thrown myself into college and then work. My closest friends were those I'd kept through school and who were now lucky enough to have email. Part of me wanted to rescue Gabi, like I had with the bully and even with the glasses, because we shared some unbreakable bond. Part of me thought whatever connection I'd once felt had been wishful thinking."

Viola's voice curled upward as she asked, "You think you loved her or were in love?"

The noises of the ocean and the boat seemed to quiet as Wend said, "I've loved a lot of people a lot of ways, and I'm still not sure if I've been in love. I would have given a lot to keep Gabi close if she'd wanted me. Losing her still hurts. That's true of Mathew, too. They're different kinds of hurt, but parts of those connections felt the same. Some sense of connection drew my interest to you, before I even knew your birthday. I haven't figured out how it all fits together."

"If it fits together. Are all of your stories sad?" Viola slouched back on the cockpit seat, but eased closer to Wend as she relaxed.

Wend pulled their arms in tight, feeling the words like a slap. "The one with Mathew wasn't."

"It was full of alienation, adults being unhelpful, and losing each other at the end."

"But Mathew was good. There was a lot of happiness in that story and Gabi's." The long ago pull of connection and comfort they'd felt with both Mathew and Gabi, at least in their better moments, reverberated in Wend's mind with what drew them to this boat and this ocean crossing. Wend wasn't sure if that sense or their old insecurities told them not to push any further now. As Viola was shaking her head again, Wend added, "The story about finding the sea cucumber was happy."

That made the corners of Viola's mouth twitch up. Wend counted it as a temporary success even as the connections Wend had revisited threatened to tear them apart.

9.

WEND WOKE from the accident shaken and disoriented. Not a real accident; no car they'd ever driven had such a smooth steering wheel. They rubbed their rough hands together. Wend didn't like to revisit bad dreams and risk the memory sticking, but the massive intersection intruded on their thinking, larger than life. They'd been driving, smoothly, quietly—until a tanker truck came out of nowhere and crashed into their car head on.

Wend tried to remember the last time they'd driven a car. It had been years. And they'd never been in a head-on collision.

Being wrung out and twitching all over was familiar. Adrenaline spiked and plummeted, but usually for a reason.

For a moment, Wend worried the boat was about to crash. But they'd never believed in prophetic dreams. They refused to consider breaking the laws of time and physics while in this state. The dream that shook them up didn't even involve flying. It barely involved driving. Wend had been gliding along, alone on a wide road, when someone crashed into them.

Like Viola, who had finally started a conversation last night. Viola, who asked for a story but questioned its relevance and emotion. Even if Wend supported the questioning, wanted Viola to draw her own conclusions, it left Wend exposed, skin prickling, and none of their usual protections were available. They didn't have a room of their own to hide in nor work of their own to dig into. They couldn't consult friends through email, and while they had been learning to accept touch from Viola, they weren't ready to initiate touch for comfort.

They had three layers of sleep sack surrounded by the raised edge of the quarter berth. Waves pounded outside, making the boat rock and creak. The additional sounds of items being moved and set down in the galley suggested Aljon was awake and nearby, which meant Viola probably had the helm again.

Wend pushed the dream away and struggled out of bed, determined to move on with the day despite failing to relax and rein in their natural hypersensitivity to touch.

After lunch, the wind died and Aljon declared, "Laundry and bath day."

The way he said it made Wend grin, and they turned away momentarily so he wouldn't misinterpret. It just sounded so ... jovial. Like hearing a call for recess, they thought with unexpected relief, before turning back to acknowledge the call.

Wend washed three sets of rash guards and board shorts that they'd been wearing over and over. The washing used salt water, and Wend didn't think they really needed to waste fresh water on the final rinse, but Aljon insisted they could use the same rinse water multiple times and then he'd use it for cleaning other items where salt tended to build up otherwise.

Viola asked them both, "Don't you get tired of feeling damp and salty all the time?"

Evidently that was one more thing they didn't have in common with Viola. Wend found humid air almost as comforting as being in water, and they were careful to wipe off salt or grit when it dried. "Better than being cold."

As Aljon ran a line for laundry, he added, "I'm used to it."

As soon as Wend secured their clothes on the line Aljon had strung across the stern, they brought the sample bot out, appreciating how easy it was to collect a proper sample now that the boat was mostly still.

Viola spotted them at the bow and called up from the starboard side already in the ocean, "Come on in, the water is fine."

The water was cooler than in the Marquesas, but it was indeed fine. The first time Wend immersed, their whole body relaxed as if held, supported by a strength they could always trust. Their spine released and resettled without strain or pinching, and the nerve endings on their skin recalibrated to discern the constant shifts of wave energy.

Wend wanted to swim far and fast, but knew enough to keep track of the boat and an eye out for sharks. Still, there was joy in moving freely within the sea.

When Viola swam close, offering something from a string around her neck, Wend treaded water beside her long enough to hear, "It's biodegradable salt-water soap. You can even use it on your face and hair."

Wend held out a hand and let Viola squirt a bit into their palm.

It slid like slime between Wend's fingers, but it left their bristly hair and scalp less greasy. They'd washed their face and neck that morning, making the effect less noticeable there. Still, washing in the ocean felt amazing. The rubbing of hands over skin, even after the soap rinsed away, gave a sensation of coming clean.

Viola ducked underwater nearby with something other than soap in her hands. Only then did Wend realize another string around the photographer's neck held an underwater camera.

Reckoning even the most dedicated photographer wouldn't go underwater to photograph sharks without at least warning those nearby, Wend focused from above and spotted the white-ruffled oral arms of a large jelly before tracing them to the golden-brown bell.

Dark red tentacles trailed for more than a human body length. They pulsed in the ocean, like arteries pumping blood to an immense watery organism.

Wend wasn't wearing a wetsuit but recalled that the 24 maroon tentacles on a Pacific sea nettle couldn't sting a person to death, assuming they'd identified the jelly correctly. It looked like the sea nettles back in the Pacific Tech Aquarium. With a red-trimmed bell half a meter in diameter, there weren't many other candidates. But contrary to the beliefs of excitable young students, Wend wasn't an expert on jellies.

With small hand motions and longer undulations of their entire body, Wend tried to back away while keeping their head above water and the jelly in view.

The jelly mostly floated with the current but seemed to squeeze its bell to curve toward Wend as they retreated back toward the boat. If Wend made a sudden move or splashed, the jelly might dart away. With the vortex propulsion of a bell that size, it could certainly swim against the weak current. But any sudden movement might as easily swish tentacles toward Wend as away.

Taking a chance to glance back toward the boat, Wend spotted Viola near the bottom of the ladder, now wearing a mask and snorkel while Aljon watched from above. Despite their reduced risk assessment, Wend preferred to leave the enormous jelly with plenty of free space.

With their opposite arm, Wend motioned for Viola to head up first. The stubborn photographer dove under instead and swam away from the boat, albeit keeping her distance from Wend and the jelly.

Somewhat reluctantly, Wend made their way to the ladder and up. The jelly didn't follow past that first adjustment when Wend had started to back away. Up on deck, Aljon asked if they'd been stung and then double-checked every inch of their visible skin after they said no.

When Viola finally climbed back up, Aljon inspected her the same way. Then he said, "The solar shower is set up over the rinse bin. I'll wash quickly at the base of the ladder, since you both seem unscathed by stray tentacles. I assume that species is fairly safe?"

"*Chrysaora fuscescens*, AKA Sea Nettle," Viola said. "Toxins are non-lethal to humans but can be painful. I only saw one and it's drifted away now. I didn't see any broken-off tentacles, but you can never be sure."

As Aljon headed down the ladder, Viola turned to Wend and said, "Whether you're magic or not, I guess it's good I brought a camera along for our bath." The words were accompanied by the barely there smile Wend increasingly associated with Viola's better moods.

Later, Wend might ask to see the photos. For now, they accepted their turn to rinse in the solar shower. With their sense of touch calmed from the ocean, the brief pour of fresh water felt feather soft.

Viola's tone, more than her words, had shaken Wend. Ever since the plastic island, Wend felt suspended between possibilities, left hanging. When they volunteered stories or tried to open up discussions of flying dreams, Viola shut them down, didn't respond, or even expressed doubt.

If the photographer required more time to gather her thoughts, Wend wanted to give her that. They appreciated when people gave them time and tried not to overwhelm them, but they couldn't pin down what Viola might be waiting for or need before sharing her puzzling thoughts. Even after their first swim in days, the way Viola hinted and then pulled away left Wend nervous, like fingers might poke at them from any direction at any time. Like they were still missing something critical.

Sounds of shouting and someone being slapped drew Wend from sleep and the bedroom they'd once shared with Gabi. As soon as they opened *the door to the hall, they smelled smoke. In their tiny tract house the other two bedrooms were mere steps away. Both doors stood open.*

The smoke and noise, now escalating to gunshots, came from the spare bedroom where Mom watched TV.

Sure enough, the sounds of escalating violence were a show. The flames spreading across scattered papers and envelopes were real. Mom had long used the guest bed as extra desk space or an area for sorting bills. She'd often fallen asleep on the couch with the TV blaring, a drink and ashtray by her side.

Now fire crept from one bill to another on the guest bed. The blankets were smoldering. An ashtray sat at a precarious angle. A fallen cigarette butt had finally done more than singe the cloth.

The spreading fire unnerved Wend, but years of waking in the middle of the night to real or televised shouting helped them hold panic at arm's length.

They'd never used a fire extinguisher, and there wasn't one in the house.

The heavy quilt hanging on the back of the couch was within arm's reach.

Wend lifted it and against all instinct stepped toward the fire. They dropped the quilt over the flaming mass of papers the way they might have draped it over their mom.

Then out of nowhere, a massive wave arose, sweeping over Wend, following the path of the quilt. It swamped the spare bed. Smothered the fire in one fell swoop.

Wend woke shaking, the way they'd shaken their mom that night after the fire was put out. In reality, there had been no wave, only a mixing bowl Wend filled again and again with water from the kitchen faucet. They'd doused the fire thoroughly, ruining the mattress underneath, before waking their mom.

Mom had said not to call the fire department, not to tell anyone. With the smell of cigarette smoke that clung to the couch and carpet anyway, no one would ever know.

Only Wend knew. After a while, they were pretty sure Mom forgot.

Fifty years later, it was only a dream. Nothing anyone else living could verify. Wend pulled their sleep sack tighter until they stopped shaking.

After several deep breaths, they appreciated the layers of fabric, then wood, then water that surrounded them.

The roll of the ocean was gentle as Wend poked their head out and found the cabin empty.

Up on deck, Viola had the tiller. Beside her sat a pan with breakfast bread and dried fish.

Aljon had climbed up near the top of the mast, both legs and one arm wrapped around it, as he checked for damage or tangling.

"Problem?" Wend asked.

"All lines in good repair," Aljon called down. "Radar reflector still full of foil." He pointed to a short length of PVC tube high on the mast.

With a tilt of her head and a half smile, Viola explained to Wend, "Since we don't have radar, we make sure all the ships that do will see and avoid us. A bunch of foil shoved in a pipe works better than any high-tech device. Breakfast?" She motioned to the pan beside her.

"In a minute." Wend rushed to bring the sample bot up for a quick test while the *Nuovo Mar* sat virtually stationary. Then they ate a hunk of breakfast bread. Alongside the embedded carrots and fruit, Wend appreciated a warm cheesy flavor from Aljon's nutritional yeast. Looking up, they further admired the strength and agility he employed to hold himself steady with one arm while checking for wear on the lines or loose fasteners.

The wind barely blew and the sun sat thirty degrees above the horizon. When Aljon climbed down he'd sweated through his light tee shirt. He also favored his left arm.

Once they'd rigged the sails to take advantage of what wind there was, Wend asked Aljon, "Are you hurt?"

"Nothing bad. I pulled something a couple days back."

Wend felt bad for not noticing, especially with all the care Aljon showed for others, setting up laundry lines and offering comfort foods. "A couple times in my life I've been told I give good backrubs, if you want me to try."

The look Aljon gave them might have been the most honest and assessing they'd ever seen from him. "I know you said you're something like gray or demi, but you also implied you're touch averse. You sure that wouldn't be weird one way or the other?"

"Touch averse doesn't quite translate from my experience. I'm hypersensitive to touch if I'm not prepared, but that's mostly about others touching me." Wend wondered if their touch sensitivity might make them better at giving backrubs, but judged it more important to say, "I'm not sure the rest matters when I'm offering to help because you're injured, but you're the age of a child I helped raise and many others I've taught. Not to say I see you as a child, but I don't think I could ever have sexual or romantic feelings for someone your age. I just don't like to see you hurting."

"Sitting or lying down?" Aljon asked matter-of-factly, hauling off his shirt and wiping away the worst of his sweat.

Viola watched from the helm without comment as Wend replied, "If you're comfortable lying down somewhere, that lets me use part of my weight, but my hands are pretty strong either way."

Aljon laid down with his shirt under his bare chest on a clear spot of deck close to the helm. Wend wondered if he felt better with Viola watching over them and appreciated that if he did.

While Wend rarely volunteered to touch people this way, the conversations they'd had with Aljon made the situation more comfortable than most. Being outside with warm sun and a breeze helped. They started by setting both hands at the top of Aljon's back, firmly enough not to tickle, and simply stroking down the long muscles to build a mental map. His remaining sweat made the move easier. They slid both hands out and up his sides, coming back under the shoulder blades to follow his spine up to his neck.

"There's strain on the left under your shoulder blade and by your spine. You're also holding a lot of tension in your neck. Do you mind if I push up into your hair?" They repeated their long stokes as they asked and waited for an answer.

"Anyplace uncovered is fine. What you did already felt good."

"Do you want me to talk you through it or would quiet be more relaxing?"

"I'd love to hear the story of the child you helped raise, if it's something you want to share. I'm comfortable either way." He relaxed under Wend's hands as he said it, which caused Wend to relax in turn.

They'd intended to offer a narration of their movements, but it seemed fitting for Aljon to request this piece of their history instead. Realizing Avery would be Aljon's age now gave Wend a new perspective on a story they'd held close and not shared for many years. Tuning in to Aljon's calm and steady breathing, Wend began working on smaller, circular strokes.

They kept their arms almost straight beneath them as they leveraged some of their weight into the massage and began their story.

"In 2019, I was helping teach school groups at the Pacific Tech Aquarium. I'd stalled out on my PhD but surprised myself by actually doing okay with kids. The head of our education program was savvy and always assigned me with a co-teacher who handled more boisterous or aggressive children well. Other teachers joked that the lost souls flocked to me. Before I even knew what to look for, the shy, scared, or nervous kids would gravitate to any station I ran or wherever I'd be explaining about sea otters or kelp. I always signed up to help with special needs groups and on days the aquarium hosted sensory-friendly hours.

"On the day Avery came to visit, I was an explainer at the touch pools. They're like fake tidepools set up indoors at a height that allows children, anyone shorter, and visitors in wheelchairs to gently touch animals like sea stars, crabs, anemones, and sea urchins. At night, the pools received fresh ocean water but during visiting hours they were filtered for clear viewing. We rotated the animals to make sure none were overstressed by too much human attention.

"It was a sensory-friendly morning, which meant fewer visitors, basic lighting, and no announcements or audio over speakers. Avery was nine and wore noise-canceling headphones amid jet black curls, a long-sleeved sweater, and long pants made of soft purple fleece. They stood by the side of the pool for a long time watching. Then they put two fingers into the water at the very edge, as if testing the temperature. They could have touched creatures in the pool without getting their sleeves wet, but it was a large pool. While everyone present stayed calm in that moment, there was always a chance someone would splash or make a wave. Avery, whose name I only learned later, kept glancing my way as they skimmed their fingers over the surface of the water.

"I had a couple animals pulled out into clear plastic tubs. One was a hermit crab with a small mound of rock it could crawl on, but many kids aren't comfortable with the way crabs skitter about. The other tub held a bat star, and I scooped water out until only two inches remained, barely covering the plump orange sea star. The next time Avery looked my way, I pushed those two bins forward on the low table beside me.

"Avery spent the next half hour at my table. They were incredibly careful, first petting the bat star and later working up the confidence to touch the hermit crab. Their mom, Mira, followed along and ended up asking me all sorts of questions about the two animals. I wasn't sure how much Avery heard, although I suspected Mira's interest was partly feigned, in order to be a good role model.

"I was more than surprised toward the end of their visit when Mira asked if I'd come to their house for dinner. I'd been told many times I was oblivious to people flirting with me, but I was wary of invitations from near strangers. Mira said, 'Avery might want to talk about this aquarium visit later, once they've had time to process. I wouldn't want to make you work extra hours, but I cook a pretty amazing minestrone, if I do say so myself.'

"I went for dinner, and sure enough, Avery peppered me with dozens of questions and a fair amount of knowledge they'd garnered from books and nature documentaries. They were enthusiastic and open in their own home and asked me to move in that first night. I didn't take the invitation seriously, but Mira invited me for another dinner, and within two months I rented their guest room in exchange for tutoring Avery eight hours a week.

"Avery was homeschooled and treated me like a co-parent as soon as I moved in. It was easy to learn their food and touch preferences. They had a black-and-white cat kigurumi that was amazingly soft both inside and out. When they wore that with slippers and mittens and the hood pulled up, they wanted to be treated like a cat. They'd curl up beside me or on my lap and want to be petted or nap, and they never talked when they were like that.

"When the great pandemic closed down the aquarium in 2020, I became even more a member of their household, since we were together 24/7. For my birthday, Avery gave me an adult-sized leopard kigurumi and asked if I'd like to be a cat with them sometimes.

"I spoke with Mira, who told me she'd explored a lot of 'alternative' scenes before. She explained what 'pet play' meant with people other than her child and the different forms that could take. I decided to follow Avery's lead and agreed Mira could also treat me like a cat when I dressed that way.

"After that, Avery latched onto me even more. There were times during the pandemic when we'd both be cats for entire afternoons and evenings. It was easier for me to feel like family that way. I still watched out for Avery as a child and was aware of their boundaries and tells, even when we were both nonverbal. It made me more relaxed about touch and cuddling in general, with both Avery and Mira.

"When people started going out again but the aquarium remained closed, Mira left me alone with Avery the same way I thought a family member would. She didn't ask or plan ahead as we'd handled tutoring hours. We kept on that way even as society drifted back toward normal. Mira convinced me to apply for a research position at Pacific Tech and to try to finish my PhD rather than going back to work in the aquarium.

"At the end of 2022 Mira asked me to move out. She said another single parent with a kid needed the space more than I did. I was confused and hurt, although I suspected, or maybe rationalized, that Mira had started a relationship with the other adult. I convinced myself that I should put the needs of the unknown parent and kid above my own. When I asked about getting together for dinners or to spend time with Avery, Mira insisted that would be too stressful. With a new parent and child joining the household, Mira asserted a clean break would be best.

"She asked me to only tell Avery I was moving away and wouldn't be able to see them anymore.

"It all happened disturbingly fast, and I was dealing with a lot of insecurity and social anxiety. No matter how wrong it felt to me, at that point I didn't dare challenge Mira's decisions on behalf of her own child. I regret that now. The time I spent with Avery and Mira added to me accepting myself and demanding to be more openly myself in the years that followed, but I never saw or heard from either of them again."

Wend ached with the loss of Avery, stirred up by revisiting the memory. Whatever good may have come from that time, they wished they'd fought harder about keeping in touch. After losing their mom, supposed dad, his mother, and the biological father they never knew—after wondering why or if those adults in their life didn't care—giving up Avery severed something inside Wend, leaving them raw and unsettled to this day.

It was only after they finished speaking and the silence stretched that Wend remembered Viola's remarks about only telling sad stories. They were suddenly viscerally aware of Viola listening the whole time, watching as Wend massaged Aljon's back.

Aljon had relaxed almost to the point of sleep during the story and massage, either missing the sad ending or accustomed to Wend's stories by now. The knots along Aljon's spine and the tight muscles that ran around his left shoulder blade had loosened. His skin was surprisingly smooth despite weeks at sea and months living on a boat. He had almost no hair on his back, few scars, and no tattoos. While his back and shoulders were nearly all muscle, he was lean enough that Wend's strength and stamina were easily equal to the task. Being able to share pleasant touch in such an uncomplicated way relaxed Wend as well.

To finish up, they stroked his neck and up a few inches above the hairline. He was sweatier there, but thoroughly washed from the day before. The cords in his neck gave under Wend's touch, and Aljon let out a sigh. Reluctant to move too fast or remove their hands completely, Wend slowed their fingers until they were still. Then they gradually shifted away.

"Thanks," Aljon said softly without otherwise moving.

As Wend stretched and took the few steps needed to reach the cockpit, which at least offered back support, Viola asked, "Did any of the animals in the aquarium act differently around you?"

"What do you mean?" Wend asked, reluctant to be drawn in and left hanging again, but unwilling to discard any opportunity.

"You said shy or nervous kids gravitated toward you. Were you ever near an exhibit or even touching the water when something unusual happened or animals came to check you out?"

Wend shook their head. "There were a couple of sea otters who liked me, but sea otters are widely known to play favorites among aquarium staff, especially with those they see delivering invertebrate snacks. That's all."

"It didn't surprise me when the giant manta ray spent time checking us out, but that sea nettle yesterday seemed attuned to you, too." Viola's gaze had shifted toward scrutiny again, as she watched Wend for any reaction. "It angled toward you when you first moved away. I studied the series of pictures I took."

"I thought you didn't want to consider magic." Wend tried for a joking tone but knew they'd probably failed. "I don't know what else would cause a jelly to seek me out. Not that I can claim to understand the perspective of an invertebrate with distributed cognitive processing and sensory systems, but jellies are large plankton that eat smaller plankton. I'm too big to be food."

"We don't know how jellies think. That's the point." Viola tapped the tiller in a way Wend had never seen before. It made her loose batik tank top shiver in blue and green ripples that caused Wend to picture jellies as Viola continued. "Swarms of jellies have clogged up cooling pipes and shut down nuclear reactors more times than makes sense. I've photographed them for articles that jokingly called them anti-nuclear protesters. On at least two occasions the plants they closed down were found to be leaking contaminants that had to be dealt with before the plants could restart. While contaminants and radiation are obviously harmful to jellies and other sea life, they sure seemed drawn to those plants."

Much as Wend wanted Viola to open up, they disliked her focus on influencing sea life. Knowing Aljon was still sprawled on deck behind them helped a little. Wend leaned back. "I don't see what that has to do with me."

"I don't either," Viola said. "Think of this as my version of storytelling or working out the puzzle. Have you experimented to see if sea animals are attracted to you or if you could call them? You are officially a scientist. Did you finish that doctorate?"

"Yes, but it's in education, focusing on STEM education. That's not the same as a science degree."

"And your genetics degrees?"

Wend didn't want the conversation derailed after Viola had mentioned working the puzzle. "I'm not denying I'm a scientist. I spent years working as a researcher and then a field scientist, first in genetics and later in marine biology or related fields. But I couldn't objectively run an experiment to see if animals react to me personally. I'm not sure that would even be ethical."

"What about small or simple animals? You pointed out jellies are plankton. You designed a bot to sample the ocean's microbiome. How often has that bot been used in the same place but with or without you present? What about over a period of time where your continued presence might change a local area?"

Wend appreciated Viola's show of interest, even as their insides writhed. They wanted to creep away or hide, but didn't want to reject Viola's preferred mode of communication, if this was in fact her version of puzzle-solving or storytelling. "The microbiome of the ocean is complex, shifting and mixing over kilometers of open water, but almost none of it can move with volition. It wouldn't surprise me if genetic traces of the giant manta ray we saw, and whatever microbiome accompanies it, show up in my samples from a hundred kilometers away. The microbiome census is testing to see what's present, what might be feeding on what or otherwise be necessary to an ecosystem. The sort of effect you're suggesting might as well be magic."

Viola leaned forward, still sounding determined, "You're claiming it wasn't your intent, but you agree it would be ethical to check samples for any bias attributable to your presence?"

That much, Wend could offer. "Of course, we have to rule out introduced components from the human biome anyway."

The moment of reprieve slipped drastically sideways when Viola asked, "Good, and have you run any experiments with your flying dreams?"

"Experiments?" Wend asked.

Viola leaned in close enough to touch for the first time in days. Her loose blue and green tank top that rippled like a jelly brushed along Wend's bare knee. "Have you tried active dreaming or going to bed intending to fly someplace and map an area you don't know yet?"

"As an adult, I've at least glanced at maps of most places I've visited, so it wouldn't have been a fair test. Anyway, I've never been able to control my dreams. For months at a time I'll have nothing but anxiety dreams with people yelling or with me experiencing failure after failure at every task I undertake. If that wasn't sufficient motivation to fly away, I don't know what would be."

Viola's expression softened. "Have you been having those sorts of dreams on this trip?"

Not specifically mentioning the fire or car crash dreams or the one with everyone shouting that Aljon had woken them from, Wend said, "Some, but not every night, which is good."

Viola stared at Wend for long moments, as if anxiety dreams sounded more unusual than out-of-body experiences.

Wend felt compelled to elaborate, trying for full disclosure and a lighter tone. "At times in my life, I've had nothing but anxiety dreams for weeks and weeks. In most of those I'm human, or some variation thereof. In flying dreams I'm always invisible and incorporeal, able to pass through walls and solids, but sometimes my movements are more like water, sea creatures, birds, or inanimate objects. Other times, I enjoy highly realistic dreams in which I'm various sea creatures."

"Did you experiment with psychedelics at any point?" Viola questioned more seriously.

"I didn't see a need. At an early age I decided to avoid most drugs and alcohol." Wend shrugged and then scanned the horizon, needing a chance to look away from Viola's sustained focus. And suspicion.

"That part, at least, doesn't surprise me," Viola said, eyes back on the water. "Still, it wouldn't hurt to try falling asleep hoping that you could fly ahead and see anything interesting we might encounter tomorrow."

Wend didn't expect it to work, but would agree to anything that helped Viola reconsider Wend's flying dreams and that some of the pieces Wend suggested in her story might be part of a larger whole. "Fine, I'll try. Anything else?"

"I can't believe you never ran any experiments. Even I experimented when I thought I could detect lies. I lost a fair amount of money at poker proving myself wrong." Viola looked out to sea as she said it, but it didn't take special lie detection abilities to hear that part was true. It might be what motivated this whole line of questioning.

Wend took a deep breath and offered the response they would have wanted, a personal experience that might fit with Viola's. "In college, I let myself be roped into a game of 'two truths and a lie' to see if I could always tell. I couldn't. But since I perceived negative emotions as well, it seemed possible I only sensed lies if they were accompanied by guilt or a particular emotional profile. That wouldn't necessarily apply in games."

"You tried something else, didn't you?" Viola watched Wend intently.

Half flattered by the attention and half annoyed to be read so easily, Wend admitted, "I once set out a plate of cookies in the kitchen at my undergrad house, knowing that I had a work-study shift as a security cadet that night and would be able to access the footage. Once the cookies were gone, I hung out in the kitchen asking people if they'd gotten any and if they'd been good cookies. I pretended that they'd been left as a thank you for a parents' weekend display I'd helped set up but that I hadn't visited the kitchen in time to get any cookies." Wend cringed at the memory, how socially awkward and underhanded their tactics had been. "I thought that might trigger enough emotion that I could tell who was lying. When I later checked my list of who I thought lied against video footage, I was right fifteen times out of the eighteen people. But I suspect a lot of people would be able to tell lies from truth at that rate, and I felt nauseous from the lying and spying I'd employed. What I'd done had been unethical, and even a perfect accuracy rate wouldn't have proven anything. I swore off ever trying that again."

When enough time had passed that Wend didn't expect a response, Viola muttered while facing away, "Other than lying, we choose rather differently which things to give up."

After that, the closest to conversation was some soft snoring coming from Aljon, curled peacefully on the deck like a cat.

10.

WIND LIFTED WEND above the boat and over a landscape of shifting white-peaked waves to reach a steady dark sky. They glided forward from the bow, low enough to smell fish and feel ocean spray on their underside and feet. They rose and wheeled and swooped. Thin clouds accented the horizon. A whale blew below, punctuation interrupting the whistle and roar of air and water.

Wend's invisible arms stretched wide and flat, like a kite slicing the air, carrying them back to their point of origin for reasons they had already forgotten. Senses they couldn't explain but recognized guided them infallibly, like iron filings to a magnet. Sharp eyes targeted a human figure leaning by a stick, face wet with salt water, but not from the sea. The human clutched a shiny prize in hand, connected to a chain that looped around their neck. New drops of water dripped from human eyes.

Wend woke in their nest—no, their sleep sack in the quarter berth. The dream memory brought sympathetic tears to their eyes, even if they didn't know why Viola had been crying over the necklace she always wore. Then their stomach roiled, and they stumbled to the head and threw up. In that moment, alone, in the middle of the night, Wend knew what they'd seen in their flying dream was real, and it was a hundred times worse than checking surveillance videos of cookies in a college kitchen.

What privacy could be found on such a small boat was precious. Wend had violated Viola's privacy in a moment she would never have chosen to share.

It didn't matter that Wend had fallen asleep focused on flying because Viola badgered them into it. They'd ended up spying in a way they'd promised never to risk again. Now they'd have to dodge Viola's questions to avoid upsetting her more. This experiment needed to end, and they hadn't spotted anything extraordinary or identifiable for the next day's sailing either. Wend slept fitfully for the rest of the night.

As soon as all three crew sat down together for breakfast in the cockpit, Viola asked, "Any luck planning a flying dream?"

Wend took a large sip of water to force down the bite of fruit bar they could barely swallow. "I tried, but I don't think I can do this as an experiment. In the end, I dreamed about being an eel hiding deep in a reef." The last part was true. The final dream they remembered before waking involved ducking in and out of endless tunnels as an eel.

The look Viola gave them expressed skepticism and disappointment, but she said nothing more as the winds picked up to fifteen knots and the sea grew choppy beneath them. They all had plenty to do until mid-afternoon when the winds settled to seven knots and steady.

Viola passed up her turn to sleep saying, "I'm not tired yet. What about you, Aljon, think you could sleep?"

"Always." He stretched both arms upward toward the sun and smiled before heading below.

For a long while, Viola sat at the tiller without looking in Wend's direction. At one point she muttered, "Tighten the foresail."

After Wend did so, they came back to the cockpit but couldn't stand the silence anymore. "Did you want to talk or should I tell a story?"

"You lied to me." Viola's voice was flat. She kept her gaze fixed on the horizon.

"What?" Wend asked, even though they'd heard—even though they should have seen this moment coming and prepared.

"When I asked about you flying last night, I could feel you were lying. It was the first time I ever felt that with you, no way I could miss it."

"Technically, I said I couldn't do this as an experiment." Wend swallowed hard. Viola had acknowledged sensing lies with such confidence, this should have been a moment of triumph. Cause for shared celebration. It wasn't. "I'd guessed what I felt as static wasn't the lie itself, but the emotion someone felt around it. You pushed me to try for a flying dream last night, and I felt terrible afterward, guilty for spying and then needing to obfuscate. What you're accusing me of isn't lying but feeling awful."

"What did you see?" Viola pressed.

"You know."

"I need you to say it."

Wend's stomach clenched, but a deep breath helped them force the words out. "I dreamed I spread out like a kite and flew toward misty clouds on the horizon. I saw a whale blow but nothing useful for sailing or as proof. When some inner sense pulled me back, I saw you crying."

"Is that all?"

"You were clutching something shiny on a metal chain around your neck."

At that, Viola sucked in a deep breath of their own. "You could have seen that by climbing up the stairs."

"You know I didn't, but honestly, I'd feel better about that." A pressure that had been building in Wend's head all day descended to their belly as they spoke the thoughts they'd hidden.

"I don't see why." Viola's tone rang hollow, but there wasn't the static associated with emotions, or with lying, as they'd been discussing. "People accidentally see private moments all the time, especially on a boat this size. It doesn't matter to me if you see them from your own two feet or flying on invisible wings above me."

That made sense in a way, but not in any way that consoled Wend. In all their life, they'd never seen anything they regretted while flying in their sleep. Maybe they'd been lucky. Or maybe whatever triggered flying dreams in the past had better timing. Now, Wend felt sick about the special ability they'd treasured before.

They couldn't explain why, and it didn't seem fair to put that burden on Viola, the person they felt bad for spying on in the first place. Wend couldn't ask what Viola believed about flying dreams or the ability to sense lies. They couldn't speak.

"When you told Aljon about your experience during the great pandemic, I gathered there was a lot you didn't say, which is fine," Viola was quick to say. "I know you were focusing on the child and not the other adult when you told him. Still, it reminded me of how I spent that year."

Viola stopped talking abruptly and set the lines for self-steering sheet to tiller, before sitting down in the same spot with her hand still resting on the tiller. "One of my younger cousins from the Philippines was staying with me at the time, in a little house I owned by the bay in Foster City. That part of my family counts dozens of people as my cousins. Rosamie is related to me through an aunt's husband. Not a blood relation, if that helps. She was 29. I was 48, old enough to be her mother, but I've never been anyone's mother. Rosamie was already widowed and brought her ten-year-old son and seven-year-old daughter with her. With all she'd been through, she was a mess of contradictions—hunched shoulders, exaggerated smiles—I felt a connection. Not like a distant cousin. Someone . . . like me."

Viola demonstrated the posture and then a huge, awkward smile. "My family in the Philippines don't view me as truly adult. It's complicated . . . It was even more complicated for Rosamie." Viola raised her eyebrows and rolled her eyes, but the levity felt forced.

Wend reeled in their own emotional backlash and tried to smile. They couldn't guess why Viola wanted to share this story now. Whatever the reason, Wend forced themself to pay full attention and nodded for Viola to continue.

"She'd come to the Bay Area hoping to work as a graphic artist. I'm sure she knew her chances of finding work that could support her and two kids in the States were slim. But I'd said they could stay with me for a year rent-free, and with the pandemic, I promised her an extra year."

As her tone grew more serious, Viola stroked her right hand along the tied tiller and looked out to sea more than she looked at Wend.

Wend sat frozen in place on the bench across the cockpit, desperate for this chance at connection but still feeling queasy from the confession that led to it. Nonetheless, they tried to be a good listener, and when the silence dragged too long, asked, "How'd that go?"

"You can guess the day to day. It was probably much like any other house with cooped-up kids, although these were dedicated to improving their English alongside their mother. They both looked just like her." Viola shook her head slowly as her gaze went vague, and Wend could tell the photographer envisioned each scene as her story reeled out. "I spent hours reading with them or to them. We found scripts online and each voiced a part in various plays. We were close enough to walk to Baywinds Park, a nature reserve with marshlands and plenty of birds. I taught them photography and birdwatching, because it was something to do outside, even if kids that age often scare birds away or fail to hold a camera steady. I thought I did pretty well by them in my own selfish way.

"I couldn't get together with most of my friends during that time. I'd been between lovers, and most of the lesbian community I interacted with in the Bay Area took shelter in place and then social distancing guidelines very seriously. I didn't make the cut for anyone's bubble or pod."

Viola blew out a long breath, "It's going to sound self-serving and ridiculous, but Rosamie came on to me. I didn't know if she was experimenting or if she'd come to stay with me because she'd realized she wasn't straight. But I knew I was older, wealthier, in a position of power as a US citizen and someone who, if not white-passing, at least passed as some indeterminate mix with Asian."

With a roll of her shoulders, Viola slouched back in her seat and frowned. "It was easy to be the best lover she'd ever had. There's a thrill to showing someone what their own body can do, and giving that pleasure with the rest of the world falling apart around us was . . . intense."

Whatever movie rolled through Viola's mind softened her expression to something clearly private. Wend looked away.

"I wasn't in love with her, but I refuse to be ashamed of our relationship." Viola's voice grew stronger again. "That year would have been a lot worse for both of us without it, and I think kids pick up on adult stress, no matter what people say."

Wend looked back and nodded, agreeing in principle, even if they both recognized this as a rationalization.

"To make a long story short, she asked me to marry her and adopt her kids. I knew it wouldn't work but considered it anyway. Maybe we could have stuck it out long enough to get them all citizenship, but it would have been a sham marriage. However awful this makes me sound, I know I would have come to hate her and the kids, because I never wanted that with them. Maybe I'm not made to want that with anyone." Viola pulled the charm at her neck from under her shirt and fingered it, saying, "Rosamie gave me this for luck when she moved back to the Philippines. At least she didn't hate me."

Wend nodded. The next stretch of silence felt comfortable. Viola stared vaguely into the distance, caught up in her own recollections. Wend tried to empathize and understand Viola's perspective as presented. It was a conscious way of remembering others' stories that Wend had practiced since childhood, wanting to preserve every reference for how other people thought.

Nevertheless, in a matter of minutes Wend's own associations began to latch on, as Wend tried to make sense of the story in their own way. It seemed only fair to offer some of what they were thinking to Viola, but Wend's insides were still unsettled both physically and emotionally.

With more uncertainty in their voice than they liked, Wend said, "I could tell you more about my relationship with Mira during the pandemic, if you want to know."

With a raise of her eyebrows, Viola said, "I assume it involves sex, which is why you didn't tell Aljon. And probably bad sex, but I'll admit I'm curious." Viola's tone was definitely teasing by the end.

"Mira would probably claim she's the best lover I ever had, but I'm not any good at telling those kinds of stories. Sex for me is all about touch and emotion. The words don't exist in any language I speak to describe even my nonsexual experiences with touch, and I'm still working out how to put my emotions into words. A lot of my thinking involves associations. I have placeholders for what would be words in my own language, but there's no way to define them for other people. Even if someone listened to hundreds of my stories and tried to appreciate my perspective on them, I'm not sure they'd grasp how certain moments connect in my mind, in my language."

"You have no idea how seductive the idea of being that person is, do you?"

Wend sat stunned, frozen in place again.

"Don't worry, I'm not hitting on you," Viola continued, "but the idea of knowing someone better than anyone ever has, knowing how they want to be touched, coming close to knowing their secret language and how their mind works, for that I could fall in love and into bed with someone. Not you, because I'm already sure we'd make each other miserable, but I can see how some other person would find that seductive in you. Now tell me about Mira."

Wend pushed Viola's confession and perspective on Mira's interest far back in their mind, to process later. With a shudder they didn't try to hide, Wend fixed their gaze on the horizon and said, "Mira considered herself adventurous. She showed me her eight-page kink checklist. That's what she called it, owning the word 'kink' and proud to say she'd tried to explore each activity back when she was in a poly relationship. She admitted some of what she'd tried had been a mistake in retrospect. She'd started out seeing herself as submissive and grown into a mostly dominant identity. Along the way, she developed strong opinions on enthusiastic consent and safewords. Most of what she said made a lot of sense to me, and I liked having things explained with all the words carefully defined. But whenever I hedged about judging relationships from my past in the context of their own place, time, and experience, she told me I'd been gas-lighted or was defending abusers. In at least one case, I came to agree with her on that, but mostly her strong emotions, and possibly her dominance, made it hard for us to discuss such things. Instead, she decided to make a safe space for me."

Viola interrupted with, "I don't know that world well, but when you say she decided for you, do you mean she took you as her submissive?"

"This is another area, much as with the millennial vocabulary, where discussion helped me identify new perspectives, but I still feel like too much of an outsider to fully apply their words to myself. Mira said out-right that she read me as submissive and wanted to help me explore that. She pushed me to clarify my boundaries and coping strategies, to deter-mine which needs were satiable and how to reset in a positive way when overwhelmed or hypersensitive.

"I'd been exploring other sensory materials anyway. In addition to the leopard kigurumi that Avery gave me, they were happy to let me try their weighted blankets and squishy toys. In a way, Avery started me explor-ing before Mira explained how other people used pet play and sensation play. Because of that association in my mind, I decided I didn't want to combine pet play with anything sexual or submissive with Mira, and she made sure she had my full and enthusiastic consent for anything we tried. At the very least, the eight-page list of options was informative."

"I bet," Viola said with a wink. Then she waited.

"I'm not sure I know how to tell this as a story," Wend said. They'd never shared more than small pieces of it before. "She mail-ordered a bunch of sex toys for me to experiment with on my own, but then she told me what order to try them in and even what to try doing. Usually, she'd be there with me the first time I tried something. She liked to watch, but we quickly realized I couldn't handle being watched without being touched, and bondage alone didn't work as touch for me. Honestly, a lot of what we explored together helped clarify what increased or decreased my touch sensitivity and how to make that pleasurable and safe. There were times I felt safe enough to enjoy sex and touch in ways I never had before.

"But I also had some panic attacks, one extremely bad flashback, and clarified some things I'd already known about what other people might call 'triggers.' I had zero interest in pain or humiliation. And while I might accept the way she used the term submissive in relation to me, I was never a good fit as her submissive, and I didn't care enough about that aspect to seek out any sort of dominant-submissive relationship again. Mostly I discovered which sex toys suited my needs when I wanted a touch that could be sexual or I wanted to overwhelm my sense of touch completely. And while it was nice to have another person as part of a safe space, for most of my life I've been finding ways to keep myself safe. That realization came later, when I went to therapy partly at Mira's urging, as well as finishing my doctorate."

"Wow," Viola said, "That may not have been your idea of how to tell a story, but it sure packed a punch for me."

"Is that a good thing?" Wend asked.

"Honestly, it makes me want to hold you or touch you in some way, but I get that you mostly don't want that. To be honest, after a long dry spell that I mostly didn't mind, all this talk about sex is a little arousing."

"Talking about touch kind of makes me miss it, but not sex," Wend said. "Would it be strange to hold our feet together?"

"I don't think either of us has a problem with being strange."

They both slipped off their shoes. Viola leaned back and adjusted a cushion on the starboard bench seat to support her back as her feet pressed alongside Wend's. By shifting sideways, Wend arranged their feet so they had one foot held between both of Viola's and one of Viola's feet held between theirs.

The sun shone warm overhead, but the steady breeze as they raced forward kept the cockpit pleasantly cool. After a few minutes, Viola said, "If I fall asleep, you have the helm." Then she closed her eyes and was asleep in a minute.

Wend kept a hand on the tiller and an eye on the ocean as they settled into sleepy foot cuddles and the moment of connection with Viola.

It happened in the early morning, a couple hours before dawn. With the wind steady, Wend kept watch. Aljon had the helm as they sailed through the night.

Viola came up the stairs, speaking fast, "I had a flying dream."

"Is there something to watch out for?" Wend scanned with binoculars as they wondered what might have spurred Viola's first flying dream.

"No, I fell asleep aching to fly like you do, and it worked! I saw the Big Dipper rising ahead of us in a clear sky." She waved toward the horizon where the constellation was visible for possibly the first time in their journey, definitely the first time Wend had seen a truly clear sky when the constellation might be visible.

It wasn't proof, as Viola could easily have predicted that well-known northern constellation and knew the sky was clear when she went to bed, but Wend believed her instinctively. A warmth spread under Wend's skin. Viola shared their ability to fly while asleep. This pushed beyond Wend's longing to be believed. Wend felt known. No longer solitary. No longer isolated by this strangeness that shaped their entire world view.

Viola waited at the top of the stairs, looking pleased with herself in a way she hadn't before.

"I'm glad you can fly. That you're happy and want to share this." The words had no sooner left their mouth than Wend's own misery from spying on Viola the night before surged in their gut. Fear sparked at what Viola might do or ask Wend to do in the name of experimentation or later plans. Wend squashed those concerns as far down as they could. Only time would tell, and they wanted to trust the connection that drew them to Viola in the first place.

"Hey, I barely glanced at the boat," Viola added quickly, either seeing or sensing the darkening of Wend's mood. "Now we know this can happen, we should all think of the deck as a place others might see. We always knew someone could wake up and come on deck at any time."

"What if this isn't how we're meant to use it?" Wend asked.

Viola's voice rose hard and loud. "Meant to? Why do you assume there's meaning or intention behind such an ability?"

"I don't know." Wend blinked against stinging eyes and fidgeted with the binoculars. They didn't want to spoil this for Viola, but they refused to be shushed and they'd promised not to lie. "Whenever I do something differently from others, I can't help trying to understand why. There's so much I don't know. I don't want to screw up."

"I thought you'd decided to stop adapting to others' wants and be yourself?"

That stopped Wend for a moment. They had decided that after nearly drowning, and it resonated through them now.

Viola continued to argue. "The flying dreams you described from your childhood didn't seem to carry a warning or show you anything in particular. Even the plastic island you led us to wasn't something we could fix, only what caught your eye. You were exploring, enjoying. Let me have that, too. And let yourself. Don't you agree, Aljon?"

Wend froze in fear of Aljon's rejection for the first time in days. He'd been quick to excuse himself after the initial story about Mathew and flying dreams, but that was before they'd built what Wend thought was a strong foundation for connection. Now Wend's brain flashed through memories of Viola's rejections, questions, and suggestions related to flying dreams and odd animal behaviors, trying to piece together Aljon's perspective.

Unaware of Wend's near-panic, Aljon shrugged, seeming completely at ease with the revelation. "I heard a sailor back home claim he found the best fishing spots by scouting ahead in his dreams. He believed the Austronesians and maybe earlier people found the Philippines the same way."

Not for the first time, Wend admired how much their younger crewmate knew and how freely he offered such insights. "How old was this sailor?"

Aljon's nose scrunched up, making him look even younger as he tried to remember. "Older than me by at least ten years, but not old enough to be called grandfather."

"The people I've noticed were all close to my age and birthday. I wondered if birthdates are part of the pattern or if it repeats in other generations." Wend spoke their thoughts aloud.

"I wouldn't mind a test. If either of you wanted to set something out while I slept, something I couldn't guess but couldn't miss seeing." Viola sounded excited again.

"You're going to keep trying?" Wend asked.

"Isn't this what you wanted, for me to understand and learn from your stories? To see if I'm part of your puzzle? Well, I believe in your flying dreams, and I want to test if I can do the same."

The truth shook Wend. Viola not only believed but admitted it aloud, in front of Aljon, who seemed to believe, too. Even Wend's previous aversion to experimentation couldn't dim the thrill of this moment. Their stomach swooped as if flying in its own dream.

Wend had taken matters into their own hands by seeking Viola out and trying to form this connection. Despite the hard feelings over the past few days, Viola was excited and supportive now. Wend felt suspended in tiny bubbles, excited and barely contained.

They reined themself in; part of collaboration was letting everyone own and follow their personal ways of understanding. Wend wanted to give back. "You're right. I'll try to think of something unexpected you can spot. I'll pay attention if I fly as well, if we're all okay with this."

"I'm going to try, too," Aljon said with a grin. "I may have never spotted lies or auras around people, but this could be separate, a matter of wanting or knowing it's possible. Even if I only change a regular dream, I'd like the experience of flying."

It was Aljon's eagerness more than Viola's success that filled Wend with social relief, like clean water flushing through them, head to toe. They were believed, their experiences accepted. In Viola, they'd found a connection that couldn't be denied, characteristics the two of them shared that they'd never found in any other person. Beyond proving the flying dreams were real, Wend no longer wondered alone. In the tiny society of the boat, Wend and Viola were in the majority, contributing pieces to the same puzzle. While the third person, Aljon, didn't act excluded or doubtful, but fully accepting and supportive of that effort.

Wend sat with their waterproof notebook in hand as they shared evening watch with Aljon, unwilling to commit to paper anything about the flying dreams, but unable to stop musing on this gift they now shared with Viola.

"Usually you write frantically fast when you have that book out. Is it a journal or a logbook?" Aljon asked from his place at the helm, face golden as he gazed at the sun setting off to port.

Wend smiled and closed the book. "Something in between. I keep notes about sampling locations and observations to write up for articles in one section. But the stories I write about my daily life I'll later mail to my friend Lisa, who's kept every letter I've written since we were kids. When I'm working through darker thoughts or ideas around engineering or philosophy, those mostly become letters to Ashok. I believe he burns them after reading."

"Those are the two friends you thought would miss you if you drowned?" The way Aljon spoke, it was barely a question.

Wend nodded. A burst of images and emotions flashed through their mind, memories of Avery watching in fascination as Wend wrote nearly daily to Lisa and Ashok throughout the great pandemic. No one else in the years between had cared enough to learn the names of Wend's two most enduring friends. Alongside their recent realization that Avery would be about Aljon's age now, Wend felt a pang for the child they'd lost as well as increased affection for the young person showing interest now.

"Did you tell either of your friends about me?" Aljon raised his chin and grinned, like it was a joke.

Wondering what answer he wanted, Wend gave the truth. "I didn't share anything personal about you. But Lisa will know all about your cooking, how you fixed the bilge pump, and the times you've offered me hot chocolate. Ashok will know which musicals we've shared and some of what we discussed around them."

"Does he like musicals?"

"Yes, but he'd call a lot of what I liked before knowing him cheesy and predictable. Over the years, he made sure I saw *Les Misérables, Rent,* and *Hamilton.*"

"Live?" Aljon asked wide-eyed.

"Yes, but he made me sit through the movie of *Les Mis* later, specifically so he could rant about it afterward. He'd read the book as well and would have made me read it if he could. 'Unabridged,' he'd always remind me."

"I read the book and saw the movie." Aljon sat up tall and puffed out his chest as he said it. "Unabridged."

"Of course you did," Wend couldn't help wishing Aljon could discuss both with Ashok, preferably while Wend listened. "What did you think?"

Aljon hesitated long enough that Wend considered retracting the question, but then he said, "When I first read the book, I was struggling with my family, Catholicism, sexuality, the general unfairness of life. I was caught in between in a lot of ways. The original includes several chapters about the bishop, who'd felt guilty about hoarding the silver, especially the candlesticks. In the musical, he's rather 'holier than thou' and says that he's bought Valjean's soul for God. To my understanding, that represented more of a gray area in the book, with the bishop and Valjean both seeking redemption and helping each other in different ways. I liked my reading better."

"You generally like books better?"

Aljon shrugged, settling deeper into the bench seat as he kept a firm hold on the tiller. "I appreciate taking my time with the words. In a book, it's easier to focus on complex relationships and romance rather than the over-the-top sexuality and use of sex to sell I see in most visual media. It might be different if I saw a live performance. I enjoy music and singing. I find them soothing, especially at sea when books and electronics aren't practical. There's a long tradition of sailors singing while they work. It leaves your hands and eyes free for other things."

Wend hadn't considered singing as one of their self-soothing strategies, tending more toward the physical with tapping, petting, swaddling, swimming, drinking hot chocolate, taking deep breaths, or counting inputs from each of their senses. Only as they spoke did they realize, "I used to sing whole musicals to myself, silently in my mind, when I couldn't sleep or couldn't deal with the noise around me. There were certain lines that popped into my mind like reminders during the day as well."

"From *Les Misérables*?" Aljon asked.

"I didn't learn that until later. I built a lot of understanding around *The Wizard of Oz*."

"Please tell me you at least read those books? And not only the first one?"

"Not that I remember," Wend shrugged. "But I must have seen the movie a dozen times. I liked the Tin Man, which seems obvious now with him having so many emotions but thinking he missed out by not having a heart. At the time I thought it was because I liked robots. Still, the part about how he'd be tender and gentle, while showing an appreciation for 'love and art,' seemed like good advice for offering socially acceptable opinions and not getting people mad at me. When I discovered *The Wiz* in middle school, I was disappointed that the Tin Man's song became 'Slide Some Oil to Me.' Of course, I didn't see the innuendo in that, or understand the larger connections to Black American art, until much later. But I was old enough to appreciate 'Ease on Down the Road' rather than 'Follow the Yellow Brick Road.' Then *Wicked* came along with a whole new spin on discrimination against witches and talking animal people. I loved those parts."

"I haven't heard *The Wiz* or *Wicked*. Do you feel like singing one or both?" Aljon asked, and then, "Should I make hot chocolate first?"

"Hot chocolate isn't great for singing and I don't need cheering up, although I would almost never say no to it. I'm happy to sing whatever you want, but would you rather do *Les Misérables* or something you know?"

"I like hearing new songs, but I'll make us both hot chocolate first."

"Could I try your version, with macadamia milk and coconut oil? Maybe it will prove better for singing."

Aljon's soft smile settled Wend in a way chocolate never could. "Take the tiller and keep us on course while the wind holds."

It amused Wend that while both Viola and Aljon were reluctant to give the helm to Wend, given their greater experience with sailing, Aljon showed even less inclination to let others use the galley. He probably would have banned Viola if she'd let him. Not that Wend minded. Someone else providing hot chocolate made it even more of a treat.

"Either I didn't manage a flying dream last night or I don't remember it," Viola announced over breakfast, as they all wolfed down a sprout and veggie scramble. "I don't know which would be worse."

Wend hadn't either and was vaguely relieved, although they had tied a life jacket on top of the dinghy as a test object for Viola to spot during a flying dream, as requested. Aljon had known to remove it by the time Viola woke. It was likely he'd set up some other indicator that Wend wouldn't know about without a flying dream. They found it easy not to care about that.

Aljon didn't say anything but served fish cakes with lunch.

WHEN THE WIND died down, Viola ordered them to heave to, even though they could have made a couple knots with the prevailing current and low wind.

"Lower your bot and check the water here." Even as skipper, Viola hadn't previously tried to dictate when Wend took samples or not, but it didn't seem worth arguing. They were only a couple days out from Hawai'i if the weather held, and the bot still held dozens of empty containers. All their samples would soon be processed and the containers sterilized for reuse.

After bringing the bot out and lowering it over the side, Wend noted, "We didn't need to stop for this."

Viola had changed from the romper she wore earlier into her shorty wetsuit. "Next we're swimming. You can take more samples to see if the microbiome changes around you, and I'll bring a camera. Just in case."

Swimming sounded better than flying to Wend right then. Although they'd rather have been asked than told, swimming promised pleasure for their skin, muscles, and mind. They stowed their water sandals and strapped the bot over the short-sleeved blue rash guard they were already wearing.

"Is all your clothing amphibious, or only what you brought on this trip?" Viola asked.

"Amphibious." Wend liked the idea and wondered why they'd never dreamed as a frog or newt. "In the Marquesas, I worked in the ocean half my waking hours. Besides, with the right board shorts and rash guards, I don't need much else." Wend paused as they pulled on fins and grabbed their mask and snorkel. "Well, not much other clothing. I count my scuba and snorkeling gear as equipment, like my bot." They patted the bot on their back before heading over the side.

Once in the water, Wend didn't need words or any interaction beyond keeping track of Viola and the *Nuovo Mar*. Viola brushed against them once, trying to get a better angle for some photographer reason Wend couldn't fathom, given they were in a randomly chosen patch of open ocean.

As it held little that was visible to humans, Wend relaxed into the constant motion of water, which caressed them like a loving touch. At first, their skin sensitivity shot up, as if starved for it. The almost scratchy overwhelming rhythm was aggravating and deeply satisfying at the same time. Wend swam forward and back, pacing the boat, rising and falling with every small surge of water.

They'd forgotten all about Viola's motives for stopping.

Then something over a meter long shot by in Wend's peripheral vision. They triggered a water sample instinctively. While their personal projects focused on the ocean's microbiome, large species in the vicinity could also be identified and might be significant to other parts of the Marine Census.

While the first pass happened too fast for Wend to worry about sharks, the second and third large bodies moving in the same direction suggested danger. Wend wasn't that well-educated about larger sea creatures, but three animals close to human size moving fast conveyed a threat.

As a fourth and fifth raced even closer to Wend, although still many meters away, Wend had a clear view of a large dorsal fin, probably the second, far back on the fish, followed by spiky finlets leading out to a tail like a crescent moon.

They recognized tuna. Fierce predators moving fast, but not ones that would attack Wend. Each stretched as long as Wend but larger and wider. More flashed by in the distance, hints of silver catching the sunlight close to the ocean's surface. All Wend could do was watch in awe, with enough atavistic fear to keep them very still.

When the school had passed, they took another water sample and looked to see if Viola had captured the migration. The photographer still had her face and camera underwater. Aljon stood at the boat's railing above, mouth open. He must have seen plenty of live tuna in his time, yet still shared Wend's sense of wonder at the visit.

Reluctant to go back to the world of speech and humans, Wend floated and swam until Viola called them in. They took a couple more samples before climbing out.

Not until the blades on the hydro turbine were adjusted for their slower speed and the sails set to catch what wind they could, did all three crew gather in the cockpit.

Viola passed her camera to Aljon, already displaying a clearer image of a tuna than Wend had been able to make out with merely human eyes. She'd captured the yellow of the finlets and the tuna's open mouth and eye. It looked majestic and less like a giant predator, because the photo showed its face and hid its motion.

"Definitely a Pacific bluefin tuna," Aljon said, as if asked a question.

Perhaps Viola had asked with a gesture or expression. She responded as if two steps ahead in a conversation, "But have they ever been seen here? Maybe their range broadened with climate change and the presumed extinction of wild southern bluefin?"

Aljon shrugged. "Didn't Japan and the US claim they'd brought the Pacific bluefin back?"

Viola waved a hand dismissively, her words spilling out faster than usual. "Along with Korea and Mexico, they vowed to restore twenty percent of historic levels by 2034. Of course national leaders and commercial fishers claimed success. The Pew Trusts didn't agree. But I haven't heard reports of changed migration patterns."

"They looked post spawning," Aljon said.

Wend smiled in appreciation. "There was a time when I would have been embarrassed to be so outmatched in this conversation. Now, I'm incredibly impressed and honored to be sailing with you both."

Viola flicked her fingers to fluff wet curls. "Good, I worried you'd want a percentage on my photos from this trip. I'm now convinced something about you summons sea life."

While Wend could have used the income, they were more concerned about the rest of the comment. They didn't like that suggestion at all. "I wasn't in the water long enough to draw tuna off their migration route— and I'm glad."

"Presuming the effect starts when you enter the water." Viola held up a flat palm to halt Wend's protest. "I'm proposing they swam slightly closer to check you out, which was my guess with the sea nettle and the tiny fish by the waterfall. The trash island with the giant manta ray already connects to your out-of-body flying, so I won't count that one."

Not sure how to express the mixture of disturbed, amused, pleased, and skeptical swirling inside them until they felt a little woozy, Wend held their head very still. "Maybe we shouldn't specify where we saw the tuna."

"What kind of a reporter are you?" Viola threw both arms open wide. "That's the whole story."

Swallowing hard, Wend forced out their argument. "Wasn't there some kind of tuna that commercial fishers targeted based on scientific publications about migration routes and feeding activities?"

"The Atlantic bluefin, but they were also bycatch on longlines and juveniles were caught in seine nets." Viola counted out factors on her fingers before adding, "Research on migration and feeding led to mapping and conservation plans. Now we have bait-to-plate tracking, DNA field kits, and mass spec test pens. NGOs and that aquarium you worked for issue warnings and recommendation lists based on restaurant and supermarket supply chains."

"Plenty of boats still change or block their vehicle identifiers," Aljon added in a measured tone, "and many countries don't enforce UN or High Seas Alliance protections."

Viola ignored him and spoke faster and louder at Wend, "As a scientist or an educator, I can't believe you'd argue to hide data because it might be misused. What if they set up marine protected areas that left out crucial migration routes because scientists hid their data? That would be worse than the commercial interests that hide FAD tech and migration groups they discover."

The tone of Viola's lecture and the implication that scientific ethics were so binary grated, but Wend had a more pressing question. They resorted to waving a hand up and down to get a word in edgewise. "Wait. What's FAD?"

"Fish Aggregating Device," Viola clarified, still talking faster than usual. "For the last twenty years seine fishers have been setting up solar-powered buoys designed to attract tuna. In the twenties, over half the world's tuna supply was caught that way. Although there's some evidence that certain schools or individuals learned to avoid the FADs, even alerting others to the danger. It would be interesting to compare documented instances with the jellies gumming up nuclear plants." Viola's eyes had drifted to scan the sea, but they suddenly fixed back on Wend as she tossed out, "Of course, we can't compare anything if data is hidden or research never published."

No longer hiding their irritation, Wend responded in a low, measured voice, "I guess it doesn't matter what I think, since you have your photos and clearly know much more than I do." They crossed their arms over their chest and kept their head up. "But if you won't even listen to my concerns, I'm not acting as your human FAD."

"That is not what I said." Viola tapped loudly on the tiller. "And don't say I'm trying to use you." Wend could see they'd hit a sore spot but couldn't fight past the annoyance mixed with guilt that poured from Viola as she ranted. "I'm a photographer sailing a route I planned before we even met. Taking pictures is what I do, and you practically forced your presence on us. You said you wanted help solving some puzzle that might involve both of us and that has effects you can't clearly explain. Now I more or less believe you can scout ahead using astral projection and possibly attract interesting sea life, and you're blaming me for wanting to publish the photos I took along the way?"

With a sick fascination, Wend realized this was the closest they'd ever come to being understood and accepted, but Viola was treating them like a useful gadget or a lesser human with inferior ethics. Their heart raced and stomach sank, but they had to respond. "I feel like you're twisting my words, either on purpose or by accident."

"No, you're the one who's all about words. You choose words to control the world around you, and if that control slips, you want to add more and more words until you get the effect you're looking for. Look at this." Viola brought up the impressive tuna picture she'd shown Aljon to begin with, the one that captured the yellow in the fish's finlets but hid all the ferocity of its motion and strength. She jammed her finger toward it. "This is how I communicate. Like the samples your bot takes, this photo captures location. That's all I want to share with the world, this picture and the location data captured with it. If you want to write about the experience, I guarantee my picture will get you better pay and publications. If you don't want to write about it, the publishers can find a dozen writers to fill in why it matters that we saw this fish exactly where we did." She lowered her arm, glaring Wend's way.

Futility stole the last of Wend's energy. "I know." They didn't have any more words.

"Dammit, at least my ex-lovers would fight back. I know I can be selfish and overbearing, but I don't think that applies right now. You make me feel like I kicked a puppy." With a toss of her head toward Aljon, she said, "Take the helm, Aljon. I'm going to make the hot chocolate this time."

As Viola stomped away, Aljon slid in beside the tiller. Once she was out of sight and hearing, he said in a soft and level voice, "You know, I didn't think well of you at first. When you pulled yourself on deck listing reasons you should join this crew, I thought you were an entitled know-it-all." He turned his head sideways and smiled to soften the blow. "Now I think you're struggling as much as the rest of us. That makes me like you more, but I think it's harder for Viola."

"Thanks." Wend loosened their crossed arms but couldn't manage eye contact. After a couple of long slow breaths, they added, "I didn't expect you to like me. We didn't seem to have much in common, and you barely spoke. I was going to keep my distance. But as soon as you talked, I was impressed with how well you knew yourself and paid attention to others. And your cooking abilities, fluency in multiple languages, and knowledge about boats and fishing are amazing."

"For someone my age?" he asked.

Not sure how to answer, Wend said, "For anyone, but especially for someone your age?"

Aljon chuckled and leaned back. "And if I'd been to college? If I had a PhD in marine biology, would your expectations have been different?"

"Different? Sure. Maybe unfairly so. Is this one of the places you don't want me to say I'm sorry? Because I am. I am struggling, every day, and expect I always will be. I think I like people who struggle to understand more than I value college degrees, if that helps." Even as Wend's insides squirmed with uncertainty and the apology they hadn't quite voiced, they realized how much calmer they felt after talking with Aljon, even if the topic was the opposite of soothing. "You're good with people, or at least with me. And . . . that isn't easy. With me, I mean."

"Thanks," Aljon said. The lack of qualifiers seemed like a good sign, and Wend was too overwhelmed to say any more.

They sat together watching the relatively calm sea until Viola emerged with three steaming mugs. She didn't try to take the helm back from Aljon. She didn't speak as they all finished their hot chocolate.

Wend wondered if they were being humored and handled. They weren't sure how to distinguish that from kindness in the current situation.

Finally, Wend broke the silence. "Your tuna pictures are amazing and you should offer them wherever you want. I could write something to go with them once I do some research, but there are probably people better qualified for that. I clearly don't know much about anything larger than plankton and some invertebrate reef dwellers."

Viola shrugged and said, "I have issues with people trying to control my work. I stand by everything else I said, but this is also how I make my living, pay for this boat, and pay Aljon enough to send some home. You lived it with us, whether or not you believe you influenced what we saw. I know you could write a point-of-view piece I'd be happy to see beside my pictures. Before we left the Marquesas, I did look up your published writings. I like how you appeal to kids or people new to your areas of interest. I want your perspective to accompany all my photos from this trip. If publications want something else or something more, it's up to them to provide it."

Wend clutched the still warm mug in their hands like a lifeline. "Thanks, I think. I definitely didn't mean to insult your work or you."

"You never mean to, do you?" Viola slouched back in her seat.

Wend had no idea what to say to that. It sliced them open, exposing the heart of their alienation, like they were being dissected. Despite the horror, there was a thrill at being seen. And at the compliment to their writing. While they would have preferred to exchange apologies and work through lingering aggressions, that clearly wasn't Viola's way. Wend raised their hands, palms up. "Aljon says we're all struggling, so maybe I'm struggling with what I mean to do."

Aljon smiled at that.

Viola pushed a hand back through her now dry hair and said, "That's more profound than I can handle right now. I think I need a sleep shift."

Wend woke with all ten fingers fanned outside their sleep sack like gills, red with hemoglobin, surrounded by warm mineral rich water. In their dream, there had been no way to see their lower body, to know if the mucus they secreted supported symbiotic bacteria that protected them from the extreme heat of a hydrothermal vent. They hadn't processed much during the dream, but respect for Pompeii worms filled their thoughts as they woke.

Once on deck, bright sun and good winds greeted them, as well as chattering birds. At least a dozen hovered above the boat as if trying to guess what it was and whether the mast would be a safe place to land.

None of them landed. After a while, Wend concluded the birds were riding the air pushed up by the sails the same way dolphins sometimes played in the water pushed along by the bow.

"Do you know what they are?" Wend asked Aljon, who tugged at something by the dinghy as Wend carried their sample bot forward and to the leeside.

He called back to Viola, "Wend asked me about the birds."

They laughed at some private joke and then Viola called out, "The small ones with long wings are Bulwer's Petrels. They eat surface plankton. The others are Wedge-Tailed Shearwaters. They eat fish, mostly goatfish. Both nest in cliffs around Hawai'i."

"Cool, thanks," Wend called back. Then they asked Aljon, "What are you doing there?"

"Checking the algae." He gestured to the clear five-gallon jug stored to the side of the dinghy with the emergency bag.

"While spirulina looks like verdant algae, it's actually cyanobacteria. Viola warned me early on not to ask about your stash or how you grew it," Wend said as they crept closer to look. The jug was filled to the brim with green, to all appearances healthy, cyanobacteria and water. "May I ask now?"

With a shrug and a raised eyebrow Aljon said, "There's not much to it. I make sure to keep a starter culture from each batch. Put that in with a small portion of growth medium, seawater, and some baking soda to adjust the alkalinity, and a couple weeks later we have this." He patted the nearly full container.

"And you use it in bread and soups?"

"Almost any mixed food you've eaten while aboard."

Appreciating the spatter of green light that passed through parts of the jug, Wend asked, "Is it kept on deck for the light?"

"It needs sunlight and carbon dioxide, but I keep it here as our emergency food supply. If we ended up with no other food in our lifeboat, this would last long past when we ran out of water."

Wend thought of the desalinator that had been bundled with the hydrogen generator but only said, "Good to know."

"Would you show me how to work your bot?" Aljon asked as he followed Wend to the side rail where they'd been preparing to lower the sample bot.

"There's not much to it," Wend echoed Aljon's words from moments before. He noticed and laughed, and Wend was pleased to have successfully shared a small joke. "You can see how the straps attach." They turned the bot over to show the straps anchored near each end of the cylinder that they'd already tied to two separate lines from the boat for redundancy. "The tricky part is securing the lines so the bot doesn't break away and you can pull it back up when we're moving like this." They looped each line around a different stanchion and tied stopper knots where they anchored the ends. Then they handed Aljon the bot. "All you have to do is lower it into the water and push this button on the remote. Then wait a minute and push again for a comparison sample." Wend had chosen to collect samples now because the North Equatorial Current aligned with the boat. It was pushing as hard as ever, but at least wouldn't pull the bot away. At around ten knots, the wind moved the boat faster, and they'd still have to fight that to pull the bot back from the water.

Aljon had no trouble lowering the bot and pushing the button twice. As he hauled the bot back up, Wend said, "The location, time, temperature, and other factors were tagged when you pressed the button. The samples sealed automatically and are kept safe inside. Sample bots are meant to be used by students and citizen scientists; therefore, I tried to design them to be foolproof while still making a serious contribution to research."

"So you build and sell them?"

"No, I published the design and instructions through a university press with a Creative Commons license allowing for free noncommercial use. All the parts are fairly common, except for the certified self-sealing sample containers. Various universities and labs make those available for specific projects. If people substitute or reuse their own sample containers, then we can't use them for official research, because we can't prove they weren't contaminated beforehand or when cleaned for reuse. But if kids want to do that for a science fair project or similar, it's fine. I've worked with all sorts of groups that assembled their own bots and then signed on to help with local projects. We rarely have problems."

"Are there projects involving sailboats cruising around the world?" Aljon asked.

Wend guessed he meant it as a joke, but their mind insisted on following through. "I justified this trip as providing reference samples between two research sites, since I was coming from a project on Nuku Hiva in the Marquesas, and I've been guaranteed a place in Hilo with one of the five projects underway in the Hawai'ian Islands. I'm not paid for working right now, but I count as a continuing employee. If the data I'm bringing in is as interesting as I expect, I could probably get a microgrant to send more bots out with sailboats like this, if any sailors want to do it as citizen scientists. What do you think? Would you take care of a bot as well as your spirulina and sprouts?"

Aljon patted the bot. "I think I could manage it."

That night, Wend took the early watch with Viola at the helm. A quarter moon shone bright in the surprisingly clear sky and the wind held constant at seven knots.

"We'll reach Hilo tomorrow if this holds," Viola spoke softly, leaning in conspiratorially, as if afraid to jinx their progress. "Did you get through all the stories you wanted to tell?"

Wend held up fingers to count, although not counting stories. "You accepted the plastic island as evidence for my flying dreams, are trying to verify flying dreams of your own, met me halfway with my lie detecting theory, and convinced me to consider effects on sea life that I never suspected." Only their thumb remained tucked. "We're well past what I hoped to learn, although the puzzle I'm trying to solve appears larger than ever."

"There's plenty I don't understand about you." Viola still spoke softly, and Wend settled in to see if this meant trouble. "It's like your appearance, the way you look much younger from a distance than close up. Every story tells me more about you, while pointing out how much more I don't know."

"Is there something in particular you want to know?" Wend asked, almost fearing the answer.

"Yes, several things. But I'm not going to ask." The silence stretched. Wend thought that might be the end of it, and wasn't going to press, no matter how curiosity riffled pages in their mind. Then Viola said, "I'm willing to tell you a story from my life that I don't usually share, mostly because I trust you not to tell anyone. Is that fair?"

"I don't think I can tell ahead of time what's fair, but I want to hear it. I'll keep it private." Wend didn't add a qualifier like 'unless you murdered someone,' because they fully believed they'd feel anything that dark radiating out from Viola. Living on a boat with only two other people made them much more aware of and comfortable with such feelings.

"Well then," Viola began, "in the early two thousands, as the internet was booming, I had a friend in the travel industry who set up her own 'hot deals' site online. She was good at finding discounts, packaging opportunities, and cultivating contacts. We'd been lovers off and on and traveled together. When she offered to make me a partner in her business, she promised me a lot of free or heavily discounted trips." Viola shrugged broadly enough that her shoulder nudged Wend's. Wend nudged back but stayed silent. Listening.

"I mostly contributed photos, for her site and some of the operators she partnered with. They were quality photos, but sometimes trite." Viola shrugged again, but smaller, and without a glance at Wend. "This was before I became well known as a photographer, and my family didn't consider anything I'd done up to that point a real job. Finally in my thirties, I was able to save money, send balikbayan boxes, set up a retirement account, visit my dad who had moved back to Italy when my mom died. By 2010, I had a mortgage on the house in Foster City I told you about.

"I felt grown up and successful. I wasn't getting rich, but when I visited locations for work, they tried hard to impress me. I stayed in suites with hot tubs and enjoyed private cottages right on the beach. That's when I learned scuba and sailing and picked up passable French and better Spanish." Viola sucked in a breath that sounded pained, but Wend couldn't yet guess why this story bothered her. "I encouraged everyone I met to travel more, to better understand the world, to appreciate nature. I believed travel was broadening and that the deals we promoted offered people insights into other lives and international policies. I rode the waves of social media, promoting the business, my opinions on travel, myself.

"Then it all shifted. The smaller hotels and services we'd help to publicize and build up could easily list their offers on a dozen different sites, had to in order to compete on a world stage. We profited more from selling cruises and tour packages than our custom itineraries. Meanwhile, living close to the bay and knowing Bay Area liberals, I heard more and more arguments about pollution, global warming, and sea level rise. As I flew to international destinations several times a year, I started to feel like part of the problem."

Wend nodded, finally catching on, but Viola rushed ahead with more words than ever.

"The travel industry expanded with the internet. More people traveled. But local businesses earned less while providing more. Tourist destinations filled local landfills, and exposés showed cruise ships regularly dumping oil and plastic waste. Coral reefs bleached and died. I talked to my business partner about going green, promoting carbon neutral travel, or sailing vacations. She told me I had no head for business and should be grateful she kept me on."

Viola rapped on the tiller in an almost violent way, but when Wend opened their mouth to comment, Viola quickly continued on. "I'd like to say I walked away then. But no, I kept that job past the great pandemic, dumping scandals, sea level rise, and glacial retreat around the world. At the same time, my nature photography took off, making my name as an eco-advocate even as I supported myself on other people's international air travel and conspicuous consumption. I changed all my handles on social media and kept a much lower profile. I lived in fear that one of my activist friends or publishers would call me out for the sort of travel I'd spent two decades promoting. Only when my own house flooded and the travel industry imploded did I pull out of the business. I invested everything I had along with the flood insurance payout to buy this boat and literally sailed away."

Staring out at the starry night, Wend let the story filter through their mind, waiting to make sure Viola had finished. "Is this what you were worrying about that first day, when you made me promise not to write a biography or exposé about you?"

"Well, I already told you about Rosamie, and I know how people would see that. It's not like there's something worse I'm trying to hide, more a series of small decisions I'm not proud of. I'm not making up for it either. This zero emissions lifestyle is my version of 'do no harm.' If my photography can be something better than that, I want it to have that chance, free of me."

"Are you trying to free yourself from your past?"

Viola barked a harsh laugh. "No matter how often I reinvent myself, there's no being free of me. I don't think I'd choose it, even if I could."

"Me neither," Wend said. "After all the people who rejected me or tried to change me, I can't do that to my prior self."

Viola tapped the side of her foot against Wend's and said, "There you go then, something more we have in common."

ACT TWO:

ISLAND

12.

WEND NOTICED the first light of dawn in the east right before Aljon pointed out specks of red light in the west, off the port bow.

"What's that?" Wend stood up to see better.

"Lava. I've never seen it before, but the southernmost tip of the easternmost island, Hawai'i, has active volcanoes." Aljon sniffed the air and added, "Smells like land from out here."

"Our first sight of land is lava," Wend said in awe, not sure if it smelled sulfurous or if that was their imagination. "Should I wake Viola?"

"I'm awake," the skipper's voice came from below. Moments later she stood between them, all staring at the red glow amidst a lightening gray mass of land.

Viola broke the silence, voice low and sleep rough, "We'll soon be passing Cape Kumukahi." Then she handed Wend a folded paper from one of many pockets in the shorts she'd chosen that day. "While I've been here before, and picked up some chatter on the local SSB net, I don't think even my subconscious could know the names, configuration, and exact locations of boats anchored in Radio Bay last night. Hold onto that and tell me later if I had a legitimate flying dream."

Wend met her eyes for a long moment and said, "I'll keep this safe."

Viola turned to Aljon and added, "I saw the two lifejackets strung out to make an 'A' on top of the cabin, using their waist cords for the center line. A for effort."

"You should have seen my eight-ray sun the night my shift was calmest." Aljon smiled.

"Lucky you flew on his shift." Wend couldn't help but smile, giddy their journey could lead to such a conversation. "All I managed was to tie a life jacket with the shoulder straps pointing different directions each night."

The thrill of seeing land and gathering evidence for dream flight gave way to the needs of the boat, especially as the wind dropped off shortly before they reached Hilo Harbor on the east coast of the island of Hawai'i. As they turned to port around the breakwater and brought the reefed mainsail to windward, Wend boggled at the lush trees and bright white houses down near the water. It was strange to think they were back in the US, with the distinct possibility of standing on dry land today. Excitement warred with anxiety until Wend pushed both down and focused on bringing the *Nuovo Mar* in safely.

Under Viola's direction, they slowly made their way between land and breakwater before tacking carefully into a very sheltered bay at the far end. Commercial vessels lined one side. The other held a US Coast Guard station, six sailboats similar to theirs, and a dinghy dock.

The sounds of jackhammers and heavy machinery competed with the warble of songbirds as Viola told them, "Radio Bay is mostly commercial, but it's the safest bay on the island this late in the year. For a few years after the great pandemic and again during the second pandemic, it closed completely to cruising boats like ours. But crews were lost to rough weather and poor anchor-holdings in other parts of Hilo Harbor, and environmental groups complained about anchor damage to ecosystems out there. It reopened a few med-moorings and this space in the center where we'll be dropping anchor. Ready, Wend?"

Viola turned the bow into the wind and brought the boat to a dead stop with a quick "heave to" to Aljon before she told Wend precisely how much anchor chain to play out. Once the anchor hit the seabed, Wend tried to keep the line straight and send it out evenly from the anchor winch as Aljon backed the mainsail to drive it in. They tested with a chain hook until convinced the anchor was secure.

"Drop the main," Viola ordered. The words echoed in Wend's mind with more weight than carried in the skipper's voice.

Viola checked Wend's work and barely finished showing them how best to set a snubber before a yellow quad-drone with domes for 360 cameras on both top and bottom buzzed in from the shore.

"Welcome back to modern life and government bureaucracy," Viola muttered.

Wend had endured plenty of confrontations with government bureaucracy, but they couldn't help smiling at the flying bot. It was a sturdy model, at least three kilos. With the latest battery technology, it could probably fly for over an hour and was clearly sealed and designed to float after an amphibious landing. Wend would have loved to use such a high-end bot for difficult to access but fairly low-wind sample locations, but suspected it cost ten times as much as their sample bot, not to mention requiring orders of magnitude more maintenance and tuning.

As it approached the helm, a deep voice came over the drone's speaker, "Aloha, this is Akana Mahiʻai from Hilo Customs and Immigration. If you wish to stay anchored in Radio Bay, please give permission for this drone to land and conduct initial assessments."

"Permission granted by owner," Viola said.

The drone landed on the deck and Wend noted drop claws, currently retracted, that could easily deliver an inflatable flotation device, and textured rubber landing spikes beneath each rotor, to help it land securely on a wet or shifting deck. Its label read "US Customs" with an ID number Viola photographed, presumably for verification purposes.

After confirming the *Nuovo Mar's* registration information and departure from Fatu Hiva seventeen days before, the voice over the drone said, "Please present passports, visas, and other relevant documents for each person aboard. Display them to the camera under this drone."

After living out an isolated, timeless reenactment of seafaring for over two weeks, it was exciting for Wend to interact with a form of high-tech border control they'd never seen before, despite their thoughts on border control in general. From the way the voice read off registration information, Wend suspected they were dealing with a simulation of Akana Mahiʻai and not a real-time human interaction, but in many ways Wend was more comfortable with programs and bots than with real-time people they didn't know.

When their turn came to feed documents under the drone, Wend pulled their US passport from the waterproof pouch they wore around their neck. They carefully opened the old-fashioned booklet and slid it forward, under the drone.

Viola and Aljon had been told to remove their papers after less than twenty seconds each. Wend worried when the silence stretched over a minute.

The voice sounded slightly different as it said, "Gwendolyn Taylor, your US health coverage through the Multi-State University Consortium expired on October 31, 2039. To re-enter the United States, you must provide alternative proof of coverage or apply for public-option emergency coverage and prepay the first month with a deposit of $2200 in US currency. Which option do you select?"

Wend choked for a moment, but found it easier to confront the drone than if they were face to face with an unfamiliar human, even if that human might be actually present in real-time conversation now. "There must be some mistake. I am still employed by the University Consortium and should still have US health coverage through my existing plan."

"Please contact your insurance provider and have them submit proof of insurance to US Customs and Border Protection with reference to your full name and passport number. Until you confirm receipt and clearance, you are not cleared to set foot on United States soil and may not remain on a boat anchored in a US port for more than 48 hours. Is that understood?"

"I understand," Wend said, voice tight.

"Gwendolyn Taylor may continue health screening with other crew and passengers. To continue remote screening at this time, you must each submit blood samples via the test kits provided by this drone." A panel opened beside the upper dome camera to display three black boxes that looked like pencil sharpeners, except the hole on the side of each was large enough for a fingertip and currently sealed beneath a clear plastic flap with a green arrow printed on one side.

Wend had used similar test kits before and reached for one as the drone's instructions continued. "Please keep test kit in clear line of sight to cameras at all times. Our nanopore technology will test only for contagions listed on the Hawai'i Department of Health official website. No personal genetic data will be tested or retained. Pending results, your travel time will be documented as quarantine time shared with only those present on this vessel. We will initially test a pooled sample of all persons quarantined together. Is that understood?"

Each of them in turn confirmed they understood and completed their blood test. While several countries had taken steps to limit future public health crises after the great pandemic and a half-global scare a decade later, this was the first Wend had heard of blood tests being required within the United States. Hawai'i was in a unique position to do so, and in the moment, Wend's concerns around genetic privacy foundered beside their panic about health insurance.

After a few more questions about agricultural products on board, which Aljon answered, and how to contact them with test results and clearances, which Aljon and Viola each answered as well as agreeing Wend could be contacted through either of them, the drone flew away.

"Well, that was unpleasant," Viola complained as she started tidying up the cockpit.

"Most places we had to arrange our own transport, report to an office, and sometimes were sent back to the boat to quarantine," Aljon remarked as he wound up lines to prepare for extended time in port. When Wend moved to help him, he said, "Shouldn't you be contacting someone about your health insurance?"

"I was supposed to check in with my new supervisor at UH Hilo, but I'd planned to do that in person or from an internet café. I don't have anything with me to access the internet." Wend's voice sounded small in their own ears.

Aljon set down the line he'd been gathering and said, "Wend, are you okay?"

When they didn't answer immediately, he said, "Let's sit down together. There must be something we can access from my phone."

Wend sat down beside Aljon, right on deck. "I could send an email to the Marine Census Project supervisor, Betta Acosta. She would know who handles health insurance, and she usually responds quickly."

"Wouldn't it be faster to call?" Aljon sounded impatient or perhaps skeptical.

"I don't want to panic her. She knows how strongly I prefer email." Wend had to clamp down hard on their distrust of phones and Wi-Fi security to risk even the password to their work email on Aljon's phone, but they typed and sent the necessary request.

Wend clutched Aljon's phone, appreciating the squishy smoothness of its case and wondering how close it was to fully waterproof. The calm bay around them meant they were barely rocking, and the sun was pleasantly warm. Nonetheless, Wend felt nauseated and shivered with a chill.

"Would you like some hot chocolate?" Aljon asked.

The offer brought tears to Wend's eyes, a pretty good indication that they needed to employ calming strategies. Usually hot chocolate promised both calm and comfort, but they weren't sure their stomach would accept it at the moment. "No thanks. Give me a minute to take stock, and I'll be fine."

Very deliberately, Wend breathed in deep, smelling salt, sulfur, plumeria, and bird droppings. Four smells meant they needed to find three sounds next. The jackhammer had stopped, but there was a power drill or similar whirring across the water. Lots of little birds still sang, and people were chatting over on the breakwater. For two things they could see, they counted a child in red swim trunks and a gray and white seagull, both standing on the breakwater. The smooth warm deck Wend sat on was the final item needed for the sensory inventory, and they felt calmer.

By the time they finished, there was already a reply from Betta. "She may have panicked anyway. She's concerned and looking into what went wrong but says I should contact Lorelei Kahale, Head of Marine Science at UH Hilo, my new supervisor." Wend took two more deep breaths and tried to mentally prepare an email about her employment and insurance status.

Aljon said, "Would it help if I dial and put the call on speaker, or would you like to go below for more privacy?"

Wend wasn't concerned about privacy at this point, but they usually avoided talking on the phone. "Speaker, I guess." Viola stowed the foresail and pointedly ignored them as Aljon dialed and the phone started ringing.

"Hello, this is Dr. Lorelei Kahale. I'll be away on vacation the week of Thanksgiving and will be unable to respond to messages until Monday. If you need help before then, please contact my assistant, Miko Yamamoto at . . ."

Aljon typed in the new number as it played on the recording. Wend tried to remember when they'd last been in the US for Thanksgiving. Two rings later, a high-pitched and youthful-sounding voice answered, "Aloha, this is Miko Yamamoto. Can I help you?"

Closing their eyes to concentrate, Wend said, "Hello, this is Dr. Gwendolyn Taylor. I don't know if you can help, but Dr. Lorelei Kahale's message said to call this number. She's supposed to be my supervisor now. I just arrived in Hilo, and immigration won't let me off the boat because they say my insurance was canceled at the end of October."

"Oh, Dr. Taylor, we didn't know when you were arriving."

"Betta Acosta pre-approved and just now confirmed that I'm listed as a continuing employee. I was taking samples in transit between two research sites. She said Dr. Kahale could fix this." Wends words were running down at the end, both in pitch and speed.

Miko responded by speaking even faster and at a higher pitch than before. "I'm sorry about that. Dr. Kahale's not here, but if I can put you on the work schedule this month, I'm sure HR can fix the insurance matter."

Nodding automatically, Wend said, "I'm available to work, but I only have 48 hours to fix the insurance issue with immigration."

"Oh!" Miko practically squeaked. "And Thanksgiving is two days away. I see why you're worried, but this might work out well for everyone. I had an instructor cancel for this Saturday for an onsite training at Hilo Harbor. Are you staying near there?"

Wend didn't know whether Miko desperately needed someone to fill a weekend slot or only saw one alternative to fix the employment situation. Either way, Wend would take it. If they could. "Right now, I can't get off the boat. I'm literally in Hilo Harbor at Radio Bay."

"Good, good. You're the sample bot specialist, right?"

"Yes, I designed them."

"Oh, I didn't know that. Terrific!" Miko's enthusiasm sounded real over the phone, but Wend had spent too much of their life pretending enthusiasm to trust that. "I can meet you at Reed's Bay Park at 9 AM Saturday. That's only a mile from Radio Bay. I'll bring three sample bots and take care of check-in and the course intro. All you need to do is explain the parts and purpose of the bots and answer any questions. It's a half-day workshop: nine through noon. Will that work for you? If so, send me a quick photo and bio and I'll get the announcement out today. Oh, I'm so glad I don't have to cancel it. I already had to cancel one and was worried they might get defunded."

Exhausted from even this minimal interaction, Wend said, "I'm sure that will be fine, but what if I can't get my insurance cleared up with HR and immigration before Thanksgiving? I'm stuck on a boat using a borrowed cellphone for all this."

"Oh, no!" Miko sounded like someone who would use a lot of exclamation points in text messages, but Wend was grateful for even a pretense of concern. "I'll see if I can get a department phone issued by Saturday. Is this a number I can call you back at? We had all your papers and knew you were joining us sometime. Let me call HR. Either they'll call you back or I will, okay?"

Wend could barely keep up with the verbal onslaught. They couldn't speak in exclamation points right now if they tried. "That would be great. Thank you."

"No problem. I'm looking forward to meeting you Saturday! Bye!"

The call ended and Aljon shook his head at the phone before smiling at Wend. "If anyone can get this done fast, I'm betting on Miko." Then his smile turned to a frown as he looked at Wend, probably mirroring whatever showed of Wend's discomfort. "I'll admit, I don't understand the problem. I thought everyone in the US had health insurance."

"Everyone is required to, and there's a public option that's supposed to fill in gaps. That works if you live here full time and know your status during open enrollment periods. In a couple more years, I'll qualify for Medicare, if it still exists and they haven't rolled the qualifying age back any farther." Wend stopped, realizing they were rambling and Aljon probably didn't want to hear about the challenges of being part contractor, part gig worker, as well as owing foreign taxes for tiny one-time publications. "Basically, if I can't clear things up, I'm going to be charged more than I'll earn this month for insurance that I won't have a chance to use."

Aljon waved the phone in his hand such that it flashed sunlight like a signal mirror. "My family treats health insurance as more prestigious than income. You make it sound like a burden."

Wend sighed, feeling embarrassed in a detached way, as if their emotional reserves had run dry. "We used to call them first world problems, but I think that's insulting now."

"Post-problematic." Aljon pointed a finger at himself. "I was born knowing all of that. Don't worry."

"I can't help worrying, even though I know I'm privileged to assume any sort of health coverage. I had access to doctors and some physical therapy for my spine issues, but struggled with serious debt after. If I'd been fully disabled, I would have qualified for Social Security early. And even then there's a wait before Medicare kicks in." Wend realized they should be thanking or possibly reassuring Aljon, who'd made do with far less for most of his life. Shaking their head to clear it, or at least start themself moving again, Wend managed a more steady tone. "I get overwhelmed sometimes, but that's my issue, not yours. Whatever happens with health insurance or my new job now, I'm glad for the time I spent on this boat with you."

Aljon stretched and leaned back to pat the deck with one hand. "This boat? With a grouchy skipper and a cook who feeds you cyanobacteria?"

Wend felt muscles from their jaw to the shoulders relax in response to Aljon's teasing. "The best cook who feeds me cyanobacteria."

For lunch Aljon served vegetable soup made with spirulina, tabbouleh with sprouts, and generous mugs of hot chocolate. Wend hadn't been hungry, but their stomach had settled enough to find the food comforting, even more so for being distinctly Aljon's cooking. All three crew sat together, eating in the shaded part of the cockpit, when Viola said, "I think it's time you checked my dream map."

Flustered at having forgotten something so significant, Wend scrambled to spread the folded note from that morning across their knees. They turned it to align with the harbor based on their current orientation. The commercial pier on their starboard side was marked with two black boats and two white. Another white boat had arrived after they set anchor, and it was easy to believe the one missing boat had left before they arrived that morning.

The six cruising boats docked ahead and to port of them were clearly labeled with names on Viola's sketch. All were predominantly white, but one was additionally labeled "blue awnings," two as "catamarans," and another with "no mast" for the only non-sailboat moored there. All six matched Viola's descriptions and placements. There was no doubt in Wend's mind when they said, "I don't think we could ask for better proof that you flew ahead and scouted the bay thoroughly. Congratulations."

Viola smiled and kicked a foot against Wend's. "You're an inspiration. I'm sure whoever you're teaching Saturday will be happy to have you."

That was when it started raining. Aljon looked delighted as he brought three bins up and set them out on deck to catch rainwater. Then he disappeared below and came back wearing swim shorts and carrying a washcloth and the soap they'd previously used in the ocean. "Who needs onshore showers when I have warm Hawai'ian rain?"

13.

WEND HOVERED in deep water, the suspension not unlike their hammock, but even closer to swimming. Their whole body rippled—no, those were long fins extending the length of their mantle. Inside, their cuttlebone stored pockets of gas, allowing them to float while in this cuttlefish form.

The huge shrimp drifting before them in the water column were at least a quarter their own size. A pang from their stomach signaled hunger and all three hearts sped in preparation for attack. Wend-cuttlefish had two large eyes with w-shaped pupils that let them watch in all directions for threats. They undulated fins to steer and adjusted the buoyancy of their cuttlebone to rise by balancing gas and liquid. Then Wend-cuttlefish lunged forward and grabbed with two tentacles mounted in front of their eyes. They pulled the shrimp into their beak to feed. Delicious. Filling.

Wend-cuttlefish sank back to the seafloor, their benthic home. They scurried, using two large lower arms and a portion of their mantle that projected like legs. Their fins rippled as they moved, six upper arms waving ahead. At present they were mostly brownish gray and white, a flamboyant cuttlefish in camouflage mode.

Another of their kind cascaded black lines, like dark clouds passing up their body, as Wend-cuttlefish rushed into a rock crevice the two of them sometimes shared. They might be siblings, hatched from nearby eggs at nearly the same time. Despite their superior intelligence among invertebrates, it was hard to recognize family when parents died before your birth, leaving a couple dozen eggs hidden along rocky crevices or reefs. The familiar other was larger, five centimeters perhaps, if Wend-cuttlefish was four. The other was more social, more drawn to where *several of their species were staking out dens, territories in which to breed and lay eggs.*

Their possible sibling darted across an open expanse of seafloor. W-pupils wide, Wend cowered under cover. Their sibling had no place to hide as a carnivorous fish ten times larger advanced.

The fish shadow passed over the expanse. Wend braced for trauma—preparing to see a friend die—a large nebulous fear alien to their cuttlefish body. The other flamboyant cuttlefish froze in place, holding their ground as they suddenly switched their chromatophores to a threat display. Wend interpreted colors surprisingly well from the black and white but polarized signals their cuttlefish eyes provided.

The other's suddenly violet mantle sported bursts of yellow around the edges, spread wide around eyes and arms. The tips of their arms turned bright red. Those colors warned of toxins that permeated the body of the diminutive flamboyant cuttlefish, the most poisonous of its kind. The predatory fish veered sharply in its dive.

The exposed cuttlefish released a burst of ink and shot away, colors already subdued to brownish gray.

Wend-cuttlefish followed quickly, imitating the color and texture of sand, pulling gracefully across the ocean floor in the confusion. They settled under a rock ledge where dozens of their kind had already gathered. The tiny currents made by other rippling fins elicited a brief show of their own chromatophores, mostly purple with hints of white and yellow, as Wend-cuttlefish shivered with pleasure at the nearness of others.

Several small cuttlefish were creating long, glorious displays in color or with rings of black that appeared to slide along their mantles and mesmerized Wend-cuttlefish. A few picked fights with each other, turning a whiter side to those they fought while still flashing showy patterns toward those watching. Wend-cuttlefish controlled their own desire to display, not wishing to fight. They sought a quieter group of observers, many even larger than Wend's possible sibling. As arms began to wave in tentative touches, they sensed this gathering was important, a ritual near the end of life to create a new generation, but something more as well.

Wend exchanged brief touches of many arms and other parts while appreciating the individuals performing movements like bows or obeisances amid eye-catching chromatophore displays. When a neighboring cuttle-fish spread wide three pairs of arms to allow one of the smaller fighters in, a thought in the back of Wend's mind noted the gametes carried by Wend-cuttlefish matched those of the fighter. Wend-cuttlefish bypassed the dangers of confrontation by suppressing their own display for now. Beneath that rock ledge, they were surrounded and embraced by a group both like and unlike Wend-cuttlefish, amidst an ocean full of life forms no one individual could fully comprehend.

It wasn't until nine the next morning that all three crew on the boat received notice their blood had tested negative on all counts. Aljon and Viola were cleared to disembark.

Wend's hammock still hung where they'd spent the night on deck, and they wanted to crawl back into their sleep sack and hide from the world. They fondly remembered the gathering of tiny cuttlefish in their dream. "I'm fine staying here alone if you two want to get real showers or go out to eat or something."

"I'm clean enough," Aljon declared, "and I have a whole month of data to use up." He waved the phone that had been in his hand almost constantly since anchoring, aside from a couple bursts of rain. "Should we try calling Miko back?"

"I guess. You don't think it's too soon?" Wend asked.

"We could find a number for HR." As he spoke, his phone vibrated and Aljon said, "Or we could wait for Miko to call back." He hit speaker and held the phone out while Wend was still processing what had happened.

"Hello?" Wend said a beat too late.

"Hi, this is Miko. I got your paperwork from HR. They filed an official proof of insurance for you with customs and sent a copy to the Hilo immi-gration station as well. Should I send copies of the forms to this phone or to the email we have on file for you?"

That sounded better than expected, and Wend wondered if Betta had intervened or if bureaucracy on Hawai'i ran smoother than elsewhere. Not likely. Wend looked to Aljon, who shrugged.

"Could you do both?" Wend asked.

"Sure!"

Wend found the speed and pitch of Miko's voice more reassuring than overwhelming this time, even as they worried about fairness and others struggling through health insurance and employment issues. "Thanks, for that and dealing with all this paperwork."

"You spared us the greater hassle of canceling the weekend class, but you're welcome. Do you need anything else before Saturday?"

After a full day of cowering in uncertainty, Miko's helpful competence lulled Wend's anxieties into submission. Thoughts quickly shifting to work, Wend said, "If I'm allowed off this boat today, I was hoping to drop off filled sample containers from my bot and pick up replacements."

"I'll send you our lab address and processing details," Miko offered, "but honestly, I don't think anyone's going to get to it until Monday. I'd be happy to bring your samples in with whatever is collected during the training. Do you want me to bring fresh containers for you on Saturday? You could show the class how you take the old ones out and process them for shipping when far from a lab. I'll bring some typical shipping supplies. How many do you have filled?"

"Nearly five hundred."

"That's great! I'm sending you our lab details and your insurance forms now. And I'm setting aside five hundred fresh sample containers with all the other materials for Saturday. I'm glad you arrived this week!" Miko sounded less squeaky and more sincere, although that might have been Wend's imagination. After a brief pause, when possibly Wend should have spoken, Miko continued, "I'll be here until four this afternoon. Give me a call if you need anything else or if you don't get immigration clearance in the next couple hours."

Wend said honestly, "I'm looking forward to meeting you in person. Thank you for all your help. Mahalo."

"'A'ole pilikia."

The call ended but left Wend standing taller, ready to face the day.

As it turned out, Aljon preferred to stay on the boat. Wend let Viola cajole them into coming to meet her friend Doreen who "always knows the best places to stay with locals." It was unclear if Viola wanted a place to sleep other than her boat, but Wend understood they were expected to find someplace else, now that they'd reached Hawai'i and were permitted ashore. That was fair. They had a job and health insurance. Today they'd deal with meeting Viola's friend and finding housing, maybe grocery shopping and laundry. It sounded like a lot. Wend wished they'd asked the exuberantly helpful Miko if there were any university subsidized housing options they might qualify for, but there had been too much else to sort out. Wend couldn't ask for more right before a long weekend.

With each step away from the boat, Wend focused on learning their way around Hilo. Viola walked ahead with a relaxed gait that suggested she knew the area well or wanted people to believe she did. They passed surf shops and breakfast places along the coast, then turned away from the ocean, toward a residential neighborhood. Wend wondered if people on Hawaiʻi used makai to mean toward the ocean and mauka to mean toward the mountains or center, the way people on Oʻahu did. Half-remembered words from their childhood bubbled up, but Wend worried they'd sound ridiculous saying "slippers" or "keiki". They practically vibrated between positive associations from walking freely on dry land in a part of Hawaiʻi much like their childhood home and the insecurity of not having a true home and leaving behind the familiarity of boat and crew.

After twenty minutes of walking, Wend's legs and inner ears acclimated to being back on land. They'd only traveled ten blocks mauka, but here tall trees and broad-leaved plants surrounded well-spaced houses painted in whites, grays, or pastels. The smell of soil and growing things almost covered the salty tang from the sea.

Adventure Treehouse Bed and Breakfast displayed stained wood walls rather than painted. It sported solar panels on the roof, a rainbow flag in one window, and a trans flag in the other. Three large wooden treehouses rose up behind it amidst palms and other trees. Viola slipped her sandals onto a low shelf by the door, then tapped before entering without waiting for a reply. Wend followed barefoot behind.

"Well, look who finally washed up on our fair shores." A well-muscled younger woman, who Wend presumed was Doreen, rose from a reception desk in the entryway and stepped around to hug Viola. She wore an aloha shirt patterned with broad-winged birds of prey on a silver-blue background. "Aloha, sistah. You need to call Shelly. Today. I don't need your drama on my island."

Viola kept a hand resting at Doreen's waist, but Wend saw how Viola's posture stiffened. They remembered Viola struggling to hand off the generator Shelly had left her, but never commenting directly on that relationship. Whatever Doreen's stake in the matter might be, Viola tried to deflect. "What? No lists of who's single or looking for scuba instructors or boarders?"

Doreen side-eyed Wend and rather than answering asked, "This someone new for you? Is that why you're ignoring Shelly's messages?"

"You have no idea how many messages hit my phone when we arrived. Makes me want to stay at sea." Viola waved a hand in Wend's direction, saying, "This is Wend, they're crew. That's all. Aren't you glad I came to see you first thing?"

Wend kept to the farthest corner of the room where a sliding glass door overlooked a large lanai and beyond that a climbing wall, zipline, and rope bridges as well as the treehouses they'd spotted from the road. Their fingers flexed with the urge to climb as well as the need for distance from this conversation.

"Good to meet you, Wend. I'm Doreen. If you want to step out and explore, feel free. But stay out of the treehouses. They're guest rooms."

"Thanks," Wend managed before taking the offered escape. They crossed the broad lanai with barely a glance at the surrounding bulletin boards, bookshelves, and coffee and tea supplies. Instead, they made their way up a climbing wall, which wasn't much of an adventure at barely four meters high, but the grips came in four different colors. Wend decided next time they'd try not using any green ones. The top connected to a hanging rope bridge, which was bouncy and fun. That led to a zipline that Wend gleefully rode back to ground level. The layout was simple but not childish. They wondered why no one else was out enjoying any of it in the sparkly warm morning sun. Never in their life had they stayed someplace so whimsical or with such pleasant tactile options, let alone surrounded by tall trees and songbirds. Wend was about to climb across an upward sloping rope net to reach the hammock chair dangling beneath it, when one of the bulletin boards they'd previously rushed past caught their eye.

The board showcased a glossy poster advertising flights over volcanoes in open-sided helicopters alongside paper fliers for waterfall rappelling and "aquatic acrobatics," which seemed to involve jet boots that could fly in and out of water. The same shop that advertised "aquatic acrobatics" also had a flier advertising "Frog Paddler" rentals for "unique and inclusive" ocean explorations. The "Frog Paddler" appeared to be a modified kickboard with small water jets that would allow someone to lie on their chest, see ocean life through a round viewing window at the front and activate jets on each side to turn, travel faster, or return to shore. While seeing "Frog Paddler" in four-inch-high red letters had reminded Wend of their mother's name for their preferred swim stroke as a child, the name of the company in one-inch white letters at the bottom drew them closer. It said, "Matthaios Water Wonders."

Doreen and Viola came through the sliding glass door at that point, strained but comfortable together.

Viola sidled up beside Wend and asked, "Find anything interesting?"

Wend pointed to the name Matthaios. Words were too small for the realization sweeping through Wend, so they pointed again and again. When Viola's forehead wrinkled in concern, Wend managed to say, "The only person I ever knew with that name was the boy I told you about, Mathew. The one I also told about frog paddling."

Without pause, Viola took a picture of the shop's address. Then, glancing at their phone, they said, "It's a couple miles further, but we could try there, if you want."

"I know Matthaios," Doreen volunteered. "He's not at the shop much." She stared pointedly at Wend and quirked an eyebrow, as if weighing her own curiosity against sharing intel with someone unknown. "He travels between here, O'ahu, and Maui where he has other shops. You think you know him?"

"If he grew up in Sacramento and went to Walnut Tree Preschool," Wend said.

"You think he'll remember you from preschool?" Doreen asked in a tone that hurt more than she could know.

"I remember him," Wend said.

"Hey, I'll send him a text." Doreen was already typing on her phone. "At Walnut Tree Preschool did you go by Wend, W-E-N-D?"

Reacclimating to the inclusion of cellphones and reliable cell service throughout every conversation would take Wend longer than getting their land legs back. But they nodded and waited, wondering how it would feel if Matthaios had attended Walnut Tree but didn't remember Wend at all.

"Shit, Matt's invited you to his place for Friendsgiving this Saturday. Preschool friends forever, I guess." Doreen sounded more than a little shocked before discomforting Wend with the perfectly normal question, "What's your phone number?"

Wend couldn't meet Doreen's gaze but managed to hold their head up as they admitted, "I don't have a phone at the moment. I can barely access my email."

"Give him my number," Viola offered. "I'll make sure to pass on the address or other details."

"What about all those messages that swamped your phone when you arrived?" Doreen's tone made Wend uncomfortable, even if the teasing was directed at Viola, who didn't seem to mind.

Then Doreen pulled a pen and paper from the nearby bookshelf and wrote an address, date and time. "He says you can bring whoever you're traveling with." Her tone was softer when addressing Wend, but the look she gave Viola as they left carried all kinds of judgment.

Wend clutched the written address as if it were a talisman and tried to breathe. Today was Wednesday. Tomorrow was a national holiday. They needed to find a place to live, take care of necessities, and be ready by Saturday to teach a class and attend a special dinner with a friend they'd been missing for half a century. Wend had walked three blocks before the solid ground under their feet registered.

Viola set a brisk pace beside them and never once checked her phone. Shortly before they reached the boat, Viola stopped at a small grocery and picked up the freshest salad ingredients available for Aljon.

When they paddled the dinghy out to the *Nuovo Mar*, Aljon swooped the groceries up from their hands before Viola or Wend made it on board. Then he called back over his shoulder, "I can tell you haven't checked messages, or at least not any that count. You really should." He took off below decks.

Wend wondered about the phone messages Aljon and Doreen kept mentioning. The scowl on Viola's face convinced them not to ask.

Instead, Viola led with, "Do you have plans for where you'll submit articles based on this trip?"

Wend had expected a question about when they'd be leaving the boat or how they'd find lodging, since that hadn't come up with Doreen. They breathed a sigh of relief as they secured the dinghy. "I owe a couple updates to a blog for Pacific Tech's marine education site, but they don't expect me to provide pictures, and they probably couldn't pay your going rate."

"If you can either wait to post or add pics later, it's the first run that makes me a living. After I've negotiated any exclusive rights, I often donate photos for educational purposes."

Wend shrugged, unsure how the offer was meant. "I probably won't have internet access until I can visit the university campus, Monday at the earliest."

"We could submit articles and photos together from my phone."

Wend stiffened at the brusque tone Viola used but suspected they weren't the real target of her irritation. "If you want."

"Are you the sort of person who never asks for a raise?" Viola's tone grew sharper. The small boat felt smaller.

Taking a deep breath Wend said, "I haven't had those sorts of jobs."

"You have a PhD!" she practically shouted.

Wend froze, not knowing how the confrontation had escalated so fast.

Luckily, Aljon returned with huge salads for each of them before Wend attempted to explain the various pitfalls of their chosen career.

Aljon stared pointedly at Viola across the small cockpit as he munched huge bites of salad.

"Tell me already," Viola finally grumbled.

"What? Oooooh, thank you for doing the shopping." He smirked.

"What have you discovered in your infinite phone time that tells you I'm not checking my messages?"

The way Viola asked made Wend's stomach cringe. They hid behind their salad and took a large bite.

Rising to the challenge with apparent ease, Aljon sassed once his mouth was empty. "I am neither your secretary nor your business manager."

"Wait, this has to do with business? Then it's not whatever Doreen was hinting about."

"Oh, it probably is. You may be the last person in your entire social network to know. For that matter, you should search the internet for mentions of your own name in the last week."

At that, Viola set down her half-eaten salad and searched on her phone.

"No way." Viola kept reading even as she said, "Hans Mehta, the fancy boat guy, is going into business with my ex, and he credits our crew with saving his father's life. This guy has serious assets and no problem with repurposing some factory where he used to make medical equipment to make ten thousand or more miniature hydrogen generators. Holy shit." Viola's mouth stayed open in something between a gasp and a smile.

"Congratulations. You're internet famous. Again." Aljon rolled his eyes.

"They credit the whole crew."

"I found five mentions with the *Nuovo Mar* but none with my name or Wend's. We are but your humble servants." Aljon bowed slightly over his bowl and rolled one hand in an overdone flourish.

Wend sighed in relief at not being part of the drama and managed to appreciate the crisp greens and tangy radishes they were chewing.

Viola focused on her phone again. "I'll tag you right now."

"Don't, don't, don't." Aljon shot his hands out to cover her phone screen. "I'll have relatives popping up everywhere with schemes to cash in on my fame."

A severe raise of her eyebrows communicated Viola's thoughts about that.

"What about you, Wend?" Viola waved her phone free of Aljon's clutches. "We could co-publish an account of how you spotted smoke and a distress flag while I was sleeping on the job."

Wend wished they had enough comedic timing to respond with a joke about having to wait for Aljon to wake Viola, but they didn't want to risk the joke falling flat when Viola had come close to shouting at them minutes before. After another bite of salad, which was remarkably satisfying after over two weeks at sea, they said, "Whatever you think best, but I don't care about getting credit. Maybe we should talk to Hans Mehta and whoever else is involved first."

"It so happens," Aljon said, waving an empty fork, since his enormous salad was completely gone already, "Someone involved messaged me not to plan anything for lunch or dinner tomorrow, since we're expected at a Thanksgiving feast the likes of which I've never seen. I don't think our host realizes what a low bar that is. Do you think I should bring a salad?"

"Wait." Viola's eyes went wide. "You mean here, on this island, and I'm guessing you don't mean Hans Mehta."

"You knew she was flying back to the US from Saint Lucia."

"But why would she end up here?" Viola's body language altered in a way Wend had never seen before. Her back curved and shoulders pulled in to make her look smaller, less self-assured.

Aljon's voice softened in response, either to the posture or whatever context he had for the entire conversation. "You'd know if you read the messages I'm sure she sent to you before contacting me. Seriously, you two bring out the worst in each other."

"Which was a fine reason to make a clean break." Viola's words sounded false, slightly staticky, but also rising at the end like a question.

"I'm not your kid. You two weren't even married. I refuse to be caught in the middle of your messy divorce." With that Aljon took his and Wend's now empty salad bowls down to the galley. He looked more openly annoyed with Viola than Wend had ever seen him.

14.

WEND SWAM toward a luminous fissure.

No, they were flying over a red glow, like embers far below them in a cranny within a crater surrounded by miles of blackened land. An active volcano. They swooped lower and felt the heat. The tiny cranny turned out to be a crescent-shaped half crater deep within a larger crater. The warmth drew Wend, but smoke in their eyes turned them aside. They flew to the less smoky side and heard a hum approaching out of darkness, opposite a stripe of dawn on the horizon.

Sunlight broke through as reverberations from the doorless helicopter pushed Wend further back.

They hovered at the northern edge of the crater watching humans in a helicopter photograph the glow below. Then they turned and flew fast without even moving their arms. They pointed their hands out in front, as if cutting through air in a smooth dive, past burnt land, past tree-lined shores.

Fat drops of rain pelted them. Their palms rose instinctively to deflect the insubstantial drops and slowed their flight to a calm glide.

Back in their body—their sleep sack, their hammock—the rain poured down from above.

Warm and safe, Wend burrowed deeper to sleep until the deluge ended.

By noon the sun shone high overhead. Wend had taken the opportunity to partially wash all three layers of their sopping wet sleep sack once the rain broke. The layers now hung nearly dry from the lines that connected the hammock to the shroud and backstay as well as one extra, set up astern where Aljon had once hung a clothesline.

It had been a quiet morning with Aljon and Viola barely speaking to each other, although there'd been no further arguments since lunch the previous day. Due to the US holiday, the commercial pier was quiet. Surprisingly loud frogs had given way to chattering birds. Wend was afraid to ask if they could stay on board through the long weekend, for fear Viola would notice they had no right to be there now.

Then a voice through a megaphone called out, "Viola, don't make me swim out there to talk with you."

Wend hid a smile at the threat, remembering how they'd first come aboard to gain an audience with Viola.

"My apologies to everyone else anchored here," the voice over the megaphone said, "but the closest person to family I've got for this feast day is ignoring their phone messages, and I already have dinner in the oven."

Aljon let out a snort, before ducking below.

Viola had been napping on her stomach on deck in a bikini. She gave up pretending to sleep and grabbed the binoculars to stare at the person with the megaphone, presumably the mysterious Shelly, who stood with hands on hips at the dinghy dock. "Well, shit."

When Viola lowered the binoculars, her pout took on an entirely different meaning beneath wide-open eyes and elevated eyebrows. Wend thought a cartoon version would have had hearts popping out of her eyes. They finally understood Aljon and Doreen's frustration with Viola over this relationship, and they definitely knew better than to comment.

As the figure raised the megaphone again, they heard, "I'll give you twenty minutes to get your dinghy over here, or I'm swimming out. Bring your work, your laundry, your whole crew. Just get your butt over here and let me feed you dinner."

Aljon reappeared on deck with a packed duffel over his shoulder and carrying a sealed container filled with sprouts and the vegetables left over from the previous day's salad. He ignored Viola but said to Wend, "If we're not leaving anyone to guard the boat, you should bring your passport and anything of value. I'm sure she means it about laundry, too."

Fifteen minutes later their dinghy bumped to dock at the feet of an unassuming person of about Wend's age, who wore several beaded necklaces and a loose dress, with long black hair flowing free in the breeze. Aljon clambered out with all his stuff, leaving Viola to tie the dinghy and Wend to take in the scene.

The previously reticent young man emptied his arms to wrap them both around the person who must be Shelly. They were both the same height, and Shelly kissed each of Aljon's cheeks before wrapping skinny, spotted arms tightly around his back. They held each other for a long while, and Wend thought the quip about not wanting to be in the middle of a messy divorce might be more poignant than they'd realized.

By the time Viola climbed out carrying a duffel and three camera bags and Wend managed to unload all their earthly possessions onto the dock, Aljon and Shelly finally let go of each other.

"Viola." Shelly stepped forward carefully to clasp her ex-lover's shoulders and lightly kiss each cheek.

Viola returned the greeting without a word.

Before the silence could stretch, Aljon said, "Shelly, this is Wend. I think you two will like each other."

Wend appreciated the vote of confidence as they offered a brief wave. "Good to meet you."

"Likewise." Shelly picked up her megaphone from the dock and said, "Let's drive back to the condo before trying to sort out anything else."

A bright green, driverless electric carshare vehicle waited in the nearest parking space. The trunk could barely hold all their belongings, but the inside had plenty of room for four adults. Wend was fairly sure Hawai'i, along with California and several western continental states, required all new cars to be electric now. Hawai'i's power grid had been one of the first to go completely renewable, and even on the largest island, no single trip was long enough to require recharging. It certainly made the streets quieter and less smelly than in the past.

Aljon sat up front and cheerfully asked Shelly how she'd spent the last few months.

"On my flight back from Saint Lucia, I met a local couple working to expand the marine protected area around the island. They were set to meet with a larger coalition that's trying to protect thirty percent of the world's oceans by 2040, the goal we failed to reach by 2030, but should meet by most measures this time." Shelly sighed dramatically.

"To make a long story short, I ended up working with a US chapter of that coalition."

As they pulled into a driveway after traveling less than two miles, Aljon asked, "Were you here all that time?"

"No," Shelly answered. "Mostly in Seattle, which is already a mess, with rising sea levels and extreme weather leading to all sorts of flooding and infrastructure damage. I'm happy to spend the winter here rather than there."

Shelly led them all into a two-story condo. The outside sported modern solar paneling, smart security cameras, and keyless entry. Indoors, sunlight streamed across hardwood floors, an eight-person dining table, and an open-plan kitchen with a window garden full of recently planted herbs. The whole place smelled of garlic, onions, cinnamon, and nutmeg.

As they stowed their shoes near the door and set down their belongings, Shelly ducked away and came back with three yellow flower leis hanging from her arm. "The landlord greeted me with one of these. When I showed interest, they offered me a lei needle and a bundle of plants to practice with." She placed one around Aljon's neck first, then Viola's and Wend's.

While Wend had plenty of warning to prepare for the brief touch, they'd forgotten how flower leis surrounded them with smell. Their brain spun with associations, half-formed memories dating back to their own childhood on Oʻahu. They had no words to describe the scent. Using the backs of their fingers they carefully lifted the lei to below their nose.

"It reminds me of sage," Shelly said, "So I figured it would complement today's feast. Even if we're not having turkey, I used sage in my taro stuffing."

The scent tended toward sweet, even tangy, and didn't remind Wend of sage at all. They realized they might not know what sage smelled like by itself, but they knew this flower. "What is this?"

"Kahili ginger. It's invasive, and the locals shear it down or dig out the bulbs to keep it from taking over. But most people are happy to see the flowers enjoyed in the meantime." Shelly drifted into the large open-plan kitchen as she talked and was checking pots simmering on the stove.

"Everything smells wonderful," Aljon said. "Can I help?"

"Why don't you set up your salad on the table and then take a look around?" She uncovered a tray of rising rolls before adding them to the oven with a couple of covered casseroles. "I don't know the best order to explain everything, but you're each more than welcome to a room here if you want to choose. The only closed door is my bedroom."

As Viola opened her mouth to protest, Aljon caught her by the hand and tugged. "You can explore with me."

They took off upstairs. Wend wanted to give them privacy but wasn't comfortable alone with Shelly yet. They skirted the edges of the open-plan room they were in, which contained the too shiny, black and white kitchen but otherwise appealed with plenty of wood tones and sand-colored rugs and walls. Paintings showed sailboats and windsurfers. The prosaic subject matter suggested they came with the condo, but the style was quirky with thick globs of shiny, overly bright paint. That texture made Wend want to touch, or at least tilt their head to check another angle. Shelves displayed a miniature wooden surfboard, a well-crafted 'ukulele, and a multi-strand shell lei. Despite the clichéd nature of the items, each was beautifully crafted and Wend would bet locally made.

Following the walls took Wend past the dining table and a large but overly tidy sitting area to double doors with several small glass panes and wooden slat blinds. Beyond those doors Wend discovered their favorite room. They knew without having to look upstairs.

The walls on all three sides were glass, over two meters long, and each had a large section that opened like a floor-to-ceiling sliding glass door. The wood floor displayed wider boards than inside. Broad ceiling beams extended outward, supporting a small overhang. All Wend could think was how perfect those beams would be for hanging their hammock, like sleeping in the garden without the chance of rain. A patterned blue futon under one beam could easily fold out into a guest bed. The futon and its armrest would also provide easy steps to reach a hammock hung close to the ceiling above.

Large potted plants in each corner made Wend wonder if the room doubled as a greenhouse, but they didn't think that word applied when there was a solid roof. They doubted the term 'lanai' would fit either, for a deck room with walls on all sides, even if three were glass and could be opened halfway. Enclosed patio was the best they came up with, but it didn't do the room justice. Beyond the glass, planter boxes to each side looked freshly planted. A mass of plumeria and other bushes Wend could no longer name crowded toward the back fence.

Aljon arrived, still dragging Viola by the hand. He took one look out from where Wend stood and called back to Shelly, "Did you plant a winter garden?"

"Yes, but there's still more to do if you're interested," Shelly responded, followed by, "Why don't you wash up and we can sort things out over salad and appetizers?"

When they sat down, with Viola choosing the seat next to Wend and across from Aljon, there was plenty of space at the large table. A bowl of whole fruit as well as a fancy fruit salad landed opposite Aljon's green salad. In between, a cutting board held dark bread, a hard white cheese, and a pot of spread with bits of green onions and purple cabbage.

"Eat up. Everything's vegan," Shelly invited as she joined them carrying a basket filled with warm twists of fresh bread. "I can either answer questions or try to tell you where things stand with Hans at the moment."

"You're on a first-name basis?" Viola asked.

"I've probably spent twenty hours on the phone or teleconferencing with that man in the past week. He insists that all four of us will be his partners in this venture and that he's not taking over *our* project."

"I didn't claim any part of it," Viola was quick to say. "I told him to contact you when he got back to land."

"He certainly did. Hans tracked me down about ten days ago. He said you and the crew of the *Nuovo Mar* saved his father's life and he wanted to pass the gift on to others as soon as reasonably possible."

"So you started calling him 'Hans' and moved into his condo in Hawai'i?"

Shelly leveled a glare at Viola that would have sent Wend running from the table. "No. Also, you gave up the right to flip innuendo or accusations my way. You're the one who said you could be attracted to men ten percent of the time. I almost turned this opportunity down because I didn't want you imagining I'd moved and switched jobs because of you. I certainly wouldn't do that for any man. I'm doing this for a project I believed in before we even met."

Viola dabbed spread onto one of the warm rolls. "Someone forwarded me a news article about Mehta converting a factory he already owned to make ten thousand—Is he calling them miniature hydrogen generators?"

"He called them that in the one press conference he held after the rescue." Shelly served herself salad and said to Aljon, "This looks wonderful."

She continued to the rest of them, "Anyway, the contract his legal team drew up promises us a final say on naming and advertising, as private independent contractors. They strongly advised we file as a non-profit or make arrangements for the Green Energy Alliance to sponsor us under its umbrella. Hans wants to give us this condo and grant money for the next two years to figure out an efficient and fair distribution and marketing system. His marketing people sent suggestions, including a 'buy one, give one' campaign I favor."

"We met this guy two weeks ago, and he's already moved you out here and decided the four of us should run a nonprofit?" Viola waved the remains of her roll through the air.

Shelly waved back with her fork. "You are intentionally unreachable on your boat and then refuse all my messages when you land. You're hardly in a position to complain because other people communicate."

Aljon shot Wend a look they couldn't interpret. Thinking it might be a request to change the subject they said, "I like your salad with all the sprouts." To Shelly they said, "Your rolls and spread are delicious."

One corner of Shelly's mouth tipped up more than the other, and Wend wondered at the significance of the expression or if that was how her face worked. "Thank you. I based the spread on a family recipe. I'm not sure how you know Viola and Aljon, but I'm happy to have you join us for Feast Day. And unless you want to sign over your rights to someone else, it looks like we may be working together."

Wend tried not to choke on their salad. Still reeling from the chance to reunite with Mathew on Saturday, Wend wasn't ready for Viola's ex to offer them a business partnership. "I'm not really part of this, just some- one they let tag along from the Marquesas to here. I do think your system for filling hydrogen fuel cells will help a lot of people, either with zero emissions boating or in coastal areas. I like the idea of desalinating water as a side benefit, and I'd love to learn more about it all."

"I noticed you had scuba equipment in your bundle, and some other device?" Shelly waved down Viola when she tried to interrupt. It was amazing to see Viola so easily quieted.

"It's a sample bot," Wend said quickly. "I designed them for low-cost research and education."

When Wend didn't say any more, not sure of what was wanted, Shelly spoke. "I thought I was prepared for whoever showed up as the mysteri- ous third crew member. But you're saying you designed a bot and then hitched a ride from the Marquesas with one of the stubbornest, least communicative skippers I know. Please, tell me that story."

"They like telling stories," Viola said, as she peeled a rambutan from the fruit bowl.

In truth, Wend preferred to prepare ahead of time and know their audience better before sharing stories, but in this case they'd been feeling adrift. Explaining the situation to Shelly might prevent further misassumptions.

Wend told about their microbiome research for the Marine Census Project with the Multi-State University Consortium that included Pacific Tech and the University of Hawai'i. They explained about discovering Viola's photographs alongside one of their recent publications and then hearing from other sailors that the *Nuovo Mar* planned to sail to Hawai'i. Perhaps they downplayed the effort and money required to catch a ride from Nuku Hiva to Fatu Hiva in time to swim aboard the boat.

By that point in the story, Shelly laughed so loud Wend couldn't continue. There were tears at the corners of her eyes as she gasped out, "You swam aboard in full scuba gear and Aljon was holding a knife and tried questioning you in French first?"

"We were in French Polynesia," Aljon protested. "I should have tried German next. Most of the extreme scuba types I've met were French or German."

When Shelly only laughed harder, Aljon volunteered, "My finest moment was the first time Wend braved the galley to ask me for a favor. I insinuated they wanted me out of the way so they could seduce Viola, and they looked at me like I'd sprouted tentacles. It turned out they wanted some of the hot chocolate they'd brought on board to share with everyone, but we had a good talk about boundaries and individual differences later."

This was a side of Aljon that Wend had never seen before. He was making fun of himself to make Shelly laugh, or maybe to communicate that Wend had no romantic connection to Viola. Wend wondered how different Aljon might be around his family, or how different anyone might be when not crewing on a small boat.

Shelly leaned against Aljon's shoulder as she announced, "Okay, you're an extreme scuba person with academic connections. That might be more useful than I expected."

When Wend opened their mouth to protest, Aljon shook his head and said, "This business makes less sense for me, but let's enjoy this first course of our meal. Then all three of you can help me understand the contract proposals and marketing plans."

After a long silence with everyone eating, Wend said, "I notice you call this Feast Day. When I was last in the US I knew people who observed it as a National Day of Mourning or Takesgiving. I can't remember when I first learned the Thanksgiving story was fiction, only how powerful that fiction seemed to me. Anyway, since you've invited me into your home and are feeding me, I wanted to ask what Feast Day means to you."

Rubbing a hand behind her neck, Shelly set down her fork and said, "I used to like the name Thanksgiving, even when I hated the history it represented. I worked with food sovereignty initiatives after the great pandemic. There were times before that when I wasn't sure where my next meal was coming from or if I'd have enough to eat. Being thankful for food came naturally. I looked forward to Thanksgiving most years, because some person or organization would always feed me a good meal on that day. Long ago, my father, a Russian immigrant, called Thanksgiving and two different days around New Year's feast days. When I met an Ohlone woman and some others who used Feast Day to refer to the November holiday, I began using that."

Again, Wend thought about Mathew's invitation for Friendsgiving and wondered if people's chosen holidays and ways of celebrating could represent another form of storytelling.

When Shelly looked to Wend for a response, all they could think to say was, "Thank you, and happy Feast Day."

Reading legal documents after bread, cheese, and salad probably worked better than reading them before.

Wend made it through to the end on a laptop Shelly lent them before saying, "I don't think I'm prepared or useful for any of this."

Shelly had been fussing back and forth between the sitting area and the kitchen as they all read. Now she perched on the sofa beside Aljon who was still reading and said, "You read fast. Didn't you say before that my device would be useful for zero emissions boating and scuba?"

"Yes." Wend nodded.

"Have you worked anyplace or on any project where it might have been useful?"

As Shelly leaned forward, Wend sank back into the cozy armchair they'd chosen and set the laptop on a side table. "Sure, half the places I've been in the last decade and lots more that use my sample bots."

"Great, you could help us communicate with those groups." Shelly tried to make eye contact.

Wend looked out the window. "I'd do that anyway. It's a good invention. I'm glad it's finally being made."

"They write part of a marine biology blog, too," Viola offered.

"See, you have all sorts of useful knowledge and connections. This won't interfere with the academic job you came for, but you'll have housing. The grant money may not be much. It's not meant to be a competitive salary for any of us."

Wend and Aljon both snorted at that. Wend had no problem making eye contact with him in the moment. He took over the conversation. "And what useful knowledge and connections will I contribute? You want me to call my old employers with the superyachts?"

"Half the people I've worked with in the non-profit sector start with fewer qualifications than yours. Besides, I've seen how hard you work and how easily you pick up languages. If we need to connect with local relief organizations, I'm betting most of them will find you more relatable than the rest of us."

"I'd rather be sailing." Aljon looked up at Shelly as if sharing an old joke.

"Stay here a few months and see if there's any part you like. I started the winter garden first thing because I wasn't sure you'd stay long enough to see things grow otherwise." Aljon looked gutted at that, and Shelly pulled him into a side hug. "No pressure. I understand you might want to live on a boat as much as I don't."

"There you go," Viola said, "Working up some fantasy in your head and trying to fit us all into it."

"You're the one who rescued some rich guy and told him to call me."

Viola raised both hands and countered loudly. "You talked him into setting up jobs and a house in Hilo."

"Listen to yourself." Shelly tried to jump up, but Aljon clung to the arm she'd wrapped around him. "You told Hans where you were headed. In our first call he told me about this condo he barely used. I wish I'd recorded that first conversation. You would realize how much of this was sprung on me when I didn't know what was true."

"Are you sure this is real? I'm not a lawyer but—"

Shelly had no problem interrupting Viola and talking right over her. "I had one of the attorneys with the Green Energy Alliance look it over. They don't claim any rights in this, since it was patented in my name and they're mostly an incubator, but they said the paperwork looked legitimate and the terms more than generous."

"I'd want to seek an outside opinion."

"I assumed." Shelly tightened the hand still on Aljon's shoulder, and he squeezed back.

Viola shook her head and stared at her ex. "Do you want me involved in this? You think we could share a house any better than we shared a boat?"

"I have no idea. Hans didn't realize we'd ever been involved or had a falling-out. I didn't think it was my place to explain. He presented this condo as having room to invite people over for discussions or networking as well as four bedrooms if we count the lanai."

Wend's mind reeled from unexpected developments and human interactions. They latched onto the use of the word lanai for the room that verged on living outdoors and offered such a perfect spot to hang their hammock. They stared at the double doors with their many smaller panes of glass, but they figured Aljon would want it, too. He should be living here with his aunt and this person who seemed even closer to him.

Aljon called them out. "You want that room, don't you?"

"I can get a place on campus, probably Monday," Wend said.

"Correct me if I'm wrong, but the way I read this"—Aljon waved his phone with the contract displayed in smaller font than Wend could possibly read—"a quarter of this condo was given to you as surely as to any of us. You could at least stay a few months and try it out, like I'm going to."

Shelly wrapped him in a tight hug.

"Don't you want the lanai?" Wend asked.

"No way, I like sleeping where it's dark. The room upstairs with a view over the back garden and heavy blinds suits me fine." He stared at Wend as if their opinion mattered.

"Why?" they asked. "You barely know me."

"I want a chance to know you better."

Wend hesitated, speechless. That morning they'd worried about being cast off and forgotten by the weekend. Now they not only had amazing housing promised for up to two years, but Aljon actively wanted to know them better. Time and again, Wend had found that people who were friendly when stuck in close quarters didn't make an effort to keep in touch with someone like Wend once they had other options. Even if Aljon's interest only lasted a couple months, they wanted to know him better, too.

Perhaps seeing how overcome Wend was, Aljon tugged at Shelly and added, "Besides, I won't let myself be outnumbered by these two again if I can help it."

"I haven't said I'm staying," Viola complained.

"Yeah, tell me about it tomorrow morning." Aljon shook his head. "I noticed the room you chose has an adjoining door to Shelly's."

The comment prompted a quick change of subject from Viola, who asked about the garden and if anything already growing there had made it into the night's feast. Wend relaxed into the discussion of food, which led naturally to eating far too much taro stuffing, cranberry relish, squash casserole, sweet potato, and three kinds of pie. Cleanup went quickly with four people helping, before Shelly insisted they should all settle into their new rooms.

Wend strung up their hammock first thing. They set the wooden shutters at a forty-five-degree angle slanting upward, allowing them to see the night sky without feeling exposed. For a long while, they stood staring out at the stars and still-flowering plumeria, not sure what to do next.

Aljon showed up at their still-open double door and said, "Any chance you want company for a while?"

Wend blinked at him in confusion until they heard a suggestive squeal from upstairs. Despite Aljon's quip about Viola choosing the room that adjoined Shelly's, Wend hadn't expected them to make up so quickly—or so loudly. "Did you know I play the 'ukulele?"

"Seriously?" Aljon's grin widened as he followed Wend's gaze to the instrument displayed like a decoration in the main room.

"My mom learned in Hawai'i and kept one in the house throughout my childhood in California. I could teach you some very childish hula dances as well, if you're interested."

"That would be perfect." Aljon sounded more relaxed already.

There was a loud thump from above as Wend grabbed the 'ukulele from the living room shelf. They decided to make some noise.

The same pull with their arms that rocketed Wend through deeper water offshore now shot them up into curling waves, like a surfer passing through rather than riding the rolling water. They were board and body, with force but no resistance, and occupying no real space. Soon they pulled out and upward, flying over a park filled with large-leafed tropical plants, squat or tall, many surrounded by circles of stones. A patch of dark sand and a pond drew them downward before a stream led them under a concrete car bridge.

Further upstream, beside a second bridge, a light-colored pickup truck stood out stark and growling in the dark night. It stopped, reversed, and turned. Tires spit gravel in all directions.

Wend feared the truck would plummet over the cliff by the bridge, but the wheels stopped in the nick of time. Two darkly clad humans jumped out. They lowered the back hatch all the way down and yanked hard on a tarp. Plastic containers rattled louder than the truck engine or the stream below. A fall of plastic, like a waterfall but out of place, plummeted over the cliff, into the water.

Moments later, the tarp was folded back. The truck's tailgate latched up.

The vehicle sped away as Wend soared down, viewing the mess humans had left at the bottom of the cliff. The rubbish had landed in nearly still water, an inlet beside the bridge and the narrow gravel road.

On each side, the road bent sharply back toward the coast, while the main body of the stream snaked away and upward, toward a mountain that could only be another volcano, a taller one than Wend had visited before.

They couldn't intervene in this flexible and insubstantial flying form. Something in their mind whispered to remember and find where the truck had gone. They followed the gravel road, but it was too late. There wasn't a single car in sight, not even headlights.

Wend traced the coastal highway back the way they'd come, past a giant graveyard, with row on row of stones. Past planted fields and quiet night-time neighborhoods.

Wend poked their head and arms out from their sleep sack, like a barnacle extending its feeding arms. Warm sunlight shone through slanted wooden shutters from three directions. Only blue sky and wooden ceiling beams were visible. For a moment, Wend lay still, perfectly content.

Then the stillness reminded them they were no longer at sea. That compounded with their flying dream and all the drama and revelations of the day before to break through their sleepy complacency.

Climbing down from their hammock, Wend used the futon below like a stepstool and glanced down at themself. The freshly washed purple rash guard and board shorts they'd slept in were presentable enough. They opened the double doors to the main room.

A clang drew their eyes to the kitchen as Aljon pulled two cast-iron pans from the oven. He quickly poured thin white batter into both before shoving them back in the oven with more clanging.

"Are you trying to wake the others?" Wend glanced toward the ceiling beneath where Viola and Shelly presumably slept.

"I'm giving them time to prepare for breakfast. It should be ready in twenty-five minutes."

Feeling even weirder about Aljon cooking for everyone now that they'd left the boat, Wend asked, "Anything I can do to help?"

"If you'd like, you can set the table." He motioned with his chin toward a cupboard above the opposite counter.

Wend gamely sought out plates, glasses, utensils, and cloth napkins and set them at the center places on the large table they'd used the night before. Four people could have comfortably eaten at the kitchen island, but it only had two stools. Aljon sorted and dismantled fruit across it.

By the time Wend had the table set, Aljon had a pineapple sliced open the long way, hollowed out, and half filled with fruit salad. "I'll use the other half later, possibly for pineapple fried rice."

"Fancy," Wend said. "What's in the oven?"

"The breakfast that shall not be named." Aljon smiled as if he'd made a joke.

Wend smiled back and asked, "Does that mean the recipe is a secret and further questions are unwanted?"

"I modified a recipe from online, because I wasn't sure I remembered well enough." Aljon tilted his head toward where his phone lay on the counter. "They're basically large popovers baked in cast iron pans. I love the texture, but they're completely impractical to make on the *Nuovo Mar*. I originally learned the recipe in the midst of an argument over whether they should be called Dutch babies, German pancakes, or hootenannies. I jokingly called them 'the breakfast that shall not be named' and later discovered that was close to what hootenanny meant in Appalachian slang."

The explanation reminded Wend of how they'd once loved following semi-random trails of information online. It also reminded them of the laptop Shelly let them borrow the day before that was still sitting on a coffee table. "I need to look up a map."

Aljon jumped from that near non-sequitur to asking, "Did you have another flying dream?"

Wend gaped at his insight. A month ago, they'd been alone in knowing and doubted anyone would ever believe them. "Yeah, but this time I'm kind of hoping it was my subconscious mashing up a new location and thoughts of 'Alice's Restaurant.'" As Wend brought the laptop to the table, they said, "I'm looking north of here for a large graveyard followed by a black sand beach, a pond, and a bridge. Then the creek leading inland from the bridge should have a road that traces up one side, crosses a second bridge, and curves back down the other side. It's a gravel road, and there's an inlet on the near side of the second bridge where a pick-up truck may have dropped garbage down a steep slope into the water."

"What would this have to do with thinking about a restaurant?" Aljon asked, as he set his fruit salad on the table and started tidying his work area.

Viola's voice rang out from the top of the stairs. "Oh, that's a song, even older than me. My mom used to play it for Thanksgiving."

"You should have mentioned that yesterday," Shelly said as she made her way downstairs. "I haven't heard that in years." With a glance at Wend she added, "What are you looking up?"

Wend had found the area they'd dreamed about and zoomed in on a satellite image. "Have you been to Honoli'i Creek by Honoli'i Beach Park?"

"Nope, but I've heard of it as a surfing spot. You planning to do some sightseeing?" Shelly asked with a yawn.

"Not exactly." Wend hesitated, not quite ready to explain their flying dreams to another near-stranger, and relieved Shelly hadn't heard Aljon's earlier remark.

"Her birthday's within a day of mine, if that matters." Viola slid into the seat next to Wend and pulled over the laptop. "That beach is three miles from here. Is this time-sensitive, or can it wait until after breakfast?"

Giving up any pretense of normality, Wend said, "Probably illegal dumping, but what would I even tell the authorities? And how would it look for haoles like us to show up saying someone else did it?"

"Um, you might not want to use that word," Shelly said.

"What, haole?" Wend asked. "As a kid I heard it all the time, either referring to me or asking if I was haole or hapa haole. It didn't seem any worse than being asked if I was 'American Indian' when I moved to California. Although I guess that term fell by the wayside. Thanks for letting me know."

Shelly nodded and brought pitchers with juice and water to the table, then claimed her own seat. "Doreen told me to avoid local words until I knew which people are big umbrella thinkers, but it sounds like you might count as some sort of local."

Wend squirmed at the way Shelly studied them from across the table and took a while to recognize the feeling and the implied question. "I lived on Oʻahu the first four years of my life, but at least half my parentage is unknown and most of my heritage questionable. I can't make any claims."

"Huh, I guess it was you playing ʻukulele last night," Shelly muttered before Aljon served up his fluffy, buttery creations.

He'd brought lemon and powdered sugar to the table, but Wend was happy alternating bites with fruit. They closed their eyes and tried to focus on smooth textures and rich flavors, but couldn't escape their uncertainty. "What should I do about the trash?"

"Up to you," Viola said. "But we'll help you get out there and even call Doreen for advice if you want."

Looking around the table, Wend saw the others were fine with Viola offering for all of them, like following her directions as skipper. "Okay," Wend said. "Maybe we can play 'Alice's Restaurant' as we get ready and go. Aljon's never heard it."

Viola only raised an eyebrow, but Shelly said, "I'll bring it up on my phone."

15.

AS THEY ALL stood glaring down at the pile of trash, mostly plastic, in the water, Shelly said, "You want to call Doreen or should I?"

"Feel free," Viola answered. "She's probably still pissed at me."

Wend crept closer to the edge of the gravel road where the truck in their dream had backed to drop its tailgate and dump trash ten feet straight down into the creek. Despite wanting others to believe in their flying dreams, part of Wend struggled to accept this sequence of events. Even as a kid, they'd never wanted to be a detective or solve crimes. While they didn't feel guilty about spying on strangers committing an illegal act, Wend didn't feel qualified to deal with this either and worried about involving the others.

Aljon moved in beside them as the other two shifted away to check the view from the bridge and call Doreen. Looking down at the pile of garbage, he said simply, "People suck."

Surprisingly, his matter-of-fact declaration made Wend feel better.

The exclamations Wend overheard from the phone conversation suggested Doreen might not be pleased with any of them. But as soon as she hung up, Shelly said, "She'll be here in ten. She also asked the obvious question about how we came across this mess. I told her we were taking a walk up the creek from the beach."

They had in fact taken their carshare to the Honoliʻi Beach parking lot. If they were going to get the authorities involved, route records might be checked, and Shelly wasn't sure driverless carshares were allowed off paved roads anyway. They'd walked up the dirt and gravel road that paralleled the creek. Wend wondered if they could avoid explaining or lying and said, "I'd be happy to watch the surfers when we're done here."

That was when Viola, who had been snapping occasional photos since they arrived, said, "I'm going down for a closer look."

"Are you sure?" Shelly asked. "Maybe we should wait for Doreen."

Viola didn't respond as she made her way to the water. Either animals or humans had worn a diagonal cut through the moisture-seeking plants that grew thick around the inlet. Wend followed Viola's lead, needing to do more. They'd brought their sample bot with the idea that testing here and all the way downstream to the beach might be useful. Now that suited Shelly's cover story.

Aljon and Shelly stayed up by the road. Wend missed whatever was said when Doreen arrived. The first they heard was, "You want me to call in a report or bring a net to haul that up?"

"You have a net?" Wend asked in surprise, not sure those above could hear.

"I was joking." Doreen's head shook as she stepped into view, wearing another aloha shirt with birds, this time on a pink background. She peered down at Viola and Wend knee deep in the water. "I'll call it in. But don't expect a quick response."

Sure enough, it took over an hour for the island patrol to arrive. Wend collected water samples down to the beach and back. They didn't stay long to watch the surfers, feeling bad about dragging everyone out and making them wait around for this. At least the way the trash had fallen outside the main water flow stopped it from floating out to sea, meaning their delay from the night before and waiting now didn't hurt anything.

The others were down by the creek with Viola by the time Wend returned. They were taking turns looking at the trash through Viola's camera with a long lens attached.

"We're not making a story about finding this trash, are we?" Wend asked.

Viola handed them the camera and said, "It might fit into one we already have."

Wend looked at a close-up showing the ragged edges of a hole in a plastic bottle obscuring the last digit in the "best by" date. If it made an artistic statement like the dead fish on deck at sunrise, Wend missed the symbolism.

When Viola took the camera back, she pulled up a picture from an hour earlier showing the same bottle in the same location, but the hole next to the date was noticeably smaller. The last digit clearly showed as "5."

"It changed that much since we arrived." Viola stared at the photo as if trying to convince herself.

"Maybe we should call someone else, like a scientist from the university?" Wend shuddered. While the dumping made them angry, this rapid breakdown of plastics worried them more. They felt a little nauseous as their stomach clenched and their brain raced.

"Could start a cover-up if someone released engineered bacteria from a lab there." Viola's suspicious tone implied criminal activity well beyond illegal dumping.

"Weren't you suggesting this matched what we found by the giant manta ray?" When Viola only nodded, Wend continued, "If it's spread that far, I don't think anyone could cover it up. More likely, someone at the university knows more than we do."

"It could provide background for your story," Viola said.

Wend inhaled sharply, about to explain in excruciating detail how that wasn't the point, but caught the corners of Viola's lips turning up as she tried not to smile. The internal panic Wend had barely recognized dissipated. "I don't know if Miko will even answer the phone today." Wend looked to Doreen and said, "I don't suppose you have local contacts for marine science?"

"I regret answering my own phone already." Doreen's tone was flat. If she was joking, Wend couldn't tell.

Aljon handed Wend his phone with the contact page for Miko already displayed, but the call went to university voicemail.

When the island patrol arrived, Doreen greeted them with, "Hey, Jessica, Bruce." They talked about family, kids, and at least once mentioned high school before Doreen introduced the rest of them. Viola explained what they'd found, even though the dumped plastic sat in a wet heap right beside them.

Bruce looked to Doreen rather than any of the rest of them as he said, "We can write it up as littering, but really, we have no way." He turned his hands out as if to say it was pointless.

"Someone will clean it up, right? And watch to see if it happens again?" Viola asked.

"Sure, sure," Jessica said as she started filling out a form with their information.

"Could I collect samples for the lab?" Wend asked. Viola's explanation had included Wend collecting water samples, implying that was how they found the dumped plastic. Now Wend added, "There's some evidence of plastic-eating bacteria."

Jessica took a step back, and Bruce frowned. "Maybe we should contact the Maunakea Rangers for advice." When Jessica looked at him sideways, he puffed up his chest and said, "Stream came down from Maunakea. They deal with this environmental stuff."

"You could send a copy of the report to the UH Hilo Marine Science Department as well, since the stream feeds into the ocean," Wend said.

Bruce heaved a put-upon sigh and side-eyed Doreen. "Fine, you have contact info?"

Aljon shared contact information for Miko and Dr. Kahale from his phone, since that was all any of them had.

Wend gestured downward. "Is it okay for me to collect a sample of the plastic, or would that be interfering with a crime scene?"

When no one answered, Wend looked up to see Jessica and Bruce exchanging pointed glances with Doreen. Finally, Doreen said, "I have a glass casserole dish in my car. Will that do?"

Pleased Doreen had a suitable container, Wend eagerly collected a sample, ignoring any not too quiet comments from the island patrol about garbage collectors and how not to spend a holiday weekend.

Two hours later, they were back in the condo and Shelly joked that she'd serve up "another Feast Day dinner that couldn't be beat."

Aljon went to wash up at the kitchen sink. Wend left their sample bot, shoes, and the glass container with their plastic sample by the door. Still processing the events of the morning and not sure what to do with themself, they followed Aljon into the kitchen to ask if they could help with anything.

Plopping down on one sofa in the great room, Viola announced loudly, "I'd planned to spend today catching up on business and choosing the best publications to approach with new photos."

"Sorry," Wend said, then bit their tongue wondering if Aljon or Viola would call them out for apologizing. When no one did, they continued, "It's barely past noon. You still have plenty of time."

"Before I do, you and I need to talk about joint submission strategies." Viola looked pointedly at Wend. "But first, I need to know if this is part of something bigger. Are we likely to stumble across new context for my sea nettle or tuna pictures?"

"I doubt it," Wend said, going to wash up in the first-floor bathroom after being shooed away from the kitchen. They suddenly felt dirty although, having showered and washed clothes the night before, they were cleaner than they'd been for most of their time at sea.

When they came back out, they started setting the table before Viola asked, "Why did you decide to work in Hilo this winter?"

"The Marquesas project failed to acquire funding past the end of the year. Everyone involved applied for other jobs, and the Marine Census Project had openings on Hawai'i, O'ahu, and Moloka'i."

"And you chose this one because?"

Wend didn't look at Viola as they said, "I wanted to meet you and travel with zero emissions if possible. I can switch between projects and islands at a later point, if I want to."

"You didn't dream about that creek or anything here?" Viola said it casually, but Aljon froze in the kitchen. Shelly pretended not to notice, but they both kept unusually quiet while heating up leftovers.

"Only last night." Wend took a seat at the table and pulled their knees to their chest.

"Why did you seek me out?" Before Wend could repeat what they'd already explained, Viola said, "Beyond seeing my photos with your article and having similar birthdates."

Shelly watched them openly now.

Wend tensed under the scrutiny. "It felt right. I told you that after the pandemic I wanted to be myself, and that included following my interests and instincts within reason."

Suddenly Aljon stood at their side. He carried a bowl with salad and a platter with breads and spreads, but he leaned right into their personal space and whispered, "Did it change then or when you almost drowned?"

Wend stopped breathing. Stopped moving. They weren't reliving their near-drowning. Quite the opposite. Their face flushed hot.

The restlessness of being alive and working to unlock a mystery heated their blood like a hydrothermal vent. The night after their near-drowning, Wend had dreamed they were a *Riftia* tube worm thriving by a deep sea vent. The pulse of water across spongy tissue and a symbiotic connection to bacteria colonizing their trophosome felt as welcoming in Wend's memory as any moment in their real life. They'd awoken with renewed energy to learn and educate others about the ocean.

Wend hadn't noticed amidst all their other life changes, but both their flying and ocean dreams intensified after almost drowning. They'd sought personal connections with friends and through teaching more than ever before. Now they followed their instincts more readily than they had since early childhood. They'd chronicled the changes as self-acceptance and focusing less on the expectations of others, but they hadn't associated the full scope of those changes with their tumble in the ocean until Aljon pointed it out. He'd brought forward a puzzle piece Wend had overlooked for too long.

The next thing they knew, Aljon was crouched in front of them holding their hands and saying, "Sorry, sorry, sorry."

Wend sucked in a deep breath.

Aljon said, "Good, breathe slow and deep."

He bit his lip, and Wend knew he was biting back any further apology as Wend had minutes before when speaking to Viola. The next deep breath brought both smell and taste, taro stuffing and squash casserole. Wend's mouth watered, and they didn't need to focus on other senses to notice Viola and Shelly tentatively pulling up seats at the table filled with leftovers from the day before.

Wend squeezed Aljon's warm, rough hand and said, "Thank you. I'm okay now. I needed to realize that."

"I could have given you more warning or said it better. Or ... not mentioned it in front of the others." Aljon's eyelashes were wet as their eyes met.

"No." Wend breathed deeply again before they said, "I'm reacting as much to all that happened this morning as to what you made me realize. Seriously, I'm glad you listened and remembered and helped me put those pieces together. Now don't let me keep you from eating." They squeezed his hand again and let go.

He stood and walked around the table to what had become his spot. It amazed Wend how quickly they'd all settled into their own places at the table and in each other's lives. Then Wend looked at Shelly, the only one who hadn't heard any of their stories. "I should probably explain."

"You don't owe anyone explanations or your stories," Shelly said stiffly.

If Wend hadn't guessed before, they'd suspect from that reaction that Shelly had trauma and therapy in her past.

Wend consciously relaxed their posture, still a bit shaken, but wanting to reassure Shelly. "Oh, you can ask either of these two, I constantly offer to share my stories. Although if Viola wants to tell you about the dreams and Aljon wants to explain what he realized, I wouldn't mind simply eating and listening for the first bit."

So each of the others shared in Wend's storytelling. Viola disclosed with striking visual details her own hypotheses and experiments involving flying dreams and sea life. Aljon gently explained how Wend had gone back to grad school after almost drowning, and why drowning might have been the real turning point in how they made decisions.

It warmed Wend deep inside to feel so known by two people they'd met less than a month before, to have them understand enough to help Wend understand more. Viola no longer resisted storytelling or discussing phenomena they couldn't fully explain. Aljon accepted it all and seemed as interested in Wend's life and perspective as in any of the bizarre events he'd witnessed. Now they welcomed Wend at their table and helped them explain the unexplainable to Shelly.

Content to listen, Wend took small bites of squash and sweet potato, focusing on the myriad tastes and smells that no one would ask them to translate into words. Hearing their stories retold helped Wend understand which parts mattered most to them or looked different from an outside perspective.

When Aljon finished his part, Viola asked Wend, "How many of your major decisions since almost drowning were ocean- or research-related?"

"Most of them?" Wend tried to remember. "I'd already moved back to the coast. My earlier two degrees came from Pacific Tech as well. I told you that I swam before I could walk and most of what I'd call my career as opposed to making money to survive involved either research or teaching. That didn't change, I just became more myself."

It surprised Wend when Shelly asked, "Do you ever feel a pull in your gut like a magnet?"

"Only in my dreams."

"What about when you're falling asleep?" Shelly's expression intensified, but for once Wend had no trouble meeting her eyes. "Does something nag at you sometimes, like you're headed the wrong way and need to change course?"

Shelly's description launched a series of emotional memories, layering atop Wend's previous realization in their mind. "I may have felt that before setting out to meet Viola. And before a couple jobs that involved travel, including to the Marquesas."

"That's why I left the *Nuovo Mar*," Shelly said. "I needed to work with more people, to spend time in Seattle helping negotiate marine protected areas, before ending up here."

"You left me, too," Viola said with a huff.

"You chose the boat over me." It sounded like an old argument, the way each of them recited their parts. Shelly continued, "I couldn't escape the feeling that I was going the wrong way. I've learned to trust that feeling ever since I almost died"—she looked at Wend—"as a teenager."

The juxtaposition of Shelly and Viola's relationship issues with whatever drew Wend to the *Nuovo Mar* and dragged Shelly away left Wend lightheaded. They'd barely accepted Aljon's observation or that nearly drowning amplified Wend's dreams and instincts beyond their growing self-acceptance. Now Shelly wanted to contribute her own near-death experience, another possible piece in an ever-growing puzzle.

"That was a little different," Viola said, grasping Shelly's hand.

"I tried to drown myself after getting pregnant from being raped," Shelly said.

Wend thought they should feel panic at this admission of Shelly's trauma, as they did at their own, but they didn't know Shelly that well yet. Wend could barely set aside their own feelings in the moment. "I hate that you went through that, but I'm glad you're here now."

"Thanks, me too." Shelly continued, "I convinced myself I'd learned to listen to my instincts, but sometimes it feels like an outside force is nudging me in certain directions."

Wend hadn't experienced whatever drew her to Viola and led to swimming aboard the *Nuovo Mar* as an outside influence. While trying to solve a puzzle, clues had pointed to Viola as a missing piece. Wend's own curiosity provided enough motivation—that and the desire for connection they'd previously experienced with Mathew and Gabi. Whatever the driving force might be, it felt completely internal, part of Wend for as long as they could remember. After all, they'd searched for Mathew long before their near-drowning, and finding him on Hawai'i now came down to their puzzle-solving mind picking up clues in his poster.

Shelly continued before Wend could respond. "I haven't experienced flying dreams like yours or Viola's, but I have no problem believing they're real."

"Whatever we each believe," Viola said, "Wend led me to two different places with something breaking down plastic in ways I didn't think possible. It may be the story of the year, but I don't think we can move on it until Monday. Do we go ahead with the story about Pacific bluefin tuna showing up in unusual places or wait to see if you're guiding us someplace new tomorrow?"

"I don't think flying dreams usually connect that way, and to be honest, I don't feel guided by an outside force. I wouldn't even have noticed the plastic being eaten away without you and your photos." Unfortunately, that could explain an outside force pulling them toward Viola, if Wend cared to admit such possibilities. They felt tired just thinking about it. "Anyway, I have a class to teach tomorrow and Friendsgiving to attend."

"With Mathew or Matthaios or whatever his name is," Viola said. "He forwarded me his address and included me and whoever else you want to bring in the invitation." Viola pulled up the message on her phone to show Wend. Glancing at Shelly, she added, "A childhood friend of Wend's invited us for a meal tomorrow."

"I'd be happy to have any or all of you along." They suddenly realized it was more than just happy. As desperately as they wanted to see Mathew again, Wend had already had to deal with multiple new people and could only hope they'd wake up with enough energy: physical, social, and mental. It would be easier to brave a group gathering—whatever Friendsgiving entailed—with someone familiar by their side. And not sixty-years-ago familiar.

"I plan to spend tomorrow back on the boat," Aljon said, "but I could make a salad or dessert for you to bring if you want."

Wend grimaced. "I hadn't thought about that."

Aljon rolled his eyes and said, "How about a fruit tart? I'll make one for us tonight and a larger one you can bring tomorrow."

"Thank you." Wend offered him a grateful smile, and he returned a wink.

"Do you want us along?" Viola asked. "He was the basis of your birthday theory, wasn't he?"

"Yes." Wend nodded and said, "Mathew and Gabi. If you're interested, I'd rather not go alone."

Shelly shrugged, and Viola said, "Sure."

Viola and Wend spent the rest of the afternoon writing up notes on possible publications. Wend logged in to and painstakingly triaged their personal email on the laptop Shelly had lent them, and prepared envelopes for their paper letters to Lisa and Ashok. Shelly led them all through mocking up a press release and sorting other paperwork for Hans Mehta, which they completed and sent. Aljon helped with the latter while also making lentils with pasta marinara for dinner, as well as the promised tarts.

By the end of the day, Wend collapsed into their hammock, exhausted. Nevertheless, a satisfying rush soothed their skin and beneath, as if they'd started building something important with these people in this new place.

Saturday morning, Wend woke mostly ready to teach. Aljon walked to the edge of Hilo Harbor with them. Miko waited at Reed's Bay Park as promised.

"You must be Dr. Taylor. I'm Dr. Miko Yamamoto, postdoc with the Marine Science Department at UH Hilo, pronouns they/them in English. I'm pleased to meet you." They held out a hand that Wend managed to shake before Miko started running through their plans and everything they'd brought. In person, their speech poured out as fast and high-pitched as on the phone. While Miko wasn't a large person, they loomed larger than their voice suggested and filled a huge volume of space around them. Their haircut was asymmetrical and their clothing included layers of interesting textures from silky to netting, but all in neutral tones.

Reed's Bay Park encompassed a relatively calm stretch of beach and an adjacent lawn beside a cluster of hotels. At nine in the morning, most of the tourists on the beach were families with small children, whose parents glanced nervously at the cloud-filled sky, which promised rain at any moment. No one local seemed concerned about rain. The air and water remained as warm as in the Marquesas, and Wend wore their usual shorts and shirt that doubled as surf wear. They'd chosen the least tattered set, which happened to be aqua and gray. With clean clothes and two showers in two days, they felt professional enough to be teaching on a beach.

Miko set their supplies up beneath a huge banyan tree, beside hundreds of aerial roots that reached down to become accessory trunks. It reminded Wend of a bloom of jellies, if their tentacles reached the seafloor, but they knew the term bloom came from plants and many tourists mistook the single banyan for a grove of tightly nested trees.

On a sturdy folding table, Wend displayed their sample bot ready for servicing. Miko unloaded three extras for students to practice with and plenty of new sample containers. "I also brought you a department-issued cellphone," Miko said as they tried to hand Wend a relatively small device in a supposedly drop-proof case.

"I don't have a great history with phones," Wend said, not taking it.

"Don't worry, we're marine scientists. We lose at least one a month to the ocean or other damage. Plenty of staff check out school phones rather than risk their own. That's why it's two years old. We get discounts and accident coverage. Obviously, it's not private, but texts and calling are unlimited. No one cares about non-work use as long as nothing violates school conduct codes. Data is regulated, so keep web searches and media vaguely work-related. We need a way to contact you when you're not on campus or co-teaching. You follow?"

"I'm going to turn it off when I'm not working," Wend said.

Miko sighed and pushed the phone into their hands. "Try to check at least a couple times a day. I reached out to people on that plastic-eating bacteria you messaged about. I can't have them contacting you through your friend's phone if anyone bites. I'm doing you a favor, even if it is a crappy cellphone."

"Okay, thanks," Wend said. When Miko didn't move or look away, Wend added, "You have been a great help."

At that, Miko smiled and half turned away to grab a tablet. "That's what I'm here for. Let's get this show on the road!"

Miko called roll.

Fourteen students were present, four either absent or late, and one late add. Miko flipped to a different screen on the tablet and called out, "Avery Mlakar."

Wend froze. A hand rose toward the back of the cluster of students, and Wend looked. Close to the banyan roots stood a tall young person in sky-blue leggings and a smooth long-sleeved tunic in spiraling sea tones. Chunky headphones around their neck barely touched the short black curls that framed a familiar face above. Even if that face had grown more angular and lost all its baby fat—even if Wend was terrible at recognizing faces—the deep-set brown eyes and almost flat nose between high cheek bones were more familiar than Wend's own face.

Avery's raised hand soon lowered but they gave a small wave directed at Wend, not Miko. In that moment, Wend knew the child who'd mattered more to them than any other had somehow found them and come to this class on purpose. A swallowed sob sliced through them, almost broke them. Whatever sense of self Wend had managed to assemble splintered into misty pieces while trying to reach across time and space to Avery.

Their body surged as if to take flight in a dream, to swoop out and touch. Wend vibrated as a thousand memories of Avery—watching ants on a windowsill, patting wet sand to form a moat, sharing a story in a patch of sunlight—displaced the here and now.

Whatever Miko said by way of introduction was completely lost on Wend. Only when Miko stepped up to the table and tapped the sample bot laid out there did Wend snap back into teaching mode. Enough of their mind coalesced to say the words they'd used many times before in such workshops.

"Having signed up for this class, you probably know something about the microbiome, sampling bots, or research protocols. But I'm going to start with an explanation I'd give a kid in an aquarium, because you might encounter questions from anyone while you're out in the field. Listen. It never hurts to learn about something you think you know from a different perspective."

A couple of eager nods drew Wend's eye, although they didn't make eye contact. They avoided even a glance at anyone toward the back of the class, standing tall among the banyan roots. Wend never did well with remembering individuals in a large group, but that mattered more in regular teaching situations than a one-time workshop like this.

"The microbiome most people care about is their own. We're all full of bacteria, fungi, protozoa, and viruses that include hundreds of times as much genetic information as humans themselves do. Some parts can harm us, but overall, we can't live without our personal biome. If it's thrown off by illness or medications, our friends and doctors may recommend anything from yogurt to prescription supplements as a remedy."

A quick scan below face level showed a quarter of the class already checking their phones. Wend also noted a trend toward brightly colored surf shoes.

"The ocean microbiome is the largest and most dilute biological system on Earth. A single liter of seawater contains millions of marine microbes, but they are so small they fill less than one percent of that volume. The sample bot filters out excess water to concentrate the microorganisms for more compact samples. Later processing in the lab splits each sample into two, keeping one for reference and amplifying whatever exists in the other. Dr. Miko Yamamoto will tell you more about that process and where to hand in samples for processing locally."

Wend nodded to Miko, who smiled encouragingly at the class. They met several students' eyes. One even slid their phone into a back pocket and smiled brightly as Miko gave hours for the lab on campus and mentioned they worked there part time. Throughout it all, Wend avoided looking at Avery, not sure they could handle that while teaching.

When Wend's turn came again, they said, "Remember that over two-thirds of the planet is covered by ocean. Each microbe you collect is working with millions of others in the nearest liter of water as well as the microbial community here in Reed's Bay and out into Hilo Harbor. This microbiome varies predictably with season, depth, weather, and climate changes. The microbes pass through the gills or guts of larger species and change or disappear as those species go extinct.

"Anywhere from fifty to eighty percent of life on Earth may live in the oceans. It's estimated ninety percent of ocean species haven't yet been identified. But we've lost half the diversity in our oceans in my lifetime. I know I seem pretty old to some of you, but I'm not that old." Wend stretched out the last two words trying for humor, which they knew helped in teaching. Younger students often found them hilarious. This group remained unimpressed. "In the ocean the primary producers are microbial. Discoveries involving the ocean microbiome allow us to unravel microbial alliances based on the exchange of vitamins, hormones, antibiotics, and nitrogen. But there are still material exchanges and signaling networks we can't begin to understand.

"If we study multiple samples over time, collected by multiple humans"—Wend gestured to the class—"we can move beyond simple remedies that only address the local ecosystem at best, to prepare multipart remedies."

"Wouldn't it be better not to break the system in the first place?" A student in loose black swim trunks and a tight white tank top advertising board wax asked.

"Yes." When Wend didn't continue immediately, the class laughed. They counted that as good teaching humor, intentional or not, and added, "I won't pretend we can fix all the damage humans have done or continue to do. We share our samples with other projects, and they're dealing with a worldwide system where ninety percent of sharks, tunas, cods, and other large fishes are already gone. Some of you must be working with coral reef projects that share our data. You'd know better than I do how much of the Hawai'ian reef ecosystem is dead or threatened. This part of the Pacific experienced some of the same bleaching events that killed over half the Great Barrier Reef in Australia. Models predict we'll lose all but the deeper mesophotic reefs by 2100, mostly due to a warming ocean rising over a meter while corals weakened by acidification can't grow that fast."

The group went eerily silent. Wend gave them a moment to settle with their own feelings and then said, "Yes, that's depressing. I suspect I'm preaching to the converted here, but we need one hundred percent green energy and zero emissions yesterday. You're here today to gain certification to use one of these babies, and yes, I've carried this sample bot tied to my body both walking and swimming for enough miles to think of it as my baby."

Miko eagerly supplied, "For any of you who don't know, Dr. Taylor designed and introduced these bots sixteen years ago."

There was a smattering of applause that Wend found amusing, not sure how many in the class thought they were humoring Wend and how many were clapping ironically. One older student, the only one even close to Wend's age, clapped exuberantly. Avery's fingers snapped inaudibly, a familiar gesture that warmed Wend beneath their skin. "Thank you, but it's really not the bots but what you do with them that matters. There are instructions online if anyone or any group wants to assemble a sample bot of their own. The sample containers are all sealed and self-contained. Let me open this up and show you how 600 of them fit inside a single sample bot." Wend demonstrated the click and twist needed to open the body of the bot. "It's no harder than opening a childproof cap on medicine. The sample panels pull out to reveal batches of 100. These all have red seals showing on top, meaning they're already full."

Wend led the class through their demonstration, urging them to come closer where they could see better, and then had them break into groups and practice servicing and replacing sample containers on their own. When the groups made their way down to the beach to take samples, Wend followed those farthest from Avery. Miko adjusted accordingly.

"Try to collect one sample before you enter the water if possible," Wend called out. "While there's an over-abundance of humans at this particularly location, it might help to rule out your own microbiome from other samples."

They tried not to think of Viola's theories about Wend attracting sea life. While they kept an eye out and made the few corrections needed to be able to certify each student on their end of the beach, they couldn't help noticing when Miko interacted with Avery.

Avery had literally rolled their leggings up to their knees but was staying in very shallow water. They were passed the sample bot last, as most of their group had gone in deeper, but they didn't seem to mind handling the wet bot. Miko remained mindful of personal space with all the students and kept to the other side of the bot from Avery. Something Miko said made Avery laugh. Their nose wrinkled the way Wend remembered, and in that moment, Wend desperately wanted to know what was said. They settled for watching from afar.

At the end of the workshop, Wend answered another round of questions, a couple of them quite detailed regarding the construction of the bots. Miko assured everyone their certifications would be online by noon Monday, and asked them all to help load the bots, samples, and folding table back into the school SUV.

Most of the class left directly afterward. When Avery lurked to one side, Miko asked them, "Do you need a ride back to campus?"

"Oh, no thanks." Avery rolled their head sideways and didn't meet Miko's eyes. "I'm at UH Mānoa, actually. I was hoping to talk with Dr. Taylor while I'm here."

Miko pointedly looked at Wend until they nodded. "That's fine. I'm happy to talk with you."

As Miko left, Wend sat down on the nearest bench to see how Avery wanted to proceed.

It took half a minute, but Avery sat at the other end of the bench looking at their feet. "So, I guess you remember me?"

That nearly broke Wend wide open. "Of course. I just couldn't— Not communicating with you was one of the hardest things ever asked of me."

"I realized, eventually, that Mom told her exes they had to make a clean break. She calls it detaching with love."

"I barely think of myself as her ex," Wend said. "I was your tutor and whatever else much more than I was ever anything to Mira."

Avery closed their eyes and sniffled.

Wend longed for the time when they were one of the people who could comfort Avery. The urge to reach out was practically hardwired into Wend despite eighteen intervening years. "I'm sorry. It had to be your choice to contact me. I thought you might hate me now."

"I didn't know your last name. Or your first. If you have anything online under 'Wend' I never found it. The announcement for this . . . had your photo."

The urge to apologize burned through Wend but a terror of saying the wrong thing froze the words in place. They weren't panicked or unable to breathe. Instead, they shook with adrenaline as their mind raced. For all they talked about trying to be whoever they actually were, a lifetime's worth of wanting to do things right and be accepted by others bore down on them in that moment. Then Avery sniffled again, and Wend realized that however grown up the person beside them appeared, they were still Avery.

"If you can tell me what would help, I'll do it." Wend waited and then said, "As a kid, you may have thought I knew more than I did, but I never had much confidence with people, and I don't now. Still, you're as close to a kid of my own as I'll ever come. I know you didn't have a lot of choices before, but I'll try to be whatever you want from me going forward."

Every muscle in Avery's body tightened as they said, "I want to know you again. You just need to be you."

The quiet words practically tore Wend's insides out. They shuddered under the strain of being asked something impossible and wanting to give it. "Okay." Wend had to swallow to continue, "How soon do you need to get back to Oʻahu?"

"I have class on Monday, but I should call my housemate if I'm not coming home tonight."

Wend closed their eyes, already overwhelmed by their plans for the day and ready to admit it. "I have to go to a Friendsgiving thing tonight that I really can't miss. I don't know how many people will be there, and it might be a sensory nightmare. You could come if you want or stay at my place. I'm sharing a condo with three other people, but I have my own room with a spare futon. It's sort of under my hammock, if you don't mind that."

"Can I decide later?" Avery asked, hands tucked under their knees and gaze fixed on the ground.

"Definitely. Do you want to come home with me for lunch? Or we could try to find someplace near here."

"I'd like to see where you live." Avery stood up and went to retrieve a messenger bag and duffel from where they'd stood, partially obscured by banyan roots.

Wend worried about Avery leaving their stuff only half hidden and how willing they were to go home with Wend after eighteen years of separation. But Wend had said they'd do whatever would help, and Avery was an adult now.

Neither of them spoke while they walked. Avery pulled their headphones on when they passed through a noisy area around one hotel and some shops. Wend tried to maintain a clear space around Avery, despite the child growing up to be as big as Wend. Walking together felt the same.

By the time they reached the condo, Wend had calmed considerably. Avery removed their headphones and settled into an easier posture.

When Wend found Viola and Shelly in the sitting area as they ushered Avery in, it felt almost natural to say, "Viola, Shelly, this is Avery. I knew them a long time ago in California and invited them for lunch and to maybe stay the night."

"Avery?" Viola asked immediately. "As in the kid from the aquarium?"

Avery looked up and smiled at that but only said, "Hi."

16.

LUNCH STARTED OUT stressful, but after ascertaining that Avery was a graduate student in Marine Biology at UH Mānoa, Viola and Shelly realized Avery didn't appreciate questions or being the center of attention. As they passed around leftovers from Feast Day and last night's marinara, Shelly asked Wend about the class that morning and then talked more generally about things to do around Hilo. When they mentioned helicopter flights over active volcanoes, Wend thought they'd had a much better experience flying there silently in their dream and wished they could show Avery that way. But they didn't say anything.

When Avery headed toward Wend's room after lunch, Wend followed and was amused to see Avery take charge by closing the wooden blinds to block the view from the main room.

"Whatever makes you comfortable," Wend said.

Avery opened the stuffed duffel they'd brought and pulled out the leopard kigurumi they'd given Wend over half their lifetime ago. Avery set it carefully on Wend's lap without otherwise touching.

Then Avery pulled out a black and white kigurumi. At first, Wend expected it to be an adult version of young Avery's cat kigurumi. But it had a yellow beak and turned out to be a penguin.

When Avery stared mutely for most of a minute, Wend asked, "Did you want to do this now, with me?"

Avery nodded vigorously and started to pull the furry outfit over their leggings. When it was halfway up, they pulled off the tunic they'd been wearing, briefly revealing a tank top underneath, before pushing into the arms and hood of their penguin. As Avery fastened up buttons, Wend got with the program and pulled the familiar leopard fur over what they were already wearing.

After that, Avery didn't crawl or meow. They didn't waddle or make whatever noises a penguin might either. Instead, they shuffled sideways on the futon until they were just barely leaning against Wend.

For Wend, the kigurumi had never been about acting like a real cat. The furry costumes conveyed permission to touch and to not speak. They realized Avery understood perfectly. That was exactly what they were offering.

Wend relaxed, leaning into Avery as well. Soon Avery was petting their knee, and Wend reveled in how soft the kigurumi still felt and how comforting a simple touch through costume fur could be. They reached up to rub the back of Avery's neck the way they'd liked as a child, and Avery practically melted against them.

From there it came naturally. They ended up huddled together on the futon for most of the afternoon.

In the end it was Avery who pulled away and stripped off their kigurumi. After they pulled their blue tunic back over their head they said, "I need to use the bathroom. Then we should talk, when you feel like it."

Wend hesitated to take off the leopard outfit once Avery left the room. The fur and cuddling reminded Wend of how little touch they'd enjoyed in their life recently and of a whole other level of comfort they'd mostly forgotten. It was hard to give that up in the moment.

Even harder was imagining that Avery might take the kigurumi away. This might be a one-time thing, and Avery might not even visit again.

Despite that, Wend peeled off their kigurumi.

When Avery settled again, there were a few inches of space between them on the futon, not as much as before the kigurumi, but more than enough to create a separation.

"Let me know when you're ready to talk," Avery said.

"You went into marine biology." The statement sprang from Wend without forethought.

Avery smiled. "That can't surprise you."

"But you didn't seem very comfortable by the water today."

"I wasn't dressed for it. I like it fine with my scuba gear or a full body swimsuit I have that makes most people think I'm either Muslim or extremely sun-sensitive." Only when Avery's shoulders tensed and they looked to the far corner of the room did Wend realize how relaxed they'd become. More slowly, Avery said, "I didn't have much time to plan for today. Yesterday morning, I was considering research groups I might collaborate with next term. I saw your name and picture beside that workshop and signed up before I'd figured out how to get here. When I first left home, I'd searched for you and failed. Now it seems marine biology isn't that large of a field after all."

"The University of Hawaiʻi and Pacific Tech collaborate and are part of the same consortium."

"I know. That's part of why I ended up here, after starting at Pacific Tech." Avery tensed and ran their hands back and forth across their own knees. "I remembered that you were going back to school when you said goodbye to me. You said you wouldn't be able to see me or write. I thought you must be impossibly far away. I should have reevaluated later, when I heard how my mom told other people to stay out of my life and hers."

"Are you okay, Avery?" Wend realized a new fear. "Will it cause trouble with your mom that we're in contact again?"

For a long while Avery shook their head, rocking back and forth with the motion, caught up in their own thoughts. "My mom can live her way. I will live my own way. You were one of the people who taught me that."

"I struggle to know what my own way means," Wend admitted. They felt another pang of worry. They'd not wanted to cause Avery any more trouble, but of course, they were an adult. Wend was asking about their mother like they were a child.

"You always did." Suddenly Avery seemed much older, and Wend realized they were the one comforting Wend. "I don't know what exactly went on between you and my mom, and I still love her and believe she means well. But she breaks a lot of hearts and sometimes worse."

Wend didn't want to think or talk about Mira now. This conversation already made them impossibly nervous, but there was one confession Wend needed to make. "I was pretty broken when she met me, and I learned a lot in your house. If anything broke my heart, it was leaving you."

"Me, too," Avery said. In a moment, they were scooching closer. Wend opened their arms to make room. Holding Avery without their kigurumi brought tears to Wend's eyes. They tried not to hold too tight.

A knock on Wend's shuttered door preceded Viola saying, "We should leave soon if we're going to Friendsgiving. And Aljon's back if you want to introduce Avery."

They'd talked off and on for hours. Wend felt mostly settled, if a bit worn out from all the intense emotions and being social for the last three days. "Do you want to try Friendsgiving? The host is someone I haven't seen since childhood. There will probably be good food but I don't know how many people."

"If you don't mind, I'd rather stay here." Avery's eyes flicked to Wend's face, not quite making eye contact, but they shared a small smile. Both knew a party would be asking a lot right now, but Wend had to go. They wanted to go. Simultaneously, they wished they had more time with Avery and more time to prepare before facing Mathew.

Wend nodded with greater understanding than they usually felt. "Sure. Let your housemate know, and tell me if there's anything I should set up before I leave."

While Avery pulled out their phone to make arrangements, Wend unfolded the only pair of real pants they currently owned. The travel pants were a gray linen blend and advertised as suitable for any occasion. The best shirt they had was a long-sleeved black rash guard.

They crossed the common room to change in the downstairs bathroom. When they came back out, Avery was being introduced to Aljon by Viola and Shelly, both of whom were much more colorfully and nicely dressed than Wend. Shelly wore a dress that hung down in three diagonal layers of forest green. Viola wore black pants and a batiked blouse similar to the mottled blue tank top she'd worn sometimes on the boat, but in purple jewel tones.

"Would you like to borrow some party clothes?" Viola asked.

Vaguely wondering what sort of wardrobe Viola carried with her, Wend started to say, "I doubt—"

Then Avery came back from a quick dash to her bag holding out a tunic cut much like the one Avery had worn all day, but in rose tones with swirls of slightly sparkly white. Wend had never worn anything like it. Avery offered enthusiastically, reminding Wend of how well the leopard kigurumi had worked out. Wend decided to think of it as another sort of costume; that's all party clothes were anyway. Besides, wearing Avery's tunic implied a promise that Avery would be here when Wend returned.

And a promise Wend would return, they realized.

Wend went back into the bathroom and changed again.

Matthaios' house was only a mile's walk from the condo, but the yards on his street were so densely packed with trees and broad-leaved ground plants that it was hard to make out the structures behind. Sweet smells of fruits or flowers blended into mossy or moldering scents with so much variation that no one scent could be isolated, let alone what was rotting.

The house itself first appeared as a sprawling half-hidden outline, more in the shape of a farmhouse than a mansion. The traditional wood architecture displayed no obvious smart tech, although Wend knew how easy that was to hide.

As they approached a single wide front door with a traditional key lock, accessed by a ramp rather than stairs, Wend noticed the tall panels of stained glass that flanked the entry portrayed more vegetation, what looked like bamboo. Wend had drifted to the side to study the neatly soldered seams when the door suddenly swung open.

"Welcome," a deep voice boomed. Then after a moment, "Is that you, Wend? It's me, Mathew, pronouns he/him."

Sure enough, the large stranger was looking straight at Wend. He wore a woven vest over a dark purple shirt, over a rather expansive belly. If his salt-and-pepper beard and hair had been white instead, he would have resembled Santa Claus. Wend realized they might be primed to think that on the weekend after Thanksgiving. He reached out with both arms, clearly signaling that he wanted to hug them.

Wend said, "No, I mean, I'm Wend, they/them, but I'd rather not hug."

He reached out a hand instead. When Wend tried to shake it, he brought his second hand to clasp the other side. "Do you remember when we held hands and sang that TV jingle?"

"Not hard to remember, all the words were 'meow.'" Wend tried to smile, but the two hands holding theirs were distracting. Yet the rough palms grounded Wend, warm and insulating. The hands of an adult stranger clasped in a familiar way, a yielding pressure that connected through nerve, muscle, and bone. They couldn't manage eye contact.

"I'm glad you remember." He spoke those words softly, making the prolonged touch bearable.

Wend wondered if it could be a test. Their mind flashed between memories of Mathew in preschool and the person in front of them now. Stabs of rejection from their last encounter with Gabi started to intrude and Wend blurted, "I remembered your name and you remembered my frog paddling."

"I would have given you the first one if I'd known how to find you." His words carried an unexpected weight, reverberating with the way Avery had said nearly the same thing. While it was hard to connect either voice or appearance to the childhood friend Wend remembered, they felt this Mathew's sincerity and attachment.

Wend marveled at two people trying to find them after all this time, both reaching them on the same day. Mentally and physically, Wend felt supersaturated, overfull in a way that left them vulnerable and needy. Consumed and consuming. Reintegrating the missing parts of their history that Mathew and Avery embodied.

Wend managed to recover their hand from Mathew and, with open-palmed gestures, said, "This is Viola Yang and Shelly Svoboda, both use she/her."

"I'm very pleased to meet you. Most people call me Matt now, but Mathew or Matthaios are fine, too. Please come in."

The entryway was flanked by a dim library and a sitting area that might be called a sunroom earlier in the day. Matt led them to a large living room with two palm-like potted plants in the far corners by a wall that was almost all windows, looking out on a wide lanai and four long planters, one covered by a makeshift greenhouse. The room held three couches, at least five other chairs, two beanbags, and several large pillows tucked neatly to the sides. There was at least one cat and half a dozen people lounging about.

One person scooted up in a motorized wheelchair, saying, "You must be Wend. I've heard so much about you! I'm Verilyn, she/her, originally from Kāne'ohe."

"I used to live there," Wend blurted. Focusing on a single individual was a relief. Trying to deal with such a large event, especially after teaching and reuniting with Avery, had probably been a mistake. It demanded more social resources than Wend could muster.

"For your first four years, same as mine, I've been told." Verilyn smiled, and Wend made an effort to focus and meet her eyes.

A purple-clad arm—Matt's—came to rest around Verilyn's shoulders.

Wend said to Matt without looking further up, "You remembered I came from Kāneʻohe."

"For a long time that was the only place name I knew in Hawaiʻi," Matt said. "Only when I learned state capitols for school did I discover Honolulu shared the same island."

Verilyn looped an arm halfway around Matt's waist and pulled him closer.

"He couldn't remember if you were kanaka or only born there." Wend noticed Verilyn didn't volunteer if she was part native, but Wend thought from word choice and appearance she might be.

"I'm not very good with faces," Matt said.

"Me neither, and lots of people have trouble guessing my ancestry. I don't know all of it, and I make no claims." Wend wanted to focus on only the two people in front of them, because the room felt too crowded. They could barely track this conversation. Their eyes kept darting out to see who was watching.

Matt turned to the room at large and started a long list of introductions, as overwhelming as expected. No one was specified as a relative or spouse, and none of them looked related, not that Wend was any good at recognizing that either. Two were clearly younger, maybe in their thirties. One of those was nonbinary, introduced with they/them pronouns, and wore a tunic similar to the one Wend had borrowed. They wondered if it was a fashion signal for nonbinary people here. Wend had been told about a couple such options in the past. By then they'd decided to be and wear what they wanted, so they'd never bothered to keep track. Wend failed to process the tunic-wearing person's name but thought it was Hawaiʻian, and their deeply browned skin and laid-back posture certainly supported that. They caught Wend looking and smiled in an easy, possibly flirtatious way, even if they were half Wend's age.

As the introductions wrapped up, another younger person, possibly under twenty, came calling out, "Dinner's ready." Looking at the three new people they asked, "Which of you is Wend?"

With that question, Wend realized they'd completely forgotten Viola and Shelly standing behind them. Wend lifted a hand and forced out the single word, "Me."

Matt caught the young person with an arm around their waist before Wend realized they'd been about to be hugged. "Wend's not a hugger. Wend, this is Greta, she/her, and my grandchild."

"He named his first fun invention based on something you told him. Did you know?" Greta asked, settling against Matt with his arm still holding her.

"That's half of how I found him," Wend managed.

"Shoots!" Dark eyebrows arched almost to points as Greta's mouth opened wide, talking through an enormous smile. "You can tell me stories later. Right now, there's spanakopita!"

Bodies moved all around them. Wend concentrated on not getting jostled. They accepted a seat at a heavily laden table that made the one in the condo look tiny. It was made of dark thick wood with obvious grooves between boards but fitted tight together and covered with thick varnish. Wend quickly counted eighteen chairs, although four were unoccupied. Verilyn sat at the head of the table with Matt to her left. Wend ended up between Matt and the other person with a tunic, whose name they had forgotten. Shelly and Viola sat together but across the table and toward the other end.

The lights in the room dimmed, and Wend noticed four lighted candles, each set within a circle of greenery.

"Friends, welcome," said Verilyn from the head of the table. "Does anyone have words they wish to say before we eat?"

Three people took turns. One offered a fairly non-denominational prayer in English that ended in "amen." Another spoke what was almost certainly Hawai'ian, which Wend could recognize but not understand. The third sang a Hebrew blessing.

After that, Verilyn invited people to tell about the making or origin of any food they brought. Most dishes were vegan, and a few with eggs or dairy were clearly marked. Viola did a nice job of naming the ingredients in the vegan fruit tart and appreciating Aljon who made it but didn't feel prepared for a group activity this evening. Greta explained the spanakopita, including that it was "part Greek like papa." People began serving and eating during the discussion of the food. Wend tried some of each dish passed their way and found them all at least interesting. The wine and beer on the table turned out to all be Hawai'ian, and there were plenty of fruit drinks, as well as iced and hot tea, that seemed to be popular.

Most people had finished their first servings by the time Verilyn asked, "Would anyone like to share a story from the past year?"

Shelly looked at Wend in a way they couldn't interpret before Viola glanced at both of them. It occurred to Wend that the wording about sharing stories was something they might have said, but they didn't consider it particularly Hawai'ian or related to the time and place of their birth and Verilyn's, although that was an interesting coincidence.

Greta told about meeting her new roommate at college in Seattle. Someone around Wend's age told about finally learning to hang glide over the summer. After that, Viola looked Wend's way and when Wend only shrugged, she told the story of Wend swimming onto the *Nuovo Mar*, including all the quotes in other languages and descriptions of what Aljon was holding and doing. People laughed in the right places, and Wend wasn't as embarrassed by the way Viola told it as they had been by the actual event.

Matt took the next turn. "Tera arrived in our lives this year, showing up on our doorstep holding a potted ti plant with two stalks." He nodded to the person seated two down from Wend, who had almost the same terra cotta skin tone as Wend, and was clearly younger than Matt but older than his grandchild. Wend locked in mind the name Tera to go with the ti plants and the person, making the name easier to remember. They should have recognized the ti plants in the living room, with leaves that were a favorite for leis and hula skirts. Matt continued to say, "She said spirits in dreams told her to bring us the plant for luck and the wellbeing of our own spirits. We couldn't say no to that and invited her in for lunch. Less than a week later, she arrived carrying another pot, saying the dreams hadn't stopped, and she thought maybe she was supposed to bring two pots, not two stalks in one planting. It was on the second visit that she met Kai and discovered they had the same birthdate and year, which of course seemed significant to us."

Set to remember Tera, Wend latched onto the name Kai for the same-age person sitting between Tera and Wend, as the last sentence caught up to them and jumbled their other thoughts. Birthdays, dreams, feeling driven to meet certain people—it all hit a bit close to home.

Shelly glared at Wend, who didn't know why and could only shrug.

"Excuse me, I need to use the bathroom." Shelly left the table and Wend bristled, perturbed by something in her tone.

"Perhaps we should adjourn to the living room," Verilyn said casually, but with a speaking look to Matt. "Everyone help yourselves to desserts or beverages and bring them along."

As they all changed locations, Wend made sure to claim a chair out of reach of any others and with a good view of the room. Despite forming generally positive impressions of everyone present, the casual mention of dreams and birthdays had set them on edge even before Shelly's hasty departure. They'd need time later to sort through the intensity of this evening. For now, they mostly wanted to observe and learn all they could about Mathew, his life, and his friends.

Once everyone was settled, Verilyn looked to Wend before saying, "Who would like to share a story next?"

Wend almost spoke up to tell how they'd rediscovered Avery that day. But they felt a little raw with that and everything else. As they clutched their hands in the tunic they'd borrowed, Wend was glad to have something of Avery's with them. The more they thought about explaining Avery's place in their life, now or before, the less coherent the story became.

As others around them began to share, Wend failed to take in one story and part of another before they realized how rude they were being and how much they truly wanted to hear what these people were saying.

The current speaker expounded on his work at an octopus farm where researchers spent years determining what to feed octopuses in every stage from birth to maturity. The octopus farm turned out to be on the Kona side of the island, and the storyteller went on to tell how the octopuses reached out to him from his first day there, how calmed he felt by them grasping his fingers or hands. It made Wend wonder if they could visit to meet the octopuses and if the grasping would soothe them the same way.

After that, Wend felt compelled to tell about the dream they woke from before spotting the trash island. They kept the dream details vague but went into detail describing the giant manta ray's stomach eversion and what Viola noticed about the plastic disappearing. They were halfway through telling, again in a vague way, about their latest dream leading them to the peculiar plastic dumpsite near Hilo, when Shelly interrupted.

"I think I need to go home." Shelly faced Wend, as if speaking specifically to them.

Startled mid-story, Wend realized Shelly had been in the bathroom for quite a while and possibly wasn't feeling well. Furthermore, Wend had invited Shelly and Viola and then ignored them, which they knew could upset people. Even if Wend no longer felt required to conform to societal norms and compensate for all their differences, they could admit when their actions were hurtful. "Okay, we can go if you need to."

Viola said, "It's okay. I can see her home and come back if you'd like."

"No, I think we'd all better go. Please." The way Shelly said it didn't leave much room for negotiation.

"I could get you a ride," Matt offered, standing up.

"No, I think I better walk. Thanks anyway." Shelly headed for the door.

Viola rushed to help, saying over her shoulder, "Yes, thank you. It was nice meeting you all."

"Thank you," Wend said, standing up but thrown completely by Shelly's abrupt exit and their unfinished story. "Really, I appreciate being invited and all the shared food and stories."

"Don't worry," Verilyn said. "See to your friend. You're welcome back anytime."

Matt already stood by the door, saying hasty goodbyes to Shelly and Viola. He said in a rush to Wend, "Please, keep in touch. At least let me know if everything's alright."

"I will," Wend promised as the other two were halfway across the yard. "I'm really glad I found you and that you invited me to share this."

Matt kept his hands by his pockets, clearly holding himself back from hugging or reaching out, even as Wend met his eyes for the first time all night. They'd never believed you could see someone's soul or truth in their eyes, but the lines around Matt's reflected years of laughter and their dampness expressed more devotion than Wend could reciprocate in the moment. All they could offer was a small but honest smile.

They rushed to catch up with Viola and Shelly even as Matt was saying, "Aloha, good night, and take care."

Shelly didn't say a word all the way home, but she kept up a good pace for someone not feeling well. From the static sparking off of her, Wend suspected this wasn't an issue of illness.

As soon as they were inside the condo, Shelly turned on Wend and said, "Do you realize what's going on there?"

Wend's eyes darted around the room, taking in the empty plate where the last of the smaller tart had been and the light in their lanai room where

Avery and Aljon sat on the futon. Both looked startled at the threesome's sudden return.

"Most of those people weren't visiting for a meal or a weekend. They live there. There's a room upstairs with a couple of large beds and all sorts of clothes and equipment strewn around, like an orgy room. And several other rooms that are clearly lived in, with full dressers, and plenty of signs of use."

Even back when Wend tried to blend in and pass as more 'normal', they'd refused to put up with certain types of gossip. "It's none of our business. So what if they're polyamorous, kinky, or like group sex. I'm pretty sure even Greta was an adult, not that Matt would be involved with his own grandkid. Seriously, why were you upstairs or looking in people's bedrooms anyway?"

"Because the whole thing felt off. Like a cult or something." Shelly raised both hands along with her voice. "You say you follow your instincts. Well, I followed mine."

Wend drew back. "I wouldn't follow my instincts if they told me to snoop in your bedroom. You can ask Viola how hard I'd try to avoid doing that, even by accident." When Shelly took a deep breath as if to shout her arguments more loudly, Wend held up a hand and asked, "Did anyone mistreat you or suggest anything inappropriate?" Much as Wend wanted to trust their own instincts, they felt obliged to ask. Shelly had been as much their guest as Matt's, and they wanted to know if anything had actually happened to trigger this reaction.

"No, but they were talking about spirits and magic without even the reticence you usually show, and they've got you doing it, too. It's insidious, and you shouldn't have been telling them our business or about the island patrol investigation."

"One. Argument. At a time." Wend enunciated, as their teeth and body shook. They took a calming breath.

When Shelly looked about to protest, Viola bumped her shoulder and took her hand. It wasn't much, but it gave Wend time to corral their thoughts into words.

"First, you were fine with me calling Miko and letting them tell whoever, so I doubt an island patrol investigation into littering is the issue here. Second, while I'm skeptical of anything I can't explain and don't tend toward religious or magical interpretations, I don't think anyone there sounded like they were brainwashed or in a cult. Now, either cite some evidence of wrongdoing on their part or give me one clear and true reason why you objected to me sharing that story."

"I felt uncomfortable and didn't trust them. I did what I thought best." Shelly's loud words bordered on shouting.

Wend shivered but couldn't express the emotions tangling inside. They'd struggled all night between their discomfort with the large group setting and having waited decades to see Matt again. To find out Shelly had gone snooping after Wend had worried about not paying her enough attention left Wend embarrassed and ashamed. That collided with their indignation at being dragged away under false pretenses, by someone they'd hoped would make the situation easier, although Wend couldn't at the moment remember why they'd expected that support. Their thoughts spun on and on, leaving them frozen in place and unable to act.

Viola finally spoke up, still holding Shelly's hand. "Why don't we go upstairs and sort this out." They glanced meaningfully at Wend. "Both why you reacted so strongly and why you insisted Wend leave as well? Further discussion with anyone else can wait until morning."

Wend didn't miss the pointed look Viola gave Aljon before practically dragging Shelly upstairs. They weren't surprised when Aljon appeared in front of them, trailed by Avery, and said, "How about hot chocolate?" Wend nodded gratefully, and he turned back to Avery. "Any nut allergies?" Avery shook their head.

Sinking down onto the sofa Wend exhaled and said, "Thanks, I never got around to dessert." They appreciated Aljon's small smile as he returned to the kitchen.

Avery joined them on the sofa and said, "Can I touch you? I could be your personal penguin if you'd rather."

"I'm fine with your touch now." As Avery carefully scooted in closer, leaning in without grabbing, Wend added, "I'd totally forgotten the *Personal Penguin* book and song. How could I forget?"

Avery started singing the childish song. They kept it going until Aljon served them all hot chocolate.

Overwhelming as the day and evening had been, Wend felt pretty good by the time they fell asleep in their hammock with Avery sleeping on the futon below in their almost outdoor room.

17.

AVERY WOKE with a gasp that woke Wend, too.

"Need anything?" Wend asked as soon as they peeked out of their sleep sack.

"Not great with new places." A moment later Avery asked, "Do you want to sleep more?"

"Not really."

"Great." A swooshing sound suggested Avery sat up.

By the time Wend climbed down from their hammock, Avery had grabbed their messenger bag and headed toward the bathroom.

Wend dressed in their usual swim-ready clothes and realized they'd have to do laundry the next day if they planned to wear a completely clean outfit every day.

Being first into the kitchen was new for Wend. They looked around to see what food was available for breakfast but were relieved when Aljon came down the stairs.

"I think I heard Shelly and Viola waking up," he said. "If you and Avery want to take off for the day, I'll keep things from blowing up."

By that point Avery was out of the bathroom. They said, "You don't have to rearrange your day because of me."

"But you're only here for the weekend. Is there stuff you want to see?" Wend asked.

"What? Like flying over volcanoes in a helicopter? Not even with headphones."

Wend wished in a way that wrung them out like a dishtowel that they could take Avery dream flying to see the volcanoes without helicopter noise, but they were used to hiding emotional reactions they couldn't possibly explain and only nodded in response.

"There are hikes around lava fields, or Rainbow Falls is famous and only a couple miles from here," Aljon offered, looking stuff up on his phone.

"That sounds fine," Avery said. "But I can come back. Also, Wend, your phone buzzed this morning."

It took a moment for Wend to remember the phone Miko gave them. "I didn't know it was turned on."

They went to check for any messages from Miko, and Avery followed to put their messenger bag away.

"Huh," was all Wend could say after reading through a long stream of texts from Miko.

"Good or bad?"

"I'm not sure. Are you okay with eating breakfast with everyone here? I can't promise there won't be shouting."

"Would it be okay to put my headphones on or come back in here if it gets loud?"

"Definitely."

"Then let's go see what Aljon's cooking." Avery managed to bounce on the completely not bouncy futon.

"You like him?" Wend asked, then watched Avery's body language switch from bouncing to curving head and spine sideways to follow a thought.

"He was very kind last night. And he's calm. Like you."

Wend jerked back in surprise. "I'm calm? Like him?"

"I barely know him," Avery said, straightening up their head and shoulders. "But I don't think either of you is likely to start shouting, slam doors, or storm out."

"That's a pretty low bar."

"You should see the other people my mom brought home." After a pause Avery added, "I should have realized you came for me, not her, at least to start. You were different from all the others and so good to me."

Wend wanted to say she'd never loved Mira, only Avery. But being open and honest had its limits. Avery had suggested they would come back to visit again, and Wend didn't want to rush or overwhelm them.

Aljon seemed to have summoned breakfast out of nothing in the short time they'd been out of the room. Wend set the table with Avery's help as Aljon slid two large frittatas into the center beside something like breakfast potatoes made from leftover sweet potatoes and mango. Shelly followed Viola down the stairs looking reluctant, but when they sat,

Shelly said, "Waking up to breakfast on the table is really nice. Do you like having a full-sized kitchen to work with?"

Wend considered that opening a good sign. While they could not forgive Shelly for her deception last night, it helped to be reminded of her caring relationship with Aljon. They'd like some closure on what happened yesterday, but they wouldn't mind a reprieve at least long enough to eat.

"I enjoyed the challenge on a boat, but having unlimited fresh ingredients is a nice change." Aljon waved a forkful of frittata with bits of zucchini and leafy greens.

The others all dug into their food, but Wend noticed Avery poking at theirs, separating out bits of tofu or sweet potato. Not wanting to embarrass them, Wend said, "I forgot the fruit bowl." They refilled the one on the counter and set it on the table between Avery and them.

Avery took a banana immediately.

By unspoken agreement, they all finished eating and mostly cleared the table, aside from Viola who was still picking at a long slice of papaya as she said, "Are we going to talk about last night now, or wait until later?"

"I got a message from Miko before breakfast that might be relevant, so maybe now is better," Wend said, with an apologetic glance toward Avery.

"I'll go check on my flight back," Avery said, taking off for Wend's room and closing the door.

"What was the message from Miko?" Shelly asked, slouching against the table. "I assume this is about whatever's eating the plastic."

"I don't think you'll like it," Wend said, before rushing through the next part. "The one faculty member who replied about the plastic issue told Miko they met me last night but didn't get a chance to talk shop. They had Miko forward their personal contact info. It was the person I sat next to, Kai, who is evidently an environmental science professor at UH Hilo and claims to know something relevant."

"They may not know anything and be luring you in." Shelly planted her elbows on the dining table and leaned forward.

Wend closed their eyes and flattened their hands to keep them still. "Why? We barely even spoke." After last night's duplicity, Wend needed to draw a firm line between Shelly as a business partner, sharing a condo that was also their home office, and Shelly as an interfering manipulator who had no place in Wend's personal decisions let alone those of Matt's household.

"It's too coincidental," Shelly said. "Everything about that place feels like a set-up, if not for a cult or sex club, then for something else."

Wend's eyes opened wide, but they managed not to let their mouth fall open. The blunt statement shocked them, even if Shelly's negative assumptions no longer did. "One of my closest childhood friends fell into what many would describe as a cult, and no one at Matt's party gave off that kind of energy." The only person who made Wend feel staticky and wrong last night had been Shelly at the end, although they might have been too overwhelmed to read the entire larger group. They'd definitely interacted with enough creepy people over the years to gauge their own uncertainty. "You didn't freak out about my dream leading us to that dump site or whatever force steered you to Seattle or me to the *Nuovo Mar*. What if Matt's people are exploring the same things?"

Shelly leaned back, unfazed by anything Wend had said. "How do I know you aren't part of the setup? If you were told ahead of time about the trash island and the dumping here, or if you had a hidden sat phone or some tech we don't know about, you could have set up this whole magical dream thing and led us to Matt's group as part of a long con." Shelly spoke louder and sat up straighter as the words poured out, until she ended up almost shouting and pulled far back from where she'd previously been slouched against the table.

Wend opened their mouth to say how out of bounds that accusation fell, but Viola jumped in faster, interrupting.

"What?" Viola gripping a fork, white knuckled. "You didn't say any of that last night. And what about my flying dreams?"

"I don't know for sure," Shelly said. "And no offense, but you are kind of suggestible."

"I thought I was stubborn and only thought of myself?" Viola matched Shelly's tone and volume.

"You know what happened with your stint in the travel industry, but you still can't see how your partner manipulated you from beginning to end." Shelly gestured broadly and knocked her empty plate to the floor where it shattered.

Wend startled. Their neck twinged in protest.

Viola ignored the crash and mess. "Oh yeah? What about you and men with beards? How much of your distrust last night started with Matt's facial hair?"

"Enough," Aljon said, looking up from the broken ceramic on the floor to Shelly and then Viola. He spoke tightly. "We all have issues. What matters to me is seeing the four of us get along well enough to work together through the winter, get the hydrogen generators where they can do some good, and maybe deal with manufactured bacteria that could be either helping or hurting the planet. Do any of you disagree with those goals?"

When no one else spoke, Wend said, "I want all of those to happen, but if the best way to reach the last two is for me to go elsewhere, I'll do that." Not that Wend wanted to give up free housing to make Shelly's life easier, but Wend would have to set and defend hard boundaries if they decided to stay.

"But what are your goals?" Aljon asked quietly.

Wend answered easily in the momentary calm. "To help the planet and not make things any worse by what I do or don't do personally."

"And for yourself?"

Wend shrugged. "To be as true to myself as I can be, within reason."

The smile in Aljon's voice as he answered led Wend's eyes up to see the soft expression, not quite a smile, on his face. "Does that include figuring out this dream stuff and whatever you have in common with Viola and maybe Matt or others?"

Wend saw Aljon lining his arguments up in a row but wasn't sure where he was headed. "I'd like to, but it's not worth upsetting what the three of you have or are doing."

Aljon leaned forward on the table, clasping his hands. "What if I think we're better with you around?"

Wend was stumped. They'd felt several times like they were building something with Aljon and Viola. Both the boat and the condo had begun to feel like home. Viola had made them doubt those feelings a couple times, and then Shelly had driven an ax into all of it. But since their first real conversation with Aljon, he'd treated them more than fairly, better than many of their past friends. The way he defended Shelly, as a son might, seemed misguided to Wend. But it was sweet, as sweet as what he'd just said to Wend. Did they want to leave him here? And for how long? "You don't plan to stay here long term anyway," they reminded.

"So stay while I'm here," Aljon smiled and added softly, "and don't assume your goals aren't worth rocking the boat. Working through challenges is good for us. Who's next?"

"My overriding goal is to see 10,000 hydrogen generators distributed to those who need them." Shelly crossed her arms and glared at Wend.

"I don't want the complications of whatever hugger-mugger Wend's involved with, and honestly, I'm not sure I want the complications that follow Viola around like a pack of sick puppies, but I can't quite kick that habit."

"No kicking puppies," Viola said. "I already miss the simple life on my boat." Viola traced small circles in the air with the fork she still held. "But if we're wintering here, I'm ready to stir shit up and have a try at all those goals, including Wend's weird hugger-mugger."

Wend had never used the term "hugger-mugger" in their life and the part of their brain that treated all communication as translation spun around the combination of contradictory nouns, even without having some hugger-mugger assigned as Wend's own with Viola's support. On the other hand, Shelly's insult to Viola and by extension Wend, if they were included as a complication or sick puppy, pushed Wend close to vomiting. Or as close as they came to shouting.

Before Wend could frame any response, Viola added to her goals. "I'd also like to get at least one major sale out of the pictures from our trip. Should I send off my sea nettle and tuna photos with the proposals we prepped on Friday, or am I needed for one of these other projects?"

Wend pushed back from the table and stood, not up for arguing about the sea nettle or tuna articles and photos at this point. "Go ahead. Have you all accepted that I'm setting up a meeting with Kai to discuss suspicions about whatever is eating PET plastics?"

"If we don't accept it, will that make a difference?" Shelly asked.

"If you can't accept my decisions and plan to continue voicing it, I will at least find someplace else to live," Wend said, "and Aljon can visit me there if he wants."

Viola rolled her head sideways to stare at Shelly. "You're right. They're like a kicked puppy, but I don't want you kicking them out."

Wend decided they were done with being compared to a puppy, but before they could make their feelings on that clear, Shelly said, "Fine, do whatever you want about the plastic. Leave me out of it, and don't bring anyone who was at that party back here. I'll try to work through my own issues and keep them from sticking to you. Just don't do anything that could reflect badly on whatever startup we launch for this. Have you thought how it might look to outsiders that you brought a student home from your class yesterday and let them sleep in your room?"

Wend's mouth literally fell open.

Aljon said, "It's not like that."

"I know. I'm saying, we all need to think about such things." Shelly nodded to herself, and her mouth settled in a satisfied line.

Aljon raised both eyebrows at Wend and waited.

"You're out of line, Shelly. If we're going to live and work together, then you're going to have to respect my boundaries. No talking about me or my friends as puppies or anything less than competent adults. If you don't want to see my friends here, then you don't offer any unsolicited comments about them. That's the deal." Wend took a deep breath, but found they weren't at all panicky. "I'm not only too old to self-censor for other people's comfort, I regret having compromised so much in the past. Avery is as close to my own child as I'll ever have. Not only am I pretty sure cis straight people share rooms with their kids all the time, but you have no right to question either of us or our decisions. I would do anything for Avery, including moving out of this place, losing my job, or defending my actions in court. I trust Avery, and probably Aljon, would support me in that. You don't get a say in that part of my life. Do we have an understanding?"

Aljon nodded and looked pleased, but Shelly only tightened her glare.

"You'd have my support, too." Viola turned to face Shelly and added, "I bet you'll agree once you think that through, because seriously, you and I are a much hotter mess than they ever could be. Now, can we get back to our own business?"

"You realize we're merely checking my spirulina and confirming everything is safe and secure onboard, not sailing around the harbor?" Aljon asked as Avery boarded the dinghy in Radio Bay. Avery had expressed more interest in seeing the *Nuovo Mar* than visiting Rainbow Falls or other tourist destinations.

"I want to see how you all lived and made it across the Pacific." Avery addressed Wend, who held the tiny boat still while Avery clambered in.

"When I was a kid, I learned the original Hawai'ians sailed here from the Marquesas, using the same route we took," Wend said from the side of the dinghy. "Later research favored Tahiti, but I always associated the Marquesas with the people who built the fishponds where I learned to swim."

"I didn't know that," Aljon said, motioning for Wend to get on board.

Wend shrugged and asked Avery, "Are you thinking about living on a boat for part of your graduate work?"

"I'm reevaluating what I want my thesis to be, but I doubt I could live on a sailboat for two weeks." Avery paused before adding, "I'm still easily overwhelmed by noises, and I like things to be predictable."

"You really put yourself out by showing up yesterday, last minute, on a whole other island." Wend sat close beside Avery as Aljon untied the dinghy.

"I wanted to find you so much. But if you'd reacted badly . . ." The way Avery's voice trailed off broke Wend's heart. Again.

"Never," Wend said quickly, before offering, "The noises on the *Nuovo Mar* took a bit of getting used to, but I liked the constant motion and only dealing with two people each day. Other research vessels I've worked on were larger with more human unpredictability and noise."

As Aljon rowed, he said, "It's nice and quiet here, but on the weekdays there's a lot of noise from the commercial dock. I'd take the sounds of the sea, even during a storm, over that any day."

"I probably wouldn't do well with the commercial noises either. That's why I have these." Avery motioned to the noise-canceling headphones around their neck, which they hadn't used during the entire walk from the condo.

"You don't need them as much as when we first met," Wend said.

"It got easier to compensate, even aside from all the training. Mom would be shocked I made it here on my own." Avery smiled, then grew somber. "I didn't do well my first year in college, even living at home."

"I was a mess my first year in college," Wend said, "and most of it had nothing to do with my neurodivergence or touch sensitivities."

"How did you cope with not showering for two weeks at sea? Didn't you use to get rashes really easily?" Avery asked, again remembering more than Wend expected.

"I mostly get rashes when my skin is dry. Warm humid climates and seawater suit me better." They didn't want to discuss the therapy they'd gone through after being forced away from Avery and Mira, or what they'd learned about anxiety and autoimmune reactions during that. It might be useful for Avery to hear that story sometime, but not today.

By silent agreement when they reached the *Nuovo Mar*, Wend climbed up to deck first with Avery second and Aljon last, just in case. But

Avery walked across the almost still deck fearlessly to rest a hand on the mast. "One mast means it's a sloop or a cutter, right? Is there a way to tell without seeing the sails?"

"On this boat, the easiest clue is right here." Aljon sprung forward enthusiastically and tapped the bowsprit. "Do you know what this is?"

"Something to attach an extra sail further forward, so this a cutter?" Avery half-asked.

"Excellent." Aljon looked sincerely impressed, and pleased with Avery's interest in the boat he clearly loved. "This is the bowsprit with the forestay and line for what we call the foresail." He gestured as he explained the rigging and even opened the cover around the mainsail enough to show Avery the gaff when he got around to explaining that.

Avery focused intently on every explanation and all the new vocabulary, reminding Wend with a pang of when they first started as Avery's tutor. Wend followed along mostly silently as Aljon grew more animated than usual and gave more and more detailed explanations in response to Avery's careful questions.

It was only belowdecks when Aljon explained their sleeping arrangements that Avery turned to Wend and asked, "You slept in the quarter berth?"

"Yeah, it's what they had available for a third crew member."

Avery ran their fingers along the time-worn wood. "I like the way it's enclosed except at the top. But is it noisier and bumpier?"

"On a boat this small, I'm not sure any one part is noisier or bumpier. But I liked it being enclosed, and I had my sleep sack besides."

"It is rougher, if you're prone to sea sickness," Aljon said, then explained, "I slept there while Shelly sailed with us."

"I guess you couldn't hang your hammock anywhere." Avery sounded sad as they said it.

"In port and once when we were mostly stopped at sea, I could hang it between the shroud and the backstay. Viola was actually sleeping in it when we spotted the superyacht with smoke and a distress flag."

"And that's separate from whatever plastic story caused the argument last night?" Avery asked. "You did have an exciting trip."

"That's less than half of it." Aljon's eye roll was audible in his grumbling tone, but Wend could tell he was pleased with Avery's interest as he waved to the stairs leading up. "If you want to sit on deck and catch up on some stories, I was thinking of making fruit bars with some of our leftover dried fruit from the Marquesas."

"We could talk down here if you'd rather," Wend offered.

"Not like I won't be able to hear you. I'll join you once snacks are ready."

Surrounded by sunlight that made the bay shine, Wend told stories of their trip to entertain Avery rather than point out odd connections and inexplicable dreams.

Avery explained their shifting interests throughout graduate school. "I came to UH Mānoa imagining my doctoral research would involve propagating and reattaching coral that were found to be resistant to bleaching. Remember when you and I talked about the bleaching events of 2015 and 2019, when people were starting that research?"

"I do." Then Wend covered their face in only slightly exaggerated embarrassment. "When I spoke about coral at the workshop, I realized others there would know far more than I did, but I had no idea you were specifically studying coral."

By the time they looked up, Aljon sat on the opposite side of the cockpit and Avery nibbled at a fruit bar from a tray he'd brought. They seemed to find both the taste and texture agreeable and hummed their pleasure. Aljon basked in the sun, clearly pleased Avery enjoyed the simple snack.

"You did a fine job explaining what I now see as a losing battle. In the last decade, Hawai'i saw five coral bleaching events worse than those in 2015 and 2019. Someone in the media has reported every year since that we've reached a carbon emissions peak or plateau, but we never see the decrease we need to keep temperature and sea level in check. Instead of the 1.5 or 2 degrees Celsius increase by 2100 that those trying to save the reefs were planning for, we're probably looking at 2.5 or 3 degrees. Twice as many heat waves, twice as much bleaching, and more than twice as much sea level rise accompany that extra degree. No coral we transplant will thrive and grow fast enough to keep up with that. Even if it did, the coral ecosystem is poised to fail in a dozen different ways, probably by 2050."

The predictions weren't news to Wend or anything they could refute, but hearing Avery lay it all out tore at Wend's heart in a way they suspected most parents understood. "That's a hard realization. Do you think the reef surveys and microbiome census are pointless as well?"

Aljon hunched forward, brow furrowed in a way that made him look older as he glanced between Wend and Avery.

"No," Avery was quick to correct. "Learning as much as we can before we lose more diversity is near the top of my list of worthwhile goals. And you have projects sampling mangrove forests and seagrass beds, right? Those we might still be able to save or transplant. We'll need them for carbon capture and protecting the 80 percent of coastal areas that are going to see worse flooding and storms, if they don't end up underwater. They might be better candidates for artificial propagation or replanting."

Wend felt compelled to say, "The oceans are resilient to some extent. If we lessen other pressures, some species and systems will find ways to adapt."

"Exactly!" Avery flung their arms wide, just avoiding Aljon's knee. "I've been trying to find a way to study that. The closest I've found are suggestions for marine protected areas, how connected they need to be for different species, and what percentage should be 'no catch' versus other restrictions."

"Shelly was working on that before the hydrogen generator project restarted. She might have contacts or advice for finding research ideas," Aljon said.

Avery bit their lip and didn't respond.

"Let me ask her," Aljon volunteered in a gentler voice. "Is it okay to give her your contact info?" Wend hadn't realized Aljon and Avery had exchanged contact details, but it made sense and Wend was glad Aljon took the lead on this. "Shelly likes to help, especially for causes she cares about. She's good at keeping her drama to her own personal life. She might not hesitate to make a scene in front of you, but she'd never blow up like that in a work or community action setting."

Wend considered again if moving out would be a better choice, but they'd agreed to stay with Aljon for now. They'd stand by that decision until new data challenged it.

"Okay," Avery said. "Can you pass on that I prefer written communications?"

"Sure. At least you like your cellphone." Aljon glanced indulgently at Wend as he said it.

Wend hadn't noticed that, but had noted Avery checked in with their housemate and arranged their flight home readily enough. If they weren't checking their phone every five minutes, that might be a kindness to

Wend or a matter of focusing on one thing at a time. "That reminds me, I should give you my email and cell number."

As they took care of that, Aljon said, "You're welcome to contact me if Wend doesn't check often enough." He clearly meant it in a friendly way, but Wend vowed to themself to catch up on email and other communications the next day.

Avery said, "These fruit bars are yummy, and I loved the fruit tart. Have you thought about going to chef school?"

"Not sure he needs it at this point." Wend picked up a fruit bar and sat back to savor one last taste of the Marquesas as Aljon shrugged, a small tilt to his smile. Wend was glad to see the question didn't bother him.

"I've had about enough of the service industry, although I might come back to cooking and sailing from time to time. I wasn't raised with the ideal of having one career for life or necessarily working within a formal economy." Aljon looked down shyly as he said, "I'd like to do something to protect the Philippines' ecosystems, especially if it could also help with storm protection and fresh drinking water. As sea levels rise, so do ground water and pollutants. I know that is happening other places, but the Philippines is far behind on monitoring, and three-quarters of the population never had a decent sewage system."

Wend's heart twisted as it had when Avery spoke about the dying reefs. "I didn't realize. I mean, I've heard about similar issues in Oakland and Marin, near where I used to live." Wend could barely imagine the challenges Aljon might face in the Philippines if such wealthy areas were caught unprepared. "If you want to take classes at UH Hilo next term, I could ask about visiting student programs."

"No, I think I'd favor apprenticeship over college, more like what I had on the boat with Viola. And it looks like I'll be learning how to handle a non-profit and marketing campaigns."

"I'm glad you're working with Wend on that," Avery said.

"Shelly and Viola are going to be much more helpful than me." Wend still wasn't sure how they'd fallen into the business arrangement or whether their contributions would be valued.

"But this way neither of you is the odd one out and you have each other." Avery stared into the air as if working through their own series of conflicting images and thoughts. "I wish I could stay here, too."

"Don't you like your housemate and whoever you're working with at

UH Mānoa?" Wend asked, feeling worried and parental and then worried they didn't have a right to feel parental after so much time apart.

Avery simply shrugged and leaned into Wend's shoulder, scattering any worries. "They're fine. I just don't want to lose you again."

Aljon smiled quietly to himself, as if reading Wend, or perhaps both of them, far too well.

"I will do everything in my power to keep that from happening." Wend slowly put their arm around Avery and held them close until it was time to go to the airport.

18.

ALJON WAS WEEDING the garden outside the open doors of the glassed-in lanai by the time Wend returned to the condo after seeing Avery off. He took one look at Wend and said, "You miss Avery already, don't you?"

Wend nodded.

"Want to talk about it or take your mind off it?"

"Not talking," Wend said.

Aljon chuckled. "It seems the tart pan I sent with you three last night was left at your preschool friend's house. We could go together to retrieve it, and you could introduce me."

That certainly jarred Wend's thoughts out of the rut they were digging. "I thought you didn't want to go?"

"I didn't want to deal with a party last night, but now I'm curious what all the fuss was about. Besides, I made too many coconut lime cookies, and you need to follow up with the environmental science professor."

"Kai, right." Wend pulled out their phone with the contact info Miko had sent, wondering about why Aljon had made cookies. "I guess I should at least reply to their message."

Aljon smiled as he plucked another weed.

After a quick text exchange and a short walk, Wend and Aljon were seated at a small table on the broad, shady lanai in Matt's backyard sharing tea, coconut lime cookies, and vegan pinwheel rolls with Kai.

"If you prefer cashew cream or rice milk to oat milk"—Kai gestured at the tiny porcelain pitcher set out beside the sugar bowl—"we have two more vegans in the household with different preferences than mine.

Given your amazing tarts and cookies, it's the least we could offer in return." Kai wore a simpler tunic than the day before, in a muted shade of purple that made Wend picture stone, although it hung as if made of silk. Behind Kai, a bush bloomed with white flowers and a tree hung heavy with guavas that appeared to be ripe.

"If it weren't so warm and humid, this would feel like sitting down to afternoon tea in Britain or Canada," Wend said.

"Guess that would have been one benefit to British rather than American colonizers." Kai raised their teacup as if in salute.

Matt brought out a plate of freshly cooked samosas at that point and chided, "You could argue that out with someone from India. Aren't you both on the same side with saving the island's ecology or whatever you're meeting about?"

"I'd invite you to join us," Kai said before selecting a samosa, "but I'm curious how much food you'll bring out in your efforts to listen in."

"I could hear you fine through the open windows." Matt waved toward the house and Wend noted his shirt was also made of light breezy fabric, although probably not silk. Something soft. "I'm trying to be a better host than last night."

Wend couldn't help protesting, even though they'd already reassured him when he first brought out tea and pinwheel rolls. "You were an excellent host. I told you, Shelly has her own issues. Nothing you need to worry about."

Matt took the seat that Kai had joked about not offering. "Listen, we knew Shelly only pretended to feel sick last night. As a kid, you said you could see or feel when people had certain emotions or were lying." There was a question implicit in that.

"You remember that, too?" Wend asked, caught between feeling touched and exposed. They swallowed back the decades-old hurt. "But you didn't believe me."

"Maybe I partially believed you? I didn't appreciate how special you were until much later." Matt's hand made an awkward half motion, as if he wanted to reach out to Wend, but held himself back.

"Umm, Matt?" Kai glanced at Aljon.

Matt looked to Wend, as if assuming they'd understand. For once, they did. "Aljon knows what I told you back then about sensing emotions and flying dreams. He knows I still feel static when people lie in certain ways, but I couldn't always convince myself that was more than intuition or the remnants of childhood synesthesia. He also knows how I found both patches of plastic, and he hasn't abandoned me yet."

Matt looked to Kai.

Slouching back in their chair, Kai raised an eyebrow at Aljon, "All that, he's cute, and makes excellent vegan cookies and fruit tart. Guess he can stay."

"Thanks for the compliment," Aljon said, but he looked a little uncomfortable and sat up straighter in his chair.

"Now look who's moving too fast," Matt said, as he took a bite from one of the samosas he'd brought to the table. "You should try these while they're still warm."

As the rest of them picked up samosas and made appreciative noises, Matt said mostly to Wend, "We know Shelly poked around upstairs and probably concluded correctly that our household is polyamorous but maybe labeled it as something worse. If you want to ask questions, we won't be offended."

Kai tipped their chin toward Aljon and said with a wink, "If my flirting makes you uncomfortable, tell me and I'll stop. We're all careful about consent and negotiating limits."

"I'm ace," Aljon said, then closed his mouth and waited.

"Okay, but not aro or touch averse?" The way Kai asked made it clear how comfortable they were with the topic. They still sounded flirtatious, but as if they were redefining the terms of their flirtation.

The shift intrigued Wend, but left them uncertain of their own limits in this social interaction, especially with the rapid shifts between usually sensitive topics. At the very least, the standards for more open communication piqued Wend's curiosity.

"I haven't explored much, but I don't think so," Aljon finally answered.

"Shoots," Kai said, giving a friendly nod. "I'll back off a bit, but let me know if you want to explore more. I'm extremely flexible, not only in my gender presentation and sexuality but also romantically and for negotiating activities in general. Most of us are somewhat flexible, or we wouldn't end up in this household." Kai sat up straighter and raised one of Aljon's cookies in a salute of sorts.

Matt spoke softly to Wend, "You want to state any limits on touch? Other than not wanting hugs?"

Wend had never been asked so directly by someone they barely knew. Then again, they'd known Matt their whole life, and he'd known their greatest secret all that time. The unique sense of connection Wend had never shaken flared now, like the sparklers they'd waved in both hands as a child. They wondered if Matt experienced anything like it, if he'd take it for granted, like knowing Shelly was lying. "Make a logical extension from being demipansexual to what demipantactile should mean and add in that I have touch sensitivities that can be unpredictable."

"Good to know. Sensory sensitivities and synesthesia may often go along with sensing deception or guilt and possibly whatever led you to the plastic," Matt said as he picked up a pinwheel roll. "Please, don't let me keep you from eating."

Wend let out a deep, shaky breath. "What about you?" they asked, and then, realizing that was unclear, stammered out, "I don't know how to ask back."

"I'm a very tactile person, also pan, poly, kinky, whatever words you know, and willing to answer any question you care to ask," Matt said, licking his fingers after finishing the tiny roll. "Right now, you're unlikely to bump into any boundary I would set, and I'm used to letting less tactile people decide when to initiate touch with me."

While Wend hadn't wanted to hug Matt yet, they felt like they would want to sooner than with most people, and hoped that he'd keep offering. "It isn't that I'm less tactile. I very much want to touch both your shirt and Kai's. It just takes a while with people." Wend felt ridiculous but a little bit brave, like they were taking another step toward being their true self.

Kai gave a delighted chuckle, crossed their arms, reached down, and in one smooth motion pulled their tunic off over their head before tossing it across to Wend. They leaned back in their chair, chest bare. "If you like it, I can tell you where I shop in Honolulu, although what you wore last night looked like the same brand."

"That was borrowed. And this is softer." Wend focused on the luxurious fabric, running it through their fingers and fully appreciating the cool slide, rather than comment on Kai's solution or observation. "Most of my clothing is wash and wear and ocean-ready, but there are many textures I avoid."

"That's my favorite vegan silk, washable, but not ideal for swimming."

They hadn't considered silk to not be vegan, something they put aside to think about later. Wend stood to hand the tunic back across the table and said, "Thank you." As they sat again, they realized Matt had removed his shirt and was holding it out to them.

"You really don't have to do this," Wend said, even as they accepted it. This fabric was feather light and smooth, like a scarf. They sat back down and held it to their cheek. "What is this?"

"Bamboo, and I like that you can appreciate the feel of it, even if not while being hugged. Many of us here are sensualists." Matt seemed completely at ease sipping tea in nothing but a pair of shorts. He carried his age and his weight well and unapologetically. The hair on his chest was as curly and graying as the hair on his head and his beard, which in a way made him look fully clothed without the shirt.

Wend handed the soft bamboo clothing back to Matt and asked, "Do you know anyone who wears kigurumi? The really soft kind?"

"Some of us here wear those as well, for various reasons," Matt said.

Wend heard Aljon choke on his tea and hurried to say, "I didn't mean to imply anything. Just mine's a leopard, and when it was first given to me I thought of you, because you used to love cats so much."

"I am still very much a cat person." Matt's voice slid low as a purr while he slid his shirt on, petting it smooth. The motion called up a rarely revisited memory of a chilly winter morning when young Mathew couldn't stop petting his soft new cat sweater and insisted Wend pet it, too. The similarity across time reassured Wend, even if they weren't ready to mention it.

"Leaving that for later discussion," Kai said ostentatiously before focusing on Wend, "should I tell you the information I have as an academic, or a story that might help you understand what's going on here?"

Wend met their eyes directly for the first time to say, "Both. Please?"

"Could sincere curiosity be some effect like the lie detection but opposite?" Kai asked mostly to Matt before continuing to Wend, "I bet people love to tell you their stories."

"It's pretty hit or miss actually. A lot of people can't stand me."

"Join the club," Kai said, with a shimmy that made the lavender-gray tones in their shirt ripple like smooth granite beneath a creek. "For the record, I didn't want to like you. But I will own and get over my biases. Let's start with my story."

The offhand comment stung for a moment before a cascade of social relief washed through Wend at their implied acceptance now. It was a cleansing sensation that Wend could get lost in, especially after periods of high anxiety, but they didn't have time to fully process in the moment. They filed the feeling away as Kai prepared to tell a story Wend needed to hear.

Resting both hands on the table, Kai began. "Until five years ago, I was doing perfectly well at pissing off my family and getting into trouble on my own. I thought anyone who'd been here less than my whole lifetime was a tourist and all white people were colonizers. I used drugs, had lots of sex, sometimes accepted money but mostly kept pretty safe. I wasn't safe about surfing, diving, and scuba. Oh, and I picked up a master's degree mostly to piss off my dad. Radical, right?"

Kai took a long sip of tea, practically daring anyone to interrupt after that brutal beginning. Wend would have readily listened to them for hours.

"I found an unexplored lava cave underwater while diving. I wasn't officially dive certified, let alone trained for cave diving. But even knowing how reckless it was, I started exploring all on my own. The first day, I didn't make it far. I wasn't carrying any sort of light. When I returned the next morning, my dive light wasn't strong, but I was sure I saw something glowing inside.

"It got away." Kai shrugged and paused.

"I got stuck in a tight spot." Kai shrugged again and made a pained face.

"I tried to readjust the scuba tank on my back, thinking I could maneuver backward and get unstuck, but I cut off my air supply. I remember trying to fix it, being panicked and then confused, and thinking I saw dark shapes or glowing dots moving around me.

"When I felt something tugging at both my scuba fins, my foggy brain imagined it was a shark. I remember thinking in an almost drugged way that at least I'd have a good story to tell if a shark pulled me out, even if it bit off my foot for payment. I gave in, relaxed, put my arms forward like Superenby to make myself as narrow as possible, and let myself be tugged backwards out of the cave. Imagine my surprise when I reached the surface to find a robot that looked like a UFO with four grasping limbs had rescued me while out for a practice run." Kai sketched an oval slightly larger than their plate and then mimicked grasping hands snaking out.

"The glowing object I'd seen had been the intended practice target. The guy in charge of the robot hauled me aboard his boat and apologized profusely before asking me questions about his robot like I'd volunteered for a focus group. When I finally asked him how he knew about the cave, he said he saw it in a dream the night before and felt a strong urge to check it out right away."

Kai paused, probably to let the mention of dreams sink in, or possibly to catch their breath. Wend needed the break to process a cascade of emotions from fear to relief that had hit hard despite Kai sitting alive and well in front of them to tell the story. Matt glanced over with a sympathetic frown, as if he could sense how the story affected Wend, but Kai continued without checking on their audience.

"The target robot came back with video footage of the cave. We watched that on his phone while he ran another test where the rescue robot got to hunt down and rescue the target. The video footage didn't show anything exciting from either run. The cave grew narrower and narrower the deeper the robots went. In short, the discovery wasn't going to make either of us famous, and it wasn't well designed for human explorers.

"But my rescuer invited me out to dinner, and it was a good dinner," Kai raised their eyebrows and gave Matt a lopsided leer. "I might have blown him for it afterward, but he bored me with a long talk about power dynamics and believing his dream sent him to me for a reason."

Wend checked for any reaction from Aljon, but he listened attentively with no sign of judgment. "I kept coming back for dinners and whatever else with him and eventually drifted into this big poly family. You've probably already guessed that guy was Matt. What you might not have suspected is I started having my own dreams that led to useful discoveries after that."

"Environmental science discoveries?" Wend asked, eager to see how this all tied together but not ready to dissect various near-drowning experiences today.

Kai tapped their nose. "One of them might be of interest to you. I found an illegal dumping site that led back to a company called IdeoBios. They were trying to modify bacteria to recycle plastic bottles into a sealant that could fill cracks in concrete or asphalt. They got as far as signing contracts for test sites on actual roads, both here and on Oʻahu. Turned out, their sealant dissolved fast when exposed to salt water. They couldn't get another round of funding and decided dumping their entire supply into the nearest available salt water provided the easiest way to dispose of it."

Wend couldn't believe even a struggling company would risk that, although they reasoned waste disposal fees might be high on the island. "Did the island patrol investigate?"

Kai lowered their eyebrows and gave Wend a flat look. "I reported what I found to local and regulatory authorities two years ago in July. Nothing ever came of it. Nothing ever will."

"I'm not always good with subtext," Wend said, choosing blunt honesty as the way to deal with both Kai and Matt. "Are you saying no one cared enough to investigate or someone actively suppressed the investigation?"

The look Kai gave Wend didn't grow any warmer. "I'm saying I've got nothing else to give you. I wouldn't even have replied to Miko's request if you hadn't started telling that story last night. But I don't think either of us should pursue this, certainly not through regular channels."

Setting down a samosa they'd forgotten they were eating, Wend leaned into the table and spoke directly to Kai, "You're saying whatever brought Matt to rescue you also helped you find out about the earlier dumping and led me to both the shrinking plastic island and the new dump site here. But you don't want to do or say anything about whoever or whatever might impede a formal investigation."

"I didn't say any of that." Kai rolled their head forward in what looked like a conscious effort to relax. "But I wouldn't disagree with anything you said."

Wend suspected they were still missing subtext but changed tack rather than poke at whatever bothered Kai. "I don't suppose anyone sequenced the original IdeoBios bacteria?"

Kai's head popped up and their eyes went almost comically wide, as if they hadn't considered that idea but wished they had. "Not the authorities I called, I'm sure. IdeoBios probably did, but they'd have no reason to tell, even if you could track down whoever owns the rights now."

"Would the island patrol have collected evidence from the crime scene that we could test?"

"No one official is going to help you," Kai said with a shake of their head, as if Wend were being completely unreasonable. "Anyway, you probably couldn't get a usable sample after so long."

"Would you show me the dump site you found?" Wend didn't understand Kai well at all, but they'd said something positive about Wend's sincere curiosity earlier.

"How would that help?"

"I'm working on microbiome research for the Marine Census Project. I already used my sampling robot at the two sites I came across before. I could collect samples from the site you know and see if there's anything still there that matches." Wend picked up the samosa they'd set down and finished it in two bites.

Kai and Matt exchanged a long look loaded with meaning Wend couldn't pretend to interpret, but neither of them felt staticky. If anything, Wend felt more and more settled.

All four of them ended up in a green carshare heading up the coast. Wend had stopped by the condo to drop off the tart pan from the night before and pick up their sample bot and another glass kitchen container like the one the plastic bottle from Honoliʻi Creek still floated in. Whatever bacteria were in that water appeared to have eaten away at least an inch from every edge of the bottle in the last two days. Wend asked Viola if she could take a new picture. Since Shelly wasn't around, Wend and Aljon let Viola know their plans and that they wouldn't be back for dinner.

Sitting up front with Matt, Wend encouraged him to tell about his life, all the usual biographic details that would normally be filled in before discussions of kigurumi or sea cave rescues. That reversal made it easier for Wend to prioritize and absorb the mundane details. Matt had been a successful businessperson, or what he jokingly called a "marine lifestyle entrepreneur," since his mid-thirties. He'd gravitated toward Hawaiʻi as more resorts wanted to offer customized adventure sports with water jet boots and backpacks or uniquely accessible surf, snorkeling, and scuba alternatives. He never promised anyplace more than two years exclusive rights, and the publicity from high-end early users launched several products into mainstream popularity. "By the time I started making rescue robots, I didn't need the money. I identified a non-profit that could better manage requests for sending free robots where they'd do the most good with enough oversight. I don't want to be responsible for anyone dying due to a bungled rescue attempt. I could barely handle that with the extreme sports crowd."

"People have died using your stuff?" Wend felt gut punched on his behalf.

"Yeah." Matt sucked in a breath, but kept his eyes on the road.

"A lower percentage than die from surfing or scuba," Kai volunteered from the back.

"I didn't mean—" Wend began, then started over, "I can't imagine how I'd feel if my sample bots harmed anyone. I don't know if I could go on training people to use them or make more. I wish you didn't have to deal with that."

"Occupational hazard."

As Wend wondered how to change the subject, Aljon asked, "Can you explain how you chose a non-profit to distribute rescue robots and what they did? We're supposed to help with something like that, at cost rather than for free, on a project our friends started."

Matt slid easily into volunteering his insights. Wend listened, impressed again with Aljon's social skills. Not only had he changed the subject neatly, but his interest showed through as obvious and real. He'd also tactfully left out Shelly's name or mention of details she might not want discussed with people she didn't trust.

The last part of their drive had them headed toward the ocean, on a barely paved road that passed between forested areas and farmland. That gave way to a dirt track with a turn off for a "spiritual retreat" before dead ending at the top of a cliff.

"This is the dump site?" Wend asked.

"Yep," Kai answered.

"Are we allowed to be here?"

Kai rocked their hand back and forth in a "so-so" gesture.

"Kai's related to the people who own the land," Matt volunteered.

"But don't expect a fond welcome if anyone finds us. We should head down." Kai threw a coil of rope over their shoulder.

Wend grabbed their bot, and Aljon took the empty glass container.

Kai led them down a steep but well-maintained path. When they reached a calm rocky beach at the bottom, Wend wondered if visitors from the spiritual retreat came here and possibly maintained the path. Plenty of shade blanketed each side of the small bay. One side was anchored by mangrove trees that Wend recognized easily by their claw-like roots. The other featured a different species with large spoon-shaped leaves and what appeared to be nuts.

"Are those edible?" Aljon asked, following Wend's gaze.

"Both the nut and the fruit," Kai answered. "They're tropical almonds, and they're an invasive pest. Not that the mangrove trees are native either, but the almond trees will crowd them out as well as any natives. Then their seeds float out to sea and land elsewhere."

Wend wondered if Kai spoke as an academic or as a local in that moment, and how much they differentiated between the two. "Where was the original dumpsite?"

Kai led them behind some mangroves near the base of the cliff. There was no plastic left to be seen, but Wend hadn't expected it two years later.

It wasn't high tide, but there was enough water for Wend to take samples. Aljon collected water, soil, and detritus in the glass container afterward.

Wend walked along the edge of the bay, taking samples where waves occasionally splashed up past their knees. Matt joined them, walking slightly up shore. "This isn't a safe spot for swimming. Do you need to go out any further?"

"I'd planned to." Wend looked wistfully out into the ocean, then back at Matt. "But it doesn't look that inviting here. And my sample bot doesn't do rescues." With a wince, Wend checked to make sure Kai was out of earshot and Matt hadn't reacted poorly.

They scooped up their bot as a honu rode the surf into shore. Although usually referred to as a green sea turtle, it was gray and brown with dark scaly flippers, but Wend thought it was beautiful. "Look at that. Guess this must be a good beach."

They couldn't see past the cliffs on either side of the small bay, couldn't guess why a honu would choose such a place. Viola's theory about Wend attracting sea life came to mind unbidden, but Wend wasn't ready to discuss that. Instead, they considered honu visiting this spot as vectors to carry PET-eating bacteria across long distances, much as the giant manta ray could.

Wend and Matt kept still and gave the local life space. Behind them, they heard Aljon pointing the honu out to Kai, and both of them chuckling as they shared some joke.

After a few moments in the sun, the honu made its way back out to sea. Wend took a couple of final water samples post honu.

As they headed back to the others, Matt asked, "Have you had a bad experience with the ocean?"

Wend refused to guess what they'd done to elicit that sort of question now. "A few, but many more positive ones."

As they headed back up the cliff trail, Matt said, "There's never a good way to ask, but did you ever have a near-death experience, like Kai's?"

The way Kai had described their cave exploration and rescue, Wend had experienced a flash of fear, but not reflected on it afterward as a near-death experience. That had probably been Kai's intention as the storyteller. While they had mentioned accidentally cutting off their air supply, the entire tale had rolled out smoothly like a cocktail party anecdote, the kind Wend could never manage. But the tone had shifted when Kai mentioned being directed by dreams, echoing how Shelly had mentioned feeling steered in certain directions after her drowning attempt as a teenager. Wend hadn't noticed that sort of change in their own life, and this didn't feel like the right moment to share the story they'd already told Aljon.

Wend appreciated that no one could see their face as they hiked single file up to the waiting car. "Yeah, 2015, on the California coast. But it's not a story I want to tell right now."

"Always your choice," Matt said. "One more question if you don't mind, did anything like that happen when you were a kid in Hawai'i?"

"After this, you should tell me why you asked, because I hadn't connected those events. Yet." Wend's stomach filled with ice. "Supposedly, I was rescued from the underside of a pier near my house when I was a toddler, between one and two years old. No one even knew I was missing. I'd never gotten into trouble at the bay near my house before. By the time my step-brother spotted me, I'd wrapped my arms and legs around the last support beam at the end of the pier and closed my eyes. The pier was at most ten meters long. But I was facing toward shore and taking breaths after each wave came in. They said I couldn't catch my breath enough to scream, and I'd swallowed a lot of water. But I clung like a barnacle and never lost consciousness. I'm not sure it counts as a near-death experience."

"You wouldn't know if your flying dreams started before or after that, would you?" Matt asked, already shaking his head as they reached the car but not looking Wend's way.

"No. Is that your theory? Near-death experiences lead to flying dreams? Along with certain birthdays?" Wend tried not to dismiss the idea, remembering how Aljon had helped them connect their second near-drowning to an increase in their dreams and intuition. If Matt's suggestion applied to more than flying dreams, Shelly might feel the influence as more external because she'd grown up without it, before nearly drowning as a teenager. Whereas Wend experienced their flying dreams, feeling guilty lies as static, and being drawn to particular people or places, as inherent to their truest self. They wondered if what came before could be any truer than whatever changed in them before they turned two. They also wondered how it all related to shared birthdates but came up blank.

They'd thought boarding Viola's boat might be their last chance to unravel the mystery of their flying dreams. Now the dreams they'd struggled to understand their whole life appeared to be only one path into a puzzle that increasingly resembled a maze. Matt sounded confident and one step ahead at every turn, while building partly on childhood conversations Wend thought he'd doubted or dismissed. Caught between the sting of past rejections and the remembered terror of nearly drowning, Wend felt both drawn to and uncertain of Matt now. Moreover, they were unsure about whatever factor, internal or external, drew them to Matt.

Wend came back from their thoughts to find a car door open in front of them after everyone else had piled in. They hurried to catch up as Aljon quietly asked Kai, "What was the rope for?"

"Just in case."

Wend reinterpreted Matt's concern about swimming from an unsafe beach.

Matt plugged a destination into the carshare and explained, "Kai isn't the only one who started having flying dreams after almost drowning. Every time I've been able to verify someone's flying dreams, that person had survived a near-death experience that involved the ocean."

"Verified? How many people could prove what they saw came from a flying dream?" Wend asked.

A staticky feeling grew between them and made Wend think Matt was going to lie. Then he took a deep breath and said, "Six that I've tested and proved to myself personally. More that I can't verify, and none of that is really mine to tell."

Wend wasn't sure if the static dissipating meant Matt had decided to tell the truth or if he'd learned to hide lies from people like Wend. If they were right and the emotion involved mattered, people might train themselves to block the relevant emotions. But Matt had made it sound like multiple people at Friendsgiving sensed Shelly's lie. It seemed likely that more of them had flying dreams than just Kai. If so, Matt probably knew more about those aspects of Wend than Wend did.

As the driverless carshare pulled over and parked by a cluster of trees and a circle of benches, Matt said, "I thought we should visit at least one viewpoint before dark. Not that we're on the right side of the island to see sunset, but the coast here is striking, even in evening shadows."

Stepping out of the car, Wend heard ocean all around them, or at least on three sides. They walked past what seemed to be a gathering or outdoor teaching area and watched waves crashing less than twenty meters out to each side. Ahead of them a narrow strip of land stretched into the sea.

As they walked forward, Matt said, "The Kauhola lighthouse used to stand here. Long before that, King Kamehameha I used it as a family retreat. Some say he taught his wife to surf nearby."

There were cliffs and crashing waves on all sides, but no people aside from the four in their group. The wind ruffled their hair like gentle fingers but smelled salty and fresh; Wend could have been back at sea.

"Tourists mostly go to the Pololu Valley Lookout. It's worth seeing, but better when you have time to hike down to the black sand beach," Kai said.

Wend realized the light was fading and the sun setting even as they studied the curving bay to their left. "Where were we before?"

Kai came to stand beside Wend, studied the coast and then pointed confidently. It wasn't that far as a bird flew or a turtle swam.

Wend looked down at the rocks and crashing surf beneath where they stood and decided there was no safe way to collect a quick water sample, even with the rope Kai had carried before. "What's it look like to you, as someone who grew up here?"

"This part hasn't changed like down by Hilo." Kai stilled as they studied the coast. "I don't remember visiting this exact spot as a kid, but I've taught kids and college students here recently. Right now, I appreciate not having to watch out for anyone."

Wend recalled a few stunts they'd witnessed while working with students in recent years, especially the ones who would have tried to collect a water sample from these cliffs at night, no matter what Wend counseled. They shook their head and sighed. "I know exactly what you mean."

By the time the sea sank into darkness, only the foam of the waves reflecting any light, Wend's stomach growled eagerly as Matt said, "Now on to that dinner I promised you."

The large restaurant in Kohala, near the northern tip of the island, surprised Wend with its quiet comfort once inside.

When Matt found out Wend didn't drink, he suggested they try a
liliko'i daiquiri mocktail. Wend loved that fruit in any form and readily
agreed. Aljon and Matt ordered the same, but Kai asked for a margarita
instead.

As soon as their beverages arrived, Matt collected his and stood. "You
can bring the drinks upstairs and see some recent creations by my favorite
artist."

He seemed to enjoy playing host or tour guide. Wend and the others
followed him up a wooden stairway hung on all sides with colorful quilts.
Wend felt incredibly out of place with the extravagant—but delicious—
drink in hand as they entered an art space they never expected to find
above the small-town restaurant.

A quiet gallery surrounded the stairs, crowded with paintings on the
walls and wood carvings and ceramics on shelves. Matt led them to a rear
wall where fanciful glass sea life, some made into lamps or nightlights, sat
below the paintings. "Aren't they amazing? Verilyn created all of those."

"Wow." Wend didn't know what to say. They stared at a nautilus made
from marbled blue glass and could only ask, "How?"

"You should come by sometime when she's working, and it will make
a lot more sense. That's called copper foil technique, or some say Tiffany-
style stained glass. Each little pane is cut, sanded, and wrapped in a strip
of foil. I can't begin to explain how complex fitting it all together gets,
especially for three-dimensional shapes like these. But she solders, stains,
and polishes, and somehow it all works out for her."

Aljon asked about a lighthouse with a tiny nightlight at the top, "Is
that based on the one that used to stand where we visited?"

"I don't know," Matt said.

Kai shook their head, clearly not knowing either, but perhaps feeling
they should know.

As Wend studied a panorama with seaweed and fish, recent images
raced through their mind forming a sort of gestalt. "Did she make the
bamboo stained glass by your front door?"

"Absolutely, although she used a different technique for that."

"I really admired that, and this," Wend said, still studying the fish.
"Please tell her."

"I will, but I hope you'll come visit more. She's home most of the time. You can tell her yourself and ask her all the questions I can't answer."

Wend nodded. "How many people live there?"

Before Wend could worry about how that might sound given Shelly's tirade, Matt answered without missing a beat, "Four full-time, and two more whenever they're on this island. I have an apartment in Honolulu, because I do so much work there. A couple other people are in relationships with one or more of us and stay at the Hilo house whenever that's most convenient. Greta visits twice a year, and others have guests like that regularly. You'd be welcome to stay with us anytime. You too, Aljon."

"We can't really have you over to our condo, at least for now." Wend hated to mention that, but preferred to have it out in the open. Matt nodded, probably intuiting the situation with Shelly. As a way of reclaiming their personal agency, Wend offered, "I'll give you my email and cellphone number. The cell is for work, and I hate phones anyway, so that's mostly for scheduling. But you can have my permanent email address. Even if I drop off the map for a couple months, I'll always check it when I come back. I promise I will reply eventually."

Matt smiled and took the contact information like the gift it was.

19.

BY THE TIME they'd finished dinner and driven home the night before, Wend had been exhausted in every possible way. Matt filled the silence by playing favorite music from his phone over the carshare stereo. He turned out to be a huge fan of geeky, humorous songs and introduced Wend and Aljon to Jonathan Coulton, Mega Ran, and Molly Lewis.

On Monday morning, Wend woke from dreaming they were a black shelled limpet with their mind replaying a song about an octopus. It was not as humorous in the new context.

They pulled on their relatively nice clothes, the outfit they'd originally intended to wear to Friendsgiving with the long-sleeved black rash guard and the gray travel slacks. They packed their drybag with their latest samples, the phone they'd been issued, the laptop Shelly had lent them, and their ID before setting out to find the Marine Science building at UH Hilo. Based on Miko's directions to the class on Saturday, they located a low white building with a roof full of self-adjusting solar panels on the makai side of campus, an easy walk from the condo.

Wend spent the first two hours completing forms and mandatory virtual trainings. They'd barely begun digging into real work when they were summoned to meet their new boss, Dr. Lorelei Kahale. Her office was small and institutional tan, but contained a large window overlooking trees and lawn, as well as students loitering in a parking lot.

"It's good to finally meet you, Dr. Taylor. Never before have I been copied on an island patrol report before receiving intake paperwork for a new staff member." Kahale spoke without standing from her desk. Her dark hair and darker expression, along with her squat frame and hunched way of sitting, put Wend in mind of a small dark storm cloud. This cloud crackled with static, like there might be lightning at any moment. Wend couldn't tell if Kahale was being deceptively polite to hide much greater anger or duplicitous in a more standard managerial or academic manner. Even if they trusted their ability to sense lies more than they ever had before, it wouldn't help them decode people who lived a façade full time.

Wend closed the office door behind them and sat without being invited. "I filed the report because I found a dump site while collecting water samples. Does policy here suggest not reporting such things?"

"You should at least notify PR about any matter involving island patrol." Kahale lifted a printed page with notes scribbled on it from her tightly filled in-box. "The island patrol copied the Maunakea Rangers on this, and Miko copied me on a query to university staff. Most irregular."

"Irregular" was a word Wend heard frequently from supervisors, although the tone wasn't always so cold. Shivering vulnerability succumbed to a surge of righteous indignation. Sincerely wanting to get to work tempered that. This university was the only game in town with the Marine Census Project and they'd hitched a ride across an ocean to get here. "I only had contact information for you and Miko, but I'll let PR know right away."

Kahale set down the island patrol report. She leaned forward and seemed to be taking Wend seriously as she said, "You realize tons of plastic washes up on our shores every year?"

"I remember plastic collecting in an ancient fishpond in Kāneʻohe Bay, where I learned to swim as a baby." Wend knew they lacked subtlety but thought their boss should realize Wend had some local stake. The condescension annoyed them, but mostly they wondered if Kahale talked down to everyone as a power play or specifically wanted to unnerve Wend. "The site I found Friday was an inlet beside a stream where someone had dumped a truckload of plastic from the road above."

"Why were you sampling there anyway?" Kahale asked.

"I arrived in Hilo before a holiday weekend. Part of my contract is for my sample bot to travel with me. As the designer of the bots and manager for the microbiome portion of the Marine Census Project, I take samples from any waters I visit that connect to our oceans." Due to Kai's warnings, Wend didn't elaborate on the unusual bacterial activity they suspected. They'd never have mentioned their dream to an academic or work contact in any case.

After a long moment during which Wend tried and failed to maintain eye contact, Kahale said, "I noticed your contract requests accommodations for group teaching situations. I trust working with Miko was acceptable."

"They were extremely helpful in all ways." Wend believed in giving credit where credit was due but wondered if they were missing subtext.

"Good, we're primarily an undergraduate department. Sometimes you may have to work with less experienced assistants." Kahale made it sound like a threat, but Wend had no age bias about who they worked with or taught. Humans presented so many challenges to Wend that age mattered relatively little.

Wend's head ached already and they wished they could unravel if their new boss disliked them for being older, having accommodation requests in their contract, or solely for filing an island patrol report about local dumping. Whatever the case, Wend struggled to improve that initial impression. "I understand. I'm happy to be here."

Kahale tapped a keyboard and glanced aside to her computer screen. "It appears you've switched locations frequently with the Marine Census Project."

"Yes, my doctoral work focused on citizen science and I travel between sample sites to conduct trainings, validate procedures, and assure adequate sampling."

"Well, Miko is in charge of those bots and the sample lab here. They'll be your direct contact for logistics and scheduling. Let me know if you need anything else." Kahale inclined her head toward the door in dismissal.

Once finished, the meeting didn't seem as terrible as first contacts with some of Wend's past supervisors. Wend was only a little chilled and shaken. They warmed quickly walking between buildings to track down a university PR person, who seemed amused by the awkward new hire showing up in person, but was willing to take a report about their island patrol interaction.

Wend returned from making their PR report to find the lab Miko had mentioned on the far side of the Marine Science building. The sample processor was tucked into a rear corner of the tightly packed, white-walled lab. A counter on the other side supported a centrifuge, sink, and fume hood. Miko stood at a counter near the entrance, quality checking new entries for the Marine Census database.

"Aloha, Dr. Taylor. I'm uploading data from your samples right now."

"Thanks, I brought more." Wend pulled the new set of samples from their drybag. "Do you know how long it will take to process these?"

"Is it urgent?" Bright red sneakers and leggings poked out from beneath the white lab coat Miko wore as they stepped around the counter.

Wend hoped there wasn't a rule against open toed shoes in the lab, or that any such rule wouldn't be enforced. They didn't own anything but water sandals at the moment. "Not exactly. I want to compare a couple of new locations with something I saw elsewhere."

"Guess we each enjoyed our weekend in our own way." Miko cheerfully took the samples and loaded them into the processor. "I can have the results online in a couple hours. If you're going to analyze large amounts of sequencing data from different data sets, you might want to work in the Marine Science Library across the hall. Otherwise, the lag time for remote logins can be a problem."

"You are the very model of a modern marine postdoc," Wend said. They didn't expect Miko to catch their musical reference, but were glad to see them smile anyway.

Wend set up in a quiet corner of the single-room Marine Science Library. A grid of small windows along one wall saved the room from being overly institutional, but a wide awning made the sunlight subordinate to LED panels in the ceiling. Four rows of semi-enclosed, matching wooden desks paired off with a haphazard assortment of unmatched chairs. Wend chose a desk with an ergonomic chair probably handed down from someone's office space and a desktop computer already set up to access the Marine Census Project.

They analyzed the results from the plastic island and marked genetic sequences that increased sharply in concentration after the giant manta ray everted its stomach. One unidentified DNA sequence showed a 94 percent overlap with a known sequence for *Ideonella sakaiensis*, higher than with any other known member of the genus *Ideonella*, which reminded Wend of the company name Kai had mentioned, IdeoBios.

Ideonella sakaiensis turned out to be the original PET-eating bacteria discovered in Japan in 2016. Its genome was publicly available, along with a great deal of analysis on the two enzymes it used to break down PET plastics into environmentally benign substances. Wend caught up on the available research while running an analysis of the Marine Census data to create possible phylogenetic trees based on either the similarity or alignment of genetic sequences related to the plastic island sample or the 99 percent similar sequence from Honoli'i Creek. To search the entire data set would take weeks, so Wend set the parameters to search recent samples first, starting with those taken around Hawai'i and the Central and South Pacific. Whenever Miko loaded Wend's new samples, they would be included in the analysis automatically.

Settling deeply back into the work, Wend lost track of time. They noted references and wrote up introductions for both scientific and popular reports delineating what they might have found. Once they knew to look for the previously unidentified PET-eating bacteria, it showed up not only at the beach Kai had led them to but all around Hawai'i and surrounding islands.

Other than Wend's samples from the *Nuovo Mar*, the Marine Census contained next to no data from open ocean, and Wend regretted that more and more as they attempted to trace the spread of the novel bacteria. They tried mapping currents, migration routes, and travel patterns for sea turtles and other ocean megafauna to connect the tiny dots of data they had from isolated island research posts.

Based on the preliminary phylogenetic analysis, Wend knew what the rest of each article needed to explain. An aggressive new plastic-eating bacteria had spread across the South Pacific in the last couple years. While it could have existed in small reservoirs before, the bacteria alone couldn't have survived and spread in open ocean. Until they understood the dispersal method, Wend couldn't prove it was engineered or released in Hawai'i, but the local concentrations hinted as much. Not enough was documented for Wend to do more than pose suggestions and questions, but they intended to use what they knew, both officially and unofficially, to promote further research.

Only when Miko knocked on the desk next to them did Wend look up and realize the windows had grown dark and the building silent.

"Time to lock up for the night," Miko said. "You can stay and work with the doors set to auto lock when you leave, but I didn't want you to accidentally lock yourself out of the library when you took a bathroom break."

"Thanks," Wend said. "And thanks for getting my new data online. It's been very useful."

"Well, feel free to mention me in your blog or any future publications," Miko suggested in a dry tone, as they shut down other workstations in the room. "I sent a workshop schedule for your approval. Tomorrow will be soon enough for that."

"How many roles do you fill in this department?" Wend asked, as Miko shelved some paper journals.

"I'm the only postdoc in a department without grad students. Elsewhere, a lot of grunt work to keep grants and file necessary documents falls on grad students. Here, I do everything that's not teaching or administration."

"You handled administration and teaching with me," Wend pointed out.

Miko pressed a finger to their lips. "Shh. Don't give anyone else ideas. It benefits my research and future publications to start more locals collecting samples nearby. I'll see you tomorrow, okay?"

"Thank you."

"'A'ole pilikia."

Wend finally made it home to an empty condo around eight that night and relished the time alone. They ate canned soup, took a shower, and started a load of laundry before Viola and Shelly burst through the door laughing.

"Oh, Wend, you're home," Viola said. "Aljon's spending the night on the boat. I've got an offer for our tuna pics and story that you are not going to believe."

"I take it you're celebrating?" While a bit put out by the sudden noise, Wend was glad to see both Shelly and Viola pleased about something.

"No, we went out to dinner," Viola said.

Shelly looped an arm around Viola's waist. "Yes, we're celebrating. Our contracts with Mehta were finalized today, too. We're all set for the next two years."

Even Wend caught the way Viola stilled at those words, her expression hardening, despite Shelly using Mehta's last name rather than Hans.

Shelly stiffened beside her, and Wend missed the raucous good cheer of a moment before. The silence stretched.

"I made progress on the plastic-eating bacteria, too," Wend offered belatedly. Both Shelly and Viola approached, looking interested, or at least seeking a distraction.

Setting out their borrowed laptop on the dining room table, Wend pulled up their most polished draft for a popular science article, and walked Shelly and Viola through the graphs and phylogenetic trees. "The new *Ideonella* species doesn't show up before 2037 in any samples I've found so far. It's 94 percent similar to the wild form reported in Japan in 2016."

Wend paused to let both Shelly and Viola scan the introduction but started again before either could voice questions. "There's another sudden jump to a new variant in 2038. Most of that shift is linked to a third enzyme that already existed in related bacteria, and probably came from an extremely lucky genetic exchange. I suspect that enzyme accelerates the breakdown of PET plastics at local ocean temperatures. Whatever it does for *Ideonella* must be extremely advantageous, because it dominates almost immediately."

Shelly picked up on what Wend hadn't included. "You said this was 94 percent similar to the wild form found in Japan in 2016. But you've found no natural link from there to these new forms in 2037 or 2038. Isn't that suspicious?"

"It is, and I think I know the missing piece, but I can't prove it. If we publish this first, it's less likely to be suppressed or cause trouble. I thought you'd appreciate that." Wend waited while both Shelly and Viola processed what Wend wasn't saying.

"You'd better tell us the rest," Viola said.

Wend risked a glance at Shelly who had her arms crossed but didn't look like she was about to shout or storm out.

"In 2037 Kai reported illegal dumping by a failed company called IdeoBios. They'd been allowed to test engineered bacteria that were supposed to break down PET plastics to make a sealant for roads here and on Oʻahu. But the sealant dissolved with relatively minor exposure to salt water. I haven't tried to track down who might own rights to any of that. Right now, there's no proof I even know about IdeoBios, and current laws say they can't patent or copyright a genetic sequence, only their production and application techniques. Otherwise, the imperative to make public all data from the Marine Census Project would be impossible. If I publish data based on multiple samples legally obtained by researchers and citizen scientists, everything I share about the sequences will be publicly available."

Much to Wend's shock, Shelly started laughing and shaking her head. "I assume your new friends don't want to be associated with any of this either."

Wend decided that comment didn't count as disparaging their friends, since Shelly seemed amused by their similarity to her. "No, but there's a very helpful postdoc who said they'd appreciate a mention in anything I publish. I thought I'd thank UH Hilo, among others, for supporting the Marine Census Project in the scientific paper and give a shoutout to Miko in the blog and educational publications, for their help with local classes and sample processing."

By that point, Viola had finished reading the popular science draft and plopped down with the laptop to scan the potential journal submission and blog posts. Instead of arguing over submission strategies or how the data came to them in the first place, Viola smiled up at both Wend and Shelly. "With my photos of the giant manta ray and the plastic island, this bacteria story won't get buried, flushed, or swept under the rug."

On Tuesday, Wend brought in larger sample containers. Some included chunks of visible plastic the bacteria were consuming. They'd carefully labeled the contents from the glass container Doreen provided at Honoliʻi Creek and the one Aljon carried for their excursion with Kai. While the sample bots around the Pacific collected a great deal of useful DNA, sequencing and imaging live organisms remained the gold standard and might provide clues as to how the bacteria survived and traveled between known plastic feeding grounds.

After all they'd seen, Wend wasn't surprised to find Miko working alone first thing in the morning in the lab across from the library.

"Aloha." Wend tentatively greeted Miko, who hunched over the sample processing machine at the back.

"Aloha! Good to see you, Dr. Taylor!" Miko came forward immediately. Peeking out above their white lab coat, Wend counted three layers of tops with different necklines in pale yellow and two shades of blue. That caused them to look down and notice Miko's sneakers were yellow today, before they disappeared behind the counter and the larger sample containers Wend had brought. "What do you have here?"

"I need to get full sequencing and lab analysis for a tentative identification of new organisms from yesterday. Can you do that here, or is there some other lab on campus with a sequencer?"

"Sadly, no." Miko frowned with their full bottom lip pressing out, but only for a moment. "You'll have to file a request for processing at UH Mānoa. I'll help you get it expedited. You should have approval in time for our intercampus transfer at noon."

Miko brought up the necessary form on the computer at the front of the lab and made sure Wend filled in every section correctly to avoid delay. Instead of feeling patronized, Wend tried to go with the flow of Miko's enthusiastic work ethic, already unable to imagine the Marine Science Department without them.

Two hours later, Miko burst into the library as Wend huddled at the computer in the corner where they'd worked the day before. "I don't know what happened, but your sequencing request was denied!" Their voice rose too loud for a library, but the two students working there both had earbuds and barely looked up at Miko's theatrical entrance. Wend realized they'd never seen such strong emotion from Miko before. While their usual cheerfulness didn't register as staticky or fake, their outrage on Wend's behalf—over denied paperwork—struck like a force of nature.

"Quick, is there another project code you could file the request under? Does it relate to work you did at a previous location or while traveling here?" That force of nature tapped a yellow sneaker on the floor, waiting for Wend to get over their moment of awe at Miko driving full speed ahead in defense of Wend's sample.

"The fresh samples are from Hawai'i," Wend said slowly, wondering what the problem could be. Wend had double-checked the request form and included links to all the cataloging they'd done in preparation the day before. Kai's hints about suppressed investigations shadowed Wend's thoughts, but faded in light of Miko's determined assistance. "The documentation for the new variant and its spread drew on data from across the Pacific, including samples I took while traveling here."

"Great. Bring up the sequencing request form again." Miko gestured impatiently at the computer station Wend used in the library. As Wend brought up the form they'd filed earlier, Miko continued, "I found a code for Marine Census Project samples that relate to more than one project site. It will go through the project headquarters for approval instead of UH Hilo. Let's see if we can get that response by noon."

Wend entered the code for the new request as Miko suggested.

After Miko rushed off to cover a lecture for a professor, Wend kept their account window open. Less than an hour later, their request with the new code went through with Betta Acosta signing off on it. Wend relaxed and wondered if they could introduce Miko to Betta someday. Both impressed Wend with their unflagging energy and ability to find a solution to any problem. The Marine Census thrived due to researchers like them, and so did Wend.

For the time being, Wend set up their next blog entry to better acknowledge the postdoc and sent a quick thank you email to Betta. If Wend stayed on Hawai'i and wanted to pull their own weight, they'd need to figure out the bureaucracy and why such a basic request had failed the first time. It seemed paranoid to blame the initial rejection on Kahale's apparent dislike for them or whatever Kai hadn't quite said. Wend set the thought aside and sank into running deep analyses based on recently added microbiome samples.

By Wednesday, Wend had put in more hours than they could be paid for, given their part-time assignment through the Marine Census Project. They'd been up at dawn, taking their sample bot around Radio Bay and up Hilo Harbor to Reed's Bay Park and beyond. Wherever they worked, Wend liked to establish a daily or weekly baseline for their local marine biome. A quick rinse in a beachside shower allowed them to walk directly to work, carrying their bot alongside and wearing their usual rash guard and shorts, which had dried by the time they reached UH Hilo.

The computer in the corner of the Marine Science Library had become their office in the absence of any assigned space. Several people involved with the microbiome aspects of the Marine Census Project sent excited questions and requests as Wend poured out new analyses. While researchers assigned to each location tended to do deep dives into their own local projects, the overall data set was expansive enough to provide a multitude of research opportunities for academics and graduate students. Wend had a broader view across geographic areas than most. They could connect findings and draw out interesting comparison data and hypotheses, which they described with plenty of notes for others to pursue as thesis work or the basis for new proposals and grant submissions. Wend enjoyed that work and knew it catalyzed the microbiome portion of the Marine Census. As a side benefit, it usually appeased supervisors who found Wend "irregular"—or worse.

20.

BACK AT THE condo over a tasty dinner of Mediterranean vegetable stew and cornbread, Shelly laid out her latest ideas, complete with mission statement, business plan, articles of incorporation, bylaws, and application documents. There were paper copies spread across the table, and Viola, Aljon, and Wend each received digital copies as well. Shelly tapped a paper. "We'll name the non-profit 'Seaward Generation' and then the hydrogen generation systems can be 'Seaward Generators.'"

"Love it," Viola said. "I'll design the business cards. Do we have job titles yet?"

"Whatever you want." Shelly pecked Viola on the cheek.

Aljon slurped his stew noisily, but he seemed to be teasing the two, not objecting to the show of affection. Wend smiled at his goofy happiness and tried to stay positive in the moment.

"Creative Director," Viola declared, posing as she framed her face with her hands. "Do you want to be Executive Director or Founder?"

"Neither of those sound like they do anything. On paper, I'm already the 'incorporator' and you're all 'members of the board.' But I'm keeping the minutes." Shelly briefly raised the tablet in her hands, "So how about Non-Profit Administrator?"

"That's no fun," Viola complained. "We should call you the idea rat."

"Rats on boats are bad for publicity," Aljon said in an overly serious tone.

"Ideas are more like worms anyway," Wend said without thinking.

With a whoop of delight Viola tapped into her phone, "I'm all for putting 'Idea Worm' on your business cards."

For some reason, that caused Shelly to glare at Wend and Aljon. "Clearly Aljon should be the 'Maritime and Shipping Director,' since he knows the most about boats, and Wend should be 'Head of All Microbiomes.'"

Wend raised their soup spoon to Aljon and said, "I think you have more influence on the microbiomes within this organization, since you do most of the cooking." Wend thought the joke was funny, but it only caused Shelly to purse her lips further.

Viola seemed not to notice. "Head Chef, Chief Bottle Washer, and Supplies Coordinator," she suggested to Aljon.

Shrugging as he sliced more cornbread, Aljon said, "Not like I have anyone to give a business card to, but I'm happy to be Head Chef."

Wend attempted to reset the sails, as it were. "Is there something for education or keeping a blog? I'm still not sure what I'm doing here, except enjoying free housing."

"Education Director? Outreach Specialist?" Shelly suggested.

"It's not likely to matter to my resume. But Aljon should have a scientific title in addition to whatever else. Maybe he should be the Outreach Specialist?" Wend suggested. "What would help later if he wants to work with local environmentalists to provide clean drinking water and storm protection for people in the Philippines?"

Viola's eyebrows rose. "Is that what you want to do, Aljon?"

Wiping up the last of his stew with a chunk of cornbread, Aljon winked at Viola. "If I can't stay on your boat forever, I've been thinking about it."

"You should definitely be involved with the fundraising aspects, build a philanthropic network." Shelly typed more into her notes than she spoke aloud.

"Invite them over for dinner. I'll cook." He smiled as he said it, then added, "Anyone want tea or hot chocolate? There's fresh mint growing in the planters that I could probably make into tea or mint hot chocolate."

There were enthusiastic nods all around.

Wend cleared the table as Aljon took a brief trip to the garden. After several minutes of making the condo smell minty, Aljon served Wend mint hot chocolate while the other three tried his new tea.

Shelly added lemon to her cup and said, "This is perfect."

"I like it fine without the lemon," Viola said.

"I think I'll try an iced tea next time," Aljon offered, sipping his own.

"I like this version of hot chocolate. Thanks for suggesting it." Wend sipped slowly, appreciating the faint trace of mint with their favorite drink. The scent lingering in the air might have been enough to change the taste, but either way Wend appreciated the deep chocolaty overtones and the warm mug in their hands.

Shelly picked up her tablet again. "I think our business meeting is officially over, but Mehta forwarded some questions from a reporter. It's a public relations piece for his company as they convert an older factory in Aotearoa to produce our hydrogen generators. They asked, 'How was the Seaward Generator originally developed?'"

Wend noted the reporter had been told the new name before they were, but didn't complain. They listened to Shelly read her answer, explaining how four friends dedicated to a carbon neutral lifestyle had realized they needed carbon neutral supply chains, green power grids, and zero emissions transportation options to achieve that goal. Wend hadn't heard Shelly call her previous partners friends before, but knew that sort of intro was good for marketing, even if Wend found the distortion staticky and unpleasant.

Shelly continued reading aloud. "The developers settled on hydrogen fuel cells as the most promising option in the 2020s and saw marine shipping as lagging the farthest behind in phasing out fossil fuels. They experimented with existing ideas for electrolysis from seawater, using nanomaterials and adjusting nickel compounds to improve longevity and prevent the decay of underlying metals. Their solution managed ten times the electric current by stacking multiple layers of three different carbon compounds between charged layers doped with nanomaterials. When that optimization turned out not to scale beyond a generator powered by two to three square meters of solar panels, they brought their solution to small-boat fishing organizations and long-range cruising businesses and clubs. At that point, fuel cells cost between four and ten thousand dollars. The Seaward Generator prototype cost that much again, but if mass-produced, it could be much cheaper. Unfortunately, the economics at the time didn't support commercial sales. Shelly Svoboda was the only member of the group who transitioned to the non-profit sector. It wasn't until the lucky rescue of Hans Mehta's father that Shelly found the partnership needed to mass-produce the Seaward Generator for both private and humanitarian use."

Setting down her tea, Viola slow clapped at the end of Shelly's recitation. "And the unnamed three friends from the twenties cheered silently from the sidelines."

"They should be glad I don't call them out as the back-stabbing scum they are." There was a sudden, grating harshness in Shelly's tone.

"What?" Wend asked, too intrigued by the sudden burst of honesty to bother with false politeness.

Jaw tight, but voice more level, Shelly said, "The two men in the group bailed as soon as it became clear there was no high-value first-market niche to exploit. The other woman stuck by me until we failed to strike a deal with a couple of the larger NGOs or the emissions credit start-up fund du jour." Shelly made a face. "And she was dating one of the guys by then."

Wend wondered if she wrinkled her nose at the idea of dating a man or the possibility the romantic partner influenced the other woman's decisions.

Holding up a finger, Viola said, "She got them to sign all rights over to you." Viola's motives for defending the other woman were similarly obscure to Wend, and lacking context was annoying.

"Which does simplify things now. Always good to have a lawyer in the group." Shelly took a deep breath and flicked to another document on her tablet. "Our registered agent for this non-profit is a lawyer I know from the Green Energy Alliance who's based in Honolulu."

Following their own train of thought, Wend asked, "Did one of the early developers have a beard or look like Matt?" They worried once they said it that this had been too direct, but Shelly didn't look upset.

She shook her head and let out a noise between a cough and a snort, "That was Ned. He came long before. Yet another man on the take who destroyed a group of friends. I should have learned then not to trust friend groups with men." Before anyone else could speak, Shelly realized what she'd said and reached out to clasp Aljon's hand across the table. "You don't count. You're family and better than all of them."

Wend's stomach twisted as they cringed on Aljon's behalf. They steadied their hands around their remaining half cup of Aljon's special mint hot chocolate and said, "I haven't seen much difference among genders as to greed, loyalty, or who destroys friend groups. Someone always leaves, usually belittling me and others in the process."

"Congratulations. That's much more optimistic than my take on men." Shelly thumped the table. Wend glanced again at Aljon, but he was keeping his eyes on the table.

"I guess a lot of the people I've known were neurodivergent, queer, or otherwise outside the mainstream to begin with, but larger systems are naturally more chaotic. Destroying part of any ecosystem may destroy the rest, if there isn't a good replacement available. I don't see that it has to be about gender. Saying any gender is bad, even with a couple exceptions, harms everyone, including named exceptions." Wend hid behind their chocolate but couldn't drink any. Thoughts of all the groups and friends who'd disregarded or abandoned them weighed heavy in their chest. Moments of gender discrimination they'd lived or witnessed stacked up like one jammed lane among many within a chaotic intersection of roaring, honking memories.

Shelly stared at Wend for most of a minute, frowning. "Yeah, you're entitled to your trust issues, and you probably end up in different sorts of groups than I do. Back when I was relatively young and idealistic, I entered a communal living situation with half a dozen women in Seattle. We fixed up a house and garden and practiced the 90s equivalent of free love, mostly by pairing up." Shelly shook her head, probably signaling some level of self-deprecating amusement. "There was always pressure to form relationships between whoever was available or left out in any given month or year, but it never felt forced. I was happy there until Ned came along with his beard and his crystals and his striving to find balance with his so-called feminine side."

Viola placed a hand on Shelly's knee and said slowly, "I will never defend Ned, but think about how that sounds."

"What? I'm a TERF because I criticize one guy who played on 90s sensibilities about sensitive new age guys?" Shelly sounded honestly confused for a moment. "You know I dated Doreen and staffed a clinic that provided HRT when insurance wouldn't cover it for twenty and thirty-somethings."

Wend tried not to show how weak that defense sounded to them, half wishing they'd never asked about Ned in the first place.

"I know." Viola tilted her head toward Wend, who didn't understand why until she added, "First you're raging against men, then singling out Ned who might be seen as sincerely exploring his gender."

"Ned was a swindler who couldn't be sincere if he tried. Which he didn't."

"Rant against him all you want. I believe you, but you're not just talking to me or other women now."

Shelly's drawn-out sigh had Wend cringing again, on both Aljon's and their own behalf, even before Shelly said, "If I have to check every word, I just won't tell this."

Aljon, ever the peacemaker, reached across the table to take her hand this time. In a voice barely above a whisper he said, "Say however much you want. I hope you'll never see me as a swindler, or even insincere."

With a pat to Aljon's hand, Shelly squared her shoulders before continuing. "Yeah, you're nothing like Ned. I'll keep it simple and say, I wasn't the only person in the Seattle group that Ned pressured into relations I wouldn't call consensual, partly by saying we shouldn't be hung up on the fact he was a man. I told him to his face that he wasn't a man so much as an abusive patriarchal prick. Others were more indulgent or couldn't handle confrontation. The whole arrangement fell apart within six months of him moving in, and it's true, I haven't been able to see men with beards, especially bushy beards and bushy hair, the same way since."

When Shelly finished her rant staring at Wend, all Wend knew to say was, "I'm sorry. I know what it's like to be pressured into sex you don't want and to see a friend group or even people you view as family fall apart over sex and relationships." They were trying to frame a further response about how treating Aljon as an exception didn't help anyone, especially if Shelly implied he was less like a man because he was ace. But Wend didn't want to speak for Aljon and knew they had to choose their words carefully.

"Yeah, I bet you do." Shelly pressed her lips together and curled her hand on the edge of the table.

Wend came up short, replaying the conversation in their mind, they wondered if Shelly intended the threat that Wend heard or to disparage Wend's demisexuality. Whether threatening to expel Wend from this group or implying Wend threatened the existence of the group, the edge to Shelly's voice seemed to place them in the Ned category rather than safe with Aljon. Maybe it was guilt by association with Matt, who Shelly apparently judged as a swindler and insincere because he reminded her of Ned. Even if Wend could excuse some lingering trauma responses, they weren't signing on as Shelly's therapist or to take her abuse.

Aljon set his teacup down with a clatter and said, "We've all had bad experiences with being misunderstood and pressured."

Viola blinked at him and then glanced in Wend's direction. "So, we try to do better. This time, we've all been thrown together a little abruptly. Even if it doesn't last for the two-year contracts Mehta offered, we can try to respect each other and not leave anyone feeling used or deserted. Agreed?"

They all agreed, even Shelly. It didn't make Wend feel much better in the moment, but they would appreciate the housing, shared food, and friendships for as long as they lasted. The mint hot chocolate Aljon had given them was amazing, even if they had to leave the table to reheat it.

After finishing up with a few more questions and tentative responses for the public relations piece, Shelly added, "The journalist also wanted a picture of me with the prototype and of you three on the boat. Perhaps our new Creative Director," Shelly stretched the title out while tilting her head toward Viola, "could arrange for that tomorrow."

"Care to spend your lunch break on the *Nuovo Mar*, Wend?" Aljon asked.

Sighing as they finished their last sip of hot chocolate, Wend said, "So long as I'm done by two. Miko and I are training a student group from Waiakea High School."

"No problem. Meet at the boat at noon." Viola turned to ask Shelly, "Is this supposed to look candid or do they want a certain image?"

"Human interest, authentic," Shelly scanned whatever correspondence she had. "Wear the sort of clothing you wore the day you met Mehta."

Wend cradled their empty cup. At some point they would need to expand their wardrobe, but evidently not yet.

Aljon tried out a new recipe for lunch the next day, a variation on Cornish pasties filled with jackfruit, mushrooms, and radishes. Wend accepted one as Aljon picked them up in the dinghy.

"Might as well eat, Viola has her shots all planned out and the sails ready to go."

Raising the sails for a picture while still at anchor seemed a little silly. Luckily, there was nearly no wind in Radio Bay, and at least for the moment, they had sunshine and blue sky.

Wend took two bites of the pasty and said, "This is amazing. I didn't even think I liked jackfruit."

The way Aljon laughed made paddling look like nothing more than a shrug of his shoulders. "You were missing out then, because jackfruit is high in fiber, vitamins C and A, several minerals, and antioxidants. Besides, it's a great substitute for meat in old recipes, because of the texture. The mistake people make is not respecting that it's sweet. I used barbecue sauce and mustard to flavor this. Glad you like it."

As soon as Wend and Aljon were back aboard the *Nuovo Mar*, Viola sent Shelly out in the dinghy with a camera to a prearranged distance and angle. As Wend hastily wiped their mouth, Viola goaded them into position. She instructed both Wend and Aljon on where to look for the best lighting on their faces as she raised the sails and kept calling out photo instructions to Shelly. No one complained; Viola in skipper-mode blended perfectly with her approach to puppet mastering a photo shoot.

Shelly took several more posed shots once the sails were positioned to look right without moving the boat anywhere. Wend suspected they were photographed more times in half an hour than in their entire life up to that point.

Afterward, they had plenty of time to stow the sails and relax on deck enjoying the sun. At least, Aljon and Wend relaxed. Viola and Shelly busily sorted through the digital photos, deciding which to send.

Before Wend left to teach their class for high schoolers, Viola handed them a small stack of business cards with an abstract background of blue and green tones that conveyed the motion of waves in conjunction with a flowing font that announced "Seaward Generation."

"These are gorgeous," Wend said sincerely.

"Thanks." Viola looked pleased.

Shelly said, "We'll all need to start networking. Maybe you can find connections in academia as our Education Director."

Wend froze. They doubted they'd be useful at networking but avoided shaking their head or arguing. They believed in Seaward Generation. If they didn't understand how to do the job now, that gave them more room to try out creative approaches.

Surprisingly enough, at the end of a three-hour joint training for the sailing team and environmentalist clubs from Waiakea High School, Wend ended up listening to a shy and serious student talking about an islanders' association that spanned not only the Hawai'ian Islands but others across the Pacific. "They, um, coordinate efforts by governments and non-governments for ocean stuff and land stuff. They have, um, liaison units for each island, and lots of the people are field reps for big international groups."

When the student, whose name Wend had totally forgotten, as they tended to when working with large groups, appeared to be waiting for a response, Wend tried, "Do you think some of them would like to work with the Marine Census Project?"

"Yeah, I mean, I posted about this training and linked the page for other projects but, you know, this isn't on every island."

"There's an interest form at the bottom of the page. Someone might be able to visit and do a training or even hook them up with a microgrant to assemble a bot and run a local project." Wend had been packing up sample bots as they spoke. The student wasn't trying to make eye contact. Went kept their gaze on the now sealed bag.

"Oh, yeah, that's good. And if someone sails to a larger island where there is training, maybe they could take a sample bot back home with them?" The kid kicked at the ground. Wend really wished they were better with names.

"Taking a bot back might require making special arrangements ahead of time, but encourage them to fill out the form. It would be great to have more people take samples while sailing between islands. I recently took samples all the way from the Marquesas to here."

"You said. I want to sail to Tahiti when I graduate."

"Maybe you can apply for a grant or set up a project."

That got a big smile.

Wend thought about this kid sailing all that way, hopefully with a more experienced skipper. Then they remembered their new business cards and pulled one out. "Here, you can tell your group about this new opportunity as well. For those who want to sail long distances or live someplace where they use hydrogen fuel cells but don't always have a reliable supply of hydrogen, there's a new generator that might help, and pretty soon there will be ways to apply for one to be donated or to buy one and give one to others in need."

"Thanks, I'll look that up and pass it on."

After a few more minutes of hesitant conversation, the student left. Wend looked around to see the others had already gone, but Miko quickly closed the distance between them.

"You do attract the earnest ducklings," Miko said. "Did you give Keanu a business card?"

"Oh yeah, I received them today for a non-profit I'm helping with." Wend wondered if they should offer one to Miko but shied away from the idea. "Did you hear their questions about someone sailing to an island that offered training but wanting to take a sample bot back to their local area?"

"I was too far away to hear any details," Miko frowned as they continued, "but you probably shouldn't give out material for your other jobs at this one. I don't want you to get in trouble."

"Oh." Wend wondered if they'd broken some department or school policy or another one of those unwritten rules they only learned by stumbling over them. They remembered Miko's upset about Wend's first request to transfer larger samples being denied and thought Miko might be a little uptight about proper procedures, but possibly in a good way overall. "I didn't mean to cause trouble. I would have offered them information on any relevant organizations, especially any non-profits. If it helps, I haven't been paid anything, for that job or this one, yet."

"No worries. Not like I'm one to say anything." Miko held their hands out, palms open, and Wend wondered at their intention before Miko asked, "What happened with the late add student from last time who stayed after. Avery?"

"Oh, I knew Avery from over a decade ago. I was their tutor for a while in California." Wend didn't mean to hide that they'd rented a room in Avery's house and all the rest, but that felt private, and Wend wasn't feeling that comfortable with Miko at the moment.

"Did they late add the class to see you?" Miko asked.

"Yes, they'd only known me as Wend before and hadn't known how to contact me."

"I guess that's sweet," Miko said in a not-sweet voice. "It wasn't one of those student-teacher crush things, was it? Not that I'd judge what goes on between two consenting adults, but that sort of thing can definitely land you in trouble."

Wend pulled back, shaking their head. "Avery will always be like a kid to me, as will anyone your age."

The way Miko tilted their head didn't show belief or understanding. Wend couldn't imagine what Miko was thinking, to ask about a student-teacher crush in the first place, but since Shelly had warned about the same idea, it was probably another blind spot in how Wend saw the world.

"I don't know what other people do, but I assure you I'm not looking for any sort of relationship with a student, regardless of age. I won't give out business cards or even mention other organizations either, if that's a problem." Remembering Shelly's suggestion that Wend might network with academics they asked, "Is it okay to talk to other staff or faculty about my non-profit work, if they're interested?"

Miko waved their still-open palms in a too fast movement reminiscent of jazz hands. "Sure, sure. I'm not saying you did anything wrong. I'm all about spreading information and one group helping another. Right?"

"Great," Wend said. They didn't feel great at all. "I hope you'll share with me if you have any concerns or if there's something I should know." Wend left it at that, wanting time to process and take stock.

21.

WEND LIFTED their arms and a stiff breeze buoyed them up, like a topsail or a glider. Instinctively, they rode the wind, scenting sulfur, salt, and fish.

First, they floated to the boat. Aljon had elected to spend the night there, but Wend didn't look below decks, only checked that the *Nuovo Mar* rested safe at anchor as they circled Radio Bay.

They broadened their circuit and swooped across the foggy expanse of Hilo Harbor, following the breakwater along the eastern side and then darting back to explore the dark silhouettes of banyan trees and quiet parklands where they'd taught their first workshop at Reed's Bay.

As the sky lightened, gold reflected off ribbons of cloud over the ocean. A gray mass poked up mid-bay. Curiosity drew Wend closer. In the next moment, a whale pushed high out of the water, displaying the whitish pectoral fins of a humpback.

Wend recoiled as if hit by a bus. Or an iceberg. They quickly rose ten meters higher.

The immense creature rested, content to stay below water after that. One eye occasionally rose above, as if looking for something. No animal had ever responded to Wend's invisible presence before, so they assumed the whale watched for something else. Wend and the whale watched together, but nothing of note occurred.

Making their way up the shore to Honoli'i Beach, Wend spotted a pair of early surfers catching choppy waves. They observed the ocean and inhabited it as naturally as the whale.

Tracking upstream, Wend scouted the previous dump site. The plastic had been fully cleared away. They floated higher, observing that all was quiet and healthy as early birds woke and sang or squawked at the new day.

Clear skies over the land led Wend to Matt's neighborhood. The houses hidden by vegetation at street level stood out clearly from above. Nearly every roof shone with solar panels. It took only a moment to identify Matt's long two-story with four perpendicular planters in the back, one glassed in like a greenhouse, all windows hidden beneath the eaves.

A single bird on his roof greeted the day with a series of cheeps like high-pitched chatting. For a moment Wend remembered a person, Miko, then they were wholly focused on the bird again.

It stood five centimeters tall, blue and tiny, but made by far the loudest sound on the sleepy street. Wend drifted higher, eyes fixed on the bird like a pointer in a presentation, arrow-shaped with wings poking slightly outward and a forked tail behind. Its steely gray-blue feathers grew brighter and bluer as the sun rose above the horizon. There were dabs of white atop the wings and tawny orange surrounded a dark beak.

Then the bird issued a slightly lower tone followed by a sharp chirp and an explosion of flapping wings.

The now silent bird swooped away as a gold and white cat leapt from a thin tree branch onto the roof.

Wend watched the cat sniff about for only a few moments before they flew off to the university. Although the marine science building was still closed up for the night, its solar panels rose to nearly vertical to catch the early sun. Seeing all was well, Wend glided back home, slipping through their patio roof directly into their hammock without spying on any part of the condo.

It rained and then stormed for most of the day. Living in swim clothes meant always being dressed for Hawai'ian weather. Wend took another round of early morning samples, then hid away in the Marine Science Library following up on user requests and searching for emerging or endangered species in the overall microbiome.

Wend couldn't help but smile when Matt both texted and emailed to invite Wend to learn about stained glass, help make gingerbread houses, and stay for Friday night dinner. They agreed and set an alarm to avoid getting lost in their work for too long.

"I thought you should know this room is here, and you're welcome to it anytime," Matt said, opening what looked like a closet door beside a washing machine and shelves full of laundry supplies. "No one will bother you or presume to interact if you come in here. At most, someone might look in to make sure you're alright. If anyone else wants to use this room at the same time, the standard is to not interact. It's meant to be a quiet, safe space."

Wend stepped onto dense carpet over what must be twice as much padding as usual. The carpet contained mottled tones of moss green and tan. It was the only carpeted room they'd seen in the house. The ceiling was twelve feet high, as in other rooms, but a wooden loft covered half the room at about eight feet. Two heavy-duty ceiling hooks with swivels attached supported double lengths of silky fabric that stretched to the floor, like something in a high-end circus performance. One was tied in a knot a couple feet above the floor, making a sort of hanging chair or cocoon that someone could huddle inside. The other hanging lengths puddled where they met the ground, suggesting at least five yards of fabric on each side. The silks were a deep blue, the walls closer to sky blue. Pillows and beanbags around the room displayed various shades of blue, purple, or green, with a few accents in yellow or gold, but nothing large in those bright warm colors.

Stepping in to stroke the sheer cloth, Wend slid their fingers and then their hands and arms along the smooth, hanging folds. Looking up, they noticed two stained glass windows whose patterns suggested birds flying through clouds and sky. The windows were placed high up on the wall opposite the loft. Behind the loft ladder stood a bookshelf and a low table with an assortment of colored pencils, complicated coloring books, Sudoku and other puzzle books, as well as plain paper. There were gauzy curtains that could be pulled around the loft, a low couch, and a huge pile of blankets in one corner. Wend wanted to run their hands across each blanket, which seemed to vary from velvet, to satin, to something plush like their kigurumi fur, but they feared they would never let go once they started.

"This is amazing," Wend said.

"I'm glad you like it," Matt spoke softly, standing barely inside the door. "I want you to know you can come here anytime. There are guest rooms above that can be a retreat if needed. They have doors that lock from the inside if you ever want that, and you could take blankets or whatever from here to there."

"Why?" Wend asked.

"Any reason you have." Matt shrugged.

"I mean, why are you offering all this to me? You barely know me. I can't even remember the names of all your housemates. Are they okay with this?"

"We're a chosen family, Wend. I chose you before I chose any of them." Matt ran a hand though his hair with his brow lowered and then looked up at Wend. "I don't want to scare you away, but the truth is, at any point you could have shown up in my life and I would have shared whatever I had. Everyone here knew at least that much about you by the time they negotiated relationships with me."

Wend knew such a declaration would scare away many people. Possibly Wend should be alarmed, but Matt was at least self-aware enough to acknowledge that. Honesty meant a lot to Wend, and nothing about Matt felt dishonest.

The truth was, Wend would have welcomed Matt into their home whenever they'd had one. At some point they'd learned not to trust most people that way, but Matt had been their first best friend. In some ways they'd let each other in closer than any reasonable older person ever would. What he said sounded uncomfortably close to a love confession. But part of Wend's discomfort in speaking about love was that their emotions formed differently around each person they'd ever loved. By their own definitions, Wend had loved many people in their life, including Matt at one point. Struggling to respond, they could only say, "That may be the sweetest thing anyone's ever said to me, but I'm still uncomfortable. I don't know how to bridge the gap between you as a little kid in a sandbox and all of this now."

"I'm not asking you to negotiate any sort of relationship with me, not even friendship," Matt said. "I know I can be intense about people and ideas I believe in. I don't want to mess this up. But I can't help caring for you and wanting to show that caring in ways you might accept. I've wanted to show you this room since you enjoyed touching my shirt and Kai's."

"That's fair." Wend couldn't help but smile remembering. The connection between that potentially awkward and socially aberrant moment and what was being offered here made intuitive sense to Wend. A lot of what Matt expressed made sense to Wend on a gut level, if they could open up to trusting that. "Who was this made for?"

"I believe we're all somewhat neurodivergent or neuroatypical in our own ways, although I won't speak for anyone else here, and there are almost as many terms for this stuff as there are people," Matt said. "I have some touch sensitivities, although I'm not sure how they compare with yours. But I've always been drawn to textures like these for comfort." He gestured at the coloring nook. "I draw to relieve anxiety, and I'm guessing from your mention of kigurumi that you might know about pet play and age play, both of which I enjoy in a non-sexual context. This room is ideal for both. Tera added the aerial silks recently. Verilyn made the stained glass, although she takes refuge in her workshop rather than here. We've made this room as accessible as possible, given its contents, but she finds more joy in nature and art. Speaking of which, you were invited to see the project Verilyn is currently working on, if you're ready?"

Watching Matt close the door on what might be the most inviting room Wend had ever seen was hard, but the lure of learning about Verilyn's glass creations motivated Wend to move on. "Thank you for showing me that. For offering."

Matt smiled and blinked, looking more like his younger self in the sandbox. As they walked down the hall, he said, "That quiet room and Verilyn's workshop are the two rooms we try to keep the cats out of and therefore have to close the doors."

"Do you have a white and gold cat that goes outside?" Wend couldn't help asking.

"That would be Wheatley. Did he get out again?"

"Actually, I saw him on your roof around dawn. I guess you're one of the few people who won't freak out if I mention dream flying around Hilo at dawn and noticing a bird singing on your roof?"

"Oh no. Wheatley is a scoundrel, but Verilyn is very protective of birds." Matt raised his eyebrows and asked without a hint of disbelief, "Come tell her what you saw, if you don't mind?"

He ushered Wend into another high-ceilinged room with windows along one side. In this one, the window glass was clear, but sheets of colored glass stood on end, like giant books arranged along shelves with vertical dividers. They were sorted by color, but in two sets, one set possibly more opaque or fancy than the other. Three tables stood away from all walls, the center one half-covered with drawings on paper or transparent film. Verilyn sat there, tracing from a pattern onto golden brown glass.

"Wend, I'm glad you came!" Verilyn turned her wheelchair from the table to greet them.

"Thank you for inviting me."

As Verilyn started to gesture toward the table, Matt cut in to say, "Before diving into shop talk, Wend had something to say about Wheatley and a bird, around dawn. I thought you should probably hear the rest of the story with me."

"Well, we already knew he'd gotten out last night." Verilyn shook her head. "Come sit down. Do you know how he reached the roof?"

"He jumped from a tree branch, probably over there?" Wend pointed toward the back right corner of the house, having always mapped locations from their dreams to ground viewpoints easily.

"I'll trim that right away," Matt said, pulling up a chair for himself and one for Wend.

"Can you describe the bird?" Verilyn asked.

Cupping their hands together to show how small it was, Wend said, "Blue, maybe blue gray, in the early light. There was a tawny orange color around the beak and dabs of white above the wings, which weren't tucked tight to its body but poked out a bit, making it a little triangular in shape. Then it had a forked tail that fanned out when it flew away."

"So it got away?" Verilyn asked.

"Yes. It made a sound like this when it startled." Wend tried to imitate the two-tone sound.

Verilyn beamed at them. "Are you a birder? That's a surprisingly complete report. I don't suppose you saw the underparts."

"No, I saw it from above, in a flying dream."

"I figured."

"Really?"

Verilyn laughed so hard it shook her whole body. "Sorry. I hope it doesn't seem like an invasion of privacy now you're here in person, but Matt told me everything he remembered about you from his childhood. As we learned about each other's dreams and extra abilities, you were the reference point. Of course, we had doubts and sought ways to confirm what we suspected. But what you realized about yourself and found words to express as a small child—it's amazing to me even now. You're the seed this family grew from."

Wend's silence reflected shock but not panic for once. They'd known many kinds of families, including several found families, but being the seed for a family they'd never known existed jolted them.

They thought back on the conversation at the condo about friend groups and how cynical both they and Shelly had been in different ways. It made Wend worry that this too would end, that what Verilyn and Matt offered was too good to be true.

"While we're on the subject of privacy"—Verilyn shot another look at Matt—"we're generally careful when talking to outsiders or about one-on-one confessions, but if you tell a story to two or more people in this household, we'll tend to treat it as part of our oral history unless you say otherwise."

"Okay," Wend said. Their mind was already racing ahead to other privacy issues before Verilyn continued.

"So Matt and Kai told me about you being rescued from the last support under a pier in Kāneʻohe. As I mentioned, I was raised there, too. While I still don't know if we met in person as kids, I grew up with that story looming over me, along with constant warnings not to go to the beach alone." Verilyn sounded straightforward, until she rushed to say with a laugh at herself, "I must have been ten before I stopped hearing warnings about something that happened before either of us turned two."

"At least they cared enough to worry?" Wend offered.

With a deep sigh, Verilyn said, "Yeah, I understand why you'd say that. I had your step-brother pointed out to me as the one who rescued his baby sister. I'm guessing the man shouting at him in public that day was your step-father. Can't say I envy you that start in the world."

"My mom was a good person, pretty damaged by the time she left him, but some of that probably predated the marriage."

Interrupting those serious thoughts, Verilyn said, "Enough of that for now. The bird you described sounds like a barn swallow. I'm glad Wheatley didn't kill anyone and that Matt is going to trim that branch." She gave Matt a pointed look before continuing, "But barn swallows are one of the least threatened birds around. They're not native to Hawaiʻi but have been seen here plenty. Over a hundred years ago, a ringed barn swallow from Britain was found wintering in South Africa. They're a cosmopolitan bunch. Much heartier than old Wheatley, who probably shouldn't be leaping off trees at his age."

"Like any of us do what we should at our age." Matt ran an affectionate hand across Verilyn's shoulders.

"He's your cat, through and through." Verilyn rested a hand on Matt's knee. "I'm holding you responsible if he kills any birds."

"Oh!" Wend said, suddenly remembering the privacy concern they'd meant to bring up before. "On the boat, we agreed that with flying dreams we'd try to not snoop, but we couldn't really consider anything done outside to be private from one of us flying in our sleep. Last night I was drawn to check on the boat, the plastic dumpsite, the university, and here. Do you all have rules about this? If I stay outside, is it okay?"

Matt and Verilyn, who had received information from a flying dream as if hearing about someone's day at work, both went a bit wide-eyed for some reason. After a few long seconds, they spoke simultaneously.

"Viola has flying dreams, too?" Matt asked.

"You've already latched on to a territory?" Verilyn gasped.

Wend took a deep breath as they felt a surge of adrenaline and all their muscles tensed. They took a slower breath and mentally listed five things they could see: Matt's purple paisley vest, a black velvet scrunchie holding back Verilyn's hair, the golden-brown glass, a black marker, a pen-like cutting tool probably meant for scoring glass. The room smelled of oil and faintly of gingerbread. That only counted two scents, but Wend was calming fast and didn't want to take too long to respond.

Without meeting either set of eyes fixed on them, Wend said, "I probably shouldn't comment on Viola, except that she knows at least as much about all this as Aljon. And I'm not sure I've ever had a territory, but I get attached to people and places kind of fast."

"If I could, I would hug you," Matt said.

Verilyn playfully swatted his knee before saying, "He's telling you because it's a primary emotional response for him, wanting to express care that way, not because he wants to pressure anyone for physical contact."

"I get that," Wend said. "I always liked watching people hug to greet their friends or hug on TV. Even when I didn't want that sort of touch myself, I liked the sentiment."

"Virtual hugs!" Verilyn chuckled before switching to a dropped topic and a more confidential tone. "My first flying dreams were checking on the homes of everyone in my family, my school, and the places my parents worked. It took over a year after I moved to this island before I started checking around here that way. Sometimes now I need to see the members of my family sleeping safely. I try not to see if they're doing anything else, but I've warned them, so they realize it could happen."

"We're not a prudish lot." Matt smiled, big and brazen.

"Being a prude is not the same as wanting privacy," Verilyn retorted, then added to Wend, "I don't even know where you live and probably wouldn't fly there without spending considerable time in person first. But if I ever do, I'll try to stay outside. From what you're describing though, I'm not sure I have as much control while asleep as you do."

"I may have improved my control while sailing," Wend admitted. It was an odd achievement to realize and feel proud of, but it helped to process their realizations out loud. "I'd appreciate you trying to give me and my housemates privacy if you can, and it makes me feel better to know you talked with your household about it."

"Being around others like ourselves seems to make us all stronger. I don't know if living in the same town counts or if it's more of a personal connection." Matt patted Verilyn's shoulder and removed his hand. "If you want to teach Wend to make stained glass, I should get out of your way." Then before she could remind him, he said, "I'll take care of the branch before setting up for the edible gingerbread houses."

As Matt left the room, Verilyn smoothly shifted back toward the table and picked up a sketch from below her glass and transparent templates. "As you might have guessed, I'm making a gingerbread house out of stained glass. It's for a charity auction this weekend to support affordable housing. The base is safely over there." She waved to a shelf above a desk Wend hadn't noticed before, where four walls of a glass house complete with door, windows, and even shutters stood waiting. "I'm tracing out the roof and chimney now. Then I'll score the glass, break it along the lines as marked, grind the edges to get rid of any jags, wrap them in copper foil, and solder them into place."

In the time that explanation took, Verilyn managed to mark and score a line. Then she tapped the edge of the glass against the table, and it made a clean break. "While you're welcome to watch, it's generally more fun to try a project of your own. Can you think of a flat design with maybe four or five simple shapes you'd like to put together? You can see some examples of ornaments I've made in the box on the desk. Most of them have too many pieces for a first project, but they might give you ideas."

Wend watched as Verilyn scored and snapped another line with ease. As she switched to tracing a new template, Wend went to investigate the box of ornaments. There were plenty of birds, cats, Celtic knots, leaves, and one highly detailed pinecone. But the shape that drew Wend's eye first and that they kept coming back to was a penguin in profile that made them think of Avery. It was the simplest of all the bird ornaments, using only five pieces of glass: orange beak, orange foot, white belly, black wing, black back that included the head in one shallow S-shaped curve. Wend picked it up carefully and brought it back to Verilyn's table.

She looked up as she finished scoring a piece for her chimney. "The S-curve is the hardest on that. Draw yourself a pattern and start with the other four pieces. There are glass scraps in the bin beneath the full sheets. They're sorted roughly by color. Help yourself."

Wend easily selected plain black and orange pieces. In a bin of white and tan scraps, they found an iridescent white piece only slightly larger than what they needed. They brought it back and asked Verilyn, "Is it okay to use this?"

"Oh, that should be lovely, but I'll warn you, it might break when you try to split off the other bits. Let's start with a wing in black." Verilyn set Wend up to trace and cut a pattern then handed them a silver marker that would show up on black glass.

Scoring and breaking the first line for the wing went well. Then Verilyn showed them how to use breaking pliers to split a smaller piece of glass. Wend's first attempt took the tip of the wing with it.

"That's okay, there's plenty of glass. Try again."

Wend ended up making the wing twice. The beak and foot each worked on the first try, but they were nervous for the iridescent white belly.

"Don't worry," Verilyn said, looking up from a grinder with a spinning metal wheel and a reservoir of water to wet the stone. "I'll find you another piece of pretty glass if that one goes awry."

After a few deep breaths, Wend made the three breaks for the penguin's belly without incident.

Verilyn said, "Well done! Let me show you how to grind the edges and put that much together. Then we'll know if we need to adjust your template for the final piece."

While the sound and grit from the grinder were unpleasant, having water involved made it tolerable for Wend. Wrapping the edges of each piece in copper foil tape was simple and something Verilyn could do right beside them, their projects most similar in that moment.

Then Verilyn demonstrated how to use flux to paint the copper and apply a smooth seam of solder. While Wend had done their fair share of soldering with electronics, that had been more about precision dotting than smooth floating. Their seams came out slightly flat or uneven, but after a couple tries Verilyn said, "It's fine, no one who doesn't make the stuff will care."

Wend retraced and tried to cut the S-shaped piece for the body. It took three tries, but they finally came close to the right shape.

Verilyn smiled at their imperfect piece. "It will fit after grinding."

That left Wend grinding for several minutes as Verilyn put the final pieces of her gingerbread house together in three dimensions. Watching made Wend glad their penguin lay flat. As Wend soldered their last piece into place, Verilyn said, "Look at that, a masterpiece on the first try."

"Not really," Wend said. It was nothing compared to Verilyn's creations. "But I'm glad you helped me make it."

"We should wash and then head up for dinner and the next art project." Verilyn showed Wend how to clean the glass and their hands.

Wend carried their little penguin along to dinner.

The pounding of rain and wind on the roof and walls proved more distracting in the kitchen than it had been in Verilyn's workshop, where Wend had forgotten the weather as they focused intently on Verilyn and the penguin. Now half a dozen people prepared pizzas or assembled gingerbread houses, all the rest familiar with each other and the large kitchen.

When Wend sat down to eat the personal pizza they'd loaded with pineapple and mushrooms on a cornmeal crust, they barely heard the hunched-over person across the table say, "I like your penguin. Do you have a plan for where to put it?"

Wend vaguely recalled that the person asking used he/him pronouns and had mentioned his fluffy blond hair was Melanesian, suggesting that constituted at least part of his ancestry. His light hair with even lighter wisps of white offered a striking contrast to his darker skin, and the laugh lines around his eyes were memorable despite Wend's trouble recognizing faces. Wend remembered him choosing cauliflower crust for his pizza but could not place his name to save their life.

Instead, Wend sputtered out a name they hadn't shared on their previous visits. "It's for Avery, the closest to a kid I've ever had."

The whole table looked expectant. Kai and Tera came from the kitchen to sit together, close enough to steal bites of each other's pizza. Wend knew conversations here tended toward longer turns and sharing stories, but the collective attention disoriented them as the person across the table said, "How's that?"

"I'll explain, but first, can you remind me of your name? I can't remember, and I'm really trying." They'd had no problem remembering Tera and Kai's names and had caught that the absent member of the household was named Yasu. For some reason, they couldn't tell this story without at least knowing the names of those at the table.

"People call me Tanny. I call him Matty." He tilted his head toward Matt on Wend's left. "I won't call you Wendy, because that's another name. This group is sadly lacking in nicknames, but what can you do?"

Wend liked listening to Tanny and suspected he'd be full of stories and eager to share. His easy manner was enough to help Wend open up for this more personal story.

"Well, Avery already ends in a 'y.' I started out as their tutor, then rented a room in their house and ended up staying and taking on a more parental role during the great pandemic. They taught me a lot about accepting my touch sensitivities and neurodivergence, both of which they have in different ways." They turned mostly to Matt to say, "Avery introduced me to kigurumi and a very simplified form of pet play. At the time they had a black and white cat kigurumi and gifted me a leopard one. Now they're a penguin." Wend tipped their hand toward the penguin ornament they had made. "And they're studying marine biology at UH Mānoa. They loaned me the tunic I wore to your party after making their own way here from Oʻahu to reconnect. They saved my kigurumi that whole time, like a security blanket, until they found me again and gave it back."

"Like a selkie story in reverse," Tera observed.

"You're not wrong." Tanny wiped his eye.

"How long had you been separated?" Matt asked.

"Eighteen years." Wend felt tears rising in their eyes as they said,

"Their mom told me to stay away and I did. Now I regret it. I should have left Avery a way to find me, at least made sure they knew my full name."

"You didn't meet Avery in the water or rescuing them, did you?" Verilyn asked.

"No." Wend pulled back a bit, not sure what the question implied, but suddenly feeling protective of their connection to Avery. "I was helping with a sensory-friendly morning at the aquarium."

Verilyn hummed.

Kai asked, "They wouldn't happen to have a birthday close to September 4th, 2010?"

"Why do you ask?" Wend stilled, wondering if their original impulse not to mention Avery had meant more than they knew. The fact that Kai possessed even partial information about Avery suggested either a setup, as Shelly had suggested, or a disturbingly thorough background check after Wend arrived.

Matt stared hard at Kai for a long moment.

"It's not private if I learned it online." Kai leaned forward and said, "Aljon's birthday is listed in his social media as September 4th, 2010. I mean, some people fib, but I don't get the impression Aljon would. I felt drawn to him, and within two weeks of meeting you told him all the things we tend to keep secret."

"But he hasn't—" Wend stopped, relieved Kai had simply found Aljon's birthday online, but figuring it wasn't their place to comment on what Aljon, or Avery for that matter, could or couldn't do. "And why would Avery—" They broke off again, remembering the part about people coming into abilities after almost dying. "I don't know what you're implying, but I will never forgive anyone who encourages either of them, even slightly, to risk their lives for this."

"First, we all agreed long ago that no one should risk dying for this." Matt spoke slowly, leaning in the same way Kai had. He took his time to meet the eyes of each person around the table, one by one, starting with Wend and ending with Kai. "Second, two people with close birthdays being drawn to you is weak evidence, as Kai knows."

Kai opened their mouth, and Tera tenderly wrapped a hand around their arm to stop them. Kai sighed loudly and spoke anyway. "I suspected after that first conversation with Aljon. Matt must, too. With four of us together that way it's hard not to feel the pull. If Wend has a strong enduring connection to someone else, someone they've practically admitted shares a near birthday, that's solid evidence. Aljon deserves to know whatever we suspect."

Wend's mind raced. What they felt for Avery had nothing to do with any of these people or Aljon. They'd shared stories with Aljon due to the constraints of life on a boat, nothing more. Except Wend couldn't explain how easily they'd conversed one on one with Aljon or why they'd connected to him much more easily than Viola. Whatever drew them to the *Nuovo Mar* could have been drawing them to Aljon as well. If Kai were right and Aljon was born only a day before Avery, that was a striking coincidence. That didn't mean Wend wanted to admit it could be anything more. "Slow down. We have no evidence. I'm not quite alienated enough to believe anyone I feel close to has to share a birthday with someone else I feel close to. Haven't you heard of the birthday paradox?"

Tanny, Matt, and Verilyn simultaneously said, "23." That reassured Wend more than it probably should that this wasn't some elaborate scam or cult-like confidence game.

"Statistically, you have a 50 percent chance that two people share a birthday in any group of 23 or more." Tanny winked at Wend. "I hit Matt, Verilyn, and Yasu with this right away. It's a classic demonstration of false logic."

"Which would be relevant if I started out knowing Avery's birthday. What I'm saying is I felt the same pull toward Aljon as with Tera, and Wend may have felt something similar with Avery." They clasped Tera's hand on the table beside them as they told Wend, "I barely believed in birthday clusters and being drawn to other people a year ago, but I learned from finding Tera. And I feel a stronger pull to Aljon than I do to you."

Steadying their own hands on the table, Wend said, "How sure are you? What constitutes a birthday cluster and how many do you know about? I couldn't convince myself the birthday part mattered based on only Matt and G—one other person I was drawn to. How does this even make sense?"

Kai raised one shoulder, a rather weak concession. "There's plenty we don't understand. Tera and I were born two days apart. Everyone else involved is your age, give or take a day, but to be fair, that's all Matt knew to look for until he rescued me."

No matter how many people's flying dreams Matt claimed to have verified or how much his chosen family thought they knew about the rest,

Kai's evidence for Aljon—or Avery—being like them felt inadequate, at least to Wend. But they flashed through memories of Viola objecting, denying, going silent for days as Wend offered what clues they had in their stories. They wouldn't shut Kai down that way. "I need time to process and then possibly more information, but definitely not tonight."

Before the silence could build into a knot in Wend's gut, Verilyn said, "Perhaps we should move on to the dessert construction for the evening?"

Dinner dishes were whisked away. Tera, Kai, and Tanny each brought out an already assembled gingerbread house and spaced the bare structures evenly along the table. Matt stayed close beside Wend, silent and steady.

"Letting the frosting that holds the walls and roof together solidify first makes the decorating a lot easier," Kai said in a tone that passed as cheerful.

"We learned that last year," Tera added, with a playful nudge to Kai's elbow.

"Lollies and icing for all," Tanny announced as he passed bowls of each around the table.

"He's gone full Aussie on us." Matt tossed a red candy that Tanny caught easily.

"Not until I bring out the extra biscuits!" Tanny called as he turned back toward the kitchen.

"How long ago did he leave Australia?" Wend asked.

"Thirty-three years," Verilyn said with a snort. As Tanny returned, giving Verilyn a quick peck on the cheek and setting gingerbread cookies that varied from people to star shapes on the table, Verilyn explained to Wend, "When my glass house is auctioned to support local housing charities, they'll also need gingerbread houses for door prizes. We'll give one to them and the extras to local groups, so we do our best to keep them sanitary, and any cookies added as decorations are given away with them. If you want to decorate a few spare cookies for yourself or friends, you can do whatever you like with those. Just wash your hands between eating anything and touching the houses."

"And while we decorate," Matt said, "maybe Verilyn will tell the story of how this household came to be."

"I'd like to hear that," Tera said, smiling toward Verilyn and then toward Wend with unexpected fondness. In that moment, Wend realized their birthday cluster not only included Tanny and Yasu, but Kai and Tera felt connected as well. For Wend, it wasn't a pull that would lead to polyamory, but Tera's looks stirred a warm, protective reaction in Wend.

The full day of intense social interactions was beginning to wear on Wend, but they thought listening to a story while patterning candy onto a house might be soothing. They picked up a spatula full of frosting and a bowl of flat candy disks and began to tile a gingerbread roof.

Verilyn unwrapped rectangular chocolate mints that resembled roof shingles as she said, "Back in the nineties, I was fresh out of law school and determined to pay back my student loans and make my own way in the world. I didn't dare fall into the trap of representing pro bono anyone related to me or brought to me by a relative, so I stayed on the East Coast after finishing law school. I disliked the weather and being treated like a novelty, but I made a lot of money, and the closest I came to Hawai'i was representing this guy." Verilyn leaned into Matt affectionately.

"I never wanted to practice criminal law, but cases involving discrimination or social justice flowed to me naturally. It wasn't until after the second pandemic that I joined a legal movement to fight climate change by going after large corporations in court. The traditional cruise line industry was failing already, and we drove out two big name airlines that circumvented carbon regulations despite having the money and technology to meet emissions targets. I finally sought a license and office to practice law in Hawai'i as we fought to be the first US state to require zero emissions planes and boats for travel within the state and faced legal challenges from airlines, other businesses, and the last federal administration before I retired."

By the time that part of the story was finished, Wend had settled into a calm, productive mindset. They located some tiny rectangular candies to brick up the chimney and felt pretty good about their gingerbread house renovations.

Matt cut thin strings of black licorice to make louvered window shutters on the other side of the same house.

"Those of you who haven't heard this story before are probably wondering how all of that led to the house we share now." Verilyn scanned her audience and focused in on Tera, who was decorating a roof with squares of butterscotch but easily made eye contact anyway. "I'd known Matt from early days, and I'd stayed with him a few times at his place in Honolulu when I didn't want to stay with family there. But I had a grandmother and more distant family on this island, and every time I came to visit, I ended up here. Now, Grandma Maile had always been my favorite grandparent. I wasn't her favorite grandchild until I came back to the islands, not rich, but a little bit famous for my climate work. Grandma Maile kept a scrapbook with every news article that ever mentioned my name. She had friends clipping articles in Japanese for her, and the couple times a paper or magazine printed a picture that included me, she framed it and put it on the wall." Verilyn paused and then pointed at a wall now filled with family pictures, mostly of people in this room. "That wall. When Grandma Maile died, she left me this house and told me to fill it with people I loved, those with whom I wanted to share the rest of my life."

"To her credit," Matt said, raising a cup of coffee, "Grandma Maile knew Tanny and I would be two of those people, and she left the house to Verilyn anyway."

"But she liked Yasu plenty," Tanny said with a chuckle. "That ol' lady knew more about our kind of family than she ever let on. She sure never needed my chosen name and the slur I'm reclaiming explained."

Wend didn't get it at first. When they did, it felt like the moment in their childhood when they first understood pink triangles displayed on pins and stickers. Not only were they pleased as punch to be in the know, but seeing others proudly own their identities still made Wend feel bubbly and warm inside. They smiled across the table at Tanny, who might or might not have observed their slow realization, but who smiled back regardless.

"Speaking of Yasu," Verilyn added, "she won't be back in time for the auction. Anyone else interested in a weekend in Honolulu?"

"I already offered to give up my place if anyone wants it." Kai piled the finishing touches of precision-placed candy onto the best-dressed gingerbread person ever.

"I've got work," Tera said with a shrug.

"Not a chance." Tanny shook his head with mock vehemence. "I'm here to hibernate for the holiday."

"What about you, Wend?" Verilyn didn't try for subtlety. "We fly out at noon tomorrow, and the charity luncheon isn't until noon on Sunday. You could meet up with Avery and give them your glass penguin. There's a spare room at Matt's place. You're welcome to stay with us and invite Avery over if you want. Network with a few NGO types at the auction who might be interested in your Marine Census Project. How long has it been since you saw Honolulu?"

The last question was easy. "I haven't been back to Oʻahu in over thirty years." The rest was complicated. Inviting Wend had clearly been planned ahead of time, before they knew about Avery at least. Visiting Avery sounded great and only fair after all the effort Avery had made to reach Wend. But what if this was too soon or Avery had finals? Affordable housing was a cause that spoke to Wend, and they'd be interested to learn more about local efforts. The charity auction might also be Wend's best chance to network on behalf of Seaward Generation, but they hadn't told any of these people that story yet. At the very least, they should ask Shelly what they were and weren't supposed to tell. Wend selected a gingerbread person to decorate for Shelly, having already finished a couple for Aljon and Viola, and focused on that.

"Honolulu was an early adopter for a lot of green tech. I could show you some of my favorite examples, if you want," Matt offered with hands clasped together on the table, completely ignoring the side of the gingerbread house he'd been fussing at before. "Or you can spend all your time with Avery, or doing whatever you want. But I bet you'll enjoy seeing the other houses at the auction, both art and gingerbread, and I can run interference if any of it seems like too much."

Even if Shelly refused to trust these people and Kai's assertions made Wend nervous, everything said tonight had sounded sincere and true. Wend felt welcomed and wanted to know everyone in the room better. They could check in with Shelly and Avery as soon as they left tonight. For now they said, "Okay, I'd like to come. Where and when should I meet you?"

22.

THE STORM either calmed or hit a lull as Wend walked home. Warm rain plopping almost straight down soothed Wend, as did walking alone. One sideways gust sent water and debris splattering onto Wend's arm, but they wiped it off with their free hand and didn't miss a step.

By the time Wend reached the condo, Avery had texted saying they'd be delighted to meet up anywhere in Honolulu the next day. Wend read the text while slipping off their wet shoes outside the front door.

Full of good feelings, Wend opened the door as they uncovered and held out the plate full of gingerbread people they'd decorated. "I come bearing cookies."

Everyone froze, their annoyed expressions enough to make Wend cringe back. For a moment, Wend wondered what could be so terrible about bringing cookies. They looked down at the plate of gingerbread people then up at the people they'd made them for.

Shelly bent over the table, teeth grinding, a collection of printouts and her ever-present tablet in front of her. "I'm going to need my laptop back."

Viola stood behind Shelly, either rubbing her shoulder or clenching it. "Maybe you should have Wend look this over with you. They designed that sample bot."

Aljon unfroze where he'd clearly been distancing himself in the kitchen area, scrubbing already clean counters. He went back to wiping but didn't speak. The tension in his shoulders suggested he needed a back rub at least as much as Shelly did.

"I can barely wrap my brain around schematics I haven't looked at in years while incorporating suggestions from two of Mehta's engineers. I don't have time to bring anyone else up to speed on this." Shelly spoke through her teeth, clearly trying not to lose her temper. "And I need another screen."

Wend set the cookies down on the table and said, "Just a minute. I'll get the laptop and clean my work off it."

They collected the laptop from their room and started it powering up even as they moved back to the table. They'd kept their documents all in one folder. All their real work for the university had been online anyway. Wend checked that the latest versions of all written work for microbiome projects, the Pacific Tech blog, and various publications were saved online. Then they sent quick notes to Lisa and Ashok saying they might be out of touch for a few days.

"I'm sure the university could issue you a laptop the same way they gave you a phone." Viola's tone sounded helpful but the words felt staticky and were clearly an excuse.

"You could just buy one." Shelly tapped her fingers impatiently. "If all you're doing is writing and sending email, they're dirt cheap."

Wend's brain connected "dirt" to some half-remembered joke about investing in land because they weren't making it anymore. Before they knew it, a song from *Oklahoma!* about belonging to the land ran on repeat in their head as they erased all evidence of their recent work and handed the laptop over to Shelly. Instead of being annoyed by the earworm, Wend found it centered them enough to speak calmly. "I would like to help, and I'm used to bringing myself up to speed on new projects."

Shelly nodded even as she opened a new browser on the laptop. "I'm sure you'll all help in time, but I've seen more NGOs than I can count that were embarrassed or ruined by one small mistake, especially early on."

"Okay." Wend itched to explore every detail of the Seaward Generators right away, to find ways they could be useful and contribute. While technical aspects appealed to Wend as more concrete and knowable, it sounded like Mehta already had two engineers stirring up Shelly's possessive issues there. Instead Wend offered, "If you don't want me looking at the technical stuff for now, maybe I could hand out business cards or find interested collaborators at a benefit in Honolulu this weekend."

"What?" Shelly practically screeched.

That wasn't a good sign. Wend took a deep breath and studied their own knees. "I've been invited to a charity auction to support affordable housing on Oʻahu. There should be people from all sorts of local organizations and some larger NGOs."

"You're going to Honolulu for the weekend with Matt?" Shelly stopped typing, and Wend could tell she was glaring without having to look up.

She was on the verge of crossing the line Wend had drawn, but Wend still tried to steer the conversation in a more positive direction. "And Verilyn and Kai," they answered, in as calm of a voice as they could muster. "Verilyn made an amazing stained glass house for the auction, and I helped make a gingerbread house that's meant to be a door prize." Wend looked up when Shelly tapped a knuckle loudly on the table.

Shelly slouched, appearing more overwhelmed than ever with the papers, tablet, and laptop all arrayed in front of her. "I'm sure you mean well." The words didn't match Shelly's flat delivery at all, and Wend knew they'd failed to break through her preconceptions. Even if Shelly wasn't giving them a fair chance, it brought old doubts flooding back. Maybe someone else would have known how to present the idea better, maybe someone who'd be better qualified to promote the Seaward Generators as well. Shelly continued, "We need to wait until there's a public announcement, possibly until we start production, to add more voices promoting this. For now, let me handle it."

"Fine." Aljon stood at the end of the table, although Wend hadn't seen him leave the kitchen. "I'll go live on the boat until you need me in another photo." His voice softened as he picked up a gingerbread person in a red tank top and blue shorts. "Thanks for the cookies and for trying, Wend."

When Aljon left through the front door, Viola crossed her arms and opened her mouth, but Shelly started pounding the keys on her reclaimed laptop, pointedly ignoring her. Wend suspected they'd be yelling at each other within minutes.

Wend seized the opportunity to flee the room and follow Aljon outside.

He was halfway down the street to the harbor by the time Wend caught up, reds and blues from candies running down his fingers in the rain as he ate his cookie. "I'm sorry you got caught up in that. I probably should have managed it better."

"That's not your job or mine." Aljon sounded calm, but there was a new tension in his tone. "You're still going to your thing in Honolulu, right?" He looked like he had more to say, and the familiarity of the reaction was oddly calming. The urge to fix things. The urge to make peace. Knowing ... knowing that they were not the problem, doing the work anyway, and then not knowing what to say about it.

"Yes," Wend said, trying to let the warm rain wash away their anxieties, to keep them from spilling over onto Aljon. "You could come too, if you want. Kai said they would gladly give up their ticket if anyone else was interested."

"No, thanks, I'll be happier on the boat. Give my best to Kai and the rest." He waved with his half-eaten cookie, ignoring the sprinkle of water running from it onto him.

Wend understood he needed time alone.

Suddenly, spending time alone, burrowed deep in their own sleep sack and hammock, sounded like the best thing in the world to Wend. They returned to the condo and found their way around back to sneak into their own room.

ACT THREE:

EARTH

23.

WEND LEANED into the rush of water and formed the bristles on their front legs into baskets. They strained food from the flow before cramming it into their mouth, savoring the rich variety long hidden by excess salt. The sudden flow of fresh water called them upstream after months at sea as a floating larva. Now they wielded maxillipeds by their mouth—the front legs they were using to scoop in their feast, as well as six walking legs and two sets of antennae. Every appendage tingled and tightened, welcoming the forgotten rush of freshwater. Curling and catching sight of their own translucent, gray and brown mottled carapace and tail, something in the still human part of Wend's mind remembered the handful of freshwater—technically amphidromous—invertebrates native to Hawaiʻi and identified the mountain shrimp, ʻŌpae kalaʻole, or *Atyoida bisulcata*.

In that moment, Wend-shrimp surged upstream, clutching onto pitted black rock even as water surged forcefully in the opposite direction. A white and red menace twice their size grabbed at them with gnathopods like skeletal fingers with serrated inner edges and two large spines.

Fleeing for their life, Wend-shrimp scuttled up the nearly vertical black rock, water rushing against them, food ignored in the need to outclimb the invading skeleton shrimp. Beside them on the rock, a dozen other mountain shrimp climbed, all newly returned from the ocean. Half-grown, they struggled to ascend the steep rock.

A distant part of Wend knew mountain shrimp were famous for climbing the precipitous creeks and waterfalls of the islands. Wend-shrimp only knew a chance to escape, as the mountain shrimp beside them was yanked away, grasped and devoured by the looming invader.

The skeleton shrimp's long antennae grazed Wend-shrimp's tail and they hauled farther up, drawing out of the water for several strides before a new cascade hit them. By now, only half as many young mountain shrimp struggled by their side. The skeleton shrimp rallied below, feasting on the stragglers, unable to climb any higher.

Wend-shrimp held fast while raking in more food with basket-like bristles. They would climb again after feeding. The upper stream would be theirs, a place to feed and breed and in time send larvae out to the sea. Hopefully the skeleton shrimp would not grow too numerous before the next generation of mountain shrimp had to climb their way home.

By two o'clock Saturday, Wend sat beside Matt on the elevated, electric Honolulu Rail, riding past high rises covered with plants. The drybag Wend used as luggage fit under their seat. Matt held a box containing a carefully packed gingerbread house, and Verilyn carried an even larger box on her lap that protected her glass house for the auction. Kai had stowed a backpack and duffel, which presumably held everything else the three of them needed.

"What is that?" Wend pointed at what could have been a steep hill with thousands of windows.

From the seat beside them Matt said, "Eco-architecture. Parts of the living walls with edible plants are fed by captured rainwater. The rest use processed wastewater."

Wend remembered a time when that was considered a joke, but Matt spoke without any humor. Attitudes tended to change faster than budgets, and Wend was surprised by the local predominance of eco-development. "Last time I was here, people argued about the cost of this rail project alone." The window Wend leaned against was half the height of the car with air rushing through ventilation ducts all around.

"When was that?"

"2015."

"Ah, *Back to the Future*. I like to think Marty McFly would get a kick out of some changes we've made here in the last quarter century." His smile wavered. "A lot of people barely believed in climate change back then, or at least the imminence of the threat, but Hawai'i had already signed the Majuro Declaration. By the time these trains started running, the state had reduced greenhouse gas emissions by twenty percent and was planning for completely renewable energy by 2045. We'd started to legislate a managed retreat, to limit new building on this coastline, and were pushing for carbon neutral air travel."

"Lots of islands where I've worked started planning and signed Majuro, but none of them jumped to this. It looks like science fiction," Wend said, still staring makai.

Matt coughed. "I'm sure you heard about the storms that hit Honolulu and especially Waikiki in 2026 and 2029."

Wend had heard. They'd mostly heard people in poorer countries complaining that Hawai'i received disproportionate aid and funding. "2026 brought the worst heat wave and ocean warming since 2016 and destroyed half the remaining coral reefs in the Pacific, but I didn't hear about hurricanes or storms here that were worse than the new normal."

"Miami in 2030 caught the world's attention with the devastation from the hurricane, but the king tides before that weren't nearly as photogenic. The news cycle buried them. Hurricanes tend to dissipate or shift around Honolulu, but every inch of sea level rise magnifies the flooding. Waikiki flooded eight feet deep in 2026. The storm surge backed up rivers and drainage channels. A third of the population, over 100,000 people, had their housing damaged and over half the local businesses closed." Matt lifted the box holding the gingerbread house for the benefit in a sort of shrug as he mentioned the damaged housing.

"Were you here?" Wend asked, drawn away from the window by a hitch in Matt's voice.

"Yeah. The first time. I sent my employees home or to evacuation centers. Only smart choice I made." Matt shook his head but kept talking, soft enough that no one else on the train would overhear. "I singlehandedly dragged fifty- and eighty-pound boxes upstairs to my office and apartment when the first surge hit. Pure luck I wasn't caught on the ground level. I'd been so busy saving inventory, I hadn't told anyone what I planned or where I was. We lost electricity and several cell towers first thing. I had no idea if anyone else was alive within a block of me. No way to communicate. No emergency radio. No news on whether the water would rise higher or how long the flooding would last. I'd never felt so alone. I can't even speak to what I put Verilyn and others through." Matt let out a deep sigh as he looked across to Verilyn and Kai, heads leaned close together and absorbed in their own private conversation.

"The shop downstairs flooded to the ceiling and water soaked up into my carpeted floor until it squished beneath my feet. The building settled such that the windows wouldn't open. I had some food but no water filter. Childhood earthquake training back in California helped me realize my safest water supply was in the toilet tank. Not that flushing the toilet would have worked anyway. For about 24 hours, I lived like a survivalist, without the benefit of training. My head filled with apocalyptic shit. I started throwing up in a corner, probably from nerves. I'll never know. Not like there were any doctors I would have bothered with that in the days right after. I could have broken a window and used one of the paddle boards or scuba sets from my shop to get away. I considered and reconsidered that the whole time, but I didn't know where to go. What was coming next. What might be in the water."

Matt shivered, and their shoulders were close enough for Wend to feel it. They offered their open hand palm up, but Matt either didn't see or didn't want the contact. He continued. "It turned out every wastewater facility shut down at least for a day, if not for weeks. Creeks backed up. Water and sewage pipes shifted, cracked, burst. Roads, fire stations, hospitals, communications—the whole region fell apart. Twenty percent of locals lost their homes and belongings without compensation. At least I had insurance, other shops, another home, a fortune and all the security money can buy. Emergency services shipped me out to Hilo."

He closed his eyes. Wend turned back to the window to give Matt some privacy before he said, "Three years later, when people were arguing it was a once-in-a-century event, it happened again." His hand reached in front of Wend and pointed out the window at a hotel where the bottom stories had been gutted to leave a metal support structure with open-air wooden platforms shuffled in, like Escher's idea of a treehouse. "It took a second catastrophe to convince owners and investors. Businesses that wanted to rebuild in the flood zone after that had to meet a slew of new disaster resilience regulations, not to mention the carbon neutral building codes that new construction faced. Times being what they were, the business community dove into eco-tourism and eco-architecture. By the time investors gave up on Miami, we'd rebranded Honolulu as the city of the future and won a pile of green building grants and architecture awards along the way."

As the train slowed for its next stop, Matt said, "This is ours."

Wend picked up their drybag. Kai scooped up the backpack and duffel. The other two still carried their respective boxes.

Verilyn led them out, onto an open-air platform with screen doors that opened every place a train door did. The platform roof consisted of solar panels that tracked the sun and one wall composed of a latticework filled with vines. The air smelled of salt and kiwifruit, although Wend didn't see any fruit on the vines nearby.

Where Verilyn stopped and pressed for an elevator, a clear view between taller buildings opened up all the way out to the ocean. It couldn't be more than ten blocks away, but everything in that space appeared reimagined into a sort of green-salvage chic. A pair of tall buildings sheltered mangrove trees among arched openings near the bottom and hosted futuristic wind towers in bright colors at the top. "Those draw warm air out while funneling ocean breezes across a cold-water reservoir down below," Verilyn said before the elevator arrived.

"Even the retrofitted buildings have cut back on traditional air conditioning," Matt added. "Most need at least two-thirds natural cooling to come out carbon neutral. Energy costs were always higher here than on the mainland, and natural cooling fits with ancient Hawai'ian ideals."

"More branding?" Wend asked.

Matt shrugged unapologetically. "Does it matter if it gets us this?"

They emerged onto a pedestrian roadway lined with tiny cafes and snack shops. Light awnings and colorful umbrellas shaded outdoor seating. Charging stations at the edges offered community-use electric bikes or scooters. The walking surface consisted of interlocking pavers made of a sand-toned composite Wend couldn't identify but suspected was water permeable, carbon neutral, and locally sourced. A security bot rolled smoothly across the accessible pavers as did a smaller sweeper bot. Several of the city trees had fruit growing in them, possibly lychees, and there were dozens of small white birds perched among the fruit. "I bet you know the names of those birds," Wend said to Verilyn.

"You want a list, or shall I tell you about the little white ones in the closest trees?" Without stopping for an answer, Verilyn continued. "They're called white fairy terns, or manu-o-Kū, and they're the official bird of Honolulu. It's said that sailors used to follow them in to land at night, as a clue to both time and direction."

"I'll have to ask Aljon if he knows them."

"I can do that," Kai said, as they snapped a picture and typed into their phone one handed.

"Oh, he said to give his best to you, and everyone," Wend blurted.

"Yeah, he texted me last night." The resigned smile on Kai's face suggested they weren't happy with whatever else they'd heard from Aljon, probably about heading back to the boat to avoid Shelly's bad mood, since Wend trusted Aljon wouldn't mention Seaward Generation. "I'm coining the term boatbody instead of homebody for him. I've never known anyone that happy to stay on a boat, even alone and at anchor."

"It's a nice place to sleep, like a hammock," Wend said.

"Should we pick up a hammock for the guest room? I wouldn't mind having one anyway," Matt offered.

"I can sleep in a stationary bed for one night. Or on the floor. Probably not a tree anymore. I haven't tried that in a while." Wend tried to make a joke out of it. They were already a little uncomfortable accepting the free flight and guest room, even if they would have gone unused with Yasu absent. But they didn't press too hard to pay, given they might need to buy a laptop before receiving their first paychecks.

As they turned mauka, the quaint shops of the pedestrian zone gave way to more standard businesses, including grocery stores, real estate agents, and bike repair shops. Some looked older and not at their best, but a surprising percentage of buildings were brand new. Wend guessed those had been rebuilt after the flooding in 2026 and 2029. A whole block on their right was taken up by a two-story mall half covered in plants, with what sounded like a small waterfall somewhere inside. It sported deep overhangs above the shopfronts that stretched toward a perimeter of trees and planter boxes.

Verilyn turned, leading them into that mall and a central courtyard with water flowing down walls lined with mosaics and small plants, some of which Wend recognized as parsley, arugula, and cherry tomatoes. Small enclosed pools at the base of each wall provided the waterfall splashing sound effects and probably protected the vertical plants as well. Wend marveled at the architectural magic used to conjure this oasis in the middle of an urban landscape.

"Do you like it?" Matt asked. "It's where we live when we're here."

"In a mall?" Wend asked. Then, realizing they probably sounded more judgmental than confused, they added, "I mean, it's an amazingly nice mall."

"It is," Kai said, pointing to one side. "That's 'Comfort,' the store with the tunics and soft shirts we both like." Pointing the other way they said, "And that is where we will eat chocolate for dinner as well as trying out flights of local hot chocolate." Based on a wooden sign too large to miss, the restaurant was literally named "The Best Hawai'ian Chocolate."

Wend didn't know what to say, staggered by new sights and noises while surrounded by a mall full of people.

"One hundred percent passive cooling. Instead of thick walls and tiny windows, we rely on air flowing over skin to provide evaporative cooling." Matt waved toward the open windows at the top of the sloped ceilings. "The ventilation is healthier than the overly air-conditioned buildings that used to dominate this area. Software modeled sunlight and wind currents before construction started. We leaned into traditionally wide roof overhangs and strategically planted trees to provide deep shade where windows can stay open all day to pull cool breezes through."

He paused and looked to Wend, either checking for questions or permission to continue. Wend recognized the joy behind his enthusiastic ramble and nodded for him to go on. "Solar panels shade parts of the roof garden and a bus stop while providing additional power. The cool water used for the wall gardens and ambient noise comes from a shared community underground system. It's based on heat exchange from a deep ocean water system that we finally completed after thirty years of fits and starts. That pipes water from 1700 feet below sea level, and a couple of beachfront hotels are powered by turbines connected to the micro-grid. There's a similar system back home on Hawai'i. Have you visited the Ocean Science and Technology Park yet?"

Wend shook their head, beyond responding verbally, although they appreciated Matt sharing what must be a second home to him.

"This way," Verilyn said, heading for an elevator to the rear, equally spaced between the two water garden walls.

Inside the elevator, Matt waved a gray card over a sensor before pressing the second-floor button. He handed a similar gray card to Wend and said, "You'll need this for our apartment door as well as elevators or stairs to this floor."

"Thanks," Wend managed, staring at the key card for a moment before following the others into a partially open hallway and then an apartment on the makai side with a sparsely decorated common room.

"Guest room is over there." Kai waved to the right as the rest of them veered left.

It was a relief for Wend to be alone and to close the guest room door behind them. They stood frozen with their back to that door, letting their bag drop to the ground, not yet ready to touch anything. The room was huge, with a roof that sloped from a normal height by a covered balcony up to at least fifteen feet on the opposite side. A door on that wall led to what must be the bathroom. The wall by the balcony was mostly glass doors that opened inward. Each of the other three walls was a different color, muted tones of brown, green, and blue that worked soothingly together. Wend had never stayed anyplace half as nice or as large.

Two enormous beds dominated the room, with bedspreads patterned in slightly darker versions of the walls' color scheme. To the sides and between the beds stood three light wood pieces of furniture Wend thought would be called armoires. They had drawers on the bottom and double doors at the top. Two were latched and locked. The one nearest the balcony had a door ajar, displaying extra blankets and terry bathrobes.

Wend sank down onto the floor and remembered to check their phone. Sure enough, there was a message from Avery saying, "About to board train at UH Mānoa. Where should I meet you?"

Remembering the tunic they'd borrowed from Avery and the shop Kai had pointed out, Wend wrote back. "I know how to find the Comfort store in the mall with two waterfall walls. Is that a good place to meet?"

The almost immediate reply was, "Great! Be there by four." A box at the bottom indicated Wend's university phone didn't accept custom emoji, but Wend figured that part of the message probably wouldn't matter. They sat and breathed for a full ten minutes before checking out the balcony. By then the view of quirky buildings with a touch of ocean in between, the tropical scent from the roof garden and walls, and what they guessed was passive cooling from the balcony air being sucked across the sloped ceiling, all seemed amazing—and only a little overwhelming.

Wend arrived early and had memorized every detail of the window display at Comfort by the time Avery walked up, already removing their headphones.

"You're really here." Avery reached out slowly to squeeze Wend's shoulder. "My favorite person at my favorite store. Have you been here before?"

All Wend could do was shake their head and blink for a moment. "Someone I'm traveling with, Kai, pointed it out as the place with the tunic you lent me."

"Come on, I need to show you something." Avery literally tugged Wend's shirt to steer them inside. Then they let go and led the way to a rack full of pajamas in fuzzy animal prints. "Look!" Avery pulled out a light blue set with big-eyed cartoon penguins. "Touch!"

Squishing a handful of fabric, Wend said, "It feels thicker than it is, like silky thin fleece. What's it made of?"

"One hundred percent cotton," Avery said. "These just came out. I love them. I love this store." Their hands fluttered in excitement.

True to its name, the store was more comfortable for Wend than any clothing shop they could remember. No pumped-in music distracted from the sound of falling water in the courtyard. Water also burbled along a narrow line of clear window planter boxes at the front that didn't involve any soil, only hydroponics. Wend wondered if hotels near the source pipes grew seaweed in saltwater window boxes.

"Hey, hope I'm not interrupting." Kai appeared suddenly in front of them. Wend startled and momentarily resented the intrusion into their time with Avery, but they'd told the group upstairs where they were going and who they were meeting. Kai may have taken that as an open invitation. "Matt sent me with these." They handed Wend a rainbow-striped Comfort gift card with $200 printed on one corner, kept one, and held another out to Avery. "Hi, I'm Kai. I'm guessing you're Avery."

Avery glanced at Wend before saying, "Hi, glad to meet you." They glanced again at Wend before accepting the gift card.

Wend had accepted their gift card reflexively, while wondering if Matt sent Kai in order to seem less intrusive or because Kai loved the store and shared in the gift. Now Wend was caught holding a gift card for what seemed like an outrageous amount, although maybe not in a place like this. They had no idea what to say or do and suspected their blank expression and lack of reaction would become a problem in a few more seconds.

Instead, Kai simply raising an eyebrow, the way they once had while flirting at Aljon, and said, "Don't worry, no strings attached. Matt swaps these things like business cards, or maybe like holiday cards? Not part of either tradition myself, but Matt seriously enjoys giving people stuff, and then people give him stuff and . . . We end up with Comfort gift cards." As Wend finally managed to nod, Kai further explained to Avery, "Matt's Oʻahu shop is at the end of this mall, Matthaios Water Wonders."

"Oh, I've been there," Avery volunteered. "They have snorkeling and scuba stuff for people with sensory sensitivities."

"Yeah." Kai's eyes flicked to the chunky headphones around Avery's neck. "Wend gave him the idea for the Frog Paddler back when they were kids."

"Really?" Avery glanced at Kai's face for a second and smiled. Kai seemed to have that effect on all the young people in Wend's life, whatever the reason. Looking between the two, Wend realized both Kai and Avery were dressed almost identically in soft tunics from the store they stood in, although Kai's was jade green and Avery's a deep wine color. Avery turned their gaze on Wend. "You certainly make an impression on people."

Wend was still reeling from that interpretation, the revelation that Avery already knew Matt's shop, along with the family seed comments from the day before when Kai said, "We're meeting for an early dinner, six o'clock at The Best Hawaiʻian Chocolate. You'll both come, won't you?"

After a deep breath, Wend said, "Can I let you know in an hour? I'll text."

"Sure," Kai said stepping back. "I'll leave you two alone now."

"Thanks, and thank Matt for the gift cards." Wend didn't know if that was the right thing to say, but Kai accepted it with a smile.

Once Kai was gone, Avery asked, "You want to take a break in the roof garden? It's officially a 'safe and quiet refuge.' It says so on the doorway and everything."

"But you wanted to buy pajamas, and now you have a gift card."

Avery hung the penguin pajama set back on the rack and led Wend to the roof. "We can come back."

As they sat on a bench that swiveled to stay in the shade of a pivoting solar panel, Avery asked quietly, "You still write to Lisa and Ashok all the time?"

In the middle of a densely planted rooftop farm with miniature hills arranged to channel warm air rising from below, Wend accepted that the world and people in it might keep surprising them at an alarming rate. The fact that eco-architecture and Avery remembering Wend's constant correspondents counted as good surprises made little difference. "I mailed them each several pages of waterproof journaling from my trip across the Pacific. We've exchanged a few emails this week, catching up on daily life. They're both fine. I need to find a cheap laptop to replace one I was borrowing to do email, blog posts, articles, et cetera, et cetera, et cetera."

"*The King and I!*" Avery smiled proudly at recognizing the reference. Wend's cheeks hurt with how wide they smiled back, even as Avery switched tacks. "There's a shop downstairs that might have a refurbished laptop. I can go with, if you want."

"Let me see." Wend checked their phone for alerts they'd set up. "Not this week. I haven't been paid by either job or for any of my writing."

Avery paused. "Is it that bad? I might be able to lend you enough for a cheap laptop. I used to spend a lot of time wishing that you'd send me letters like you sent to Lisa and Ashok."

Wend leaned closer, and Avery reached out, tugging Wend against their shoulder. "No. I'm sorry. I'd do anything to make those years up to you."

"Bit late to adopt me, even if my mom seems to think it's possible." Avery's arms gently encircled Wend, even as they tensed at the mention of Mira.

They wanted to tell Avery how many times they'd dreamed about adopting child-Avery but couldn't move past the fact they hadn't even sent letters, no matter their reasons at the time. "I don't want to cause trouble between you two. Did something happen?"

Avery held on tighter. "Anyone who's ever come close to me, she perceived as a threat. Sometimes I wish she'd apply her detach with love routine to me."

Wend wasn't sure if Avery had told their mom about spending time with Wend, or if it was a more general statement but, flustered, they managed to get out, "It has to have been hard. I do believe she loved you." The last had been added without consideration. Wend couldn't believe they'd just defended Mira to Avery.

"Yeah, I know." The love and hurt in Avery's voice triggered a cyclone of feelings intermixed with those Wend still carried for their own mother.

They tried to listen past their own emotions as Avery continued, "Maybe she could detach partway? I'm all grown up, fully fledged, on my own. She had a fit when I told her I found you and struck up a friendship again. But I don't want you to worry or do anything about it. You can remember I'm a grown-up now."

"Yes," Wend said, but admitted, "I still want to take care of you, but you always seemed to take care of me back. We can work it out." Avery telling Mira so soon suggested they were still in close communication and there would be all sorts of hazards to navigate. Wend was ready to pledge their support in whatever way Avery wanted, but Avery was already responding.

"Yeah, you were never like other adults. You were more like me but with the bonus knowledge and abilities of an adult." Avery leaned their head against Wend's, and Wend suddenly realized how wrapped up in each other they were in a public space.

When Wend pulled away, Avery let them.

Their gaze indicated they thought Wend distanced themself to say something important. "It might be the emotional equivalent of growing upside down, but I don't think I perceived my mom as much of a parent. So I didn't question Mira's role with you, because I didn't believe I knew how parenting worked. But I knew I loved you and wanted whatever was best for you. I just wish that when Mira kicked me out I'd stuck up for you, and myself, better."

"I understand," Avery whispered even quieter to cut off Wend's rising spiral of worry. "I'd still rather be your kid than Mira's."

"Please don't idealize me," Wend sputtered. "If I'd been around all those years, I'd have made a million mistakes. You might not want me in your life at all."

Avery pressed the back of their hand to the back of Wend's in the small space between them. As they chewed on their lower lip, Wend recognized the mannerism and the struggle to find words from when Avery was small. They waited until Avery responded, "I barely understood what idealize meant when you first told me not to idealize you. Even as a kid, I knew you didn't have all the answers. I couldn't imagine what else you meant."

Wend hadn't remembered using that phrasing when Avery was young. "See, I'm full of mistakes."

Avery shook their head hard and their hand pressed to Wend's fluttered even more rapidly. "I see you. Or I want to. If as an adult I see you as a parent, doesn't it make sense that I'd want to take care of you as much as I'd let you take care of me? Maybe you see yourself as worse than you are and it would help to see yourself through my eyes sometimes."

"I struggle every day to decide who I am," Wend said. "Do you ever feel that way?"

"All the time."

Wend wanted to fold around Avery again, but not here, in the middle of this roof, no matter how safe and quiet the refuge was meant to be. They forced out words instead. "Sometimes I want to become a hermit, or at least retire and not have to deal with so many people. But I'm not sure I'd be recognizably myself if I weren't trying to balance other people's perspectives and my interactions with the outside world. I think I started too late to really know who I am."

"No. It's never too late." Avery's childish tone dissolved, and the words were spoken with the confidence of a young adult, perhaps repeating a therapist. "You seem more confident now, maybe older and wiser." Avery's voice rose and lightened, as if daring Wend to accept the compliment, to see themself though Avery's eyes.

"I don't feel that old. Definitely not wise." As they let the observation about confidence sink in, Wend realized how out of touch with their true self they'd been when they left Avery before. "I'd be honored to try being a parent for adult-you, the way you described, but you know you can have any number of parents, right?"

Avery shifted their hand until one pinkie overlapped with Wend's. "Okay, but right now, I'm glad to have you."

By dinner, Wend was all talked out. Avery had donned their headphones more and more once they returned to shopping. But they both wanted to try the chocolate café, and Avery wanted to meet Matt and the others.

"Looks like someone went shopping," Kai teased as Avery and Wend were shown to the table with Comfort bags in hand. "Can I see?"

Avery eagerly sat beside Kai and started showing them the penguin pajamas and a new two-layer tunic.

Wend sat down beside Avery and across from Matt. They self-consciously pulled out the expensive tunic Avery had convinced them to buy. It had a super soft inner layer, like the tunic they'd borrowed before, and over that was a semitransparent layer of breezy bamboo fabric shading from deep indigo at one shoulder to a pastel aqua at the lower point of a diagonal cut hem. "Thanks for the gift card," Wend said as they held the tunic out to Matt. "Do you want to touch?"

With a smile at the reminder of their interaction over tea a week before, Matt carefully took the tunic and said, "It's wonderful. One layer like the tunic you borrowed"—he glanced at Avery—"and one like my shirt. Are you going to wear this to the luncheon tomorrow?"

Despite the casual delivery, the remark felt intensely personal to Wend. They were surprised to find they didn't mind, perhaps even liked it. "Do you think it will fit in?"

"Do you care about that? You can wear anything you want. If this feels right to you, then wear it." He stroked the back of his hand across the outer bamboo fabric before handing it back.

Not for the first time, Wend felt challenged in a good way by this new group of friends. The openness of the conversation hung like a weighted blanket, like hyper-focused reality. It helped Wend cope with being social.

"How do you do that?" Wend asked. "Every conversation with you is supersaturated. I used to say I was oversaturated when my senses were overwhelmed or there was too much new information to process, but you somehow step past all that."

"Is it good or bad?" Matt asked. The rest of the table's conversation had paused around them, although Kai still made a show of admiring Avery's purchases.

"Strangely comforting, like that store, the roof garden, this whole mall. I usually can't stand malls."

Verilyn laughed. Verilyn had a beautiful laugh. "Ka 'ike kuhohonu. We draw on the deep knowledge of living with the land. We try to create living buildings and to live more truly as ourselves. But in your words, it sounds like an improved 3-D printer."

"I always struggled with words," Wend said, liking Verilyn's take on their supersaturation.

"I'm glad you make the effort," Verilyn said with no sign of static or teasing. "Your words are worth hearing."

The Best Hawai'ian Chocolate's restaurant menu offered a diversion in the form of incredibly detailed descriptions of local ingredients and where exactly they were grown, many on the walls or roof of the mall itself. Each recipe included chocolate, cocoa, cocoa butter, or nibs. Wend craved each in turn while fighting down a jittery sense that they didn't belong in a restaurant like this. Matt suggested they order family style so everyone could try more dishes. Wend breathed a relieved sigh and ordered the spinach salad with walnuts, nibs, starfruit, and liliko'i.

Kai bantered with the server before saying, "I'll add the butternut squash mole to share and a flight of your vegan hot chocolates. Wend, you want a flight to sample?"

"Have you been plotting with Aljon?" Wend joked, and then worried that Kai wouldn't catch their humor.

"I wish," Kai answered with a wink. "When I mentioned the story Viola told that first night, he revealed that the ingredient options he had aboard failed to sway you toward vegan hot chocolate."

Wend melted a bit inside, imagining Aljon sharing that tidbit and Kai remembering and building on it. They ordered the vegan hot chocolate flight.

Avery ordered last, after thoroughly considering the drink options, and chose a flight of vegan white hot chocolates with homemade marshmallows as well as chickpea pasta for the table.

As the server left with their order, Matt fell back into tour guide mode. "Most of the cocoa here comes from the island of Hawai'i, and cashew nuts are only grown on Maui. Almost everything else comes from O'ahu, plenty from urban farming right here in Honolulu. In the last few years, grants to develop damaged or economically depressed sites often required urban farms or public roof gardens along with rain harvesting, solar water heating, and reclaiming wastewater."

"Stop saying it like you didn't have a hand in setting up half of those grants." Verilyn reached out to muss the back of Matt's hair as if he were a kid.

"Hey, I'm bragging about the buildings, not myself." He leaned into her touch and chuckled.

"They're really great buildings," Avery chimed in. "This is by far my favorite mall, too."

Their flights of hot chocolate came and Avery asked, without looking at the server, "Could we get a bunch of teaspoons, so everyone could taste?"

Wend made an effort to look at the server then, a person who couldn't have been over thirty but nonetheless smiled at Avery with parental fondness and brought them a dozen teaspoons.

"I have so many spoons, it must be a good day!" Avery joked before pushing four toward Wend. There were four small cups in each flight, and Avery clearly didn't want any spoons reused. "You try each of mine and I'll try each of yours. Does anyone else want to taste?"

Matt and Verilyn shook their heads, eyes squinting with amusement as they shared a pot of tea.

Kai dismissed them with a casual wave. "They've probably tried it all before. While I usually prefer dark chocolate, I'd love a taste, if you don't mind."

Avery passed them another four. They all had plenty of spoons. "Clearly I was meant to sit in the middle."

As Wend's side of the table began sampling each other's beverages one spoonful at a time, Verilyn asked, "What are your interests, Avery?"

"Nutty," Avery pronounced, presumably commenting on the second dark chocolate, which did have a nutty aftertaste, not from a nut milk but from the cacao bean itself, since the curation card said it was made with rice milk. "I've been studying some of the same Marine Census data Wend works with." As they dipped a spoon into the third dark chocolate, they faced Wend to say, "I'm a bit jealous someone else got to sequence the PET-eating bacteria you found, but I might build my thesis on something else in your samples."

"What?" Wend asked, setting down a spoon and barely noticing the hint of vanilla in the white chocolate they'd sampled.

Avery closed their eyes and hummed, focusing attention on their latest taste while making Wend wait. Kai chuckled and took up their next spoonful.

"Your giant manta ray sample set includes unusual mRNA," Avery said. "If the same correlation shows up with other samples that contain the new *Ideonella* bacteria, wouldn't that be interesting?"

Wend savored a spoonful of a creamy white chocolate made with cashew milk. They nodded for Avery to continue.

"You remember teaching me how some squid, octopus, or cuttlefish species can edit their own mRNA to produce different proteins in proportions needed for new environments?" Avery waited for Wend to nod again. "Most research back then focused on helping humans with neurological disorders. But recent studies have shown those edits can be passed between squid via certain microbes. One species of saltwater rotifer threw off research on squid in an aquarium until the researchers realized the rotifers they were using to clear water and detritus could transport and expel squid mRNA between tanks in the aquarium."

Waving a spoon, Kai added brightly, "I heard about that fiasco."

Avery smiled uncertainly in the face of Kai's enthusiasm. "It's possible some species with complex editing of their own mRNA, like squid, adapted to favor your new PET-eating *Ideonella* bacteria and that adaptation is spreading through the ocean via microbes, like those rotifers. Or the intact mRNA could be showing up through some other mechanism. If we already knew, it wouldn't be an interesting research topic."

The idea sounded unlikely to Wend, but could be revolutionary if proven true. It would offer a more direct route for certain macrofauna to influence others of their species and the oceanwide microbiome. Wend couldn't help noticing how rapidly Avery's focus shifted, from marine protected areas a week before and coral attachments earlier in graduate school, but in the moment they'd encourage wherever Avery's interests might lead them.

"If I'm understanding correctly, based on science from the twenties we could hypothesize that squid-A might edit their mRNA to produce whatever proteins in their gut support a thriving colony of the new *Ideonella*, because that helps them break down PET plastic they've swallowed." When Avery fluttered their hands in excitement, Wend spoke a bit faster. "You're proposing microbe-A passes through squid-A's gut, collects not only the new *Ideonella* but some of those mRNA instructions for building better housing for the new *Ideonella*. Then microbe-A passes both instructions and bacteria on to other microbes and megafauna until microbe-Z happens to pass them on to giant manta ray-Z?"

"Microbe-A would have been microbe-Avery back when you were my tutor." Avery sighed beneath a white chocolate mustache. "Who knows how the story ends? Maybe ray-Zoey ingested both microbe-Zoey and *Ideonella*-Zoey right along with their first meal of plastic. Even if rays can't use the mRNA instructions to benefit *Ideonella*, after that stomach eversion trick, they've delivered everything squid-Xavier needs to better host the new *Ideonella* picked up with their next plastic meal." Avery lifted their fourth spoon and said, "Now pay attention to our current experiment. These drinks are too good to go unappreciated."

Matt stage-whispered to Verilyn, "I didn't follow half that, but I'm still rooting for microbe-Avery's protein-building plans to make it through and somehow help squid-Xavier."

Wend decided to appreciate the story as well, no matter how improbable. They finished sampling the white chocolates and tried their own dark chocolate flight while the others exchanged clever invertebrate stories, mostly from online videos. Wend could have offered several firsthand accounts from their own dives, but appreciated not having to entertain anyone at the moment. Kai had been right, the chocolate at this place was amazing. The third cup in their dark chocolate flight might be a contender for Wend's new all-time favorite.

"We've lost Wend to chocolate bliss," Kai said eventually.

"What a way to go," Matt answered as if it were an old joke.

"This one," Wend pointed at their third cup, now empty.

"That's my favorite, too," Kai said. "It uses oat milk and extra cocoa butter. We already have the supplies upstairs and you're welcome to share."

Wend might struggle to accept gift cards and fancy restaurant meals, but they loved the idea of sharing this new favorite hot chocolate. "Thanks, and with that, I'm full." Wend leaned back in their chair and folded their hands across their middle.

"I hope not," Matt responded. "That looks like our dinner arriving."

Wend groaned.

Everyone laughed, but as dishes were laid across the table, Wend's awareness grew of how their recent meals had mostly been compensation for their work on the boat and then with the condo provided for Seaward Generation. The fact that Matt and his household kept feeding them more and more elaborate meals was a little disconcerting. "I don't think I was ever meant to live like this."

"Why not?" Verilyn asked after the server departed. "That sounds like impostor syndrome. Kick it in the ass."

Wend preferred "alien" to "impostor" but knew both had at times been offensive to others in queer, neurodivergent, or racially-marginalized communities. They still didn't know what to say when faced with such luxury and abundance.

"Listen," Verilyn said, and it was impossible not to. "We can have whatever moral or ethical debate you want later. But the housing and meal we're enjoying here is one hundred percent sustainable. It may take decades to bring the whole globe to zero emissions, net zero or negative carbon, post-scarcity economics, and respect for all human and other life. But I believe that possibility is exactly what we're modeling here." She met Wend's eyes as if reading their mind. "There have been whole decades in my life where I never saw a meal like this. Never surrounded myself with as many friends as I have here. Heck, there were years when I didn't have time for entertainment, relationships, or following the news. I can't regret those times, because I wouldn't be who I am now without them. But no previous version of me would want to give this up now that it's offered. Appreciation is at the heart of all good things."

"Let's eat." Kai served themself chickpea pasta and squash mole then lifted a fork in salute. "One wai."

The expression was new to Wend, but they recognized the Hawai'ian word for water and the sentiment that probably encompassed sharing much more. Dishing up a small serving of salad, Wend caught Verilyn watching. Wend gave her a smile and a shrug, but felt a little flutter inside. They were getting caught up in Verilyn, what for some might be akin to a crush and for others a form of fascination. For Wend it began as an undifferentiated flutter that could grow in different directions. Or not. It felt good. The hot chocolate and salad tasted great. Appreciating who they were with and what they had in this moment seemed like a step in a positive direction.

24.

THAT NIGHT, Avery insisted there would be no problem with them staying the night and sharing a room. Wend sat cross-legged on one of the enormous beds, still in their usual day clothes, when Avery emerged from the bathroom in their new penguin pajamas with long sleeves and long pants. They held a shorts and tee shirt version of the same pajamas. "These are for you, if you want them. They came with the set, but I won't wear shorts or short sleeves. They are super soft."

"Are you sure?" Wend asked.

Avery bounced on the balls of their feet. "Very. I'm glad you like the fabric, because I wouldn't want the short set to go to waste."

"Thank you." Wend went to change and brush their teeth as songs from *The Pajama Game* ran through their head.

When they returned, they unpacked the stained-glass penguin they'd made and carried it to Avery, who now sat on the far bed. "I wasn't sure whether this should be a holiday gift or not, but I never found anything to wrap it in. I made it for you."

"You made this?" Avery's eyes opened wide as if the simple ornament were an amazing work of art.

"Yeah, it's my first stained glass ever. Verilyn taught me."

"It's the nicest thing anyone ever made for me," Avery said. Then they padded across the room to set it safely on their bag, before returning to ask, "Can we pretend I'm in my penguin kigurumi and you can hold me for a while?"

Wend didn't try to unravel if Avery asked that way to improve their own mindset or Wend's. They didn't want to spoil the moment, and Avery looked very cuddly and in need of a break.

Propping up pillows at the head of their bed, Wend sat where there was room on both sides and said, "I'd be happy to hold you anytime. Do you want me to tell a story?"

Avery nodded and crawled up on the bed before curling against Wend's side. Wend stroked their back and told a story that child-Avery wouldn't have been old enough to understand.

"I met Ashok when I was barely eighteen, my first day at Pacific Tech as an undergrad. He was twenty-four, entering the PhD program, and I saw him as the first adult to ever treat me like an equal. We spent twenty minutes trying to find the linen supply station in what seemed like a maze of basement hallways." Wend remembered how they'd recently reframed the puzzle they wanted to solve as a maze with different entry paths. The memory of a new friend working through a maze with them seemed especially apt.

"We found a room that housed two club libraries, one for what they called the Gay and Lesbian Club back in 1990, and the other for the campus Science Fiction Club. We both thought having those two libraries share a room was funny, although there was probably more overlap than either of us guessed at the time. Ashok told me he was gay and had assumed it was obvious from the pink paisley shirt he wore that day. I told him I couldn't imagine caring what gender any person I liked was, but that I wasn't yet sure if I wanted sex or kissing with anyone. He took that totally in stride, not making the assumptions other people would have back then. Even though we'd just met, he was the first person I ever spelled that out for.

"My roommate transferred out at Spring Break, and I was distraught thinking I'd lose the dorm room that felt more like my home and a safe space than any I'd ever known before. Ashok pointed out that grad students could live in the undergrad dorm if an undergrad invited them into a room. He'd had a bedroom of his own in grad student housing, but he was willing to move in and share a dorm room with me. He claimed he did it for the shock value. He longed to see all those horrified undergrad faces when sweet little me picked flaming old him over any of them. I'll admit he played that up for all it was worth, but I knew he really moved so I could stay in a place where I felt comfortable. I think that's when I knew I loved him and never wanted to lose him." Wend wished they'd been available when Avery started college, if only to offer comfort by email or letter. They petted Avery's hair and tried to let go of that regret.

"Ashok's family had money. He could have moved someplace better than campus housing, gone out to fancy clubs or restaurants every night, had much more exciting friends than me. But neither of us left campus most weeks, except for groceries to supplement our ten meals a week from the college food service. We didn't go to movies or watch TV. We rarely even borrowed books from the libraries downstairs. There was this sense that if we didn't learn every last thing then we would have wasted our time at Pacific Tech and wouldn't be able to solve whatever needed solving later. I don't know if we both thought we had to be better to make up for being different or if we were simply idealistic about making a difference and saving the world. But we were in it together. And we've stayed friends ever since."

"I'm glad. That sounds exactly the way I imagined Ashok," Avery said, slow and soft with their eyes closed. "Or maybe you told me parts of that before."

"Maybe parts." Wend hadn't expected Avery to speak. In their kigurumi they never spoke. That clarified for Wend that Avery didn't need the release of pet play tonight so much as the comfort of being held.

Avery asked, "Now that you've found Matt, do you feel closer to him than to Ashok?"

"Ashok was my first real adult friend. We've stayed friends through so many changes in our lives that nothing could ever challenge that relationship. No one who cared about me would try. Whereas, I never stopped feeling connected to Matt. I'm amazed by how the core person remains the same, but we missed all those life changes." Something inside Wend warmed, but couldn't settle, like a cat on top of a heating vent. "You should see the safe space in his house. It has giant beanbags, blankets with different textures, sheer fabric hanging from the ceiling, a loft, and a coloring nook underneath. He told me I could use that room as well as a guest room above it anytime. Then there's this place." Wend waved at the spacious bedroom suite in the fancy living building.

"Have you had any home or safe space since you lived with me?" Avery asked.

"I've had my own room several times, at universities or research stations. I had a super plush blanket at first and then my hammock and sleep sack."

"Maybe Matt senses you want a home and some comfort. Is that so bad?"

"But it's not mine." Wend didn't want to talk about it, but their stomach knotted up at the thought.

"What is?"

Wend hesitated. "I don't know how to answer that."

"That's okay. I don't either." With that, Avery fell silent. Wend kept petting their back until they were sound asleep. Then Wend tucked Avery under the covers and went to sleep in the other huge bed in a room that wasn't quite safe and wasn't quite home.

Wend wriggled in the night air as they flew through the balcony doors and then shot high up above the city. There were fewer city lights than they'd expected, but those lights spread far and wide in all directions except over the ocean. Car headlights traced neat lines and curved beneath regularly spaced streetlights.

Rolling onto their back, Wend drifted beneath familiar stars. Vague memories of childhood stargazing in Kāne'ohe merged with later nights on the California coast. The physical distance made less difference than the time of year.

A shape tussled across Wend, made of wind and starlight, but material enough to roll them. They whipped into a twisting somersault trying to identify what could touch them in a flying dream. The shape of webbed feet and a long tail distorted the lights below, like viewing the city lights through a clear plastic balloon, if the balloon were supple and frenetic like a seal at play. No, a sea otter, Wend corrected as their visitor half curled onto their back clasping transparent forepaws together.

They raced off, a mile in a minute before looking back to see if Wend would follow.

Wend chased at that incredible pace, barely noting the massive solar farm beside an industrial park on the way out of town or the huge bands of windmills as they crested the mountains and rushed toward the windward coast. They didn't need to follow a freeway to find Kāne'ohe. From their earliest flying dreams, they could recognize the peninsula that made Kāne'ohe Bay into an ear with a string of ancient fishponds dangling like an earring.

They took the lead to dive into each fishpond, slowing down but still skipping like a stone, past resting birds that didn't startle or notice. The transparent flying otter followed them through the fishponds and as they dipped into tidepools and ponds all along Kāneʻohe Bay. If there weren't as many sea creatures in those pools as Wend remembered, they were too exhilarated with flying and company to mind.

Then their company took the lead and explored underwater along the barrier reef and sheltered inner reefs. Wend had known of the reefs as a child, when people wanted to save them from human sewage, but they didn't dive there until thirty years ago, when the reefs were battling acidification and invasive algae. Now the algae barely disrupted the coral, thanks to urchin farming efforts. Much of the reef remained muted or bleached, but there were bright spots. The astral otter nosed at portions where new coral had been attached and some form of local ecosystem appeared to be recovering. Then the barely-there otter came to loop around Wend, and there was sadness radiating though the playful maneuver.

After a long time spent swimming together and inspecting the reefs, Wend followed the flying otter down the coast, around the point, past Diamond Head, and back to Honolulu. They floundered back into their room and their overlarge bed then slept straight through until morning.

Wend woke to find Avery sitting up in bed, poking at their phone. "Good dreams?" Avery asked when they noticed Wend's eyes were open.

"I dreamed about the Kāneʻohe reef restoration you talked about."

"Oh, what sort of dream?" Avery still held their phone, but Wend knew from their unmoving stare that they weren't seeing it anymore.

In that moment, they knew too much.

Even anticipating what would come next, Wend couldn't lie to Avery, couldn't even deflect. There were tears already forming in Wend's eyes as they said, "A flying dream, with an almost invisible sea otter leading the way and swimming around me, both in the air and in the water. I led them through some fishponds and tidepools. They made sure I saw where coral had been grafted on and where the native coral demonstrated the greatest resilience."

Avery looked up with a wide-open smile, only to see the tears escaping down Wend's cheeks. "Are you upset about the corals? Wasn't some of it fun? If I told you the other otter was me, would that make a difference?"

Wend couldn't help the sound that escaped them. It emerged between a sob and a squeak, filled with pain.

Only then did Wend realize how completely their life had changed. They fully believed in their own flying dreams, that other people they knew shared the experience, and that each of those people had paid the price by nearly dying.

Crossing the distance between the two beds, Avery climbed up next to Wend and rested a hand on the bedspread, inches away from Wend's own. "Please." Wend took their hand and Avery continued, "I'm sure the bay looks different from when you were growing up, and you know I'm upset about the coral. But I was mostly happy in that dream. I felt safe and accepted imagining you might be the one flying with me. Now I know you flew with me. We somehow shared a dream and flew to Kāneʻohe. There's never been anyone else in my flying dreams before, no matter how real they seemed."

"I want to be happy to share this with you." Wend managed to gasp around tears. "But it means you almost drowned or died in the water at some point. When?"

Avery's lips sucked in and their brow wrinkled. Their grip on Wend's hand tightened. "Don't worry. It was before I met you. I ran away and fell off a cliff."

At Wend's sharp gasp, Avery corrected, "A little cliff. I was only seven or eight. I didn't break any bones, just bumped my head and swallowed a lot of water."

The words chilled Wend all the way through. It was good Mira wasn't in the same building or even the same state, because Wend was suddenly furious. "Where was Mira? Why didn't she ever tell me?"

"I don't know. The boyfriend who scared me into running probably distracted her. I think she felt really bad afterward. Maybe that's why she didn't tell you. Or maybe she let the past be the past, as she does." Avery sounded calm, reminding Wend of Aljon always trying to soothe people. That reminded Wend of Aljon being the same age with the same potential if he ever survived nearly drowning, because this strongly supported Kai's theory. Oblivious to Wend's cascade of realizations, Avery continued, "I never thought of it as almost drowning, but they did call an ambulance.

The ambulance upset me worse than the fall. I had a fit, I think. I didn't understand what was happening."

"And after that you had flying dreams?"

"I remember a few before I met you, but more after you started tutoring me. I usually flew out to sea or along the coast. Will you tell me about them? The dreams? I'd like to know." Avery sounded desperate, the reality of it all only now catching up to them.

Taking a deep breath Wend said, "I'll try if you want. But anyone else in this apartment could probably explain it better. If you're okay with telling them, they might know how we traveled together."

"You trust them?" Avery asked.

Wend was surprised to find they truly did. They nodded and let Avery lead the way out to the common room, still holding hands in their penguin pajamas.

Matt, Verilyn, and Kai sat fully dressed around a glass table with steaming cups in their hands and a basket of rolls and spreads between them.

"Love the pajamas!" Kai greeted them.

"Good morning," Verilyn said, eyes tightening in concern at whatever signs she noticed. "Help yourselves to juice or hot beverages in the kitchen, and join us."

Matt had begun to stand, but sat down again at a look from Verilyn. "There's tea in the kettle or hot chocolate in the saucepan if you want either of those."

Wend made a beeline for the hot chocolate, needing the comfort more than they cared to admit, despite all the chocolate and comfort they'd been given the day before.

Avery pulled a glass bottle with strawberry guava juice out of the refrigerator and asked, "Want any?"

"No thanks." Wend gestured to the chocolate, but Avery shook their head.

As soon as they sat down, side by side at the table, Matt asked, "Did you sleep well?"

"Amazingly well," Avery gushed with more meaning behind it than Wend could ignore.

"Do you want to tell them, or should I?" Wend frowned at their chocolate as they asked and cowered under everyone else's gaze, as if they were predators and Wend or Avery the prey.

"I can, if you're sure you're okay with this." Avery sounded half cautious and half exuberant.

Wend nodded.

Avery kept one hand on their juice and grabbed a roll with the other, wrapping their fingers around it the way they clutched squishy toys as a coping strategy. "Last night Wend and I shared a flying dream in which we were transparent sea otters and flew to Kāneʻohe Bay. I've had flying dreams since I fell and maybe almost drowned as a kid, but Wend didn't know about that until a few minutes ago, and I didn't know there was any connection or that other people might be involved in this. Wend seems to think I should ask one of you to explain."

Wend noticed at least one indrawn breath and a prolonged pause as the others absorbed the rapid summary, but couldn't manage to look up from the warm ceramic mug they held without sipping, the scent of chocolate enough to steady them for the moment.

"Well," Matt said in a slightly choked up tone, "being able to fly together is amazing and rare. I've only managed it twice with others, when both people involved were trying. You two must share a profound connection."

The reverence and hint of jealousy surprised Wend. They closed their eyes and decided they didn't need to deal with anyone's emotions except Avery's for now. But Avery seemed to enjoy hearing each of the others explain pieces Wend already knew. It helped for Wend to hear all of them sounding intrigued together, but the thought that Avery could have died before Wend ever knew them pounded relentlessly in Wend's head.

Verilyn finally said, "Wend, none of us like to think about a kid almost dying. But knowing that it happened to each of us, I have to believe it was meant to be. Like going through puberty or menopause, it's part of life's journey, at least for some of us. Those who grow up near the ocean learn to respect its power."

Wend clenched their teeth, tense and angry in a way they couldn't verbalize as their mind roiled at the assertion that near-drownings should be part of life's journey, regardless of birthday clusters. Instead, they imagined rare algal blooms releasing toxins or microbes that affected the brains of human children exposed during a critical period and activated on re-exposure. Nothing they'd learned about genetic predispositions or microbiome effects on mental health could justify their connection to

Avery or explain the birthday clusters. But focusing on science comforted Wend. They didn't need to justify what they shared with Avery.

Kai added, "Matt freaked out several times wondering what happened to you before preschool. If you'd been able to see his face when you told your story about that pier, you would have seen him flinch. We all get it."

Wend took a deep breath, not sure that was the same, but wishing they'd known to comfort Matt in the moment.

"Was it a pier in Kāneʻohe?" Avery asked, sounding more tentative than before. "Was it still there last night?"

Opening their eyes and shaking their head at how differently they weighed their own experiences, Wend admitted to Avery, "I didn't think to look for it." Then they focused on Kai and said, "Anyway, I admit you were probably right."

Kai nodded in acknowledgment but didn't choose to say more in front of Avery. The tension in their jaw suggested they took the risks of near-drownings seriously, at least when considering Avery, and possibly Aljon.

Wend asked instead, "What else do you know about shared flying dreams? How do you try for them?"

Matt answered first, "Some people meditate and plan. I allow my desire for the person and the journey to fill my mind as I'm falling asleep. Tanny's the best at it. He and Yasu do guided meditation and can fly while in a trance. All I've managed is a sort of lucid dreaming."

"Sleeping in the same bed helps," Kai said.

"We weren't," Wend said.

"But you were with me when I fell asleep," Avery added with a frown. "I was hoping we could fly to visit each other when we're on different islands."

"That's quite a distance," Matt said.

"If this is real, I'm pretty sure I flew back to Hilo last Sunday, right after my first visit with Wend."

"They moved really fast as an otter," Wend couldn't help saying, pride winning out over their unease.

"I was a falcon, last time. They can fly 180 miles per hour, but I bet I flew even faster in my dream. Faster than the plane I flew home on." Avery set down their juice, pulled a chunk off their roll, and studied it. "I saw all the islands along the way, despite some clouds. Molokaʻi was bigger than I expected, maybe that should have clued me in that it was real. I didn't go into your room. If I had, maybe I could have jumped on you like my otter did last night, and gotten you to join me."

"I guess I'm okay with you trying if you want, if you find me asleep in my room sometime. But only come in through the back, and don't spy on the rest of the condo. We have an agreement about that."

"They all know?" Avery suddenly sounded very young, and more upset than they'd been by talk of drowning. "Am I the only one who didn't know?"

That led to an explanation about birthday clusters, how Wend targeted Viola's boat, and how they found the trash island with the PET bacteria in the first place.

"Maybe that's why I want to study it." Avery practically bounced in their seat. "Or maybe the microbes or whatever is spreading gene edits around the ocean can also save us from drowning and influence our dreams."

A shiver crept up Wend's spine and they froze, as if caught in a predator's shadow or the deepest coastal fog.

"Don't count on it," Kai said sternly.

At the same time Matt said, "That's a big jump."

Kai won some silent negotiation telegraphed by raised eyebrows and continued in a grave tone. "You're not immune to drowning. We knew at least one person who survived to be like us and drowned later. And when a dream first led me to a plastic dump site, it got me in trouble with some shady people. I'm pretty sure they graffitied my parents' house. Someone ran a smear campaign against me at work that may have cost me a promotion. I figure that's getting off easy. The guy who engineered the new PET bacteria, Randal Simonian, disappeared at best, and I doubt that was his choice."

"It was engineered?" Avery asked.

At the same time Wend gasped. "You think they killed him?"

Kai threw their head back, hair swooshing dramatically. Their next words sounded low and strained, forced through a tightly clenched jaw. "We live on a small island, and this one isn't that big or that far away. Let it drop."

"It seems like whatever's sending the dreams and leading us places wants something done that involves that bacteria," Avery said, their voice small but steady.

"You're leaping ahead of the evidence. If there's any force that sends, leads, or wants involved, we've yet to identify or interpret its motives," Verilyn said, tapping the table to emphasize each point. "As someone who used to be a lawyer, I'd advise you not to plan your thesis around any topic associated with illegal activity or coercion."

Matt added, "After years of trying to figure this out, I haven't seen evidence of a coherent narrative behind one person's dreams or all the dreams we know about taken together. The fact some people can guide their dreams through meditation or what we're thinking when we fall asleep suggests, at the very least, that we bias our experiences. Any hypothesis in your mind may influence what you dream. Remember that."

Avery nodded solemnly. "I'll agree that tying my thesis work to something I might have reasons not to publish would be risky. I should maintain a skeptical and scientific mindset. But seriously, you can't expect me not to research something three of us had dreams about."

"You dreamed about it?" Wend asked.

"Kind of. Not in a flying dream. I dreamed I was this giant worm, like a sandworm from *Dune*, watching a swarm of tiny baby worms gobble the edges of a huge donut. After I woke and realized the huge donut was the opening on a plastic water bottle being swarmed by bacteria, I started checking samples in the census database that Wend had flagged for the new PET-eating bacteria. Those bacteria are each about a micrometer long, and I was several hundred times longer, so maybe half a millimeter. If the tiny baby worms were the new *Ideonella*, then I was the right size to be a rotifer or other tube-shaped multicellular microbe. But the one previously identified in the squid lab didn't show up in those samples. No rotifers have image-forming eyes, but my perceptions could be a characteristic of the dream state. I'll need to search more data to rule out thousands of other microbes or possibly identify a microbe that hasn't been cataloged yet."

"You started looking for a microbe that could transport mRNA as well as the new *Ideonella* because you dreamed you were a larger microbe?" Wend asked, not sure whether they were horrified or impressed.

Avery waved their hands frantically. "I didn't think these dreams were real at the time. I thought I was problem-solving in my sleep."

"Wait," Wend said. "Do the rest of you have incredibly vivid dreams about being invertebrates or microbes? Are those real? Real time? Like the flying dreams?"

Matt raised a hand. "Let's get breakfast. Sounds like we have more to discuss."

With a full breakfast set around the table, and everyone happily sipping their beverage of choice, Wend wondered if they were supposed to re-ask the question. Then Kai spoke.

"I'm not sure I've ever been microscopic, but I've had a few dreams inhabiting sea creatures." They punctuated the words with a fork holding a piece of pancake. "Mine usually happen around dawn, both for me and whatever lifeform, and I sometimes learn details I can verify later about a species I haven't studied. For me they feel more real than flying, like I'm inside a specific living being. I'm never invisible or passing through objects as I do in flying dreams, and I discover abilities and senses I wouldn't imagine or know about ahead of time."

"Me, too," Verilyn said.

"Me, three," said Matt, leaned back with a coffee, "except I haven't worked to verify those. I'll leave that to the marine and environmental scientists."

On some level, Wend must have known, because they didn't panic or feel overwhelmed by this latest reveal. Perhaps they'd been fiddling with this puzzle piece since Aljon accidentally triggered the panic attack about their second near-drowning, and they'd realized their dreams had intensified afterward along with other motivating factors in their life. "Maybe we share an awareness of the ocean because we're part of that ecosystem." Wend picked up a grainy roll and added a layer of creamy spread with green flecks. "That doesn't mean we're supposed to fix anything or are part of some greater plan."

"Do you know how many ways those ecosystems have changed in the last two years?" Avery asked. "From what I've read, scientists can't agree on how many species go extinct each year on land, let alone in the oceans where eighty-five percent of species probably aren't identified yet."

"That estimate was ninety percent when we started the Marine Census Project fifteen years ago." Wend sighed, looked around the table and asked, "Are the other beings in the sea creature dreams also people I might know? Have any of you been decorator urchins, flamboyant cuttlefish, or mountain shrimp in the last few weeks?" There were headshakes all around, even as Wend prepared for a false or coincidental positive.

"You have an impressive dreamlife, especially if those are all astral transfers," Matt said.

"Is that what you call them? Are yours always sea creatures? You had such an affinity for cats." Wend knew they were talking too much, skipping ahead, and missing implications. Their mind used to run away like that all the time, especially when stressed or hyperfocused. Now at least they could own it and didn't feel ashamed. Much.

"As far as we know, we're all connected to the ocean and sea creatures. My affinity for cats is a separate but enduring part of my personality." When Matt smiled slowly, the phrase "cat who got the cream" came to mind.

Pretty soon, Wend might be ready to hug or pet him.

"But if humans are destroying the ocean, what does that make us?" Avery asked with a frown and only crumbs left on their plate.

Wend had worried about that with their flying dreams, another set of expectations they didn't know how to meet. They couldn't think of anything to say.

More gently than Wend could ever manage, Matt offered, "People who are trying to save the oceans. Most of us before we even realize our full connection."

Avery didn't look appeased. They turned to Wend and demanded, "Have you looked for microbes in people who dream this way after almost drowning?"

With a slow shake of their head Wend managed to say, "As recently as a month ago, no one had ever believed me about my flying dreams, at least not since preschool." Wend glanced at Matt, who frowned in apology. "When someone suggested sea life might be attracted to me, I couldn't find any clear shifts in the ocean microbiome around me to connect the incidents they suggested. I don't have the right background to compare the microbiomes inside each of us with other people. Ocean samples are easier, because it's all one great soup." After all the early years Wend had spent trying to understand their differences through genetics research, they'd been almost relieved not to find a clear-cut answer. "Even if someone studying the human genome found something common among all of us, it would probably show up in people without such abilities. There are still people who believe the gut microbiome predisposes kids to autism, but if so, that's one of a thousand factors that matters for some people and may affect other neurotypes as well."

Avery nodded along. "Finding out microbes influenced my dreams for years wouldn't mean they were the cause, or the only cause. And it doesn't fit with the birthday clusters."

"Everyone we know about was born near the ocean." Kai pushed aside their breakfast plate. "Maybe we had to be in the water on a certain day when our brains were in a particular phase of development and the relevant microbes were blooming or dividing."

Wend remembered their earlier conjecture about the timing of algal blooms and that Kai was an environmental science professor. Not suggesting it themself hadn't suppressed the idea for long.

"It could have happened in utero, from our mothers—or whoever was pregnant with us—swimming in the ocean and being at a particular stage of pregnancy on that day." Matt looked a little sad as he said it.

Wend tried to remember what he'd volunteered back in preschool about his mother and wondered what ever happened to her. "We're a small, self-selected data cluster trying to solve an equation with too many unknown variables. Until this month, I considered being raised by a single parent, neurodivergence, spine issues, or extreme flexibility as possible factors. Now they're clearly not all applicable for each individual who has these dreams, but if this turns out to be more of a syndrome or spectrum, not everyone would have to check all the boxes."

"Wonder where I've heard that before." Kai laughed in a communal way. Wend guessed they'd been on the other side of this realization recently and wondered what factors they'd considered.

Verilyn reached a hand to rest at the juncture of Kai's neck and shoulder. "We're stronger once connected and when we're close together." She paused before turning her attention to Avery. "If you ever need help after a dream, you can call us. We'll give you all our numbers." Kai held out their hand and Avery passed their phone silently, even as Verilyn continued, "While I've retired from practicing law, if you have anyone threaten you, physically or legally, about this plastic-eating bacteria research, call me immediately. I will find you the right legal counsel for any situation." She made a point of looking at Wend after Avery.

"You say that like you know who might threaten us," Wend said. They slightly regretted it, as the puzzle-solving mindset they'd regained over breakfast shifted again.

Verilyn's sharp glance indicated she noticed the shift, in some fashion, but chose not to alter her response. "I'm not sure the bacteria engineer Kai mentioned represents an isolated incident. He may have drawn the wrong attention for more than illegal dumping." Verilyn paused. Wend felt a short pulse of static before she said, "There might be other groups like ours out there, connected to each other and the sea. I believe one of them went after Matt in the past. It's been a while, and I could never prove it, but you should keep alert."

25.

THE MAKAI SIDE of the ballroom stood open to the sea with only a sloped half wall and a dozen pillars tiled in stone to break up the view. A steady stream of cold water flowed down a trough atop the wall, gurgling like a minimalist fountain as it cooled the air blowing inward. The sloped ceiling with hanging fans to pump hot air up and out no longer surprised Wend. It felt nothing like the air conditioning they remembered from similar venues in the past, but the cooling compared to outside was appreciable. The scent of salt and the sounds of the ocean soothed Wend.

The event had little in common with charity auctions Wend had previously attended or the more formal affairs they'd imagined. Short sleeves predominated and no one wore a suit, but that might say more about Hawaiʻi than eco-architecture. There were abundant variations on aloha shirts and muʻumuʻus in evidence, as well as tunics or sash-legging combinations, worn by people of all genders. Wend's new tunic provided excellent camouflage.

The fabric, especially where it brushed their arms when they moved, reminded Wend of the caress of the ocean when they swam.

The mini-houses donated by artists to be auctioned held pride of place on a long table toward the back of a raised platform. The ginger-bread house door prizes, each in a reusable transparent cake carrier, lined a shelf above a table heaped high with canvas gift bags. The servers, circulating trays with finger sandwiches, lettuce wraps, fresh rolls, and fruit, were dressed the same as other attendees and had name tags identifying them as event volunteers, sometimes with job titles from organizations sponsoring the event.

Avery had laughed off any suggestion that they attend. Wend would have at that age, too. It took years of academic presentations and mandatory university fundraisers for Wend to develop all the compensating and self-soothing tricks they needed for large events, and they'd never experienced Avery's level of noise sensitivity. With age and practice, Wend had become more easily overlooked, a sort of invisibility they usually enjoyed.

Today, Verilyn conscientiously introduced them to people who supported marine research as well as housing initiatives. Wend struggled through a few explanations of the Marine Census Project and received invitations to present at a local college and an Elks Lodge.

Matt appeared at Wend's elbow, saying, "They're about to start the auction. Kai's saving us spots."

As they reached their seats, Kai held up a heaped plate saying, "I told one of the servers that my friends had been too busy talking to eat. Anyone want some?"

Wend wondered how they stumbled upon so many people determined to feed them but simply said, "Thank you," while choosing a three-layer finger sandwich and a fruit kabob.

The auction began with several short speeches, focused more on praising and thanking various people than sharing new innovations or project plans. By the time those were finished, Wend concluded ninety percent of the people in the room knew each other and either worked together or had attended similar events in the past.

The art houses brought up for display and described in loving detail during the auction turned out to be much more interesting. Wend's favorite was a clear glass greenhouse purported to be a self-sustaining ecosystem. The glasswork couldn't rival the one Verilyn made, but it contained mosses, ferns, and plants that resembled miniature mangroves. Matt was the only one of them bidding in the auction. He ended up buying a wooden puzzle box house that he claimed Yasu would love.

The door prize drawing followed, and Wend was shocked to win a gingerbread interpretation of the candy house in Hansel and Gretel. Kai laughed so hard their eyes watered as they said, "Of course you'd win the house with every surface coated in caramel and chocolate before someone added more candy on top."

"I'll depend on all of you to help me eat it," Wend replied.

Matt groaned playfully, and Verilyn mussed the back of his hair.

When everyone switched to milling around and saying goodbyes, Wend finally had a chance to look at posters that explained the housing initiatives the auction supported. In addition to learning more about natural cooling and urban farming, Wend was excited to read project site evaluations comparing water rights, carrying capacity, and standards for reuse of materials. There were organizations providing locally manufactured solar panels produced with a "buy one fund one" model much like Seaward Generation planned to use. Other groups helped with site-specific designs for water, solar, and agricultural installation.

"Hi, I'm Ali, are you new here?" An unassuming person, wearing a short-sleeved plain white button down with tattoos of molecules peeking out on their upper arms, surprised Wend by starting a conversation after reading silently beside them for a while.

"Um, hi. I'm Wend. I'm new to this event and recently returned to the island. I was born in Kāneʻohe. How about you?" That barely articulate response represented the culmination of decades of social learning for Wend, and they counted it as a success when Ali smiled and took over the conversation.

"I grew up on Maui and still have family there. I studied material science at MIT and ended up focusing on green and sustainable architectural supply. Moved back in 2030 when Honolulu became an international center for eco-friendly planning. Those pavers are my design."

Wend encouraged Ali to explain beyond the caption labeling the grid-like pavers as "permeable with local and recycled content only."

His explanation wound to a natural end as someone in a bright aloha shirt that even Wend assumed no local would wear interrupted by asking, "You're Dr. Gwendolyn Taylor, aren't you?"

Wend startled but recovered. "Yes, have we met? I'm terrible with faces."

"No, I'm Dr. Andrew Perez. I wanted to ask you about Seaward Generation."

Luckily, Wend's initial surprise had put their guard back up. Aware of their promise to Shelly not to mention it at this event, they asked, "How did you hear about that?"

"This news article hit the AP feed an hour ago." Raising a cellphone the way an old-time government agent might flash a badge, Perez displayed the photo from Thursday with Wend, Aljon, and Viola posing on the *Nuovo Mar*. "Perhaps we should talk in private?"

"I was about to head out anyway. Good talking to you," Ali said, suddenly looking as awkward as Wend felt.

"Yes, thanks, nice meeting you, Ali." Wend counted remembering the name as a success. It helped if they focused on small accomplishments when caught out in social situations.

Numbly, they followed Dr. Perez across the hall outside the ballroom to a small hotel business center containing a fancy printer and a VR conferencing station.

As soon as the room's clear glass door shut behind them, Perez said, "I'm curious as to how you found a billionaire's stranded superyacht a full day before emergency services arrived."

Now every red flag went up. Wend considered excusing themself, but realized that could also draw unwanted attention to Seaward Generation. Unsure if Perez represented a business interest, press, or some sort of law enforcement, Wend did their best to answer succinctly. "We happened to be nearby. I spotted smoke and an orange flag."

"Spotted while you were awake, or spotted in a dream?"

While not sensing static from Perez, Wend's apprehension ratcheted up an order of magnitude, along with their mental defenses. They searched for a way out, but Perez physically blocked the only door, and Wend wasn't sure what sort of mind game he was playing. Never at their best with strangers, and generally more successful at freezing than fighting or fleeing, Wend's anxiety slowed their response as if they'd swallowed a boulder. "Awake. It was mid-morning. There's not much to tell."

"The article says it took a long time for your sailboat to reach Mehta's yacht due to minimal winds. But why would a sailboat with no backup motor be carrying a hydrogen generator, especially a prototype to be presented to a potential manufacturer?"

Sometimes Wend missed clues others found obvious in conversations like this. In the past, they'd been easy to manipulate as they tried to play along and avoid conflict. They still weren't noticing any staticky deception in this case, but they stepped closer to the clear glass wall and kept an office chair between Perez and themself, just in case. Cool air entered through openings in the glass at ground level. If they screamed or shouted, someone in the hallway might hear, but a quick glance showed no one in sight. "Why exactly are you questioning me?"

"I'm a busy man." Perez pushed closer to Wend, stopped only by the chair Wend now clutched in desperation. "I have a news reader that flags articles of interest. Your name came up twice this weekend, and there you were, right in the same town as me." Wend fought a bubbling playground instinct to hurl the chair at the imposing man. Their defenses prickling, Wend tried to harness that aggressive instinct, at least until they came up with a better plan.

"So you're not here for the auction?" Their tight grip on the chair was all that stopped Wend from shaking.

Perez crossed his arms and smiled. "I find it interesting that you teamed up with Viola Yang to sail across the South Pacific and along the way chanced to rescue and form a business alliance with a billionaire and, let's see," he tapped at his phone before holding up another picture Wend recognized, "discovered a new migration route for Pacific bluefin tuna."

A flash of non-verbal associations had Wend broadening their stance and freeing their arms like an octopus preparing to defend a festoon of eggs. Then they consciously connected "spotted in a dream" and "teamed up with Viola Yang" to what Verilyn had said about other groups of people connected to the sea—people who might be a threat to those Wend cared about.

Wend shoved the chair to force Perez farther from the door as they raised their voice to demand, "Are you the one who killed the bacteria guy?"

Perez stepped sideways, as if to stop Wend from reaching the door while protesting, "What? No. I never killed anyone." His voice remained strong, but Wend felt a hint of static and noticed his face reddening.

Caught between the glass wall and the chair but sidling their way closer to the door, Wend rephrased, "I'm not very good at euphemisms. Did you disappear him or manipulate someone else into killing him?"

Only as Wend reached back for the door handle did they realized the breeze through the room had shifted because someone else had forced the door wide open.

"Yes." Verilyn wheeled around the corner in a tight curve and ended up right beside Wend. "Please tell us, Dr. Perez, where do you draw the line? Illicit trading? Corporate espionage? Blackmail?"

"What's your involvement with this one?" Perez practically crashed into the office chair as Wend made a desperate grab to block his lunge with it. His voice rose in anger as he continued without waiting for an answer. "Is Matthaios behind Seaward Generation as well?"

"I don't answer to you." Matt strode in and claimed a position on Wend's other side, standing closer than usual in the confined space. "But whoever you're targeting, it would be in your best interests to stop."

Balling his hands into fists, Perez focused on Wend again. "Strange how these two take your side when you seem to have lied to them, at least by omission."

Matt snapped back, "You seem to confuse a person's right to privacy with lies of omission. Can't say I'm surprised, with how little you cared about my privacy and how easily you've lied in the past."

Privately, Wend drew strength from the way Matt and Verilyn took Wend's side on faith, without knowing the situation or how much had been kept from them. That trust helped to dissolve the boulder that had formed in their stomach and slowed all their reactions.

"Careful, Matt," Verilyn said while staring long and hard at Perez. "Don't give him an opening or say anything you might regret."

Perez's jaw tightened as he complained, "I didn't come here to speak with either of you. I was having a private discussion with Gwendolyn."

"That's Dr. Taylor to you," Wend responded with squared shoulders and all the condescension they could muster.

Verilyn followed up in a conspicuously casual tone, "From outside we heard a loud argument about someone being killed and saw Dr. Taylor apparently forced against a wall. We couldn't ignore someone threatening a guest. What is your business here?"

"I spotted a public figure, someone pictured in today's news, and stopped to congratulate them on their success and ask a couple questions," Perez answered with sarcasm so thick even Wend couldn't miss it.

"And talk of killing someone?" Verilyn pursued.

"They brought that up. I wondered if Matt had started some new libelous accusation against me, but you two interrupted before I could clarify the matter." When Perez glanced toward the open door, Wend realized a small crowd of semi-familiar faces from the auction had gathered in the hallway. Several shifted uncomfortably or pulled out phones as the situation intensified again.

Perez glanced to the hallway. "I think I've heard all I care to for today." Wend stood tall, jaw clenched, as Perez finished his sentence with a glare in their direction. "Don't worry, I'll be in touch."

He edged past the tight cluster of Matt, Wend, and Verilyn to make his way out through the open glass door. Those gathered in the hall made way and took the resulting calm as their cue to disperse. Only Matt and Verilyn remained when Wend muttered, "That was a threat."

Verilyn sighed so deeply her shoulders sank inward. "Perez knowing you exist is a threat."

No one elaborated further until they were back in the common room of the apartment above the mall, where they all sat down with the candy-encased gingerbread house on the table between them.

Kai said, "I picked up several more pounds of the hot chocolate Wend and I like best, if anyone wants some."

"Just water, please," Matt answered, and Wend nodded along.

Verilyn asked for coffee.

Clasping his hands together on the table, Matt leaned forward and spoke softly, "I meant what I said about respecting your privacy, but if you want to tell us what happened with Perez, we'd like to help."

"Was he involved with the IdeoBios trouble?" Wend asked.

From the kitchen, Kai turned around fast with their mouth wide open, only to close it before saying, "Not that I know of."

"Is that the killing Perez claims you mentioned?" Verilyn followed up, sounding a bit too much like a lawyer for Wend's peace of mind, but that might be what they needed. The image of Perez pushing closer, blocked only by an office chair, refused to leave their mind.

"I might have drawn a wrong conclusion and asked if he killed the bacteria guy." Wend closed their eyes as heat swept their face at the magnitude of their possible mistake. But part of living honestly and accepting who they were included making mistakes. Sometimes, big embarrassing mistakes. "He was directly threatening me, blocking my way out. He asked if I'd spotted a billionaire's boat while awake or in a dream, flashed a news article about a new tuna migration route Viola and I discovered, and insinuated something about Viola and I traveling together." Wend raised their hands, fingers spread in front of their face, grasping for some way to explain. "All at once, I was certain he knew about the birthday clusters and dreams and that he'd gone after the bacteria guy for related reasons. I don't usually go on the offensive like that, but there was a bit of static and . . . I think I channeled a brooding octopus maybe?" Managing a glance up at Verilyn, Wend added, "You'd mentioned other people like us just this morning; maybe my brain jumped in the wrong direction."

Verilyn chuckled as Kai handed her a steaming cup of coffee. "No, you got that last part right, and I trust your instincts as much as my own on the rest. I agree he was hiding something."

Tears came to Wend's eyes, as relief washed through them.

Continuing as if she hadn't noticed, Verilyn explained, "Andrew Perez was born in the same month as you, Viola, Matt, and me. He seems to be part of a similar group born around the Atlantic, and he hounded Matt for over a decade, during which time I was Matt's lawyer among other things. I'm sorry I didn't warn you about him by name, but I didn't anticipate this encounter. My training makes me cautious about dropping names. Speaking of which, did you name IdeoBios or anyone else involved to him?"

"No, after Kai's warnings, I only told Shelly and Viola that name and why we probably didn't want to share it around." Kai set water in front of them, and Wend took a long sip before asking, "Should I warn Shelly and Viola about Perez? He knew Viola's full name and showed me an article on his phone that tells a lot about Shelly and her current project."

"Definitely. I wouldn't be surprised if he goes after them next." Matt hesitated before adding, "Twice now, you've mentioned news articles Perez found. Is this something the rest of us should know about?"

"Oh, yes." Wend forced themself to look up and meet Matt's eyes as they realized they still hadn't shared that key piece of information. "I only promised Shelly I wouldn't mention Seaward Generation until the information was public, and I had no idea it would post today. Perez said it's on the AP feed, so you could probably search my name or Seaward Generation or Hans Mehta." While all three of the others pulled out their phones to read the article, Wend used theirs to message Viola, Shelly, and Aljon about Dr. Andrew Perez ambushing them with a copy of the article and asking odd questions about Viola and the nonprofit. Wend added that they'd heard mentions of Perez going after people and businesses in a questionable manner, but they'd rather discuss details in person. Then Wend pulled up the actual article and quickly skimmed to see what it included before putting their own phone away.

"That's very exciting," Matt said. "Congratulations on saving a life and launching a new product as well as a nonprofit."

"Both the generator system and the nonprofit are mostly Shelly's. The rest of us are being rewarded for landing in the right place at the right time and offering help any reasonable person would have given." Wend eyed the gingerbread house as they felt their energy ebbing. Sugar wasn't the best solution, but it was hard to win a candy-covered house and not want to eat it. Wishing Avery were still around to share the winnings, Wend wondered how they could eat something that fancy.

Kai tilted their head as if facing the same dilemma. "We should celebrate by devouring this house. No nibbling. We know that only led Hansel and Gretel into heaps more trouble."

"You take one side of the roof and I'll take the other?" Wend laced their fingers under one set of eaves as Kai matched their motions opposite. Together they pulled up and cracked the house open like a coconut.

As they feasted on an overabundance of sugar and chocolate for the second day in a row, Verilyn said, "Don't sell yourself short. Many reasonable people would not offer up one-of-a-kind multi-thousand-dollar technology to help a stranger, and perhaps Viola wouldn't have, if you'd argued against it." Verilyn broke off a toffee-coated gingerbread front door and devoured it in two tidy bites. "The article says you were the one to spot Mehta's boat. If Perez were already watching for news about Viola, which is my best guess, I can see how he became suspicious enough to check your birthdate. If it won't spoil your enjoyment of your winnings, I'd love to hear anything you're willing to tell about that rescue or your encounter with Perez."

Not sure if it was the sugar rush or this group of people that made them feel comfortable with the difficult topic, Wend poured out both stories. Between bites of chocolate, candy, and gingerbread, they volunteered everything they could remember from both awkward social incidents. Every truth revealed lifted a weight from their shoulders, until they sat up straighter, more comfortable in their skin than they'd been in a while.

When Wend ran out of words and they had all eaten their fill—Wend and Kai a bit more than that—Matt said, "If you'd like, I could share my story about Perez. It's not pleasant, but it turned out okay."

Wend nodded, eager to know more, and neither of the other two objected.

"At eighteen, I had a regular gig playing mandolin in a band that attracted a lot more groupies at renaissance festivals and pagan celebrations than most people would expect. I also took classes in computer programming at community college that I believed would make me rich someday, and I was pretty free about sex, drinking, and drugs." Matt raised one eyebrow toward Kai, perhaps acknowledging shared history or a previous conversation. Kai shrugged one shoulder and winked. "My mom had passed away two years before, and while a couple aunts pitched in, they didn't care much for me, especially my first year as a legal adult. On my nineteenth birthday, June 15, 1991, we were celebrating at a beach bonfire when my good friend Skye told me she was pregnant and planning to have my baby, whether I wanted anything to do with it or not. Part of me panicked, because I'd always believed I'd take responsibility and support any kid of mine. I also knew I wasn't ready and that my life as I knew it was about to come crashing down around me.

"I honestly can't tell you what went on in my mind or how much intoxication played a part, but that was the night I almost drowned."

Wend nearly dropped their water glass, setting it down with an awkward clunk. They'd been picturing Matt's teenaged band, imagining creatively arranged medleys of songs from *Cats* and then a toddler dancing along. The shift to almost drowning made them choke, all images fading to black, half-imagined music overcome by static. The idea of a world without Matt carved an aching pit through the center of Wend.

Struck by a burst of unfamiliar panic, like heat burning their face, Wend looked up and caught Matt's gaze. On his face, they saw guilt at the admission but mostly a deep understanding of that carved-out space inside. Matt had carried that emptiness for years as he searched for Wend. He didn't need them for sex or pet play or as a marine science educator. All he wanted was to see Wend alive and doing well. Wend knew it with a confidence in their empathy they rarely experienced, because all they wanted from Matt now was the same.

Wend reached a hand across the table. Matt took it. When Wend curled their fingers inward, he wrapped his other hand around the outside. They both held on tight for a long moment. Wend could almost hear the "meow, meow" song of their childhood looping through the silence. Whatever each of them had been through, they'd found each other again and were sharing stories now. Their hands exchanged warmth, both very much alive.

Matt nodded before releasing Wend's hand and continuing. "In the following weeks, as I recovered physically and had far too many heartfelt talks with professionals and family, the eruption of Mt. Pinatubo made it the most notorious volcano of modern times, not because it displaced tens of thousands of people and rerouted whole river systems in the Philippines, but because its ashes traveled around the world, created a global layer of sulfuric acid haze, lowered global temperatures, and further damaged the ozone layer. In my mind, Pinatubo became synonymous with my birthday and the day I drowned. I dreamed repeatedly of the explosion and all the dust that settled into the ocean. In the dreams, I inhabited a hungry mass below the water's surface, feasting on that dust and what grew from it. Those were by far the most vivid dreams I'd had in my life."

Matt shrugged and with a half-smile half-frown said, "So sue me, it played more like a cheap horror flick than a nature documentary in my adolescent mind. It wasn't until 1999 that someone suggested my dreams were visions of carbon sequestration and that Mt. Pinatubo had been sent as divine inspiration. By that time, I was living in the outskirts of Boston, where Skye had family. They'd trained me as a plumber, and I managed to support Skye and my daughter, Kayla, even though Skye didn't believe in marriage and refused to put my name on the birth certificate."

"Is that what you wanted?" Wend asked in surprise.

Spreading his arms wide, Matt said, "It seemed right at the time, but wait 'til you hear what happened instead. First, Skye and I considered ourselves pagan and poly. Our friends went to Burning Man or preached Hellenic neo-paganism. Next, we became vegetarians and environmentalists. Eventually, we joined a radical environmental activist group that some later called an eco-cult, in which I became a sort of prophet figure. The group wanted to release iron filings into what they called desolate ocean regions. They were well-educated and taught me about the Redfield ratio, explaining why we'd need an area rich in phosphorous and nitrogen in order to fix carbon atoms and remove a significant percentage from the atmosphere. I read and fact-checked and fully believed my dreams about gobbling up phytoplankton that grew around the ashes from Pinatubo had set me on a mission to seed iron filings in the ocean to save the planet."

Matt held one hand to his chest in a self-deprecating gesture that made Wend's heart ache for him. They knew how it hurt to be duped by those you'd trusted, but they'd never found any words that made it better. And they sincerely wanted to hear the rest of the story.

"Our group enjoyed a minor flurry of media attention. Someone mentioned my dreams in an article, and my birthdate would have been easy to find online. About that time, Perez started a campaign against us and stirred up panic about toxic algae blooms, which others in the group had been concerned about already and planned for in our site selection. We led rallies, protests, and fundraisers. By 2005, we'd made a deal with someone who owned a large enough boat and believed our theories enough to take the money we'd raised and prepare for the trip.

"That's when Perez stepped in with his lawyers, operating under the auspices of a much larger and better funded environmental organization. They'd snuck one of their members into our group, and she had recordings and copies of financial records that showed we'd violated permit and tax laws at the very least. They shut us down and took all the money we'd collected. But Perez seemed to have a special hatred for me. He painted me as a charismatic cult leader who meant for the group to die at sea, as well as poison the ocean.

"One of our pagan poly friends was involved with Verilyn at the time, and convinced her that I never knew enough to lead that group and certainly hadn't intended for anyone to die. They raised money to mount a legal defense and keep me out of jail. But Perez got to Skye's family and convinced them I was nothing but trouble. Skye wouldn't speak to me or let me see Kayla. Skye's uncle, who'd trained me as a plumber, let me know I'd never find work in that field in his city again."

Matt let out a long sigh, and Verilyn rested a hand on his shoulder.

"Skipping forward a bit, I managed to make some money as a marine plumber in various boatyards up the coast. That eventually led to being dubbed a marine lifestyle engineer and ending up in Hawai'i. Verilyn helped me with legal stuff and more. Work done by Perez and others led to widespread condemnation of iron fertilization culminating in the London Dumping Convention and a UN moratorium in 2008.

"In 2012, Russ George ended up doing about what my group had planned, and Perez supported one of the groups that went after him, although probably not as personally. Since then, more and more evidence has accumulated that the supposedly 'excess' nutrients from those 'desolate' regions in the southern oceans are carried by global currents to eventually feed three-fourths of the phytoplankton in northern oceans."

With a nod to Wend, Matt said, "I'm sure you understand more about iron distributions in various parts of the ocean than I do. With the benefit of hindsight, I realized iron fertilization didn't sequester any additional carbon, merely moved it around and undermined fish populations and the food web. Evidently, there's a whole microbial system transporting iron across oceans, and at this point I agree with Perez's opposition to most geo-engineering. It scares me to think what damage a slightly misguided group like the one I belonged to thirty years ago might do in the near future, with private space flights and satellites, let alone with a profit motive for stirring up panic via social media."

When Matt's words ran out, Verilyn leaned into his side and pulled him closer.

Wend hoped they could offer such comfort eventually, but were glad to leave it to Verilyn for now. "That sounds awful. I dislike Perez even more now than I did in person, which is saying something. But what makes you think he knows and has a group of people like us?"

"He was born in June of 1972, as was his wife, who was a major force in UN biodiversity circles until she died four years ago," Verilyn answered. "I've tracked his legal and personal activities over the years, and similar birthdays are overrepresented among both his colleagues and those he attacks in court. I'm pretty sure he filters his media stream for ocean or environmental news involving people our age, especially if there is any mention of dreams. His background is in biology, focusing on crustaceans."

"Meaning he's always been crabby," Matt said.

Before Wend realized how much they needed the release, they snorted and threw a hand over their mouth, meeting Matt's sparkling eyes as if they were four years old again.

Verilyn looked to the ceiling and then gave Matt's nearest hand a playful slap. "Perez is especially opposed to bioengineering and for-profit efforts. As with Matt, I may agree with some of his concerns, but I can't condone the way he attacks people financially and personally. We've tried to keep younger clusters off his radar. Kai and Tera aren't listed on any documents with our address and try to avoid media associations with us, but we refuse to live in fear of Perez or anyone else. I've seen no evidence so far of him targeting other birthday clusters, and would like to keep it that way."

Wend thought of Aljon and Avery and turned back to Matt. "What about Greta? Is she Kayla's kid? How is she connected to all of this?"

Ducking his chin and smiling fondly, Matt said, "Greta is indeed Kayla's kid. By the time she was born, Kayla had grown into a strong, independent person who thought I should at least know I had a grandkid. I did everything I could to be a good grandfather and mend what rifts I could with Kayla. But as far as Kayla or Greta know, the dreams that led to my portrayal as a cult leader were nothing but dreams."

Wend bristled and hunched inward at the mention of cults, yet considered the alternative for a moment. "It does sound cult-like, whether you instigated it or not. Did they attempt to test if your dreams had some basis in reality?" Wend asked, trying to tamp down their negative associations.

"Maybe it wasn't the healthiest organization, but there was no religious component, other than a lot of us already being pagan and believing in Earth magic," Matt said. "No one ever accused you of starting a cult?"

"No." Wend drew back in horror at the thought before realizing how rude that might seem.

Instead, their reaction seemed to amuse Matt, who sat up straight again as he choked back a laugh. "Well, your belief in your own flying dreams and in understanding people through stories formed the basis for what we have now, although I prefer to think of it as a chosen family, mutually chosen by all involved."

Wend wanted and worried in equal measure, which collided in a full body shiver. "I had some issues with a cult, or something like one. My best friend at fourteen ended up marrying her mother's boyfriend, who said we all arrived on the same spaceship in a previous life. A few months before that we'd both agreed he felt creepy. I thought Gabi felt that the same way I felt lies. After the wedding, I lost her completely. When I saw her again as an adult it was like whatever had connected us had been erased. She wouldn't tell me her new name and didn't want anything more to do with me."

Matt buried his head in his hands before saying, "Let me guess, her birthday was close to ours, and losing her broke your heart."

That summary brought tears to Wend's eyes, but they nodded.

Matt reached across the table and rested his hand where Wend could easily clasp it. They accepted and held tight as Matt said, "I'm sorry you lost her. That situation sounds extremely messed up, whether or not there was a cult involved. But you have to know we're nothing like that."

"I know," Wend said. What others might see from the outside didn't matter. Wend knew what they believed at their core. "I think I'm ready to hug you now."

Matt stood slowly. Wend joined him, still holding his hand. He didn't make a move except to hold his other arm out in invitation. Wend stepped forward and slipped their arms around him, letting go of his hand. He returned the embrace, and they stood there, by the end of the table, with both Verilyn and Kai watching. It was a very patient hug, gentle enough that Wend knew they could pull away at any moment. Solid enough to feel secure. As Wend relaxed into the touch, Matt's warmth fused with Wend's own. They could hear and feel Matt's steady breathing, smell both sweat and herbal shampoo from the puff of salt and pepper hair by their face. The hug settled something deep within Wend, something that connected back to the little boy in the sandbox who had been their first close friend.

When they stepped away, it took a while for Wend to find words. "I liked that, but I might not always be ready for hugs."

"Understood. That one was amazing." Matt's eyes were a bit damp.

After a long stretch of silence Verilyn said, "The rest of us will follow your lead, but I give pretty good hugs too. And I already think of you as part of the family. That said, we should be heading for the airport if we want to catch our flight back tonight."

26.

"I KNEW that auction was a bad idea!" Shelly practically shouted as Wend walked in the door.

"Hi Wend. How are you doing?" Viola asked more gently. She sat at the table beside Shelly, eating take-out Chinese food with chopsticks in one hand while scrolling through messages on her phone with the other.

Shelly pounded at her tablet.

Wend worried the tablet might crack and wondered how long Shelly had been banging away or if she'd turned it on at Wend's arrival. "I learned a lot about eco-design and natural cooling, before being accosted by Andrew Perez."

"What did he do?" Viola asked.

At the same time, Shelly demanded more loudly, "You agreed not to mention Seaward Generation."

Wend leaned against a chair at the end of the table and dropped their drybag on the floor. Keeping their volume normal but slowly and carefully articulating each word, Wend grated out, "I never once mentioned Seaward Generation. Perez approached me flashing the article on his phone. That photo of me on the *Nuovo Mar* let him stalk me in a public place. Did you know that was coming out today?"

"Not until after you left," Shelly said. "I was happy about it until I got your text. Then I started researching Andrew Perez. You know he has a history with your friend Matt?"

"A history of harassing Matt," Wend said, even more annoyed that Shelly hadn't messaged them as soon as she heard the article was coming out that weekend.

"Which he deserved! He was leading a cult that was about to dump iron filings in the ocean and possibly get a lot of people killed." Shelly slapped her hand on the tablet in a way that made Wend jump.

Wend was about done with Shelly's overly physical outbursts, but had mentally prepared themself this time. Rather than calling Shelly out for spouting her judgmental, unsolicited opinions, they had safety concerns and a list of facts to share. Then they would firmly shut their door and find refuge in their lovely lanai with their very own hammock.

"One, it wasn't a cult." Wend counted off points as they dug each fingertip into the back of the chair. "Two, Matt wasn't the leader. Three, it's thirty years later, and Matt realizes that was bad science. Four, Perez invented the part about killing people. Five, Perez wasn't just trying to save the oceans. He went after Matt personally and financially, destroyed his family, and cost him his job."

"And now you and Matt have drawn Perez's attention to us." Shelly's hand pounded on the table, displacing the tablet and causing an empty plate by the corner to rattle.

"You set Perez's sights on me." Wend clutched rhythmically at the back of the chair to stop their hands from shaking. They had to take two deep breaths to say firmly, "We think Perez was tracking news articles and associated birthdays. He mentioned Viola by name and complained about our tuna article before Matt even arrived."

"Shit. Why do birthdays have to be so easy to find on the internet?" Viola tried to reach a hand out to Shelly, but was rebuffed.

"This is too much," Shelly said. "Why couldn't it have stayed just you and Aljon crossing the Pacific?"

At least now she'd said it. They were all in their sixties; certainly they could decide as adults where to go from here. One thing was certain; Wend would not continue absorbing this vitriol. Turning to face Viola, Wend met her eyes to gauge how much she cared about the puzzle, the project, and everything Wend could contribute.

Viola looked away. "As a skipper, I prefer a three-person crew." Her voice strained as she said it.

Shelly glared at Wend. "Look, I appreciate your part in starting this deal with Mehta, and I'm trying not to disparage your belief system about dreams and birthdays and whatever, but I need you to keep your distance right now, from me personally and from Seaward Generation."

Distance from Shelly would be welcome, but distance from the project? How would that even work? "You want me to resign?" Wend asked. For the good of the project and their own mental health, they had already considered it, but they weren't going to be bullied out.

"I hope that won't be necessary," Shelly said. "But if you care about what we're doing here, you might want to have a letter of resignation ready, just in case."

It surprised Wend how bereft they felt, like along with Shelly they could lose Viola, Aljon, and the chance to help with the generator project, all at once. Trust and a fragile sense of belonging drained away and left a raw, scratchy feeling along every nerve. Wend dug their nails into the chair.

They weren't going to write a letter. Shelly could do her own dirty work if it came to that. "Anything else?"

"Try not to mention or make any statements about Seaward Generation or any of us to anyone," Shelly said. "And maybe you could make yourself scarce for a few days."

"And live where?" Wend asked, raising an arm toward their enclosed patio room.

"Won't your beloved childhood friend take you in? He and Perez are the men who started this feud." Spit flew from Shelly's mouth as she said it, but Wend couldn't look any higher.

While Matt's repeated invitations seemed sincere, Wend didn't feel comfortable accepting anything more from him right now. "Is this about your issues with men? Guys with beards? It's not clear that Perez even connected me to Matt until Matt and Verilyn came to my defense. Now you're the one breaking up this household, trying to push me off to him." Wend did not like to bring up trauma, but Shelly had tried to manipulate Wend—and by proxy, Viola and Aljon—since meeting Matt and his family. Wend was done with that.

When Shelly's fist slammed the table again, Viola managed to put in, "You're welcome to stay on the *Nuovo Mar* until things calm down. You like it there, and it might be good for Aljon to have company."

That didn't seem fair to Wend, but they didn't want to stay in the condo either. "Fine, I'll get my things and let myself out the back. But don't lie to yourself, Shelly. If anyone's starting a feud here, it's you."

"I'll pack up some of this,"—Viola waved at multiple containers of uneaten take-out scattered across the table—"for you to share with Aljon."

The lump in Wend's throat made it too hard to answer. When they heard a dish shatter as they packed, Wend couldn't tell if it was thrown or merely dropped.

One thing they knew—this arrangement wasn't going to work.

A piercing sensation raked Wend out of sleep and into the air where a frenetic puff of air-light feathers buffeted them higher and higher. It took Wend's sleepy mind only moments to realize that Avery had pulled them into a flying dream. Avery's excitement swept through Wend. Gratitude and solace lifted Wend higher as they flew together, feathers brushing and wings occasionally overlapping in a way corporeal birds could never manage.

The two of them rushed beyond Hilo and soared across forested slopes until they passed above the enormous dormant caldera of a volcano Wend knew must be Maunakea. Wend remembered their wish, before they knew Avery could fly this way, to show them the active volcanoes farther south without the annoyance of helicopter noise. They saved that thought for another night, content to follow Avery's lead for now.

On the far side of Maunakea they found a broad, grassy plain where two nocturnal birds soared, seemingly unaware of Wend and Avery, suggesting they were real and not dream projections. Bright yellow eyes in round faces rimmed in white flew past before diving to snatch prey from the ground. It didn't take much knowledge of nocturnal birds to recognize the round faces and compact bodies as owls, but picture book images of pueo, or Hawai'ian short-eared owls, sprang to Wend's mind. Their mother had told them many stories: of pueo as ancestral spirits, of pueo rescuing a girl imprisoned for riding a horse through town, of pueo bringing a princess back to life again and again after a jealous suitor murdered her.

Wend didn't know how authentic their mother's versions were, but their favorite story had always been "The Battle of the Owls," which was rumored to have taken place on O'ahu, someplace between Kāne'ohe and Honolulu. The way Wend learned the story, a man had stolen eggs from a pueo nest. When the parent owl cried out in grief, the man felt terrible and returned the eggs unharmed. Then he built a temple to honor the pueo. A local ruler grew jealous of the temple dedicated to pueo and sent soldiers to kill the man who built it. Just as a soldier was about to strike him dead, hundreds of pueo darkened the skies, surrounding both man and temple. The soldiers fled and never returned.

There was no way to share the story with Avery in their current form. That would have to wait until they could send email the next day. For now, Wend followed the swooping motions of the owls they thought were pueo, and Avery swooped contentedly beside them.

Only upon waking the next morning did Wend remember being called "keiki a ka pueo," a phrase that translated literally as "child of a pueo." They hadn't learned until much later that it also meant a child whose biological father was not known. Perhaps that explained how many pueo stories their mother had told. Regardless, Wend welcomed any association with the majestic birds they'd emulated the night before.

The success of that visit from Avery meant Wend woke surprisingly refreshed in their quarter berth. Rain before bedtime had discouraged them from sleeping in their hammock on deck, but the slight sway of the boat, even in this well-protected anchorage, proved surprisingly soothing.

Across the cabin, Aljon lounged on his stomach doing something on his phone. The way he lost himself in it, along with his relaxed posture and thumb movements, reminded Wend of how young he was—and how much good cell signal could affect some people's behavior.

"I'm tempted to swim ashore so as not to interrupt or leave you without a dinghy."

"Nah, the solar showers for this bay top off overnight and won't be warm yet." Aljon put down his phone and said, "Would you care to try a mung bean scramble made with leftover moo shu veggies? One of my favorite leftovers tricks; I call it leftovers egg foo young." He chuckled, though without his normal humor. "We have fruit as well."

They watched the sunrise as they ate on deck. Wend hated to leave when Aljon rowed them ashore. But they had samples to take and a database to mine.

Wend rushed outside. Students approaching the marine science building gave them a wide berth, but Wend was beyond caring what others saw.

In the warm afternoon sun, they felt less shaky.

Wend took a step and a breath. Then another. By the time they were crossing in front of the university cafeteria, Wend had their phone in hand. It was a university phone, but this related to university business. If they called instead of texting, the content should remain private.

Verilyn would never know that this was the first literal call for help that Wend had ever made.

"Hello?" It sounded like Verilyn, but uncertain and not particularly friendly. Wend wondered what showed up on her caller ID.

"This is Wend. Do you have time to offer advice?" Wend brought all their remaining social skills to bear on the problem at hand.

Even before her words landed, the tone of Verilyn's reply warmed Wend more than Hawai'ian sunlight. "For you, anytime. What's wrong? You sound upset."

Upset covered one minuscule aspect of Wend's emotions, but they ignored that simple label. The important goals were to keep breathing and ask what they'd called to ask. "I've been called in to HR. It could be nothing. Am I paranoid to think Perez started trouble here already? If he has, what do I say?"

"First, I'm glad you called. Remember, I'm speaking to you as a friend. I'd like to come to campus and take you out for tea after your meeting. Is that okay?"

"Sure, I guess." It wasn't what Wend had asked for, but the tone of the question made Wend want to agree.

"Good. I assume you're meeting in the auxiliary services building. I can be there in ten minutes and will wait right outside. Now listen carefully." Verilyn paused until Wend made an affirmative noise. "In a meeting with HR, you want to be honest, but the most important thing is to take care of yourself. The HR person is not there as your friend, no matter what they say. If at any point you are uncomfortable or in need of emotional support, you have the right to request a witness of your choosing, and you have to be allowed a reasonable amount of time to call that person in. You could call another staff member you trust or a union rep, but if you want to call me, I will be right outside waiting to meet you for tea. Do you understand?"

"I think so. What if I panic?"

"Set up a text you can send me with one tap. Whether you need to call me in or not, know I'm there for you. No trouble you can get into will panic me." Verilyn sounded every bit the lawyer, retired or not, in a way Wend had never expected to find reassuring.

"I'm glad I called you," Wend admitted. If nothing else, it was easier to breathe now.

"I am, too," Verilyn said. "See you in a little bit."

Wend stood in front of auxiliary services by the time they hung up. They prepared a brief text, ready to send to Verilyn if needed, and slowly set out to find HR.

A few minutes later, Wend sat across from Samantha Nagata who said, "Let me come straight to the point. You've only been here a week, and several concerns have been raised about unprofessional behavior, use of university resources for personal profit, and actions that may reflect negatively on the university and projects you're affiliated with."

Wend waited, but when Nagata didn't say anything more, Wend asked, "Could you list the specific complaints? This is the first I'm hearing about any of this."

"I'm sure you've heard some concerns from your supervisor, Dr. Kahale." Nagata grated like static in Wend's mind, the way politicians and salespeople often did.

"She's only spoken to me once, on the day I started, to say Miko Yamamoto would be my main contact for everything." Wend wasn't sure if Nagata was surprised by that information or by some social expectation Wend had defied. Either way, the long pause while Nagata checked something on her computer gave Wend a slight respite.

"Kahale reported you had an interaction with the island patrol?"

"I reported an illegal dumping situation I came across while taking samples for the Marine Census Project a week ago Friday," Wend clarified.

"This says you reported a possible new species found at the dumpsite and worked around Kahale's denial of your processing request." Nagata sat back as if having specified a problem.

"One living sample I sent to UH Mānoa came from that site, but the project has recorded the same genetics in a wide distribution of samples, including several I took on my way here. I had no idea Kahale refused the sequencing request. Miko came to me with an alternate code from the Marine Census Project for samples related to a previous assignment."

When Nagata didn't respond immediately, Wend added, "I don't know what you're getting at."

"Kahale mentioned a news release this weekend connecting you to a commercial enterprise for processing seawater called Seaward Generation?"

Wend wondered if that was bigger news than they'd thought or if Kahale had a news reader like Perez used. Perhaps locals flagged any news related to Hilo. Wend didn't like the idea of more people scanning for their name, but otherwise this raised the question of Perez contacting Kahale, which counted as more disturbing. Wend thought back to Shelly's most recent instructions and said, "I can't comment on behalf of Seaward Generation, but if you've read the article, it clearly states that it's a non-profit for distributing small hydrogen fuel generators. I'm not sure that counts as processing seawater, and I don't see how it relates to illegal dumping or the possible new species I reported."

"They all involve seawater," Nagata said seriously.

"Two-thirds of our planet is covered in seawater, and the dump site was in fresh water." Arguing might not be wise, but Wend had given up on saying only what was socially acceptable. To the extent they were talking about science, Wend wanted the facts to be correct.

"Have you used university resources in your work for Seaward Generation?"

"No."

"Are you certain? You have a department-issued cellphone."

"Only because Miko said I needed one. I've followed the guidelines they gave me. Honestly, I'm still not sure what complaints have been lodged against me. I have work I'd like to get back to. Do you have an actionable list we can discuss?"

"I'll need to collect your phone and any other university-issued property. I'm afraid you're being suspended from all work with the University of Hawai'i, the University Consortium, and the Marine Census Project pending investigation."

"Why? Investigation of what?" Wend heard the slight whine in their voice as pressure built in their head. While they could still breathe and speak they said, "I have a friend I was supposed to meet after this. She said I could call her in here if needed. I think I should do that."

"Is that one of the accommodations listed in your contract?" Nagata was checking her computer screen as she asked.

Wend pulled out their phone and added a few words to their prepared text message. "No, she implied anyone could call a witness to an HR meeting, like a staff member, a union rep, or a friend."

"I see." Nagata did not sound pleased. "If you feel that's necessary. How long will your friend need to get here?"

Wend had already sent the text and received an immediate reply. "She'd been waiting for me outside the building and is coming in now." By the time Wend opened the door and looked, Verilyn was ready to join them.

"Thank you, Wend. Sam, I hope you don't mind me sitting in," Verilyn said smoothly.

"I didn't realize Dr. Taylor was calling a lawyer."

"I'm retired and here as a friend," Verilyn said as she positioned herself next to Wend's chair, facing Nagata. "Feel free to catch me up on anything I missed, but I'm mostly here to listen. And to help if asked."

The look Verilyn gave Wend may have been meant to reassure, but the way she flustered Nagata mattered more, like a shield appearing between Wend and some power they couldn't quite comprehend, let alone fight. "She said I'm being suspended, but I still don't understand what I supposedly did wrong."

With a nod to Wend, Verilyn turned a silent and expectant expression toward Nagata.

Nagata said, "Their supervisor, Dr. Lorelei Kahale, commented on unprofessional behavior, use of university resources for personal profit, and actions that may reflect negatively on the university and related projects."

This time, when Nagata fell silent, Verilyn kept watching her, also silent. Wend decided to follow both their leads.

Finally, Nagata said, "We've been asked to open an investigation. It's policy to suspend employees from work and deny access to university facilities during an investigation."

There was another long silence. Finally, Nagata asked, "What do you want?"

Rather than answer Nagata, Verilyn turned to Wend and asked, "Have you been given any paperwork showing the accusations, the terms of your suspension, or what is under investigation?"

"I haven't been given any papers," Wend said.

"The policies are all documented online. I can send the relevant forms digitally."

Verilyn shook her head, and Wend said, "I'd prefer paper copies to look over now, please, in case I have any questions."

Verilyn gave the faintest nod.

Nagata turned to her computer saying, "Of course."

The suspension paperwork printed out first. Nagata clearly had that ready. Wend took it and held it where Verilyn could read through at the same time while Nagata frantically typed up something on her computer.

Pulling a highlighter from a beaded purse at her side, Verilyn started highlighting every policy or handbook mentioned in the suspension notice. It claimed Wend would be provided with copies upon request. They should also be given a receipt for any university property collected. Verilyn then circled the phrases "without pay" and "for a maximum of sixty days without further action" and drew question marks next to them. There was a line at the end where Wend was supposed to sign. Verilyn covered it with two fingers and shook her head.

Half an hour later, Wend sat with Verilyn at the most secluded table available outside the campus cafeteria. They were both drinking mediocre tea while looking over at least two dozen pieces of paper that Nagata had grudgingly printed out as well as sending electronically. Wend had forwarded them all from their university phone to Verilyn after checking with Nagata to make sure that was an acceptable use of university resources. They'd then cleared the phone before handing it over in exchange for a receipt, which Wend knew to ask for thanks to Verilyn's expert highlighting on the suspension paperwork. After Nagata had proven unable to provide the details required for several of the policies Verilyn had also highlighted on the suspension paperwork, Wend refused to sign. They'd all agreed to reconvene in one hour.

Now Verilyn said, "I have a local connection for contract law, but I'll need to call in a private investigator from Kona, if we want to go that route."

"What would a private investigator do?" Wend asked.

"Find out what Perez has been up to since yesterday. I strongly suspect he visited your supervisor, possibly in person to avoid electronic or phone records, which a lawyer could request. We probably should have set someone to watch Perez yesterday. I must be going soft to have expected better of him."

Wend clutched both hands around the arms of their chair to keep them still, oddly thrilled to have Verilyn affirm their earlier worries about Perez. "You think he set this up?"

"Does Kahale have any other reason to go after you, possibly risking her own reputation?" Verilyn asked openly, as if ready to take on whatever problems Wend might have. Wend couldn't process the full scope of their gratitude right now, but it cocooned them more securely than all three layers of sleep sack.

"I only spoke to her once. She didn't seem very logical at the time. Then again, most people don't." Despite the strong Hawai'ian sun and weak cafeteria tea, Wend sipped and found the warm drink reassuring.

"If you're willing to take this to court, I'm pretty sure you'd win. But you might have to deal with intrusive questions about your neurodivergence, relationships, and other issues. Perez would see that as a win, as a way to harass you and keep you from working. But if you hand this over to the lawyer I have in mind, we can probably force the university to back down and have Kahale blaming whoever misled her about you. Failing that, Yasu's back in town tomorrow and could give you sound public relations advice, maybe set up a friendly newspaper interview."

"A newspaper interview started this whole mess," Wend complained.

"Maybe. But it's interesting that Perez is targeting you rather than Viola or Shelly," Verilyn said.

"I detest being interesting."

Verilyn laughed. It was an understanding laugh that let Wend feel one step closer to Verilyn. Not just a protector, but a friend. "If I took the quick way out and retired, they probably wouldn't let me work on the Marine Census Project as a volunteer with all this hanging over my head, would they?" Wend didn't know how they'd support themself, especially if their free housing and promised pay from Seaward Generation disappeared as well. But they'd been broke before, better than going into debt for a lawyer and being torn apart in court.

"I don't know, but if you're willing, I'd much rather hire a lawyer than give Perez that satisfaction. Even if Perez isn't behind this, I'd hate to see intimidation force your hand in any way." Verilyn sipped her tea and then wrinkled her nose, as if having forgotten how bad it was.

"You know I don't have much money?" Wend had to say it bluntly. "UH hasn't issued my first paycheck yet, but your lawyer would be welcome to that and whatever else they can get from the university."

"I gather that money is a sensitive issue for you, and I respect that," Verilyn said, setting her cup of tea far to one side. "But this continues a fight Matt and I took on long ago, if Perez is behind it. If not, it's some other bully attacking you, and I have strong opinions about anyone who'd try that. Likewise, your marine census and hydrogen generators both fit with causes I'd support due to my general beliefs on ocean preservation and reining in climate change. All I want from you is permission to take action on issues I care about."

"Okay." Wend knew they were no match for Verilyn's argumentative skills or her good intentions, and it was a relief to hand off the legal aspects to someone they mostly trusted. "I'll work with whatever lawyer you think best, but please make it clear my goal is to get back to work and stop all this before it gets any worse." Wend felt hopelessly out of their depth, but not as helpless as when they'd first phoned Verilyn. "I should send Betta Acosta an email, too. She's in charge of the Marine Census Project and helped when I first arrived here. Maybe she can keep my insurance going at least."

"Have you told Viola and Shelly about being harassed by HR and bringing in a lawyer?" Aljon asked over dinner on the boat.

Wend shook their head and looked sadly down at their half-eaten mango cashew salad. "Do I have to? They kicked me out and didn't want me to have anything to do with them for a while."

"I don't think Viola's happy about that," Aljon said. "She's used to waiting out Shelly's temper the way she'd wait out a storm, but she doesn't know what to do when you're caught in the middle."

The way they sat across the cockpit from each other felt familiar, but Viola's absence nagged at Wend. They weren't ready to forgive her acquiescence in their last interaction with Shelly. Knowing Aljon sometimes filled the role of a child, however conflicted, in relation to the other two, Wend didn't voice their comments. "What about you?"

"She knows I can take care of myself." Aljon laughed and nudged Wend's bowl closer. "Eat."

"Are you Viola's confidant?" Wend asked, picking up their salad and stabbing some mango and cucumber.

"Close enough. She didn't have any choice when she and Shelly shared this boat with me, and I was the only one left after Shelly took off. Now she mostly rants via text." Aljon held up his phone to show a screen full of messages, but not long enough for Wend to read anything.

"And you're okay with that?" Wend couldn't help asking.

He nodded. "Happier from a distance, but I think they really care about each other. They may lack some boundaries I'd prefer in a relationship, but I think they're getting better together. They both love the things they love unapologetically."

"You think it's romantic?"

"Maybe, I'm ace, not aro." Aljon waved around a fork stabbed full of salad. "Mostly, I like seeing people happy, and I'm used to living in the middle of large-family and small-town drama. Speaking of which, how was your weekend with Matt's group?"

"You can call them a family, too. And it was good." After a moment Wend added, "For the most part."

"Are you only sad about the scene with Perez, or something else?"

Wend finished the last of their salad, raking together cashews, before saying, "Avery joined us, and we all found out some stuff. I should probably tell you about it. Or maybe Kai should. They'd probably do a better job."

"You know, it makes me a little uncomfortable to hear Kai has something to tell me."

Wend couldn't guess what sort of confessions Aljon worried about there but hurried to say, "It's nothing about them. It's about you and Avery, and a little bit about the rest of us."

"This sounds like a story, and I think I'd rather hear it from you." Aljon set both of their empty bowls aside and leaned back on his side of the cockpit, kicking his feet up.

Wend lowered their voice, as if others around the bay might hear. "You remember when Matt asked if I'd come close to drowning before he first met me? And the whole story about Kai almost dying in that cave before they started having flying dreams?"

"Neither is a story I'm likely to forget." Aljon answered, a worried edge to his voice.

"Good. I don't know how many more near-drowning stories I can take." Wend swallowed hard and managed to continue. "It turns out Avery fell off a cliff and almost drowned before I ever met them. They have flying dreams, too. All this time, I didn't know. As if not being there for them wasn't bad enough. I feel like I withheld part of their heritage. They had a right to know."

"You barely knew yourself. You only learned about the connection to near-death experiences when I did." Aljon sat up again, hunching forward with his elbows on his knees.

Wend shifted uncomfortably but didn't back away. "I know. And now there's another piece I have to share, but I'm afraid you'll try something rash or be a tiny bit less careful. If anything happened to you, it would be my fault."

"Are you trying to say I might have flying dreams too, if I come close enough to drowning sometime?"

Wend stared at him in a way they'd never stared at anyone before.

"Avery and I exchanged contact info when they visited the boat, if you remember? Some sites not only show birthdays but point out when someone's the same astrological sign or born the day after you." Aljon slouched back in his seat as if his strings had been cut and leaned his head to look up at the sky. "I admit, I did not consider that possibility. Not that I would risk my life no matter what you answer, but how certain are you that having a particular birthday and surviving a near-drowning are the only requirements?"

"Not at all." Wend slouched opposite Aljon. "Remember my grade school story about how Robert and I came up with totally different reasons for thinking we each might be an alien? I still think feeling alienated might be a factor in this, and that could relate to any number of other variables. There's certainly a high preponderance of synesthesia, touch sensitivities, and only children of single parents in our current sample. And the birthdays might relate to a baby being in the ocean at a critical stage during a microbial bloom."

"I don't fit any of those labels, but I could make my own claims to alienation. Cooling off in the ocean worked for babes in arms as well as everyone else in my family." Aljon tapped at his knee as if singing in his head, "Robert wasn't part of your birthday cluster, was he?"

"No. I think knowing Robert helped me identify how my connections to Matt and later Gabi felt different, even if I didn't know what it meant at the time. That doesn't make my relationships with Lisa and Ashok any less important, but they're not part of my birthday cluster either." Wend hesitated before adding the next piece. "Here's the thing. Kai suggested you represented a new birthday cluster based solely on the connection they felt for you, and I guess the way both you and Avery connected to me."

"Oh." Aljon sat still, unusually still for him.

Wend could practically see the thoughts cascading through his head or what others described as gears turning or getting in touch with themselves. All Wend knew to do was wait and keep watch, not that any waves or boats were likely to blindside them in Radio Bay.

Finally, Aljon said, "What I feel toward Kai, I haven't felt before. It's not what I feel for you, but knowing this, I might be able to understand parts of it better. Thanks for telling me."

"You're welcome? I guess that might explain why you preferred to hear this first from me rather than Kai, but I think they might know better what to say. Did you have any other questions?"

Aljon asked without hesitation, "Are you sure Avery's part of this, that their flying dreams are like yours?"

"We ended up flying together, in the same dream. That's how I found out. I hadn't even known people could share flying dreams, but the others already knew. It usually happens with people they sleep with, but Avery flew all the way here and dragged me out to see local owls last night."

Rolling his head to give Wend a mock skeptical look about the owls, Aljon started laughing, then coughing, then laughing again as he sat back up.

Pretty soon, Wend was laughing, too.

27.

A WET, flippery feeling beside them drew Wend into their own wet, flippery body and helped them reorient faster than the night before.

They swam out of the boat where Aljon remained sleeping. Wend dove and surfaced a few times, relishing the calm of Radio Bay at night. Only when Avery did the equivalent of rising out of the water and moving backward on their tail did Wend grasp they were in dolphin form, and wonder if Avery's choice always led Wend to take the same shape. Somehow, they knew they weren't a real dolphin. This was a variation on their flying dreams.

Avery's nearly vertical posture seemed natural enough in this form for Wend to copy, and while upright they spotted a lone person skulking by the Coast Guard station and carrying something to the water. Wend sank down but quickly raised their head above water for a more sustainable view. This time Avery copied their motion and where they were looking. They both watched as a burly figure in dark clothing placed an oval, platter-shaped robot with four grasping limbs into the water. As the person fiddled with a remote-control box, pulled out a long antenna, and poked curiously at various buttons, both the box and the bot lit up. A muffled curse hit Wend as an overwhelming burst of static followed by fear for their life and then Aljon's.

Wend leapt up from the water and back through to the cabin of the boat before they realized that the robot with four grasping limbs might be one of Matt's rescue robots or something similar. Whatever the case, the person struggling to operate it did not have good intentions.

Wend screamed silently and flapped at Aljon with insubstantial flippers. They noted Avery following behind, picking up on their panic, and poking *through the roof to keep watch over the robot and operator. Wend had no easy way to communicate with Avery and couldn't wake Aljon in dream form. They plunged back into their physical body thinking desperately, "Wake up! Wake up! Wake up!"*

It was a shock to wake in human form with the words forming silently on their lips.

As they scrambled out of bed they stammered, "Aljon, wake up. Now. I'm not sure, but I think someone means to hurt either us or this boat."

Aljon sat up, awake and blinking.

"There's someone on the dock with a remote control, piloting a robot they took from the Coast Guard shed. I can't prove it, but I think they mean to hurt us. Call for help. Please don't go near the water. I'm going after that robot."

When Wend poked their human head above deck, they could only make out the person on the pier as a shadowy figure, lit by a single green LED on the remote in their hands. But the robot in the water had a white light pointed straight at the *Nuovo Mar* as well as the green and red lights used to mark starboard and port.

By the time Wend stepped on deck the robot had swum to within ten meters. Without much thought for stealth, Wend dove over the side straight toward it. Salt water stung their eyes, but the lights were bright enough for Wend to close the distance and grab the robot's rear starboard limb. They held the grasper closed as they pulled it off course and away from the *Nuovo Mar*, the pier, and all the other boats.

Wend swam hard in the nearly calm water, not sure if they were towing a weapon or something meant to plant evidence or infest the boat with vermin; they only knew they needed it away. While the graspers might be able to harm them, they didn't think the robot was designed with that in mind. Being all the same length, it would be hard for any of the other limbs to reach Wend while being pulled by one at full extension. The operator seemed far from experienced, and the robot didn't start pulling away or shaking its limb until Wend had it halfway to the breakwater.

If the robot carried a bomb, that might breach the breakwater and be hard to repair, but nothing that small should threaten Radio Bay, or so Wend hoped. Most other dangers an aquatic robot could deliver relied on it being in the water or reaching a boat. They seriously doubted this one could even pull its own weight once out of water. The only plan Wend came up with as they swam away from all other people and property was to toss the bot up on the breakwater.

Every stroke of the way, they imagined they might be blown up, stabbed, or attacked with a drill attachment. No part of them wanted to die or even bleed in these waters. At least they hadn't heard of sharks in Hilo Harbor. Mostly, they hoped Aljon was safe on the boat, and they were glad Avery's human form was several islands away. They didn't want Avery to watch whatever happened next but had no way of knowing now.

The breakwater rose higher above the tide than Wend had expected. The large volcanic chunks of rock could easily cut hands and feet or be slippery in places that would cause Wend to fall. But they didn't know how long they had, only that they wanted to safely stow the robot where it wouldn't hurt anyone and might remain available as evidence.

Bracing their left foot and left hand on the rocks, Wend ignored the jagged surfaces and pulled up several feet, hauling the robot behind them. It weighed more than their sample bot, maybe thirty pounds. Holding it by one limb made the weight ungainly, but it also gave Wend leverage. They started to swing it back and forth, gaining momentum until they could lob it up onto the seawall. The robot made it almost to the top and landed with one limb wedged firmly in place.

Not wanting to remain a target, in case whoever controlled the robot also had a gun, Wend pushed off the wall and back into the ocean. Without the robot's lights, the water lay dark beneath them, but Wend felt infinitely safer. Even as salt stung their scratched-up hand and foot, the warm ocean water swirling over their skin soothed Wend, bringing them down from an adrenaline high.

Then they heard Aljon shout, "Help! Attacker making a run for it on the industrial pier. Anyone have lights? Cameras? Island patrol are on their way!"

From low in the water, Wend couldn't see the person escaping. They hoped the shouting would keep Aljon safe. Presumably someone with a gun would have used it already, or would be reluctant now that anyone on a boat nearby could be watching.

They swam back to the *Nuovo Mar* and found the ladder already lowered. Climbing aboard, the weight of their physical body dragged heavier than they remembered.

Aljon filmed the industrial pier using his phone. Perhaps he could see something Wend couldn't. They turned instead to watch the breakwater, wanting to make sure no one went near the robot until help arrived. Not that their previous experience with making a report to the island patrol had been especially productive, but it was the best they could hope for in that moment.

When Aljon stopped filming, he asked, "Are you alright, Wend?"

"Yeah, a bit shook up. And you?"

"I'm fine. I texted everyone on the island whose number I had. Viola answered first and said she'd call the patrol. Verilyn said something about a PI?"

Wend realized they'd neglected to mention that part. "I'll explain later. I think one of us should row ashore to meet whoever shows up first. The other needs to keep an eye on the breakwater, where I tossed the robot, and maybe on the coast guard building and wherever you last saw the person controlling the robot. And the *Nuovo Mar*, of course."

"Is there any chance we interrupted someone from the coast guard doing a test or something legitimate?" Aljon asked, piercing Wend with new worries Wend hadn't had time to consider. "I'd have thought they'd be the first to respond."

"I don't know." Wend wrapped both arms around their ribs as they took a deep breath. "That robot was headed straight for our boat and I sensed something nasty from the person on the pier. I don't have proof, and I don't know how I'm going to explain that, but I guess I should be the one to row the dinghy in to dock."

"I think they'll want to talk to you more than me. Are you up for it?" Aljon frowned, but his voice was steady. Wend belatedly noticed he'd pulled on a shirt and long shorts despite his abrupt awakening.

Wend nodded, knowing they could handle the short row to the dinghy dock, but not sure how they'd manage more human interaction today, especially with all they couldn't say.

Aljon waved at people on other boats who had woken to his shouts and gave Wend a knowing look. "There are headlights pulling up, and the lights on one are island patrol. Here, take my phone. Viola knows how to download my photos and video."

"Okay, I'm ready," Wend said, trying to believe it.

Aljon helped by untying the dinghy. It took Wend long minutes to row the short distance to the dock. They were suddenly exhausted and dreaded speaking to anyone. But they would do what had to be done.

At the dock, two island patrol officers waited in front of Viola and Shelly, Matt and Verilyn, as well as a small group of people from other boats who'd gathered behind to watch. Wend didn't have to tie the dinghy, as Viola and a patrol officer both moved to do it. Wend ignored the hand the officer offered to steady them as they climbed out onto the dock and then to the adjacent walkway.

"You the one called in an attack on the *Nuovo Mar*?" a second, taller officer asked.

"I called," Viola said as she finished securing the dinghy line. The slacks and buttoned blouse she wore looked surprisingly conservative to Wend's untrained eye, and there was no mistaking her measured tone and visual inspection of both the dinghy and Wend. "I own the boat. The crewmember still onboard messaged me. I guess Wend was in the water?"

"There's an aquatic robot I threw up on the breakwater," Wend said, speaking as clearly as they could. They felt shaky and cold now, as they stood sopping wet on the breezy shore. Their voice began to waver along with their jaw. "I don't know if it's weaponized or something else. The person operating it first appeared by the Coast Guard station and didn't seem too familiar with it. Maybe they stole it from there? They launched it from the end of the commercial dock closest to the *Nuovo Mar*."

The taller officer looked Wend over and then said to his partner, "Mel, close off the breakwater and call for instructions on how to investigate a possibly weaponized robot that might have been stolen from Coast Guard supplies."

That was a more rational response than Wend had expected. They were almost certain they hadn't met either Mel or the remaining island patrol officer before and decided to fall back on social scripts they'd used many times in the past. "Thank you. My name is Dr. Gwendolyn Taylor. I was the first to spot someone acting suspiciously. I woke Aljon when I became worried by how the person focused on the *Nuovo Mar* and proceeded to launch a robot at us."

"I'm Officer Sean Keli'i. Can you describe the person operating the robot or where they went?"

Wend looked around, noticed Matt and Shelly glaring at each other, but didn't have the energy to deal with that. "I'd say fairly large, my height or taller and bulkier. I think Aljon tried to take pictures or video, but I'm not familiar with his phone. He said Viola would know how to find them."

Wend passed Aljon's phone to Viola and continued to answer the officer's questions as to the sequence of events. Viola's fingers practically blurred across the screen before tapping through still images, keeping the phone where Officer Keli'i could see it the whole time. After trying with little success to brighten a couple of the photos so Keli'i could share a better description of the suspect, Viola played the first video and paused at a profile shot.

When Viola let the rest play, Keli'i called in on his radio, giving a description that included, "Suspect is believed to have fled Pier One on foot. Based on limited photographic evidence suspect appears to be between five feet eight inches and six feet in height, approximately two hundred pounds. Last seen wearing a dark tee shirt and dark ball cap. Was carrying a remote control for a robot that we'll also want as evidence."

"Roger that. We had an anonymous call reporting drug smuggling aboard the *Nuovo Mar* at your current location."

"Can we get a trace or other info on that call? Might be our suspect," Keli'i replied.

"Will try. You want another unit on site?"

"Is someone coming about the possibly weaponized robot on the breakwater?" Keli'i sounded a little stilted as he repeated the phrase.

"I'll look into it."

After that, Keli'i asked Viola if they could check the boat or if they'd need to get a warrant.

When Viola agreed, Verilyn interrupted with her phone in hand saying, "Dr. Taylor's personal lawyer is already investigating someone potentially framing them at work and asks to be present if the boat is searched and for any further actions involving their client."

Wend couldn't hide their surprise but managed to keep quiet. In the past, they wouldn't have liked someone else speaking for them or taking control of their situation without asking, but given the day they'd had, letting the lawyers take charge seemed more than reasonable. If it made Wend look more like a helpless victim, maybe that was part of Verilyn's strategy.

Shelly, who'd only been standing in a shadow with her arms crossed, now stepped forward. "Why are you even here?" she demanded, glaring down at Verilyn.

"Aljon called me," Verilyn answered calmly, which seemed to surprise Shelly into shutting up again.

Viola stared out at the *Nuovo Mar* and Aljon, but not scanning for damage the way she had with Wend and the dinghy. Or not solely scanning for physical damage. While clearly aware of the human drama on the dock, Viola looked like a skipper assessing a storm that shifted unexpectedly. Wend respected that mindset, even as they ached for time alone, or better yet, another shared dream with Avery.

"Is this lawyer local or on the way already?" Keli'i asked gruffly.

"Cynthia Shapiro. She'll be here in five."

To Wend's surprise, Keli'i laughed. "I bet. She lives for this stuff."

Wend thought, not for the first time, how strange it must be to live in a place where everyone knew each other. Since it sounded like no one would be asking them anything until Shapiro showed up, Wend sank down to sit cross legged on the walkway. Verilyn tossed them her lap blanket saying, "To sit on or dry your hair, whatever you need."

"Thanks," Wend said, wrapping the light, woven blanket all around their head and body until it formed a protective cocoon with only their face peeking out. It helped more than they cared to admit, which they tried to convey to Verilyn with one appreciative glance.

Some indeterminate time later, two vehicles arrived at once. The first was a van labeled "Hazardous Disposal Unit" that disgorged an officer already wearing protective bomb squad apparel and a tech with computer bags over both shoulders. Both headed for the breakwater and Officer Mel. The other was a sleek red electric mini. The driver stepped out and made a beeline for the crowd around the dinghy dock, where Officer Keli'i had been trying to collect witness statements. The new arrival nodded to him saying, "Sean," and then to Verilyn saying, "Which of these is my client?"

"Wend," Verilyn said, waiting for Wend to look at her, "this is the lawyer, Cynthia Shapiro, the one you consulted by phone earlier today."

"Pleased to meet you," Cynthia said, holding out a hand.

Wend reached a hand up to shake from their blanket burrito but was saved from having to say anything as Cynthia continued speaking. "I'd like to consult with you in private, but unless you have something pressing to tell me, I'll ask you to stay here for now, while I accompany the island patrol to check on the boat and wait for a preliminary report on the robot. Until we know if the nature of this attack was to plant evidence, harm you, or something else, I won't know precisely what further information I need. Are you comfortable waiting here with those present?"

The level of static coming from Cynthia, even as she outlined basic options, set Wend's teeth on edge. It might have to do with being a lawyer, although Verilyn had never affected Wend that way. Looking around at the dissipating crowd, Wend realized they experienced a peculiar contentment in having Verilyn, Matt, Viola, and even Shelly all present and Aljon in line of sight on the boat. That and the blanket wrapped around them were all they truly needed at the moment. "I'll be fine."

Keli'i, Cynthia, and Viola paddled out in the dinghy. Of those who'd come to watch, mostly from private boats wintering in Radio Bay, a few asked if Aljon was okay or might need anything. Shelly assured them he was fine and would be provided with anything he needed.

"Such a sweet young man," one said.

Another mentioned, "He taught us how to make fruit bars. So kind."

Soon the small audience migrated as far as they could toward the breakwater. Officer Mel corralled them to one side. The tech with computer gear typed frantically while talking into a radio. The officer dressed for handling bombs slowly made their way out along the uneven volcanic rock wall holding some sort of sensor stick in front of them. It made for quite the show. Wend couldn't help watching as well.

Clouds obscured a near quarter moon. Harbor lights weren't designed to illuminate most of the breakwater. Everyone tracked the headlamp on the bomb technician's helmet and various small LEDs on their sensor stick and other equipment. They couldn't see the robot, which seemed to have shut down or had its lights turned off, until light from the approaching headlamp reflected off of its metal body.

While the officer on the breakwater took sensor readings, Wend glanced to the *Nuovo Mar*. The dinghy had docked, but all the people were currently hidden below deck.

Wend glanced back to see the bomb technician kneeling to reach the robot stuck near the top of the wall by a single limb wedged into the rock. They grabbed the opposite limb and pulled it up to expose the underside of the robot. Suddenly, the bomb technician went very still.

Wend anxiously wondered if a larger city would have a bomb-defusing robot that could handle this threat, but the uneven breakwater with

ocean on both sides demanded a lot of adaptability, beyond standard programming or design features. Despite relying on such limitations when
stranding the marine robot, Wend curled tight around new worries for the
human technician now facing the danger.

There was a radio exchange Wend couldn't make out that resulted in
everyone on the *Nuovo Mar* coming back on deck. Aljon and Viola each
had their arms full of belongings that they dumped unceremoniously into
the dinghy. Then they climbed in along with the lawyer and Officer Keliʻi.
Aljon and Viola rowed together to bring them back to the dinghy dock as
quickly as possible.

Meanwhile, the bomb technician placed a box of tools where it
weighed down the second robotic limb, holding the saucer-shaped robot
belly side up.

Matt gave a shocked gasp when the headlamp clearly illuminated the
robot's shape with all four limbs for the first time, but when he opened his
mouth to speak, Verilyn shook her head and silently reached for his hand.
He gave it. As they stood there holding hands, watching a bomb technician work on what might be one of Matt's rescue robots, Wend wanted to
offer their hand to hold as well.

Instead, Wend sat frozen, huddled on the ground, looking between
the bomb technician and the approaching dinghy.

They heard a phone vibrate, and saw Verilyn check the screen and
then pick up. In brief quiet bursts, facing away from everyone but Wend
and Matt, Verilyn whispered, "No . . . I'll give you a number . . . Call and
ask them to deal with it quietly . . . You can say I gave you the number."
Then Verilyn gave a number that Wend tried to commit to memory
through mental associations, even though they weren't sure if it had anything to do with the drama of the moment.

By the time Verilyn finished, the dinghy bumped the dock.

All four occupants clambered past Wend, but Wend only watched
the bomb technician, who was moving again. At such a distance, Wend
could barely make out the tool in their far hand that seemed to be lifting
something out of the robot.

Suddenly there was a shout. It echoed from both the bomb technician and their partner at the near end of the breakwater. It might have
been: "Get down!"

Wend didn't process the words. They saw the bomb technician throw the part they'd been extracting into the darkness above the ocean on the far side of the breakwater. Then the technician braced on both hands and knees as seconds ticked by.

Curling tighter into their blanket ball, huddled around their knees, Wend heard Officer Mel shout at onlookers: "Get down!"

There was a BOOM and SPLASH.

In Wend's mind they pictured several dead fish, a dead ray, and a seawater soup of dead micro-organisms.

With their eyes, they saw the bomb technician still braced firmly in place. No damage to them or the breakwater showed on the side Wend could see, but for several long seconds, they didn't move.

Finally, they tapped their helmet and pulled a new tool from the box still bracing the now upper limb of the robot. Wend watched that person, the human closest to the explosion, pry out the robot limb that had first kept it pinned to the breakwater. Then they packed the robot into what must be an evidence case, possibly also used for bomb disposal. They collected that and their tools and made their way steadily back to shore.

Only afterward, when Wend stopped staring, did they hear their lawyer say, "The island patrol want you to come to the station. You're not accused of anything at this time, but there are safety concerns. I'm advising you to go with them and to insist that I stay with you at all times."

"Okay," Wend answered but looked to Verilyn, "Do you want your blanket back, or should I wash it first?'

Verilyn smiled, and Wend was shocked to see tears in her eyes. "I can't believe that's what you're worried about right now. Keep the blanket. We're so glad you're safe."

It was the "we" that made Wend look at Matt. There were tears running silently into his beard. Wend had no idea what to say and guessed this wasn't the right place for any discussion they might have had. "Would it be okay to hug you, each of you, before I go?"

Verilyn reached out first. She pulled Wend down into a gentle hug and to where she could whisper, "You are welcome to our safe space or guest room at any hour. At the very least, come for dinner tomorrow. We'll have a lot to discuss, I'm sure."

Then Wend stepped over to Matt, who opened his arms but waited for Wend to close the distance. He sounded half strangled. "I couldn't—If anything happened to you or Aljon and they used that robot—" Then he was shaking, his forehead pressed to the side of their hair.

Wend wanted to tell him it wouldn't have been his fault, even if whoever chose the robot did it to set him up. But they realized that might make him feel guilty that anyone could be targeted for their association with him. Wend didn't know what would be helpful to say. Words confounded them, and they decided the less said about Matt's association with any robots the better. Instead, they held him tight and promised, "I'll see you tomorrow."

Then they were bundled into an island patrol car beside Aljon, who actually waved at some of the spectators, presumably friends he'd made while staying on the boat. Wend's lawyer sat up front with Officer Keli'i.

The only person who spoke during the drive was Aljon who quietly told Wend, "I brought all your stuff off the boat. The island patrol don't want us going back there until this is settled." After a pause he added, "I'm really glad you were there to wake me up." Aljon clearly realized Wend had been dream flying when they first spotted the attacker, and he was letting them know that secret was as safe as he was, as they were.

It made Wend wonder if the boat would have been a target while empty or with only Aljon on board. They hated the idea that Aljon might only be at risk because of Wend. In that moment, they understood Matt's fears even more. They wished they could call to check on Avery, but guessed it would be a bad idea even if they'd had access to a truly private phone.

The first two hours at the island patrol station were tedious and claustrophobic. They repeated the same information over and over again with their lawyer, Cynthia Shapiro, standing quietly by. When an officer made Wend open their sample bot for inspection, since Aljon had brought it along with all their belongings from the boat, it was Cynthia who pointed them to the Marine Census Project webpage that clearly explained the purpose of the bot, complete with diagrams. She still grated on Wend's nerves and felt staticky almost all the time, but Wend was glad for her presence as a buffer to deal with the island patrol and others involved.

The first bright spot came when someone conformed to stereotypes enough to bring in donuts at dawn. While Wend tended to be fussy about chocolate, almost any other form of sugar could cheer them up, at least in the moment. Aljon commented that the vegan donuts provided especially for him were very fresh.

Viola shook her head at their shared delight. Shelly rested half asleep against her shoulder in the meeting room where they'd been left to wait.

Aljon made a point of showing Wend a donut pic that he'd sent to Avery as part of a seemingly innocent text chat. Tears stung Wend's eyes. They wanted to tell Aljon how relieved they felt to know Avery was safe on Oʻahu, now sharing a picture of their own breakfast cereal. But expressing any emotion would bring all the rest flooding out, and Wend couldn't handle that while trapped in a public building full of strangers. The best they could offer in that moment was, "Tell Avery I'd rather be there sharing breakfast with them."

At close to eight in the morning, Cynthia came in with Officer Keliʻi. As they pulled up chairs, Viola nudged Shelly to fully awake and sitting.

"I have some good news," Keliʻi began. "Based on an anonymous tip, we have a suspect in custody and found the remote for the robot."

"That was fast," Viola said. "Did they say why they attacked my boat?"

Keliʻi sighed and gave Cynthia a look as if hoping she'd answer. She gave him a tight smile and a tiny shake of her head.

The island patrol officer sat up straighter, and attempted to make eye contact with each of them before continuing. "The suspect with the remote confessed to piloting the robot and placing the explosives in its delivery compartment. He also made the anonymous call suggesting you were smuggling or selling drugs."

There was a pause before Keliʻi shrugged and continued, "Look, he's a local kid. Born when Radio Bay was closed to outsiders during the second pandemic, after an even longer closure for the great pandemic. His whole life he grew up with people arguing to limit access. The local news interviewed him recently for opposing construction of time share condos for the new longer stay tourism market, and he basically sees the cruisers wintering over in Radio Bay as part of that same problem. Or maybe someone convinced him of that recently and handed him the bomb and instructions for using it. Our bomb techs don't think he could have come up with the triggering mechanism for when that compartment opened, even if he could have stolen some marine explosives from a local construction outfit."

"So someone else put him up to this." Viola's disgust matched Wend's;

trying to harm them was bad enough, but taking advantage of a teenager made it all the more horrific.

Keliʻi nodded and said, "He's pretty much given that away, but I'm not sure he even knows who set it up, and possibly set him up to take the fall if discovered. You have any ideas?"

Everyone looked at Wend, who looked at their lawyer, who nodded. Wend carefully recounted the whole incident with Perez.

"I believe Perez could be behind accusations made against my client at their place of work yesterday as well," Cynthia said.

"And Perez came to you with a newspaper picture of all three of you on that boat promoting some non-profit." Keliʻi nodded toward Shelly at the end. "So he or someone else could be targeting any of you, the boat, or your new non-profit." He sighed and finished, "We'll keep the investigation active and keep you posted."

In all, it was an inconclusive and unsatisfying end to one of the worst nights—following one of the worst days—of Wend's life. After Keliʻi and Cynthia left, Wend forced their gaze up to meet both Viola's and Shelly's. Figuring the rest would have to wait, Wend only said, "I'll need my room back at the condo."

28.

THE DARK around them teemed with multitudes. Without color, without light, their vision was vibration. They pulsed dozens of tentacles, reading the water currents that gushed around others like them and responded to some larger force. Savory flecks sucked through their gaping round mouth. As they undulated, rigid cuticles realigning along their tube-shaped body, sticky toes held fast to a slippery indistinct wall beneath. Folding sideways they brushed their tentacles—no, not tentacles, not flagella, dozens of tiny cilia—into contact with another of their kind. They felt no bulbous head, meaning they weren't in a swarm of box jellies as they'd first guessed themself to be. Instead, tufts of cilia covered matching sides of a corona, which identified their neighbor as a rotifer and matched their own mouth-parts as well. Tiniest of animals, they relished their immensity among microbes.

Wend flailed mentally, trying to recall words spoken by Avery about this form, before Wend-rotifer sank deeply into the rhythms of cilia pulling in nutrients, water flowing through trunk and foot, any excess discharging to maintain osmotic balance.

A part that remained Wend, or something more cognizant, recognized their *Ideonella* bacterial passengers as well as mRNA messages for building proteins to shelter *Ideonella* within a future squid host. A different mRNA segment that Wend-rotifer carried came from the common octopus. When carbon dioxide acidity triggered a chemical change, this mRNA could edit instructions for protein production to adjust a cephalopod's base metabolism. Wend-rotifer remained merely the messenger, unchanged by these messages.

Octopuses and squid were masters of self-editing, but Wend-rotifer knew in their sticky toes that they were not sheltered within any cephalopod now. Whatever larger creature carried them also inadvertently carried their mRNA messages and *Ideonella* passengers farther than any rotifer ever could on their own.

Rotifers were many, replaceable, uncontrollable, unstoppable—powerful!—a source of information broadcast widely rather than targeted to specific destinations. Each carried many possible messages and several smaller microbes.

Suddenly, Wend-rotifer heaved with the very floor that anchored them. Floor became wall became roller coaster. A row of sharp white mountains passed too close to their five primitive eyes—some part that was Wend recognized multiple rows of shark teeth. Their transport had been a shark!

Two passing rotifers tasted familiar, one distractingly like home and safety. They slipped away before Wend could connect with toes or cilia.

Wend-rotifer rode on a stomach lining everted into bright sunny water beneath a plastic sky. Here rotifers floated, swam, ate, expelled. Some of the *Ideonella* Wend-rotifer expelled attached to the floating plastic island. Others were swallowed as food or passengers, beyond Wend-rotifer's care.

While drifting in open ocean, Wend-rotifer brushed a different trunk and foot. Cilia tasted the tang of distant family lines, distant ocean basins. That rotifer expelled mRNA from foreign squid to disable a pigmentation code. It seemed trivial, probably some passing fad. Wend-rotifer acted merely as a messenger among messengers, part of a larger and more important system for communication. Their carrier fee was paid as they digested portions of the organic matter they swallowed. Wend-rotifer's toes adhered temporarily to the tangy appendages of a newly arrived rotifer as both flowed together into the belly of a ray.

Wend woke in their hammock at the condo still thoroughly exhausted. Salty tear tracks crusting their eyes, a scratchy reminder of crying themself to sleep before their rotifer dream. Wend deftly rubbed away the grit. At least they'd reached the safety of their hammock and panda pajamas before the emotional storm broke. While they hadn't managed another flying dream after, they would swear they taste-touched Avery in the myriad of microbes at the end.

From the sounds in the adjoining common room, they weren't the only one awake now. After identifying mostly kitchen noises, Wend decided it must be Aljon and therefore felt safe to venture out. Still, they changed into clean daytime clothing first, black board shorts with a purple rash guard, a unique form of personal armor for facing what might be another challenging day.

"Did I wake you?" Aljon asked, dressed in his own casual but clean daytime attire, as Wend stumbled on their way to the kitchen.

"Probably not. I've gotten used to sleeping at night since we landed here. Bad habit." They leaned against a counter covered with slices of eggplant, grated cheese, and a pan of breadcrumbs. Some sort of tomato sauce boiled on the stove, but the smell in the room didn't seem to match the sauce. The room smelled like garlic with either butter or cheese.

"This doesn't smell like breakfast." Wend sniffed again, trying to figure out the dominant smell.

"How many countries have you lived or worked in to maintain such opinions on breakfast?" Aljon asked. "Besides, it's two in the afternoon. I decided to make eggplant parmigiana."

Aljon pushed a bowl of fruit in front of them. "Have some fruit. There'll be cheesy garlic rolls served as appetizers or breakfast in a moment."

Two o'clock might still be too early for Wend's sleep-muddled brain. "I thought we were keeping this kitchen vegan?"

"Kai turned me on to a vegan grocery with amazing mozzarella. It's made with cashews from Maui."

Believing in Aljon's cooking and what the delicious smell promised, Wend started to peel an orange.

Luckily, they woke further while eating the tangy citrus, because Shelly and Viola made their way downstairs as the rolls came out of the oven.

Viola bumped up beside Aljon in the kitchen, leaned her head against his shoulder and said, "You are my favorite Italian relative."

He nudged her in the ribs saying, "We've decided hot rolls and fruit are breakfast. There'll be eggplant parmigiana for dinner in a couple hours."

"Shouldn't we call this brunch then?" Shelly asked, taking a roll and then passing it between hands when it registered as too hot to hold.

"You are all very particular about naming your meals," Aljon pronounced in a pointed tone. "None of you were this fussy at sea."

"We existed only to eat and sleep on that boat," Shelly complained, rubbing red eyes with the hand not holding the roll.

Wend shook their head at Shelly's negative tone and noticed Viola and Aljon sharing a similar look. Then Aljon said, "I believe life on a boat makes people appreciate what they have. For all you two argued and were otherwise loud, you never kicked anyone out."

Wend froze with their hand halfway to grabbing a roll. They'd come a long way from the time in their life when they would dissemble or make excuses for Shelly's actions, but their gut ached in sympathy at what it must cost Aljon to brave bringing this up. Pulling their hand back and sitting up straighter, Wend ordered their thoughts to offer the best compromise they could, for both their own sake and Aljon's.

"It occurred to me that I could come and go by the back door to my room." Wend pointed toward the garden door. "Aljon could claim the futon under my hammock if he wants to stay there rather than upstairs. After all, this housing is part of our pay, the only part received so far, and it doesn't feel right to be kicked out of our own house." In fact, it made Wend's skin crawl thinking about it.

"Is that why you brought in a lawyer?" Shelly asked.

"Nakakahiya ka!" Aljon spat out, gripping tight to the kitchen counter but not facing any of them. "I don't know what your issue with Wend is, but this can't go on. Shelly, you are like a mother to me, and it is hard for me to say anything against you. Instead, I ask you to please show Wend the consideration you've shown me. You and Viola may thrive on or at least bounce back from insults and arguments, but it's obvious that Wend is more like me. We do not need or want the fallout in our lives."

For a long beat no one moved or made a sound.

Finally, Shelly said, "Wow, I had no idea—no idea you saw things that way or—I just didn't realize."

It was beyond Wend's understanding how Shelly hadn't known but also how Aljon came up with the argument that finally broke through. Or maybe that took a bombing. Wend wanted to say something on their own behalf or in support of Aljon, but they didn't know what words would help. Instead, they took a garlic cheese roll and ripped off a large bite. It was delicious.

"Maybe we could write up a list of house rules, starting with no one can push anyone else out," Viola said. "If someone's unhappy, they could suggest changes that might help and everyone could discuss options until we agreed."

Wend wondered how often Shelly would be the one asking for changes and how quickly such meetings would escalate to shouting. Aljon squeezed his eyes shut before turning away, but Viola and Shelly only watched each other.

Shelly laughed, but not in a happy way. "You'll do even worse at remembering house rules than I will."

"I know." Viola nodded. Her slight smile seemed honest but pained. "This might encourage both of us to put up or shut up."

"I guess." In an incongruously light tone, Shelly said to Wend, "Sorry if I was unfair. You came into my life at a stressful time. But it certainly wouldn't be right for you and Aljon to have to share one tiny room."

Wend nodded, surprised by the apology. As a teacher they'd been trained to say when they accepted an apology, but children's words were easier to untangle and their transgressions easier to forgive. No static suggested Shelly lied, but her words rang tinny and hollow. Her only effort at making amends was to dismiss the compromise Wend had offered in desperation. So Wend stayed silent. They looked to Aljon, who'd had the most success so far with getting through to Shelly. Wend trusted him in this as they had at the helm of the boat.

The cook was now rinsing eggplant slices, for reasons Wend couldn't guess but didn't question. Having clearly regained his calm he said to Shelly, "It's interesting how concerned you were, for appearances' sake, about Avery spending one night on that futon. But you don't mention that in my case or with Wend and me sharing the boat. Is that because I'm ace or a man or because you trust me more than you trust Wend?"

"What do you want?" Shelly asked, sounding surprised, as if her minimal apology should have solved everything.

"I want you to reconsider your assumptions," Aljon said. Each word landed like a stone. "And I was curious about that in particular."

"You think I'm biased about you being ace or Wend being nonbinary and whatever?"

"I'm asking," Aljon replied in a curt, cutting tone. Perhaps he was working through the trauma of the night before by confronting the challenges he could. Wend would never have expected the conversation to veer in this direction, or for Aljon to continue pressing.

Shelly finished the last of the roll she'd kept on eating throughout and rested her chin on one palm. "You know, I learned the word 'conscious-ness' from 'consciousness raising.' My generation, at least where I lived, were confronting our biases before grade school with *Mr. Rogers, Sesame Street*, and *Free to Be... You and Me*."

That comment and list of shows stirred memories in Wend and an awareness of unexpected congruities with Shelly. Part of them badly wanted to find a common language that would bridge their communica-tion gap, even as the part nursing emotional wounds urged caution. Wend had memorized and loved *Free to Be... You and Me* before they'd known what a musical was or what they could learn from sung stories.

"I know I have biases. Have always known it. I don't think you or Wend even push against the major ones, although I may owe Wend a bet-ter apology for my biases against Matt." Shelly looked toward Wend and said more seriously, "Sorry again. I want this project and I know you do too. If you give me another chance, I'll try to act like a decent person. Demonstrate why these two ever put up with me in the first place."

Viola looped an arm around Shelly's waist and said sotto voce, "Only some of the reasons."

Sidestepping the ill-placed innuendo, Wend's mind flashed back to familiar extremities brushing along their own, offering a sense of home. They blurted, "You didn't happen to dream about being a rotifer with dozens of cilia lining the corona around your mouth, did you?"

To Wend's surprise, Shelly choked and then said, "Fine, I'll admit to the dreams this one time, but I don't want it brought up routinely, espe-cially not at breakfast or whatever meal this is. I thought I was a worm at first. Coordinating all those cilia drove me nuts. It was dark and I didn't understand most of it, but I knew there were others present. I sensed some were familiar. Then I got spat out topsy-turvy into the ocean with more confused flailing. Happy now?"

Wend smiled, touched by the awkwardness of the admission and sensing they'd finally won a real concession in this disjointed conversa-tion, even if they weren't ready to forgive all the rest. They'd known Shelly's birthday and suspected during their discussion of being drawn to certain people and places, but Shelly had opposed any talk of flying dreams or unexplainable insights after meeting Matt. "Yes. I think we were the microbes Avery suggested co-occur with the new plastic-eating bacteria. I carried some of those bacteria as well as mRNA instructions for squid and octopuses. Did you sense that we were part of some giant information network that might help to save life on Earth?"

With a flick of her wrist Shelly dismissed the question. "I was happy not to eat or kill anything recognizable. Most of my ocean dreams are full of violence, very eat or be eaten." Then she asked more tentatively, "You don't think we were invaders from another planet trying to manipulate Earth genetics?"

More than anything, Wend wanted to ask about Shelly's other dreams, what she'd been, what she'd seen. But if they might never have another conversation like this, that wasn't the part Wend needed to focus on. "No. Some segments of mRNA I carried came from the common octopus. I've read enough about cephalopods to know they edit their own genetics and genetic expression orders of magnitude more than most other species. I don't know how these rotifers transfer those instructions between individuals, but Avery may want to study that if no one else is." Wend longed more than ever to know if Avery had shared that dream and helped carry the relevant bacteria and mRNA instructions.

"Another message I picked up originated from squid for squid. No influence from beyond Earth's ecosystems as we've always known them." They didn't feel obliged to point out that extraterrestrials could have been active in Earth's oceans for centuries or millennia or that Wend-rotifer had also passed mRNA that might benefit the new PET-eating bacteria that almost certainly reflected human interference. Whatever bioengineering Perez feared, whether guided by humans, extraterrestrials, or as yet unknown biological forces, it extended beyond Wend's comprehension or capacity to judge. What counted as extraterrestrial no longer mattered to Wend the way it had when they'd compared lists with Robert, which was a revelation in itself. "We're all trying to save the planet. We all have dreams, and it's not in any of our best interests to let our dreams overshadow or be overshadowed by anyone else's."

"You were in my shrimp dream too, weren't you? When that big white shrimp took out the one between us, practically swept right over us, you kept on climbing." Shelly took a deep breath. "I understand about the cycle of life. I guess spending your dream time as a shrimp or microbe makes dying look different. Maybe Aljon is right, you aren't as hostile as I assume people, and life in general, to be. Nor do you share our passionate natures."

The suggestion that Wend wasn't passionate, even cloaked in sameness, rankled. It echoed times when Wend had been called emotionless because their mind processed input differently and early training had them compensate by burying their feelings. A glance at Aljon and the sour lemon expression on his face suggested Shelly's words triggered similar feelings in him, perhaps from years of people conflating being ace with not wanting as much as others could. They felt so much in that moment, what they'd come to call a "belly full of tears," along with a cold and stinging sense of rejection.

But Viola rubbed Shelly's shoulders, as if she'd overcome a major personal challenge. A flash of empathy, whether others believed Wend possessed enough or not, urged against pressing the issue right now.

Aljon cleared his throat loudly. From the counter, where he was setting up a sort of production line that involved slices of eggplant and three shallow bowls, Aljon said, "Moving on, whoever might ultimately have been behind last night's attack, it seems intrusive to base Seaward Generation on this island if no locals are on the staff or on the board of directors—not that it would be any better if the only local took my role as cook, I'll point out. That means my place in this operation is secure at least."

"My agenda for our next board meeting specified recruiting new board members," Shelly responded, sounding much more confident. "I want to ask Doreen."

"From the Adventure Treehouse Bed and Breakfast?" Wend asked, ready for the time being to shift the conversation to their efforts.

"She's not only local, but guests come to her place from around the world. She's connected to small businesses in global tourist destinations, many coastal with boat harbors."

"You're stacking the board with people who like you better than me," Viola accused, her tone playful.

Aljon rolled his eyes from across the kitchen in a way only Wend could see. Viola's teasing, if that's what it was, hadn't landed well with Wend either. Or perhaps it was poorly timed.

"If it wouldn't make you too uncomfortable, Verilyn seems like a good person to have on a board of directors." A small voice in Wend's brain shouted that their suggestion and timing wouldn't land any better, but Wend increasingly believed that Verilyn was a good person to have on your side in general, and Shelly was at least listening for the moment. "She knew everyone at the charity auction on Oʻahu and introduced me to useful people, even though all she knew about was my work with the Marine Census Project. Her skill set is totally different from mine, or any of ours, I think. She used to be a lawyer and knows a lot about contracts, human resources, and who to ask for what. She's the one who found me a lawyer yesterday when I almost lost my job here and with the Marine Census Project."

After a sharp inhalation, Viola said, "Shit, you really had a bad couple of days."

Across the kitchen, Aljon nodded over his eggplant slices as he dipped them in dry ingredients then wet ingredients then dry ingredients, carefully coating each side.

Shelly started to say, "I'm willing to consider Verilyn, but could we talk to Doreen first? She might have useful—"

A loud knock at the door rapidly escalated to pounding.

The events of the previous night had everyone in the room on edge. They all froze and fell silent at the pounding. Shelly recovered first, creeping over to peek through the peephole on the door. Whoever she saw outside didn't worry her much. She shrugged and pulled the door open, admittedly with the chain still engaged. "Can I help you?"

"I'm here to see Wend. Don't try to tell me they're not here."

"Could I have your name?"

"Mira Mlakar."

Wend jumped up from their chair. Both Aljon and Viola looked at them with concern, seeming to have recognized the name.

Being the only person in the household who had no idea about Mira's former relationship with Wend, let alone Avery, Shelly asked, "And you're here about?"

"What are you, Wend's chaperone or some new lover intent on protecting them from the big wide world? I came to speak to Wend. Either let me in or call them to the door."

Wend knew they weren't obliged to talk to anyone, but the last thing they—or Avery—needed now was more disruption. Wend offered the others a quick wave and made their way to the front door. Seeing Mira through the inches allowed by the chain didn't stir any fond memories or longing for touch or care. Wend hadn't been sure before, but it made them more confident about standing up to Mira now.

Mira had barely changed. Fine wrinkles framed her eyes and gray shot through her dark hair. She stood fit and tan, wearing the same sort of brightly colored ruffled blouse that Wend once viewed as cheerful. Despite so much shared history, a coldness crept through Wend. Where they would normally feel a tug of friendship or familiarity, there existed only a loose tangle of associations, some positive, many neutral, a few bad.

Resentment for being cast out, separated from Avery, and never trusted with the story of Avery's near-death bubbled up instead. "You can let her in. She's someone I used to know."

As soon as Shelly shut the door, removed the chain, and opened it again, Mira pushed her way inside. "Used to know? Is that all? And what right do you have spending time with my child?"

"Would you like to sit down?" Shelly asked, hovering beside the angry mother for reasons Wend couldn't fully comprehend.

"No. Butt out of our business." Mira planted her hands firmly on her hips, shoulders square.

"It seems to me you're butting into our home, which is also our place of business," Viola said. "I'd appreciate if you wouldn't yell, and not pushing people around is a house rule."

Wend would have laughed at that, if they weren't caught up in a more cutting anger than they'd felt in years. "I would like to resolve this without shouting," Wend said, forcing a quick breath before adding, "You realize that Avery found me and came all the way here to see me? That was their choice, and they are an adult."

"It was a bad choice. They didn't tell anyone where they were going. What if they'd run into trouble along the way? What if you'd turned out to be an ax murderer?" Mira nearly shouted. Her accusations stung enough that Wend nearly failed to notice the staticky feel of deception and negative emotions tangled in with regret.

Much to Wend's surprise, Aljon stepped up next, wiping his hands on a kitchen towel. "You realize Avery is twenty-nine years old? They are perfectly capable of choosing who to see and where to go. Seriously, I thought my nanay and titas were overprotective. I had no idea."

Wend had never before felt any sort of static from Aljon. They realized he was pretending to understand less than he did, probably to help Wend, but the whole situation was confusing.

"That Avery can choose their own relationships with whomever they want is beyond question. If you only came about that, and to suggest I could be an ax murderer, I'll ask you to leave me alone." Wend tried to keep their tone steady.

"I didn't come all this way to be pushed aside, when this is about my child. I changed my holiday plans and flew out early when I heard you'd reentered Avery's life and were having such an impact. You know I don't approve of presuming on old relationships. The power differential based on knowing Avery when they were a child—there's no way this can be healthy."

Wend bristled, again, at the assumption their relationship was anything but proper, especially from someone who knew the sort of parent they'd been to Avery. Well, Mira should have known. Either way, her argument was entirely based on her own expectation of maintaining power over Avery, but Wend wouldn't repeat what Avery had said about wishing Wend were their parent instead. They knew Mira could outmatch them with words and emotional displays, but this time, they didn't have to compete. They let their relief settle over the rival emotions, at least for the moment. "I'm not sure what you're trying to imply, but I don't think it's honest. Whatever issues you have about letting people in close to you, or by extension, close to Avery, are not my problem. I'm fine with you choosing to detach and stay detached from me. Avery is an adult now, a very capable adult. My interactions with them are not your business."

"What has happened to you? You never spoke to me this way." That reaction from Mira felt honest at least.

Wend wondered how much they were following Aljon's example in confronting the problems they could. "I'm not negotiating with you. I'm not anything with you. And I don't think Avery will like it when I tell them you showed up here."

"This is none of Avery's business—"

"No, it's none of your business." That might have been the first time Wend ever interrupted Mira.

The look on Mira's face went from flat shook to blushing outrage. "How dare you. I'm their mother!"

"Which is why I'm trying to be civil, because I don't want to cause trouble between the two of you, something I already told Avery." Conflicting emotions and images from Wend's own complicated relationship with their mother swarmed in their brain, but didn't overwhelm them.

"Then you'll butt out of their life?" Mira asked.

"No." Wend resolved to repeat it calmly as many times as necessary to prevent having to do this again. "Avery can decide what part each of us plays in their life. I will try not to interfere in whatever they share with you. Ideally, you'd extend me the same courtesy. But I know we don't live in an ideal world, and so I'm telling you, this is not your business and I have nothing further to discuss with you."

Mira huffed and thrust her hands out at shoulder level. She gestured toward Wend with the other three all standing close behind, blocking the rest of the condo. "You won't win."

"We're not competing."

"I'll take this up with Avery." Mira's voice grated loudly.

"You might at least wait three days until term wraps up," Wend said, not wanting to pass on any of this unpleasantness, but knowing Avery would have to specify their own boundaries. At best, they could offer Mira time to cool off without jeopardizing any school deadlines.

"Out of curiosity," Shelly unexpectedly spoke up, "did anyone new contact you, encouraging you to make trouble for Wend or the rest of us right now?"

"I have no idea what you're talking about," Mira snapped. That at least felt true. Sudden confusion and being forced to reconsider the situation served to calm Mira down.

"That's good," Viola said. "But if you're worried about bad people finding your kid, you might want to take a more circuitous route, do a little sight-seeing before heading back. Someone tried to blow up my boat last night, with two of us on it, and I'd hate to see you or anyone else tangled up in an ongoing investigation." The notes of insincerity around that speech only heightened when Viola said, "There are some active volcanoes you could visit, maybe hike around, a way south of here."

"Yeah, you could pick up some nice volcanic rocks as souvenirs," Shelly added, as she moved to open the door.

With a "humph" Mira headed out. "Don't treat me like a fool. I know as much about local taboos as any of you."

Wend hoped Mira was far enough from the door not to hear when they all burst out in exhausted laughter. Together.

29.

CYNTHIA SHAPIRO stood in Matt's living room, barely past the entryway in a pencil skirt and heels that seemed entirely out of place. The lawyer had insisted on driving Wend over and on Wend asking someone else to see them back to the condo later—which was thoughtful, but Wend still bristled at her presence. They gladly chose a seat across the room, beyond where the rest of the household had already gathered. They noticed a new face, but sensing the group's comfort and lack of static, they said nothing.

"I gave Wend a detailed report on the drive over, and they preferred that I brief the rest of you," Cynthia began. "There haven't been any significant developments in the bombing investigation since the arrest this morning," she said simply, indicating that wasn't surprising and she didn't expect anything more.

"For the original contract dispute, the incident last night provided additional incentive for the university to agree to terms today." She smiled sharply. "The supervisor for the Marine Census Project, Dr. Betta Acosta, expressed deep concern for Wend's wellbeing in this new location, citing previous issues with lab paperwork and health insurance. She deemed this a wrongful termination and intends to review how the Marine Census Project is administered locally. Acosta offered a contract whereby Wend would be employed directly by the Project, under terms used for local contractors on smaller islands or isolated research stations. The offer includes guaranteed health coverage and other benefits, regardless of what location they work from. In addition to their current salary, there's an allowance to cover office space, computer, phone, and other needs. Wend would have the option of contracting separately to teach classes or run trainings specifically for the University of Hawai'i. I can negotiate for that or for the university to reinstate the existing contract, if Wend chooses. Any questions?"

There were none, but Verilyn made a point of escorting Cynthia out, and took several minutes to return.

During that time, Matt came to sit beside Wend. His eyes looked puffy and tired, but he smiled as he said, "Wend, let me introduce Yasu, the member of our household you haven't met."

Yasu raised a hand but didn't rise from the couch or offer to shake hands. "I've heard a lot about you. Bet you've heard that from everyone here." At Wend's nod, she laughed, and settled from a gentle slouch into an impressive sprawl deep in the corner of one cushy couch. In warm brown pants and a top made of stretchy velour, Yasu looked entirely relaxed as she said, "I work in marketing and PR, mostly for green products and causes. If you want help spinning what happened last night to benefit Seaward Generation, I'll share my thoughts for free, but I understand your business partners don't trust us much."

"That was mostly Shelly, and she's softening." Then Wend remembered the bag they'd brought in and lifted it from the floor by their feet. It had the blanket Verilyn had lent Wend, handwashed as well as Wend could manage, but also a gift for their hosts. "Aljon and I made peppermint fudge. He may also have asked in passing if he could help prepare a high tea here, possibly with a winter holiday theme, if he's invited back sometime soon."

"Anytime," Kai said from across the room.

"Aljon is more than welcome, and you can always bring your friends here," Matt added gently, "including Shelly when she's ready."

Wend appreciated how antithetical that sentiment was to Shelly wanting to control who entered the condo, including Wend. While it might not work to bring Shelly here anytime soon, they were trying to work past that. Matt hadn't seen Shelly at her worst or heard the stories underlying her biases, but he clearly understood some of her issues and felt much safer welcoming people into his own home with his chosen family around him. The way Wend longed for that sense of safety made their skin itch.

Seeing Matt waiting for a response, wearing a festive blue-green shirt and silver-blue vest but with eyes still red from worry, Wend could only say, "Thanks." They reached out a hand and Matt held it, as he had when they were little and singing "meow" all across the schoolyard.

When Verilyn returned, she settled next to Matt and said, "This next part is for family and shouldn't leave the room." Family clearly included Wend as Verilyn continued without a pause, "The tip last night that led the island patrol to the robot remote and operator came from Avery. They called me, but I redirected them through the private investigator I'd already hired." Wend remembered Verilyn's brief phone conversation as the dinghy returned from the *Nuovo Mar* and thought they should have guessed. Verilyn kept right on speaking, "He's already confirmed communications between Perez and Wend's supervisor at work, Lorelei Kahale, but hasn't yet verified any communication with the bomber. However, Perez is flying back to Europe tonight at eleven. I'll be notified when his departure is visually confirmed by our investigator's colleague watching in the airport. Unfortunately, I don't expect we'll find hard evidence to connect Perez to any illegal activity. On the plus side, I don't believe anyone can trace the tip on the bomber back to Avery, which is good, because they were calling from Oʻahu with their eyewitness account of following the attacker from Radio Bay. I guess that means you two can link up in dreams from quite a distance."

At Verilyn's knowing look, Wend nodded. "I'd told Aljon the night before about my previous flying dreams with Avery." They hesitated before adding, "I covered the birthday and drowning aspect again. He said he wouldn't risk drowning for flying dreams, and I know he meant it." The mere thought of Aljon's life being at risk again, under any circumstances, made Wend's throat go dry.

"I'll follow up," Kai said. "Do you think he'll guess about Avery's involvement?"

Aljon had commented casually on several texts he and Avery exchanged after the bombing. They'd used his phone to let Avery know about Mira's visit as well. "I'm sure he guessed that Avery and I spotted the bomber while flying together. That reminds me, Avery's mom showed up at the condo today. At first I thought Perez had gotten to her the way he got to Kahale and the person who tried to blow up the boat. But Mira's timing appeared to be coincidental. Well, not coincidental. But because I arrived and Avery found me; not the rest."

The dryness of Wend's throat as they rushed through that speech must have been audible, or Tera had otherwise excellent timing, as they carried in a pitcher of water with slices of lime and some other citrus just as Wend finished speaking. Wend eagerly accepted a glass, but declined tea when Matt offered. Verilyn and Yasu agreed to share a pot of tea as

Verilyn delicately reviewed recent events to bring everyone up to speed. Then she and Yasu dissected the players involved, which led to Yasu commenting sternly, much to Wend's gratification, on how anyone mentioned in a press release should be notified when it went live.

Matt only chimed in with ideas for keeping everyone safe, especially Aljon and Avery. He mentioned to Kai, "Now that Aljon knows the rest, he might benefit from your cellphone security tips. Could he pass those on to Avery, or does that need to be handled in person?"

Kai tilted their head and shook it fondly. "Aljon's making me feel old already. Taught me a couple of privacy tricks he picked up from activist friends. Avery, on the other hand, is a devotee of the new unemojis, and I had to update software before they'd even play on my phone. But don't worry, we're all playing safe.'

Before Wend could ask what a unemoji was, Tanny called from the kitchen, "Soup's on!"

The soup turned out to be chili served with additional roasted chilies on the side. Tera brought out brown rice, quinoa, and cornbread biscuits, in addition to salad and the ubiquitous bowl of fruit.

Matt sat beside Wend again and took the opportunity to say, "No pressure, but I know where there's office space available with the fastest internet on the island. It's above a charming store called 'Matthaios Water Wonders' and next door to the best shave ice this side of the island."

"This just happens to be available?" Wend asked, trying to sound light and teasing and to keep their issues out of it.

"The landlord is very particular, but you'd probably have adequate character references." Matt blinked at them with such undisguised hope that Wend wondered how anyone ever said no to him. "I have spare office space on O'ahu, too. Whatever you want."

"Let me think about it?" Wend asked.

"Of course." He passed Wend the salad with a cautious smile.

Verilyn's phone buzzed, and all eyes turned to her as she said, "I only had it on for emergencies. It's from the private investigator. He says someone's approaching our house. Someone he can't identify." After a pause and another buzz, Verilyn said, "They're approaching our front door."

Matt shared a look with Kai and Tera that had the younger two collecting their full plates and heading out of the room. The others rearranged the table with practiced ease as the doorbell rang. "I'll get it," Matt said as he stood.

Tanny got up with a huff, shaking his head. "Interrupting my dinner. I'm going too."

So it was that the two largest people in the room opened the door, completely blocking from sight the person who said, in a high and proper British accent, "Truce, I come in peace. My name is Gillian Ainsley, pronouns she/her, birthday June 23, 1972. I believe I traded messages at sea a few hours ago with one or two people here. Anyone know about tiny microbes with cilia around their mouths that travel in the bellies of sharks?"

"Um," Wend said, afraid to say more.

Matt turned his head and raised his eyebrows, but at Wend's shrug he said, "We should probably hear her out."

"Would you care to join us for dinner?" Tanny offered roughly. "It's spicy."

As Gillian stepped inside they could all see she was willowy and tall, if a touch stooped in the shoulders, but moved gracefully in light gray pants and a soft pink blouse that didn't overwhelm her light skin and hair. "Can't refuse an invitation like that. If I enjoyed English food, I might have spent less of my life traveling."

Yasu added a new place setting at the end of the table where Tera had sat before, and Verilyn performed minimal introductions. Much to Wend's surprise, further questions about their unexpected dinner guest and her allusion to shared ocean dreams and birthdays were dropped until everyone finished at least their first servings, and Gillian appeared to have finished completely. That gave Wend plenty of time to reflect on their last dream and on what they were willing to say about the species of rotifers that Avery had first proposed were transporting the new plastic-eating bacteria. Among other issues, Wend hadn't told anyone here about Shelly's presence in the dream, and didn't feel that information was theirs to share.

Finally, Gillian set their napkin on the table and said, "In the interest of full disclosure, I'll state that I'm acquainted with Dr. Andrew Perez and am taking over his position as the Atlantic Liaison for the Ocean Planning Committee, effective tomorrow. He does not know I'm with you now, nor do I believe that is any of his business. I heard about the bombing last night and certainly hope he had nothing to do with it. However, his public interaction with Dr. Gwendolyn Taylor on Sunday prompted my journey and his replacement on the Committee. He knew of that by midnight Sunday, local time. If he engaged in any problematic activities afterward, he will be held to account, one way or another."

The way she rattled it all off sounded like something out of a spy movie. Wend could only guess that Gillian didn't expect to find legal proof of Perez's involvement but might know people who would act through other channels. What Verilyn had suggested about a group around the Atlantic had been so vague that Wend couldn't react with horror or contempt to the implied extrajudicial punishment. They still weren't sure Perez would face any consequences, whatever he had done.

"Your honesty is appreciated," Verilyn said. Only then did Wend realize they'd sensed no deception from Gillian, during that recitation or before. Matt and Tanny had probably made a similar evaluation before letting her in. Others at the table may have been assessing Gillian throughout the meal while Wend reflected on ocean dreams and microbes. Gillian nodded at the allusion to others potentially sensing lies before Verilyn added, "What is it you want with us?"

"While recovering from jetlag and having a lie-in this morning, I had a fascinating dream about ocean creatures smaller than any I could name. I'm assuming this won't surprise anyone present and there aren't any secrecy protocols I need observe." Gillian glanced around the table. "Perhaps some of you have had such dreams, where you experience yourself fully embodied in another lifeform while still retaining much of your own identity and knowledge? Perhaps you've learned to identify other individuals, whether known to you in daily life or not, who are inhabiting the bodies of sea creatures in a similar way?"

On her next scan of the table, Gillian focused on Wend longer than on anyone else, but Wend couldn't meet her eyes or even shift positions. They were glad they'd already finished eating as their insides sloshed about unpleasantly, a sensation they couldn't name and had rarely felt before.

"So be it," Gillian continued. "Let's say I dreamed I was a microbe in the belly of a shark. That shark somehow disgorged both stomach and contents, myself and other microbes, beneath a spill of garbage. The other expelled microbes and I took in smaller microbes and biological material that I somehow knew to be genetic instructions. There were distinct variations among my microbial companions. Some traveled from the Pacific Ocean and others from the Southern Ocean by Antarctica, although this dream took place in the Atlantic. I'm not sure what all the microbial messages were for. One definitely facilitated the digestion of plastic and another conveyed a greater tolerance for acidification. I knew that because someone else inhabiting a microbe recognized those genetic messages for what they were. I have to wonder what part our human knowledge is playing in a larger information exchange. What I took away from the dream was that different groups from various parts of the globe must work together, especially those who share such dreams for our oceans."

The sloshy feeling inside Wend had shifted to a rippling, almost a fluttering. They could admit the fascination and sudden draw they felt toward Gillian, at least privately, in their own mind. There were no words to express that connection, a compulsion born of dreams that shared scientific understanding. Out loud they managed, "I couldn't have explained it. But how did you know who was also a person and where they were from?"

The smile Gillian gave Wend grew warmer than they'd expected. "Oceans taste different to me in many forms, as do those riding along in dreams. I suspected you might be involved. You are a microbiome specialist with a background in genetics after all, and you had reason to be sleeping past noon local time today."

Clearing his throat, Matt said, "I was there."

That no longer surprised Wend, as they'd placed the taste of home and safety they'd noticed from the rotifer alongside Shelly, before encountering the one who taste-touched like Avery at the end. Wend wondered if mentioning Matt's presence in such dreams to Shelly would help or hurt, and how they could ask Matt's permission to share without violating Shelly's privacy first. It was possible Matt had already guessed in rotifer form, although Shelly didn't seem to have picked up on much. Then they thought about the octopus genetics they'd seen within their microbe but first described to Aljon when discussing reefs in the Marquesas and an octopus Viola had photographed there. The tangle of possible connections expanded. For the time being, they asked only, "Are you suggesting my work specialty has something to do with inhabiting smaller organisms?"

"We all have our affinities," Gillian said. "I tend toward shoaling fish. If I had ended up in a whale, I would have sought out a cetacean specialist I know. I can't give you any hard and fast rules. Maybe one of us draws others to a species where we can communicate useful details. Or maybe we're drawn there for some larger reason or by our own curiosities. Did you want to connect with other people or share insights with those microbes?"

Wend didn't think they should comment on the rotifers they'd first learned about from Avery. Whether they wanted to connect with other humans was beyond complicated at the moment, but might explain why Matt was drawn into their dream along with Shelly as well as Gillian, someone who could offer protection against Perez. If Wend could somehow connect those forces to support each other and possibly ocean life, they'd work to strengthen that collaboration. Remembering Verilyn's question from earlier, Wend repeated, "What do you want from us?"

"An exchange of information and ideas. That's all." Gillian bit her lips together, looking as insecure as Wend felt in that moment. "I don't mean any of you harm. I promise." Given that Gillian knew they could sense deception, she genuinely wanted to reassure them. That must be why she came to this house in person tonight.

Before Wend could think of anything to say or how to admit they'd only learned such dreams could be shared a couple days before, Verilyn cut in with, "I hope you will be staying nearby for the time it takes to build trust and understanding."

"Of course," Gillian said smoothly, lowering her eyes and clasping her hands. "Please accept my visit today as a gesture of good faith. Once I'm settled on Oʻahu, I would be pleased to host any of you for a meal in my home. Thank you for sharing this with me tonight." She left several cards with her contact information before offering brief goodbyes and leaving.

"I feel like we should do a security sweep after that visit," Kai said, as they reentered the room with their now empty plate.

"Contrary to appearances, we're not living in a spy novel," Yasu responded.

"Speak for yourself. You haven't spent a night and a day trying to figure out who maneuvered a local kid to almost blow up our friends while possibly implicating Matt." Verilyn's voice held an edge Wend hadn't heard before, as she felt around the table and chair where Gillian had sat and inspected the business cards thoroughly.

"Sorry. I've been so focused on the details—I missed what it meant for you." Yasu made her way to Verilyn, who accepted her apology with a warm hug.

Tera carried in a large magnet from the kitchen and ran it over and under the end of the table where Gillian had sat.

"Anything I can do to help?" Yasu asked. "Besides PR and spin if it comes to that?"

"You can help clear the table!" Tanny joked in a booming voice, playfully bumping Yasu's shoulder as she immediately set to it.

"Gillian felt honest to me," Wend offered as they stacked their own dish with Matt's. "Did you know all that about affinities and tasting different origins before?"

Seeming to finish her search, Verilyn turned and said, "She appears to be offering new insights, and I'd like to trust her. That only makes me more cautious." She rubbed the side of her head.

"Feeling drawn to others similar to yourself or identifying as part of a group makes you more vulnerable to manipulation," Tera said.

"Nice to see you identify with our group skepticism," Kai offered with a fond smile.

Wend couldn't help noting that the people urging caution were the people they'd relied upon and trusted most in the last few days. On the other hand, Verilyn suggested Gillian stay nearby to build trust and understanding, and that seemed to be what Verilyn herself did by showing up at the university HR meeting to support Wend, directing Avery on how to safely call in tips on the bomber, even lending Wend her own lap blanket last night. Kai shared insights on IdeoBios and showed Wend the original dumpsite they'd found as well as reaching out to Aljon repeatedly. Matt's entire chosen family had offered Wend food, shelter, and honesty from the start, while allowing Wend to reciprocate on their own terms.

"Take some time. It's free." Tanny gave Matt a gentle nudge.

"Shall I set out dessert?" Matt asked.

"Aljon's fudge or the cake you're going to pretend you didn't spend all day baking?" Tanny teased.

"I'm not pretending anything. I'm proud of my cake, and there are far worse behavior patterns to fall back on than stress baking." He carried out a rolled cake decorated to look like a log. The swirls in the bark were clearly made by the tines of a fork, with powdered sugar sprinkled to suggest a dusting of snow, but Wend found the idea of a cake formed into a log endearing.

"Can't have too much chocolate," Kai said, as they set Wend and

Aljon's fudge out beside the log cake on a coffee table in the living room. After Tera and Verilyn finished searching for spy tech, they brought tea as well, and the whole group settled down in the living area.

"Are we keeping watch together until eleven when we know Perez has left our state?" Matt asked.

"Not like he had to act in person to do damage before," Tanny noted, serving himself a big slice of cake. "It's a beaut."

Wend first tried the intense dark chocolate frosting used for the bark, then the dark cocoa flavored roll cake, and next the nutty filling with telltale speckles from vanilla beans. Finally, they tried a bite with all three together and told Matt, "This is amazing. I'd be willing to bake for a day to make more, but it probably wouldn't come out like this."

"Glad you like it," Matt said. "The recipe may be the best thing I kept from my pagan days in Boston, although I've modified it for local vegan ingredients. Some people call it a Yule log, and Yule started out as a pagan festival in honor of the winter solstice."

"Isn't the solstice still three weeks away?" Wend couldn't help asking.

"This is a practice cake. I like to practice." Matt laughed at his own joke and half the room laughed with him. The rest were too busy eating cake.

Wend wasn't sure they got the joke, if it went beyond making lots of desserts. "Well, I'd be happy to help, although Aljon would probably do better."

Matt raised a forkful of cake as if in a toast. "I'll make sure to invite you both."

While they enjoyed the cake, Wend didn't think they could deal with this many people until eleven, even if they were too tense to fall asleep. "I should probably head back to the condo."

"I'm happy to walk with you." Kai looked concerned, as if reading something in Wend's body language when they said, "Or you can stay here, in either the safe space or the room above it. You can message Aljon or whoever to let them know, if you want." Kai held out their phone.

Matt said, "You're always welcome here." Others around the room nodded.

Wend took the opportunity to message Aljon and also Avery. If they told Avery precisely where they'd be, describing the exterior of the house and the side door that led to the laundry room and the safe space, that was a reasonable precaution.

No one said much when Wend said goodnight. They let their hand rest against Matt's when he handed them a spare toothbrush and showed them the cupboard where such supplies were kept.

After doing the minimum they could tolerate to prepare for sleep, Wend made their way into the soft-floored room with its beanbag chairs and coloring nook. They held tight against the length of silky fabric hanging unfettered from the ceiling and let it soothe more than the warmth in their face. Then they chose a blanket the texture of their favorite teddy bear as a child and climbed up to sleep in the loft.

The rush of wings through their face, through their own wings, pulled Wend from sleep into the air. They followed Avery past the wall beside the loft and up into the damp night air before registering their nearly invisible pueo form with strong wings, round face, and short owl ears. Even if Wend hadn't known it was Avery who woke them up, they were beginning to associate these well-defined flying forms with Avery dreams. But the energy shared between them had changed.

Tonight, Avery was not playful as they'd been in sea otter, dolphin, or even pueo form before. They followed the main road south, driven and tense. Rushing at full speed through the sky still brought relief to Wend. They felt safe in this noncorporeal form with Avery protected and known beside them. Warm air rushed under their wings, barely ruffling their feathers. With keen night vision, they spotted small bursts of movement from animals below. The movements of humans appeared more blatant and prolonged, in cars and walking home, drinking and laughing, pleasantly inaudible to Wend in dream form.

Avery followed a road to the left, clearly with some destination in mind. In no time at all, they circled two craters. One emitted only steam, a vent. In the other, a small speck of red glowed, and heat rose in thermals Wend thrilled to ride. They remembered wanting to share this with Avery and thought they could easily find the more spectacular eruption they'd flown over before, if it was still active. They tried to veer west to investigate, but Avery dove down toward a small hotel at the edge of the larger crater.

Following Avery's lead, Wend slowed and took in the cluster of red buildings surrounded by a low stone wall and red picnic tables. A sign in front read "Volcano House," and Avery unabashedly swooped through the wall at one end by a parking lot.

Wend's stomach sank with a weight alien to their bird form. The fact they stayed airborne despite the weight surprised them, until Wend remembered they were only an observer. They had no physical presence in this place. When Avery darted in and out of the hotel wall, clearly beckoning Wend, they had no desire to observe inside. Wend didn't want to use this gift to spy, especially now that they'd confirmed how real it was.

Avery darted in and out of a specific window. They flew in tight circles around and then through Wend, until Wend conceded and perched on the windowsill with them. Open curtains and a light inside revealed an ordinary hotel room, with pleasant wood fixtures, and a red and white motif Wend considered a bit overdone.

At the far end of a king-sized bed, studying a tablet on her lap, sat Mira.

Wend was not surprised. They couldn't even blame Avery for invading their mother's privacy after finding out she'd come to Hawai'i to interfere after their choice to reconnect. But Wend couldn't spy on someone who'd once been their friend, their lover, in some ways their teacher. They flew to the roof to stare out at the black immensity of Volcanoes National Park, at the slight glow and steam from a crater within a crater.

In Wend's mind's eye, the scene overlay the glimpse they'd caught of Mira, sitting calmly alone, late at night. The page open on her tablet represented the marine biology department at UH Mānoa, a detailed map. A mother staying up late to research her twenty-nine-year-old's graduate studies program seemed reasonable. If Avery wanted to read over her shoulder, Wend couldn't object. At least they hadn't found Mira with a lover or writing a diary entry. Thoughts of how their dream flying could be misused made Wend want to fly back to bed.

Except, they couldn't leave Avery that way. They waited. Afterward, they led Avery to the more active volcanic site. Clearly impressed, Avery circled and swooped. But Wend's heart wasn't in it anymore.

The next morning, Wend woke in the loft of the safe space and shivered. Burrowing deeper beneath pillows and blankets didn't help.

They stumbled into the living room and then out to the backyard where Matt and Kai sat. At the table where they'd once shared tea, there were now coffee and croissants.

"I saved you a chocolate croissant," Kai said, setting aside their phone.

The way Matt pursed his lips suggested the snappy retort or contradiction he didn't voice. Instead, his look grew serious as he studied Wend. "You sleep alright?"

With a shake of their head, Wend pulled out a chair and said mostly to Kai, "Does anyone here worry about dream people reading over their shoulder? Or anything written you leave lying around? And not just at night?"

"Nah, I worried about someone watching me have sex at first. Then I embraced my inner exhibitionist." Kai raised their coffee cup as if in a toast.

"You were never shy," Matt said with a soft shove to Kai's knee. Then more seriously to Wend he said, "Our household talked about intentional spying before, but decided none of us want to live with that level of paranoia. Until Avery proved us wrong, we imagined someone would have to be on the same island and have exemplary control to target us that way. I'm guessing Avery had no problem collecting you from the safe space last night and then wanted to look around?"

"They didn't look around here!" Wend found that idea appalling. "But they knew where Mira was staying and found her reading something about their university department."

"Anything interesting?" Kai asked.

"I didn't go in to look!" Wend took a deep breath and tried to calm down.

"So how do you know? You and Avery can't talk or hear anything when you dream together, can you?" Matt sipped his coffee and responded calmly, even as he blatantly fished for more information.

"No." Wend had assumed none of them could hear in flying dreams and hoped that was true, or no conversation they had would ever feel safe again. "I caught a glimpse through the window before going to wait on the roof." As an owl, it had felt natural to perch up there, although they hadn't made that connection at the time. Back in their own body, they realized how much safer they felt while invisible and insubstantial. While they agreed that living every moment as if someone might be watching would be unbearable, they wondered how their childhood had been shaped by flying free in their dreams. But many sorts of dreams must offer people escape, even if they didn't believe they were real. "That reminds me, how well defined are your forms in flying dreams? Mine were always vague before, but with Avery they're very specific. I was a pueo and could tell Avery was too, even without really seeing them. Are there affinities involved in flying dreams?"

"No idea," Matt said. "Maybe Avery's ability to travel so far and fast has to do with their forms being more detailed? They said they'd been a falcon the first time they flew between islands, right? And they mentioned dreaming themself into those microbes. They already knew that was a different sort of dreaming."

"Do some of us only have one kind?" Wend asked.

A soft smiled grew on Matt's face before he said, "It's good to hear you say 'us.'"

Wend's defenses melted like wax. They almost reached out to hold Matt's hand, but they already felt too exposed. They reached for the chocolate croissant instead. Swallowing the first bite felt intimate in its own way, like being touched inside. While Matt and Kai knew each other far better than Wend knew either of them, they'd saved Wend breakfast. They'd expected Wend to join them. More surprisingly, Wend felt perfectly comfortable doing so and speaking about worries and dreams without any fear of rejection or scorn. This might be the first time in Wend's life that they'd felt that comfortable with more than one other person at a time, felt like part of an "us" without reservation.

"I wish I had more to tell you," Matt said. "Some of us rarely have dreams of either sort. But as with any form of dreaming, we may forget. Some certainly have more control than others, and standard techniques to improve lucid dreaming may help. Still, I've practiced a fair amount, and I've never had much control in flying dreams, not even as much as you described back in preschool."

"But you've shared flying dreams with others?" Wend thought they remembered Matt saying that back on O'ahu.

"Only with Verilyn, and only twice."

"Did she pull you in? Was it different from your own flying dreams in any way?" Wend asked.

Matt blushed. "She sort of carried me. I was small, and she was much larger with huge wings. Rather than a predator and prey thing, I thought of it like the eagles rescuing Bilbo."

"That is perfect." Kai busted up laughing and said to Wend, "That is totally their relationship in a nutshell."

Wend had already guessed Matt was submissive with Verilyn as his dominant, and he'd mentioned non-sexual pet play and age play before. Wend could easily imagine that mapping onto a hobbit being rescued by a giant eagle.

Wend liked the idea of Matt having someone to rescue and carry him. "What about flying dreams on your own?"

Matt held his coffee without sipping for a long moment as he thought. "I'm more like a spirit that floats around, drawn to certain places rather than planning a destination."

This suddenly seemed more personal than Wend had realized at first, and they decided not to ask Kai.

Kai volunteered on their own, waving a piece of croissant in an arc that suggested a smooth gliding launch. "I'm some kind of human when flying on my own, maybe a merperson or someone with wings or part dragon. But yeah, my head and shoulders at least feel like my own. I'll leave it to Tanny to speak for himself, but every dream I've shared with him worked by his rules. With Tera it can go either way, my forms or hers, and I don't think it's a matter of who pulls the other in. But the one time I flew with Verilyn, she was definitely huge compared to me." They smiled wide with admiration, so Wend figured that must have been a good thing.

"Speaking of Verilyn," Matt mentioned as Wend finished their croissant, "she took off for Oʻahu this morning. The private investigator watching Perez at the airport said he never boarded his plane. And not to make you paranoid when we were cautioning against that, but he supposedly dozed off at the gate. When he woke up, he seemed agitated and started checking something on his phone. Then he got up and left the airport."

"What? When were you going to tell me?" Wend didn't push away or hide their agitation.

"As soon as you ate?" Matt tucked his chin as he answered.

Not sure what to think of that, Wend blinked as their mind raced. "Is there any chance he knows about Avery or the samples in the UH Mānoa lab?"

"I don't see how," Kai said.

"You said you had office space there?" Wend asked Matt. At his nod they continued, "Maybe I could set up to work from there for a while? Just in case Avery needs me?"

Matt's eyes went wide before focusing in tight on Wend's own. "I'd like to come, too. It would be easier to sort out office space that way. You could stay at the apartment with Verilyn and me again, and you know we'd also want to help Avery. Or you, right?"

It was obvious even to Wend that Matt worried for them almost the same way they worried for Avery. They looked to Kai for any additional insights.

Kai shook their head and said, "Some of us still have to show up for work." With a glance at their phone they added, "I'm teaching Enviro 101 in an hour. But I'm happy to relay messages and keep an eye on things here while you're gone. Don't take all the fudge."

 **30.**

WEND PAID FOR their own roundtrip ticket to Honolulu, and it was their largest non-essential purchase in years. At least zero emissions travel was not only available but standard here. "Was Verilyn involved in any legal battles against local airlines?" They turned to Matt, seated beside them. He wore a brilliant vest of woven reds, pinks, and purples, but kept his arms tightly crossed in front of it. "You can use the armrest or overlap my space. I don't mind," Wend said.

Matt shrugged, arms still crossed. "I can't stand playing into those stereotypes. Anyway, within Hawai'i, we had enough solar power and hydrogen fuel production by 2035 to make the changeover for local flights mostly a matter of marketing. International service may lead to legal battles by 2050 if the US lets their requirements for flights over 500 miles slide." Matt chuckled softly, mostly to himself. "Every small business association meeting ever includes someone complaining that we'll make Hawai'i uncompetitive, no matter that a circular carbon economy with open air recapture makes no sense long term, especially with international air travel."

Wend enjoyed hearing Matt intertwine science and business concerns, but they couldn't work out if the stereotypes about armrests that he wanted to avoid involved simply being large, acting entitled as a man, or something more. Wend didn't think the quiet plane was an appropriate place to ask, but tried to let their concern show as they purposefully made eye contact. "Seeing your arms boxed up like that makes me uncomfortable, and I'm not that shy of touch, at least not with people I know." When Matt relaxed his arms a little, hands still clasped but with elbows on the armrests, Wend tried asking, "What would it take for Hawai'i to stick to the 2050 goal for zero-carbon flights at international airports? More natural disasters?"

"Maybe, but I'm betting on California."

That surprised a laugh out of Wend, and neither of them startled when Wend's arm brushed Matt's elbow. He continued in a lighter tone, "If California holds the line for net-zero emissions by 2050, along with Europe and Japan, Hawai'i should align with that standard. If the rest of the US won't lead, they can follow."

Matt relaxed as he spoke, and Wend realized they hadn't spent much time with him alone. "You still think of yourself as Californian?"

"No, but they have as much pull for climate change as any country outside the US. Hawai'i can't change the aviation market on its own, but California ranks in the top ten world economies year after year, no matter the forecasts of doom and gloom."

"Where California leads, the nation follows?" The tagline was almost a joke now, but Matt's smile showed he understood the sentiment.

"Spoken like a true California kid," he said.

That led to Wend sharing a story of being disqualified from a 'California Kids' writing contest back in grade school because they'd been born in Hawai'i, and how it confused them because they'd already been told they didn't count as Hawai'ian.

"I always thought of you as both Californian and Hawai'ian." Matt leaned his head to almost touch Wend's as he said it, and a tension inside Wend finally eased, fully accepting the graying man beside them as the kid from the sandbox at Walnut Tree Preschool.

"I tried to teach myself Greek in high school, because I thought I wasn't Greek enough," Matt admitted in turn. "As it happens, I'm not good with languages, but I enjoy etymology. I found it cool that 'genealogy' came from the Greek 'genea' and 'logia.' Then I tried out Hellenic neo-paganism, which eventually led me to that group in Boston. Paganism had a much greater impact on how I defined myself than my Greek heritage did, in the long run."

For the rest of the flight, Wend and Matt caught each other up on the life stories they were comfortable telling in a semi-public space. If their arms rested together as they each leaned into the conversation, Wend didn't mind at all.

At the airport, Wend bought a burner phone and immediately texted

Avery: "Back to where we first swam as sea otters. Don't want to interrupt your end of term. Let me know if you need anything."

A minute later they read: "Mostly done. Still here Friday?"

Seeing it was Wednesday already, Wend thought that was likely. As they exchanged a couple of brief messages, Wend found the communication reassuring. For them, a few words on a screen were as real as a voice on the phone or even video. Another shared flying dream would be better, but Wend tried not to be greedy.

Realizing others might appreciate a similar reassurance, Wend sent their new number to Aljon and let him know they'd arrived safely in Honolulu.

As promised, Matt took them to see the office space available above Matthaios Water Wonders in the mall where they'd stayed before. Matt's personal office was small and crowded with a drafting table desk, computer desk, and a filing system equipped to hold large blueprints in the bottom drawers. The walls were covered with overlapping schematics and sketches, but Matt guided Wend to a tidier office in front of his own with a series of framed blueprints on the wall. He pointed proudly at one labeled "Frog Paddler." "I would have called it 'Wend's Frog Paddler' if I'd had a way to ask permission. As you can guess by the name of the store, I thought of that as a bonus at the time. Now I'm pretty sure you wouldn't have liked it."

With a shake of their head Wend said, "I appreciate the thought." Glancing around the tidy room they stood in, Wend asked, "Is this the unused office?"

"It's meant for an admin; that's why it's right in front. But the company isn't structured that way anymore. Those less involved in retail mostly telecommute. If people walking through bothers you, the internet wiring to our apartment here is equally good. We could move this computer to the room you stayed in before," he waved to the desktop model with two large flat screens and an office-sized printer.

"But other people stay there sometimes, right?"

"Some of the financial people have been using it once a month and around tax time—" He was clearly about to suggest they could stay someplace else when Wend cut him off.

"Don't worry about it. You know, the Marine Census offer includes an allowance for office space and equipment. You don't need to give me anything."

"I know." Matt held up his hands in surrender. "I'm hoping you'll want your main office back on our island. I can offer you a much better view there." This office didn't have a window. Even Matt's offered only an obstructed street view behind the mall. "You could rent or buy whatever equipment you want, and we'll make the necessary arrangements to move it. Are you officially working this week?"

Wend hadn't signed a new contract since their suspension. Technically, they had until Monday to decide on the Marine Census offer, and whether they wanted to work something out with UH Hilo. Either way, they'd intended to mostly work from Hilo. Despite their whole itinerant history, Wend had started to feel at home. Not sure what to do with that realization, they quickly shifted gears. "I should get a cellphone or laptop to follow up with the genetics lab here and finish some articles and paperwork I had in progress."

"I have a gaming laptop I'm no longer using that I would happily lend or give you," Matt started, but with a glance at Wend's shaking head he finished, "Or I could go with you to the computer shop downstairs to see what they'll pay for it. And you can see if they have something better suited to your needs."

When they entered the computer store Matt was greeted with an immersive holographic ad describing a completely automated honeybee hive that could be delivered complete with a Hawaiʻi-raised queen bee. Wend wondered if he'd consented or opted in for such ads, and if there was some way for bystanders to opt out. A moment later a chirpily enthusiastic employee offered to help Matt find whatever he was seeking. He glanced back to Wend who waved him off, relieved when the honeybee ad disappeared.

The room buzzed with demos for other holographic applications, voice recognition software, and XR devices including haptics and gaming rooms. The salespeople shot about like a cloud of static electricity making the brightly colored room seem impossibly crowded. More than a minute passed before a slouchy employee with floppy blond hair and skin tanned just short of a painful burn said to Wend, "Sorry, your ID and devices aren't reading right. You wanna clue me?"

"My name is Wend, pronouns they/them. My dive wallet is waterproof and signal-blocking, for chip security. I'd like to explore my options for laptops and cellphones, preferably refurbished."

Ten minutes later, Wend was ready to retreat to the apartment. And possibly hide under a bed. It wasn't that they disliked the models they'd been shown; touchscreen security and auto-encryption options were available on relatively affordable laptops, although they'd need a more serious computer to perform complex genetic analysis. Their young surfer-type salesperson could not understand Wend's dislike for newer cellphones that assumed the user would constantly wear an ear accessory for silent prompting, but the condescension when Wend asked about cheaper options was minimal.

As soon as possible, Wend said, "I have enough notes to look over. I'll get back to you when I've made my decision."

"I'd be happy to answer more questions. Used inventory turns over fast. Hate for you to miss out."

The name tag on the floppy-banged helper said "Cece." Wend tried, "Cece, I appreciate your help. I'll ask for you or do what I can to see you get credit for any sale, and I'll understand if something sells before I get back. But I'm not ready to buy anything right now."

Matt, who had been waiting quietly after a quick discussion with another store employee at the trade-ins desk, joined Wend almost instantly. "Ready to go?"

"Definitely." They fled the store with only a perfunctory, "Thank you, Cece."

Once they'd escaped to the courtyard beside the waterfall wall with the plant mosaic, Matt asked, "Would you like to get dinner at The Best Hawai'ian Chocolate or eat back in the apartment?"

Exhaling one slow breath, Wend said, "I'll head back to the apartment. But you can do something else if you want."

"Nah, I've spent plenty of time at all the places I like here. Let's head up and see what Verilyn's plans are for this evening."

Verilyn, it turned out, had ordered a big box of vegetables and sat chopping them at the dining room table. "I hoped you two would show up before dinner. I need stir fry. Anyone interested?"

"Sure," Matt said. "Should I start the rice cooker?"

Verilyn nodded assent. Then to Wend she said, "You're welcome to join us, unless you'd like time alone. We could let you know when dinner is ready."

With someone else, Wend would have second- and third-guessed whether Verilyn wanted Wend out of the way or would think Wend rude if they didn't help. In the present circumstance, Wend said, "I could chop vegetables or research computers on my own. Do you have a preference?"

"I would love your company whenever you're ready," Verilyn replied.

"Let me put these papers away." As Wend headed to the room they'd stayed in before, Matt passed them the quote he'd been given for his laptop. "Consider it with the rest. It makes at least as much sense to sell it to you as to the store, and you'd avoid a huge markup."

Without any further explanation or even looking up from her chopping, Verilyn said, "Retailers are allergic to paying retail."

Wend accepted the paper but barely glanced at it before leaving the whole stack on their bed to study later. Instead of dealing with that, they washed their hands and asked Verilyn, "How can I help?"

Soon they were chopping carrots on a cutting board beside Verilyn's as she brought them up to speed on reports from her private investigator. "Gillian Ainsley appears to have flown back to Oʻahu last night, taken over Perez's apartment lease, and reported to the head of the Ocean Planning Committee this morning, as planned. It's unclear whether she realizes Perez never left."

In the kitchen, Matt nodded along without comment as he started the rice maker and pulled out a package of extra-firm tofu.

"Should we tell her?" Wend asked.

When Verilyn stopped chopping, Wend looked her way. Verilyn motioned for Matt to join them, and he settled across the table with a calm but serious expression as Verilyn continued, "No. I know you want to trust Gillian, but it's useful to wait and see what information she offers. After Perez's abrupt departure from the airport last night, he went directly to Kewalo Harbor. He was observed making a heated phone call from there. We don't know who he called or why. Our Oʻahu investigator is checking if anyone of interest received a call at eleven last night or has a boat or slip there. All we know for now is that he seemed angry during his phone call and then close to tears afterward. He spent the night in a nearby hotel where he'd not made a reservation."

Before Verilyn said anything more, she pulled out her phone and gestured for Wend to move the cutting board aside. Realizing they were still holding a knife, they set that down, too.

"I've been exploring what Perez might have seen on his phone. What would send him haring off to Kewalo Harbor? Nothing in the news last night matched. But the bombing at Hilo Harbor was trending in the news here, and I found a link to a previous bombing at Kewalo Harbor. It happened nearly two years ago, and involved marine explosives and a marine construction robot rather than a rescue robot. I have a couple of calls out to see if there might have been a similar trigger mechanism or anything else to connect the two incidents. I haven't heard back, but I tracked down a local yacht club article about helping the family. A mother and child were asleep on the boat at the time of the blast." Verilyn passed her phone to Wend with the article open, "Their last name was Simonian. I verified that they were the spouse and child of that engineer from IdeoBios, Randal Simonian. There's no mention of him being present during the bombing. There's no mention of him at all in this article asking club members to help the family. He seems to have disappeared at about the same time as that bombing."

The article didn't offer anything more. It was a brief, almost formulaic request for members to help a woman and child who'd suffered a traumatic experience and damage to their boat in the harbor. Wend's heart raced, and they could only ask, "Do you think he was killed that night? Do you think he died in the blast or Perez killed him separately?"

"Neither," Verilyn answered with surprising calm. "I don't believe the investigation after the blast would have missed human remains. But Perez going there last night and making an emotional phone call suggests new information. What if he was allied with someone else, both in whatever happened with Simonian and in harassing you? That other person may have orchestrated both bombings."

"Someone new is out to get me?" Wend asked, handing back the phone and pulling the cutting board with carrots closer. They weren't panicking. Rather, they felt tethered by a string that was gradually reeling them farther and farther away from whatever was happening. At least the cutting board and carrots stayed mundane and present.

"Probably to scare you. The Simonian bombing didn't cause injury or sink the ship, even though it seems to have gone to plan." Verilyn tucked her phone away and pulled her own cutting board back into place.

When Wend stayed quiet, Matt asked, "You think the first bombing was intended to scare Simonian into hiding?"

"The kid recruited to target the *Nuovo Mar* seems to have wanted

Wend and Seaward Generation off his island or maybe the Hawai'ian Islands in general, but he doesn't profile as a murderer. The previous bombing could have been a message for Randal Simonian and his family to leave as well. There's a lot we still don't know. Even if Perez concluded that both bombings were related, we don't have any evidence. This is all speculation."

"Do you think Gillian is involved?" Wend asked

"I don't have a sense of that yet." Verilyn sat up taller in her chair. "Should we get back to making dinner?"

Matt returned to the kitchen and turned on soft guitar music. Wend and Verilyn returned to chopping, neither of them in time to the music.

31.

WEND DRIFTED from the too large bed up to the sloped ceiling. They twisted around, reaching for an air-light touch, searching for a barely seen image. There was none. Wend's body flowed, amorphous, projecting arms or flippers to steer through the air, but they didn't recreate any of the marine mammals or birds they'd been with Avery. They wondered if they'd emerged into this dream form too early and Avery might still come.

The clock read half past three. Avery could have stayed up late or upset their normal sleep schedule to finish something for school. It wasn't like they needed to fly to another island tonight.

Or maybe they'd chosen to fly to Hawai'i to check on their mother instead. Wend tried not to think of that as spying. They tried not to feel left behind or left out. The way Avery had pulled Wend into flying dreams four nights in a row was extraordinary compared to everything Kai and Matt described. There might be limits or constraints on the ability that Avery wasn't aware of yet, or they might need to focus on school for now.

Still, Wend waited around the room for half an hour. The papers from the computer store were scattered over half the bed. Wend found them easy to read in this form despite the low light.

Matt's laptop was the logical choice, at least as a personal, portable computer for writing and communications. The graphics card that made it a reasonable gaming computer could support the design and analysis software Wend used as well. What they negotiated with the university would determine if they could visit campus occasionally to access large chunks of Marine Census data, but that shouldn't be necessary too often.

Eventually, Wend ran out of things to read or do in their room. The clock passed four.

They'd always loved flying in dream form and weren't going to waste the opportunity on moping.

Wend surged up through the roof. A single pull of their limbs shot them higher into the air than the first pull underwater after diving into a pool. The lights of Honolulu dazzled, no dimmer than on the weekend, although less traffic marked the roads. Instead of heading to Kāne'ohe, Wend soared over the beaches. They people-watched along Waikiki Beach, but neither rowdy partiers nor couples necking interested them much.

Tracing along a parkland led Wend to the famous Ala Wai Harbor. A burst upward offered a view of a newer harbor filled with rows of cookie cutter modern yachts, and Wend circled until they found the sign saying "Kewalo Harbor." They realized that had been their destination all along but didn't know if their own curiosity or some outside force had led them there.

They barely recognized the man standing at the end of the outermost dock.

Perez stood alone in the dark, inches from the calm harbor water with something bunched up at his feet. When he bent to lift it, Wend could see by the hunch of his shoulders that it was heavy. He tried once slowly and then squatted and jerked in a way that must have jolted his spine.

Wend only had a moment to interpret Perez dumping the heavy object off the end of the dock before they saw him yanked underwater after it.

A chain around his ankle linked Perez to the sinking object. No noise intruded on Wend's dream flight, but their mind knew the clank of chain and the heavy splash of an anchor.

The scream Wend let out didn't form a sound either. They spun in place, seeking watchers—whether someone forcing Perez to kill himself or someone who might call for help.

Wend needed to locate other witnesses to his drowning.

People strolled along Ala Moana Boulevard, but they were too far away to hear the clank of chain or the splash. Wend seemed to be the only one watching. In this non-corporeal form, what could they do?

Whatever they felt for Perez, Wend couldn't stand by and watch him die. They dove into the water, down to the bottom of the harbor where Perez

stood as if balanced on one foot, limbs suspended in a parody of ballet.
He didn't thrash or try to break free. Bubbles left his mouth in a slow
trickle, like tears from his eyes if he'd been crying. He looked remorseful,
or maybe that was Wend projecting. He certainly wasn't fighting to live.
Wend remembered their second near-drowning and how they'd initially
believed they were ready to die. They wondered what Perez experienced
before, and why he'd chosen this form of suicide now.

Not sure how Avery had pulled them into dream flight or what such an
attempt would do to Perez while awake but drowning, Wend dove at his
chest. They clawed and pulled.

Their touch passed through him. There wasn't the faintest sense of shared
space the way Wend sensed when their wings overlapped with Avery
in dream form. Wend flailed and focused, but nothing they tried had
any more effect than when they flew through the roof of a house. Perez
showed no awareness of their presence. The water around him seemed
strangely devoid of fish or any macroscopic sea life. As far as Perez knew,
he'd died alone.

There were no more bubbles. Wend had no idea how much time had
passed.

A single pull with their arms carried Wend up above water. Above the
dock. Above Kewalo Harbor.

No activity suggested anyone realized a person had drowned.

Not knowing what else to do, Wend flew back to the apartment where
their body lay asleep in a too large bed covered with meaningless papers.

Wend awoke shuddering and staggered out their bedroom door. They
made their way across the common room and pounded on the door
behind which Matt and Verilyn slept.

By the time Matt answered in only a robe, Wend was sobbing. The
emotions they usually held in check during a crisis flooded out. In a way,
the crisis was over. Wend woke the others because they couldn't bear it
alone.

"What's wrong?" Matt asked, reaching out his arms but stopping a few inches short of Wend's shoulders.

"Perez drowned himself at Kewalo Harbor," Wend gasped out, falling forward and trusting Matt to catch them. "I watched in dream form and couldn't help him. I don't think anyone else saw."

"Are you sure he's already dead?" Verilyn asked matter-of-factly.

Wend nodded.

"Bring them here," Verilyn said from the bed. She'd pushed herself up to sitting against the headboard with a couple pillows wedged behind her. She wore a light-colored satiny nightshirt that shimmered as she turned on a bedside light.

Matt guided Wend to sit on the edge of the bed beside Verilyn and sat down beside them, keeping an arm around Wend's shoulders. Wend couldn't stop crying, but their breathing evened out as they leaned into Matt's shoulder.

"I followed him under. I tried to pull him out, like Avery pulls me into dream forms, but I couldn't do anything. I saw the bubbles stop. I don't know how long I was down there, but the docks were still quiet when I flew up. I don't think anyone else noticed. It was just past four when I left here."

"And it's barely past five now, so not that long. You say he drowned himself. How?" Verilyn asked.

Wend felt compelled to answer. It was a relief to follow Verilyn's lead. "There was a chain around his ankle and something heavy he could barely lift. He had to try a second time to heft it off the dock. I think it was an anchor, at least sixty pounds from the way he struggled with it. When it held him to the bottom, he didn't fight. He didn't want to live, even at the end. I knew how he felt, and I couldn't even show him that he wasn't dying alone."

Matt held Wend a little tighter and said, "You did all you could. We can let someone know. See it's handled with respect."

Wend couldn't see whatever silent conversation or knowing looks Matt and Verilyn exchanged. Verilyn picked up her phone and told Wend, "I think it's best to call in an anonymous tip about a suicide. I'll check with the private investigation firm first. Someone was supposed to be watching Perez. Is there anything else you want me to do or that I should know?"

All Wend had to do was shake their head. Matt kept an arm around them as Verilyn made the phone calls.

By the time the sun rose around seven, Wend, Matt, and Verilyn had all showered, dressed, and eaten. The island patrol collected Perez's body from Kewalo Harbor and confirmed his identity. Verilyn's private investigator reported Perez had not left his hotel via the front door, so they hadn't known to follow him. He'd had a single guest. The investigator sent a picture of the visitor leaving the hotel before midnight. It was a terrible photo taken in the dark from a distance, but it was enough to distinguish a short dark-haired person.

"Definitely not Gillian," Matt commented from the corner of the couch he'd taken over, "but could be half the island."

"Probably less than a quarter," Verilyn replied from where she'd parked her chair by the dining table. She'd shifted into work mode and kept busy with her phone and tablet.

Wend had been lazing in an armchair, watching Honolulu rooftops catch the morning light as the business district came to life in the shaded streets below. Both the dreamlike quality of the morning and their sorrow from the night before had faded with the sun. Not knowing how to help with other investigations, they decided it was time to return to their regular work. "I guess I'd like to buy your laptop, if you seriously want to sell it. What's a fair price?"

Matt's mouth opened, but he took longer than usual to answer. "I know everyone deals with grief in their own way, but selling you anything four hours after you saw . . . what you saw, just doesn't feel right."

"I need something to do," Wend admitted. "Maybe I'm trying to escape into work, but I can't process any more emotions right now. I'd rather do something useful and normal. I looked over the estimates and ratings for different equipment last night before . . . and even with a fifty percent markup, your laptop would be the best deal. I'm assuming the price they offered you for it was low and you'd never really sell it through them. So let me buy it."

"I almost certainly would have given it away. I hate dealing with that stuff. Large contract negotiations I can handle, but I'm more of the 'what's mine is yours' school with friends." He sighed and let his head fall back on the couch. "I realize that may sound entitled or privileged or make people uncomfortable or like I'm trying to buy their affections, but I'm stating how I feel."

It surprised Wend to hear so much hurt and stress pouring out of Matt over gifting. Wend had rarely had much to give beyond their work or their stories. But they'd been shamed or called out multiple times for trying to protect their personal belongings in settings where others borrowed without asking. Matt's worries, about seeming entitled or like he was trying to buy someone's affections, filled Wend's mind with a cascade of imagined lectures and insults directed at him for the opposite reason. "I'm glad you told me. We all set different boundaries around our belongings and I want to respect yours, but it matters more for me to be very clear on what's mine."

Verilyn held out her tablet already opened to a personal payment app with Matt's information displayed. "How about this? You transfer whatever the store quoted, which I'm certain is the most anyone could get Matt to accept." Matt nodded and turned wide, hopeful eyes to Wend as Verilyn continued, "I already heard you won the argument to pay for your own plane fare this time and am suitably impressed. We can deal with the office space issue later."

Wend took the tablet and typed in their account info and the price as quoted.

Once the transfer completed and they handed the tablet back, Verilyn told Matt, "Now give them their computer, and be done with it."

"Thank you," Matt said to Verilyn with wide-open, grateful eyes. She patted his shoulder as he passed on his way to their bedroom.

In the brief time Matt was away, Wend turned to Verilyn and wondered if they could get a pat on the shoulder for saying thank you, but they weren't ready to ask for that. Instead they said, "Thanks for helping with this and, well, everything this morning."

"You're welcome, and I'm truly glad I could help." Verilyn's kind words landed much like a reassuring pat for Wend. The silence that followed felt safe, as if they'd reached a larger understanding.

Matt came back with the laptop, power cord, laptop bag, and a backup battery that he handed to Wend in a tidy pile. "It should be all cleared out and ready to use, but let me know if there are any issues. I think a six-month warranty and service agreement is standard."

Verilyn laughed.

Wend smiled. "Thank you. I'm sure it will be fine." Then they got to work sorting through two days of missed communications and mostly meaningless campus and project updates.

They stopped short an hour later when a message from UH Mānoa that should have contained a link for the full report on the PET bacteria listed the documents as "withheld." Searching for more information led Wend down a rabbit hole of bureaucratic doublespeak until they discovered that someone from UH Hilo had marked the report as no longer needed on behalf of the entire Marine Science Project. All the work had been done, but Wend couldn't see the report because someone had blocked the final transfer of funds for two hours pay to a lab tech.

Wend was willing to pay out of pocket. It would be less than the fifty percent extra they'd tried to give Matt for the laptop they now owned. But the site wouldn't let Wend pay as a private individual. "Verilyn," Wend asked, "do you know how I officially accept the offer to work directly for the Marine Census Project so I can authorize paying a UH Mānoa lab tech?"

In the end, accepting the new position involved multiple explanations, decisions, and gathering advice from not only Matt and Verilyn but the lawyer, Cynthia Shapiro. Wend visited the office above Matthaios Water Wonders to print, sign, and scan physical documents. Only after completing the equivalent of a crash course in HR could Wend fully claim their new position as a local contractor for the Marine Census Project, leaving them independent of, but free to negotiate teaching or lab time with, the University of Hawaiʻi.

Then, after two hours of untangling bureaucracy to cleanly switch positions, Wend discovered they couldn't change the payment code for the report without waiting two business days for account verification or visiting the lab in person.

"Is this really 2039?" Wend grumbled to Matt and Verilyn, who had both followed them to the tiny windowless office. "I guess I might as well visit UH Mānoa, since it's just down the train line."

"Sounds fun," Verilyn said. "One of our favorite coffee shops is right at the edge of campus. I'm sure we could all use a snack given our early start this morning."

"You don't need to waste more of your morning on this. I'm pretty comfortable with college campuses and labs." Wend tucked the papers they'd signed into their new laptop bag and looked around for anything they might be missing.

It was Matt who said softly, "You realize we're no closer to identifying whoever sent a bomber after you two nights ago?"

"But we're pretty sure they only intended to scare me." In truth, Wend had somewhat forgotten while caught up in bureaucratic minutiae. Their shoulders tightened into a higher position as they remembered all the rest.

"I doubt they planned on you jumping in and taking their bomb for a swim." Matt shivered, and Wend realized his shoulders were more tense than theirs. "Could you accept that Verilyn and I would feel better staying at least as close as the coffee shop? It truly is one of our favorites, with cats and board games even."

"Sounds nice," Wend said. "Let's go."

Wend walked alone from the coffee shop to the marine biology genetics lab. They carried the laptop bag over one shoulder and a chocolate muffin that should have been called an unfrosted cupcake in their opposite hand. The hot humid air melted away much of Wend's tension, although they knew the grief from what they'd witnessed would circle back given time.

Buildings on the Mānoa campus crowded together, taller and mostly older than at UH Hilo. Students everywhere turned frenetic this time of year. Wend loved sunny college campuses with plenty of outdoor activity and instantly oriented to the rhythms of this one. Even being older and unfamiliar with the campus, Wend felt comfortably anonymous. They took their time, enjoyed their muffin, and read the signs on every door. They found the campus IT center and an office for the National Weather Center. They noted fliers for a band called "Hello Honu" and a science talk titled "Ocean Hazards: Deep Subject."

When they finished snacking, Wend entered a three-story tan build-ing and made their way to the basement. A helpful sign pointed them toward the "Ocean Genomics Lab." The door opened onto a large chilly room with three separate "clean" areas enclosed by clear interior walls, a machine Wend recognized as processing samples from their bots, and oth-ers Wend could identify as fairly high-end genetic sequencing equipment. At the front counter, a deeply tanned, large but short man whose name tag read "Lou Chan, Marine Genomics Lab manager, he/him" stood arguing with none other than Wend's former supervisor, Lorelei Kahale. In plastic and metal chairs to one side sat Avery, who removed their headphones as Wend entered, and Mira, who wore a white visitor's badge that noted she was "Avery's mom."

Mira jumped up saying, "What are you doing here?"

At that, Kahale looked over her shoulder and then turned to say in an even harsher and more disturbing tone of voice, "What are you doing here?"

Wend snapped to a place beyond panic that they usually reached only when someone was injured or they had to speak in front of a non-student audience. "I'm here to clear up a payment issue that caused a report I ordered to be withheld."

That shut everyone up except Kahale who practically shouted, "You're suspended!"

"You realize a lawyer challenged that and the Marine Census Project is now reviewing the local administration?" Wend asked, almost but not quite meeting Kahale's gaze. From the corner of their eye, they saw Avery doing something with their phone behind Mira's back. "Anyway," Wend continued, shifting sideways to better see Lou Chan behind the counter, "I've accepted an offer to work directly for the Marine Census Project. I'm all set up with an independent billing account as of this morning, and I was informed I could come here in person and show ID to avoid a 48-hour online verification process before receiving results from the sample I submitted."

Wend held their ID out toward Chan while keeping more than an arm's length from Kahale and Mira.

Unfortunately, that was when Mira regained her power of speech. "Wait, you were suspended? Is it your sample Avery's trying to study? Because they received a notice their report was being withheld. I thought this lab was either incompetent or placing unreasonable barriers in their way. Which is it?" The last seemed to be directed at Chan.

Chan accepted Wend's ID and said with stilted politeness and a blank expression, "If you could all relax a minute, I will check on all requests."

While Chan ran Wend's ID through a scanner and clicked through tabs on his computer monitor, Kahale leaned across the counter saying, "That sample and all reports derived from it belong to my department, a department with which this employee is no longer affiliated." She pointed an accusatory finger in Wend's direction.

Wend took a deep breath and focused on the chill lab air, the smell of ammonia, the hum of machinery, and the white of Chan's lab coat.

He stood at the counter a moment later and said, "Dr. Gwendolyn Taylor's name is on the original sample with requests for sequencing and full reports." More slowly and a little more sternly, he said, "They were previously listed as working for the Marine Science Department on Hilo but all billing went through a Marine Census Project account not affiliated with the university. Your previous hold only worked because Dr. Taylor was affiliated with your department. Now they are not." He shrugged as if he gave these sorts of speeches to department heads every day. "Our system already updated to show Dr. Taylor has full authority as a local contractor with an account directly authorized by the Marine Census Project. The additional report requested by student Avery Mlakar is billed to a graduate research account on this campus. At this point, only Dr. Taylor could deny that request."

"I can have my reports?" Wend realized they hadn't expected to be given their results today, not after seeing Kahale there in person to argue. "Thank you."

"I'm releasing electronic copies now." Chan tapped a single button.

"You can't do that," Kahale protested, voice rising along with one pointed finger.

"I just did." His steady voice and still body language contrasted neatly with Kahale's drama.

"Thoughtless actions have ruined greater careers than yours," Kahale threatened Chan. "I won't let this stand."

"Take it up with my union. I'm a professional, not an academic." Chan did a convincing job of sounding unconcerned, although Wend could sense a mounting irritation.

Kahale spun around to confront Wend, "You, I can ruin. Ask your little friend in Environmental Science."

Oddly enough, that was what started alarm bells ringing in Wend's mind. They only knew one person in Environmental Science but still managed a semi-credible, "Who?"

"Someone who lost their shot at department head after making an island patrol report much like yours. Did you think I wouldn't connect the dots?" Kahale waved a finger near Wend's face, causing them to take a step back.

With one deep breath, Wend managed to ask all in one go, "How were you involved with an island patrol report filed by someone in Environmental Science two years ago?"

That was when Kahale shut up. She strode out the lab door, but it opened to reveal two island patrol officers. Wend noted that the officers' badges were slightly different here on Oʻahu and these two wore campus ID as well. They could hear Kahale arguing as the officers recited a statement of rights and the doors swung shut.

The louder and closer voice of Mira overrode the noise in the hall. "What have you gotten yourself involved in now?" Wend glanced back to see if this was aimed at them or Avery. Mira was completely focused on Wend, to the exclusion of Avery and her camera.

Rather than try to justify anything to Mira, Wend took one step farther from her and closer to the end of the counter. "Thanks a lot, for your help with that," Wend said to Chan. "Can you tell me if the report this student requested is with the materials I was sent and whether I'm allowed to share it?" They nodded toward Avery but felt they should keep a professional distance with all that was going on. They didn't want to bring any further attention or stress Avery's way, since they'd been listening to the whole encounter without headphones. Unless Wend missed their guess, Avery was also recording or sharing either video or audio of the entire incident from their phone.

"They requested a separate report on a microbe found concurrently in your sample." He looked between Wend and Avery as if trying to figure out their connection. "You technically have a complete data set already with genomic analysis, but you could purchase a copy of the additional report they requested for twenty dollars. I don't see why you couldn't share it with whoever you want, but I'm not a lawyer. If you've really got one already, you might ask them."

"Thanks again," Wend said. They tried to smile and look in the general vicinity of his face, but they were close to needing a break. "I'd like to purchase that additional report." They offered their ID again.

He said, "Initial here." He held out a smaller device.

Wend initialed without reading what the screen said and repeated, "Thanks."

They turned to leave and were glad to find neither Kahale nor island patrol in the hall.

Mira and Avery followed them out, which wasn't a surprise. The fact Mira stayed quiet until they were all outside and standing under a nearby tree was.

"I deserve an explanation," Mira said. "You both told me not to come here until at least tomorrow, and now I find you're both here working on some shared project? And what's this about being suspended by UH Hilo?"

Avery answered before Wend could. "How would you feel if someone was hounding me the way you're hounding Wend? They solved a problem neither you nor I could, which was evidently blocking their request too, and they totally stood up to that jerk from UH Hilo who was taken away by island patrol. Who do you think was in the right?"

"Avery—" Mira began, visibly startled by Avery taking that stand. They turned to face Wend and started again. "Wend, I'm trying to stay calm and respect both your boundaries, but some of this is understandably disturbing from my perspective. Maybe we could all sit down for lunch together and talk things out."

"I think Wend has other friends to meet up with," Avery said to Mira. Then leaning toward Wend they said, "It's your call. I did stream all that video to Verilyn. I can send you a recording if you want."

Wend didn't think either they or Avery should have to deal with Mira right now, but also understood Avery needed to work through issues with their mother at their own pace. Wend would either have to invite Mira along, or leave Avery to her after all that had just happened. They hummed a few notes from the personal penguin song and forced a smile. "If you're already chatting with Verilyn, you could ask if she and Matt want to join us for lunch."

The five of them ended up at an outdoor campus food court. Since it was barely noon, they had no trouble claiming a large accessible table where they could have a mostly private conversation. Matt and Verilyn gave no indication of the rough morning they'd shared or of anything they'd heard about Mira before or seen in the video Avery streamed. They exchanged introductions with the pleasantries expected when meeting someone's parent.

Wend managed to say very little and to settle themself by focusing on the fresh rolls they'd chosen, made with smooth tofu and crunchy cucumber, sprouts, carrots, mango, and papaya all wrapped up in rice paper.

Somehow Verilyn steered the conversation away from Mira bragging about her hard work as Avery's mother, and led with, "You must have loved having the ocean nearby to float in during the last trying stages of pregnancy."

"Hah," snorted Mira, "like I'd dare venture out in a bathing suit by then. But the first day it got above 80 degrees that September, I slipped back into a pre-baby one-piece, and I had the cutest little swim diaper for Avery. They were barely three weeks old."

Matt and Verilyn exchanged a knowing look, presumably at gathering specific details on Avery's earliest visit to the ocean, which might help develop their theory on critical times for first exposure. Mira proudly opened her mouth, probably to tell more "baby stories," but Avery interrupted.

"I have an image of the new rotifer I plan to study." Avery showed Mira a sketch on their phone asking, "Does that count as cute?" Without waiting for an answer, they went on to explain how it coexisted in samples with the new PET-eating bacteria Wend was studying, specifying that they hadn't expected to see Wend or to even need to visit that particular lab today.

Realizing the mention was intentional, Wend followed Avery's lead and added that they hadn't expected to see Avery or visit that lab today and hadn't known Kahale was on Oʻahu.

Matt raised his eyebrows in an interesting way at that, but Wend decided any side discussions could wait until later. Angry about Kahale's tirade in the lab and at Mira for making the situation worse, Wend explained, "Until now, I thought Kahale had been approached by someone else who orchestrated the attack on Viola's boat, among other things. I'd been trying to keep Avery separate from all that, which was why we suggested you be circumspect after your appearance at the condo." Wend managed a quick glance at Mira's face, but didn't see any remorse or acceptance of responsibility. "From what Kahale said in there today, she may be more involved than I realized and could have been suppressing research into these PET-eating bacteria since they were first reported on Hawai'i two years ago."

After voicing their frustration and concern, an elaborate mosaic of manipulation and deceit assembled within Wend's mind. If Kahale had been involved two years ago, she could have been working with Perez the entire time.

Oh. That changed everything.

Kahale could be the mystery figure behind the bombings. As a marine biologist, she'd be familiar with the sorts of drones used, and possibly with marine explosives. Given Kahale's presence on O'ahu today, she could be the person in the picture, the one who visited Perez last night before he committed suicide. "Excuse me," Wend said.

They walked away as calmly as they could to hide behind the largest tree available and then crumpled as they struggled to breathe.

Matt leaned beside the tree a moment later, further shielding them from view. "I couldn't let you isolate yourself for what looks like the start of a panic attack. But I'll stand by quietly if you choose. Otherwise, I'm here if you want me."

Wend grabbed his hand without thinking.

"Squeeze twice if you want me to keep talking." After Wend squeezed twice, Matt crouched beside them and said, "Okay, do that again if you want me to shut up or if you need anything else. I'm pretty sure Verilyn was a full step ahead of us both on what you're worrying about. She's taking care of it and making sure we're all safe. Let's both focus on this safe, pleasantly warm day, with a light breeze in these slightly scraggly trees. By visiting in December, you're really not seeing the best of a campus reimagined as a botanical garden. Come back in a few months, and you can walk beneath this canopy barely noticing the boxy buildings all around. They have a plant finder app that explains which plants are native, Polynesian cultural heritage, or cosmopolitan."

Matt kept talking about the campus plants' biogeography as Wend focused on his hand, his voice, even his breathing—then on the larger world around them both, including the fresh, woodsy, and floral scents of the plants surrounding the food court.

"I don't usually fall apart this easily," Wend said, when they could speak normally again.

"Easily?" Matt shook their hands chidingly where they were still clasped together. "Are you kidding? I watched you take down your former boss while ignoring Avery's mom and however much you'd already guessed about Kai. You were totally badass in that lab."

"Sometimes my emotions get put on hold." The words came easily now, to Wend's surprise. "I guess my thoughts did too, because I didn't connect Kahale with the photo from last night or the bombings until I was spelling things out for Mira. I wouldn't have thought to call the island patrol. I'm assuming Verilyn managed that?"

Matt gave Wend's hand a gentle tug as they started to stand. "I think we all did pretty well today. The best work requires a team."

32.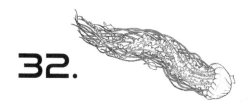

TAP DANCING around truths about dreams, the nightly life of microbes, and fortuitous sampling near plastic dumpsites elevated a socially awkward situation to teeth-grindingly painful for Wend. The only redeeming feature of the three-way video chat that afternoon with Cynthia Shapiro and Verilyn was the conclusion that Wend could send lab reports to Avery without creating further problems or drawing undue attention. They then set the Marine Census Project tools in motion to incorporate the new genetic information and analyses into the main database. No matter how they tried to streamline the process, it took effort to make new data easy to access with all the different search criteria and grouping methods various researchers needed.

Wend improved several cross-referencing factors for other new data sets before Verilyn said, "This sounds ominous."

That grabbed both Wend's and Matt's attention.

Verilyn continued without looking up, "Gillian wrote asking if we might join her for dinner tonight. She apologizes in advance for having to order something in and for her accommodations not yet being fully prepared for guests. Then she says she has documents of a 'sensitive and delicate' nature to share with us and congratulates us on reaching out to the authorities about Dr. Kahale at almost the same moment as she spoke with a different division."

"What led her to suspect Kahale?" Matt asked.

Verilyn half frowned before asking, "Shall we go tonight and find out?"

Wend would have preferred hiding out with their work and their new laptop for several days, but they knew Matt and Verilyn wanted to keep them close and realized that might still be wise. "Okay, do we need to bring anything?"

Matt rolled his shoulder and said, "I'll pick up a gift box from The Best
Hawaiʻian Chocolate."

"What a lovely box, thank you." Gillian accepted the gift from Matt when
they arrived and went on to ask about the locally produced chocolates
and the eco-friendly packaging. Wend glanced around the room trying
to determine which aspects weren't prepared for guests. Gillian had art
on the walls that showed dancers moving with a stop motion effect that
Wend couldn't imagine came with any apartment. There were books and
photos on display shelves and plants hanging by the front window.

Despite the upheavals of recent days, Gillian spoke about nothing
of consequence until they'd finished the pleasant Italian dinner she'd
ordered. That suited Wend, who hadn't eaten since their early and light
lunch. They enjoyed their salad, minestrone, and penne pomodoro while
letting others carry the conversation. Despite Gillian's protestations about
having to order in, the table was set with matching dishes and a white-on-
white embroidered tablecloth.

Only when tea and the chocolate gift box were set out, still at the dining table, did Gillian produce a flat box filled with papers.

"There's no easy way to lead into this. While I can't help but grieve
Perez's suicide, what he left behind makes me—makes me regret not saying harsher words to him years ago. Perez left a suicide note, and a box of
what he called 'evidence.'" She pushed the box across the table to Matt,
unopened. "This box contains photocopies of items I handed over to the
island patrol, most of which relate to Dr. Kahale or to Perez himself. There
are also photographs that appear to have been taken through windows into
your home, presumably without permission. I'm giving you the only copies
I have, but of course other copies or digital versions might be uncovered as
the investigation proceeds. Now, if you'll excuse me for a moment." Gillian
left the table for another room, possibly her bedroom, since it wasn't the
bathroom door that had previously been pointed out.

During dinner, they had each been sitting on their own side of a table
configured for four people. Now Matt pushed the box in front of Verilyn
and shifted his chair right up against her wheelchair. He motioned for
Wend to do the same on the other side.

As Verilyn opened the box, she revealed a photocopy of Perez's handwritten suicide note on his own monogrammed stationary. It read simply: "I have long believed that we are all responsible, even for the unintended consequences of our actions. I leave the enclosed documents as evidence of my missteps and my poor choice to associate with Lorelei Kahale. I hereby bequeath all of my remaining assets to the family of Randal Simonian, formerly of IdeoBios." Perez had signed and dated it early that morning.

When they'd all finished reading, Verilyn set the note face down in the lid of the box, on the table in front of Matt, and shook her head without comment. Tears came to Wend's eyes, but they had little energy left for sorrow, and Gillian's parting comment left Wend coiled too tight for emotions or tears to escape.

The next few pages included photocopies of handwritten notes and printouts of phone messages between Perez and Kahale.

"They both worked on the Ocean Planning Committee together for at least three years," Verilyn pointed out, a few pages in.

"It doesn't look romantic or otherwise intimate. More like two fanatics trying to control other people's lives." Matt held up one of the earlier messages from Perez saying, "Stirred up appropriate outrage. Told a couple of orgs that I'll donate. Cover expenses if they take IdeoBios to court. Withhold final payment if not."

"Oh my," Verilyn said, reading silently. "You might not want to read this. It can't be unseen. This appears to be another suicide note, signed by Simonian, the lead engineer at IdeoBios, dated two years ago and addressed specifically to Perez and Kahale."

Wend needed to know. When they reached out, Verilyn handed it over without further comment. The note covered a full page, in tight neat handwriting, and ended with, "I do not expect you to believe my good intentions. I write to take full responsibility for any damage done by IdeoBios or the bacteria I engineered. By the time you read this, I will have thrown myself from the cliffs at Palea Point. I trust you will call the authorities to verify my death. All I ask is that you spare my family and co-workers after this. I alone bear the responsibility. They are innocent and should be left in peace."

Verilyn shook her head. "If Perez had handed that over to authorities, both he and Kahale would have been implicated." Verilyn passed the note to Matt's outstretched hand as she searched frantically on her phone. "No one reported Simonian's suicide. There's nothing listed for that night or even that month at or near Palea Point. I wonder if Simonian's family ever knew."

At first, Wend reacted more to the grief in Verilyn's tone than to that past injustice. They'd assumed someone murdered Simonian since their first conversation with Kai. They'd accused Perez of that crime, and now that accusation twisted back on itself. Perez had known about Simonian's suicide but apparently not the attack on his family that may have provoked it. When Perez connected Kahale to both bombings, Simonian's note and Wend's accusations must have added to a burden Perez could no longer carry. Wend couldn't forgive Perez for what he'd done or overlooked before. But they empathized more as the way their own words might have contributed to Perez's suicide sank in. It filled their stomach with stones and their legs with lead.

They'd never wanted Perez to die, not even when they'd felt frightened and trapped after the auction. Certainly not when they'd watched him drown and been unable to help. Now they knew his death and Kahale's arrest would keep Kai, Verilyn, and Matt safe. Knowing that didn't comfort Wend, but it reminded them that no one person could foresee all the consequences of their words and actions. Wend could only keep trying to do their best with what they'd learned.

"It's a good reminder"—they realized they were speaking aloud—"to reach out to each other. When we need help, and to check in with our friends."

Wend didn't look for a response; instead their eyes fixed on the next page in the box, which they couldn't help grabbing and reading. "This is about—" Wend didn't say Kai's name given where they were. Instead they restated Kahale's reference, "the environmental science professor Kahale mentioned earlier. She bragged to Perez about the faculty members she'd swayed against them when they were being considered for department head."

Verilyn's tone turned crisp and back to business, as if her thoughts traveled a similar route to Wend's before snapping back. "If Gillian gave all this to the island patrol investigating the bombing, I suspect Cynthia's already on it. I'll ask her if another labor action or possibly a lawsuit is in order, if they want to go that route."

"I can't believe Perez kept all this," Matt said with a sigh.

Wend could. To Wend, the collection suggested Perez planned for this outcome, one way or another. He'd been weighing his responsibility before the final drop tipped the scale. They didn't voice those thoughts.

"As a lawyer, I've said that so many times." Verilyn shook her head. "Perez probably believed he was fighting the good fight right up until the end. There's no mention here of the drone bombing two years ago. Perez must have remembered that from news coverage at the time when he saw the report from Hilo Harbor. He was honest enough to hold himself to his own twisted standards."

"Don't forgive him just yet," Matt said, looking down.

At the bottom of the box were several eight by ten photos. The first showed Matt in his Hilo living room, mostly naked but with cat ears and a tail. He knelt with his head on Verilyn's knee as she petted his hair. She was fully clothed, and looked every bit the stereotype of an older woman who adored her cat.

"Your privacy has already been invaded enough," Wend said, as they tried to shift their chair away.

"I don't mind if you don't," Matt said.

Verilyn lifted the top corners and quickly shuffled from bottom to top to glimpse each picture. "They're all in our living room. You won't see anything explicit there, and I'd rather show you now than have you confronted with images in the street or in court. Although it's always possible he had more."

Wend nodded and kept their place beside Verilyn as she paged through pictures that were slightly more suggestive, some with Matt wearing a collar and leather-like accessories with Verilyn in a tight red outfit of her own. One showed Yasu and Tanny in gear that implied their roles as well, but all the photos centered on Matt.

As she set the last one aside facedown and then shut them all back in the box, Verilyn said, "If Perez were still alive, I'd question exactly what sort of interest he harbored. His attacks on you as a charismatic cult leader may have been an expression of attraction."

"You suggested that long ago," Matt answered softly, "but that's not what I see in those pictures."

"No, that was stalking," Verilyn said. "But it doesn't mean the other is untrue. Misguided attraction wouldn't cause him to leave those with his suicide note and evidence exposing Kahale. Right to the end, he attempted to exert his power over both you and Kahale."

"But Kahale was responsible for preparing bombs, risking lives, and driving both Perez and Simonian to suicide." Matt choked, as if questioning his own culpability.

Despite Wend's earlier self-recriminations, or perhaps because of them, they couldn't bear to see Matt compare himself to Kahale. "You would never do anything like that, but he targeted you and sided with her." Wend meant it and hoped they sounded reassuring, but human motivations tangled beyond their understanding in that moment. They'd assumed the problem with their health insurance upon reaching Hilo had been an honest mistake and Kahale had only targeted them later because they collected samples that included the new *Ideonella* bacteria, a subject Kahale wanted to suppress to hide her past misdeeds. Wend doubted that the scientific inquiry alone worried Kahale enough to risk hiring someone to bomb the *Nuovo Mar*. Only after Perez discovered Wend independently through flagged news articles, and said something to Kahale—Wend couldn't guess what Perez had mentioned to Kahale. Perhaps Perez uncovered Wend's connection to Kahale and thought Wend knew more about Simonian. Wend had no idea and preferred to focus on the microbes involved. "Both Perez and Kahale crossed lines we would never cross."

Gillian chose to re-enter the room at that point, carrying a photo in a silver frame. "These were my partners in dance and in life when we were younger. I know it's not the same, but Perez never approved of us either." The picture showed three slender young women, the palest one almost certainly Gillian, entwined in a modern dance pose. They wore matching skin tight unitards while one straddled the other and the third arched close behind. Wend looked again at the art on the walls. None of it included these dancers, but it reflected a continued love, of dance at the very least. Gillian set the frame on the counter, not pointed their way, but visible.

"That box is yours to do with as you will," she said. "I hope to demonstrate through my actions that I am not at all like Perez and wish to work with you amicably. To that end, the Ocean Planning Committee is also reviewing the documents relevant to Perez and Kahale's illegal and ill-advised actions. At a minimum, Kahale will be removed from her role on the committee as the representative from the Island of Hawai'i. I can't make an official offer, but others on the committee showed interest when I put forward Verilyn's name. Would you possibly be interested?"

Wend couldn't help contrasting Gillian's easy acceptance of Verilyn and Matt's lifestyle with Shelly storming out of their house initially. Now both were considering Verilyn for a supervisory position.

"Do others on the committee realize I could be involved in a scandal?" Verilyn smiled as she said it, as if she might relish the possibility. Oddly, the reaction lifted Wend's spirits a small amount.

Gillian answered blandly, as if Verilyn had asked a detail about benefits. "Without sharing any details, I mentioned that Perez seemed to have been collecting blackmail material on you and Matt, but that as far as I'd seen, neither of you had done anything unethical."

Verilyn met Gillian's eyes, and the two appeared to study each other. "I'll research the scope of the committee and the time involved. It's not as if I need more work."

Gillian nodded along. "That I knew, having seen your impressive list of community activities and board positions. I appreciate your willingness to consider the post."

"Whatever happens with that, I look forward to getting to know you better." Verilyn added with a slightly predatory smile, "Our meetings so far have been most interesting."

"I wouldn't mind if our next was less so," Gillian responded without missing a beat, one corner of her mouth tilting upward.

"A fine sentiment to end on," Verilyn said. "We've all had a long day."

As soon as they reached the apartment over the mall, Wend's body flooded with relief but also jangled with nervous energy. That combination hit in the aftermath of social anxiety more than true fight or flight. Wend didn't have a name for it but knew from long familiarity that they wouldn't be sleeping anytime soon. They either needed a repetitive physical activity or something warm to hold.

"Do we have the makings for hot chocolate?" Wend asked.

Matt answered as Verilyn tucked the box away in their bedroom. "Kai left a full bag of the kind you both like. Top cupboard on the left."

As Wend pulled out ingredients, they asked, "Anyone else want some?"

"I'd love some," Matt said.

"I'd prefer a glass of cold water." Verilyn appeared to instantly relax as she settled in her favorite spot by the couch.

"I'll get three." Matt darted to the sink as if he felt more like Wend.

Soon after, they all converged in the sitting area with water and hot chocolate. Matt leaned against the arm of the sofa far enough that his arm grazed Verilyn's. She took his hand and asked, "Are you doing okay?"

Matt said, "Yeah, I'm mostly glad none of the pictures showed Kai or Tera. They have more to lose."

"They're more careful, sad as the need for that is. If we're still going home tomorrow, we can wait to discuss our visit with Gillian and this evidence of someone trespassing in our backyard. Kai saw Avery's video earlier. It's not worth risking additional communication to warn them about this." Verilyn's thumb stroked the top of Matt's hand as she spoke; Wend thought that gesture expressed more intimacy than anything shown in the photos. "I didn't have any sense that Gillian meant to lie or imply she could blackmail us in the future."

Wend hadn't considered that, although they hadn't picked up any static. They were even less suited to work in spy-craft or diplomacy than in education. That suited Wend fine. They'd rather get back to analyzing data, sampling with their bot, and doing what they could for the planet. Wend focused on their cup of hot chocolate. They'd chosen a heavy round ceramic mug that fit their hands perfectly, ignoring the handle. Even heat soaked through their fingers and palms as each sip coated their mouth in warmth and rich flavor.

"You look like I feel as a cat," Matt said.

Wend sighed. "If I had my kigurumi here, I might try being one."

"With us?" Matt asked.

"With you as a cat, maybe. I'm not ready for other people to pet me or anything." Wend knew it was true as they said it, even if they hadn't thought about it much.

"I'd be honored. I often wear more for pet play than in those pictures." Matt picked up the hot chocolate Wend had made him, his expression soft and almost reverent.

Wend sipped their chocolate, letting the idea of pet play with Matt settle, and finding they had no objections. "I don't care much what other people wear, but it has to stay strictly non-sexual for me."

"Me too, for that," Matt said.

"You two should negotiate this when you're less worn down," Verilyn suggested.

"Yeah, yeah, just talking," Matt said, leaning his head against Verilyn's shoulder briefly.

"In that case, do you know why you'd be comfortable with touch as a cat now but not as you are?" Being the focus of Verilyn's nonjudgmental curiosity eased Wend's jitters despite the topic.

A cascade of images, emotions, and moments fell through Wend's thoughts, but with few attached words. "I'm not up to explaining that, but it's related to why Matt could hold me this morning when I panicked. I don't think it's what others mean by submissive headspace, but maybe a different headspace." Wend thought for a moment about what they wanted or wanted to say and offered instead, "Would you like to hear about the friend who taught me to appreciate hugs?"

"Definitely." Matt tucked his feet beside him on the couch and curled up, more cat-like, halfway over the padded armrest.

Verilyn nodded and reached out to play with the hair above his neck.

Wend watched the soothing motion as they began, "Lisa started out as the friend of a friend in high school. I had no real understanding of gender back then, but I might have called her a girly girl. She always wore dresses and makeup. Her favorite book was *Little Women,* and one of the first things she told me was that I reminded her of Jo. I read the book when we were better friends and took that as a compliment, although I had trouble getting through the story, and this was long before anyone suggested to either of us that Alcott might have been trans."

Finishing their hot chocolate, Wend held onto the cup while it remained warm. They took a sip from the water Matt had poured them before continuing. "Anyway, my second year of high school was rough. The clothes I wore were a concession to societal norms in that I couldn't get over how uncomfortable jeans were, even though I wore them every day at that point. I'd swapped my sneakers for open-toed sandals and cut my hair short, which I think was moderately in style in the late eighties, but I wasn't trying nearly as hard to fit in as I had in junior high. I took my lunch to eat in the biology room every day, because that teacher had made it into a safe space long before anyone used that term.

"Lisa was there every day as well. I don't know if she got bullied for her dresses, her behavior, or for her mom being from Mexico. I didn't think of her as a friend until she started hugging me every time I stepped into the room. That sounds intrusive now, but I had no context then. There were other people Lisa hugged every time she saw them. I accepted it the way I put up with shaking adults' hands." Wend considered explaining how they learned to shake hands or why that bothered them less than being hugged or kissed by aunts and uncles they saw once a year at most, but decided that wasn't part of the story they wanted to tell right now.

"As I grew to know Lisa better, I was surprised to find I liked being hugged. If I could make my body relax fast enough, it felt more like being accepted than anything I'd experienced before. Lisa learned to hold on longer with me, not long enough that anyone noticed, just a few seconds. By high school, I'd learned to pass in more ways than I could explain, but I was still bad with eye contact and made a lot of small repetitive movements with my hands and feet. Lisa never cared about any of it. She encouraged me to return compliments with compliments and to acknowledge other people's ideas before spouting my own contradictory thoughts, but she never disparaged my efforts. I didn't trust the emotions I sensed from people or my own understanding of teenage social interactions, but I came to trust Lisa's hugs. She never stayed upset with me long enough not to hug. I honestly don't know how other people saw it, but Lisa could sign her letters with X's and O's and people smiled like she was everyone's little sister." Lisa still signed emails to Wend that way, no matter how her life progressed or the world changed around her.

"I don't think she ever dated in high school. On a trip home from college I told her I was bisexual. We didn't separate romantic from sexual feelings then or have terms like 'pan' or 'demi.' She'd entered a relationship with a man, and she told me she'd only felt that sort of attraction to a couple people, both men. Thinking back, that was probably my first discussion about the gray-ace spectrum. I balanced on the verge of working through a lot of trauma, which I didn't even recognize as trauma, involving various sorts of touch and sex. But none of it changed Lisa's hugs. While most of our communications in recent years have been electronic or by paper mail, I have no doubt that she would hug me the same as always if she walked in that door right now. I think she and Avery might be the only people with whom I can't imagine circumstances where I wouldn't want to hug or be hugged by them."

"Wow," Matt commented, followed by, "I grew up with a lot of family and family friends who hugged. But I still remember being jealous when your mom picked you up from preschool, because she'd literally pick you up and hold you in her arms."

Wend viscerally remembered the shape of their mother's body and the strength of her arms when Wend clung to her, how safe that had felt at the time, so different from any other touch. "My mom taught me about unconditional love and understood when I wanted soft clothes and pulled the tags out. But she struggled with boundaries and had plenty of trauma and mental health issues of her own. And alcoholism. I don't know if all that grew worse or if I simply became more aware as I grew older." Wend didn't want to dig deeper right now. "Much about my mother was amazing, but there were times I couldn't stand her touch, especially later."

"You don't have to feel just one way." Verilyn's eyes skated across Wend's face and stiff shoulders before saying, "I understand feeling unconditional love for a parent but not feeling safe with them. Whether you maintain a relationship or not, it remains complicated. Inside."

Brightness burst, a good sort of pain, deep in Wend's throat. Verilyn offered words Wend hadn't come up with on their own, but they fit perfectly. Wend relished having Verilyn in their life now, even if uncertain what role she'd play. They almost reached out to hug or touch her, but could only sit and nod.

After a quiet moment of processing, perhaps for all of them, Verilyn spoke again, "I'm wondering, if you're willing to say, what do you think Lisa and Avery have in common?"

Wend's shrug at that required their entire back and shoulders, a release that reminded them to set down their hot chocolate cup, no longer warm. "I could call it unconditional trust, or as close as I have for anyone. My other lifelong friend, Ashok, I love as much and have probably shared even more with, but he's almost as anxious about touch as I am. We do hug, but it's complicated. Despite our best intentions, sometimes our anxieties feed off each other. Why that doesn't happen with Avery, I can't say. Maybe because I knew them as a child? I don't think I'll ever stop wanting to take care of them. Whereas Lisa more often takes care of me and is close to my age, but not birthday cluster close. I can't think of anything Lisa and Avery have in common that they don't share with someone else in my life." Wend half-laughed. "After all these years, I can't understand my own social stuff, let alone other people's."

"Most people imagine they understand more than they do, about themselves and others. I hope we'll find plenty of opportunities to know each other better." Verilyn glanced toward Matt, curled up by her arm. "For now, we should sleep."

At that Matt's eyes flashed open, like a kid about to protest bedtime. "I have a question, if you don't mind."

His eyes fixed on Wend. Thinking it would be a question about hugs, they asked, "What?"

"Would you try to bring me along if you go flying tonight? Whether you're with Avery or not? I mean, if Avery agrees?"

Wend had no idea if they could pull someone into a flying dream. So far it had always been Avery pulling them in, but they hadn't tried except with Perez, who wasn't even asleep. They considered sharing dreams the way they shared stories or touch, how pleased they'd felt discovering Matt had been a microbe in the belly of a shark with them. "I'm willing to try. I'll leave a note asking Avery, in case they show up. Are you both okay with us possibly entering your room unseen, whether it works or not?"

"We'll keep it decent and wear pajamas," Matt promised, which wasn't what Wend had meant. They tried to roll their eyes the way Aljon did and were reassured when Matt smiled in return.

The tilt of Verilyn's head suggested her amusement. "I'm not only fine with this, I'd be happy to tag along if you want to try for me."

"I can't promise anything," Wend said.

"We know," both Verilyn and Matt said at once.

This time, Wend woke fully aware of their tail and webbed feet. They tussled and tumbled with their invisible companion in the dark of their bedroom, so excited to be a sea otter again with Avery that it took a minute to remember the note. They couldn't speak or point Avery toward it in this form. Instead they wafted, like one air current shifting another, although they weren't real air currents and therefore didn't affect the paper note Wend had left out. It simply read: "Matt and Verilyn would like for us to try to bring them along, but only if you want."

In the next moment Avery rushed through one bedroom door and then another, to where Matt slept curled on his side, next to Verilyn who slept on her back. Avery dove onto Verilyn's chest, like an excited child breaking into a bedroom and jumping on the bed, earlier than first thing in the morning. It took Wend a moment to try nudging Matt's shoulder with one webbed foot. Realizing how little effect that would have even in a solid form, they tried swimming through his shoulder, flapping their tail while thinking "come on, come on, come on."

A shape rose up to meet Wend. In a moment, it formed webbed feet that brushed gently against Wend's own. Four touching four, and then a tail flapping gently, as Matt explored his form.

Next, a great shape swam around them, at least as large as all three of them put together and larger than Wend thought any real sea otter could be. Verilyn took naturally to her new shape, looping and twisting and gathering the three smaller forms together as if they were riding a raft as they flew out over the sleeping city. Wend recalled pictures where sea otters carried a shell or toy this way, or a mother carried a single pup. They remembered both Kai and Matt reporting that Verilyn was larger when they dreamed together. Wend didn't know how it worked, how Verilyn held them together as less than a breeze, rushing over Diamond Head and Spitting Cave to Hanauma Bay, another place Wend hadn't seen in over fifteen years.

The four of them dove into the famous bay together, separating underwater. Wend had snorkeled in the enclosed, shallow reef flat as a child and later as a researcher, when concerns about overuse as well as climate change threatened the oldest marine life conservation area in Hawai'i. They knew most of the live coral here now had been transplanted into cracks and crevices to save the bleached and damaged reef. Still, they gloried to see all the black and white or bright yellow fish, easy to spot at night with their spectral vision.

Wend wriggled excitedly in otter form before falling in with a honu, what some called a green sea turtle, although this one's shell was yellowish on the bottom and mostly brown on top. As another honu joined and then another, Wend flew up, circling around and above the water to see several honu converging by the northern point that sheltered the bay—Palea Point.

Wend should have realized. Whether Verilyn had chosen their destination consciously or not, they'd both read about Palea Point in Simonian's note. While the reef at Hanauma Bay would normally hold Wend's interest for hours, they couldn't turn back now.

Wend rushed ahead, in the directions the honu pointed, to find a low shelf of dark rock, the last sheltered area inside Palea Point. Wend glided onto the land, studying the waves that lapped at the mouth of the bay. No part of them wished to explore the seafloor, to search for any traces that might remain of a human who'd drowned two years before.

At first Wend overlooked a scuttling swarm of crabs, as they were dark brown or gray on the nearly back rocks at night. But Wend's flying dream forms always had exceptional night vision.

The crabs crawled over each other, forming lines rather than spreading across the flat empty spaces in between. While individual crabs continued to move, the lines made up of crabs remained more of less constant, forming letters: RIP.

Wend jerked back, confused and upset. A larger form they recognized as Verilyn, despite being invisible with little more presence than warmth from a heating vent, encircled Wend.

They stilled but could not close the eyes they didn't truly have. When staring at the message, RIP, became unbearable, Wend twisted their attention as well as their spectral form, to focus on the cloudy sky. A few bright stars or satellites glimmered unchanged.

Soon the smaller forms Wend knew to be Avery and Matt pressed to each side of them. They floated together beneath the gray sky and let Verilyn carry them back to the apartment. Avery split off with Wend and saw them back to bed, a gentle sea otter breeze when Wend would have preferred a solidly furry cat or penguin, but there was comfort in the barely there touch.

33.

WEND WOKE LATE, hesitant to leave their warm bed. But thoughts and questions barraged their insistently awake brain.

They shuffled their way into the common area where Matt and Verilyn sat eating and already busy at the dining table. Matt set his phone aside, but Verilyn kept poking at her tablet. Wend joined them but ignored the fruit and baked goods in the center.

"Do you know Randal Simonian's birthday?" Wend asked.

"Good morning," Verilyn said, "and yes, we already checked. He was two years older than Kai, not sharing birthdays with anyone we know, and we haven't seen clusters that close together." She shrugged and smiled, appearing comfortable with the remaining uncertainty.

"Whereas Perez studied crustaceans," Matt offered. He pushed the box of rolls and muffins closer to Wend.

"I saw him die. The island patrol collected his body." Wend closed their eyes and realized they had a headache. "Much as I usually like flying dreams, I don't want to interact with ghosts or become a ghost in that form after I die. Do you think Perez was trying to alert us, in case we hadn't seen the suicide note he kept from Simonian? Or was that some sort of memorial for the scientist he helped harass to death?" Wend's voice choked off at the end.

Verilyn asked very gently, "Did you have any sense last night of others in that form besides the three of us and Avery?"

"No." Wend tried to calm down and think in a more rational, awake manner. They stumbled into the kitchen and downed a glass of water before refilling it and returning to the table. Despite it being neither warm nor reassuring, Wend clutched the tall glass tightly. It grounded them and helped them link facts together in a more reasonable way. "It wasn't like he was sharing a body with a single crab either. Do you think Perez, after dying, could control hundreds of crabs and maybe a few honu, all at once?"

"What if it wasn't a purposeful act?" Verilyn suggested. "Gillian said she recognized the genetic messages being exchanged while inhabiting a microbe because some other human inhabiting another microbe contributed that insight. What if Perez passed along his knowledge or regret for Simonian's suicide at that location with an image of 'RIP'? Although, if Perez is now part of some collective consciousness that we connect with in dreams, he might have meant for us to see."

"I still don't like it," Wend said.

"Neither do I." Matt sipped his coffee. "But I like the idea of a larger consciousness guiding Simonian's actions even less—which I was worried about before checking his birthday. If all the charismatic cult leader hype Perez created about me were true, I'd endorse a belief system wherein if one of us died, some aspect could continue within Earth's ecosystem. Beyond decomposing, I mean."

Wend couldn't help giving a twitch of a smile at Matt's remark. "Looks like we don't need a cult for that." They selected a lumpy roll that made them miss Aljon and his breakfast bread. "My research into the PET-eating bacteria showed significant changes after the bacteria were released into the ocean. There are reasons why a particular strain might predominate and proliferate, but if we're sharing knowledge through dreams, whatever Perez learned could have combined with another person's or creature's bioengineering abilities."

"Are you saying he might have inadvertently helped with bioengineering?" Verilyn set her tablet aside, giving Wend her full attention.

Wend nodded. "Unless this system we don't understand had direct access to Simonian's expertise when he drowned, even if he wasn't part of a birthday cluster. Everything I learn raises more questions. Am I supposed to act on what I see in dreams? Should I be hunting down the infestation of skeleton shrimp I saw in one recent dream? Is it better to publish findings about the new PET-eating bacteria or help cover up their existence? Are we tools or consultants or observers in whatever's going on?"

"We are who we are," Verilyn said. "I had my issues with Perez, but I'm willing to believe he meant well in his own way. If he had to share a message with us after death, regret for what he did to Simonian could be a sign of progress, in this life or whatever comes after. My chosen family are among the best people I know. If they're part of something larger, I'm willing to give it the benefit of the doubt, not because their choices will always be right but because I believe in those people."

"At least Kahale doesn't appear to be one of us. Her birthday doesn't fit," Matt said before heading toward the kitchen and asking Wend over his shoulder, "Do you want some tea or hot chocolate?"

Wend shook their head, mouth full of hearty bread with bits of fruit but no mint, head swirling with concerns about Perez, Kahale, and their motives, not to mention the mystery now encompassing all their dreams, the world ocean, and unknown numbers of people born in various years.

Verilyn's thumb swiped across her phone. "Avery messaged asking how you were, whether you'd checked your new phone, and if all or any of us wanted to spend time at a beach today with them and Mira."

Wend sighed. They'd checked their new phone several times after seeing Avery yesterday and even put in an order for a cellphone on their new work account. Nothing they did with phones ever amounted to enough. "Did they send all that just now?"

"Their first message came over an hour ago. Do you want to reply from your phone, or shall I pass on that you're awake at least?" Verilyn raised her phone, looking eager.

"Fine, feel free to communicate on my behalf." Wend waved the hand not holding their roll. "Is either of you interested in beach plans or seeing Mira again?"

Matt practically bounced back into his seat, holding a fresh cup of coffee. "Mira wasn't that bad—when she was busy eating. Think we could convince her to keep a snorkel in it?"

Verilyn raised both eyebrows and looked down her nose at him, refusing to laugh but not disagreeing.

"Seriously," Matt continued, "I'd be happy to check out a Water Wonders van with equipment. You could try out the Frog Paddlers or some aquatic acrobatics."

"The Frog Paddlers are quiet, right? I'm up for trying quiet stuff." Wend longed to be back in the ocean and to swim with Avery in person. "I wish I'd brought my sample bot and scuba gear."

Before Wend knew what was happening, Verilyn messaged, read, and raised her head proudly. "Avery offered to bring a sample bot."

Matt busied himself arranging for rental equipment and lunch.

Wend wondered if they should even bother checking their phone at this point. They decided after breakfast would be soon enough and took a long sip of water.

When they reached Queen Kapiʻolani Beach, there were fewer people than Wend expected, even for a weekday and well before noon. The sky hung heavy with gray clouds, but the water gleamed bluer in contrast. Although they'd chosen the location for its convenience to the university, Avery and Mira were late.

"Why don't I get you two set up with Frog Paddlers while I unpack the rest." Matt's voice sounded tight.

Wend realized he was worried they wouldn't like the invention he'd named after their earliest swim stroke. They barely managed not to laugh. Realizing how much Matt remembered from their preschool conversations could never yield anything but appreciation from Wend, but they didn't know how to convince Matt except by showing him. In that spirit, they decided not to comment on the powder blue electric van painted with cartoon fish and bubbles that bore the logo for Matthaios Water Wonders and came completely stuffed with provisions and equipment for what was meant to be a few quiet hours at the beach. It seemed only fair to let Matt show off his creations and the company he'd built.

First, he helped Verilyn into what looked like a floating lounge chair atop giant wheels clearly designed for beach sand. It was even a sandy color. Then he loaded two green Frog Paddlers on the back, and they all made their way across morning cool sand to reach the water. Once they were about knee deep, Matt locked the wheels on Verilyn's beach chair, and explained all the options with the Frog Paddlers.

"Obviously, this main part floats. There are optional straps to help with certain motor issues, but neither of you need those. You can mostly position yourself by resting your face above the viewing circle. That's designed to give a clear 180-degree view beneath you. Your shoulders rest here." He pointed to the sides of the section that resembled a kickboard and then started demonstrating various ways to manipulate the flippers using arms and hands. "Based on your descriptions," Matt said to Wend, "the basic motion is a modified breast stroke. The blade naturally shifts to the position of least resistance when you reach forward. If you want to back paddle or turn by shifting one arm backward, you squeeze the handle. Once again, there are other options for different accessibility needs, but I'll spare you the full pitch for now. I know you're both strong swimmers, so we can skip that part of the safety lecture." Motioning to the lower part of the board that narrowed to form a tapering tail like a sting ray, Matt said, "There's the option to kick or steer with your legs at whatever ability level, or the finger triggers can fire small jets of water that add a power assist when activated repeatedly. You can trigger those on one side or both. Verilyn trained some of our trainers on best practices with the Frog Paddler, and well," Matt looked at Wend with huge, eager eyes, "you may come back with inspirations I never considered. Assuming you're both fine as swim buddies for this, I'll meet you back here when you're ready to come in, okay?"

"I'm excited to try it out," Wend said. Matt's need for reassurance shone through as clear as the morning sunlight through a break in the clouds. "Thank you, Matt."

He laughed at himself and said, "I always imagined you trying this someday. Is it okay if I take a few pictures? Just for us?"

Wend couldn't object in this case. They nodded and found a comfortable position on the Frog Paddler as Matt helped Verilyn with hers. Just floating with their feet and hands trailing in shallow water eased Wend past their earlier upset and headache.

Then Verilyn and Wend headed out from the beach. The fisheye viewers provided an amazing perspective down into the water, much broader than the edges on most scuba or snorkel masks. Swirling sand gave way to clearer water. The arm movements came instinctively to Wend, a fine tribute to how they'd learned to swim. They didn't really like having something between their legs but imagined how that might help with some physical limitations and how it could provide a feeling of security for other mindsets. When they finally tried the finger jets, the tiny bursts of current made them laugh.

"Having fun?" Verilyn asked.

Wend realized another advantage to swimming this way was easy conversation. "It's still hard to believe Matt invented these and called them Frog Paddlers."

"He would have included you on the patent if he'd known how to find you."

"That wouldn't have made any sense," Wend said. "I didn't even invent the term. My mom did."

"I once saw a comedian included on a patent. They joked about a ridiculous combination of features for a kitchen gadget and someone in the audience came away inspired to make and sell it. Be glad he doesn't call you his muse." The way Verilyn said it suggested personal experience, but she changed the subject, saying, "There's a channel over here where we should see fish on such a calm day."

Sure enough, the channel ran ten feet deep with dead coral or rocks along the sides, providing hiding spots for colorful fish. One darted out, several inches long with blue and yellow bands. Wend thought it was the state fish, with a really long name that they ought to remember. Several smaller fish kept out of its way. Not for the first time, Wend wished they could identify more marine vertebrates, but for the most part they believed the names didn't matter. They drifted with Verilyn, appreciating whatever they saw together. At one point they drifted so close that their flippers touched. Wend startled and shot out a hand instinctively to hold their position, wrist lightly resting across Verilyn's hand and flipper.

"Is this okay?" Wend asked.

"Of course," Verilyn answered before adding, "hold tight and press your left jet as I push mine."

Wend followed instructions and intuited how to align their legs as they became a slowly spinning pinwheel, or pressurized water ballet, along with Verilyn. Soon they were both giggling like little kids.

Then Verilyn exclaimed, "Look!"

Wend followed her gaze as a group of fish with electric blue lines near their tails, shaped much like the large fish from before with the yellow and blue markings, circled beneath the two frog paddlers. The cloudy sky meant the humans weren't casting the menacing shadows from above that often frightened fish, but Wend was surprised when the fish arced up to swim within a foot of where Wend still touched Verilyn's hand. They remembered the pool by the waterfall on Fatu Hiva and the line of tiny fish with iridescent blue stripes that had circled around Wend, a behavior Viola later cited as odd.

Checking that no one swam nearby, Wend asked, "Do fish ever seem attracted to you, or maybe to you and Matt if you're together in the water?"

Now Verilyn laughed. "The fish whisperer theory. Kai and Matt suggested something like that before. I'm not usually so lucky."

"Viola suggested it partly based on an incident like this when she first went swimming with me. We were kind of testing that theory when we encountered the Pacific bluefin tuna. It doesn't seem very consistent, and I didn't find any bias in my data from the sample bot. But what if it only happens when two of us swim together? The dreams work a little differently when we're together."

"By that logic, we could have affected the crabs last night by watching together."

Wend wasn't sure whether they preferred that to the ghost or collective consciousness ideas or not. "I guess all we can do is pay attention and observe. But maybe we should head back for now."

"If you want." Verilyn didn't sound disappointed, but the stillness of her hand in Wend's suggested something else. "Can I lead you around the long way or are you worried about influencing whatever we might see?"

Wend hid their face in the bubble window looking down. "I promise I'm not going to go overboard worrying about unintended consequences." Verilyn laughed, and Wend realized what they'd said. They laughed, too. "I just want to understand as much as I can."

"I'd already picked up on that." Verilyn's voice softened. "And I admire it."

Wend warmed inside and worried less as they let go and followed where Verilyn led. They spotted a surprising number of small fish after that, but none of them showed any particular interest in the Frog Paddlers or them.

As they approached their original launch point, Avery and Matt swam out to join them. Avery wore swim goggles, a full-body swimsuit, and had a sample bot strapped to their back. Matt swam in shorts and a rash guard much like Wend's. Rather than Frog Paddlers, they swam with colorful innertubes sporting an extra layer on top and bottom, like a donut frosted on both sides.

"What are those?" Wend asked as they approached near enough to speak.

"Spin Tubes Matt invented!" Avery shouted louder than Wend had ever heard them. "A friend of mine calls them 'hug tubes.' See how tight mine's pumped up? I can drum on the top to make the bottom ring tighter." They demonstrated pounding gleefully on the green ring atop their tube. "Then I squeeze these valves to shoot air out making me spin!"

Avery played with different leg positions, pointing their toes straight down to spin the fastest. They stopped, facing Wend, and started drumming again. "Fun, but I really like the hug part in between. You make great toys, Matt."

"I agree," Wend said.

Matt beamed as he thanked them both.

Then Matt and Avery spun, seeing who could go the fastest, until they were both dizzy.

Wend looked up the beach toward the light blue van decorated with fish and saw Mira relaxing in a beach chair, hat pulled down over her eyes. "Mira didn't want to swim?"

Matt spun slow enough to answer, "Said it wasn't beach weather." But on his next rotation, he crossed his eyes and puffed out his cheeks, offering silent commentary on Mira's opinion.

"Why do you think I suggested the beach?" Avery called out while spinning fast.

Wend choked back a laugh, appreciating that Avery could, when needed, manage Mira just fine.

When Avery calmed their twirling and pumped their Spin Tube full again, they asked, "Where's the best place to see fish?"

"Possibly wherever we all come together," Wend answered.

Verilyn added to Matt, "Wend reinvented the fish whisperer theory you and Kai proposed."

"We could never get consistent results." Matt sounded eager to try again.

"I know that feeling," Wend sighed, but led them all back along the channel to a likely viewing spot. After a few minutes of only seeing two to four fish at a time, mostly staying close to the walls of the channel, Wend asked, "How would you all feel about holding hands?"

As one they looked to Avery, who held out both hands saying, "Yes, I am absolutely in for this. But I'll have to let go sometimes to take samples with the bot." They took a sample then, demonstrating how quickly they could press the remote attached to a wrist strap.

Wend nodded, silently pleased to let Avery take charge of samples for this experiment.

The four of them reached their hands together forming a rough circle.

Within seconds of their hands touching, a swirl of smaller fish spiraled up to see them. Those scattered moments later as four larger fish, with electric blue lines by their tails and bright yellow above their mouths, came out to circle beneath the strange human island. They didn't come as close as when Verilyn and Wend had been floating on the surface with just the Frog Paddlers, but they circled three times, each circle slightly larger than the last, until they passed directly between Matt and Avery's dangling feet.

"I think the same group of fish came up after Verilyn and I touched. And there might have been a similar moment with Viola in Fatu Hiva."

"Do they have lagoon triggerfish in Fatu Hiva?" Avery asked.

"Maybe? I saw similar fish in Nuku Hiva, a few islands over. But the ones I'm talking about in Fatu Hiva were smaller and their blue stripes ran horizontal. They looked more translucent and their stripes more iridescent from what I remember. Viola took a picture. It's just—Viola had a theory about me and sea life, and now I'm wondering if it's any two of us being in close proximity or touching."

When the triggerfish vanished from sight, Wend let go of the others' hands and checked to see if anyone was watching. While people swam above the channel, no one seemed to have noticed the fishes' odd behavior or the four of them.

"What happens if we try again?" Avery asked, reaching out for Wend's hand. They held for a minute or two while nothing happened, before Matt reached out as well. The triggerfish didn't return, but a few smaller fish came from down the channel and curved beneath them before heading back where they'd come from.

"I sense many interesting beach days in our future," Matt said.

"I wish my mom wasn't taking up all of my winter break," Avery complained.

"I seriously don't want to come between you and her," Wend reiterated, giving a squeeze with their still-linked hand. "You're going to need to make your own choices. If you'd like her to stay, make the most of that time. I'll find time for you whenever you want. Unless there's some other problem I should know about?"

"She forgets I'm a grown-up and makes me feel small, but nothing terrible." Avery ducked further back inside their tube, letting go of Wend's hand and squeezing the upper tube to pump it fuller as they continued. "I wish she'd asked instead of telling me she'd be here all month and then showing up early."

"You can tell her that," Matt suggested in his gentlest tone. "My grand-kid orchestrated major negotiations to arrange when she'd visit me, her mom, and her other grandparents. I came away with even more respect for how much she'd grown up." He glanced over, pausing. "You have no obligation to spend time around anyone; these are all your decisions."

Avery's mouth twisted. "Yeah, I had a pretty big battle to convince my mom I could move to Hawai'i on my own. It took her a while to adapt, but I should take the next step now that she's here for a month."

Wend nodded and fiddled with a flipper on their Frog Paddler.

"You're welcome to join us for Solstice, or anytime that you'd like, with or without Mira," Verilyn offered easily.

"I'll keep notes on anything we try with Kai or others, then we can see what replicates later with you," Wend promised.

"And I'll keep you posted on my rotifer research," Avery volunteered eagerly. "With the extra analysis on the sample you shipped from Hawai'i, I was able to confirm the full genome and document everything needed to verify a new species."

"That's great," Wend said. "You might get to name it."

"How about Microbe-Avery? Rotifer-Avery?"

Everyone laughed.

"I can always fly to you now," Avery said mostly to Wend.

Suddenly worried, Wend asked, "Does anyone know what happens if someone tries to wake Avery if they're flying far away?" It seemed an odd place for such a conversation, but Wend didn't know when they'd next have the chance. Matt didn't seem to mind, and Verilyn appeared to be keeping watch to make sure no one swam within earshot.

"I woke myself up in a panic after following the person who tried to bomb your boat," Avery said. "I snapped back to my body, and it didn't feel any worse than waking up from a nightmare."

Wend reached out a hand that Avery accepted. One small fish angled closer. "I'm sorry you had to witness that."

"I'm not," Avery said. "I'm glad I had phone numbers from Verilyn and others, though."

"Sorry I'm still so ambivalent about phones," Wend said.

"It's okay. Check when you feel like it. You really don't mind me butting in when you sleep?"

"Not at all." Wend meant it and that led to a realization. "I might do better with a phone only people who knew me well could call. Maybe I'll keep the current flip phone just for messages from you three and Aljon."

The three present smiled, not at all bothered by Wend's idiosyncrasies around phones. They headed back to the beach for lunch with Mira, distracted only a few times along the way as they tried goofy tricks with the Spin Tubes and Frog Paddlers.

 # 34.

WEND PICKED UP their new work phone and checked in with Aljon on their burner phone before leaving Oʻahu, so they weren't surprised to see Doreen at the condo when they returned for dinner. Her aloha shirt featured sea birds Wend recognized this time, although they wondered why anyone would print albatrosses across a sunset background of oranges and reds.

"Join us," Shelly called as soon as Wend was in the door. "We're celebrating! Doreen agreed to join the board!"

Shelly poured wine, which Viola and Wend declined. Aljon agreed to a small taste while handing Wend and Viola juice in stemware for a series of toasts to Doreen and Seaward Generation. Then they all sat down to a stew full of local vegetables and a cucumber salad that was mostly fruit.

"Our first order of business," Shelly said as soon as people were done complimenting the food, "is to decide whether our main office should remain here or move elsewhere."

"Hey, I joined. You can't move!" Doreen protested, pouring more wine for herself and Shelly. Aljon covered his glass with one hand.

"We have free housing and a convenient harbor here," Viola said. Something in her tone caused Wend to look up. They were surprised to see Viola wasn't making eye contact with anyone.

"True, but the attempted bombing can't be good publicity." Shelly waved her full glass until the wine almost spilled then took a sip. "If the locals don't want us, I wouldn't feel right staying."

Doreen made a scoffing noise deep in her throat. "All publicity is good publicity. There's no such thing as 'the locals' in this case. The kid who piloted that bomb embarrassed his family. He crossed a line between island pride and terrorism that even island patrol officers reluctant to arrest a local kid can't ignore. None of them would dare say anything publicly against you now. A lot of the older generation wants to whip those kids into shape, even if those same elders have mouthed off in front of them about too many transients passing through since the brats were first stealing candy."

"So what do people think of us and how do we make it better?" Shelly asked.

"I, for one, appreciate neither of you landing on my couch yet," Doreen said with a mock stern expression directed at Shelly and Viola. "You've been here two weeks and your personal drama hasn't made the news, only your boat and your business."

Wend reflected on why they'd been staying on the boat with Aljon but knew better than to mention it now. It had only been a couple weeks, and they'd just instituted house rules. They remembered Aljon's previous allusions to Viola and Shelly's drama and its fallout and wondered if the house rules and agreement not to kick anyone out signified more than Wend had realized.

After pausing to appreciate the food and some more wine, Doreen continued, "Supportive factions will like you for being environmentalist or queer or a woman-led business."

"Does it help I'm not white or from the USA?" Aljon asked. Wend thought he might be poking fun at how the older generation delineated factions, but no one laughed, so Wend wasn't sure.

Doreen shrugged. "We still have work to do on environmental justice and indigenous representation, but the rescue at sea is an okay start. As long as your manufacturing remains elsewhere, you're not having much impact on the local economy. I want to seize the opportunity to present this island as a leader in both environmental efforts and the new economy. You're sure the bombing was a one-time thing?"

"Up to your island patrol now," Shelly said with a wink, raising her glass.

"Our island patrol," Doreen corrected. "Stay here and share in the good and bad of our little island."

"Shall we vote?" Shelly asked. "All in favor of keeping our headquarters in Hilo, at least for now?"

Wend raised a hand along with everyone else. The only other place they'd consider would be Oʻahu. But Avery still struggled to defend their space and independence from Mira, and Wend wouldn't want to intrude on Avery's choices or crowd their growth. Besides, the free housing here was hard to beat. And Matt was here. Verilyn. They found each person in Matt's family intriguing at least. Several seemed interested in sharing stories and getting to know Wend better. Running down the list in their mind, Wend realized they needn't justify their decision to stay. From the microbes to the people, in all their adult life, this was the first place to claim Wend.

"Aljon?" Shelly asked, as she served herself more cucumber and fruit salad, "Do you know anyone in the Philippines called Keanu?"

"Of course, because I am personally acquainted with everyone in the Philippines." Aljon's snark earned a chuckle from Doreen, and Wend couldn't help smiling. More seriously, Aljon asked, "Isn't that usually a Hawai'ian name?"

"Huh." Shelly pulled out her phone before continuing, "This email came from the Philippines liaison for an international NGO who said, 'Excited to hear about Seaward Generators as well as other ocean tech from Keanu. Consider bundles? Joint training? How soon?'"

Wend set down the strawberry carved into a rose that they deemed too pretty to eat in that moment. "I heard about an interisland association from a kid named Keanu and handed off a business card that first day—before you told me not to. It's the only one I've given out."

"You gave out one card and someone in the Philippines saw it?" Shelly asked.

At the same time, Doreen was saying, "You have business cards?"

Viola pulled hers out and proudly displayed their subtle blue and green background.

"I like." Doreen said pointedly to Viola, "Careful. You'll end up in the business card business." Then to Shelly she added, "You better not plan on telling me how to network."

Holding both hands up in mock surrender, Shelly only said, "Is the other ocean tech mentioned your sample bots? Is there someone in charge of distribution for those who might work with us?"

Wend took a moment to appreciate Shelly's offer. She wanted to collaborate with the Marine Census Project, involving Wend's sample bots in particular. Wend wondered if they could stretch their role as a local contractor to facilitate such a program, but thought that might represent a conflict of interest. They hated to ask Betta for any more favors, but she could authorize someone to oversee such an alliance.

Aljon took the idea one step further. "I bet the nonprofit distributing

Matt's rescue robots would partner with us, too. I could sail around carrying demo models and teach people about all three."

Wend froze at the thought of Aljon sailing without Viola, possibly drowning without any radio or radar, and none of them would ever know. But Aljon would have a Seaward Generator he could use to power communications as needed. And a rescue robot. As skipper he'd choose a crew he trusted, and this plan could lead into the work he'd described, protecting people and ecosystems in the Philippines.

Viola and Shelly exchanged a series of looks along the same lines as Doreen leaned back to enjoy her wine.

"Aren't we getting ahead of ourselves?" Shelly asked.

"No!" Doreen answered decisively. "We have all three inventors right here in Hilo. Take that, Honolulu and Silicon Valley. We could rebrand as Silicon Bay!"

Wend had opened their mouth to explain about sand being mostly silicon dioxide when everyone around them started laughing, and Wend realized, they were in on the joke. Glad to see everyone finally on the same page, they laughed along.

After dinner, Shelly unveiled the biggest surprise as she pulled large blueprints from a mailing tube. "Mehta sent physical drawings for the new Seaward Generator schematics and the revised factory layout. There are materials lists and cost estimates that I'll send each of you digitally."

Wend ran their hands over the generator schematics as if they could absorb the knowledge through touch. In a way, they could. Physically mapping sizes and distances had always helped them remember details. They touched each line and studied dimensions until they thought they could reproduce the diagram from memory if needed. The chemical and filter specifications were beyond their experience; the design, significantly more complex than the sample bots they knew well. Nonetheless, they looked at the specifications for seals around tubing at several junctures and brought their laptop to the table to compare with those used in sample bots. "If you care, we could save a couple dollars per generator with a part rated for marine use that I think is better. I'll reply to all with a link and details."

It was a modest contribution, but Wend embraced the success when no one disagreed. They longed to make more tangible contributions to the project and incentivize Shelly to share information and design details going forward.

As the evening wore on, Shelly and Doreen finished the bottle of wine and opened another. Wend made sure to refill the water pitcher and move it close, but by that point, Wend had had enough.

When Aljon and Wend excused themselves to Wend's glassed-in lanai, Viola asked, "Can I join you?"

"Sure," Wend said, even more surprised when Viola closed the door to the main room behind herself.

Wend cleared their sample bot off of a pile of spare bedding so they could use that as a seat, leaving the futon free for Aljon and Viola. Having three people in their room at once wasn't something Wend had anticipated.

As soon as everyone sat down, Viola said, "I owe you an apology. I could have been a better listener on the boat, and I shouldn't have let Shelly push you around once we landed. I'm sorry."

Wend hadn't considered Viola the type to apologize, especially not in such a broad manner. And in that moment, a disconnection Wend hadn't quite noticed healed. They had grown close to Viola on the boat. They were glad to see her happier now, despite all the complications that came along with Shelly. "Apology accepted. For what it's worth, I have no regrets. I know I can be annoying or confusing to people, but since swimming onto your boat, everything has worked out better than I ever imagined."

"You certainly changed my life," Viola said, then seemed to choke on any further words. Aljon leaned against her and pressed his lips together tightly.

Wend followed Aljon's lead and stayed quiet.

After a long silence, Viola said, "There's a story I should have told you. But it's hard." When Viola stopped again, Aljon took her arm and wrapped their fingers together. Wend wondered if he already knew the story or could guess. "I had a flying dream once before. After nearly drowning on a kayaking trip with my first serious girlfriend"—Viola opened her mouth to say a name but couldn't—"someone who you and Aljon both remind me of in some ways. She always wanted to learn, explore, discuss. I loved her, but I made her cry too often. It was always my fault. I admit that. The night after we almost drowned, we shared this unbelievable dream where she pulled me back to the river, diving in and out to explore the choppy white water where we lost control. We spotted the pair of sunglasses I'd lost. They lay there, peaceful under the water, snagged in a tangle of downed branches not more than a hundred feet downriver from where we flipped. I could have gone back to see if the sunglasses were truly there."

Viola shook her head, and Wend was about to say she didn't have to explain, when Viola continued. "When we woke up, she told me what she'd dreamed. I could have said I experienced it with her. We could have filled in complementary details until we convinced each other. We could have gone back to look for the sunglasses in that tangle of branches. Instead, I lied. I didn't admit to anything. Eventually I snapped and told her to 'stop talking about the stupid dream!'"

Wend cringed at the words, spoken in a grating tone as Viola imitated her past self. Hard memories flashed through Wend's mind: Viola challenging Wend on their storytelling, insisting on experiments to test if flying dreams were real, making them cry on at least one occasion. It all flipped upside down with what Viola told them now.

"We didn't break up that day, but I should have known that was the end. I knew she would have taken the shared dream as a sign, believed we were soulmates or had some quest we were meant to fulfill together. Instead, I convinced myself the shared dream wasn't real, that my mind filled in details to let me imagine we'd both shared the same dream. I told myself we'd both been recalling a traumatic experience."

Viola closed her eyes for the next sentence. "After that, I drank to forget. She drank to keep me company. I lashed out and said terrible things that eventually pushed her away. Bad shit happened to her after that, and I told myself I wasn't responsible. She was too soft. I should never have gotten involved with someone that dependent and vulnerable. That part might have been right. I'm better suited to someone like Shelly who refuses to be scared off and can be every bit as selfish as I am. But I shouldn't have lied and denied what I knew about that dream, to her, to myself, or when you started dragging it up again."

With all the long pauses and the pain practically strobing out from Viola as she told this story, Wend had no idea when or how to respond. Their skin broke out in goosebumps even as they felt drawn to Viola, wanting to offer comfort or absolution.

Aljon eventually asked, "Was that the only flying dream you had before this trip?"

"As far as I know," Viola answered.

"Have you had more since arriving in Hilo?" Wend asked.

"No," Viola replied immediately. "I don't think I have the sea creature dreams or feel the pull to places or people that you and Shelly mentioned either. Maybe I'm not very good at this."

"Or you like being in control," Aljon said. When Viola turned to look at him, he loosened his grip and said, "As a skipper, you're reluctant to let me take the helm. As a photographer, you observe, but you also tell anyone with you where they can stand and how still they need to stay. You say Shelly has trust issues, but you've pretty much stated that you only trust yourself with her because she'll fight back and stick up for herself. You don't think Wend or I or most other people can handle you. I think you apologized to Wend and told us this story to protect us, because you don't trust yourself not to hurt us."

With a tense shrug Viola said, "That's one way of putting it. I could point out that Wend offers stories in about the same way and you used to apologize all the time. We all have some issues with relationships and possibly with denying ourselves. I'm impressed that Wend swore off drinking and lying so much earlier than I did."

"Life's not a race," Wend said. "I had different issues with trauma and neurodivergence that influenced my decisions from the start. Aljon's twenty-nine and just explained interpersonal dynamics I barely understand at sixty-seven. Like I told you before, I see life as a puzzle, probably the kind without edges. You found your own way back to flying dreams, and I bet you could have more or manage to dream as a sea creature. Is that what you want?"

"Maybe not," Viola said, squeezing Aljon's hand and bumping his shoulder. "Still, for all my limitations, I'll help where I can. Maybe the point of discovering all this is that we have to help each other. If this involves the world ocean, biodiversity, and climate change—a few tiny problems like that—we're going to need all the insights and skill sets we can muster."

At that point there was a loud knock on Wend's door. Shelly opened it a moment later with a sway that left her hanging from the doorknob, "The wine's all gone. Doreen went home. This doesn't look like much of a party."

"It will be, as soon as I make some cookies." Aljon stood and dragged Viola along with him.

"I could make hot chocolate," Wend offered as they followed.

Shelly raised an eyebrow but said, "Why not? Time for a cookies and cocoa party!"

A long shallow coast stretched outward beyond a broad continental shelf. Nutrients ran rich off the land into the sea. The upwelling of iron, phosphate, and silicic acid added spice to the mix. Some part of Wend thought they recognized Monterey Bay. As cyanobacteria, they simply feasted, multiplied, and sank, sequestering methane and carbon dioxide as they fell. Wend-cyanobacteria spread from millions of bodies to billions more, dividing, fissioning, exploding to fill all available space. With every division, more of their surface area pressed into the soothing water, energized by warming sunlight.

Some humans would call it a blue-green algae bloom, although cyanobacteria were not truly algae. They understood blooming. Bursting. Creating. Becoming more than they were before.

All of Wend-cyanobacteria was one, all the way back to the first photosynthetic organisms that brought oxygen to Earth's atmosphere. Their time was not only now, but always. They bloomed in the warm surface waters of a coast that had always existed in some shape or form.

Seawater became less viscous with heat, and all the Wend-cyanobacteria moved more freely. They rose up through the water column into the warmth of day. In the sun-warmed surface waters they gorged themselves. They multiplied and absorbed extra sunlight until they could further warm the water, increasing their own claim. The deeper waters grew so dense by comparison that wind could barely mix the layers. This stratification helped Wend-cyanobacteria to proliferate, succeed, overcome, and overwhelm the competition from diatoms and larger algae that they trapped in lower, oxygen-depleted waters.

Some species within the Wend-cyanobacteria floated languidly on the surface, benefiting directly from increased carbon dioxide in the air. They tugged at a distant memory in Wend's mind of a sea otter that was also a dolphin or a different kind of breeze. That was too confusing for Wend-cyanobacteria to process.

Other microbes formed gas vesicles that allowed them to migrate higher and lower—tiny balloonists delving for nutrients or ascending to their place in the sun. A few released toxins that killed a colony of bivalves and produced harmful vapors for some creatures who breathed air. Still others inadvertently poisoned fish being farmed in underwater cages, but those fish were ill-suited to the warmth of this cyanobacteria-prolific autumn anyway. Wend-cyanobacteria understood how the cycle of life must include death for larger, more individualistic lifeforms as well.

An algal bloom of *Pseudo-nitzchia australis* that had proliferated up the coast took out seals, sea lions, and even whales through domoic acid exposure. Wend-cyanobacteria marveled as the large corpses became mobile feasts as they sank. The whale that ate the krill that ate both *Pseudo-nitzchia australis* and cyanobacteria was eaten in turn by scavengers, opportunists, and eventually by sulfophilic bacteria.

When the *Pseudo-nitzschia australis* intruded at their edges, Wend-cyanobacteria fought to supplant them. They flowed over their smaller cousins, seized the sunlight from above. They relished their victory, engaging in extra bouts of photosynthesis and reproduction. But the currents were not in their favor for long.

Domination was not their goal.

Ancestral cyanobacteria had started the carbon cycle, taking carbon from the air and incorporating it into their bodies, to be consumed by larger lifeforms or sunk to the ocean floor. They had gifted their abilities to their descendants, the chloroplasts that made algae, like the pesky *Pseudo-nitzschia australis*, and had made all plant life possible. As a lifeform, cyanobacteria were as generous as they were self-serving.

Wend-cyanobacteria connected to all life on Earth. They might supplant, suffocate, or otherwise eliminate their neighbors, but across time, they knew they were all one and the same.

Waking with a long indulgent stretch on Saturday morning, Wend remembered to check both phones and their laptop for messages first thing. They were surprised to find an email from Miko, sent late the night before, to their Marine Census Project address.

Either their startled noise or their fussing with electronics woke Aljon, who'd ended up sleeping on the bed beneath their hammock after Viola and Shelly made their way noisily upstairs. "Is something wrong?"

"I don't know. Miko wants me to meet them. To talk." Wend didn't want to go, but knowing where they stood with Miko could help with decisions they needed to make for work.

"They weren't very nice to you recently." Aljon had only heard Wend's side.

Wend wanted to hear Miko's perspective, even beyond the useful aspects. "They say they're sorry and are willing to meet me wherever is convenient."

Aljon tilted his head. "I should check on the *Nuovo Mar*. When were you next planning to take samples at Hilo Harbor?"

Wend didn't have a plan but hadn't taken any samples since they'd been suspended. "I guess now is good."

"Breakfast first," Aljon said. "See how soon Miko can meet us at Radio Bay."

"Us?"

"You, but I'll be nearby if needed."

Miko met them at Radio Bay less than an hour later. Wend took a water sample off the dinghy dock. Aljon inspected the dinghy more thoroughly than it had probably ever been inspected before. The commercial dock was quiet in the early morning on a weekend, but several people from neighboring sailboats waved to Aljon and asked how he was doing.

"Aloha, Dr. Taylor," Miko said from the walkway beside the dinghy dock.

"You can still call me Wend. Have you met Aljon? I know you've communicated by phone."

"Good morning, Aljon." Miko stopped. They looked at Aljon, who held up an oar for significant inspection. Miko turned quickly to Wend. "Please, I'm sorry if I treated you unfairly and listened to gossip. Could I speak with you alone for a minute?"

"I was going to take a sample from the commercial dock next," Wend said. "Could we talk as I go?"

Miko bit their lip and nodded. As soon as they passed out of earshot of Aljon and others, Miko started in on a high-pitched explanation with a lot of literal hand wringing. "You know I worked for Dr. Kahale, and she could have dismissed me, probably easier than she dismissed you. I tend to give people the benefit of the doubt, as I did for Dr. Kahale several times. But she asked me questions about the work you did, who you shared data with, how you managed students in classes. I didn't recognize her manipulations for what they were. Every question seemed like something the person in charge of the department could reasonably ask. Then she said you changed locations because there were problems with your work or interactions with students. I shouldn't have believed that. You worked hard and did so well in the workshops I saw. But she was my boss, too."

"Apology accepted. You didn't mean any harm," Wend said as they reached the end of the commercial dock and lowered the bot to take a couple samples. As they realized their sample location was within feet of where the bomber had stood with his remote control, Wend took a steadying breath.

"But I did harm." Miko continued quickly, "Dr. Kahale didn't know the Marine Census System well enough to track what you did. If I hadn't told her about your lab requests, she might have allowed the sequencing without issue. I think she blocked that twice, but I didn't realize until she went to O'ahu Thursday after finding out you'd sent samples there. She found out from me. I heard she was arrested for harassing you there. I feel terrible."

"Honestly, she was worse to the person at the front desk, and that wasn't the only reason she was arrested." Wend didn't know how much to reveal about Kahale. Miko had been kind to them from the start and was easy to forgive. Wend wanted to work with them in the future, not serve as confessor or confidant. They pulled the bot back up and started toward their next sample location automatically.

Miko followed, talking soft and fast. "I gathered. Island patrol from Honolulu came to campus yesterday. They asked me if Dr. Kahale ever worked with marine explosives. I pulled up the hazardous materials paperwork I'd filed two years ago and again on Monday. I don't know if Dr. Kahale even realized that accessing secure storage required paperwork, but I knew and filed it and still didn't suspect when I heard some terrorist tried to blow up a boat you were on. If anything, I might have suspected you. I'm so, so sorry."

Wend stopped on the far side of the pier. From there they could look out across the calm harbor, protected by the breakwater and undisturbed by wind or rain this morning. Thus far, they hadn't felt the need to make eye contact with Miko at all. "I'm glad you filed the papers and shared that information with the island patrol. But why did you want to meet with me today?"

"There's inventory control on the explosives. The island patrol confirmed those were the explosives used in this attack and one other. I don't know how any court could fail to hold Dr. Kahale responsible now. But I feel like an accomplice. Even if I didn't know. I should have guessed or asked more questions." There were tears in Miko's eyes when Wend finally looked.

Setting their sample bot on the ground, Wend tried to get Miko to meet their gaze. "I don't think anyone will blame you for that. I know I don't. Is there something you need from me?"

"I want to keep working with you. I miss seeing you in our computer room. I feel like I chased you away when you were maybe the nicest prof we had." Miko cried harder.

Wend stood stunned. No one had ever suggested they were the nicest professor out of any set, or the best in any way. But Wend couldn't see what Miko had to gain from manipulating them now, and nothing Miko said registered as a lie.

Even if Wend were the sort of person who hugged, they thought a hug might be inappropriate now. It was hard enough to look close to Miko's crying eyes, but they wanted to offer what comfort they could. "Thank you. I enjoyed leading workshops with you and would be happy to do so again. I'll have to see what works out with my new contract, but I'd appreciate your help setting things up when the time comes. Let me give you my new cellphone number." Wend recited the number for their new work phone, the one they hadn't yet given to anyone but Betta Acosta, and then only on a form listing it as a work expense. Someone else might have worked that into a joke about paperwork to make Miko laugh, but Wend couldn't come up with anything. Instead they processed aloud, "I'll tell Betta Acosta you're the person who kept the records for hazardous material and gave me the codes to process my samples when Kahale interfered. Betta already knows you helped with my health insurance and scheduling when I arrived, and she's looking for someone to improve operations for the Marine Census Project on Hawai'i."

Miko babbled their thanks and how much they appreciated the second chance as Wend lowered their bot for another sample.

35.

"GOOD MORNING, sleepyheads. You missed first breakfast, but we picked up donuts, which I am reliably informed are the best on the island. And you will never believe what Wend's stealthy morning meeting turned out to be about." Aljon set the donuts on the table as he whipped up a new veggie scramble for Viola and Shelly, who sat hunched over the table with only coffee.

Raising a donut and looking through the hole at Aljon, Viola teased, "Did you complain to Kai about the vegan donuts the island patrol provided?"

Aljon's answering smirk was confirmation enough.

At the same time Shelly asked Wend, "You had a morning meeting? Where?"

Filling their own glass with water, Wend said, "Miko wanted to apologize, and part of that was telling me they helped the island patrol from Honolulu trace the explosives Kahale requisitioned for both this boat bombing and the one to threaten Simonian's family two years ago."

"Who's Simonian?" Shelly asked. Wend noted she'd come downstairs wearing soft gray sweats that might be sleep clothes and with her hair still tousled. Whether that boded good or ill for whatever discussion followed, Wend couldn't predict.

"The engineer with IdeoBios who modified the PET-eating bacteria." Wend started with the basics.

"So this bombing wasn't anything to do with the generators?" Shelly asked.

"Perez and Kahale must have discussed Seaward Generation after he flagged the news article and confronted me." Wend tried to explain as well as they could, hoping this wouldn't turn into an interrogation. "Kahale hadn't taken overt action against me before. The fact she didn't tell Perez about either bombing and used a local kid suggests she had motives of her own."

"Such as?" Shelly prompted.

"I barely understand your motives," Wend said with a shrug. "How can I possibly explain hers to you?"

Shelly's shoulders jerked back, but rather than respond with anger, she studied Wend silently, as if finally questioning her previous misassumptions about Wend.

"Maybe you should bring us up to date on what you do know about Perez and Kahale," Viola said. "It sounds like we may have missed a few steps in some people's eagerness to celebrate last night."

The way Viola tried to pick fights with Shelly baffled Wend. For both their own sake and Aljon's they hurried to say, "Celebrating is good. It sounds like the island patrol have the evidence they need to convict Kahale for attacking us and Simonian's family, Perez died of suicide and left a bunch of notes and other evidence, and Gillian seems much nicer and has shared all sorts of information about dreams and stuff."

"Wait, who's Gillian and what have dreams got to do with this?" Viola was at least distracted from picking on Shelly. Aljon set down a plate with veggie scramble, which helped as well.

Picking out an old-fashioned donut from the box, Wend held back a sigh and set in to explain what they'd learned from Gillian and other sources. "The last time we discussed dreams together, Shelly admitted to being a microbe in a dream with me. It turns out, Matt and Gillian were inhabiting microbes there, too." Wend quickly explained Gillian and her theory of affinities and transmitting information, which had helped her determine Wend was a likely participant in that microbial dream.

Shelly's gaze bored through the wall to some point Wend couldn't see. "I can't believe they all talked like that over dinner with a stranger."

Wend's brow crinkled in a moment of doubt, but they decided that counted as Shelly opining on herself and not directly on Matt's family. "Tera and Kai left the room and hid while the others rearranged the table. Afterward, a few of them searched around Gillian's seat for listening devices or something." Taking a deep breath, they changed tacks. "I don't think any of us realized how much it meant for Matt to invite us all for Friendsgiving, and he barely protested the way you left. They all knew you were lying and had in effect spied on them and then flipped out about their poly lifestyle. Still, Matt's okay with me updating you, even though I haven't told him you were a microbe with us or that you even have those sorts of dreams. Can't you understand that Matt and his family are risking their privacy and giving you every chance to earn their trust because they care about me and Aljon and all of us functioning together?"

During a long silence, which no one interrupted, Shelly pushed vegetables around her plate and scowled as she thought.

Wend decided this more thoughtful version of Shelly, who at least appeared to listen, was preferable and hoped she'd stick around. They enjoyed the sugary goodness of their donut along with a great deal of water while allowing Shelly all the time she needed to respond.

"That sounds a bit idealistic and possibly not how Matt or others would tell it, but I take your point that other people's motivations may not be as bad as I sometimes assume." Shelly's eyes flicked to Wend, who nodded but stayed silent. "You implied Gillian wanted to work with people here and already distanced herself from Perez?"

"Gillian set out to replace Perez on the Ocean Planning Committee after he publicly harassed me. Then after his death . . . " Wend swallowed hard, still haunted by what they'd seen but needing to set that aside while dealing with Shelly. "Gillian provided copies of papers left behind by Perez. But Verilyn still wants us to be cautious and not tell Gillian too much until we know her better."

"It's good to know I agree with Verilyn on something." Shelly smiled as if to make a joke, but then schooled her expression and stated, "It may take me a while, but I accept that my life, and maybe my dreams"—Shelly shook her head with more than a hint of dismay—"make interacting with members of that household a necessity. I'm still not sure I want anything to do with Gillian or whatever group around the Atlantic, but I'll try to keep an open mind."

Wend's knees bounced with excitement, but also anxiety. "I understand being cautious about Gillian, but so you know, it makes me uncomfortable to relay information in only one direction." Wend tried not to reach for the burner phone in their pocket, remembering the other message they needed to convey. "Do you think you'll ever feel comfortable spending time with Verilyn, Matt, and the rest? And maybe admitting you were in the microbe dream and know about all of this, even if you're not quite comfortable with it?"

Shelly sighed, setting down her fork although she'd barely started on the lovely scramble Aljon provided. "I probably owe Matt and his household an apology, at least. Let me know when there's a good opportunity, and we can also invite Verilyn to join our board of directors."

Wend couldn't help smiling as they said, "We're all invited for a holiday tea today. Aljon wanted to help cook, but you can show up to eat at three."

A look passed between Shelly and Viola that Wend didn't pretend to understand, before Shelly said, "Why not? I'd hate to miss out on whatever Aljon and others prepare."

Viola only smiled and pantomimed a hat tip to Wend.

"Great, I'll let them know." Aljon pulled out his phone faster than Wend could and stood up. "Now I have cooking to do."

Wend took that as their cue to leave the table, but then turned back. "Oh, and I forgot to mention that sometimes people share flying dreams, and a couple nights ago we flew to where Simonian died and may have seen a message Perez somehow sent there when he died."

"What?" Viola squeaked as she asked. That led to Wend sitting back down for a whole other conversation.

"What did you bring this time?" Kai asked, already trying to lift the cloth covering the steamer basket. Aljon twitched it back into place without breaking step.

"Papaya and black bean mini-tamales," Aljon answered with a small smile just for Kai. "My reading on 'high tea' suggested savory dishes should be included, and tamales were popular for winter holidays where I grew up, although these are my own variation."

"We're all about variations," Kai said with a wink. "The savories we include would hardly fit with what Brits call high tea. We're probably closer to afternoon tea with extras."

"Excellent extras," Matt said. It was barely one o'clock as Matt led Aljon and Wend into the kitchen, with Kai waltzing along behind. "We have more of the samosas from last time, kept frozen, and Tera is preparing tomato bisque." He gestured to a pot simmering on the stove, although there was no sign of Tera. At the moment, there were only four of them in the large-open plan kitchen.

Matt had two jelly roll pans with chocolate cake set to one side. Wend smiled in recognition. "Are you making another Yule log cake?"

"At the slightest excuse," Kai teased, resting a hand on Matt's shoulder before turning back to Aljon. "I was about to start ginger scones. We could pair off, unless you have other dishes you want to try?"

"I haven't done much baking, but I want to learn everything." Aljon plucked the recipe card out of Kai's left hand. "Do you think your scones can outshine the donuts you recommended earlier?"

Shaking a jar of candied ginger in their right hand like a maraca, Kai sang, "Let's find out."

Matt shook his head at their antics. "My filling and frosting both use an electric mixer. If the noise will bother anyone, I can move that part outside."

Both Wend and Aljon shook their heads.

Kai pulled out a pastry cutter, and Aljon stepped forward saying, "Let's see if my knife skills transfer to rocking one of those."

Then Aljon jumped into making scones with Kai, while Wend gravitated toward the pan of melted chocolate on the stove beside Matt. It smelled dark and sweet with just a hint of natural bite.

"You can pour that into the mixer while I pour in boiling water, ready?"

Luckily, the pan had insulated handles and the chocolate poured easily into the whirring contraption. Once the frosting was set aside to cool, Matt said, "Ready to whip pistachio butter into filling?" He pushed a clean bowl for the stand mixer toward Wend.

"I've never used one of these, only handheld beaters," Wend didn't hesitate to admit. Matt showed them how to set and adjust each part of the mixer so Wend only had to figure out one knob at a time.

From across the kitchen Aljon commented, "For someone who enjoys food so much and asks so many questions about how it's made, you don't seem to have spent much time cooking."

Not wanting to lie, Wend said, "I haven't had my own kitchen since I was a kid, but I made most of the meals in my house growing up. I fried or scrambled eggs, boiled pasta, and heated stuff from cans, not what most people would even call cooking. For a long time, I got better results from microwaves than any kid or adult I knew, mostly because we didn't have a working oven. But all of my instruction came from the packaging directions on the food itself and a booklet that came with the microwave. I treated that booklet like a treasure, my very own cookbook."

Expecting dismay or condemnations of their mother or their

upbringing, Wend was surprised when Matt only asked, "What happened to the oven?"

That story, at least, didn't sting to tell anymore. "My mom wanted to help out this young couple who said they'd paint our kitchen while she was at work. When I came home from school, there was a gap in our cupboards where the built-in oven used to be. I was six and figured they took it to be modernized or something. It wasn't like I was allowed to use it anyway. I made soup out of a can for dinner. My mom ate her share when she came home without comment. A week later, we got a microwave as an early birthday present for both of us. I thought the new machine must be better, and didn't realize until years later that she couldn't afford to replace our original oven. Meanwhile, I learned to shape each food into the best curve to heat it evenly. I practiced heating milk for hot chocolate without letting it scald or boil. I had to clean marshmallow off the inside of the microwave before learning to put those in later."

"Oh no." Aljon followed that with what might have been either a prayer or a curse in Filipino, and finished with, "I concede your superior knowledge of microwave cooking."

Matt asked, "Did you know you can measure the speed of light with Peeps in a microwave?"

"I'm not cleaning it up," Wend and Aljon responded in unison.

When everyone finished laughing, Kai said, "Where I grew up, I loved everyone's kitchen except mine." They didn't elaborate, and for a moment no one seemed to know what to say.

"I felt safe in our kitchen and extended that to others," Aljon said as he added coconut oil to the scones. Kai used a fork to poke the dry ingredients inward as Aljon looked up and said, "My nanay and lola didn't let anyone insult me there, and I flipped off implied insults elsewhere. Once I could earn a living, machismo became less of an issue for me than not wanting sex in general. Attitudes were already shifting."

Kai's expression softened but their fork didn't slow.

Aljon volunteering such insights always shook Wend to the core. Even if they'd stopped being surprised by those moments, they reverberated with the undertones of hurt. Much the same as when Wend spoke about their mom.

"Good to know." Matt smiled at Aljon before saying, "I liked food, and my mom taught me to cook, same as I assumed she would with any kid she'd had. But I was rarely in charge of meals back then. I learned in Boston, and then here."

The way each person chimed in with small stories while going about their tasks did more to put Wend at ease in the kitchen than any training could. They thought they might learn to like kitchens and cooking here.

Matt glanced in the mixer and then raised an eyebrow conspiratorially at Wend. As he detached the bowl with whipped pistachio filling from the mixer he said, "Want to help fill and roll a cake?"

Shelly surprised Wend by arriving at three with a plate of clearly homemade date balls rolled in nuts and by apologizing to Matt first thing. "After what happened last time, I wanted to offer something of my own, even if they can't compare to Aljon's mini-tamales and whatever else you've all made."

They'd set up for tea outside again, and the whole household milled around and listened. Viola stood silently at Shelly's side as Shelly said, "I'm sorry for letting my temper run away with me and treating you all in a biased manner. It's my baggage. I'll own it and try to do better. Also, Wend made it clear you all know about the dream stuff. While I'm not comfortable discussing that much either, I'll admit I have a similar birthday and was a microbe in the shark dream." Shelly breathed and then let out a tremendous sigh as Viola rested an arm around her shoulders.

Watching the lack of reaction from Verilyn and Matt, Wend guessed they'd known Shelly's birthday at least. If they hadn't checked before, Perez targeting Seaward Generation would have been reason enough.

As the person most directly addressed, Matt answered, "I appreciate your honesty and that you're uncomfortable with some subjects. I gladly accept your apology, and hope we can get along better going forward."

Verilyn came next, taking Shelly's hand in hers and saying, "We've found ourselves in each other's orbits both due to dreams and through our connections to Wend and Aljon. That should be incentive enough to work past bad first impressions on either side."

"Thanks, and I really am sorry." Shelly's tone was more businesslike than reconciliatory, but at least it was a start. Matt offered Wend a knowing smile, as if thinking the same.

"Apology accepted. That's all behind us now." Then Verilyn introduced Yasu and reiterated other names.

Kai and Aljon lightened the mood by bringing out three multi-level tea trays. While each contained the same overall selection of tea sandwiches, sweets, tamales, samosas, pickled vegetables, fruit, salad kabobs, and dips, Aljon had arranged each differently. At the center of the long white tablecloth that covered three square outdoor tables pushed end-to-end, Aljon placed the most traditional arrangement, featuring symmetrical circles with desserts and frilly garnishes on top and savories nestled together in the middle tier. At the head of the table, nearest Verilyn, Kai positioned a wild three-level bouquet, with dozens of "flowers" carved from fruits and vegetables filling every gap between other tea foods. Finally, near the foot of the table, Aljon whimsically displayed triangular sandwiches and samosas turned on edge amidst tamales and salad kabobs skewered upright like pillars. To Wend it resembled futuristic architecture, but with an oddly anachronistic log cake roof. Shelly's date balls and Tera's soup found space between the tea trays, as Yasu explained the different teas and everyone chose seats.

Partway through the meal, when the soup bowls had been cleared and most of the warm foods devoured, Shelly put forward the idea of Verilyn joining the board of directors for Seaward Generation.

"I'm honored," Verilyn said, "and I'll certainly consider it. But I've recently been asked to join a committee based in Honolulu, and I don't want to overextend myself. You said Doreen recently joined your board? I think she'll do a fine job representing local interests, and I've already told Wend that I'll help them reach out to any of my contacts in the nonprofit sector."

"I'm happy to help with media or PR, if you want," Yasu offered. "That's my field, and I've worked with plenty of environmental startups."

Tanny raised a salad kabob as if raising his hand to speak. "I still have some contacts around Melanesia and Australia, many involved with ocean trades or preservation."

"And Kai is going to be the new head of Marine Science at UH Hilo," Tera put in.

"You are?" Wend realized after a moment of silence all around that they needed to clarify. "I mean, that's great and congratulations."

"Thanks," Kai said. "It's not quite official, so don't tell anyone." Kai raised their eyebrows toward Tera who shrugged unrepentantly. Kai explained, "The investigation into Kahale uncovered evidence, an actual offer letter that was later rescinded, showing I would have been the Head of Environmental Science for this campus if Kahale hadn't interfered two years ago. The university has become increasingly interdisciplinary and cross-disciplinary anyway, so the lawyers, board of regents, and others suggested I take over Kahale's position in Marine Science. I've decided to accept."

A series of congratulations and toasts followed. Aljon rushed around the table to present Kai with a small plate, nearly filled from one side to the other by a samosa pointing in toward a large round scone, decorated with extra pistachio cream and a date ball eye to look like a cartoon fish. "Congrats on becoming the big fish in a little pond." He grinned shamelessly, and Kai laughed so hard they could only clutch Aljon's hand in thanks.

After Kai made a production of shoving their mouth full with at least a quarter of the fish's head at once, Aljon announced to the table, "If this is the time for sharing good news, I heard from Avery a couple minutes ago, and I won't apologize for checking my phone at the table for this one."

Aljon caught Wend's eye briefly, but not in a way to draw others' attention. Wend leaned forward, small sandwiches, date balls, and even a slice of Yule log cake forgotten on their plate. None of their remaining food was warm; it could wait.

"Avery sent, 'Tell Wend and everyone that I'm co-authoring a paper with the grad student who did the sequencing on Wend's new PET bacteria sample. Her name is Bryn, and we're already in the lab sorting out images and scan data to show how this rotifer transports mRNA. Bryn's birthday is the day after mine, but we're taking things slow and only talking about these microbes for now.' That's followed by a series of unemojis Avery labeled as bacteria-W, rotifer-A, and mRNA-B." Aljon rolled his eyes and held out his phone so that Wend could see the tiny animated figures chasing each other around the text message window. "There's a follow-up text about planning to cite the manta ray paper Wend and Viola wrote, because rotifer-A and mRNA-B were prevalent in that sample as well."

With a final wink toward Wend, Aljon said, "They've already messaged you asking if you want to provide any 'unpublished correspondence.'"

Wend laughed even as their worry about Avery being associated with those rotifers and bacteria, as well as a new person possibly in their birthday cluster, reverberated through their bones like waves striking a cliff.

Avery made their own decisions. Wend would provide whatever supporting data they could, and their shared expertise could guide further actions as needed. They set aside their worries as their chest filled with warmth, no, pride at their child's achievement.

Their child. The thought felt right.

Whatever relationship Avery was working out with Mira—while evidently spending considerable time in a lab with Bryn—Avery had chosen Wend as a parent, so they could be one without any guilt. Avery would always be Wend's little penguin, and Wend would protect them like a leopard. A leopard who might sometimes be defended by a kickass penguin. The smile on their face must have grown truly goofy. Half the table was watching Wend, who made no attempt to hide their joy.

Matt broke the silence by proposing a toast. "To Avery's future publication." He raised a teacup and others imitated him, daintily touching teacups and laughing.

By then, Aljon had put away his phone and headed to the other side of the table, picking up another small plate on the way. This one displayed a samosa floating over a wedge of bell pepper with dips swirled underneath to form waves. As he placed that sailboat samosa in front of Viola, Aljon said, "In other news, I'm taking over as skipper of the *Nuovo Mar* for a year or two, while Viola stays here." Viola and Shelly leaned in shoulder to shoulder, for once looking like the loving couple Wend knew they could be. They both smiled, wider and wider, with perhaps the same parental pride Wend had felt moments before.

Aljon continued, "One of Doreen's nephews has applied to be crew, at least as far as Australia, where I'll be picking up a dozen of the new Seaward Generators in the spring. I have a couple of online friends who are considering sailing with me as we make our way between islands collecting local people's suggestions for how best to use Seaward Generators in each community. If anyone has an idea that might be worth applying more broadly, I can offer a development contract, to make sure those ideas are rewarded, not stolen. In some instances, where a specific idea sounds promising and could benefit people right away, I can offer them a generator on the spot. Then I'll forward the other ideas back to headquarters and the rest of the board."

Wend's satisfaction at Aljon's confident declaration settled differently than the thrill at Avery's news, but their face still twinged from smiling so wide.

"One wai," Kai said. "Congratulations."

"Good on ya," Tanny added.

Aljon waved a hand. "Wait, there's more." Everyone hushed as he said, "The first local suggestion we received was that I carry and prepare to train people to use other ocean tech, like the sample bots Wend designed and maybe rescue robots, although I know Matt's separated himself from decisions about those. I'm applying for a grant through the Marine Census Project to become a trainer and hopefully build some sample bots."

When Aljon paused, Matt slid in smoothly. "I would love to put you in touch with the non-profit distributing my rescue robots, and I'm certain some donor would sponsor a few for your next sailing." Wend had no doubts who that donor would be but didn't look to see how Shelly or Viola might react.

Rather than wonder how Aljon's idea had progressed so far so fast, Wend jolted at the sudden synergy, as if the puzzle they'd been trying to piece together turned out to have a second picture printed on the back. "It's coming together, through us. Viola first came to my attention with a photo of a common octopus, and a few days later, I was on her boat telling Aljon how that prolific species traveled between reefs sharing microbiome samples. Now I realize, we're all like that octopus. From my sample bots to the Marine Census Project to the university labs, Seaward Generation and other NGOs, businesses like Matt's, and maybe the island patrol and the Maunakea Rangers. We all interact at a societal level, but those societal structures are tied to nature and the oceans as well."

Wend realized they'd spoken on impulse, and a tea party might not be the right time or place to share such an observation. But they looked up to find the whole table listening attentively.

Kai latched their thumbs and wiggled all eight fingers, then prompted, "The octopus?"

"When we share information or perspectives, we expand possibilities for all those other groups and for natural ecosystems as well. Each announcement today drew from others present. Aljon's going to sail Viola's boat to share tech three of us developed. Avery's research builds on sites you and I found, and that work would have been squashed without Matt and Verilyn to corral Perez and eventually Kahale." They didn't mention dreams or Kai's promotion directly and couldn't ask in the moment if Matt and Verilyn, or the rest of their family, benefited from closure or otherwise. Reining their thoughts back in, Wend concluded, "Like the octopus, we don't fit everywhere but we're adaptable, and some of what we carry could lead to newer, better options."

"Hear, hear!" Matt raised his teacup and turned that into another toast. Wend lifted their cup and was relieved to see that Viola and Shelly both smiled and toasted, still curled in close to each other.

As Wend finally picked up their mango curry and cress tea sandwich, Verilyn cleared her throat and said, "As everything shared this evening demonstrates, we are better together, even if it took some of us six decades to find each other." Her gaze included Viola and Shelly as well as Wend. "I believe in the value of our struggle. There's a whole planet at stake, and I hope a new and better time approaches as we draw from many perspectives."

People around the table nodded or murmured at the words about the planet and then some chuckled, perhaps thinking of their sea creature experiences or flying dreams as new perspectives they might share, but everyone grew silent as Verilyn continued, "All life is a work in progress. I am grateful to be part of this chosen family and the larger community we are building. We gather for this holiday tea, in honor of all the winter holidays, and the shared hope that the dark and cold of winter will always give way to creation and rebirth. To our future."

Wend raised their teacup but didn't think their future could outshine this moment.

Wend helped Matt and the others move leftovers inside as shadows stretched across the lanai. Aljon collected his steamer and Shelly's tray, and he stopped to tell Wend, "I'm heading back with Viola and Shelly, but I think you should stay."

"I can go. You've done so much already. This all turned out amazing." Wend wasn't fading under social fatigue as they'd expect by this point, so they wouldn't mind staying, but that also meant they could handle what-ever comments Shelly or Viola might share back at the condo.

Aljon merely tilted his head toward the second log cake now displayed in Matt's living room and said, "Stay. You helped with that cake, too."

Wend laughed, and didn't argue further.

With only Matt's family remaining, they snacked as they tidied and gradually filtered into the living room where they set out tea and water beside the second enormous log cake. Matt settled in the sturdy armchair that appeared to be his favorite. Wend picked up another slice of cake and curled into their preferred chair, far from the center of things, but close beside Matt.

After shifting restlessly in his seat for a couple minutes, Matt said, "I really want to give you something, Wend, and waiting doesn't make sense to me, especially when gifts aren't a big part of our holiday celebrations."

Wend was about to say no. They didn't want anything, especially not anything more from Matt. But he was already saying, "Please, let me give you this, because it would make me feel better?"

Wend thought about Verilyn and Tera's skepticism toward Gillian and about what they'd already suffered through with Perez. It reassured Wend that they didn't have to trust Matt or the rest of them completely, at least not yet. But Wend already trusted these people with more than they'd thought possible, not only those present but those at the condo as well. With all the work ahead and all they still didn't understand, Wend wouldn't have to struggle alone.

That trust could prove to be a mistake, especially if everyone deserted them at once, and they had only Lisa and Ashok to fall back on. Not that it hadn't happened before. Those two had seen Wend through many rejections, albeit usually by one person at a time. Undoubtedly, trying to keep up with so many personal connections would make Wend's life harder. It might overwhelm them.

All things considered, Wend decided that even at sixty-seven, it was worth learning how to care for all these new people, and if they were occasionally overwhelmed or worse, to also accept their care.

At Wend's nod, Matt held out an old-fashioned key on a two-strand metal chain. One strand shone lighter and the other more golden, but Wend didn't think they were gold and silver, maybe two different alloys of gold or gold plate. He dangled the key until it touched Wend's right hand and they grasped it partly by reflex. Without even a touch, they could feel Matt's warmth. They could see it in his face.

Wend's other hand still held a plate with cake. The situation was ridiculous.

Wend thought they should say "no." But they'd learned to question such thoughts. They'd gone from swimming aboard Viola's boat to setting up house rules so no one in the condo could kick anyone out. By accepting Avery into their work and dreams, they'd realized how unconditional their love could be. Hesitantly, Wend began to understand how Matt could care about them so blatantly and steadfastly that everyone around him accepted Wend before Wend even realized.

"Consider it as coming from all of us," Verilyn said, "if that helps. We would have taken you in and given you a room at any point. The key is mostly symbolic, to say you're always welcome and this is your home and your family, to share any time you want."

"This is a lot," Wend said. "I appreciate it. I really do. But . . . it's a lot." They wanted to bury their head in their hands, but both hands were full. They held a key and chocolate, which possibly covered everything Wend wanted in life.

"Matt rushed things a bit," Kai said.

"As usual," Tanny added.

"But I had this ready, to welcome you." Kai stood, holding out a three-strand lei made of tiny shells. "The shells are laiki and kahelelani ʻakala pua from Niʻihau. You don't have to wear it for long if the texture bothers you, but would it be okay—" Kai raised the lei, holding it wide with both hands.

Wend didn't know the specific shells, but they knew Niʻihau shells were historically associated with Hawaiʻian royalty and carried a special luster due to the lack of fresh water on the island. That connection to both human history and the sea creatures that formed the shells grounded Wend. They said, "I'd like that."

Inclining their head slightly, Wend braced for an unfamiliar touch, but Kai barely brushed their skin as they placed the lei around Wend's neck.

"Mahalo, it's beautiful," Wend said. A shiver ran through them, from the shell lei to their fingers and toes. Wend didn't know if they wanted to cry or melt as they met Kai's eyes for the briefest moment.

"My blanket for you is finished." Tera sounded proud and almost as excited as Matt. "It's waiting on your bed upstairs, since I didn't know this was happening tonight." Tera gave Matt a fond look that echoed previous comments about him rushing ahead. Her look as she faced Wend again carried that same fondness, or at least the possibility. "I used colors based on the tunic you wore when we first met."

Kai nudged Tera playfully then said to Wend, "She makes us all blankets. They're super soft."

Wend remembered the woven blanket Verilyn had lent them after the bombing. It had looked handmade and wrapped Wend in security throughout the island patrol investigation. To think Tera, one of the people they knew least well in the household, had already made such a blanket for them spoke of an acceptance Wend could barely process. They wished they had something to offer in return but only managed to say, "Thank you."

"I'm making stained glass for you as well." Verilyn's small smile was almost a pout but full of amusement. "You look like you're getting used to being overwhelmed by us. But if you want some time alone in your room, or the safe space below it, we'll all understand."

With a shake of their head, Wend realized they didn't want to be alone tonight. They wanted to stay with their newfound family, to complete something. To start something. For the moment, this felt safe, even when they knew nothing and no place on their planet was ever truly safe.

Here they were surrounded by people who openly accepted them, who saw Wend as truly as anyone ever had. Their mind flashed back to Gabi sharing their room in junior high and a young Avery holding out squishy toys to comfort Wend thirty-five years later. They managed to shake their head and say, "I don't want to be alone. If we—we might know each other in dreams, like when Matt and I were both carrying messages in that shark. It's like we're establishing communications. Verilyn mentioned a new time beginning, and I want to know you all, your perspectives, as much as I'm personally able."

Those words sounded incoherent, even to Wend. They remembered Gillian's hints about affinities, how Wend might have always had an affinity for the microbiome. But when Avery pulled Wend into flying dreams they'd moved with Avery as an insubstantial sea otter, pueo, or dolphin. They thought of last night's dream. What they'd experienced in those unfamiliar forms with Avery meant something different to them as cyanobacteria, but they'd registered the familiarity and remembered. "Last night I dreamed I was a vast expanse of cyanobacteria. Microbes passed through me that felt familiar in that form but also from others, like we need to build our understandings together, to perceive each of our human viewpoints better, but also other forms and lives. There's so much to understand, whether or not we work with other groups of people around different oceans."

"I think I was in that dream," Matt said, "bobbing up and down like the tiniest submersible in a sea thick with algae."

The flash of clarity from when Matt handed them the key hit Wend again. They wondered if only people like them—whatever that meant—longed to connect to others this way, or if it was a common desire among humans and other living beings. A sense of belonging flooded Wend, beyond what they could contain. They'd discovered not one but two homes, two families, plus Avery. After spending so long with only long-distance friends, a wetsuit, a sample bot, and a drybag to call their own, they now floated in a sea of connections even when awake and out of the ocean. Over the last few days, they'd handled numerous revelations without being overwhelmed. That meant something. It all meant something, more than Wend could explain.

Tomorrow might not go as well. But they had time, and they weren't alone.

For tonight, Wend said, "Perhaps if I share a story . . ."

ACKNOWLEDGMENTS

Thank you, world, for the ocean.

Thank you, ocean, for regulating heat, moisture, and carbon to support life, even humans.

Thank you to the humans who protect the ocean in whatever ways they can. It would be impossible to thank every person and organization who informed the ocean research that first inspired this story, as then the story led to so much more research! Suffice it to say that it took not just a village but an ecosystem to form this book, from people I've never met, like Anne Farahi who wrote a fascinating National Park Service blog post about Hawaiian Mountain Shrimp, to those who carried on months of correspondence with me, like Mary with Conservation International. I am donating 100 percent of my royalties from this book to Conservation International (www.conservation.org), because their efforts to protect thirty percent of the ocean provided the initial inspiration for this story. Like the coral skeletons that form a reef, that foundation provided various niches for data, words, and video insights gleaned from the work of thousands of other people and organizations. Thank you all.

Next, I wish to thank the individuals and groups who helped create a writing culture that allowed me to grow as a writer and eventually see this book published. First, there was fandom, from a high school club with the fanzine *Tardis Enterprises*, to *The Dabney Collection* at Caltech, to Writer's Workshops at Baycon and WorldCon, to Archive of Our Own and NaNoWriMo. Partly through fandom, I met the first readers for my novels who became my lifelong friends, Leslie and Allen. Beyond them, there grew a whole tangle of friends and family who gave feedback on earlier works or who through discussions of other books impacted my writing: Mike, Janet, Melinda, Matt, Vincent, Deirdre, Cera, Earl, Cat, Harold, Linda, Yair, Eric, Maneesh, Michelle, my first "group" from high school, the Old Darbs, the Horde, my local speculative fiction book group, my online indie book group, my nonbinary discussion group, and many more.

At the time I am writing this (June 2023) there's media outrage about losing the diversity of viewpoints that rose along with "peak TV." However, I've always been more of a book nerd, and I'm personally outraged to see so many queer, neurodiverse, racially-diverse, and otherwise outside-the-mainstream indie publishers under threat. I want to thank Thinking Ink Press and Queer Spec for introducing me to a publishing process based on respect and understanding with my earlier short stories. I also want to thank the small presses who rejected my stories (who I will respectfully not list here), because they and others kindly ushered into being so many amazing books that I would never have had a chance to read otherwise. Thank you to small and indie presses everywhere and to every reader, beta reader, and reviewer who supports them!

Now I want to offer extra special thanks to the people who helped make *Be the Sea* so much better than anything I could have produced on my own. At the top of that list is Emily Bell, who is many things to many people, but for me and the characters in my story, she was both the editor and friend we needed and never expected to find. Thank you also to Betsy Miller and Cat Rambo, both of whom gave different but much needed early feedback and insisted that this book could find a home. Oddly enough, each of them also mentioned Emily and Atthis Arts, where I later found my publishing family! Thank you to Chris Bell for book layout and all the practical business details. Many thanks to Matthew Spencer for near infinite patience and for creating my absolute favorite cover ever on any book. Thanks to all the amazing beta readers, sensitivity readers, and proofreaders who shared their time, energy, and unique perspectives. In particular, I'd like to thank: Ava Kelly, Chris Zable, Dominique Diokno, John Danskin, Minerva Cerridwen, and Tyler. Extra thanks to both Chris and Minerva who went above and beyond their initial reader roles to offer outside expertise (and joy!). Any remaining missteps are mine.

Finally, thanks to every reader or listener who values stories. Thank you to every person who shares their stories. Special thanks to everyone who has shared stories with me from the time I was tiny up until today. A small piece of each story survives in me and inhabits this book.

ABOUT THE AUTHOR

Clara Ward lives in Silicon Valley on the border between reality and speculative fiction. When not using words to teach or tell stories, Clara uses wood, fiber, and glass to make practical or completely impractical objects. Their short fiction has appeared in *Strange Horizons*, *Decoded Pride*, *The Arcanist*, and as a postcard from Thinking Ink Press. You can view photos of felted sea creatures and find links to more of their writing on their website: clarawardauthor.wordpress.com

Printed in the USA
CPSIA information can be obtained
at www.ICGtesting.com
LVHW091106140624
783227LV00019B/78

9 781961 654044